CHRONICLES OF THE KE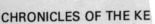

Jame struggled with an a̶n̶... tendrils of power
were slipping past her, sliding over her mind, numbing it
with their touch. It was the nightmare of that first meeting all
over again... but this time it was something else, too. For an
instant, she seemed to see the faces of the tavern audience
turned up eagerly. A bow, the first step of the dance, and
they were hers. Not the mists of desire but tongues of ice
and fire licked at her now. Still immobilised by Marc's
weight, her mind shied away from them, instinctively tracing
the first moves of a wind-blowing kantir. To her amazement,
she felt the energy flowing past her, back into its natural
channel over the tessellated floor.

The ultimate power, the ultimate dance. She had at last
found the true outlet for her strange talent.

The priest was staring at her. 'Shanir,' he said, almost to
himself. He must be one himself to wield hieratic power, but
there was no dawning welcome in his face. Rather, Jame
had the uncomfortable feeling that he was really seeing her
for the first time, not just as a plaything or a tool but as an
individual dangerously like himself who could only prove a
threat.

But there was more at stake here than their mutual hatred.
It was neither priest nor god she was being asked to serve,
but the Law and the code of honour it embodied. Bane's
abyss had opened up behind her. If she turned her back on
that empty altar, as he undoubtedly hoped she would, it
would be beneath her feet.

'Where is the scroll?' she asked in a low voice.

'Look in the temple of Gorgo. Did you think you could trifle
with a priest – any priest – and not pay for it? Swear before
our god that you will bring me the scroll that lies in the arms
of the false idol there. Your word on it, thief.'

'Priest,' Jame said grimly, 'death break me, darkness take me,
the scroll will be in your hands tonight. My word on it.'

Chronicles of the Kencyrath

P.C. Hodgell

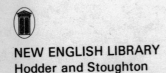

NEW ENGLISH LIBRARY
Hodder and Stoughton

First published in the
United States of America
as two separate volumes:

GOD STALK
Copyright © 1982 by
P.C. Hodgell
First published in the United
States of America in 1982
by Atheneum
Published simultaneously in
Canada by McClelland &
Stewart, Ltd

A portion of this text
previously appeared in an
altered form in 1977 in the
book *Clarion Science Fiction*
edited by Kate Wilhelm,
Berkley Publishing Corp., N.Y.

DARK OF THE MOON
Copyright © 1985 by
P.C. Hodgell

First published in the United
States of America in 1985
by Atheneum
Published simultaneously in
Canada by Collier Macmillan
Canada, Inc.

First published in Great
Britain in 1987 by
New English Library as
Chronicles of the Kencyrath

British Library C.I.P.

Hodgell, P.C.
    Chronicles of the Kencyrath.
    I. Title II. Hodgell, P.C.
    Godstalk
    III. Hodgell, P.C.
    Dark of the moon
    813'.54[F]

ISBN 0-450-42400-6

Printed and bound in Great
Britain for Hodder and Stoughton
Paperbacks, a division of Hodder
and Stoughton Ltd., Mill Road,
Dunton Green, Sevenoaks, Kent
TN13 2YA (Editorial Office: 47
Bedford Square, London, WC1B
3DP) by Cox & Wyman,
Reading, Berks.

For Mike,
with affection & gratitude
and
for my parents,
with love

Contents

PRINCIPAL CHARACTERS PAST AND PRESENT

IN THE KENCYRATH

The Past

ANAR: Jame's former tutor and Ishtier's younger brother

ANTHROBAR: the scholar who copied that portion of the Book Bound in Pale Leather which the Kencyrath used to reach Rathillien

GANTH GRAY LORD: Ganth of Knorth, once Highlord until his defeat in the White Hills and exile to the Haunted Lands

GERRIDON, MASTER OF KNORTH: the arch-traitor who, some 3,000 years ago, sold himself to Perimal Darkling in exchange for immortality

GLENDAR: his younger brother, who led the remnant of the Kencyrath to Rathillien after Gerridon's fall and became Highlord in his place

JAMETHIEL DREAM-WEAVER: Gerridon's twin sister and consort, also called the Mistress

KERAL: a changer, half-brother to Terribend and Tirandys

TERRIBEND: Tirandys's brother, who disappeared at the time of the Fall

TIRANDYS: a changer and Gerridon's half-brother, also Jame's Senethari or teacher in the Senethar

The Present

JAME

TORI: her twin brother

MARCARN (MARC) OF EAST KENSHOLD: an aging Kendar

ISHTIER: Highborn priest of the Three-Faced God in Tai-tastigon

THE HIGH COUNCIL

ADRIC, LORD ARDETH OF OMIROTH

BRITHANY: his Whinno-hir mare
PEREDEN: the last and youngest of his sons, in command of the Southern Host
BRANT, LORD BRANDAN OF FALKIRR
CALDANE, LORD CAINERON OF RESTORMIR
DONKERRI: his grandson
GENJAR: his son, who led the Southern Host at Urakarn
GRAYKIN (GRICKI): his spy at Karkinaroth
KALLYSTINE: his daughter, Torisen's limited term consort
LYRA: also his daughter, consort to Prince Odalian
NUSAIR: his son, Donkerri's father
SHETH SHARP-TONGUE: his randon commander
DEMOTH OF THE COMAN, Kraggen Keep
KOREY: his half brother and rival for control of the Coman
ESSIEN AND ESSIAR, LORDS EDIRR OF KESTRIE
HOLLENS (HOLLY), LORD DANIOR OF SHADOW ROCK: a distant or bone cousin of Torisen's
JEDRAK, LORD JARAN OF VALANTIR: patron of the Scrollsmen's College at Mount Alban
ASHE: a former randon, now a singer attached to Mount Alban
KEDAN: temporary lord after Jedrak's death
KIRIEN: Jedrak's great-great-grandchild and heir
RION: his great-great-grandson
KENAN, LORD RANDIR OF WILDEN: patron of the Priest's College at Wilden
KINDRIE: a Shanir of his house, disowned for leaving the priesthood
TORISEN, LORD KNORTH OF GOTHREGOR, HIGHLORD OF THE KENCYRATH, also called Tori, the Black Lord or sometimes Blackie
BURR: his Kendar servant
HARN GRIP-HARD: his randon commander
LARCH: one of his former officers in the Southern Host
ROWAN: his steward at Gothregor

IN TAI-TASTIGON

At the Res aB'tyrr
TUBAIN: the innkeeper
ABERNIA: his wife

CLEPPETTY: the Widow Cleppetania, cook and housekeeper
ROTHAN: Tubain's nephew and heir
GHILLIE: Rothan's younger cousin, the inn's hostler and
    musician
TANISCENT: a dancer
KITHRA SEN TENZI: a maid, formerly of the Skyrrman
SART NINE-TOES: a guard

In the Thieves' Guild
THEOCANDI: the Sirdan or lord of the Guild
    CANDEN: his grandson
    BANE: his pupil
        HANGRELL: a would-be follower of Bane
PENARI: Theocandi's older brother, Jame's master
MEN-DALIS: leader of the New Faction, Theocandi's rival
    DALLY: his half-brother
    THE CREEPER: his master spy
GALISHAN: master of the Tynnet Branching District,
    Melissand's lover
    DARINBY: a journeyman
    RAFFING: an apprentice
    SCRAMP: an apprentice from the Lower Town
    PATCHES: his sister
TANE: a former rival of Theocandi, the Shadow Thief's first
    victim
SHADOW THIEF: a temporarily detached soul used as a demon
    assassin by Theocandi
MELISSAND: a famous courtesan

In the Temple District
DALIS-SAR: a Kendar drafted as the sun god of the New
    Pantheon; Men-dalis's father and Dally's foster-father
GORGO THE LUGUBRIOUS: once an Old Pantheon god of rain,
    now a New Pantheon god of lamentations
LOOGAN: Gorgo's high priest
ABARRADEN: a fertility goddess of the Old Pantheon whose
    eyes Penari stole

In the Kingdom of the Clouds
PRINCE DANDELLO: heir to the Throne of Clouds
SPARROW: one of his attendants

From Skyrr

MARPLET SEN TENKO: keeper of the Skyrrman inn

NIGGEN: his son

BORTIS: a brigand in Marplet's pay, the sometime lover of Taniscent

HARR SEN TENKO: the Skyrr representative on Tai-tastigon's governing council (the Five), Arribek sen Tenzi's political rival and Marplet's brother-in-law

ARRIBEK SEN TENZI: the Archiem or ruler of Skyrr

From Melalondar

KING SELLIK XXI

PRINCE OZYMARDIEN: Sellik's cousin, owner of Edor Thulig, the Tower of Demons

THULIG-SA: Ozymardien's pet demon, used to guard Edor Thulig

ELSEWHERE

GRISHARKI: warlord of the Grindarks

KRUIN: late king of Kothifir, who went hunting wolvers

KROTHEN: Kruin's son, present king of Kothifir and the Southern Host's employer

MOTHER RAGGA: the Earth Wife of Peshtar, a far-hearer

ODALIAN: Prince of the Agontiri of Karkinor, a would-be ally of the Kencyrath and Caineron's son-in-law

THE WOLVER GRIMLY: a poet and werewolf from the Grimly Holt

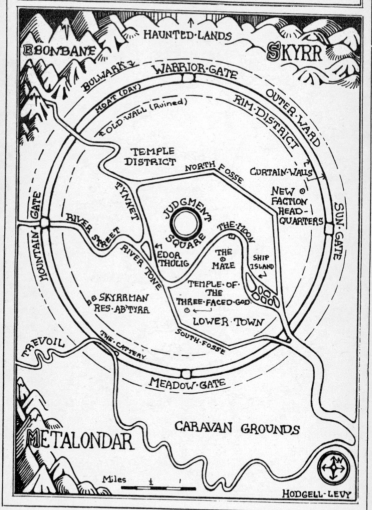

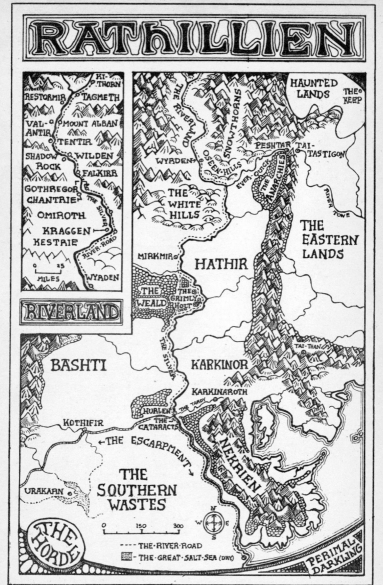

RATHILLIEN

RIVERLAND (inset map)

KI-P-THORN
RESTORMIR · TAGMETH
VAL-ANTIR · MOUNT ALBAN
TENTIR
SHADOW ROCK · WILDEN
FALKIRR
GOTHREGOR
CHANTRIE
OMIROTH
KRAGGEN
KESTRIE
THE SILVER
RIVER-ROAD
WYADEN

0   25
MILES

THE RIVERLAND
SNOWTHORNS
OSSEN HILLS
WYRDEN
THE WHITE HILLS
MIRKMIR
THE WEALD
THE GRIMLY HOLT
HATHIR
PESHTAR · TAI-TASTIGON
EVER-QUICK
THE ANARCHIES
HAUNTED LANDS
THE KEEP
RIVER TONE
THE EASTERN LANDS

BASHTI
THE SILVER
KARKINOR
KARKINAROTH
TAI-THAN
HURLEN
KOTHIFIR
THE CATARACTS
THE TARDY
←THE ESCARPMENT→
NEKRIEN
URAKARN
THE SOUTHERN WASTES

0   150   300

THE HORDE

N
W · E
S

---- THE·RIVER·ROAD
⊞ - THE·GREAT·SALT·SEA (DRY)

PERIMAL DARKLING

Hodgell '84

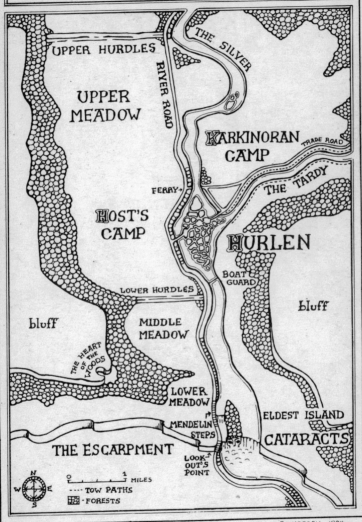

THE CATARACTS

UPPER HURDLES

THE SILVER

RIVER ROAD

UPPER MEADOW

KARKINORAN CAMP

TRADE ROAD

FERRY

THE TARDY

HOST'S CAMP

HURLEN

BOAT GUARD

LOWER HURDLES

bluff

bluff

MIDDLE MEADOW

THE HEART OF THE WOODS

LOWER MEADOW

ELDEST ISLAND

MENDELIN STEPS

CATARACTS

THE ESCARPMENT

LOOK-OUT'S POINT

N
W E
S

0   1 MILES

- - - - TOW PATHS

▦ - FORESTS

P.C. HODGELL · 1984

God Stalk

1

Out of the Haunted Lands

The hills rolled up to the moon on slopes of wind-bent grass, crested, swept down into tangled brier shadows. Then up again and down, over and over until only aching muscles distinguished between rise and descent, climb and fall. A night bird flitted overhead. Jame paused to watch it, thinking enviously of wings. For a moment it showed clearly against the moon-silvered clouds, and then the wall of mountains to the west swallowed it. How near the Ebonbane seemed now that night had fallen. The range loomed over her, an immense presence filling half the sky, blotting out the stars. Two weeks of walking had at last brought her out of the Haunted Lands into these foothills, but that in itself was no help. Clean earth or not, this was still a wilderness. What she needed now was civilisation – even a goatherd's hut – but something, and soon.

Thin, high voices called to each other behind her. Jame caught her breath, listening, counting. Seven. The haunts had found her trail again.

She tensed to run, then forced her weary muscles to relax. Flight would only weaken her. Besides, they seemed to be keeping their distance, an odd thing after so many days of close pursuit. Should she finally turn on them? They were well spread out, tempting targets for their wounded prey... ah, but what good would it do to kill something already dead? She would make one last bid for life, then, Jame thought as she started up the next slope. If only she could reach shelter before her strength gave out and they overtook her.

Then, suddenly, there was the city.

Jame stared down at it from the hilltop, hardly trusting her eyes. It lay well below her, cradled in the curve of the foothills as they turned to the southeast. Even from this distance, it looked immense. The outer circle of its double curtain wall was miles

21

from edge to edge; the inner seemed to strain under the pressure of the buildings it contained. Grey and silent it stood between mountain and plain, a stone city that appeared in the cold moonlight to be more the work of nature than of man.

'Tai-tastigon!' Jame said softly.

Behind her, the wailing began again, then faded away. In the silence that followed, a cricket chirped tentatively, then another and another. The haunts had withdrawn. Not surprising with the city so near, Jame thought, rubbing her bandaged forearm. They had followed her far beyond their own territory as it was, drawn on by the blood-scent. She shivered, remembering that first encounter in the Haunted Lands before the burning keep. Dazed by fire and smoke, she had turned to find a dark figure standing behind her. For a joyful moment, she had thought it was Tori. Then she was down with the foul thing on top of her, its fetid breath in her face.

Jame looked at her hands, at the long, slim fingers and at the gloves hanging in shreds from them. Each ivory white nail lay flush with the skin now, its sharp point curving halfway over the fingertip. They looked almost normal, she thought bitterly. Trinity knew what the haunt had thought when those same nails, fully extended, had ripped the rotting flesh from its face.

Not that that would stop such a creature for long. Even if she had killed it, nothing stayed dead forever in the Haunted Lands, just as no one could live there unprotected without changing as the haunts, once ordinary men, had changed. That was the curse that the Kencyrath, Jame's own people, had let fall on the region when their main host had withdrawn from it long ago. No longer maintained by their will, the Barrier between Rathillien and the shadows beyond had weakened. Perimal Darkling, ancient of enemies, now gnawed at the edges of yet another world, poisoning the land, sucking health from the air. Still, it would have been much worse if a handful of Kencyr defenders had not remained, Jame thought; it was worse now that they were all dead. She, the youngest and last, was getting out none too soon.

Or perhaps not quite soon enough. Though the Haunted Lands lay behind her, she could feel their evil growing in her bandaged arm even now.

It had taken her some time to realise that the wound was infected. Injuries rarely took such a turn among her people, for as a rule Kencyrs either died outright or healed themselves

22

quickly and well in the deep helplessness of *dwar* sleep. Jame had hardly slept at all in the past fortnight. Such endurance was another trait of her kind, but it also had its limits. She was perilously close to them now. There was some time left, however, enough, with luck, to find help in the city below... if the city could provide it. There it lay, Tai-tastigon the Great, just as the Scrollsman Anar, her old tutor, had once described it. Only one thing was different: nowhere below was there a trace of light – not a watch fire on the walls, not a street torch, not even the dim star of a candle in some indistinct window. All was dark, all was... dead?

Memory shook her. Two weeks ago she had climbed another hill, had found another mass of buildings spread out lightless, lifeless below her. The keep. Home. But not anymore. *He* had called her tainted, a thing without honour, and they had driven her out. But... but that had been years ago, she thought in confusion, one hand pressed against her forehead, against the ache of thwarted memory. Where had she been since then? What had happened to her? She couldn't remember. It was as if the frightened, outcast child she had been had run over the hills into the mist and walked out again half-grown to find... what? The dead.

But not all of them.

Abruptly, Jame swung down her pack and began to burrow through it, throwing its contents right and left until only three objects remained inside: a book wrapped in old linen, the shards of a sword with the hilt emblem defaced, and the small package that contained her father's ring, still on his finger. Tori, her twin brother, had not been among the slain. If he had escaped, as she desperately hoped, let him call her honourless when she put sword and ring in his hands for she would accept such a judgement from no one else. 'No, my lord father, not even from you,' she said in sudden defiance, looking back the way she had come.

Far to the north, green sheet lightning played across the face of the Barrier. A wind was rising there that would topple the keep's burnt-out towers and whirl their ashes southward – after her. Jame paled at the thought. Hastily, she shouldered the pack and set off down the hill towards the city, trying to fix her mind on the hope that Tori had come this way before her, but all the time tasting ashes on the wind.

*

A long, gentle slope stretched from the edge of the hills to the first out-work, an earthen bulwark of alarming size but overgrown with feather weed and breeched with many deep fissures. On the other side, the land ran down at an increased angle to the foot of the outer curtain. To the right, a ramp made of rubble work ascended to a gate set high in the wall. This structure and the half-ruined bulwark suggested a city once heavily fortified but now secure enough to neglect its own outer defences. Perhaps this confidence had been misplaced, Jame thought as she trudged up the ramp. Perhaps these proud towers seen first from the hill and now so close at hand were nothing but shells, gutted and empty, the home of rats and mouldering bones. Anar had not said so, but then neither had he mentioned the unnerving lightlessness of the city. The gateway rose dark and vacant before her. Nothing moved there but the weeds between the paving stones as they nodded in the wind.

Inside, the land again dropped sharply away, this time into a broad, dry moat. A bridge spanned it. Jame crossed and found the city gates on the far side gaping open without a guard in sight. She entered the city.

At first the way seemed clear enough. The avenue was broad and straight, lined with high walls set with many iron-barred gates. These opened into private courtyards and gardens, all dark and deserted. For several blocks Jame walked along this open way, and then the road disappeared under the remains of a gatehouse set in an ancient wall. On the other side lay the great labyrinth of Tai-tastigon.

Within six turnings, Jame was utterly lost. The streets here were laid out like an architect's nightmare, swerving drunkenly back and forth, intersecting at odd angles, diving through tunnels under buildings and sometimes ending abruptly at the foot of a blank wall. Nor were the buildings more reassuring. Tall, narrow, pinched in aspect, they presented face after withdrawn face to the street, each one locked and sealed into itself, all indifferent to anything that passed before them.

Jame prowled on, more and more ill at ease. The wind whimpered about her, rattling grit in the gutter, setting a wooden sign to creaking fitfully overhead. There was still no trace of light, no sign of life; and yet the more she saw, the more convinced she became that this was no citadel of the dead. There were indications of age all around her, but little of decay.

Occasionally she even saw a flowerpot on a high window ledge and once a banner restless in the wind, showing golden patterns to the moon. Clearly, if the people had left, it had been very recently; but if they were still here, they were deliberately keeping very quiet.

Or then again, perhaps not. As she rounded certain corners, the wind bore, or seemed to bear, not only dust and scraps of paper to dance about her feet, but snatches of sound. Several times she stopped short, straining to catch a thread of song or chant distorted by distance; and once far, far away, a voice laughed or cried, impossible to tell which, before it too dissolved into the rush of the wind. Was anyone really there? Something like the patter of small, running feet made her start more than once, and a dozen other lesser sounds niggled at her attention, but not one ever quite emerged from the harping of the wind. Nerves, Jame told herself at last, and went on.

Her thoughts kept returning to the city gate, now far behind, standing open to the Haunted Lands, to the coming storm. If only she had barred the way, but how – and against what? Her arm throbbed. Strength was leaving it, would soon leave her. It was foolish, of course, to think that a closed gate could shut out the wind; and as for the haunts, surely they had withdrawn. There was nothing else out there to follow her, she told herself firmly. Nothing. It was only because the pursuit had been so long, so bitter, that she felt even now that she was not free of it.

Then the sound of falling water reached her, and she went forward eagerly into a small square where a fountain played merrily by itself. This was the first clear running water Jame had seen in weeks. She welcomed its coolness as she scooped it up with one hand to drink, then splashed more on her heated face. Her arm also felt hot. Gingerly, she unwound the makeshift bandage, hissing with pain as skin came away with the cloth. Beneath, the teeth marks still showed clearly, white-rimmed against a darkness that had spread out from them like some kind of subcutaneous growth. Her fingers twitched briefly. There was still life in them, but it was no longer entirely her own. Jame swallowed, tasting panic. She had suddenly realised that if the healing process was delayed much longer, she might have to choose between her arm and the living death of a haunt. Oh for the chance to sleep, but not here, not out in the open. She must find shelter, must find... light?

Yes! Jame sprang up, staring. On the other side of the square, under a shuttered first story window, was a bright line. She crossed over to it and scratched on the windowframe. The light at once went out. All the other cracks, she now saw, were stuffed with rags from the inside. In fact, every nearby door and window was similarly secured. If this was true throughout the city, then the people were indeed here after all, but they were in hiding, barricaded inside their homes. Therefore, whatever it was that they feared, that all of Tai-tastigon feared, was out here in the streets – with her.

Jame stood very still for a moment, then cursed herself with soft vehemence. Fool, to have let her attention wander. For the first time since entering the city, she opened all six senses fully to it, and what they told her chilled the fever heat in her veins: she *was* being followed – no, stalked – and it had nothing to do with the Haunted Lands or the keep, whatever she had done there. No, this threat was new, and its source already far too close for comfort.

Then the pattering sound began again. Before, confused with distance, it had woven in and out of her hearing; now it was rapidly growing not so much louder as more distinct, like the approach of rain over hard ground. Jame couldn't tell from which street it came. When the noise seemed almost on top of her, out of the corner of her eye she glimpsed something white running close to the ground. She spun to face it, but already it had gone to earth. In the sudden silence, a pair of yellow, unblinking eyes stared at her from the deepest shadows of the street that led eastward.

A cat, Jame thought with relief.

She had actually taken a step towards the thing when she saw the cracks. They were coming toward her down the moonlit side of the roadway past the yellow eyes, shoving some cobbles apart, uprooting others. At first their progress was slow, almost tentative; but as they entered the square, the multitude of small cracks abruptly combined into five major fissures, which lunged forward, splitting everything in their path.

Jame backed up rapidly. She neither knew what would happen if one of those cracks opened under her feet nor particularly wanted to find out. Turning, she fled westward. The quick footsteps followed her, and after them came the crack of cloven stone.

She took refuge in a doorway. There were the eyes staring at her from across the street, and the lintel over her head split in

26

two. She fled again. The labyrinth should have been her ally, but turn and twist as she would, she could not lose her pursuer.

Then, suddenly, the eyes were ahead of her.

Jame darted down a side street and skidded to a stop. Before her, in the shadow of an ornate gateway, lay a broad, inky pool of water that stretched from wall to wall. She was about to splash across it when something huge surfaced with an oily gurgle. For a second, moonlight glistened on a broad, leathery back, and then it was gone again.

From behind came the sound of splitting rock. It had almost overtaken her. Swallowing hard, Jame stepped back and waited. A moment later, as the water again broke open, she sprang forward, one foot coming down on the sleek back, the other on the far shore. The fissures, however, plunged straight into the pool. For a heartbeat nothing happened, and then the waters went mad. Spray lashed the walls, soaked Jame as she shrank back into the archway. For an instant, she thought she saw a huge, blind head rearing up, gape-jawed against the moon, and then it was gone. The water gurgled down into the cracks. The pool, it seemed, had been all of an inch deep.

Across the wet cobbles, Jame once again met the yellow stare. For a moment their eyes locked, then the thing turned and rapidly pattered away. It ran not on paws but on small fat hands like an infant's, and no shadow kept pace with it on the moon-washed pavement.

When it was out of sight, Jame turned to regard the gateway. It was set in a high wall, which extended a considerable distance in both directions and appeared to set off an entire district from the rest of the city. Beyond the gate, the shadows cast by overhanging buildings lay black and unbroken across the way until far ahead faint lights appeared suspended in the gloom. The air that breathed in Jame's face was heavy with incense. She hesitated, then drawn by those distant lights went warily forward into the shadows.

It was not as dark inside as she had expected. Here the buildings fit together like a gigantic puzzle-box, interlocking in the oddest ways and yet each standing by itself with no shared walls. Moonlight filtered down from above. This, in addition to her excellent night vision – the racial legacy of far dimmer worlds than Rathillien – brought Jame forward until she came to a street where light spheres hovered at intervals by the walls.

She had had to force herself to get this far. Out in the city, her sixth sense had merely tingled with the presence of those odd beings that had stalked her. Here, she flinched under waves of raw force that gained strength with each step that she took into the district. All around her, a hundred, a thousand hearts of power were beating feverishly in the night. Anger, defiance, and fear – gigantic, inhuman – crashed down on her rapidly weakening defences. The ground and air seemed to shake. I'm a mouse caught in an earthquake, she thought in sudden panic, shying back against a wall. It vibrated under her hand. Those beings whose home this was had no thoughts to spare an uninvited guest. They could crush her flat and never know that they had killed. She must get out.

Jame fled back the way she had come, blindly, headlong. Just when she felt that she must stop or die, the gate to the district appeared before her. Gasping, she threw herself down on the damp pavement beyond it. After a moment, she sat up unsteadily and leaned back against the wall, cradling her injured arm.

Fool, fool, fool, to spend her dwindling strength so recklessly. Soon she might call on it in her need and none would come. Already she had forfeited her sixth sense, temporarily deafened by the unheard cacophony that she had just escaped. Was this the way she always behaved, rushing about like a total lack-wit? What a cursed nuisance to have mislaid so much of her past... or to have had it taken from her.

'Damn,' she said suddenly, lowering her head onto her arm. She must be mad to joke about that. Lost, lost, all those years, her home, her family, almost herself. It wasn't the frightened child she remembered who must cope with this night-stricken city but the stranger that child had become. All she had now were shreds of her Kencyr heritage. Very well. She would cling to them and, idiot that she apparently was, force herself to be wise, to conserve her strength. She got carefully to her feet, then froze.

The wind was turning. Fitful gusts of it, foul with the breath of the Haunted Lands, brushed past her face, toyed with her hair. The gate to the north was open. Through it had come the outriders of the storm, but who could say what might follow in their wake? Jame shivered and turned away. Stepping over the still quiescent fissures, she walked hastily southward along the wall with the wind catching at her heels. She did not look back.

At length, the winding roads brought her to the edge of a vast open area where every street in the city seemed to meet. Jame walked out into it towards the large marble throne at its centre, glad for such freedom after so many dark ways, glad even for the boisterous wind, which here had still more of the clean western mountains about it than the northern wastes. A flash of white caught her eye. A flurry of papers was bounding towards her across the pavement before the wind. All whirled past except one that plastered itself against her boot and refused to be shaken free. She peeled it off. It was covered with marks that she recognised as Kessic, the commonscript of Rathillien. It read:

NURK LURKS IN DOORWAYS.

Who, or what, Jame asked herself, is a nurk?

Curious to see if the other blowing papers carried the same message, she caught as many as she could. Some did, but most were as different as the languages in which they were written. After five minutes, Jame had collected specimens of Nessing, Globvenish, Skyrr-mir, and several other even more exotic tongues. She had also been warned away from streets, alleys, squares, rooftops, and even window ledges each with its own peculiar occupant. It seemed that no place out-of-doors was considered safe, although from what exactly she had no idea until one paper, covered with lines that looked like an incredibly complex knot hacked apart at random, announced quite simply:

BEWARE THE DEAD GODS.

The wind snatched the paper away and sent it tumbling off after the others. Jame let it go. Gods? Caught in the grip of the Kencyrath's own deity, it had never occurred to her that other people might think there was more than one. *Gods?* Was that what these Tastigons called such creatures as the baby-handed beast and the puddle-dwelling leviathan, for surely there was nothing else half so odd loose in the streets tonight. She began to laugh at their foolishness, and then stopped abruptly, catching her breath.

Another voice had cut across her own. For a moment Jame thought she had imagined it, but there it was again, faint with distance, screaming. Before the second cry died away, she was

29

running towards the mouth of the street from which it had come. In her haste, she did not see the small dust devil that had momentarily caught up the last of the loose papers and was now travelling slowly after her across the flagstones, against the wind.

The narrow ways closed about her again. She paused at a crossroads under a hollow crown of arches, unsure of which way to turn, then plunged into the right-hand street as the shriek sounded again, much closer this time. Broad ribbons floated from the upper windows here, silently braiding and unbraiding themselves in the air, making the entrance to the alley until Jame was almost on top of it.

Inside, an old man was backed into a doorway, gripping his staff and snarling toothlessly at two young men who stalked him. As Jame entered the narrow lane, he shrieked again. There was no fear in that sound, only pure, frustrated rage, reinforced by the heavy stick, which he swung with unexpected vigour, causing his assailants to leap back. Youth and endurance, however, were on their side, as would be the final victory if only they were patient. Their aged prey knew this all too well, as his impotent fury showed. So did Jame.

Without thinking, she darted forward and, with a Senethar fire-leaping kick, neatly dropped the attacker on the old man's right. The second man spun about to find his friend crumpling to the ground. He didn't see Jame, who was already parallel to him in the shadows, poised to strike again. The blow never fell. As Jame paused in surprise, the man stared wildly past her, apparently at nothing, then turned and bolted. Another figure detached itself from a doorway farther down and fled after him, glancing back with a pale, horror-stricken face. Then both disappeared around the far corner.

Jame had actually started after them when a wave of dizziness struck her so suddenly that she thought the cobbles had lurched beneath her feet. When her mind steadied, she found herself clinging to a doorpost for support, with the old man gleefully hammering on her shoulder and repeatedly shrieking, 'Run, you buggers, run!' almost in her ear.

'Eh, that was smart work,' he said, turning to Jame at last, his cloudy eyes almost luminous with delight. 'They'll think twice before bothering old Penari again. But who are you, boy? What's your name?'

'Jame . . . Jame Talissen,' she stammered, automatically giving a name that, up to that moment, she had not remembered she possessed. 'But I'm not a–'

'Talisman... Talisman,' the old man repeated querulously. 'Odd name, but then you Kennies are odd people. You are Kencyr, aren't you? Ah, you can't fool me, boy, not with that accent; but then it would never occur to you to try, would it?' All his wrinkles suddenly slid into an expression of extreme craftiness. 'You're a Kencyr, and that means you're so honest it probably hurts. Come see me later, boy. I may have a job for you.' And with that he scurried off down the alley, leaving Jame half-collapsed on the doorstep, weakly finishing the protest he had not waited to hear.

The effort brought dizziness surging back. Jame fought it desperately, feeling control begin to slip away. Images flashed through her mind: the darkened keep, faceless figures in the gloom, the snap of... twigs? No, of fingers breaking.

'No!'

It was her own voice, echoing sharply back from the opposite wall. Once again she huddled on a doorstep in a silent city, near the body of the man she had just struck down, far from the northern wastes and their vengeful ghosts. Trinity, another slip like that and she would be gone for good. Forget the past, she told herself; it could no longer hurt her without her consent, but the present, ah, the present could kill.

Somewhere, something was burning.

Jame's head jerked up. The alley was clouded with smoke. Ten feet away, the body of the fallen man had begun to burn.

Numb with shock, she watched as tongues of thin blue flame licked up around the still form. The skin on the back of the outflung hands blackened and fell away. The hair went up in a sudden blaze, revealing for a moment a beautiful heliotrope tattoo behind the left ear blooming in the heart of the flames. Garments, skin, muscle, and bone, each crumbled in turn as the black, greasy smoke rolled upward, teased a few feet above the body by the sudden presence of a small whirlwind in the passageway.

Then Jame saw that a large, indistinct form was taking shape before her, and without consciously willing it, she found herself on her feet again, pressing back into the shadow of the doorway. A vague head-shape on top of a long column of smoke swayed back and forth at the level of the shuttered second storey windows. There was also the hint of a very long tail, defined only by a small cloud of soot that swept from one wall to the other, leaving the dust devil in its wake. The creature fed slowly, sensuously, then belched and wandered off down the alley, leaving behind only ashes and a greasy spot on the cobbles.

At that point, it didn't matter to Jame if this was a god, an hallucination, or the local form of street sanitation; she was out of the alley the way she had come before the creature had turned the far corner.

Beyond, the wind stopped her. It had risen again and now came in sharp blasts that lifted the ribbonlike banners away from the walls and set them to warring in midair, one side of the street against the other. Ruby and amethyst veined with gold burned in the cold moonlight; silver flashed against emerald and turquoise. Then all colours dimmed. Tattered clouds, forerunners of the storm, had crossed the moon's bright disc. Behind them, rolling down from the north, from the keep, came the mighty storm-rack.

Jame stood shivering in the blast. She tasted ashes, felt them grey on her face, her lips, a death-mask for the living; but *Nothing stays dead forever*, whispered a thin voice in her mind. She dragged a jacket sleeve over her face, as though to wipe off the skin itself, and felt suddenly naked. Without her sixth sense, numbed as it still was, how could she know what even now might be searching the darkness for her? The gate to the north was open. Beyond the city, beyond the hills, among the toppled towers shadows were stirring, crawling, snuffling along the trail of blood and guilt. *He* would follow, for there were things he would want back from her, things he would come great distances to reclaim. Even now she thought she heard his tread. It shook the ground.

Dreams, all fever dreams, Jame told herself desperately, making one last effort to break free.

But the ground still shook.

It was as if something very heavy had been dropped some distance away. There was another vibration, and another and another, evenly timed, forming a slow, ponderous beat of increasing strength. It was getting closer. Then Jame saw a strange sight: all the banners down the street were tearing loose and coming towards her. They seemed, by the shape they had assumed, to be plastered against a huge form, but she could see nothing behind them. A fourth storey balcony crumpled against the wall. Ribbons caught in the wreckage. Then, briefly, moonlight flooded the street once more, and Jame saw dust mushroom up around a large, circular patch on the ground. The stones beneath her lurched again. When the next footprint appeared, twenty feet closer, she saw the cobbles at its centre sink a good three inches into the earth.

She was just thinking in a numb sort of way that whatever else this thing was, it was damned heavy, and wondering what, if anything, she should do about it, when the bone-jarring beat suddenly picked up speed and the dust surged towards her, leaving a trail of crushed stone in its wake.

'Oh, *no*,' said Jame out loud, and bolted.

She turned left at the crowned crossroads and raced on into the city through streets that echoed with her passing, around corners, under walkways, and finally over the river by a stone bridge, which gave a fleeting glimpse of steel grey water and boomed behind her as the other swept over it.

All too soon, the air began to burn in her lungs and her eyes to blur. She was running quite blindly, near the end of her strength, when her foot struck something and she fell. Training made her roll over outstretched arm and back rather than sprawl, but the pack jolted her spine cruelly, and as she came up again, her legs gave way. The thing must be almost on top of her. She scrambled to her feet, gasping and half sick, but driven by the pride of her warrior race to meet death honourably.

To her amazement, nothing happened.

The pursuer was indeed there, hardly five paces away, sweeping first one way and then the other as piles of debris, boards, and fragments of masonry all turned to powder under the heavy tread. It seemed to be pacing rapidly back and forth before her, turning with an abruptness that suggested bafflement rather than some elephantine attempt at cat-and-mouse, almost as if it had run into a barrier even more invisible than itself. Then, without warning, the huge pug marks turned and stalked back the way they had come.

Jame found herself face down on the pavement without distinctly remembering how she had got there. There were bits of broken cobblestones pressing into her cheek, and her knees hurt badly. That was it: the ground had seemed to leap up at her, and she had gone to meet it – knees first, by some miracle, not straight down like a diver. As her heart slowed, she sat up unsteadily and rested her forehead on her aching knees for a long moment. Then she looked up.

The street about her was strewn with rubble and lined by empty, half-collapsed buildings. Moreover, the farther ahead she looked, the worse the general decay became, until the roadway itself at last wholly disappeared under the debris that had flaked away, scablike, from the rotting façades that overlooked it. It was like standing on the edge of some great urban sore, born of an unknown and unmentionable disease whose symptoms were ruin and desolation. Not only that, but the source of infection itself was close by ... and it was still very, very active. Jame had thought her sixth sense numb, and perhaps it still was to such small teasings as she had experienced before, but this was altogether a different matter. She could feel the power flowing about her – cold, deep, impersonal – like a mighty river that wears the rocks in its bed to pebbles and eats away its banks. Now it began to find channels through her own mind. Unable to run, she turned at bay, at last drawing fully on that core of resistance bred into all her kind by long exposure to powers beyond their control. One by one, her mental barriers went up.

The effort left her spent, almost stripped of her will. As if in a dream, she felt herself rise and walk, drawn towards the source of the power even as its currents buffeted her. The mounds of earth and debris loomed before her. She began to climb, sneezing at the dust from boards that disintegrated under the weight of her hand. Splintered wood, chunks of plaster, a broken clay doll, and then she was on the crest, staring down at the temple.

It rose tall, stark and windowless above a sea of ruins. Those buildings farthest from it still contrived to stand; but the closer they came, the more total was their collapse, until those that had once stood beside the temple itself were now reduced to bulwarks of dust piled high against its gleaming flanks. Nothing entered that poisoned circle by choice. Bats sheared away when their flight brought them too close. Rats swarmed through the buildings beyond, but none descended into that greater desolation. Nothing moved there that the wind had not touched, and even it seemed to sicken and die in the presence of that sullen edifice, whose shadow alone had crumbled granite and reduced mighty oaken beams to a handful of dust.

The source of all this destruction, the temple itself, was not large, although it gave the impression of occupying a great deal of space. Jame knew instinctively that its interior would also seem immense, just as she knew, without ever having seen anything like it before, to whom it was dedicated.

This was a dwelling of the Three-Faced God. Torrigion, That-Which-Creates; Argentiel, That-Which-Preserves; Regonereth, That-Which-Destroys: names rarely spoken out loud and never all at the same time, names whose very mention could bring down a power that few men could now control and whose potential even for casual destruction was all too clearly shown by this graveyard of homes and hopes. This and none other was her own god, the one who had taken the Three People – Arrinken, Kendar, Highborn – and made them one against the enemy from outside, Perimal Darkling, Father of Shadows. For thirty millennia, three thousand years on Rathillien alone, the Kencyrath had fought the long retreat from world to world, down the Chain of Creation, waiting for their god to manifest himself through them in final battle. Chosen they were and proud, but bitter, too, over long delay, and angry that, the task being set, their god had apparently left them to accomplish it alone.

And finally, for what? A lie?

The power that flowed around Jame now, she suddenly realised, was different only in degree, not kind, from that which she had sensed in the puzzle-box district and again in the streets among the so-called dead gods of Tai-tastigon. Was there only one god, as all Kencyrs believed, or many? If the latter, then her people had been cruelly deceived for longer than one could bear to think. Had the Kencyrath been used? Very well. It had been created for use – but not to serve a lie. Honour would not endure it, nor would Jame. The mere suspicion of betrayal – now, when she most needed all the reassurance that her Kencyr heritage could give – acted on her like the deadliest of insults. Fists raised, wrists crossed, she silently challenged the temple before her: let it be war, then, until the truth was known. It was a mad gesture, as mad as to spurn the one place in this haunted city where she could be sure of help; but she was beyond reason now. Let it be war, or at least a clean end far from this seething abscess of divinity. As she turned away, darkness fell again and did not lift. The storm had broken at last.

Men said afterwards that no blacker night had ever fallen on Tai-tastigon. The wind roared through the city, ripping up slates, clawing at the houses until those within feared that not a wall would stand until morning. They thought they heard voices wailing high above the earth, and those who peered out swore that they saw terrible things as the north wind, the demon wind, bore southward the nightmares of a dying land.

Jame stumbled on, wrapped in feverish dreams, oblivious to the chaos around her. It seemed to her that she was back in the keep, a child again slipping silently through the hallways, looking for something. It was very late. If anyone saw her, there would be hard words in the morning, especially if *he* learned of it; but she was too anxious to care. It was important that she find... what? Her feet were very cold, and the night was very dark. Nearly everyone must be asleep. Jame hurried on, wondering why she was so nervous, wishing she could remember what she was searching for. Then, suddenly, she knew. There was a space beneath a certain staircase, a favourite hiding place, and she was not looking for something but someone. Tori. There were the stairs now. Why was she so afraid to look beneath them? It was what she had come for, wasn't it? A dark recess, and in it, yes, a dim figure.

'Tori?'

No response. Jame crouched lower, peering into the shadows, then jerked back with a hiss. Oh God, Anar. Pressed against the far wall, she fought down nausea. No time for that now. She must look in all the places that Tori might be, hoping desperately that he would be in none of them.

The dead were everywhere, huddled in doorways, crumpled in corners, stretched out on the floor as though trying to crawl to safety, tendons like taut wire along the bone, bones held together with a bit of skin and desiccated flesh. Jame made herself look into every face that sword, fire, and decay had left recognisable. She knew them all but never found the one she dreaded most to see. But if Tori wasn't here, where was he? Once Anar had told her that if she walked long enough to the south, she would come to another sort of land where the wind smelled sweet and the soil was untainted. Tori had heard that story, too. Was that where she would have to go to find him?

She was still looking for Tori; but now there was a pack heavy on her back and she was trying to find her way out of the keep. Something had frightened her – no, she had done something terrible, and now she must get away. But where was she? The passages wound on and on, twisting, turning, leading nowhere. Had she lost her way? No, don't even think that. Keep going, keep going, keep going...

There was someone walking behind her.

You were gone so long, child; now will you leave us again so soon? It was Anar's voice, faintly mocking, hardly more than a whisper.

What? No word for your old tutor? Look at me, child.

She would not. No one at the keep had been kinder to her, but never again did she want to see that face from the dark of the recess.

Then she heard other voices echoing in the hallway behind her. At first they were only a soft-textured murmur, one sound running into another, but then strands began to separate. An accent here, an inflection there... Jame felt her heart lurch. They were all coming. Shambling feet scraped on the floor, rotten clothing ripped as bodies stumbled against the rough stone walls, but the voices that called to her were sweet and wheedling.

Where are you going, child? Come back to us. We love you.

But once they had let her go easily enough, Jame thought bitterly. *He* had said that she was tainted, a thing without honour, and they had let him drive her out into the wilderness. Now they said that they wanted her back. It was a lie, of course, but to what purpose? Then she knew. They wanted her to hesitate, to delay because *he* was coming, too, coming to get her, coming to make her pay for what she had done.

She heard his footsteps overhead.

I must run, Jame thought wildly, and found that she could not move. The crash of iron boots grew louder. He was coming down the stairs from the battlements.

'It's a dream, all a dream!' she cried out loud in helpless protest.

For an instant, the city street again lay before her, with a metal sign high overhead banging against the wall. Then it faded into the keep's upper corridor. A black figure strode down the hall towards her, brushing aside the indistinct crowd that swarmed there, crumbling flesh from bone with his touch. Three broken arrows still nailed the grey jacket to his chest. His mutilated hand reached for her.

Child of Darkness! The voice was the sound of bones grinding, cracking. *Where is my sword? Where are my...*

'FATHER!'

The hated word stopped him.

Nothing stays dead forever: but 'I gave you fire!' she cried at him, at them all. 'Fire and final rites, such as I could manage.

Even when your hands twitched in my grasp. Even when I saw your dead eyes open. Did you *want* to become haunts?'

They stared at her. She could read nothing in their faces. Then they were covered with ash. They were falling apart.

'Nooo!' she wailed, clutching at them, seeing her childhood again in flames.

The wind whirled them away.

Her legs betrayed her, and she went down, too spent to remember her bad arm until she tried to break her fall with it. Pain dazed her, spiralled her senses towards darkness. 'Don't go!' she heard someone cry. 'Don't leave me alone, not again!' Yes, it was her voice, but this time no one answered. For a moment she clung to the image of that empty hallway, the last of her old home that she would ever see. Then it too slipped away.

The cobbles beneath her hand were hard and cold, glazed with ice from the bitter rain that had begun to fall. She lifted her face to it. It seemed to wash away everything – icy street, shuttered windows, even, at last, itself. Jame let them all go. Numbly, like a sleepwalker, she rose and stumbled on, beyond guilt and grief at last, moving blindly forwards until the night swallowed all.

2

The House of Luck-Bringers

The first thing Jame saw upon opening her eyes was the cat. It was rather hard to overlook, being very large, very close and, in fact, very solidly sitting on her chest. They stared at each other. It yawned, showing white teeth and a great expanse of pink ribbed gullet, then snuggled down with its nose tucked under her chin and one forefoot resting firmly in the hollow at the base of her throat. This made it somewhat hard to breathe. Jame raised her hand to shift the paw, then froze, staring at her arm. It was not only still there but almost healed, with nothing but white scars to mark the injuries that might well have cost her both limb and life. *Dwar* sleep had come in time after all.

For a moment, sheer relief made her almost dizzy. Then she began to wonder where she was and how she had arrived there.

From what Jame could see, she was lying on a cot in a small room, at the other end of which was a narrow doorway blazing like the mouth of a furnace with the level rays of the rising sun. The light made her eyes ache. She shut them for a moment, then craned backward until above and behind her a window framed with ivy leaves came into sight. Towards one edge, suddenly appearing in silhouette as a gust of wind pushed back the greenery, were several small stone heads, all frozen in fits of mad laughter.

That stirred a memory.

Jame relaxed, trying to remember what had happened after her awakening in the rain. She had slept again and dreamed that she was walking – well, clearly she had been, although out of all that time only one image remained: the façade of a house covered with small figures carved in full relief that gambolled up the walls, clustered around the windows, and clung together under the eaves, all looking like deformed children, all making gestures that bordered on the obscene. The door had opened at her touch. And beyond it? Think. Yes, now bits of it came back: a room full of faces, of eyes wide with fear staring at her. After that, it had been like sinking into deep water, alone at first but then the familiar forms had begun to slip past in the darkness, faces, hands, hair, touching, clinging, dragging her down beyond light, beyond life...

The beams overhead had white roses painted on them against a cerulean blue ground. They were not part of any nightmare, past or present. Why then was it so hard to breathe?

Oh, you fool, thought Jame. It's that damn cat.

She was trying to dislodge the beast, who only responded with a loud purr, when a woman darted into the room crying, 'Boo, you great lump!' and heaved it off her chest onto the floor, rump first.

'Oh, the wretch!' the newcomer exclaimed, shoving the offended feline out of the room. 'I'm only gone a minute, a few seconds, and he comes sneaking in. You haven't been smothered, have you? I mean, it would be a bit much after surviving the Feast of Dead Gods to be done in by Mistress Abernia's pet tabby, wouldn't it? I'm Taniscent, by the way – Tanis to my friends.' She perched on the edge of the cot and leaned forward eagerly. 'Well? Don't you want to ask where you are?'

'I seem to remember lots of tables and men with ale mugs,' said Jame slowly. 'Everyone stopped drinking when I came in, though. Is this an inn of some sort?'

'Yes, the Res aB'tyrr – that is, the House of Luck-Bringers – and as for stopping, aiee! Some of our patrons were like to drop dead of fright when you opened that door, and the rest nearly jumped out the windows. If you hadn't gone down in a heap a moment later, there wouldn't have been a full bladder in the house.'

'I'm sorry I broke up your party. But what about my arm?'

'Oh, that was a proper mess,' said Taniscent with relish. 'The healer said it would have to be amputated – bitten off, preferably, if we could find someone with a suitably tame demon – but while Tubain was trying to make up his mind, it began to mend. Damnest thing he'd ever seen, the healer said; but then he'd never tended a Kencyr before. Thirteen days it took. Yes, you've been asleep that long.'

Jame's startled reaction to this was cut short by the appearance of a large, dark form in the doorway. After several moments of manoeuvering, it came edging sideways over the threshold and turned into a big-bellied, bald-headed man.

'Every year those frames get narrower,' he said cheerfully. 'So you're with us again. We'd begun to worry. I'm Tubain of Endiscar, your host. Be welcome to this house and peace be yours therein.'

'Jame of the Kencyrath. Honour be to you and to your halls.'

'Kencyr! Well, now, so the healer was right. We don't see many of your kind here these days except for those bound for East Kenshold or west over the Ebonbane. Where did you come from? Where are your people?'

'My people are dead.' The words came flatly now, a mere statement of fact. Already the nightmare images were fading and so, she suddenly realised, was the room about her. I'm slipping again, she thought with a flicker of panic, and fixed her attention on Tubain's broad, bland face. 'I came from the north.'

'No one comes from that direction,' the face said decisively. 'The fever must have confused you. You must have come from East Kenshold. On this side of the mountains, there's nowhere else...' nowhere... nowhere... nowhere... a word echoing in the distance, then dying away. Jame slept again.

It was not a cat that woke her the second time but a great clatter. She opened her eyes just in time to see Taniscent scoop a small bronze mirror off the floor, toss it on the opposite cot, and run out in a flurry of bright shawls, not noticing that her new roommate was awake. Jame stared after her. When they had first met that morning, she had assumed that Tanis was at least in her thirties, but how could the girl who had just rushed out of the room be more than nineteen? Perhaps *dwar* sleep had dulled her senses... or perhaps not. After all, she had accepted far stranger things without question on that first night. But there would be time for answers later; now what she wanted was food, for the long healing process had left her desperately hungry.

She sat up carefully, then swung her feet to the floor and, after several tries, succeeded in standing up. There, that wasn't so difficult. With fresh confidence, she took a step towards the door, only to discover that the folds of her overgrown nightgown were snugly twisted around her legs. She stood there swaying for a moment, then lost her balance altogether and came tumbling down on the opposite cot.

A face stared up at her from the mirror beside her hand. Was that really what she looked like, all sharp lines and huge, silver-grey eyes? Certainly, no one would ever call those features beautiful, Jame thought ruefully; but were they really enough like a boy's to have fooled that old man in the alley? Well, maybe, with all that long black hair out of sight under a cap. It was a very young face, and a defiant one, she thought with an odd sense of detachment, but frightened too. And those extraordinary eyes... what memories lived in them that she could not share? Stranger, where have you been, she asked silently. What have you seen? The thin lips locked in their secrets.

'Ahh!' said Jame in sudden disgust, tossing away the mirror. Fool, to be obsessed with a past she couldn't even remember. But all that was behind her now. A new life had begun, and with it came at least the prospect of food. Spurred on by her growing hunger, she soon managed to untangle the gown and then set off gamely for the door.

Beside it, crouching darkly in a corner beneath a wall vase full of flowers, was her knapsack.

The sight brought Jame up short. It seemed to have been waiting for her, patiently, dull malignancy gathering in its dusty folds. I haven't outrun anything, or left anything behind, she thought bitterly. For two weeks she had carried the relics of her past, known and unknown, on her back like a deformity. Even now they were part of her, and so were those lost years, whatever terrors they might have contained. The latter were beyond her reach now, but as for the pack and its contents, she must find a safe place to hide them as soon as possible. Then, forcibly putting all of this out of her mind, Jame lifted the hem of her gown and unsteadily left the room.

Outside, an open gallery stretched some ten paces in either direction, connecting the north and south wings of the inn. Below, one storey down, was a courtyard bounded on the far side by a stout wall. From below came the pungent odour of manure and the sound of hooves shifting on straw, mingled with a more distant clatter of pots and a sudden whiff of something cooking. Whatever the latter was, it smelled delicious. Jame was trying to locate the source when there was a crash somewhere nearby, closely followed by an angry shout. A tall, aproned woman emerged from a side door to the left holding a piebald cat at arms' length, dropped it on the pavement and stalked back inside.

Ah, the kitchen. Now, how to get down to it?

At the northern end of the gallery she found a broad flight of stairs angling around the sides of a square well. Trailing skirt gathered up in her hands, Jame cautiously started down the steps. All went well at first, but halfway to the bottom, her foot caught in the hem and she found herself falling. Instinctively, she curled into a ball and finished her descent in this manner, in no immediate danger of breaking anything but under the distinct impression that she was renewing every bruise she had ever had in her life.

She was stretched out on the tiles at the bottom gathering her wits and admiring, in a rather dazed way, the carved rafters high above, when a head blocked her view and demanded, 'Are you *quite* finished?'

'Y-yes, mistress,' said Jame, staring up into the hard, bright eyes of the woman from the courtyard. 'I ran out of steps.'

'In well-regulated households,' the irate voice said, 'invalids do not come casually tumbling downstairs. And I'm the Widow Cleppetania, cook and housekeeper... not the mistress.'

'And I'm Jame of the Kencyrath,' the other replied rather sharply, 'not an invalid.'

The widow snorted. 'I'll believe that when I see you stand up.'

Jame did, very slowly and painfully, clutching at the nightgown as it tried to slip off both shoulders simultaneously.

'Humph!' said the widow, not quite so harshly. 'If you can walk, you can eat. Come along, young lady, and be fed.'

Jame followed her into the kitchen, a high-vaulted room with three fireplaces, two of which had large kettles hanging on rachycrokes over the flames. The one on Jame's right as she entered contained boiling water, and behind it she saw a tiny scullery tucked under the stairs. The pot to her left, which hung between the kitchen and the main hall, gave off the marvellous odour that had drawn her from the gallery. The widow gestured her to a seat on the raised hearth of the third fireplace, whose back was to the courtyard. Jame sat down beside it, grateful for the warmth of its flames, while the widow ladled broth into a bowl.

'Watch your mouth,' she said, giving her the steaming porringer. 'It's hot.'

Jame ate, too hungry to be careful or even to mind the burned tongue that her first taste gave her, while the widow finished sweeping together the remains of a dish and then returned to the bustard, which she had been preparing on the central table. The

43

kitchen filled with the fragrance of thyme, basil, and rosemary. She was dicing figs when Jame finally put the bowl aside, scraped clean.

'Cleppetania...'

'Call me Cleppetty,' said the widow, reaching for a beaker of white wine. 'Everyone else does.'

'Cleppetty, what is the Feast of Dead Gods?'

'Ha!' She started to flourish the vessel, remembered just in time that it was nearly full, and put it down with a thump. 'I told Tubain that only ignorance or imbecility could have brought anyone out on such a night. The Feast of Dead Gods is what I expect you narrowly missed becoming. Once a year, on Autumn's Eve, all the gods who've lost or outlived their worshippers come back from wherever it is they've been and spend the night wandering the streets. Some are harmless enough, but most are hungry and out hunting for sacrifices – which is fine if they happen to relish potted begonias, but not so good if their people were fools enough to raise them on baby's blood or virgin's hearts. It's said they can't enter any building without an invitation, but most Tastigons seal up their windows and doors on that night just to be sure. Not Tubain, though; it wouldn't be hospitable, he says.'

She snorted, reached for a spoon, and began to stir the mixture so energetically that part of it flew out of the bowl.

'It would have served him right if something big, red, and ravenous had strolled in that night instead of you. That man and his hospitality! We would have been ruined years ago if it were not for Mistress Abernia.'

While she had been speaking, the piebald cat had furtively slipped back into the kitchen and was now sitting beside Jame, cleaning itself. Another cat joined it, and then Boo. Jame watched them, digesting this information, while the widow seized the bustard and began to cram stuffing into it as enthusiastically as if it were a defunct enemy being dealt the final insult.

'Cleppetty...' she said at last, very slowly. 'If there are so many dead gods here, how many live ones are there?'

'Why, hundreds, thousands.' The widow stared at her over the carcass. 'Bless you, child, what island of the moon did you come from not to know that every god in the Eastern Lands has a temple here? Tai-tastigon is the holy city of them all. That's why things are so strange here sometimes: we're not just god-ridden, we're overrun. Everyone knows that except, apparently, you. Now, is there any other common knowledge I can astound you with?'

Jame considered this for so long that the widow, after a moment's wait, went back to her bird. There were any number of questions she would have liked to ask about these gods, but she hardly knew how to frame them and was, moreover, rather afraid of the answers she might get. Better let them wait, she decided, as Cleppetty manoeuvred the bustard onto a gridiron and started towards the fire with it, her back arched against the strain.

'There is one thing,' she said, getting out of the way as the woman bent to fit the iron into its fireside slots. 'About Taniscent...'

The widow froze, one side still unsecured. 'What about her?'

The sharpness of her tone startled Jame. 'Well,' she said hesitantly, 'this morning I could have sworn that she was about thirty years old. But now, just a few minutes ago...'

Cleppetty dropped the rack. The bustard plunged into the fire in a fountain of sparks as cats scattered in all directions (except for Boo, who only tucked in his paws), and the widow dashed out the door shouting, 'Tanis, you damn fool!' Jame heard her thunder up the stairs and along the gallery as she tried to rescue the bird from the flames. She was still trying when Cleppetty stalked back into the kitchen, seized a pair of tongs, and rolled the singed fowl out onto the hearth. She regarded it balefully for a moment, then turned sharply to Jame.

'There's a drug called Dragon's Blood,' she said in a hard voice. 'It temporarily restores youth – or the illusion of it – but the more often you take it the more you need, and the faster you age between times. Tanis started using it four years ago when she turned twenty and thought that age was ruining her dancing. Now she takes it because of that worthless lover of hers, who I suppose she's with now. If this goes on much longer, she'll destroy herself. I'm telling you this because we care for each other here, and that poor, foolish child needs all the help she can get. Remember that.'

Then they heard heavy feet stamping into the hall, and someone shouted for food.

'Customers already!' Cleppetty surveyed the kitchen with despair, taking in the burnt bustard on the hearth, the mound of broken crockery still on the floor, and the piebald cat on a high shelf, peering warily around a china plate that had already begun to teeter ominously.

'What an afternoon... for you too, now that I think of it. Back to bed with you and let me salvage what I can of the day; and the next time you come downstairs,' she shouted after Jame as she started carefully up the steps, '*please* do it the regular way.'

After that, Jame recovered rapidly. In a few days, she was running all over the inn, as bright-eyed with curiosity as a cat; but for all her pleasure at finding herself in a new, intriguing situation, she did not forget what brought her to this city in the first place. Now that she had seen Tai-tastigon, however, she realised that it would be virtually impossible to find news of her brother in so large and complex a place. Anyway, if Tori had come this way, he probably hadn't stayed here long, not with the Riverland – the home of the Kencyrath on Rathillien – waiting on the other side of the Ebonbane. She would have to follow her brother there, Jame decided, if they were ever to meet again on this side of the pyre.

'But how do I get out of the Eastern Lands?' she asked Cleppetty.

'Just now,' said the widow, 'you don't. The mountain passes snowed in a week ago and won't clear again until the spring.'

'But surely there are other routes.'

'Once, yes. Folk used to go overland around the Ebonbane's southern toe, but now the Mildarien Peninsula is infested with haunts – and worse. As for the sea lanes, an early storm season has closed them, too. Every year we get more and more sealed off. Someday the routes westward will disappear altogether, but in the meantime if you meant this to be a short visit, your timing's as skewed as your sense of direction.'

Jame's first impulse was to set out anyway – southward, perhaps, in search of a ship willing to dare the Cape of the Lost in storm season. The psychic attention that held the Kencyrath together tugged at her. Once she would have yielded to its pull without a second thought, but now she found herself hesitating. After all, her full strength had not yet returned, and she must not foolishly endanger the ring and shattered sword, her brother's lost birthright, which she would be carrying to him. No, she must wait either until she was completely fit again or spring made travel less hazardous. After all, what were a few more weeks or possibly even months when it had taken her years to fight her way back to that terrible homecoming at the keep? The world of her people would open up before her soon enough, she told herself. Her task now was to prepare herself for it.

Meanwhile, life at the inn whirled along, each day repeating the basic patterns and yet improvising on them endlessly. Cleppetty set the pace. Every morning she started out by scrubbing the kitchen, the tiles of the great hall, and the floor of the side room where those too drunk to go home the night before had been dragged. Then there was the marketing, then the cooking, which kept her in the kitchen all afternoon. By early evening, the central cauldron was full of soup or stew and all available surfaces were covered with brie tart, humble, galantine, and eel pie, haslet for the hunters, leek dishes for the lustful as well as meat laid out ready for the spit and an odd assortment of other viands depending on who was in town for what religious festival. Then the customers began to arrive. From early evening until the late watches of the night, the inn filled with clatter, song, and ceaseless shouts for wine. Every third day, the widow baked bread, spreading flour all over the north wing with the vigor of her kneading. Every seventh day she did the wash.

As soon as Jame was strong enough, she began to help whenever Cleppetty and the others would let her. At first, this was mainly in the kitchen. Cleppetty had a minor talent for theurgy, and, with her book of common household charms, could do a number of handy things such as kindling a fire with its own ashes, making broken china whole, and raising bread in half the normal time. At the end of Jame's second active week at the inn, she suddenly found the book thrust into her hands.

'Now let's see you try,' the widow said, plopping a lump of unleavened dough down on the table before her.

Jame hesitated. Many of her people had such talents if not far greater ones, but those that did were feared and often compelled to enter the priesthood. Apprehensively, she recited the charm. It usually took Cleppetty half an hour to ready her bread for the oven; Jame's rose in five minutes. When the widow sliced into the baked loaf, however, they discovered that its sudden expansion had been due to the growth of rudimentary internal organs.

That was the end of Jame's apprenticeship in the kitchen.

From then on, she helped with the laundry, washed dishes, and assisted in the great hall every night.

Tai-tastigon, by daylight, was a quiet place, as far as she could tell; but as dusk crept through the streets, strange new sounds and smells took root in the shadows and grew. As she darted between the tables under the three great chandeliers, Jame often heard the distant clamour of some religious festival or glimpsed the bizarre costumes and gilded faces of the celebrants themselves as they entered the Res aB'tyrr to drink a noggin to luck before some important rite. Once they brought with them a silent woman clad only in golden ornaments. Ghillie, the hostler, pointed her out to Jame, whispering that she was to be their sacrifice. Jame thought he was joking until she met the woman's haunted eyes across the table.

And so the days passed. The people at the inn continued to treat her well. Tubain was always courteous as, indeed, he was to all who entered his establishment. Cleppetty remained brusque but not unkind. Rothan, Tubain's nephew, was friendly enough but rather pompous as befitted the innkeeper's heir. More observant or less tactful than the others, Rothan's young cousin Ghillie made the mistake at first of teasing Jame about her hands, and got the scare of his life when she nearly went for his throat. Luckily, he was a light-headed, good-natured boy and soon forgot the entire episode. As for Tanis, she was delighted to have a roommate patient enough to listen to the tale of the endless fluctuations in her affair with Bortis, a handsome, arrogant bandit, come down from the hills to winter in the city.

The only member of the household whom Jame did not come to know was Mistress Abernia. Tubain's wife never left her own chambers in the south wing. Jame heard her from time to time shrilly berating her husband for some outrageous piece of generosity or other, but never saw more of her than a shadow cast on a closed curtain, gesticulating wildly. No one would (or perhaps could) tell her why Tubain's wife lived in such seclusion.

Nor was this the Res aB'tyrr's only mystery. Of more pressing concern was its relationship with the establishment across the square, an inn called the Skyrrman, run by a native of the Tenko canton of Skyrr named Marplet. Ever since her arrival, Jame had been puzzled by a series of small, unpleasant events at Tubain's hostelry. One morning, for example, she came down to find Rothan and Ghillie grimly scraping excrement out of the mouths of the b'tyrr figures on the front wall. Another day, someone tossed a sealed jug over the wall into the inner courtyard where it shattered, spraying Cleppetty's newly washed sheets with urine. It didn't occur to Jame to connect these events with the Skyrrman, however, until one afternoon something flew through the window and landed in a heap on the table that she was scrubbing. It was the piebald cat. Patches of its fur had been burned off and three of its legs were broken as well as its neck. Then Jame heard Marplet's household rowdies out in the square, laughing.

A black rage rose in her. She dropped her washbag and sprinted for the door, only to be jerked back on her heels as Cleppetty grabbed her collar from behind.

Half-strangled, she heard the widow's harsh, angry breath in her ear and, through clearing eyes, saw Rothan and Gillie on the other side of the room, both obviously furious but doing their best to ignore the taunts now being shouted in the square. Tubain had simply disappeared into the cellar. Then the voices outside faded into the distance, and Cleppetty let her go.

'Why?' she demanded hoarsely, one hand on her bruised throat. 'We should all have gone after them. Why didn't we?'

'Child, if you have any friendship for us at all,' said the widow, 'don't ask... and above all, don't interfere.' With that, she turned and stalked back into the kitchen.

Jame stared after her. Bound by the Kencyr law of hospitality, she must obey; by that same law, however, the honour of the household had become her own, to defend or forfeit. But how could she defend what she didn't understand? The sudden passivity of her new friends, whom she didn't believe to be cowards (except, perhaps, for Tubain), baffled and unnerved her. And that wasn't the worst of it, either. Cleppetty and the others knew exactly what was going on, Jame realised suddenly with growing dismay, and had probably known since well before her arrival. But they hadn't told her. Why? Because, for all their friendliness, they still didn't trust her. Because she was an outsider. Again.

At first, she pretended that it didn't matter. After all, these people had a right to their secrets and no reason as yet to trust her with any of them. But as the days passed and Marplet's growing, unexplained harassment brought the others closer together in their passive resistance, she felt her own exclusion

49

more and more. It reminded her all too vividly of life at the keep. For the first time, she realised how much being a full member of this household mattered to her, and how much she needed it.

I've got to belong someplace, she said to herself one day, and if not here, where?

She was lying on the warm tiles of the north wing roof, four storeys up, looking out over the city. Ivory spires rose in the distance, tipped with light as the sun began its slow tumble down the far side of the Ebonbane. Night always fell quickly in Tai-tastigon, and with its fall the city sprang to life. Jame longed to be down in those convoluted streets, sniffing out their secrets. She had not forgotten the subtle lure of the maze, much less the gods of Tai-tastigon and the challenge she had issued because of them before her own temple. But Tubain had requested that she not leave the inn at all. He seemed to think that if she ever did, she would become instantly and irretrievably lost. Regarding the darkening tangle of streets below, Jame thought wryly that he might well be right; but the day might come when she would have to risk it. As much as she liked these people, she couldn't stay here indefinitely on mere sufferance. If matters didn't improve soon, she would have to slip the silken collar of Tubain's concern and disappear into the night, as alone and friendless as she had come.

Below, someone made a remarkable noise, half-gurgle, half-squeak. Looking down, Jame saw Tubain at the rail outside Taniscent's room, staring up at her. There was so much horror in his expression that she promptly slithered down the tiles, jumped to the second storey roof and, catching the eaves, swung down to the gallery floor beside him.

'What's wrong?' she demanded, sudden eagerness sharpening her voice. Was he at last going to take her into his confidence?

'You could have broken your neck!' the innkeeper said, almost incoherent with agitation. 'What were you *doing* up there?'

'Oh.' Damn. 'I was looking at the city. Why would anyone have laid out the streets in such an insane jumble?'

'Well,' said Tubain, making an obvious attempt to regain his composure, 'it's partly intentional and partly not. You see, we're rather prone to disasters here, natural and otherwise. Old buildings are always getting knocked down, washed away, or trampled flat, and new ones rise wherever there's room. But that's the least of it. Ever since Tai-tastigon was built back in the days of the Old Empire, folks in these parts have loved puzzles. Once their whole culture was built on them, social conventions and all, and the highest form of art was the labyrinth. Of course, things have changed a lot here since then, but some folk still hold to the old ways. For example, when the Sirdan Theocandi of the Thieves' Guild came to power, he reconstructed part of the Palace into a perfect maze; and old Penari lives in the heart of one so complex that its own architect lost his way trying to get out and was never seen again.'

That latter name made Jame start. 'This Penari . . . who is he?'

'Why,' said Tubain, surprised, 'the greatest thief in the history of Tai-tastigon, which is as much as to say in the world, and the only man ever to know all the streets of the city. The Temple District is his manor, but he's not very active or much seen these days. Where did *you* hear of him?'

Jame hesitated, then told the innkeeper about the incident in the alley. Tubain's eyes grew wide as he listened.

'For fifty-six years,' he said at last, 'ever since that man stole the Eye of Abarraden under circumstances that weren't just difficult, mind you, but physically impossible, every thief in the guild has dreamed of becoming his apprentice. For fifty-six years! And on your first night in the city, he makes you the offer. By all the gods, *that* will make some faces red at the Palace, the Sirdan's not the least.'

'Do you mean to say,' said Jame, quite horrified, 'that he was offering to teach me how to *steal?*'

'Why, what else, and why not? Nearly everyone in Tai-tastigon does or has or wants to. It's fine work, I hear, if you can get a good master and, of course, don't get caught.' At that moment Cleppetty called him from the kitchen door. He excused himself and trotted off, saying, 'Penari, eh?' out loud to himself. 'Just think of that!'

Jame did, long and seriously over the following days.

Meanwhile, she continued to room with Taniscent, but began to find this arrangement increasingly unpleasant. Soon after her arrival, Cleppetty had wrung a promise out of the dancer never to use Dragon's Blood again. This was a relief of sorts, but it didn't save Jame from the days of brittle smiles that followed nor the nights of hysterical weeping when it became clear with the wearing off of the drug that Tanis had paid all too heavily for those brief returns to her lost youth. On the other hand,

Jame was keenly aware that she herself was not the most desirable of chamber-fellows; her own sleep still brought her dreadful shapes, and she would often wake with a start, unsure if the voice she had heard cry out was her own. On such nights she would take a blanket and go up to the fourth storey solar to sleep, if she could, and often to wake in the cold dawn with Boo snuggled warmly against her.

This large, empty loft soon became her refuge from the tensions of life at the inn. As a rule, no one bothered her there, since the whole area was much too open to serve either for storage or guests. Here she at last found a hiding place for her pack, behind some loose stones in one corner, and also the necessary open space to experiment with the Senethar training patterns.

She often wondered who had taught them to her. When her brother Tori had first begun to learn the arts of war all those years ago at the keep, she had begged to be taught them, too. Her plea had been flatly refused. And yet now the knowledge was there, as she had discovered in the Haunted Lands. It was wonderful suddenly to have the benefit of such training, but frightening too not to know where it had come from or what other skills she might have brought out of those lost years.

The incident with the bread had shaken her badly. She was different, she always had been, Jame thought, staring blindly at her hands, and her father had not been able to accept it. *Shanir, god-spawn, unclean, unclean* . . . words out of the past, shouted at her from the keep gate. That had been soon after her nails had first worked their way to the surface. How her fingertips had itched, and what a relief it had been (as well as a surprise) when the sharp points at last broke through the skin. Nail-less until then, unlike everyone else at the keep, she had been proud of her new acquisitions. The horror and disgust of the others had bewildered her. Jame realised now that they had been afraid, frightened of what she was, of what she might become, although no one had ever made it clear to her exactly what that was. Would her people always react to her this way? If so, what sort of a fool was she to long for them, for the unhappy home she had lost? A Kencyr fool. Well, now she had six months to learn if she could make a life for herself apart from the Kencyrath.

But days passed, and Jame remained an outsider at the Res aB'tyrr although virtually a prisoner within its walls. As this confinement became more and more burdensome, she spent longer periods in the loft, working eventually with the Senetha dance patterns that corresponded to the four Senethar types of combat, discovering as she went which ones she knew. Earth moving, fire leaping, water flowing, wind blowing... the second was still almost beyond her in her weakened state, and the fourth (assuming she knew it all) quite impossible, but it pleased her to at least have made a start. So she kept pushing at the limits of her knowledge and endurance, both to expand them and, often, simply to wear herself out. Exhaustion made sleep easier and certain thoughts less gnawing.

One morning a few days after Winter's Eve, she was doing the kantirs of a fourth-level water flowing pattern when she saw Ghillie, upside down from her position at that moment, staring at her open-mouthed around the newel of the spiral stair.

'Ee!' he said when she stopped rather suddenly, her back arched in a curve that from his position must have looked almost impossible. 'Why didn't you say you were a dancer?'

Jame straightened, grinning, and turned. '"Ee" yourself,' she said. 'I didn't because, strictly speaking, I'm not. This is a kind of fighting practice. But what are you doing up here at this hour? I didn't expect to see you until afternoon after last night's debauch.'

'Aunt Cleppetty got me up,' said the boy ruefully, 'and gave me a fine lecture on disappearing before all the guests were in bed. She also told me to tell you that she's going marketing just now and wants you to go with h – hey, watch out!'

But Jame was already past him, boots in hand, ricocheting down first one stair and then the other towards the front door where Cleppetty waited impatiently, a shopping basket on her bony arm.

They crossed the square with Jame hopping on one foot, trying to get herself shod without falling down, too excited even to notice the derisive hoot from the door of the Skyrrman that greeted this performance. At the southwestern corner of that inn, piles of bricks, dressed stone and timber – all waiting to be hoisted up to the unfinished fourth storey – were spread out on the pavement, partly obstructing the side street. Cleppetty marched straight through these, looking neither right nor left nor – more to the point – up, where a heavily ladened sling swung creaking in the breeze. It was typical of Marplet sen Tenko's attitude towards the general public that he should permit such a thing to hang there apparently unattended, and typical of the widow's attitude towards Marplet that she should completely ignore it. As for Jame, only stubborn pride carried her after Cleppetty through that sinister shadow as a gust of wind made it shift on the ground and set the supports high above to groaning.

Then it was behind them, and they had turned onto the small street called the Way of Tears, which ran along the west side of the Skyrrman, past the gate to its inner court and the back wing that housed the servants' quarters. Here a slim, black-haired girl leaned out of a window to stare down at them. Jame, her mind still on falling objects, almost shied before she saw that the other's hands were empty and her expression showed only curiosity. For a moment their eyes met. Then the road twisted away behind the inn, and the brief contact was broken.

Tai-tastigon by daylight proved to be a much different place from the one Jame remembered seeing on her first night. Now, instead of dark, empty ways, the streets were full of life. Men hurried past, intent on their own business. Women leaned out of upper windows to gossip with neighbours across the way, while lines of wet laundry flapped languidly between them. Children, playing in the gutter, stopped to watch and giggle as a stray dog urinated on someone's pet geraniums. All that was mysterious or menacing seemed to have vanished or to have grown as pale as the moon set high against a bright, late morning sky.

Then they passed under the arch of an old gate into a tangle of backways. The main streets had been confusing enough, but here even the residents seemed to rely heavily on members of the Pathfinders' Guild, who hawked their expertise at every crossroad. Those who weren't willing to pay a guide's fee had scrawled directions to themselves all over the walls. One had even anchored himself to his own front doorknob with a string, which stretched along the pavement for five blocks before ending suddenly in the middle of an intersection, the victim, perhaps, of some indignant guide.

Jame was just thinking that their route couldn't possibly get any more complex when the widow dived into yet another maze-within-a-maze composed of dank, rapidly narrowing lanes. Caught between claustrophobia and wall-slugs, Jame was almost ready to retreat the way they had come (assuming she could find it) when they suddenly emerged from a crack between buildings into a small square bustling with people: the vegetable market, reached by some arcane shortcut.

While Cleppetty shopped, Jame wandered around the stalls and carts, admiring the great piles of produce. She noticed that two municipal guards armed with the usual iron-headed truncheons were also on the prowl, presumably looking for thieves. It didn't occur to her that they might actually find one until a boy suddenly winked at her across a stand and made a potato disappear into his pocket as if by sorcery. Jame thought of those iron-bound clubs and went on to the next stall without a word.

Barring that incident, nothing disturbed the general air of normality about the market; and even the theft, in an odd way, seemed a natural part of the scene. Sitting on the edge of the central fountain with her fingers dipped in the cool water, Jame wondered if the exotic image she had built up of Tai-tastigon had anything to do with the true life of the city. Once a year, perhaps, the very stones went mad, but was the rest of the time passed like this, in steady industry spiced with nocturnal revels for those who desired them?

She was still wondering when someone shrieked.

Jame's head snapped up. She saw a gnarled farmer drop the turnips that he had been showing to a customer and snatch a broken scythe out of his cart. God of her ancestors, he was coming straight at her. The end of a blue ribbon curled over his arm as his blade leaped up. But surely that first wild cry had come from behind her, Jame thought in confusion, springing to her feet; yes, there it was again not ten feet away, mixed now with a great splashing. She twisted about and saw a heavyset man festooned with blue ribbons charging at her through the fountain. He was brandishing a short, sharp sword.

For a whole second, Jame simply froze, paralysed with amazement. Then she dived for cover under the bed of a tomato cart and came up again on the far side. Cleppetty, who had taken refuge in a doorway, reached out and pulled her into the recess. Together, they watched the fight.

The two men met almost on the spot where Jame had been standing, but they did not remain there long. Step by step, the older man with the scythe was forced backwards. He used his improvised weapon well, swinging in tight, vicious arcs that hissed and flashed in the sun, but he was at a disadvantage: his adversary, while a hopeless swordsman, had the dubious fortune to be completely berserk.

The farmer's ramshackle cart was close behind him now.

Beyond both men and wagon, Jame saw the guards watching with interest.

Then the older man's foot came down on one of the turnips he had dropped, and he went over backward, crashing into the cart with such force that the near wheel fell off. A torrent of vegetables cascaded to the pavement. The swordsman sprang forward with a triumphant shriek, only to stagger and fall himself on the treacherous footing. He tried to get up again and again, foam dribbling down his chin, too deep in madness to remember his weapon or look where he put his hands or feet.

The farmer rose slowly, carefully, and picked up his scythe. He touched the edge once as though to be sure of its keenness, then stepped towards the fallen man through the field of squashed vegetables. The latter rose to his knees, his voice a squeal of frustrated rage. The sound stopped abruptly as the blade caught him under the chin. Something went flying through the air and landed wetly on top of the pile of tomatoes before Jame. She stared at it. The eyelids were still fluttering. Then the farmer stalked over, grabbed the thing by the hair, and walked off with it.

Cleppetty left the doorway, muttering savagely to herself, and half dragged Jame through the wagons towards the fissure by which they had entered the square. Looking back, Jame saw the tomato-seller examine his produce, throw two into the gutter, and carry several others to the fountain. He was washing them when the wall cut off her view. The murmur of renewed business followed them for several turnings into the dank nest of lanes.

'Cleppetty . . .'

'. . . think they'd have more self-respect than to do it in public,' the widow was saying to herself in tones of profound disgust and unusual directness. 'Some people have no sense of propriety. And what a mess . . .'

'*Cleppetty* . . .'

'. . . no consideration for others, either. At least I got the salad makings before . . .'

'CLEPPETTY!'

Jerked to a halt by Jame's sudden stop, the widow turned and glared at her. 'Now what's the matter?'

'Cleppetty, what *happened* back there?'

'If I tell you, will you stop yelping at me and get a move on? We've lost enough time already. Besides, you're standing in a puddle.'

56

And so she was. Boots squelching loudly, Jame followed the widow out of the tangled maze, several times treading on the older woman's heels in her impatience. Cleppetty, however, said nothing until the road widened and they were walking side by side again.

'Those men!' she said, beginning with a sort of explosion. 'Their sects are involved in a temple war. The ribbons prove it's a legal one, and so, having paid for it, they've the right to do whatever they want or can to each other, anywhere, anytime.'

'Legal? Paid? To whom?'

'Why, to the Five, our governing council.' She gave Jame a sharp, sidelong look. 'Surely you've at least heard of that.'

Jame nodded. Ghillie had mentioned it several times, but never this business of warfare in the streets, which was odd, given his taste for the sensational. 'It's made up of King Sellik's representative, the Skyrr Archiem's, and three that the city guilds choose themselves, isn't it?'

'Of course,' said the widow, 'and they need money to pay for the guards, themselves, and especially the city charter. Tai-tastigon is half in Metalondar and half in Skyrr because of the River Tone, you know (or do you?), and must pay for the privilege of belonging to neither. So the Five levy taxes and license violence. As for the wars, there are four kinds.' The basket handle slid down to the crook of her elbow as she brandished a knobby finger in Jame's face. 'One: private, for individuals and families. Two: trade, for merchants. Three: temple, for religious fanatics like those two oafs back there. Four: guild, and very messy those can get, too. You may yet see one for yourself if the Sirdan Theocandi of the Thieves' Guild loses any more of his people to that Tai-abendran upstart, Mendalis. Praise be that my sister's daughter's son is well out of it back in Emmis.'

'Your – uh – grand-nephew is a *thief?*'

'Oh aye, and a good one too, I'm told . . . and we shall never get home if you keep stopping like that.'

'S-sorry,' said Jame, making a fast recovery. 'But why do the citizens put up with it, I mean with madmen lopping heads off in the streets and ruining merchandise? Those two back there might have killed anyone, including me.'

'That,' said the widow, 'was because you were unlucky enough to get caught between them and fool enough to stand there gaping until they nearly ran you down. You seem to have a knack for that sort of situation, by the way, which I hope you will in future try to control. As for the rest of us, the more wars there are, the less we have to pay in taxes. So we take an occasional risk. There are worse systems.'

At that point, they turned yet another corner, and Jame recognized the Way of Tears with Marplet's wall stretching out on her left. Cleppetty, like a horse nearing the stable, picked up speed. Jame was fairly trotting to keep level with her as they approached the corner. Her sodden right boot kept slipping down, however, and she entered the square as she had left it, hopping on one foot, this time tugging the boot off. Cleppetty was already among the brick mounds, several paces ahead of her. The servant girl Jame had seen at the window was just turning away from the fountain, an ewer full of water clasped carefully in her arms. She looked across at the two from the Res aB'tyrr, and the pitcher slipped out of her grasp.

Then time seemed to slow for Jame. She saw the ewer falling, falling, and the girl's face distort with a look of horror. She was staring not at Jame and the widow but above them. Simultaneously, Jame heard a rush of air overhead and saw the shadow of the sling darken across Cleppetty's shoulders. The ewer was falling, falling, and she was springing forward. Bare toes and shod dug frantically at the cobbles. Her hands struck the widow's back, and they were both falling, with Cleppetty propelled ahead, her hands in the air, her basket flying away... and the ground leaped up at Jame's face.

The ewer shattered, cobbles bit into her cheek, and then the sky fell.

Bricks crashed to the earth all about her in a deadly hail, smashing on impact, filling the air with flying shards. One grazed the arm that she had flung up to protect her head, numbing it at the elbow. Far away, a woman began to scream. Then something all too close struck the ground with a resonant boom, making the pavement pressed against her face jump. There was another crash, even nearer, and then nothing.

Jame thought she must have gone deaf. A moment passed, however, and through the savage ringing in her ears she heard dust rattling down, the fountain splashing, and then, nearby, Cleppetty's oh-so-welcome mutter, no louder, no more or less indignant than ever.

She carefully unwrapped her arms from about her head. The right was still partly numb but moved without difficulty. Not so her leg. Looking back, Jame saw the last object that had fallen.

It was a beam, some ten feet long and nearly a foot square at the head. The first end to hit had gouged half a dozen cobbles out of the ground; the second had smashed into a pile of bricks, fragmenting the first seven layers. Her bare foot was wedged between pavement, girder, and the two surviving tiers of bricks.

The widow was kneeling beside her now, but her words were only noises to Jame, for she had just heard something else, high above, which seemed to thicken the blood in her temples and pull her head back as though it were on strings. Niggen, Marplet's ungainly son, was leaning out of the third storey window, where the tackle rope had been secured, snickering.

He stopped abruptly when he saw Jame's face.

The killing madness had come on her too suddenly to be checked or controlled. She was still thinking quite clearly, but only about how to get to that window, to get at that toad-faced boy, and what she would do then with red hands, red nails. But first one had to be mobile. She began to pull at the trapped foot. Something gave in the ankle, and then it was free. She tried to stand. Far back, behind the madness, there was pain, but now only a certain weakness registered, which must be kept in mind lest it betray her. Someone was saying, 'Stop it stop it stop it,' over and over again, and then a hand gripped her hair, jerking her head around.

Eyes stared into her own, inches away, and a voice demanded, very distinctly: 'Do you want to destroy us all?'

Jame blinked. It was Cleppetty, her face dirty and scratched. Over the widow's shoulder, she saw Ghillie and Rothan running towards them across the square.

'All right?' The widow gave her a light shake. '*All right?*'

Jame nodded, speechless.

Cleppetty sighed and let go of her hair. 'Good. Now come along home, child. There's nothing more to do here, and you're hurt.'

The cousins had reached them by this time. Ghillie made a gesture as though to help Jame, but Rothan, for once showing more sensitivity, stopped him. They walked back to the inn with Jame a little apart from the others, limping badly. No one said a word, not even the servants who had appeared in the door of the Skyrrman. Certainly, no one laughed.

Once inside the Res aB'tyrr, however, the silence broke. As Jame slowly pieced her senses back together, she found herself seated in the kitchen with Cleppetty bent over her ankle and

59

everyone else crowded around them, talking furiously.

'Did you see . . . did you hear . . .' someone was babbling in the background. '. . . could have been killed,' said another voice, nearer, angrier. 'I tell you, this time they've gone too . . .' 'Just cuts and a pulled muscle . . . then why . . . I don't know.' Ah, Cleppetty and Tubain, coming rapidly into focus.

'Kencyrs are odd people,' the widow was saying, quite clearly now, 'and this child is odd even for a Kencyr. Just look at those . . .'

Jame closed her hands with a snap and thrust them out of sight behind her. 'Why did you say "Do you want to destroy us all?"'

Everyone in the room spun around and stared at her.

The corpse has sat up on its pyre, she thought grimly. Hurrah. 'Why did you say that?'

'Well?' Cleppetty glared at Tubain. 'Are you going to tell her? She's earned the right to know.'

The innkeeper raised his massive shoulders and let them drop again in a gesture of complete helplessness.

Cleppetty snorted explosively. 'Very well,' she said. 'If you won't, I will. The sum of it is that we're involved in an undeclared trade war with Marplet sen Tenko. It began about a year ago when he started to build the Skyrrman, which he had no right to do in the first place since Tubain here has the tavern charter for the whole district. We went to the Five to protest and were sent to the Skyrr representative, Harr sen Tenko. He wouldn't even see us.'

'Even if he wasn't the most corrupt magistrate in the city,' said Rothan, 'his wife wouldn't let him. We found out afterwards that she's Marplet's sister.'

'It gets better,' said a mournful voice under the sideboard, where Ghillie had gone to earth to avoid being trampled by Cleppetty.

The widow snorted again. 'You may well say so. After that the goading started. It looked odd to us from the start, and so we held back – a damn good thing, too, because pretty soon we noticed that every time Marplet's lot tried to start a fight, there were always one or two guards lurking around just out of sight. So that was it, then: Marplet had bought them; and if we reacted, they would swear before the Five that we had started the trouble in the first place, had in fact begun an undeclared trade war, and so as the instigators would have to pay. Wars are expensive. The fine for an illegal one would ruin us – *will* ruin us, if we fall into Marplet's trap. Now do you understand?'

'I . . . think so,' said Jame. 'But why didn't you tell me this before?'

'He,' said the widow, jabbing a finger at Tubain, 'didn't want you caught up in it. He seems to think that if he ignores it, the whole thing will dry up and blow away. Well, it didn't blow away, it fell down – and the gods know what it will do next. *Now* will you take this business seriously?' she demanded, turning on the innkeeper. '*Now* will you admit that something has to be done?'

Throughout this tirade, Tubain had been leaning against a post of the cellar door with his eyes closed, like a small boy pretending to be asleep in a room full of bogles. Now that they were all staring at him, he opened them, said with great dignity to no one in particular, 'I'd better go check those new hogheads,' and disappeared down the basement steps.

'He won't even *talk* about it!' Cleppetty exclaimed, hoarse with exasperation. 'Mind you, he's a good man – one of the best – but there are some things he simply can't face, and that doesn't make it any easier on the rest of us. If you stay here, child, you'll have to be especially careful because you seem to attract violence and have a potential for it that, I think, will mean disaster for someone sooner or later. That's the trace of far-seer in my family speaking. Take it for what it's worth. But remember, it would be a poor return for Tubain's hospitality to pull the inn down on his head.

'Right. That's enough of that,' she said, clapping her hands. 'The rest of you, scat. We all have work to do and no more time to waste.'

After the others had left, Jame stayed in the kitchen for a while with her foot in a basin of cold water, surrounded by a growing cloud of cinnamon, ginger, and galingale as Cleppetty attacked the ingredients of a goat's heart pie. Then Tanis, who had been out, burst into the room and so embarrassed her with praise that she was forced to flee. Although her ankle throbbed savagely with every step up to the loft, she was almost dizzy with relief. The waiting was over. She would not have to leave the inn after all. For as long as she needed it, she had a home.

And yet, somehow, that wasn't enough.

Sitting on the ledge, looking out over the city, Jame

considered this. A home, yes, but the inn could never be her whole world. She had too many questions that could only be dealt with out there in the labyrinth of Tai-tastigon, questions that no outsider could hope to answer. Only when she knew the city could she hope to know its gods. She must find a way into the heart of this larger society – as she had into that of the Res aB'tyrr – and how better than by joining the city's most powerful guild?

But to become a thief! No proper Kencyr would even consider the idea. But hadn't she been told often enough that she wasn't proper and never would be? She would probably go through life as she had begun it at the keep, with only a precarious toehold in the world of her people. Honour alone – as the Kencyrath understood it – kept her secure, and only a scrollsman or priest could tell her if such a thing as an honest thief was possible. The spirit of the law would undoubtedly be outraged, but if the letter remained intact...

Jame suddeny grinned. It seemed she had already made up her mind. In the morning she would first seek her priest's blessing (ha!) and then the killer-maze that Penari called home. If she survived both, it looked as if the Kencyrath was about to acquire its first official thief.

3

Into the Labyrinth

That night Jame slept deeply and was pleased to find in the
morning that her ankle had all but healed. After she had worked
the last bit of stiffness out of it, she went down to the kitchen to
inform the household of her plans. She expected opposition.
Instead, 'I've seen this coming for a long time,' said the widow as
she cut generous slices of bread and cheese and put them into a
knapsack. 'You're not the sort to relish life in a cage.' Tubain
also made no protest but was clearly upset as he intercepted her
at the front door and furtively slipped three silver coins into her
hand. She thanked him with a quick smile and left the inn.

Marplet sen Tenko was sitting in a window of the Skyrrman
smoking a long-stemmed pipe. His big tiger-tom, Fang,
crouched beside him on the sill. As Jame crossed the square,
both the innkeeper and the cat watched her with almost the
same expression, calculating, self-confident, and faintly amused.
Neither would relish a quick kill, she realised with sudden
insight. This man would toy with the Res aB'tyrr as long as the
game entertained him and not a moment longer. Still, his
mocking gaze teased the flicker of an answering smile from her,
and she saluted him formally with raised fist and open hand, as
one does an acknowledged enemy on the eve of battle. Then she
left the square.

Her goal was the house of her god, where she meant to ask the
priest if she could join the Thieves' Guild without a fatal loss of
honour. The many gods of Tai-tastigon had made her question
the very foundations of the Kencyrath, their belief in the Three-
Faced God; but as she had realised the night before, she could
no more separate herself from all aspects of her culture than
step off the edge of the world. That was clear to her now, far
clearer, unfortunately, than the location of the temple. On
impulse, she set off towards the rising sun.

The streets unrolled before her, twisting back and forth under a bright winter sky. They rarely led due east. Realising that she was not going to get anywhere in a hurry, Jame began to enjoy the challenge of these tangled ways. Some streets were quiet, lined with handsome houses or the back walls of gardens; others bustled with brightly clad crowds, through which peddlers strolled, hawking fermented mares' milk and honeyed locusts, while bands of penitants trotted past chanting their sins in unison. But best of all, in Jame's opinion, was a nest of spiral lanes, each arm of which was devoted to a different sub-chapter of the Glovers' Guild. Here she saw gloves made of leather, linen, and silk dyed all shades of earth and sea, their cuffs sparkling with jewels or heavy with shining threads. It was an elegant pair of black kidskin that she finally bought, however, joyfully spending all the money that Tubain had given her. With gloves on, her differences would not be so apparent. The idea delighted her.

Beyond the glovers' lanes, the buildings began to grow progressively larger and shabbier. This looked promising, she thought, remembering the abandoned structures around the temple; but while there was a growing tinge of darkness in the atmosphere, it was nothing like that which surrounded the dwelling-place of her god. Then she came to the crest of a small hill and found herself looking down over a narrow canal at the charred ruins of the Lower Town.

In a city as thick with gods as Tai-tastigon, only the practice of keeping such beings confined to their sanctuaries made a normal life possible for their mortal fellow citizens. Occasionally, however, one did escape or 'come untempled,' and that was what some people believed had happened to the Lower Town. At any rate, six years before it had become evident that something that had no right to be there was at large in this rich district; but since no one knew its name, there was no way to drive it out. At last those who could had left the area, putting their homes to the torch behind them. Even this last attempt at purification by fire had failed, however, and the destitute had thus inherited what no one else would have.

This, at least, was the story that Ghillie had told Jame. She didn't know how much of it she should believe, but there was undeniably something wrong here, even after all these years. As she passed more and more of the blackened buildings and the hovels that had sprung up like sickly growths in their shadow, she found herself moving warily, her sixth sense prickling, as though she had invaded, in its absence, the den of some unknown and unimaginable – *thing*.

It was a strange place to hear the sound of rushing water. Drawn by it, Jame continued eastward until she came to a low section of the Old Wall at the end of a street. Beyond it, there was a sharp drop down to the floor of the Rim, that relatively new district that circled the city between the old and inner walls. Some ten feet below her, a cataract of water roared out of a vent in the wall, holding a rainbow captive in its spray.

'Is that the River Tone?' she asked an old man who was standing nearby, watching the waterfall.

'Nay. That be the sewer outlet.'

'But the water is perfectly clear!'

''Course it is,' he said, spitting down into it. 'Old Sumph and his priests see to that. We puts it out, they takes it in. Eats shit, does old Sumph – among other things – and loves it. You don't believe me, go over to the inner wall sometime and have a look 'cross at his backside.'

Jame reflected that whenever she asked about the gods of Tai-tastigon, she always seemed to find out more than she wanted to know. But if this old man liked being informative...

'Can you tell me,' she asked him, 'where to find the Temple of the Three-Faced God?'

His shoulders stiffened. When he turned, she fell back a step, thinking from his expression that he meant to strike her. Instead, he spat on the ground at her feet and hastily shambled away.

What an odd reaction, she thought, watching him go. Some people, apparently, liked her god even less than she did. Nor was the old man unique. When Jame put her question to other residents of the Lower Town, most were too frightened to say anything, and some became violent. All she found as the day slid down into dusk were hostile looks, incredible squalor, and more sickly or deformed children than seemed possible. Quite a number of these urchins took to following her until, by the end of the day, she found herself at the head of a ragged, hobbling parade, unsure if she should walk slower so as not to tire them or run away from the lot.

However, the problem disappeared along with the children as the sun dipped behind the Ebonbane. Everyone was seeking shelter, Jame realised, and all around her the few feeble lights were flickering out. Clearly, this was not a place to be out in the streets after dark.

Her wandering had by now brought her to the Tone, running swiftly in its deep bed, and hearing faint music ahead, she set off along its left bank in the growing gloom.

Across the river stood rows of shining houses similar to those that once had filled the Lower Town. Beyond them, farther upriver, were the islet estates of the very rich, cradled between the arms of the Tone, separated by canals.

Music came from some of these gleaming isles, but not the boisterous strains that had first reached Jame in the darkness of the Lower Town. These she continued to follow as the two branches of the river drew closer together until the farther one disappeared behind the flank of a large, narrow island ringed with a marble wall in the likeness of a ship's side. Ahead, looming against the Ebonbane, was a huge white structure with mastlike spires from which streamed banners of scarlet and gold. The grounds around it swarmed with people costumed and plain, rich and shabby, all dancing together in the mad grip of carnival, drunkenly singing the praises of the Sirdan Theocandi and the great, the wonder thieves of Tai-tastigon.

Jame walked on along the far bank, listening, looking, catching delight like a heady perfume borne on the air. It was a long island. At its point the walls rose in a jutting prow set with the figurehead of a woman triumphantly brandishing a severed head in either hand. Their stone beards curled down her arms and the swift waters of the Tone creamed about her bare feet as though the island were surging onward into the heart of the city.

A block beyond that Jame crossed a bridge and turned back. She had gone down the other side of the island almost as far as the stern when out of the corner of her eye she saw something pale falling. There was a loud splash below, closely followed by another, as a young man on the opposite bank dove into the river, fully clothed. She saw him surface, his arm wrapped around something, and begin to struggle across the current towards her side. The racing water would have borne him away if a man on the quay below had not thrown out a line and several others run down the steps to help pull him in.

'Is it another one, Tob?' a latecomer called as he darted past her.

None of the straining figures below had time to answer: they were hauling first the pale object and then the young man up onto the dock. Jame saw that the former was the naked body of a boy. His white skin was oddly marked as though someone had drawn the diamonds of a board game on it and blackened every other one. Then she saw that the dark areas were not skin at all but rather the lack of it.

'Aye,' said a bitter voice from the midst of the group bending over it. 'Another one.' And they all looked up at the Sirdan's palace.

Upstream, the shadowy form of a man stood at the railing of a balcony suspended over the water. He was looking down at them.

The swimmer stood, white shirt plastered to his ribs, and stared back. For a moment the tableau held. Then one of the men coughed and began to struggle out of his coat. They carried the draped corpse up the steps and away, leaving the young man to glare upwards a moment longer before he turned to follow them. He passed Jame without noticing her, blinded with anger. She saw him cross one of the catwalks back to the island, then turned away and walked on.

The music died away behind her, and the lights grew dim. A chill wind was blowing off the mountains, pushing at her back. She suddenly felt very cold and tired.

The rest of the night was spent in following first the Tone and then the Old Wall away from slums and mansions alike and in several hours of sleep snatched on someone's second storey balcony.

Hovering near the wall a few feet from where Jame had taken shelter was one of the strange light spheres, which she had first seen in the puzzle-box district. She woke in the grey dawn at the sound of a voice and saw the globe darken. Below, a black-robed man paused under the next light and extinguished it too by murmuring, 'Blessed-Ardwyn-day-has-come' in a bored monotone. He disappeared into the morning mist, banishing the puffs of light as he went.

Jame breakfasted on the cheese and bread that Cleppetty had provided, then swung down to the street.

She had decided not to return to the Lower Town. Even though the violent reactions of the people there had convinced her that the temple of her god lay somewhere nearby, she no longer trusted herself to find it blindly. Better to retrace the wanderings of that first night... if she could. Consequently,

Jame now followed the Old Wall northward to the Sun Gate. From there, a two-hour's walk along the curving streets of the Rim District brought her to the Warrior Gate, now standing firmly shut against the Haunted Lands, the Feast of Dead Gods being long past.

Like all Kencyrs, Jame had received extensive memory training as a child. She knew the lengthy epics of her people by heart and could recite genealogies of leaders and important people stretching back thousands of years. This, however, did not help her greatly with visual images. It was midafternoon before she found the little square with the fountain and only recognised it because of the network of deep cracks that ran through it. Jame followed these westward until they ended suddenly before a familiar gate.

Now she had a choice. Before her lay the puzzle-box, more properly known as the Temple District, which she had previously entered and left by the same route. In that respect, it was a dead-end. Still, she felt drawn by it and curious to know if her earlier impression had been correct. Perhaps she had overreacted. Perhaps these so-called gods were not the threat that she had at first believed. At any rate, it now occurred to her that, to the best of her knowledge, none of the people she had questioned so far about her own god had been priests. That was excuse enough. Bracing herself, she stepped through the gate into the Temple District.

Moments later as Jame walked through cross-currents of incense, hearing the drone of chants on all sides and seeing the tangle of buildings that stretched out of sight at each crossroad, she reluctantly faced the truth. Although the feverish beat of power had now sunk to a steady pulse, it was still undeniably there. The threat was real after all. Damn.

The sound of loud voices nearby broke in on her thoughts. On the steps of a small temple, a round little man in hieratic garb was arguing vehemently with a plump old woman.

'What do you mean, "No"?' he was saying angrily. 'What sort of answer is that?'

'An honest one,' the woman retorted, brandishing a fistful of delicate bat bones inlaid with silver under his nose. 'Now see here: I don't read these things for the fun of it. You ask me "Will all be well"; the bones tell me that all won't. There the message ends. But as a far-seer I can tell you this much more: a deadly force is all too near you even now and will come nearer still. You will provoke it; and what it begins, you will finish. There, priest. You wanted your fortune told. Now I wish you the joy of it.' With that, she turned and flounced down the steps.

The indignation went out of her gait before she reached the bottom, however, and Jame suddenly found herself looking down into a pair of worried eyes. 'Foolish as he is sometimes, he's not a bad man,' the old woman said to her in an undertone. 'Spare him if you can.' Then she scurried away.

Jame stared at her for a moment in amazement, then shrugged. Far-seers had no great reputation for sanity. On impulse, remembering her errand, she went up the steps.

'Excuse me, sir,' she said to the priest, who had turned back to his sanctuary and already had one step over the threshold. 'Can you tell me where to find the temple of the Three-Faced God?'

The little man spun about. Jame had just time to note the desperate unhappiness in his face before he shrieked, 'Heretic!' and struck out wildly at her. As she swayed to avoid the blow, her half-healed ankle twinged in warning. Without thinking, she followed the path of least resistance, which happened to be over the guard rail, down five feet, and over backwards into a puddle. A burst of laughter greeted this performance and one of the men who had stopped to listen to the previous altercation shouted, 'Well done, Loogan!' after the priest, who had already disappeared. 'All hail Gorgo the Lugubrious God!'

'Loogan, huh?' said Jame under her breath as she got to her feet, flushed with anger. Then she limped back the way she had come, ignoring the jeering spectators.

Her temper had cooled somewhat by the time she reached Judgment Square, that vast open area with the Mercy Seat at its centre. On this visit, Jame found it full of people. As she threaded her way through the crowd, fending off peddlers, she marvelled at how different everything was from the first time she had seen this place. Then, as she approached the Mercy Seat, she saw that it too was no longer empty. At first Jame thought that the figure lolling on it was an effigy of some sort, then that it was a sleeping man clad in a tight black garment which, oddly, seemed to be moving. It wasn't until she was quite close that she saw the darkness was not cloth at all but dried blood and flies. The man's skin, still attached at the neck, hung over the back of the Seat like a strangely shaped cloak. Under the dangling right hand, someone had scrawled in chalk:

Steal a peach, steal a plum,
See to what your carcass comes.

Greatly sobered but undeterred, Jame continued on. After all, that would never happen to her; although it gave her a jolt to think that the thief in the stone chair had probably once said as much to himself.

On the far side of the square, she found what looked like the right street and soon confirmed this by coming to the crowned crossroads. Not far beyond that was the River Tone and the bridge by which she had crossed it. On the opposite side her troubles began again, for this was the area through which she had raced so blindly and one street was no different from any other to her. Dusk was falling too, bringing the prospect of another cheerless night in the open. Discouraged and footsore, she sat down on the edge of a small fountain in a dirty little square to eat the last of her food. Without provisions or money she would soon have to start home, perhaps to mount another expedition later – although it was clear to her now that she might spend the rest of her life bumbling around these streets without coming any closer to her goal. Perhaps it was time to admit that the labyrinth had defeated her and her plans.

To the west, the sun had slipped behind the Ebonbane, kindling veins of fire in its snow-locked passes. Jame was gazing up at the mountain peaks dejectedly when she suddenly remembered the Res aB'tyrr's loft with its fine view of the city. That was what she needed now: height. She jumped up and eagerly scanned the surrounding roof lines. There were several tall buildings visible above the houses bordering the square, but one soared above the rest, its upper storeys still flooded with light above the growing sea of shadows. That was the one.

Moments later, Jame stared up at its crumbling façade. The door was bricked shut. She swung herself up onto the portico roof and pulled the rotting boards away from a second storey window. Inside, light filtered through cracks and down the stairwell revealing a wilderness of dust and decay. She went up the steps quickly but with care, for many of them were rotten, until a collapsed flight some seven storeys up blocked her way. From there, she went out a window and up the side of the building for the last twenty feet, gouging fingerholds through the sour plaster to the lath.

When her hand finally closed on the eave trough, she pulled

herself onto the roof. She was climbing up the steep slope, eyes fixed on the tiles before her for rotten spots, when a foot suddenly appeared almost under her nose. Something gave her shoulder a strong push, and she found herself slithering down the incline, nails scrabbling for a grip. Then her foot came up against the gutter and the descent stopped. Heart hammering, she looked up. A young man clad all in white was smoothly crab-stepping down the roof towards her. Two other men watched from the ridge.

'If you do that again,' she heard herself say in a remarkably conversational tone, 'I shall fall off.'

'That's the idea,' said the descending man with an angelic smile, and he reached out towards her again.

Jame seized his wrist and pulled. Over-balanced, he pitched forward past her into space. She released her first hold and grabbed for his jacket as he shot past. They both went over the ledge. Jame's free hand caught the gutter and then nearly lost it again as the other's suddenly arrested weight wrenched at her muscles. She hadn't come up here to kill or be killed, Jame thought savagely, wondering which shoulder would dislocate first, and damned if she would let either happen through some stupid accident – although from the way her companion was dangling, it wouldn't surprise her if she had inadvertently hanged him with his own collar.

Two heads appeared above, silhouetted against the sky.

'Well?' she snapped.

A minute later all four of them were sitting on the roof, feet braced against the gutter, panting. The two rescuers seemed the most shaken of the lot, and Jame's erstwhile assailant the least. The latter was in fact still staring down into the void like a man entranced.

'That's the closet I've ever come to going over,' he said at last in an awed voice. 'I almost wish you'd let me fall.'

'I suppose we could try again,' said Jame, anger giving way to curiosity. 'Do you often go around pushing people off roofs?'

'Oh, all the time. Only citizens of the Cloud Kingdom are welcome up here and, of course, their guests. Incredible . . . just incredible . . .' He leaned forward, causing Jame and the man on his other side to grab his flowing sleeves simultaneously. 'I've seen a hundred, a thousand fall, and each time it seems to take longer. Seconds, minutes, hours . . . twisting, turning, dancing in the air . . . marvellous!'

71

'Messy too, I should think, when they hit the ground.'

'Oh, I never watch that long.' He sat back and looked at her with wide admiring eyes. 'No one has ever come so close to sending me over before. You must be an unusual person. You're sure you won't let me push you off? Well, in that case no one else shall have the pleasure. Come to court some day soon and I shall have Uncle grant you the freedom of the skies.'

With that, he bowed to her, rose, and seemed to float up the incline. All three men had just disappeared over the ridge when Jame remembered her mission. Eagerly she examined the patterns of the city below, but nowhere in the deepening shadows was there a sign of that desolate circle, those cold white walls.

'Hey!' she called after the trio, and the fair head popped back into sight over the ridge, looking disembodied.

'Yes?' it said, hopefully.

'I'm looking for the temple of the Three-Faced God. Do you know where it is?'

'Oh.' Disappointment washed over the features. 'Sparrow will show you.' And it vanished again.

'*Hey!* When I come to court, who shall I say invited me?'

'Why, Prince Dandello, of course,' the voice drifted back. 'The Cloud King's nephew.'

'No, I don't know why the groundlings won't discuss your god or, for that matter, the priest Ishtier,' said Sparrow, waiting on the crest of a gambrel roof for Jame to scramble up to him. 'They're a fat-headed lot from what I've seen; though mind, I've never had much to do with them. Born in the clouds, I was, and here I'll die – barring accidents – without ever touching the ground.'

Without warning, the wiry little Cloudie launched himself down the far side of the roof towards a projecting cornice, bounced off the top of it, and easily cleared the eight-foot gap across to the opposite roof. Steeling herself, Jame followed him. They had come quite a distance across the labyrinth by now with comparative ease. Obviously, this was the right way to travel for anyone with good nerves, although not even these saved Jame from a quick spasm of fear as the street flashed past beneath her, some forty feet below.

'Two things, though,' said Sparrow as she caught up with him several houses later. 'They do tend to treat anything they don't like as if it doesn't exist, and I think the Townies blame your god for whatever it was – no, *is*, that's happening to them. We Cloudies haven't been overjoyed either, what with the way these roofs have disintegrated. You'd never believe it, but this was a flourishing neighbourhood six years ago. Now watch your step. We're getting close.'

The warning was necessary. They had reached the edge of the temple's greatest influence, as the condition underfoot clearly showed. Jame went first now, picking her way carefully, hearing plaster rattled down inside as boards groaned under her weight. Then there the temple was, tall, stark, ghost-pale under the new moon. The power that flowed continually out of it buffetted her, but at the same time she felt the attraction of that monolithic structure, the sure, arrogant claim of the force that dwelt within its walls on her, body and soul, as a Kencyr. For a moment, Jame hesitated. Then, 'Damnation,' she said and, with a gesture as foolhardy as it was defiant, threw down all her mental shields. The power claimed her instantly. She forgot her guide, her resentment, everything as it drew her down from the rooftop, across the graveyard of dust, and into the dark doorway.

The moment Jame crossed the threshold, the maelstrom seized her. It seemed to her dazed mind that two currents flowed through the twisting corridors, the greater bound outward, the lesser on either side of it whirling inward along the walls towards the temple's heart. She was spun forward, whipped around faster and faster until her shoulder crashed into a door and it gave way, spilling her sideways onto a tessellated floor.

Her senses ringing in the sudden lull, she stared numbly at the patterns beneath her hand. They spiralled in towards the centre of the chamber. Her eyes followed their curve to the foot of the statue there on its raised dais, then up that towering, black granite form to the three faces of her god. The aspect of Regonereth, That-Which-Destroys, was turned towards her, its features obscured with marble carved veil-thin. Lower down, one hand reached out and upward through a fissure in the masonry as though beckoning. Each long, scythe-curved finger was tipped in ivory, honed and gleaming.

Ishtier, Highborn priest of the Kencyrath, stood in the shadow of his god, watching her with hooded eyes. His nearly fleshless lips were raised in a faint smile, and tongues of power from the outer corridors licked eagerly past her, spiralling into the centre. She got quickly to her feet.

'Who are you?' It was a thin, dry voice, not exactly rusty but like the hinges of a door infrequently opened.

'Jame of the Three People.'

'That is but half a name. Tell me the rest.'

'With respect, my lord, it does not concern you.' She did not realise until she saw his slight smile deepen that he had asked and she replied in High Kens. More power swirled into the room, tugging at her mind. It was getting harder to think.

'Very well . . . for now,' the priest said, 'Why have you come?'

Jame tried to answer, struggling with the unaccustomed clumsiness of mind that prevented her from shielding herself against this man. Much more of this and not even her namelessness would protect her.

'I-I want to join the Thieves' Guild,' she said, hating herself for the stammer.

'You, a Kencyr, wish to steal? You would sell your honour so cheaply?'

'I would sell nothing!'

'Then you are a fool,' said the priest coldly. 'Nothing comes without a price . . . not even this conversation.'

Jame caught her breath as power whipped past her face. A second bolt of energy clipped her shoulder, numbing it and spinning her around. Two more quick blows took her off-balance again. Her jacket had begun to smoulder. She ripped it off, twisting desperately, futilely, to avoid the invisible assault. Ishtier watched, the thin smile again on his lips.

'Dance, fool, dance,' he said softly.

Sudden anger made Jame reckless. Defiantly, she raised her clenched fists in challenge, not to the priest but to the statue towering above him. 'Lord, a judgement!' she cried to the three faces of her god.

Ishtier drew himself up with a hiss of outrage. Then, abruptly, his expression changed. *'Steal not from your own kind,'* said the god-voice through his unwilling lips. *'Do with others what you will, so that it be done with honour, until in your thoughtlessness you destroy them.'* The voice ceased. Wiping spittle from his face with a shaking hand, Ishtier said hoarsely, 'There, brat. You have the answer you sought. Now get out.'

Jame bowed and went, not trusting herself to speak. She had her answer indeed, ambiguous in part as it was. Now it was time to go home.

The moon rose over her shoulder as she walked westward, thinking over the day's events. Twice within the last few hours a priest had humiliated her. She had never liked the breed anyway, not since she had realised as a child that it was because of a priest that Anar had gone mad. It had taken a continual effort to protect the keep from the deadly influence of the Haunted Lands. Before Jame's time, this had been the responsibility of the scrollsman's older brother, a priest of great power and knowledge; but one night this man had fled with a female companion, leaving his inexperienced kinsman to assume the terrible burden alone. By the time Anar had become the twins' tutor, his mind had already begun to crumble under the strain. Soon he was more like a child himself, except that he still kept their home safe and continued to do so until sword's edge and arrow's point had destroyed everything for which he had sacrificed so much.

Indeed, it was a terrible thing to wield the power of a Kencyr priest, to stand between the people and their god. The best, like Anar, were often destroyed by it, while others became so warped in time that allowances had to be made for them, even with the rigid structure of the Kencyrath.

Jame, however, forgave nothing, especially not now, now that she had met Ishtier. Old grief and fresh resentment kept her simmering all that long walk home until, in the early hours of the morning, she turned onto the Way of Tears beside Marplet sen Tenko's inn.

There was a burst of raucous laughter from the courtyard of the Skyrrman as she approached its gate, and a slim figure darted out into the street ahead of her, closely pursued. Cloth ripped as hunter and hunted converged. The slighter of the two reeled into the opposite wall, clutching the remains of her bodice over small white breasts. Jame saw that it was the black-haired servant girl. Niggen was standing in the middle of the road with the torn fabric in his hand, giggling.

Before the boy even realised that she was there, Jame had spun him around. The heel of her palm caught him under the chin with a blow that snapped his head back and practically lifted him off his feet. A moment later, it would have been hard to say who was more startled – the men at the gate, Niggen on the ground spitting teeth, or Jame herself, who had acted purely on instinct.

'If you touch that girl again,' she said to Marplet's son, 'I shall gladly knock out whatever teeth you have left.'

Not until she was crossing the square towards the Res aB'tyrr and heard someone shouting for a guard behind her did she realise what she had done. Marplet had his excuse at last.

'I'm sorry,' she said, pulling her cap off in contrition to the astonished Ghillie who met her at the door. Then she turned to face the small group approaching her from the Skyrrman.

Marplet was in the lead, with two burly guards behind him, and Niggen trotting eagerly at his side. The innkeeper stopped short, however, when he saw Jame's face framed with her mane of black hair. For the first and last time, she saw him pale with anger as he turned on his awkward, bewildered son.

'Do you mean to say,' he demanded, pointing at her, 'that you were beaten by that . . . that *girl?* You spineless booby!' Without another word he whirled and stalked back to the Skyrrman.

The guards looked at Jame, at each other, then shrugged simultaneously and walked away.

'Something told me you were home,' said Cleppetty wryly behind Jame. 'Come and have some supper.'

By then, it was very late. The widow had apparently been in bed before the disturbance but showed no sign of returning to it even when Jame had finished her bowl of warmed-over stew.

'Can't sleep yet,' she said in answer to Jame's question. 'I'm waiting for something.'

'What?'

'With luck, you'll never know.'

But Cleppetty had hardly finished speaking when a shriek brought both women to their feet. It came from across the square. Jame was halfway out the front door when the widow grabbed her arm and hung on grimly.

'Let me go!' she cried, trying to dislodge the older woman without hurting her. 'I said I'd break that slime-ball's teeth if he hurt that girl again, and so help me God I will!'

'It isn't Niggen,' said the widow. 'Did you seriously think that Marplet would accept an humiliation like that without revenging himself on someone? Wait.'

They stood listening to the cries until the door of the Skyrrman suddenly opened and a figure was thrown out. Even then Cleppetty wouldn't let Jame move until it had staggered halfway across the square towards them. Then they both ran out and helped the sobbing, half-naked girl into the kitchen where the widow brought out a jar of ointment and began to dress the whip cuts on her back. Fortunately, the girl was more frightened than hurt, but there was still a great deal of blood, wailing, and general mess before Tubain arrived in his nightshirt to survey the damage.

'Tuby,' said the widow, 'we will have to keep her.'

From the moment the innkeeper had entered the room, he had been surreptitiously trying to leave it again. At Cleppetty's words, however, he suddenly stopped fidgeting and looked squarely at the weeping girl for the first time.

'Of course, we will,' he said.

Jame wondered if she herself had been adopted in a similar fashion.

The bandaging done, Ghillie and Jame helped the newest member of the household up to Taniscent's room. They had just tucked her in and quietly retreated to the gallery when the dancer herself slipped into the courtyard below through the side gate. Ghillie took one look at her and fled. Clearly, something had upset Taniscent badly, and Jame, meeting her at the head of the stair, immediately learned what it was. After weeks of cooling ardour, Bortis had finally called her an old hag and gone off with a fifteen-year-old from the next district.

Jame nearly said 'good riddance.' Instead, respecting Tanis's distress, she concentrated on putting her friend to bed. This proved difficult. She was just beginning to think that she would have to sit on the dancer until she settled down when the widow's voice rose from the courtyard in an exasperated shout:

'Now listen to me, all of you: Shut up and go to sleep!'

'Yes, Cleppetty,' six voices meekly chorused from all over the darkened inn.

Taniscent sighed and closed her eyes. With kohl running down in streaks to puddle beside her nose, she looked, if not haglike, at least thoroughly grotesque, and closer to forty years old than twenty-four.

Jame took a blanket and lay down on the gallery floor. It was hard to believe that the long day was over at last. She had a premonition that she had started something – several things – during the course of it that might have alarming consequences later, but was too tired to sort them out now. Besides, here was Boo, lumbering out of the shadows purring loudly. Knowing that if she didn't humour him the cat would probably sit on her face, she opened the blanket and let him curl up inside it against her. Dawn was just beginning to touch the eastern sky as she fell asleep.

4

The Heart of the Maze

'Penari!'

The echo cracked back from the stone walls of the entrance way, unsoftened by any furniture or trappings.

'Where are you? It's me, Jame... the Talisman!'

Something rustled in a far corner, disturbing loose debris with scurrying claws. There was no other response.

'Damn,' said Jame.

She was standing just inside Penari's home, that huge, circular edifice known as the Maze. It had been easy enough to locate from the rooftops, but now that she was here it was obvious that her problems had just begun. Many thieves before her had matched their wits against this intricate building, searching for its heart; only a handful had ever been seen again. That was what she must risk now if the old thief would not even come out to greet an invited guest. With a sigh, she resigned herself to the inevitable.

Three doors opened off the entry hall. Jame tied the end of a large spool of thread to the post of one, kindled the torch she had brought with her, and crossed the threshold. Inside, the confusion of small rooms and narrow passages began at once, choking off all outside light and sound within a few turnings. Still and close as the ways of a tomb it was, and very like being buried in one. Leaping torchlight held back the darkness, but between its flickers the walls themselves seemed to close in.

Surprisingly, there were several small streams running through the building and a number of stairways going up but none leading down. Jame wandered about the ground floor, shouting at intervals but still getting no response. Then she began to climb. The levels became less complex the higher she got, although there was still no way to tell exactly where she was at any given moment. Penari's hidden apartments could be anywhere. By the time she reached the fifth and final level, her thread, voice and patience were all beginning to run out. She had just decided to give up when the floor underfoot suddenly gave way.

She fell, the thread snapping, the torch plummetting down ahead like a falling star. Then it vanished. A moment later, the water slammed into her.

Black, choking, not alone ... her hand found the edge of the pool, and she pulled herself out in a near panic, barking her shins on the rim without even noticing it. Behind her, something surfaced with a liquid chuckle and dived again.

Jame crouched in the dark, shivering, listening. What had she just escaped? Where was it now? If only the pool would confine it. A rustle, a rasp of scales on stone ... it was coming after her.

She sprang up and backed away. A wall brought her up short. Eyes were no use in this almost tangible darkness, but her ears caught the sound of something very large, very heavy, fumbling at the pool's rim, slowly drawing its immense bulk out of the water. The close air filled with a thousand small noises, multiplying as the walls gave back their echo. With a choked cry she whirled and leapt. Her fingers caught at the rough stone blocks and she scrambled blindly upward until one hand closed on a wooden beam. She was hanging there in midair when a dazzling light seemed to explode in the room.

'Well!' said a voice. 'No one's ever done *that* before.'

As her vision cleared, Jame saw Penari standing below with a torch in his hand. Behind him, light gleamed on a huge mound of flesh, white, convoluted, and quivering. Pink, lidless eyes stared back at her over his shoulder.

'Too bad it's you, boy,' the old man said, 'Monster hasn't been fed so far this month.'

'From what I can see, Monster hasn't any teeth.'

'Being a moon python, he doesn't need 'em,' said Penari with more loyalty than truth. 'Twenty years ago he had a fine set.'

'I'm sorry I'm late,' said Jame, rather incoherently. 'I was ill. Uh ... if I come down, will I get eaten?'

'After scaring the poor bugger half to death? He'd be more likely to throw up on you ... or on me,' he added, glancing up mistrustfully at the swaying head.

Somewhat reassured, Jame dropped to the floor. Leaving the giant snake to recover himself, Penari led the way through a bewildering series of corridors to the heart of the Maze. To

Jame's surprise, this one large room occupied the whole core of the building, extending from the second level basement up to the ceiling of the fifth floor. Spiral stairways led from the bottom, where they stood, to screened alcoves and shelves of books and scrolls that extended up out of sight into the shadows. A huge chandelier full of guttering candles provided the chamber with its only light. Wax from it dropped steadily on the red and gold patterns of the carpet and on a massive table laden with manuscripts. Everywhere there were rich things dimly seen and covered with dust.

Penari showed her the various entrances to the central room and took her out into the Maze to demonstrate how one reached the outside world from each. He apparently expected her to remember every unmarked turn after one sight of it. When he had trotted her from cellar to attic and back, the old thief fished a small greasy coin out of his robe and gave it to her saying, 'Right. Now go and buy a pig for Monster's dinner.'

For the next few days, Jame went to the Maze early each morning, after a night of helping at the inn, and for the next six or seven hours ran errands for Penari. She began to wonder if she had misunderstood the nature of the job that the old man had offered her. Then, on the fifth afternoon, Penari snatched up his staff and went with her when she left the Maze. They turned north at the gate, east at the Tone, and soon were in sight of the Sirdan's Palace, already grey in the dusk, rising up behind its exultant figurehead.

The outer courtyard was again full of lights. This time, however, they shone on the nightly thieves' bazaar, where the spoils of the day were being sold or bartered to the sound of ferocious haggling. Jame felt many eyes on her as she followed Penari through the crowd. Word must have gone before them, for as they entered the Guild Hall, all faces turned in their direction and many voices stilled. The Guild secretary was at his post beside the throne dais with a small group of people waiting to see him. Penari cut in at the head of the line, drawing Jame after him.

'This is the Talisman,' he announced, presenting her. 'I want to enroll him as my apprentice.'

The secretary peered at Jame, his face an odd mixture of bewilderment and suspicion. 'Master Penari, this is not –'

'A Kencyr? Of course it is. You think I'd trust my secrets to any of this rabble? Go on, Master Secretary, record it. Under

Guild law, no one can dictate my choice, or interfere with it once made – as much as some might wish to.'

The triumph in his voice was unmistakable, and so was his determination. The secretary shrugged and wrote in the huge book on the table before him.

'Talisman,' he said to Jame, 'do you swear to obey the laws of the Thieves' Guild of Tai-tastigon, to uphold its institutions, to conduct yourself to its credit and to that of your master?'

'I so swear.'

'Very well. Bare a shoulder – uh – "boy".'

One last chance, Jame thought. If this fails, I give up. And she stripped off both tunic and shirt.

The secretary looked stunned. Penari, however, after a moment's impatient wait, picked up the brand – red with ink, fortunately, not heat – and pressed it against her skin, muttering something about dithering officials.

That was it, then. He's too blind and I'm too flat, she thought despairingly, and put her clothes back on.

The episode was apparently over as far as Penari was concerned, for he was already halfway down the hall when she turned to follow him. A hand on her arm stopped her. The nails of the index and middle fingers were filed to sharp points. A man with almost luminous grey eyes set in a dark face was looking down at her. 'Someone wants to see you,' he said softly. The grip on her arm tightened, meaning to hurt, succeeding. 'Now.'

'Go along, Talisman,' her new master called back from the doorway. 'Give my regards to Theocandi!' And he disappeared, fairly gurgling with some secret mirth.

The dark man released Jame's arm and signalled her to proceed him. They went through a door behind the secretary's desk and beyond that into a narrow, winding passage. It was rather like being back in the Maze except that here the halls were richly appointed and she was being followed by this... person, whose gaze, sliding insolently over her body from behind, made her feel acutely self-conscious. Then the corridor opened into a small, tapestry-hung audience chamber. The Sirdan Theocandi stood on the far side of it, waiting. Even without Penari's parting words and the heavy chain of office that this sharp-featured old man wore, Jame would have known him from the authority – one might even say the arrogance – of his stance. She saluted him warily with crossed wrists held low, but not the open hands of friendship.

'So,' he said in a flat, cold voice, not bothering to acknowledge the greeting. 'Penari has at last taken an apprentice. Let us hope he has chosen wisely, for himself *and* for the Guild.'

'I hope to serve him well, m'lord,' Jame said, wondering if she had been summoned merely for a lecture. Somehow, she didn't think so.

'There are many ways in which to serve. Some are more advantageous than others.'

Ah-ha! 'And what might those be, m'lord?'

'A clever person can find them out.' Confidence now ran in a strong current beneath the icy surface of his voice. Forty years of power and easy victories showed in his disdainful assurance that he could buy whatever, or whomever, he wanted. 'There are secrets . . .' he began, but at that moment the drapes to one side parted and a boy came quickly into the room, holding a scroll.

'Grandfather, look at this,' the newcomer said eagerly.

For an instant, Jame wondered why the boy's pale features were so familiar. Then she remembered: that was the frightened face she had seen in the alley the night Penari had almost died. The boy felt her eyes on him. He turned, saw her, and promptly lost what little colour he had.

The Sirdan, however, was too angry to notice this interchange. The boy's intrusion had set him badly off stride for reasons that Jame could not even guess. 'We will continue this discussion later,' he said curtly to her, still glaring at his grandson. 'Now go.'

'Very well, m'lord. Oh, by the way,' she added, turning at the door. 'My master sends his regards.' She sensed his wrathful eyes on her back as long as she was in sight.

Walking out through the hall, Jame considered the growing complexity of her situation. It was obvious now why Penari had chosen her, a Kencyr, to be his apprentice. After decades of pressure to make him reveal his secrets, he had taken revenge on them all by choosing to confide not only in an outsider but in one whose very race was to him a guarantee of her incorruptibility. Just now he had thrown her to Theocandi in hopes that the Sirdan would break his teeth on her. That he had not was only the first warning that little from now on was apt to be as simple as her new master seemed to think. As a further token of this, what in all the names of God was she to make of

Theocandi's grandson, that pleasant-faced boy who had stood by watching while two pug-nasties had tried to kill an old man?

She was descending to the courtyard when something warned her that she was being followed. The dark man came down the steps towards her, flanked by three others as richly clothed as he, in shades as sober.

'There's a meeting at the Three Legg'd Dog in an hour,' he said to her as he passed. 'Be there.'

He and his companions were several steps below Jame when she said, quietly, 'No.'

Those unnervingly bright eyes turned back to her, lighting up even more with incredulous, pleased surprise.

'What did you say?'

'I said, "No".' Automatically, she noted the position and postures of all four, the flash of a knife hilt sheathed in one man's boot, another in his comrade's belt, and took an unobtrusive step back to the stairwell. 'I belong to the Guild now and as such owe loyalty to it and to my master,' she said. 'No one said anything about jumping when *you* whistle.'

'Quite right, too,' said a new voice from the foot of the steps. A young man clad in royal blue stood there watching them. 'No one owes Bane anything he can't exact by force,' he said, still speaking to Jame but watching the four. Two others had come out of the crowd to stand behind him. Am I being defended? Jame wondered, unexpectedly amused, but then decided that she was more the excuse than the cause for this confrontation. The role didn't appeal to her.

'Carry on, gentlemen,' she said to the gathering at large and walked past the lot of them into the bustle of the market before anyone had a chance to react.

The young man in blue caught up with her several blocks later, on the south bank of the Tone.

'That was rather remarkable,' he said, falling into step beside her. 'It isn't often that anyone stands up to Bane, especially without support. You must either be extremely brave or phenomenally stupid.'

'Mostly the latter, I think, in conjunction with being very Kencyr.'

'Really? Someone told me that, but I didn't believe it. Is it true that you people don't come from Rathillien at all, and that you're able to touch minds with animals, and that you can carry each other's souls?'

'More or less,' said Jame, smiling at his sudden eagerness. 'Also, some of us can't endure sunlight – although I can; and most of us are left-handed – although I'm not. By the way, you may not remember it, but I think we've met before. About a week ago, weren't you the one who dived into the river after that boy?'

The light went out of his face.

'I thought so. Who was he?'

'No one knows,' he said with growing bitterness. 'So many young boys come in from the provinces looking for someone to sponsor them in the Guild. Bane can pick and choose. To be fair, I don't think the Sirdan approves, but he has very little control over his so-called pupil. Theocandi's general edict has protected your master so far, mostly because Penari has never much interested Bane. You, however, apparently do – and that can be very dangerous.'

'Wait a minute. Go back a bit. Why should the Sirdan protect Penari? I got the impression that they don't like each other.'

'Nor do they, but Theocandi has to have some guarantee that no one will beat the old boy's secrets out of him' – they'd kill him first, thought Jame – 'and besides, differences notwithstanding, brothers have to stick together, the way Mendy and I do.'

'Now let me get this straight; Penari is Theocandi's brother...'

'Older.'

'And you're Men-dalis's?'

'Younger. Right. The name is Dallen, incidentally – Dally to you.' For the first time since the mention of the flayed boy, he smiled. His face was surprisingly youthful. 'You really don't know much about current events, do you? I wonder if you have any idea what kind of a situation you've walked into.'

'If I did, I probably wouldn't be here. And speaking of walking, are we bound someplace in particular or are you just looking for a nice stretch of river to pitch me into?'

He laughed. 'I don't think I could if I wanted to. No, I just thought it would be a good opportunity to introduce you to some of the other 'prentices at the Moon in Splendor down the way. It's as close to neutral ground as we have left in Tai-tastigon; and since your master hasn't taken a side yet, you probably won't want to at first either.'

'Not until you've had a chance to recruit me for your brother, you mean.'

'But of course,' he said, with an ingenuous smile.

The Moon was a large, brightly lit inn facing the Tone and River Street. Inside, the noise was deafening. Wall to wall, the great hall seemed to be cobbled with the heads of apprentices, with a few older journeymen thrown in and one young master holding court in a far corner. Jame's companion was greeted with a roar of welcome and not a few eyes turned towards her, openly or covertly. She had the sense of being sized up from all directions and found reassuringly lacking. Room was made for them at a centre table.

'I don't see any women here,' she said in an undertone to Dally, taking an offered seat.

'Very few have been permitted into the Guild since Theocandi came to power. He doesn't think much of female thieves, which is idiotic considering the great ones we've had in the past. At any rate, no one can accuse you of getting in under false pretences.'

'I should hope not, but if anyone says anything about having made a clean breast of it, there's going to be bloodshed.'

At that moment, a wizened monkey of a boy scrambled up onto the tabletop, upsetting tankards right and left, and rose unsteadily to his feet. Those whose ale hadn't been spilt raised a derisive cheer and some began to clap.

'No, no, no!' the boy screeched, waving his hands. 'No dancing tonight, 'least not 'til we've welcomed our new member. You, Talisman, stand up. Fellow lunatics, Master Penari's new 'prentice!'

There was another cheer, as derisive as the first, but somehow tinged with uncertainty as well. They hadn't made up their minds about her, Jame thought, bowing to them. Among her own people, such hesitancy would quickly be followed by a challenge, and so it was here, too.

'The measure, the full measure!' someone shouted in the back of the room and many eagerly took up the cry, all hesitation gone.

The 'full measure' arrived. It was an enormous flagon that must have contained over a gallon and a half of ale. Regarding it with dismay, Jame said 'Propose something else.'

'Well! What else can we pr-pr-propose, eh?' The boy threw a broad wink at his audience. 'Something reasonably simple... like maybe fetching us the Cloud King's britches.'

'All right,' said Jame.

Dally choked on his beer. 'Talisman, you loon,' he gasped between bouts of coughing, 'Scramp was only teasing you!'

'And I've paid him the compliment of taking him seriously, or as much so as anyone can. See you later.'

She was gone before he could react, leaving behind a small but rapidly spreading ripple of shock.

Behind the Moon in Splendor was the house of an obscure lay brotherhood whose members, for reasons best known to themselves, spent their lives pushing a boulder up a ramp and then letting it fall from a considerable height on a bound chicken. In the course of a day they usually disposed of nineteen or twenty birds in this fashion. The sound didn't carry far, but one could distinctly feel the floor shake inside the Moon, and sometimes a dish fell off the wall.

Dally had anxiously noted two such tremors since the Talisman's departure, and now here was another one rattling the cups on the table. He was furious with himself for having brought her to this place instead of to his own faction's haunt, where he at least had some control over Lower Town trash like Scramp. If anything happened to his new friend, he would take it out of that wretched boy's hide. For the hundredth time, Dally wondered where the young Kencyr was.

Most Tastigons who knew anything about the Kencyrath thought of it as an exotic oddity. They laughed at Kencyr claims to a home-world other than Rathillien, and as for Kencyr beliefs, how could any reasonable man even consider monotheism, much less warnings that some monstrous evil lurked all around the Eastern Lands, waiting to devour them? You humoured people like that, especially if they happened to be the finest warriors around, but you didn't always take them seriously.

Dally, however, did. The Kencyrath had fascinated him since childhood. He had always longed to meet one of its people; and tonight he finally had, only to lose her again in a matter of minutes. This Talisman seemed an unlikely figure when set against the magnificent, vaguely sinister forms of his imagination, and yet perhaps not so out of place among them after all. He hoped desperately that he had not seen the last of her.

'I see you waited for me,' Jame said, slipping onto the bench he had kept vacant for her. 'Here.' She tossed the bundle of cloth across the table to Scramp. It was a pair of trousers, made

86

of rich fabric but much mended. 'I'm afraid the only proof of ownership I can offer is that patch on the back,' she said as the little Townie held them up so the people in the rear who had stood up on their benches could see. 'But if any of you gentlemen think I had time to embroider the royal crest there, you don't know much about needlecraft. Just the same...' the noise level was on the rise again, excitedly overleaping her voice '... *just the same*, I should tell you that I didn't steal these pants. The Cloud King gave them to me.'

And that was exactly what had happened. On climbing to the inn's roof, Jame had been amazed to find Sparrow waiting for her. It seemed that when she had not appeared in court within a few days, Prince Dandello had sent out scouts to look for her; and it was her erstwhile guide who had spotted her first, entering the Moon with Dally. He had escorted her to the Winter Quarters, which were across the river in the loft of an abandoned house. There His Spacious Majesty had been pleased to give her not only the coveted freedom of the skies but also an old pair of pants when she explained her need of them.

She tried to tell the other apprentices all this; but Scramp, after listening with incredulity for a moment, stopped her short by suddenly bursting into laughter. That set off the rest of the room. Only Dally saw Jame's face go white and understood why.

'Scramp, my dear lad,' he said quickly with an unmistakable note of alarm, 'there's one thing you must never, ever do in dealing with any Kencyr, and that's even to imply that he or she isn't telling the truth. It simply isn't healthy.'

Scramp took this warning, if not seriously, at least enough so to sit down and temporarily shut up. The racket soon regained its normal tone. Jame relaxed slowly. The violence of her reaction had surprised her, almost as much as the realisation that so many of her new colleagues were not prepared to take her or her concept of honour seriously. There might well be trouble over that later; but if so, it could be dealt with when it came.

'Do you suppose,' she said rather plaintively to the room at large, 'that I might have a drink now? A *small* one?'

A moment later seven noggins had appeared on the table before her, and an untold number were still on the way.

'Welcome to the Thieves' Guild,' said Dally with a grin.

5

Winter Days

Dally slid to the right, feinting, then lunged. Jame pivoted to meet him. Her left arm jerked up as she tried to snare his knife in the full sleeve of her d'hen. For a second the blade caught in the tough, mesh lining, then he twisted it free and jumped back. Hissing wickedly, her return strike skimmed the front of his tunic.

'Not bad!' he said, manoeuvering warily at arm's length. 'You're fast enough, but you always hold back. Come on, let's see some aggression!'

Back and forth they went over the flagstones of the Res aB'tyrr's courtyard, circling the well, avoiding the mound of manure that Ghillie had just mucked out of the stable. It was three and a half weeks after Winter's Eve, and the late afternoon air was growing chill, but still the lesson continued.

'C'mon, attack, attack!' Dally gasped, leaping in with a lateral strike, which Jame neatly blocked. 'What's the matter with you?'

'I don't like knives!'

'Well, you've got to learn how to use one anyway, unless you want every flash-blade in town picking on you. You can't take them all on bare-handed...'

Jame, with a frustrated growl, drove her knife between two flagstones and sprang at him. A moment later, Dally found himself disarmed and face down on the pavement with the pile of manure inches from his nose and his right arm locked in a most uncomfortable position over his head.

'... then again,' he said in a muffled voice, 'maybe you can.'

'Am I – uh – interrupting something?' said an unfamiliar voice tentatively.

'I am, I think, about to be stood on my head in a dunghill,' said Dally, wriggling futilely. 'By all means, interrupt, interrupt!' His arm released, he scrambled to his feet, then froze, regarding the boy at the gate with disbelief.

'Canden, the Sirdan Theocandi's grandson, isn't it?' Jame said. 'Meet Dallen, the brother of Master Men-dalis.'

The kinsman of the Guild's two bitterest rivals bowed to each other warily. Neither seemed quite sure what to do next.

'Cleppetty's just baked a damson tart,' said Jame, amused. 'Come in, both of you, and have some.'

'It really was you in the alley that night, wasn't it?' Canden asked as he perched on the south hearth, gingerly juggling a slice of pastry. 'I thought you were a ghost god. You gave me a real scare turning up at the Palace like that.'

'I'll bet I did, and for all I know, you deserved it. What in all the names of God were you doing, hiding in the shadows while those two pug-nasties tried to murder your grand-uncle?'

'Oh, they wouldn't have hurt him.' Canden gave Dally a quick, nervous glance. 'It was all a trick, you see. In another minute I was supposed to jump out of the doorway and save him, thereby winning his gratitude and maybe a chance to become his apprentice . . . or so Grandfather hoped. I told him it wouldn't work, but he never listens to me. Now he's furious with me for failing and with you for being successful, but I don't care. In fact, I'm glad,' he said with sudden, desperate defiance, quite losing control of the tart, which slid off his knee onto the floor. 'I don't want to be a thief or trick Grand-Uncle Penari out of his secrets or be the next Sirdan when Grandfather dies. No one seems to understand that.'

'Wait a minute,' said Dally, startled out of his suspicious silence. 'I thought Bane was Theocandi's chosen successor. After all, he's the old man's only pupil.'

'Normally, that would be true, but he was forced on Grandfather by his father, Abbotir of the Gold Court, just before the Guild Council meeting six years ago in return for political support. The funny thing is that I don't think Bane wants to be a thief either. He has his own interests, his own . . . amusements. Three weeks ago, on Grandfather's nameday, his followers made me watch while he mutilated that child. The things they did to him before he died – and after . . .' He shuddered, then suddenly looked up. 'I would have come sooner if Grandfather hadn't wanted me to, but to spy, to betray . . . that can't be what friendship is for . . . can it?'

Dally, who had been listening first with suspicion, then with embarrassment, now looked at that young, pleading face and said warmly, 'Of course, it isn't.'

At that moment Cleppetty appeared at the hall door. She

stopped short, staring first at the half-empty pastry tin and then at the sticky mess on the floor at Canden's feet. In the midst of this explosive pause, Dally stepped up to her and gravely kissed the tip of her sharp nose. Then with one accord he and Jame bolted out the street door, dragging Canden with them.

'Well,' said Jame several blocks later when they had stopped running, 'now that you gentlemen have arranged things so that I can't go home for a few hours – or maybe a few days – how do you suggest we spend the rest of the afternoon?'

'I hear that the Askebathes' temple has been desanctified for repairs,' said Canden eagerly. 'They might let us in to have a look around... if there isn't something you'd rather do.'

'Why not?' said Dally, smiling at the boy. 'We're free until this evening and can pay our respects to my father while we're in the district.'

'Is he a priest?'

'No. He's Dalis-sar, the sun god of the New Pantheon.'

Jame grinned, remembering how she reacted the first time he had sprung this bit of information on her. All she could think of to say, in a tone of profound confusion, had been, 'How did *that* happen?' 'Oh, the usual way,' Dally had said lightly. 'My mother was a handmaiden in his temple in Tai-abendra. Actually, I wasn't born until after she'd left to marry a local tradesman, but she arranged for my adoption so I and Mendy, who's a true god's son, would be full brothers.' 'Handmaiden' was the usual clerical euphemism for a temple prostitute.

So they visited the house of the Askebathes and then that of Dally's father. Jame was unable to see much of anything in the latter because of the blinding light cast by the wheels of Dalis-sar's war chariot. Today it was especially bad, Dally told her, because the god himself was standing in the golden vehicle.

'It would be even worse,' he added, 'if he were facing us directly. Instead, yes, he's still glaring back over his own shoulder. That's been going on for a good six years now. No one knows why.'

Jame herself could see neither god nor chariot because of the glare. When she held up her hands to blot out the heart of the fire, however, it seemed to her that behind it was not the rear of the temple but the city itself, as though seen from a great height, with the details of the Lower Town preternaturally distinct.

But the sanctuary was alive with more than radiance. Anger shook the air like the steady, immense rumble of a volcano, penetrating flesh, jarring bone, yet unheard. It was the darkness at the heart of the light. Dally had proudly told Jame that, like all the deities of the New Pantheon, Dalis-sar had once been a man, and that man, a Kencyr. She had smiled at the idea of a monotheist being drafted as a god. Now, however, the cold darkness of that rage, so like her own the day the beam had fallen, left no room for doubt. Shaken, she left the temple, her fingertips on Dally's arm, for the brightness had left her temporarily blind.

Outside, all was enemy territory. She had never felt it so much as now, walking sightless and vulnerable between the two young men. The gods of Tai-tastigon were all around her. The shadow of their power brushed her mind in the redshot darkness. If any of them, even Dalis-sar, proved to be real in the same way that her own god was, she would have to admit that the entire culture and history of her people – thirty millennia of hardship, sacrifice, and honour – were built on self-delusion. But how did one go about proving the entire populace of a large city wrong; and if she failed to do so, how could her faith in her own heritage, in herself, remain intact?

They were passing the temple of Gorgo the Lugubrious. Speculatively, Jame looked at it, blinking away the last of her blindness.

Canden left them at the district gate, and Jame and Dally walked on, discussing their new acquaintance. Dally clearly wanted to take the Sirdan's grandson at his word, but felt he owed it to his brother to keep some suspicions alive. Jame, who as yet had no stake in Guild politics, smiled at her friend's reluctant caution.

They arrived early that evening at the headquarters of the New Faction, a fortresslike house near the Sun Gate in the Gold Ringing District.

'One has to make a good impression,' said Dally as he escorted her through the richly appointed corridors. 'It isn't easy, though, competing with a man who has the whole Guild treasury as his privy purse.'

Men-dalis received them in his private study. It was the first time the leader of the New Faction and Master Penari's apprentice had met. Dally watched them both eagerly, noting the graceful formality with which they exchanged greetings. All was going well, he thought.

Jame would have agreed – at first. As fair as his brother was dark, blessed with sapphire blue eyes and movements a dancer might envy, Men-dalis was without doubt the handsomest man she had ever seen. The very room with its rich furnishings of blue and silver seemed to take on an added lustre from him. No one would ever doubt that this indeed was a true son of Dalissar, Lord of the Golden Chariot.

He began to speak of his plans for the Guild after the Grand Council awarded him the sirdanate that coming winter. Jame had heard them all before from Dally, but never so glowingly described. The eloquence of the speaker first tugged at her imagination, then swept it forward into a bright, nebulous future compared to which Theocandi's forty year regime seemed the merest dross.

Then, abruptly, something brought her back to the present with a start. A face was peering over Men-dalis's shoulder. Far back in the shadows of the room, perched on the edge of a table like an escaped gargoyle, was a tiny, skull-faced man. His hands, more bone than flesh, lay twisted together on bony knees under a sharp chin. His expression, which only her Kencyr eyes could have seen in the dark, was one of unalloyed malignity.

Soon after that, Men-dalis's monologue ended and they were graciously dismissed. Jame, glancing back from the doorway, saw the New Faction leader already deep in conference with the man from the shadows, who, she suddenly realised, must be the head of his spy network, a man known in the streets of Taitastigon only as the Creeper.

'Dally...' she said as they left the house. 'Would you say that I frighten easily?'

'Gods, no. Why?'

'Your brother scares me. I think he might be capable of anything.'

Dally looked startled, then said, 'Of course he is!' and launched into an enthusiastic description of all the glorious things that Men-dalis would do when he had power. Jame tried to listen, but her mind only saw that radiant, preternaturally handsome face, cheek to cheek with a living death's head, whose eyes, pools of hatred and envy, had not once left Dally's face.

Men-dalis did not request that Jame visit him again. Clearly, he did not attach much importance to her and was content to win her loyalty, if at all, through Dally.

Theocandi also kept his distance, but with less indifference. Through Canden, Jame learned of the life-long rivalry between the Sirdan and her new master. Theocandi had always been jealous of Penari's reputation and raged at his older brother's refusal to envy him his own position and power. All his life, the younger brother had tried to excel the elder – in skill, arcane studies, renown – and always he had failed. Now in the evening of his days, nothing was more important to him than mastering the secrets that had always made Penari superior in all things that had ever really mattered to either of them. In the end, however, Theocandi could not believe that Penari would give what he considered to be family secrets to an outsider. Consequently Jame was left alone, for the time being at least.

Meanwhile, she, Canden, and Dally were getting on splendidly together. Dally, too good-natured to hold his suspicions for long, had taken an almost fraternal interest in the younger boy, while Jame responded to his loneliness, so reminiscent of her own at an earlier age. She also discovered that Canden had in him a spirit of inquiry not unlike her own and a fascination with the past that if anything surpassed his mistrust of the present.

'Do you know what the oldest building in Tai-tastigon is?' he asked Jame one day. 'That temple of yours. As far as I can tell, it was here before the city walls went up, before the Old Empire was established, before the Kencyrath itself even arrived. How is that possible?'

'Maybe the scrollsmen and Arrin-ken know who built it,' said Jame. 'I don't. Every time we've had to shift worlds, though, the temples have always been waiting for us. The one here is probably as old as Rathillien itself. The other Tastigon priests don't even like to acknowledge its existence.'

'Maybe that's why they chose a different part of the city for the Temple District,' said Canden thoughtfully. 'I've heard that there's another even larger Kencyr temple to the south, in the ruins of Tai-than.'

He talked a great deal about this lost city, the great southern capital of the Old Empire, whose decaying towers no man had seen in half a millennium. An expedition was currently being organised to search for it, and Canden desperately wanted to be part of it. It was an announcement of these preparations that he had brought to show his grandfather the night he had interrupted the old man's attempts to bribe Jame. Theocandi would probably never have let him go anyway, but now he was too incensed by the boy's failure in the alley even to consider it. Jame felt responsible for all this. Trying to make it up to the boy, she gave him her friendship and, in an attempt to placate Theocandi for his sake, passed on to him some of the things that

Master Penari taught her.

None of these could be classified as a secret. In fact, nothing she had learned so far seemed to fit into that category, and Jame was beginning to wonder if the old man meant to keep his own council after all. This disappointed her, of course, but on the other hand the training he was prepared to give her left neither time nor grounds for dissatisfaction.

Eventually, Penari introduced an intense course on the rules of Jame's new profession, however, which gave her hope that her lessons were about to move in new directions. She learned that everything an apprentice stole over a certain value became the property of his master, whose duty it was to send the booty to one of the five Guild courts, each one of which was specialised in a different kind of merchandise. There it was assessed and the length of time determined for which its possession was punishable by law. This crucial time, called the period of jeopardy, began as soon as the object came into the apprentice's hands. In Tai-tastigon, possession was the sole proof of guilt. Complicity was sometimes punished as well, but only if the accused had been in physical contact with the stolen article. Penalties ranged from fines to the loss of a finger, hand, or the whole of one's skin, for robberies involving undue violence or the injuring of a guardsman. The worst punishment of all – public flaying preceded by whatever mutilations a mob of concerned citizens could inflict – was reserved for anyone who tried to assassinate one of the Five or a Guild-lord.

Hearing this, Jame's eyes darkened with memory. Not long before, an embittered young journeyman had attacked the Sirdan in the Guild Hall itself. It would be a long time before she forgot that pitiful figure, already blind, tongueless, and castrated, writhing under the knife and cauterising irons on the Mercy Seat.

Realising that he had lost her attention, Penari ended his lecture with a snarl. Scooping a handful of gems out of a desk drawer (along with several marbles and a mouse's skull), he threw them down on the floor before her, then immediately swept them up again and demanded to know exactly what she had seen. This was an old exercise between them, and Jame usually did very well at it. Today, however, she could only name eighteen out of thirty or so stones. Various things were distracting her, not the least of which was Monster, who had fallen asleep with his head balanced precariously on her shoulder.

Penari, thoroughly exasperated by now, snatched up the large translucent rock he used as a paperweight and threw it, nearly braining them both. Upon extricating herself from the python's sleepy coils and recovering this stone, Jame suddenly realised that it was not the piece of quartz she had always taken it for. She was in fact holding an enormous uncut diamond, the Eye of Abarraden itself.

That day's lesson ended with Penari sending her out into the Maze with instructions to find her way from one point to another and, on returning, to describe to him turn for turn where she had been. She went, knowing that the old man would detect any mistake in her eventual recitation instantly. The same was true when he had her go out to memorise sections of the city. He would name a street and ask her how she would get from it to another, sometimes insisting that her route lie over the rooftops or even through the houses themselves as if she were escaping from a very determined pursuer. In the course of these games, she had suddenly realised something very odd: for her master, Tai-tastigon was the same, structure by structure, as it had been when he had first gone into seclusion over fifty years before and nothing would convince him otherwise. This knowledge cleared up some of her confusion. It didn't help much, however, when he made her describe routes through areas long since reduced to rubble by one of the city's numerous disasters and subsequently rebuilt. Today, she was happy enough to contend only with the Maze and did so well in it that Penari, mollified, let her go early.

Standing on the threshold, turning up the collar of her d'hen against the cool evening air, Jame reflected that she was receiving an education every bit as eccentric in some ways as it was excellent in others.

A tall figure passed by the end of the street, instantly recognisable by his cream-velvet d'hen. Jame called after him to wait, and a few minutes later she was walking westward beside Darinby, a journeyman of Master Galishan. Darinby was one of the Guild's finest, a true craftsman with family tradition behind him and glory ahead according to most savants, who predicted that he would soon become the Guild's youngest master. Jame had always admired his skill, style, and integrity. He was the sort of thief she hoped to become if the length of her stay in Tai-tastigon permitted it; and it pleased her very much that he in turn seemed to like her. They walked on together, discussing the upcoming Guild elections.

'No, I haven't chosen a side,' said Darinby, 'and probably won't either. Theocandi's too corrupt for my taste, and Mendalis is too ambitious. My master will probably support the latter – if he can get his mind off M'lady Melissand long enough – but you and I, Talisman, should be glad we've no voice in the matter.'

'Huh. Sometimes I wonder if anyone else realises that.'

'Your position *is* rather peculiar, isn't it?' he said, smiling. 'Strictly speaking, Penari has no more power than Galishan, just one vote out of a hundred among the landed masters for their two representatives; but others will be swayed by his decision, and you're the only person in the city close enough to him to influence it. Bad times are coming. I don't envy you, Talisman, no, not at all.'

They parted at the Serpent Fountain.

'Oh, by the way,' the journeyman said, stopping suddenly and turning back towards her. 'There's a rumour that since you enrolled at the Guild Hall, Bane has given up young boys. I should walk wary if I were you, Talisman.'

She watched him go, his d'hen glimmering in the dusk.

Wind devils whirled about the fountain, mixing its spray with the thin rain that had began to fall. Jame spun about. Surely someone was watching her. Often over the last few weeks she had felt the sudden chill of eyes but never seen the face behind them. No more so now. Darinby's words, however, had unlocked a memory. The first time her flesh had crept this way had been in the Sirdan's Palace, walking down a corridor with the whisper of footsteps behind her. Names of God, but her nerves must be raw. The square was empty, its shadows tenantless. She set out for home briskly, not deigning to look back.

It was mid-evening when Jame reached the Res aB'tyrr after a breathless game of Follow-my-lead across the rain-slick rooftops with a trio of Cloudie friends. The first thing that struck her as she opened the kitchen door was the uproar within; the second was a large, half-roasted goose. Her immediate impression was that someone had thrown the fowl at her. Then she realised that the headless creature was in fact under its own power and making a very credible attempt to escape. After several hectic moments of being hauled about the courtyard, frequently off her feet, she finally pinioned the greasy, squirming carcass and marched it back to the door.

Inside Kithra – formerly of the Skyrrman – was struggling to hold down the lid of a pot from which a score of naked chicken wings protruded, flapping madly, while Cleppetty pursued an escaped quail about the kitchen with a broom, and Ghillie, huddled in a corner, frantically read names out loud from a book of household exorcisms.

'Look under fowls, not fantods,' gasped the widow, flailing away determinedly. 'You brought it home, you get rid of it!'

Ghillie flipped over several pages and began to read again, even faster than before: '... Afanci-Ainsel-Allisoun-Assgingel ... ah!'

A wind full of chittering sounds rushed through the kitchen and up the three chimneys. Cleppetty's bird plopped to the floor. Kithra's kettle stopped jumping. And the goose suddenly went limp in Jame's arms.

'Ah, indeed!' said the widow with satisfaction. 'But, oh, what a mess!' She ruefully surveyed her once immaculate kitchen, spattered now with fragments of pastry, goose, and bits of stuffing.

'So this is how you amuse yourselves when I'm not around,' said Jame, dropping her now inert captive on the table. 'What happened?'

'Bogles,' said Cleppetty succinctly. 'And this is nothing: you should have been here when the pigeon pie decamped. Now upstairs and off with that shirt, missy; you're better basted than that damned bird.'

The gods of Tai-tastigon were for the most part properly templed; but now and then, presumably when they slept, wisps of power escaped. These sometimes attached themselves to passers-by and were carried out of the District to become the dreaded bogles – malignant, mischievous, or simply mindless impulses that would wreak havoc until the speaking of their proper name dispelled them. Nothing had ever followed Jame home – nothing would have dared – but Ghillie, clearly, had been less fortunate.

As she changed clothes up in the loft, Jame heard clapping and cheers from across the square. Though still not completely furnished, the ground floor of the Skyrrman blazed with light. The uproar receded, leaving behind the sound of a harp running thoughtfully through its trills. Jame listened, hardly breathing. The master harpist was playing well tonight, more than living up both to his reputation and to the staggering sum that Marplet sen Tenko must have paid to bring him upriver from his home in Endiscar to perform here. With such competition, it was hardly surprising that the Res aB'tyrr was almost deserted tonight and had been for the last two weeks. The music ended, its last note dying away into silence before the storm of applause began again.

In a dark, third storey window of the Skyrrman, a shadowy figure raised its hand to Jame in a mocking salute. She returned it, one palm down in the Kencyr fashion to show appreciation, and then descended to the kitchen.

'We're still being watched,' she said, reentering the room. 'This time by Marplet himself, I think. Why do you suppose they do it?'

'The gods only know,' said Cleppetty, scraping food off the wall. 'Why, for that matter, have they been making a list of our patrons this past fortnight, and what business has our precious Bortis at the Skyrrman?'

'Bortis?' It took Jame a moment to remember Taniscent's former lover.

'That's right,' said Ghillie, coming in from the courtyard with a bucket of water, which he poured into the scullery cauldron as Kithra stoked the fire under it. 'In case you haven't noticed he practically lives there now.'

'Something's up, all right,' said the widow, sitting back on her heels. 'But what? Marplet's well on his way to ruining us as it is, what with all his grand, imported talent. Of course, he can't keep it up forever, even with his brother-in-law's support; but if we lose enough business long enough, Tubain won't be able to renew our charter when it falls due come Spring's Eve ... and if he can't, Marplet will snatch it up as fast as hot bricks in a blizzard. Without that bit of paper, the Res aB'tyrr has no legal protection. It will be the end of us. Surely that should satisfy him.'

'But it won't,' said Kithra suddenly, her voice hardening. 'He played cat-and-mouse with you, and the mouse drew first blood. After what happened to Niggen, his pride is at stake now too. No, he won't be so easily satisfied.'

Jame was inclined to believe her. If anyone knew the workings of Marplet's mind, it was his former servant. Kithra had come from her home in Tenzi canton a year ago to work at his inn, and by dint of some very skilful seduction had finally ended up in his bed. This should have greatly improved her social position, but she had reckoned without Marplet's intense misogyny. Her ploy had only earned his contempt. The girl's hatred for him now, after the way he had expelled her, was frightening in its intensity. Just the same, it had not taken the edge off her natural ambition. Jame believed she was currently trying to decide if it would be more advantageous to marry Rothan, become Tubain's mistress, or take on both roles simultaneously. She looked at Kithra askance, wondering just what her attack on Niggen had unleashed on this normally tranquil household.

And then there was Marplet sen Tenko. Slowly she was beginning to understand him better – the love of perfection that had led him to construct his inn so slowly, using only the finest materials; the almost feline quality of mind that allowed him to take such pleasure in his many schemes; his shame at having to call that lump of flesh Niggen his son. She could almost feel the sense of anger and betrayal that gripped him each time he saw that ungainly boy in his perfect house. What she did not feel, strangely enough, was any sort of personal animosity towards her whenever their eyes met across the square.

'Female or not,' Cleppetty had said in grim amusement when she mentioned this one day, 'now that he's taken your measure, I think he's rather come to like you. You'd look better sitting on his hearth next to that mangy tomcat of his than Niggen does, and more natural than you do here, for that matter. A tiger cub in a field of tabbies, that's you.'

'Meow!' Jame had said, and rolled Boo over on his back.

Now she folded up her sleeves and helped the others scrub down the kitchen, half listening to their talk, thinking her own thoughts. Finally the inn closed its doors for the night.

Up in the loft, on the edge of sleep, a sudden coldness jolted her awake, made her throw back the blanket and stand staring out. The Skyrrman was dark. She was alone and yet, somehow, as beside the Serpent Fountain earlier that evening and a dozen times before that, she was being watched.

Are you thinking of me, butcher of children? she asked the night. I am of you. Thought crosses thought, like steel in the dark. Why can't you leave me alone . . . and why am I afraid that you will?

The rain had turned to snow. White crystals fell on her black hair, on bare arms and breasts. Shivering she lay down again, wrapped in her blanket, but did not sleep until the eastern sky was tinged with light and cocks had begun to crow at the edge of the city.

6

Water Flow, Fire Leap

Mid-Winter's Day arrived, cool and clear. Jame, Dally, and Canden went to Judgment Square to see the apotheosis of the Frost King, but were driven to the rooftops when fighting broke out between two factions in a temple war and the crowd panicked. Up on the tiles, Jame first had the pleasure of preventing her friends from being thrown off and then of presenting them to Prince Dandello, who had come with his retinue to see the rites. The bloodshed below, however, made the prince ill, and he soon left. The other three soon followed.

They were becoming a common trio, one the Guild had trouble understanding. But then they understood little when Jame was in question. By now, she could open any lock in the city, go anywhere like a shadow in the night, and reach anyone from a guild lord in his hall to the meanest beggar in hiding for his life. But still her new talents made her uneasy. The closer she came to actual stealing, the more she wondered how it would be possible to abscond honourably with someone else's property, despite what Ishtier had told her. And so she hedged. The apple vendor missed the rottenest of his wares from the bottom of the pile; the nobleman, surrounded by his retainers, discovered that the smallest button on his trousers was inexplicably missing. And now a rich merchant went his way, unaware that deft fingers had slipped into his pocket, found the least valuable coin there by touch alone, and triumphantly carried it off. Surely not much honour was risked by such trifling thefts as these.

'Just the same,' said Dally, looking doubtfully at the tin coin that she had just dropped into his hand, 'they'll never understand it at the Moon.'

Jame smiled ruefully. She knew only too well what her reputation was now that she had gone for weeks without matching the exploit of the Cloud King's britches, which had brought her into the Guild with such fanfare. The other young thieves conveniently forgot that none of them had accomplished much during their first six months or, for that matter, in their first year. For Penari's pupil, however, things were different. With such a master, she must command respect or deserve contempt; her peers had left her no middle ground.

But that trial would soon be over. Winter would now be sliding down towards spring, and it was time that she make plans to leave Tai-tastigon. Her smile faded. She had suddenly realised that she didn't want to go.

There were several reasons for this, she realised later. For one thing, she hated to leave without somehow having proved herself worthy of Penari's instructions. For another, she was hardly closer to solving the mystery of the gods than she had been when she first came. And then there was the Res aB'tyrr. The business of the charter must be settled by Spring's Eve, so come what may, she would be on hand for that. But if Marplet failed in his current scheme, he would simply launch another, and another, and another, until one succeeded or he, somehow, was stopped. Moreover, if Kithra was right, Tubain would have her (Jame) indirectly to thank for anything unpleasant that befell him from now on. It was hardly honourable to desert him now and yet how could she commit herself to a campaign that might drag on for years if Marplet found it sufficiently entertaining?

But there was more to her hesitation even than this. She was no longer sure that she should rejoin the Kencyrath. She was remembering more and more of life at the keep: her father's ill-will, her brother's disapproval, all for something she couldn't help, for a cruel trick of heredity. It was said that there was no greater punishment for a Kencyr than to be cast out, denied any place among his people. But was that really worse than a shadow existence, permitted on sufferance alone to sit at some stranger's hearth? She didn't know. What had been true at the isolated keep might not be so in the Riverland. Still, as she sat on the loft's window ledge that night, more and more the face of the Kencyrath bore the features of Tori, her twin brother, whose love for her, however strong, had shone but feebly beneath the weight of his prejudices.

There was a burst of applause from the inn across the way, which quickly settled down into rhythmic clapping. Harpists were popular in Tai-tastigon, but a good dancer even more so.

Jame thought of Taniscent in her lonely room below, hiding that wrinkled face and prematurely aged body from even the kindest of eyes. Once her talent might have saved the inn. How much that thought must prey on the former dancer's mind now God alone knew.

Cruel, cruel city with its gleaming snares and velveted claws, its eyes that shone up steadily at her even now, watching, waiting. And this was the place she thought to call her home? Yes. Its temper suited her. She could make her own way here and never think of the past again.

But was that possible? Perhaps . . . if she really knew what she was turning her back on. However, not only had several years fallen out of her own life, but she had learned not long ago that she didn't even know any recent Kencyr history. It seemed, for example, that the host of the Kencyrath had suffered a major defeat some thirty years ago, which had resulted in the exile of Ganth Gray Lord, its greatest Highborn. Dally knew this much, but little more. It had been a long time since news had moved freely across the Ebonbane – which probably, Jame thought, was why her own people had never learned of these events. Nonetheless, hearing of them now, she felt more cut off from her heritage than ever and even less inclined to abandon it without knowing what she was giving up.

But was the knowledge worth the pain that gaining it might cost?

And what about the ring and broken sword? They must be got to her brother somehow, if only by messenger. Maybe Tori would even prefer it that way. But who could she trust with such a mission . . . assuming she could bring herself to delegate it at all.

Round and round her thoughts went – to go, to stay – and to make matters worse, she must decide soon. The passes usually cleared soon after the Feast of Fools, which took place just after Spring's Eve, and remained open until the Feast of Dead Gods at the end of the summer. This year, however, the readers of bones had predicted a remarkably short season, lasting perhaps a matter of weeks or less. When the high passes unlocked, she must go quickly or not at all.

Dawn surprised Jame, with no decision made. The widow, coming down early on a baking day, found her already up to her elbows in dough and pummelling away at it with all the frustrated energy of a mind at war with itself. Wise Cleppetty set to work without a word, and between them they soon plunged the kitchen deep into a floury fog that did not lift until late morning. Then came the baking, then the scrubbing, all in silence, all at a pace that even the tireless widow began to regret. She was just beginning to wonder, rather desperately, if she was about to be launched into spring cleaning two months early when Jame suddenly put aside her apron and left the inn.

The widow collapsed into a chair. 'Don't ask!' she told a startled Kithra.

Jame found herself walking eastward with no clear idea of where she was going. On Armorers Row, a display of daggers laid out on black velvet caught her eye, reminding her of her aversion to knives. That was another mystery rooted in the past. Was she never to understand the reason for that either? On impulse, she picked up a knife, closed her eyes, and tried to remember.

Nothing came.

Sudden anger rose in her. Dammit, she wouldn't go through life without a past, forever a stranger to herself. Fiercely, she summoned all her will and threw it against the barrier in her mind. The ornate hilt bit into her hand. The sounds of the market fused into a dull roar. For a long moment she was alone in the red-shot darkness behind her trembling eyelids, and then she saw the room.

It was huge, its upper regions lost in shadows. Figures moved about her, indistinct, all eyes and gleaming teeth. One of them held up something. A cloak made of black serpent skins sewn together with silver thread. They put it on her bare shoulders... heavy, heavy, and the tails, coiled together beneath her chin, twitched. She was climbing a stair. The snake heads thumped on each step at her heels. He was waiting in an alcove, the shadows a mask over his ravaged face. A white-bladed knife slipped from one cold hand to another. She went on, clutching it, up towards the doorway barred with red ribbons, towards the darkness beyond...

'Hey!'

Her eyes snapped open. A shop boy was standing in front of her, scowling pugnaciously.

'You wanta buy that?' he demanded.

She dropped the dagger and walked blindly away. Her head throbbed. The hall, the man on the stair! Red ribbons, she vaguely remembered, were usually for a lord's wedding chamber, but the Serpent Skin Cloak and the Ivory Knife, surely they were things of legend. She thought of her mother, that strange, beautiful woman whom her father had brought back one day to the keep out of the Haunted Lands, out of nowhere. The others had thought her mute, for by day she never spoke, but at night her daughter had often awakened to the sound of her voice, reciting the ancient stories or singing songs that had been old when the Kencyrath was but newfounded. That was how Jame had first heard of the cloak, the knife, and the Book Bound in Pale Leather.

It was no use, she thought: fact would not separate from legend. But still, where had that hall been and who, in all the names of God, had she been climbing to meet, knife in hand?

The parapet of the Old Wall stretched out before her. Below, beyond it and the curtain walls, the caravans were gathering on the southern plain for their dash across the Ebonbane in the spring. To leave Tai-tastigon, to remain – either way, it couldn't hurt to make some inquiries.

The rest of the afternoon did little to ease either her growing headache or her mind. The first caravan-master she spoke to told her that the fee for anyone joining his convoy at Tai-tastigon was thirty-five golden altars. 'If the price were any lower,' he said, giving her a shrewd look, 'we'd be overrun with thieves joined up for the pickings. It's no good trying to cross on your own, either; those hills will be thick with bandits come the thaws. No, without my help or that of my colleagues, you'll never see the other side.'

'What about the sea routes?' Jame asked, stung by his smug air.

'These days, that's for those who don't care what they pay, or if they arrive. You've heard of dead water? Hit a patch of that some dark night and you sink like a brick – ship, cargo, and all. The straits are rotten with it. You don't believe me? Go ask in any port and check the fares too, while you're at it. Mine will look like a bargain after that.'

'Well then, couldn't I work my way across? I can be a first-rate cook by then, and I'm already a fair hostler.'

The master laughed. 'All such positions were filled weeks ago, boy, but if you wouldn't mind working in another sort of position...' His hand dropped to her knee.

'Think about it, you scrawny bastard!' he shouted after her a moment later. 'No one else will make a better offer!' And with that he retreated into his tent, gingerly feeling his jaw for loose teeth.

Unfortunately, the master was right. His two colleagues asked forty and forty-five altars respectively, and both laughed at her request for employment. Discouraged, she started home on the path that ran along the outer face of the bulwark. It had never occurred to her that passage would be so expensive or – worse yet – honest work so hard to find, though she cursed herself now for not having realised that the shortness of the season would affect both drastically. She had virtually no money of her own. Another thief would have stolen what he needed; but even if Jame had been in the practice of taking valuable things instead of trinkets, she would still have had too much respect for her oath not to turn them over to Penari. Although he and Tubain kept her in pocket money, neither paid her for her work – which was only fitting since one had agreed to train her without the usual fee and the other was giving her free room and board. She had counted on striking a bargain with the caravan-master and working for whatever she couldn't pay outright. It seemed now that she must either come up with the whole sum or a new plan if she really meant to leave in the spring.

Just then she came to a brook cutting through the bulwark and realised with irritation that she had missed the cut that led to the Meadow Gate. There were, however, other ways to enter the city. She followed the stream until it disappeared behind a gate in the outer curtain wall, then climbed the steep, lichen-covered stairs to a postern high in its outer face. Inside, a rope walk stretched across the dry moat to a minor gate set in the inner wall. Below, on either side of the swift water, were the kennels, catteries, and mews that catered to the sporting element among the city's rich folk.

Jame was two-thirds of the way across when she happened to look down and saw a man walk up to a small back-water carrying a weighted sack that appeared to be moving. He threw it in. Instantly such a feeling of panic swept over her that she almost fell. Close, wet, no air ... she scrambled over the guide rope and dived clumsily. It was a long way down. The water hit her like a body blow, driving air out between her teeth. My God! she suddenly thought, halfway to the bottom. Do I know how to swim? At any rate, she clearly knew how to sink and was rapidly doing so in water that proved surprisingly deep and shockingly cold. Weeds rippled in the current below. Among them nestled many small sacks, only one of them still moving. Fighting down the panic that beat at her, she unsheathed the knife that Dally had insisted she carry and slashed open the bag. A small, furry body wriggled frantically through the slit. They swam upward together and surfaced gasping. The man on the bank stared at her open-mouthed as Jame waded ashore holding the shivering ounce cub.

'What in Perimal's name did you think you were doing?' she demanded, nearly inarticulate with delayed shock and rage.

'Drowning it, of course,' the man said, still staring.

'*Why?*'

'Look at its eyes.' Jame did. They were wide with fear and opaque as milk opals. 'Blind,' said the man regretfully. 'Born that way, poor mite. We kept it an extra month hoping they would clear, but this afternoon Master said, "Right. Dispose of it." So here I am, and there it is.'

'How much?'

He looked at her, puzzled. She forced herself to clarify.

'How much do you want for it?'

'Well now,' he said, rubbing his chin, 'although it don't look like much now, that's a Royal Gold, one of the rarest cats there is. If it were sound, Master would ask two hundred altars for it or more, but blind... well, Master is a hard man. He'd rather destroy it than ask less.'

'I'll get the money,' Jame said, knowing she spoke nonsense. Two hundred altars was more than half the price of Tubain's seven year charter, enough gold to keep the inn affluent for three seasons. Still, desperation drove her to repeat, 'I'll get it, somehow.'

The man looked at her, at the trembling cub in her arms. '*Well* now,' he said slowly. 'It seems to me that the tyke might as well disappear into the city as into that pool, though Master would ruin me for sure if he ever found out. I'll tell you what: promise never to tell how you came by him, and he's yours.'

There was little that Jame would not have promised at that moment. It was only as she hurried away, slipping her prize inside her d'hen for warmth, that she realised there was no way she could ever prove that the cub had not been stolen.

The sun set behind the mountains as Jame walked quickly through the curving streets of the Rim. She was still very wet

106

and fast becoming bitterly cold in Tai-tastigon's sudden twilight with the cub a shaking morsel of ice against her right breast. The mind link she had shared with it in that moment of crisis no longer seemed to exist, although the beast clung to her as tightly as before, its small claws pricking her through her shirt. Perhaps it would return. Now all she felt was the cold and the same vague sense of being followed that had haunted her for so long that she now virtually ignored it. Besides, the inn was just ahead, on the other side of that gatehouse set in the Old Wall. Soon there would be warmth, supper, companionship...

In the shadow of the gate's arch, blocking the way, stood three men. The largest was Bortis. He smiled disagreeably but with satisfaction when he saw her and said: 'I've a message for you, thief. You aren't to go home tonight... nor ever again if you're mindful of your health.'

'Oh?' Jame said, bidding for time to rouse her half-frozen wits. 'Who shall I thank for this kind warning?'

'Let's just say a friend, and you needn't bother to try going another way. All roads are closed to you tonight. Your friend doesn't want you hurt, but if you should be so ungrateful as to ignore his advice, well, something unpleasant might happen to you.' His smile broadened. 'In fact,' he said softly, 'something may happen to you anyway.'

Jame took a quick step backward. With her right arm immobilised by the cub, she couldn't fight effectively against such odds. Her only chance lay in flight. Then, simultaneously, she saw Bortis look over her shoulder and sensed too sharply for any doubt that someone was behind her. She whirled. Bane stood there, smiling at her.

'Well, well,' he said, regarding the young ounce. 'Mother and child. Very pretty. Gentlemen, this lady would like to pass. Have you any objections?'

Bortis grinned and lunged. Bane pushed Jame out of the way and side-stepped. The edge of his left hand cut down on the other's wrist as he shot past. He was behind the man with his right forearm across his throat before the bandit had time to recover. Bane's left hand, now free, came up from his belt gripping bright steel. With a gesture of great delicacy, he pricked Bortis's right eye.

Bortis staggered against a wall with hands to his face. The other two men recoiled from him, too shocked to press the attack.

'Shall we go?' Bane said to Jame, bowing. 'Theocandi's spies heard that there might be trouble here tonight,' he said as he escorted her to the gate of Res aB'tyrr. 'I thought I'd come to see what was brewing. Shall I stay in case there's more excitement?'

'No!' said Jame. Her stomach twisted at the thought of Bane involved in the hostelry's affairs, even of him setting foot inside its walls. 'No thank you,' she repeated, trying to be more courteous. 'We'll cope . . . Bane, I don't understand you at all.'

'You only think you don't,' he said with a lazy smile. 'You know me as well as you know yourself. Go in, m'lady. Your lips are blue with the cold.' And he drew a fingertip down her cheek, turning the sharp nail edge to the jawline where it left a thin line of blood.

Cleppetty was at the kitchen table, chopping meat. For a moment she simply stared at the bedraggled, apologetic apparition that had materialised on her doorstep with dripping clothes and a smear of blood on its face. Then she advanced on Jame purposefully. Minutes later the young ounce was snug in a nest of old aprons by the fire, and Jame, having been shaken out of her wet garments and into a blanket, was sitting beside it, looking rather dazed.

The widow thrust a cup of hot spiced wine into her hands, waited until she had drunk half of it, and then said: 'Explain!'

Jame did. Just as she finished, Ghillie and Rothan came in. Rothan was glaring into space with bloodshot eyes, making little whuffling noises deep in his throat. Ghillie, on the other hand, seemed half wild with joy even though his lip was split and bleeding freely.

'You should have seen him!' he crowed. 'They said we couldn't pass, we objected, one of them hit me, and Rothan here went at them like a bull with a bee up his butt. It was glorious!'

'Wait a minute,' said Cleppetty. 'Who are "they"?'

'Why, some of Marplet's pug-nasties, of course, too far from home to be protected by their precious guards. Oh, we've waited a long time for this! You should have been there with your skillet, Aunt Cleppetty. All we needed to make it perfect was a few cracked skulls.'

'I may crack some yet,' the widow said, regarding the capering boy balefully. 'This doesn't sound good.' She went to the door and shouted for Tubain, Kithra, and Taniscent.

'Kithra's out,' sang Ghillie, trying to induce Jame to dance with him. 'So is Taniscent. I saw her leave with Bortis.'

'Bortis!' said Tubain, entering from the courtyard. 'When did she start seeing him again?'

'Just about the time he settled into the Skyrrman,' said the widow. 'I thought you knew. Ghillie, you monkey, calm down. What will the customers think?'

'There aren't any.'

'*What?*' Cleppetty advanced on the boy menacing. 'None?'

'Look for yourself!' he cried, ducking behind the still immobile Rothan. 'The hall is empty.'

At that moment, Kithra burst into the kitchen through the street door. 'They're stopping them all,' she gasped. 'They tried to stop me too, but I got away and ran.'

'*Who* are they stopping?' Cleppetty demanded. 'We're all here now but Tanis.'

'Why, the customers ... all our regular people.'

'Of course, Marplet's list!' said Jame. 'Now he's making use of it, but to what purpose? Surely he doesn't mean to blockade all the streets until Spring's Eve.'

'He may not have to,' said the widow grimly. 'Ghillie, Rothan – wake up, you great lump! – go watch the main approaches to the square. Tuby ... bless us, where is the man?'

'He went out the courtyard door, madam,' said Kithra tactfully. 'I think he's gone to warn his wife.'

'Hmph! Well, let him go. In these lands, we don't tie our leaders to trees and keep them on the battlefield. Kithra, stay with me. We've got water to draw, just in case. You, missy,' she said, turning to Jame, 'get some dry clothes on fast and come back down. I've work for you, too.'

Jame dropped the blanket and, naked, darted up to the loft. When she came down again, hastily belting her spare d'hen, Cleppetty was waiting with Boo and the sleepy cub in her arms.

'Here,' she said, handing both over. 'Take them up to Mistress Abernia. They'll be safe there as long as the south wing stands.'

Jame crossed the courtyard and climbed the stairs with her charges, conscious with each step of a growing excitement. At last, after nearly five months at the inn, she was about to meet its termagant mistress.

Light shone around the edges of Abernia's door. Jame scratched on its panels tentatively, then rapped with her knuckles.

'Who is it?' the shrill, familiar voice demanded.

'It's Jame, mistress. Cleppetty sent me.' She could hear the sound of breathing now, down by the keyhole, and below, the widow's urgent voice barking orders.

'Please, mistress. I've brought the children.'

The door opened abruptly, light streaming around the broad figure on the threshold. A powerful hand scooped both the ounce and the cat out of Jame's arms. The door slammed in her face.

'I gather you met her,' said the widow drily as Jame reentered the kitchen, looking dazed.

'I-I think so ... Cleppetty, am I losing my mind, or was that Tubain dressed up in ...?'

'Hush!' The widow glanced hastily out the door to be sure that Kithra was still at the well. 'The mistress was already here when Tubain first gave me a home at the Res aB'tyrr. I discovered her secret by accident and have helped to maintain it ever since as it's clear that Tubain needs her. She can face things that he can't, and on her own ground she's a regular lion. Nobody else knows about this, not even Rothan, but it occurred to me tonight that someone else should, in case of an emergency. That's you, for lack of anyone more sensible.'

'I'm honoured ... I think.'

'You are,' she said with a sudden smile. 'Now help me get these kettles filled.'

But there was no time. Ghillie burst into the kitchen followed by Rothan. 'Marplet's men are coming!' the boy gasped. '*All* of them. Rothan figures thirty; I say closer to fifty. Shall we bar the door?'

'No,' said the widow after a moment's rapid thought. 'Whatever they have planned, they'll be looking for an excuse to make it seem spontaneous. The fewer opportunities we give them to complain, the better.'

'So what do we *do?*'

'Wait.'

They stood at the kitchen door, listening. Outside, the sound of voices, shouting, laughing raucously, was coming closer. Jame and Ghillie ran to the front windows. Men were entering the square from all directions, calling ironic greetings to each other as though they had met there by chance. The fur-trimmed clothes of some betrayed them as brigands from the hills, doubtless colleagues of Bortis, while Jame recognised others as members of Tai-tastigon's true criminal class, guildless men who would do anything for a price. A loud, mock debate ensued over which inn should be patronised. Ghillie and Jame retreated precipitously to the kitchen just as the front door crashed open and the first of them came tramping into the hall, shouting for the best wine in the house.

'Now what?' said Ghillie, white-faced.

'We serve them,' said Cleppetty grimly, 'or rather you three do. Kithra stays here with me. They may have special instructions about her.' She jumped down from the bench she had been using to reach a high shelf and handed Jame a small black bottle. 'Put three drops of this in every tankard. That should confuse them some.'

'Confuse' was a mild word for it, Jame thought as she and the others plunged down the steps to the cellar with their first load of empty vessels. Not long ago, Ghillie's girlfriend had teased him into trying some of Cleppetty's special medicine, and he had spent the rest of the day watching green marmosets scamper across the ceiling. Still, three drops wasn't much per glass, and it was a very small bottle. She climbed the steps, two tankards clasped by the grip in each hand, and her courage quailed at the roar that came crashing down to meet her.

The next two hours were a nightmare. Jame, Rothan, and Ghillie were kept continually in motion carrying food and drink to the clamorous mob and suffering everything it could provide by way of pinching, tripping, and general insults. The interlopers were still playing the part of rowdy but otherwise normal customers, except that they missed no opportunity to criticise either the food or the service and got excessive pleasure out of assuring Jame and the others that all accounts would be settled at the end of the evening. The little bottle was long since empty. Some men had taken to staring into space, grinning idiotically, but the majority seemed relatively unaffected.

'How long can this go on?' Ghillie gasped as he and Jame collided on the stair.

In the hall, someone started shouting for Tanis.

'That's done it,' said Cleppetty, looking out the kitchen door as the noise grew to a steady, pounding chant.

'Madam, it's all right!' Kithra called from the back door. 'I just saw her come in.'

'What good is that?' Jame said to the widow. 'She can't dance.'

At that moment, Taniscent herself entered through the

111

curtains below the minstrels' gallery. Candlelight shimmered on her translucent garments, on skin glowing with scented oil, and the crowd roared at the sight of her. Jame felt her mouth drop open. She thought she had never seen the dancer look more beautiful, or so young. Beside her, the widow growled deep in her throat.

'Sixteen years old, seventeen at most,' she said. 'How much Dragon's Blood did it take to do that, and who gave it to her?'

Taniscent mounted the table under the central chandelier, the applause of the audience dizzying her with delight. Oh, it was every bit as wonderful as Bortis had promised. This was where she belonged, where she would stay forever. Briefly, she wondered where her handsome lover was and why he had left her to wait for this moment of triumph alone. She would tease him about that later. Now, she would dance as she had never danced before, glorying in her remembered skill, in the youth that again burned so hotly in her veins.

Jame watched, entranced. She had forgotten how good Tanis was, or what enthusiasm she could draw from her audience. But although the men cheered, there was something half-mocking, half-expectant in the echo, and an undercurrent of pure cruelty. Turn, bend, glide... the sensual dance went on, separating planes of sense, merging them again in the flickering light... and then the change began.

Jame blinked. What place had lines in the lovely face, or flecks of grey in that dark, lustrous hair? Cleppetty gripped her arm fiercely. The waist seemed to be – no, *was* thickening, the slim ankles likewise. Breasts, glossy with oil, began to sag under the diaphanous fabric. The note of the mob had also changed. Hisses and jeers now interlaced the applause, growing in volume. The sound broke Taniscent's trance of movement. She faltered, looked down in bewilderment at the malicious glee on the faces below, and then caught sight of her own hands where the veins now ran blue and prominent under the skin. With a wail of horror, she fell to her knees. Ghillie and Jame ran to help her, elbowing a way through the jeering crowd to get her to the kitchen. Behind them the tumult grew.

Cleppetty was putting on her hat and cloak. 'Take her up to her room,' she ordered Kithra, then turned to Jame. 'Ghillie says that you know how to dance.'

'I know the Senetha. D-do you mean you want me to...'

'That's right. I'm going out of the district for help, and we've

112

got to buy time either until I return or they get enough wine in them to reinforce the drug. Thank the gods they mean to drink all they can before the burning starts or we would have been finished hours ago.'

'B-but Cleppetty, what if they don't like me?'

'That we'll have to risk. Put on one of Tanis's costumes and stand on your head if you have to, but *keep their attention*.' And with that she disappeared out the street door.

Jame stood there gaping after her for a second, then turned and fled up to Taniscent's room with the voice of the mob loud behind her.

Kithra had the dancer in bed and was trying to keep her there. Ignoring them both, Jame burrowed into the chest at the foot of Taniscent's bed, throwing gaudy clothes right and left. Was there anything there that wouldn't fall off her the first step she took? A long black scarf, a pair of diaphanous trousers ... she tore off her clothes, put the latter on with her own belt to hold them up, slipped the former around her neck, crossed it over her small breasts, tied it in back. One hurried step towards the door and the thought stopped her as though she had run into a wall: one does not dance the Senetha barefaced in public. Someone had told her that emphatically, many times. The half-memory of a face formed, was scattered by a flicker of pain. She snatched up another gauzy scarf. Knotting it around her head like a semi-transparent blindfold, she went out onto the gallery. The wind brought to her the rising clamour from below.

Inside the great hall, chaos reigned. Half the men at least seemed finally to have succumbed to Cleppetty's little black bottle and were either staring into space or stumbling about wild-eyed. Marplet's household toughs were trying to organise them. Then one man more clear-minded than the rest jumped onto the centre table, waving a blazing brand. Jame darted into the room. Vaulting onto the table, she caught the man with a fire-leaping kick squarely in the stomach. He disappeared off the other side, doubled up in mid-air, his torch flying. There was a moment of startled silence as audience and would-be performer stared at each other. Then, taking a deep breath, Jame gave the assembled ruffians a full, ceremonial bow. Hesitantly, she began to dance.

The quavering notes of Ghillie's flute came down from the minstrels' gallery. He had never played for her before and, having no idea what tune to use, had settled for Taniscent's favourite. Worse and worse, Jame thought despairingly, trying to adapt to it. All she needed now was to remind her audience of how different this was from Tanis's usual, provocative performance. In fact, the Senetha was so different that Marplet's bullies were probably still watching her only because they hadn't figured out yet what she was doing.

But the essence of the dance is concentration. Long practice soon made Jame forget her nervousness, and she began to flow through the patterns, feeling the power build in her, around her. There was more of it than she had ever sensed before, dancing alone in the loft. It came from all sides, from the men who watched her open-mouthed. Hunger lay naked on every face. For a moment, the rawness of it took Jame's breath away, and then something deep inside her responded. With a gesture at once reckless and exultant, she clothed herself in their desires. This had happened before, would happen again. In the utter intimacy of the dance, she gave each man what he wanted most, took from him all that he could give without the touch of hand or lip.

Then one by one the upturned faces fell away. In the darkness that followed, golden-eyed shadows whirled with her. *Priestess*, they whispered in her ear, *Chosen of our Lord, feed on us and give us food. Dance!* And she danced – in joy, in terror, touching and touched – until all sound faded and she was alone.

When Jame regained her senses, she was kneeling formally on the table. The room was empty except for the widow, who sat watching her intently.

'What time is it?' she asked, stretching with unaccustomed sensuousness.

'Nearly dawn. You've been sitting like that for hours.'

Memory returned in part with a rush, freezing her in mid-gesture. 'What happened? Did you get help... or was I so bad that they all jumped out the windows shrieking?'

'I found a pair of guards who would come, all right,' said the widow, 'but when we got here there was nothing for them to do. Everyone was gawking at you. Then, when you bowed and sat down at the end, it was as if they couldn't see you any more. Damnedest thing I've ever seen. We would have had them staggering all over the inn, hunting for you, if I hadn't promised that you'd dance again tonight.'

'Oh, Cleppetty, no!'

'Oh, child, yes, if you don't want another riot. But don't worry,' she added, grinning fiercely, 'we can lay in another supply of black poppy milk by then, though I doubt if you'll need it. You surprised me, missy. I don't know how you did it, skinny thing that you are, but you seduced every man in the room... and some women too. Not even Taniscent ever did that.'

'Tanis! I'd forgotten about her. How is she?'

'Gone. Kithra left her unattended to see how you were doing, and she slipped out. Betrayed, ruined, and replaced all in one night – no wonder she ran away. We'll get her back, though. Whether she dances here or not, this is her home, and now she'll need us more than ever. What you need is sleep. Tomorrow – or rather later today – we'll see about a better costume for you, one not quite so likely to fall off. Now don't make faces at me, missy; like it or not, you've got a new career on your hands.'

7

The Feast of Fools

The note was written in the flowing script on a piece of the finest cream parchment.

> *The dancer B'tyrr* [it said] *will present herself at Edor Thulig during the Feast of Fools to perform before His Glory, Prince Ozymardien of Metalondar*

'Well,' said Tubain, reading over Jame's shoulder, 'I suppose it was likely to happen sooner or later. His Glory is always interested in anything unusual, and that's you.'

'Very flattering, I'm sure,' said Jame with a grimace. 'Just the same, I don't much care for the tone of this thing. He seems to expect me to come running with my tongue hanging out because he's deigned to whistle for me.'

'When you're the richest man in Tai-tastigon, maybe in all the Eastern Lands,' said Cleppetty from the top of the ladder, 'you make assumptions. Here, catch.'

She tossed down a ball of ribbons, which dissolved in midair into a mass of multicoloured streamers fluttering down indiscriminately onto the two below, the nearest table, and into an early patron's bowl of soup.

'Damn!' said the widow, and came clattering down.

'Such a pity too,' said Tubain, mournfully still staring at the note, oblivious to his sudden, garish splendour. 'Just when things were going so well.'

'What's he talking about?' Jame asked the widow as she helped her collect the ribbons. 'Does my prospective host do after-dinner card tricks or is he just an avid anthropophagist?'

'Worse,' said Cleppetty grimly. 'He collects things. Jewels, furs, ivory, people. Last year, for example, he took to wife the most beautiful virgin in the Eastern Lands – and rumour has it he's kept her just as received. In a collection like his, you understand, there's no place for a damaged article.'

'How frustrating for her.'

'As you say, but the point is this: if you dance particularly well before him, he's liable to collect *you*.' She called Ghillie to help her shift the ladder to another part of the hall. 'At any rate,' she said, climbing it again with a handful of loose ribbons, 'you've got until tomorrow to decide. He should at least pay well . . . provided you ever get out to spend it.'

Jame watched as she reached the level of the b'tyrr figures and began to blindfold each one by stretching a ribbon across its eyes and securing it on each side with a nail. In view of their talismanic function, this struck Jame as a thoroughly inauspicious procedure. All over town, however, the minor tutelary figures were being treated in much the same way, while in the Temple District priests went about their evening duties with as great a pretence of normality as possible. They, like everyone else, were waiting for midnight and the Feast of Fools, that annual leap-day no calendar ever showed for fear the gods would discover its existence and spoil the fun. It seemed rather churlish not to let the faithful b'tyrr in on the secret, but there it was: one couldn't make exceptions.

The B'tyrr, the Talisman – now she was called 'luckbringer' in two languages, neither of them her own. Jame smiled ruefully. What a contrast to her own full name, which she never used.

'Hullo!' Dally called from the doorway. 'Ready to go, or are you still needed here?'

'Cleppetty?'

'Go, go,' came the answer from above. 'The work is well in hand for once.'

'My jacket is in the loft,' Jame said to Dally. 'Come up and see how much Jorin has grown.' Without waiting for an answer, she darted up the steps. He overtook her on the last turn of the spiral stair, and they tumbled onto the loft floor together, laughing. Across the room, near the place where the knapsack still lay hidden, two sleek heads raised inquiringly, the milk opal eyes of the ounce cub gleaming above and behind Boo's round face.

'He's grown, all right,' Dally said, bending down to stroke Jorin, who responded with one of his most unfeline chirps of pleasure. 'Pretty soon he'll be too big for the loft. A pity you had to stain his fur, though; the markings were beautiful.'

'Altogether too beautiful,' said Jame wryly. 'A common tawny I can explain, but not a Royal Gold. Someone would be sure to make trouble. There's been no trace of the mindlink, though. Maybe it will take another crisis to reestablish it, or maybe it's gone for good. That might be just as well.'

'I still don't see why,' said Dally. 'It doesn't seem right to be ashamed of a gift like that.'

Bitterness twisted Jame's smile. Why indeed? What was it that made most of her people so fear those old abilities and physical traits, which, if legends spoke true, all Kencyrs had once shared? That question lay at the heart of her expulsion as a child from the keep. With an effort, she put herself in the place of that man, her own father, who had stood at the gate, shouting curses after her.

'I suppose,' she said slowly, 'that it's partly because we no longer trust anyone to use such gifts properly. Of course, the ability to touch minds with an animal isn't all that threatening, but what about those who can weave dreams or whose blood, once tasted, binds a man body and soul? Our history is full of strange people, Dally, with strange powers. One of the strangest is the Master. When that man fell, it was as if we all had fallen, even those who fled out of his power into Rathillien. That was when honour became such an obsession with us ... and when we began to fear all Kencyrs who, like the Master, had special gifts that might be turned to the service of the Enemy.'

'Wait a minute,' Dally protested. 'That happened nearly three thousand years ago when the Kencyrath first came to this world, didn't it? But just now you spoke of this Master, whoever he is, as if he were still alive.'

'So he may very well be. After all, he betrayed his people and god to Perimal Darkling in exchange for immortality.'

'This is no good,' said Dally, shaking his head. 'You've got to tell me this story properly or not at all.'

Jame hesitated. Few outsiders knew the full history of that treacherous act, which had nearly shattered the Kencyrath's spirit forever, but then Dally, as Dalis-sar's stepson, was to some extent a member of the family. Abruptly she knelt, closed her eyes, and began to recite:

'Gerridon Highlord, Master of Knorth, a proud man was he. The Three People held he in his hand – Arrin-ken, Highborn, and Kendar – by right of birth and might. Wealth and power had he, and knowledge deeper than the Sea of Stars. But he

feared death. "Dread lord," he said to the Shadow that Crawls, even to Perimal Darkling, ancient of enemies, "my god regards me not. If I serve thee, wilt thou preserve me, even to the end of time?" Night bowed over him. Words they spoke. Then went my lord Gerridon to his sister and consort, the priestess Jamethiel Dream-Weaver, and said, "Dance out the souls of the faithful that darkness may enter in." And she danced. Two-thirds of the People fell that night. Highborn and Kendar. "Rise up, Highlord of the Kencyrath," said the Arrin-ken to Glendar. "Your brother has forfeited all. Flee, man, flee, and we will follow." And so he fled, Cloak, Knife and Book abandoning, into the new world. Barriers he raised, and his people consecrated them. "A watch we will keep," they said, "and our honour someday avenge. Alas for the greed of a man and the deceit of a woman, that we should come to this!"'

'Ouch,' said Dally. 'I'm sorry I asked. But what were those three things that got left behind?'

'The Serpent-Skin Cloak, the Ivory Knife and the Book Bound in Pale Leather. The third was the greatest loss, I'm told. Nobody ever dared to memorise it, not at least since a priest named Anthrobar turned his brain to a cinder simply by trying to copy the damn thing – and to make matters worse, his partial transcript, which is what we used to get to Rathillien, disappeared soon after our arrival.'

'In other words, you're stranded here without it?'

'That's about it ... and nice quiet neighbours you've found us too,' said Jame, with a sudden grin. 'Blood feuds every other day, wars on the weekends, and our wretched god sitting on top of the whole mess. With your luck, you may even get the Tyr-ridan before we're through with you.'

'The what?'

'The Tyr-ridan. It's another reason why mind links and what-not are considered ominous. You see, the more old abilities one has, the closer one is to the godhead itself.'

'What's wrong with that? The closer the better, I should think.'

'Not with our god it isn't. Remember, we haven't even been on speaking terms for the last twenty thousand years or so. When it wants something done, it simply manifests itself in some unfortunate Shanir – that is, one of the old blood, of the old powers. Creation, preservation, destruction ... sometimes one attribute shows up in an individual, sometimes two, or even all three under different circumstances. Things tend to happen around the Shanir. Worse, when all three aspects of the god are present at once, each one concentrated in one of three Shanir known collectively as the Tyr-ridan, the final battle with Perimal Darkling is supposed to occur.'

'But surely you should be looking forward to that,' Dally protested. 'After all, it will be the culmination of your destiny.'

'When the Master fell,' said Jame, 'I think a lot of our people lost faith in their destiny altogether. But listen, we'd better get going.' She eased her d'hen out from under the two cats and stood up. 'Canden will think we fell down a privy hole on the way.'

They descended and crossed the hall.

'Don't forget,' the widow's voice called from on high, 'you're to perform here during the Feast. Anytime will do.'

Dally saw his companion grimace. 'You still have reservations about dancing, don't you?' he said as they crossed the square.

'Yes, more so all the time. I can't get over the feeling that I'm abusing a great and terrible ability, although what its proper use is I can't guess. I knew before that the Senetha was a way of channelling power – all Kencyrs use it to generate the force behind the Senethar in combat – but this...! Dally, it's frightening. Somehow I'm vampirising my audience, men and women both. I don't like what that does to me ... or maybe I like it too much.'

'Well, it should be some comfort to know that no one can remember afterwards exactly what they see when you dance,' said Dally. 'I can't, anyway. You'll have to admit, though, that this forgotten talent of yours chose a lucky time to surface.'

That, indeed, was true. Not only had it been instrumental in saving the inn that night some eight weeks before but since then it had caused a remarkable change in the financial condition of the Res aB'tyrr. Two days ago Tubain had renewed the tavern charter and returned with a little sack containing fifty golden altars, which he had presented to her rather sadly, knowing what she wanted them for.

Marplet, with a somewhat whimsical air, had since offered her as much a week if she would work for him; and Jame had surprised herself by turning him down with sincere thanks. She now knew that she had the rival innkeeper to thank for Bortis's absence. Some said that the maimed brigand had been driven away because he had disobeyed orders. Jame suspected, however, that Marplet had done it to protect her, since Bortis clearly blamed her more than Bane for what had happened to him. In a way, Jame thought, Marplet himself was acting much like his former henchman in transferring his hostility from her, its proper object, to poor Tubain.

'Why do things always get so complicated?' she said out loud, interrupting Dally.

'It's a confusing system, all right,' he said, adding, 'the Thieves' Guild, I mean,' when he saw her puzzled look. He had, she realised, got off on an altogether different topic.

'Most people don't realise that there are actually two elections,' he continued. 'In the first, late this coming autumn, the landed masters choose their two representatives for the Guild Council. In the second, next Winter's Eve, the Council votes for the new Sirdan. The bribery market is very lively already. Even Mendy is making arrangements with someone very important for a big loan, although I shouldn't think,' he added loyalty, 'that he'll have to buy as many people as Theocandi will. But you see, all this makes a lot of extra work for the spies and, well, the Creeper told me yesterday that he couldn't spare men any longer to search for your dancer friend. I'm afraid there's nothing more we can do. She's probably died of old age by now anyway. I'm sorry.'

'Well, you tried,' said Jame. 'Word may come yet through other channels. Meanwhile, it mustn't ruin our holiday. After all, by this time next week I may be gone.'

Dally bit his lip at this, but said nothing.

Soon after, they met Canden in Antiquarians' Row, where the Tai-than expeditionary headquarters were located, then walked north together. Canden talked with great enthusiasm and considerable expertise about the maps that he was helping to collate for the expedition's leaders, the renowned explorer Quipun of Lefy. Jame gathered that Quipun had given this task to the boy originally to keep him quiet, but suspected that he was now beginning to realise his eager young helper's potential.

They came to the River Tone and walked along its bank, buying from street stalls fresh grilled shrimp and venison rolled in almond dust. The setting sun cupped between the white slopes of Mounts Timor and Tinnabin spilled its crimson light down the hidden paths by which the first caravan would travel the next week. For the first time, the imminence of her departure struck Jame. It seemed impossible that she would be leaving so soon with so many questions still unanswered and her researches in the Temple District barely begun. She hadn't even really decided what it would be like to rejoin her people. Since the night of the near-riot, events had simply carried her forward, smoothing the way to a leave-taking that now seemed all too sudden. She almost wished that something would happen to prevent it.

Just then, Edor Thulig, the Tower of Demons, came into sight on the left. Its foundations rested on the largest privately owned island in the city, which lay between arms of the River Tynnet and the River Tone. The high wall that girt it was topped with barbed spearheads and torches that threw their light on the swift water below. Its gate, however, was open, revealing the full sweep of the stairs that reached from the Tone's edge to the threshold of the Tower itself, and there too the doors gaped wide. Inside, firelight set monstrous shadows leaping over the ceiling and walls of the vaulted entrance way. Outside, obsidian sheathed walls soared up one hundred and fifty feet to the clawed toes of the four stone demons whose interlocking wings encircled the top of the edifice. Above their outthrust heads was a band of high, clear windows, this time of richly hued glass, and finally the stone tracery of the dome under which Ozymardien's great collection was kept.

'There'll be quite a party up there tonight,' said Dally, staring up at the stained glass level.

'I suppose so,' said Jame. 'I've been ordered to attend it.'

She told them about the summons. They both agreed that, intriguing as the opportunity was, it would be wisest to forgo it. At this, Jame merely looked thoughtful, and Dally, regarding her with sudden apprehension, quickly proposed that they see the Feast in with a glass of ale at the Moon.

The tavern was swollen with apprentices, but a friend of Dally's named Raffing called them over to a side table where he and several other of Master Galishan's pupils, including his roommate Scramp and Darinby, were sitting.

'Lit up like a shrine and open as a whore's legs,' a lanky, pimple-faced thief was saying. Jame recognised him as Hangrell, the apprentice of a rather disreputable master, whose territory abutted the Lower Town on the west. 'He's mocking us, he is. Tower of Demons indeed! Everyone knows he only has one.'

'One is quite enough,' said Raffing with a grin. 'Look at its record: in the thirty years since the Tower was raised, no thief has got so much as a clay pot out of it yet.'

'Exactly what does the Prince's pet devil do?' asked an apprentice new to the city.

'Mangles souls,' said Darinby laconically.

'But how?'

'How do you think? Look over there.' He pointed to a small table in the back of the room where a single man sat facing the wall. His shadow was black on the stones before him, all except the shadow that should have been cast by his head. Then there was nothing. His hair seemed to be falling out in strips with the skin still attached. Underneath, the flesh was brown and wrinkled as a rotten potato.

'Poor old Jubar won't be with us much longer,' said the journeyman dispassionately. 'He ran into the demon up in the lit levels during the last Feast of Fools. The idiot thought that because the gods slept, so would Thulig-sa.'

'Why didn't it?' Jame asked.

'You don't outwit a demon that easily, or any other being with even part of a human soul. Gods never have them; their worshippers know better. But a true demon has only victims, and therefore needs a soul as badly as we do bones. Some tear off whatever they can get through the shadow, like Thulig-sa; others suck it dry, bit by bit, like the Lower Town Monster. Either way, it means a slow, withering death for their prey.'

'Sometimes not so slow,' said the pimple-faced apprentice with a sly smile. 'Remember Master Tane.'

'Here now,' said Darinby sharply. 'That was never proved. *You* remember present company, Hangrell.'

They all looked at Canden, who was staring fixedly at his cup.

'Just after the last Guild Council,' said Dally in Jame's ear, 'the Sirdan's chief rival died suddenly. Theocandi was suspected of using soul sorcery – a shadow thief, to be exact – but as Darinby says, it was never proven. Speaking of souls,' he said out loud, 'don't the Kencyrs equate them with the shadow too?'

'More or less. With us, though, both are more... uh... detachable. Some of the Highborn and, I think, all of the Arrinken, have the ability to carry other Kencyrs' souls. The only advantage this seems to have, though, is that a man who has voluntarily given his soul into someone else's charge is very hard to kill.'

'That sounds desirable, anyway.'

'Not always. We like to keep death as an option.'

'Sometimes it's easier than running away,' said Scramp.

'Your terms are beginning to confuse me,' said Darinby, as though Scramp had not spoken. 'What's an Arrin-ken?'

'The first of the Three People, our judges. The priests give the laws, the scrollsmen record them, the Kendar enforce them, and the Arrin-ken temper them... or at least they used to. Two thousand years ago they got disgusted with the rest of us and withdrew to consult. As far as I know, they're still at it.'

'For two thousand years?'

'Time doesn't mean much to that lot; they're as close to immortal as makes no difference. I didn't say, you know, that they were human. In fact, they look rather like big cats – tiger size – can move things without touching them and, on occasion, have been known to walk through stone walls. The rest of us used to be much closer to them physically and mentally than we are now.'

'Marvellous!' said Scramp with a giggle. 'I love bedtime stories. Tell me, have you ever seen one of these beasties?'

'I think I have,' said the new apprentice unexpectedly, 'or at least its tracks. Anyone who's ever lived on the slopes of the Ebonbane can tell you about the Mount Timor Cat and how it's outwitted generations of hunters. It's even been known to help caravans caught by the snows.'

Scramp snorted. 'I liked the first story better,' he said. 'It sounded more... convincing.'

Jame regarded the little Townie thoughtfully. She was fairly certain that he had been trying to gain acceptance among the others all these weeks by baiting her – the only one more an outsider than himself – so she had tried to be patient. There were, however, limits.

'One would almost suppose,' she said mildly, 'that you didn't think I was telling the truth.'

Scramp gave her a quick, frightened look. Unlike some of his colleagues, he had never underestimated this odd, silver-eyed creature – but he also knew that whatever level of impudence he reached he must then maintain, if he was not to lose everything he had gained. Even now, he could feel the men at the other tables watching him out of the corners of their eyes, silently goading him on.

'What does it matter if you are or aren't?' he said, wondering if his voice was really as thin as it sounded. 'Who are you anyway? The penny pickpocket. The rotten fruit thief.'

There was dead silence. Everyone was staring at them now, all pretence of indifference gone. For a moment, the Talisman's eyes went very hard and metallic. Then, slowly, they cleared.

'Not a very distinguished record, is it?' she said in a brittle voice. 'Still, there's a little time left to make amends. Your master Galishan holds the Tynnet Branching District, doesn't he?' Darinby nodded, suddenly very serious. 'Very well. With your permission, I hunt there tomorrow night...'

'Don't say it, don't say it,' Dally pleaded.

'... in the Tower of Demons.'

Men-dalis's brother put his head on the table and groaned. Outside, bells began to ring, people to shout, fireworks to explode. Inside, everyone except those at his table stood up and, to the horror of the innkeeper, began with great solemnity to smash the furniture.

The Feast of Fools had begun.

From gate to gate, Tai-tastigon blazed with lights. The midnight sky bloomed suddenly with scarlet flowers, emerald vines rising, golden fountains dripping fiery sparks on the rooftops below. Candles thronged every window. Bonfires threw their fitful glare on the façades of houses, on the fantastic figures that leapt and whirled around them. Down River Street came the effigy of a major fertility god borne on the shoulders of its shouting worshippers. Its priests ran on ahead with robes tucked up, snatching flowers from passersby, weaving them into garlands, and dashing back to throw them over the figure's jutting phallus. Those who followed loudly kept score. In all that great, exulting city, only the Temple District was dark, and now the Lower Town as well where no joy ever survived the fall of night.

Two figures stood in the shadows on the shore of the Tynnet, across the water from Edor Thulig.

'If anything happens to you,' one said with considerable violence, 'I'll break that Townie's neck.'

'No, you won't,' said the other. 'You know perfectly well that he didn't push me into anything that it wasn't already in my mind to try. I've had a good master, Dally. He hasn't asked for anything but loyalty, and it won't disturb him at all if others call him a fool for having bothered with me. Just the same, the man who stole the Eye of Abarraden deserves better than a petty larcenist for an apprentice. Anyway, maybe I'll feel better about leaving Tai-tastigon if I can do it with a bang.'

'It may be with a loud screech if Thulig-sa gets its paws on you,' said Dally gloomily. 'That is, of course, assuming His Glory doesn't add you to the jade screens and stuffed fantods first.'

'Don't worry,' said Jame with a grin. 'I'd look silly under a bell jar. Just pass on my message to Sparrow, if you can find him ... and Dally, if something should go wrong, please be kind to Scramp. You don't know what it's like always to be an outsider.'

Before she realised his intent, Dally caught her by the arms. His kiss was so sudden and fierce that for a second she thought her front teeth would be knocked down her throat. Then he was gone. She stared after him, incredulous, then pushed the incident to the back of her mind. Putting on her dancer's mask, she crossed the bridge.

Inside the outer wall, beyond the open gate, a wilderness of white roses glowed faintly in the darkness. Jame followed a tessellated walk through them to the still-unguarded river steps. There really was something arrogant about all this openness, she thought as she climbed the steps, a kind of contemptuous challenge thrown down to the whole mad city, now reeling into its last four hours of carnival. The passage way was some thirty feet long and lined with a mosaic of Metalondrian devils doing unspeakable things to intruders. Ahead, an open hearth fire roared up the central well of the tower. No one, guest or servant, was in sight, all having long since either mounted to the upper levels or retreated into the honeycomb of rooms between the outer wall of Edor Thulig and the inner one of this shaft.

Jame started cautiously up the spiral stair. The wind, whistling in the open door, rose with her, tugging at her cloak, running cool fingers over what skin the Senetha costume left uncovered.

The costume ... what a time they had had making it. Tight black cloth, some leather, much skin showing in unexpected places ... how pleased Kithra had been with it in the end, and how shocked the widow was. Jame hardly knew what to make of it herself except that, for what she did, nothing else would serve. And she had worn something like it before. She was sure that part of her mind remembered where and for what purpose when she danced, but that knowledge always slipped away again when the trance ended. It was the trance itself that worried her now. If it fell on her again, here, she would be stripped of all control while it lasted. Anything might happen. Too late to fret about that, however; here was the end of the stairs and the threshold of the demon's true domain.

The lit levels varied from three to five. Ceilings differed in height, stairs sprouted in odd locations, passageways – all gleaming white – dipped and swirled in a more or less concentric fashion. It was not a true maze in the Tastigonian sense, but it was designed to confuse anyone in a hurry, and doubtless had done so many times in the past. Light spheres illuminated every corner, throwing multiple shadows at Jame's feet.

Several times as she prowled this area, fixing its major patterns in her mind, she heard something moving stealthily behind her but tried to ignore it. With the Prince's invitation but none of his property in her possession, there should be no danger. That would come soon enough.

Guests were normally conducted through this region blindfolded. One broad staircase led from the upper level to the chamber above where, from the sound of it, the party was still in progress; none, however, gave access to the servants' quarters below in the honeycomb. Intermural stairways must service that. When she had satisfied herself as to the arena's layout, Jame fitted together bits of metal taken from various pockets in her cape and clipped a thin, strong rope to the resulting spidery form. Then she opened a window and stepped out onto the broad shoulders of the southern stone demon.

The wind buffetted her in savage gusts, filling her cloak, making it tear at her shoulder. She released it. It whirled away, a boneless night bird homing. For a moment it was hard to stand. Then came a lull. Jame swung the grapnel cautiously, paid out more line, and threw it upward. It disappeared over the balcony railing above. She tested it, took a higher grip on the rope. As her feet left the stone image, the wind came again, pushing her sideways into space. Far, far below, the spear-lined wall, the steps, the river. She began to climb. An immeasurable time later, her hand closed on the railing. She stepped over it into a pool of ruby and amethyst light on the balcony floor. Inside, there was a burst of laughter and applause. Shadows moved across the magnificent windows, dark, very close. Jame retrieved the grapnel. The narrower floor of the upper gallery was perhaps twenty-five feet above her, forming a partial roof. She threw the hook over its railing and climbed quickly up. As she had suspected from the presence of this rim walk, both the outer tracery dome and the inner one of amber glass were fitted with sliding panels. One on the north side was partially open. Jame slipped through it into the heart of Prince Ozymardien's treasure trove.

The cavernous interior, dimly lit with spheres, suggested the nave of a cathedral in its dimensions and a museum in its content. The faint light fell softly on the sheen of silken tapestries, on the marble limbs of statuary arching out of the gloom, on furs, gem-encrusted weapons, ivory miniatures on black velvet, cups of gold, and feather capes, all spread out ready for the touch of their master's hand. Jame walked among them, marvelling at their splendour. She longed to spend hours here simply looking when she knew that minutes must suffice. Then, on a little table just beyond an incredibly lifelike figure reclining on a couch, she saw what she had come for: the Peacock Gloves.

Everyone knew the story of the old man who had embroidered their high, shimmering cuffs with threads gleaned over a lifetime from the floor of the city's finest textile shop and how, when they were at last finished, that Prince had bought them for his new bride. The sum he had paid would keep their creator in luxury for the rest of his life, but it was a trifle compared to what His Glory must have spent on nearly everything else under this dome. Then too, the bride must soon have tired of them to have found their way here, to this forgotten table littered with cosmetic bottles.

Jame, however, thought they were the loveliest things she had ever seen. She was trying them on when behind her someone sighed. She whirled, and saw the figure on the couch change position. It was the princess, the virgin bride, fast asleep among the ivory warriors and the stuffed monstrosities.

Well, why not? Jame found herself thinking wildly. She's part of the collection too, isn't she?

She stood there frozen, waiting for the eyes to open, for the first scream. Nothing happened. Warily, she crossed over to the couch and looked down at its occupant. The princess lay curled on her side like a sleeping child. Her lips were slightly parted and her eyelids quivered, a hint of moisture on their long lashes. Over her stood the other, the predator come in from the night,

128

tense, watchful, but slowly relaxing. Then with great care, she reached down and pulled the displaced sheet up over the sleeper's bare shoulder, turned, and silently left.

Down on the main balcony again, Jame disengaged the grapnel from above, caught it as it fell, and hooked it over the rail with the full one hundred and forty feet of line dangling from it. The wind, even fiercer now, battered her. She checked the sleeves of her costume to be sure they covered the gloves' ornate cuffs, then, fighting down a sudden tremor of nervousness, reached for the catch on one of the tall, glowing windows.

Ozymardien's chamberlain was thoroughly exasperated. Had he not transformed the entire upper chamber into this opulent forest glade? Did not the most beautiful courtesans and finest performers in all Tai-tastigon grace these silken bowers and cavort under the jewelled boughs where hidden birds sang so enchantingly? Was there not present everything that should promote a glorious celebration of this, the Feast of Fools? Yet there sat His Glory on the velvet sward beside a wandering brook of chilled wine, sulking, bored. It was so hard to find a genuine novelty to whet that jaded palate. Now, if that little tavern dancer – the Bitter? the Batears? – had come, there might have been some hope. But then again, probably not. What he needed was a miracle.

What he got was the thunderclap of a window slammed open by the wind and a slender figure standing on the sill, looking startled. On the far side of the tower, three other costly windows crashed shut, two of them shattering. The wind howled through the hall, lashing the artificial trees to a frenzy, dislodging clockwork song birds, candied fruit, and dwarf musicians from their branches, overturning candles everywhere.

'That's not a woman, it's a natural disaster!' the Chamberlain's assistant cried, making a futile grab at a passing marzipan thicket. 'Somebody, quick – catch that oak!'

The figure from the window was walking across the room through the clusters of shrieking courtesans. It stopped before the Prince, bowed and, with no prologue whatsoever, began to dance. The wind still roared, the flames leaped, but bit by bit the human clamour died away as all watched, hypnotised. To the Chamberlain, it seemed as if he was no longer in the Tower of Demons at all but in another, larger chamber with darkness pressing tangibly, obscenely against the windows. There was a curtained bed decked with red ribbons. A figure danced before it with a white-bladed knife in its hand and something like a pallid, five-legged spider crawled feebly across the floor towards it. Then both the vision and the memory of it were gone. The dancer was walking back to the window by which she had entered. His Glory, suddenly coming out of his trance, began to clap wildly, ecstatically. The Chamberlain, with a great effort, took himself in hand.

'Put out those fires!' he ordered the guards, 'and somebody, stop that woman!'

Jame, out on the balcony, heard the shout. She couldn't remember if she had performed or not and rather thought they were after her for breaking those beautiful windows. Either way, a quick retreat seemed in order. She grabbed the rope and swung over the railing. Fifteen feet down, a blast of wind caught her like the blow of a fist, knocking her sideways through a window onto the lit levels. The rope slid through her fingers. She crashed to the floor and lay there half-stunned in a confusion of broken glass.

From somewhere nearby came a confused mutter, as though many voices were whispering hoarsely together. Bruised and bleeding, Jame staggered to her feet. The rope was gone, either blown away from the tower or detached from above. Her first line of escape had been cut off.

The noise was getting closer, louder . . .

She must try to reach the spiral stair that circled down the tower's main shaft – but the stairway that would bring her closest to it was the same up which that abominable sound was coming. She should have left her soul with Ishtier, Jame thought wildly . . . but no: he couldn't be trusted to return it. Should she wait for the Prince's guards to find her? Not that either – it would mean her skin for the theft of the gloves, even if they arrived in time. Think, fool, think . . . there was another flight of stairs on the west side of the tower. She backed towards it, extinguishing each light sphere as she came to it with a whispered 'Blessed-Ardwyn-day-has-come.' The sound faded, grew again, so confused by the strange turnings of the semi-maze that it sometimes seemed behind her, sometimes ahead.

It *was* ahead. She whirled and saw Thulig-sa coming at her around the curve of the passageway, a patchwork thing of stolen shadows exuding dull malice and hunger. A dozen piping

130

voices accompanied it, all crying, 'Run, thief, run!'

She ran. The darkened corridor swallowed her and her precious shadow, concealed them both as she darted into a side passage and stood there trembling, her back pressed against the wall. The demon rushed past in the dark, trailing the moans of its previous victims. Then she was out in the open again, racing along the western wall and down the steps. No time for the spiral stair now; no time for anything but the third escape route, which must be taken without pause for thought or fear.

The window stood open before her as she had left it. Without slacking pace, Jame was through it onto the shoulders of the stone demon, in the air, falling.

It was a very long way down. The wind spun her like a dry leaf, let go in time for her to see the spear-tipped wall, the steps, her own shadow leaping up to meet her on the torch-lit water.

It was like hitting a stone wall.

Deep beneath the surface, Jame fought for her life. The air had been slammed out of her, and the current was savage. She surfaced, gasping, went down again, and came back up. A bridge soared over her head, then another one. Any minute now she would either be dashed against the Guild island figurehead or swept past it into the white water of the channel. Someone was running along the bank, trying to keep up. Dally. It had to be. If he dived in now, they would probably both drown. Where the hell was . . .

Something splashed into the water just ahead. She made a wild grab, felt her fingers close on the rope and slide down to the cork-bound hook. On the upper span of the Asphodel Bridge, Sparrow (who, it seemed, had received her message after all) gave a triumphant whoop and braced himself to take the strain. A minute later, Dally hauled her up onto the quay. Leaning against him, she shook down her sleeves, held up the Peacock Gloves, and began to laugh hysterically.

If the sudden appearance of the Cloud King's britches at the Moon could have been said to have caused a stir, it would be hard to describe the reception of the Peacock Gloves. There was a moment of stunned recognition, then pandemonium. It was as if a great insult had finally been avenged, a haughty arch-enemy humbled, and every thief there was caught up in the wild exultation – all, that is, but one.

Ever since her arrival, Jame had been surreptitiously

131

watching Scramp, whose miserable silence seemed louder to her than all the commotion that surrounded them both. Silently, she willed him to be sensible, to realise that for the first time in months nobody was goading him on, but she was the only one not caught by surprise when he suddenly pushed back his tankard, stood up, and, in a shrill voice, said, 'I don't believe it.'

The others stared at him, some puzzled, some beginning to snicker.

'I don't believe it,' he repeated, louder, as though to blot out the laughter. 'Either those aren't the real Peacock Gloves or you didn't get them in the Tower of Demons.' He took a deep, shaky breath and said, very distinctly, 'You're lying.'

A look almost of physical pain crossed Jame's face. 'Don't, Scramp,' she said very softly. 'Don't push. Please.'

'YOU'RE LYING!'

It was almost a shriek, like some small animal caught in a trap. He backed away from the table, knife in hand.

'C'mon, you – you coward!'

This time Jame followed him slowly, feeling sick. The smashed furniture had been cleared away, leaving an open space now ringed with shouting apprentices. As Jame entered the circle, she hesitated, then shifted her knife from right to left hand. Dally was appalled. Not only would this force her to depend on her weaker side, but it rendered her d'hen's full left sleeve useless for defence.

Scramp lunged. Cloth ripped as Jame sprang back. Forgetting the jacket's uneven construction, she had tried to block with her unpadded right arm. The boy slashed at her face, barely missing as she slipped aside in a wind-blowing evasion.

'Do something!' Dally shouted at her. Her reluctance to fight was so obvious that several voices had taken up Scramp's cry of coward.

'Damnation,' said Jame in disgust and threw down her knife.

Scramp leaped at her, steel flashing. She caught his hand. The blade flew out of it as she twisted, and Scramp came crashing down. Pinned, he recanted, then burst into tears. The others rushed in on her cheering. At that moment, she would gladly have gutted the lot of them.

'Good work!' said the luckless Dally, coming up half-wild with relief, and received such a look that he fell back a step. A boy slid up to him through the crowd and tugged at his sleeve. He bent to listen to the urgent whisper, then turned quickly back to Jame.

132

'You've got to get out of here fast,' he said in a low voice. 'Someone told the guards about the gloves, and now there's a full squad converging on the Moon. Here –' He handed her the articles in question, which he had taken charge of when the fight began. 'You'll be safe enough in the Maze, if you can get there. I'll stay and help confuse the trail.'

'As you wish,' she said coldly. 'Just be sure they leave that boy alone.' She disappeared out the front door, tucking the still-damp gloves in her wallet.

Penari's house was only about three furlongs from the Moon, and Jame usually reached it by going upstream a ways, then cutting due south. As she emerged from the inn, however, she found a brace of guards bearing down on her and so turned hurriedly down the side of the Moon, hearing a shout of recognition and the heavy clump of boots behind her as the chase was joined. The streets behind the tavern formed one of those sordid little tangles that all but those forced to live there and the guards assigned to the district soon learned to avoid. Jame, in fact, had never been through it before and soon found herself in difficulties, especially since the overhanging walls prevented her from taking to the rooftops. She could hear the guards behind shouting. Other voices answered them to the left and right. The squad had arrived in force and was closing in.

Ahead, the dirty lane branched in an unusual and rather slipshod way. Jame was reminded of a similar formation in the Maze, which she had often passed on her way to Point A, Master Penari's favourite intersection for some obscure reason and the one to which he most often had her find her way. If she were going there now, she would take the right fork, go past three alley mouths, turn left... well, why not? As she followed ths course, she suddenly realised that each step of the way was recognisable. Looking up to the second, third, and fourth storeys, even more familiar patterns abruptly emerged.

She was running now, aware of voices close behind her but too excited to care, when, rounding a corner, she crashed into something that she at first thought was a wall. Then it put out brawny arms and caught her on the rebound. Far over her head, a bearded face looked down at her, rather bemusedly.

'Pardon,' it said in a remote, polite rumble. The language was formal Kens.

'H-honour be to you,' she stammered in the same tongue, almost by reflex.

'Who speaks?'

'One who would have further words with you...' A guard appeared at the end of the passageway, came lumbering down on them. '... later. Meet me at the Res aB'tyrr in the Red Wax District.' She ducked under his arm and ran. Behind, there was the sound of a mighty collision, then of two voices, one swearing luridly, the other rumbling an apology.

A Kendar! She remembered his counterparts at the keep, their gruff kindness to her despite her father's disapproval. How wonderful it would be to have one of her own kind for a friend again – if only he would accept her. This might turn out to be quite a special night after all. Then, as though in confirmation, she turned the last corner and saw, just as she had known she would, Point A in all its solid glory, the Maze itself.

Penari looked up from his overflowing table as she burst out onto a ground level balcony some two stories above him.

'Sir!' she shouted down, 'I know the secret of the Maze! It's a street plan of the old city – all five levels of it plus the basements and sewers with walls instead of houses. That's it, isn't it? *Isn't it?*'

'Talisman,' said Penari, 'you may amount to something yet. Now come down and tell an old man how you young fools have spent the festival.'

She did, in considerable detail, and concluded by laying the gloves on the table before him. It was the story, however, more than the plunder that delighted the old thief, as Jame had expected it would. Hence she was not surprised when, after chortling himself dry, he made her a present of the Peacock Gloves.

'Just take them over to the Shining Court and have Master Chardin assess them,' he added. 'Tell him to put the Guild dues on my account and don't you go strutting them in public until it's safe, boy. Remember that!'

She left him grinning to himself like some ecstatic death's-head and chanting, 'I to the temple, you to the tower,' over and over again with great satisfaction.

The Shining Court, fortunately, was near at hand. To her surprise, she found Master Chardin waiting for her in the hall, a robe thrown over his night shift.

'You think I could sleep through this racket?' he said, leading her into his brightly lit workroom. 'You've set the Guild in an uproar, young man – again. No, don't apologise. It's the results that count. Now, let's see these famous gloves.'

He took them, making soft, reproachful sounds at their dampness, and stretched them out under the multiple light spheres. As he examined them, Jame regarded him curiously. She had never met this thin, prematurely balding young man before; but like everyone in the Guild, she had heard much about him. He was perhaps the only one of Theocandi's appointed officials who would have nothing to fear if the present Sirdan was overthrown: Men-dalis would never be fool enough to dismiss anyone so supremely competent. No one, however, knew how Chardin himself would vote. He was a man who lived for his work, for the pure pleasure of handling the rich things that came into his court each day, and was known to be almost constitutionally apolitical.

'I'd value these at fifty-one, no, fifty-three altars,' he said at last, straightening up. 'That's five altars, three crowns Guild duty. You say your master will settle? Very good. He or you, depending on who keeps possession, will be at jeopardy for the next thirty days. Now, in case the Prince wants them back, what ransom?'

'No ransom,' said Jame firmly, 'no bids, either.'

'How about rewards? There's an unconfirmed rumour that the Princess will pay very well for their return, perhaps as high as seventy-five altars. No? Well, I can't say that I blame you. Just look at that needlework, those colours . . . you've got a real prize there, my lad, one I wouldn't mind bidding for myself.'

After a few more minutes of rapture on one side and quiet gratification on the other, Jame left. Homeward bound through the noisy, windblown streets, one eye wary for guards, she wondered about the Princess's offer. Had it been made, as Master Chardin had implied, without her husband's knowledge or backing? What funds other than the bride's portion of her dowry would be available for her? Not very extensive ones, probably. Seventy-five altars was a great deal of money, suggesting an unexpectedly ardent desire to regain her stolen property. It was unpleasant to think that she, Jame, had deprived that child of something so valued, when she had only meant to take a trifle; but would any real thief allow such considerations to distress her? Of course not. It was time, she told herself, to start acting like a professional; but oh lord, what would that giant Kendar think of all this?

Someone very big suddenly stepped out of the shadows, barring the way. At first she thought it was the Kendar himself, then, with greater alarm, that it was a guard. Neither, however, was the case.

'Lady Melissand wants to see you,' said the burly apparition in atrocious Easternese. 'You come.'

Now what in all the names of God could the most famous courtesan in Tai-tastigon want with her? Jame was eager to get home and perfectly aware that the streets were no place for her tonight, but this brusque invitation (or was it a command?) also made her exceedingly curious.

'I'll come,' she said, and followed her lumbering guide northward into the district called the Silken Dark.

The Lady Melissand managed a small, very select establishment just off the street of ribbons, where her commoner sisters plied their trade. On the outside, it looked like quite a plain, sedate house; inside, however, there was a lush courtyard garden with fountains, flowering trees, and birds of brilliant plumage flying about freely under a lacework dome. Bursts of laughter and an occasional moan came from both the shrubbery and the rooms above as Jame and her guide walked through the green shadows of the garden.

Melissand's apartment was in the back, opening onto the court. Someone inside was shouting angrily. As they approached, a man stormed out, nearly running into Jame. He gave her one furious look, then disappeared into the shrubbery. They heard him stumble, probably over someone's feet, and go out the gate cursing. Like everyone else in the Guild, Jame had laughed over Master Galishan's infatuation with Lady Melissand, but it had never occurred to her before now how agonising it must be for so proud and jealous a man to fall so hopelessly in love with a woman whom any rival could enjoy for a price. She would have given much not to have him know that a fellow thief had just witnessed his frustration and shame. The apartment door was still open. She scratched lightly on it, then entered.

The Lady Melissand lay on a pile of satin cushions with a studied grace that went oddly with her exasperated expression. At the sight of her visitor, however, she instantly regained her poise and waved Jame to a seat opposite her. Trays of sweetmeats and thimbles of honey wine were offered, polite conversation was made, and then she settled down to bargain seriously for the Peacock Gloves.

'But how did you know I had them?' Jame asked.

136

'Ah, my dear,' said the other archly, 'I have spies everywhere. I know everything.'

Jame wondered if she also knew that the articles in question were folded up in the wallet at her side. It seemed not. The bidding went from thirty altars to fifty, from fifty to seventy-five.

'You see, I've always wanted them,' said Melissand, delicately nibbling on a candied tree frog, 'ever since I first saw them. Yes, the old man offered them to me first, but then His Glory stepped in with a better offer behind my back. One hundred altars ... you know, my dear, you have a most unusual face – such delicate bones, such unnerving eyes! One hundred and twenty-five.'

'M'lady,' Jame protested, trying to stem this tide of unwanted offers. 'You overwhelm me. I really must have time to think about this.'

'Ah, but of course! How rude of me. Take as long as you like; but remember, I asked first, and can probably better anyone else's bid. In fact,' she said, frankly appraising Jame, her smile deepening, 'come back no matter what you decide.'

'M'lady,' said Jame rather desperately, 'you'd only be disappointed. Contrary to popular opinion, I am *not* a boy.'

'My darling goose,' said Melissand, widening her eyes, 'whoever said you were?'

There must be something in the air, Jame thought as she regained the street. First Dally and now this lady. Who next? Boo?

Meanwhile, there was the growing mystery of the gloves. She didn't believe for a moment that Melissand's interest was purely esthetic, nor, she was beginning to suspect, was the Princess's. It was time she had a closer look at these trophies of hers, but not so close to the courtesan's house.

Several streets later, after she had eluded one inept follower and a second very good one, Jame stopped under a streetlight and took out the gloves. They were indeed a masterpiece of needlework. Even in this dim light, the embroidered cuffs shimmered with the iridescence of skilfully blended colours. Each 'eye' possessed subtle differences in shade and stitchery, each thread proclaimed different exotic origins and yet they emerged harmoniously together. Perhaps beauty alone was at stake here. Such richness in colour, texture, and weight ... but what was this extra stiffness, here, inside this lining? Jame found where the inner stitching had been cut, and slipped her own gloved fingertips inside. Out came several sheets of very thin paper, folded many times. The waters of the Tone had done the ink little good, but enough remained legible – more than enough.

'The fool,' said Jame softly to herself, looking over the intervening buildings at the dome of Edor Thulig. 'The incredible, little fool.'

The rose garden was as open and deserted as before. Jame hid her wallet, containing the gloves, under a bush, then followed the walk around to the back of the tower. Here, as she had expected, was another door, plainly intended for the servants' use. She scratched on it until a face appeared at the grate.

'I want to see the guard in charge of the treasure dome,' she said. 'Tell him it's about an article of clothing.'

The face disappeared. A few minutes later, the door opened, and a handsome young man emerged. He grabbed Jame by the arms and rammed her back into the entry wall.

'You miserable little thief,' he hissed in her face. 'Where are they?'

'You damned idiot,' she said, trying to get her breath back. 'Aren't you in enough trouble as it is?'

He let her go and stepped back, glaring.

'I want to talk to you and the Princess. Kindly take me up to the dome.'

He led the way up through the servants' domain without once looking back, his big hands clenched at his sides. There were several bad moments for Jame in the lit area: she had only guessed that Thulig-sa would not attack an empty-handed thief, however guilty. Fortunately, she was right. The party above had apparently ended after so many of its elaborate trappings had either blown away or burned up, and enough walls were back in place to give His Glory some privacy from the servants now busily cleaning up the mess. Jame could hear his shrill voice rhapsodising over something or someone as she and the guard furtively climbed the last flight of stairs.

The treasure dome was much as Jame remembered it, except that candles now burned around the couch and the princess was sitting in the middle of it, hugging her knees. She jumped up at the sight of them and tried to assume an authoritative stance.

'I have the reward money here,' she said, indicating a small casket on the table where the gloves had lain. 'Did you bring them?'

'No, your highness.'

The girl's eyes went wide with fear and despair, all pretence gone. She sat down abruptly on the bed. The guard swore under his breath. Stepping quickly forward, he stood beside the princess with his hands protectively on her hunched shoulders.

'Your highness,' said Jame hurriedly. 'I didn't come here for the money or to return the gloves, I played a dangerous game and have won, I think, the right to keep them – but nothing gives me the right to keep these.' She took the letters out of her sleeve. Both the princess and the guard stared at her. 'I thought you would feel safer if you could destroy these yourself,' she said, putting them on top of the casket. 'Please believe me, it was never my intent to cause you pain, much less to put your position here or more likely your very life in danger; but if you two must conduct an affair practically under His Glory's nose,' she concluded in sudden exasperation, 'will you kindly have the sense in future not to put everything down in writing?'

It had been a near thing, Jame thought as she made her way through the crowd-choked streets, bound for home at last. It appalled her sometimes how easy it was to set such a train of events in motion. Cleppetty had been right about her talent for precipitating disasters, or at least near misses. This one, however, had come out reasonably well, if with some loose ends. Scramp's part in it still bothered her, but perhaps now that he had proved his courage by challenging her, the others would be more willing to accept him. And there was still that big Kendar to consider. It had been the height of idiocy, she now realised, to tell a stranger to cross half the labyrinth by night in search of an obscure inn. If he wasn't there when she got home, she would have to go out looking for him.

She had covered about a third of the way, taking a shortcut through the dingy back streets where many of the younger thieves had lodgings when, to her surprise, she came upon Raffing sitting huddled in a doorway, his head in his hands.

'What's the matter, Raff?' she said, stopping in front of him. 'Too much young ale?'

He started violently. 'Oh! Hello, Talisman. No, it's not that. Something terrible has happened. About an hour and a half after you left the Moon, Master Galishan came in, white as a

139

priest's linens. Of course, he heard all about you, Scramp, and the gloves almost before he was over the threshold. That put the sauce on the capon good and proper. He hauled Scramp out of the corner, tore into him like a mastiff after a rabbit, and ended up by disowning him altogether.'

'Oh,' said Jame lamely. 'I'm so sorry. How is Scramp taking it?'

'That's just it,' Raffing said with a sudden shudder. 'He's not. He came back to our room before me and – well – he hanged himself.'

Several streets away, there was the sound of wildly discordant chanting. It grew closer, louder, faded as the mob of frenzied celebrants tumbled together past the end of the street, somersaulting down to the Tone where a good many of them would undoubtedly fall in and drown.

'Does his family know?' Jame said at last.

'Gods, no.' Raffing glanced involuntarily up at the darkened window above him. 'Thal's balls, Talisman, I've only just cut him down!'

'Do you know where they live?'

'As a matter of fact, yes. Why?'

'Take me there.'

'Now? Go into the Lower Town at night? Well, why not?' he said with a semi-hysterical laugh, lurching to his feet. 'I sure as hell can't go home.'

The festival was dizzily spiralling down to its end. After nearly twenty-four hours of revelry, only the heartiest were left to celebrate, and they did it with the air of survivors in sight of rescue, dancing on the bodies of the fallen. The Lower Town itself, however, remained as it had always been after sunset: dark, sullen, menacing. Luckily, their destination was near the fosse that constituted the western boundary of the area. Not a trace of light showed about the house's sealed windows. After considerable scratching, knocking, and finally subdued shouting through the keyhole, the door opened a crack and a wizened face, a younger edition of Scramp's, peered out.

'Not so loud!' it hissed and withdrew. Jame followed. The door swung shut behind her, its lock clicking.

She was in a large room dimly lit with candles. Six children, all younger than the one who had opened the door, were sitting up in beds of various descriptions, staring at her. The mother, a plain but neatly dressed woman, stared too, her face expressionless. Jame cleared her throat awkwardly. Those seven young faces, each one a living portrait of Scramp at a different age, watched her as she told them about their brother. When she had finished, she brushed off a spot on the already clean table, took out the gloves, and laid them on it.

'You can do one of two things with these,' she said to the oldest and apparently brightest of the children who, she suddenly realised, was a girl. 'Sell them to Lady Melissand, who is willing to pay at least one hundred and twenty-five altars, or give them to Master Galishan if he will promise to take one of you in your brother's place. She wants the gloves, you see, and he wants her. Tell her she'll be at jeopardy for the next thirty days ... and be sure you get the money or the promise before she has a chance to examine them.'

The girl nodded. 'I'll go to the master tomorrow,' she said, almost in Scramp's voice.

'Good. That will be best ... and by God, if anyone bothers you, they'll answer to me for it.'

Someone pounded on the door.

'Talisman!' It was Raffing, shut outside. 'In Ern's name, open up ... it's coming!'

'It?' Jame said to the girl, who only gave her a wild look in reply. A child began to whimper, then another one. She looked for a moment at the gloves lying in a pool of light on the table, then unlocked the door and stepped outside. It slammed shut behind her. Raffing, who had turned away for an instant to stare down the street, launched himself at it, to no avail. It would not open again that night, not even if Scramp himself were to come crawling home with his blackened face and swollen tongue to scratch at its charred panels. Raffing clawed at her arm, babbling something, then turned and ran. Jame stood in the middle of the street, watching the Lower Town Monster approach.

It was a darkness that crawled, a huge, sprawling form that seemed both to have and to refuse any given shape. The cobbles showed faintly through it, as did the walls beneath its questing fingers as they traced the outline of each door and window, probing delicately into the cavities where wood or stone had fallen away. Flat as a cast shadow it seemed at first, but then it paused and gathered itself like a prone figure rising on its elbows. There was the vague shape of a head, a face moulded in darkness, unearthly, unreadable.

It was looking at Jame.

She stared back, wondering why she was not afraid. It was almost as if it wanted to tell her something. *Stand, stand, and let me touch*... but to be touched was to die the death of the soul. Slowly, she began to walk away. It followed her.

In eerie silence, at a walk, they went through the streets of the Lower Town. At the edge of the fosse, the pursuer stopped. Jame, standing on the opposite bank, saw it stretch out tentative fingers towards her over the water and lose them, as though the current ran on invisibly far above its natural bed. Then it withdrew, creeping soundlessly back into the darkness of the Lower Town. The muffled wails of children rose to meet it.

'Substance *and* shadow,' said Jame softly to herself as she watched it go. 'But whose soul, demon? I wonder.'

It was nearly midnight by the time she reached her home district. The town had quietened down remarkably as the festival drew to its close, and the streets were nearly deserted. Very soon now the gods would wake, and no one with his wits still about him wanted to rouse their suspicions with any unusual commotion.

The Res aB'tyrr was in the process of closing up. Inside, a blizzard of ribbons fluttered down as Ghillie unmasked the B'tyrr, hiding for a moment the man sitting at a back table, the sole remaining customer.

He was every bit as big as Jame remembered. Massive shoulders, corded arms, hands twice the size of her own, dark red hair and beard shot with grey... at a guess, he was in his mid-eighties, late middle-age for a Kendar. Although he looked fit enough, Jame noted with concern that his air of remoteness had deepened. He was gazing sightlessly at the still full cup between his hands, oblivious to the cascading ribbons, to her, to everything.

'He's been like that ever since he came in,' said the widow, emerging from the kitchen. 'D'you think he's ill?'

'I – don't think so,' said Jame. 'Just exhausted, more likely. Look at his clothes. He's come a long, long way, probably on foot.'

She went over to his table. 'All gates and hands are open to you,' she said to him in formal Kens, then, in Easternese, 'Be welcome to this house and peace be yours therein.'

'Honour be to you and to your halls.' The rumbled answer was uninflected, almost subterranean.

'Please.' She touched his cheek with gloved fingertips. 'Come with me. I know where you can rest.'

He looked up at her vaguely, blue eyes like deep water under heavy brows, and shambled to his feet. Picking up his pack and a double-edged war axe with carefully sheathed blades, he followed her mutely up to the loft where she chased the cats off her pallet and made him lie down. He fell asleep instantly. She pulled the blankets over him, then withdrew to the opposite corner and sat down with Jorin curled up in her arms. The ounce began to purr, the man to snore.

Soon she would go downstairs and help the others, but not just yet. The events of the last twenty-four hours were rushing through her mind. She could no longer tell which were her responsibility, which the result of circumstances outside her control. She blamed herself for everything. Was it honour or pride that first made her accept Scramp's challenge, then humiliate him before all their peers? What *was* honour? What was she that lives should crumble so casually when she touched them? Bortis was perhaps as correct to blame her for his maiming as Scramp for his death or Taniscent for her shattered life. She no longer knew how to regard any of these events. And what, ancestors preserve her, would this man, this emblem of her people and past, think of them? She would tell him everything, Jame decided, all her fears, all her secrets. He would judge her. Then, for the first time in her life, she would perhaps know how to judge herself.

The sound of a bell made her start. Another joined it, then another and another, until all over Tai-tastigon they were in full tongue. A shriller, less musical note chimed in from below. The Feast of Fools had ended. Standing at the kitchen door with kettle and iron ladle, Cleppetty was helping to beat in the new year.

8

Voices out of the Past

The Kendar was still asleep when, three days later, the first caravan left. On the fourth day he finally woke, but seemed even less interested in his surroundings than on the first evening when he and Jame had met. He would eat if watched but didn't seem to hear any questions put to him and spent most of his time either in sleep or mechanically polishing the blades of his great war axe.

'He worries me,' said Jame with a frown, watching Cleppetty stir with a spring of lemon balm the warm wine she would presently take up to the newcomer. 'It's as if all the spirit had been battered out of him.'

'Maybe he's just weak-witted,' suggested Kithra wickedly.

'No,' said Jame. 'As it happens, I've seen this sort of behaviour, years ago, in my father's keep. It was a hard life there. After a while, some people simply gave up. Most of them asked for the white-hilted knife; but a few just sat down in a corner – so as not to be in the way, you see – and stayed there until they died.'

'Are you saying that if our friend doesn't rouse himself...'

'He may well die,' said Jame, taking the cup, 'by passive suicide.'

On the tenth and fourteenth days respectively, the second and third caravans left. From the loft, Jame watched first one and then the other ascend into the Vale of Tone by the River Road and vanish into the shadows of the Ebonbane. Word filtered back that they had come upon the remains of the first caravan just under the Blue Pass, scattered over a mountain field black with crows. Soon after that, snow fell among the peaks again. A few wagons, late for the rendezvous, had gathered south of the city, hoping to form the nucleus of a fourth convoy, but no one was optimistic now about their chances of starting. True to predictions, the season had closed after only two weeks.

It was an odd time for Jame. All plans gone awry, she lived without new ones, waiting to see if the Kendar would live or die. A shock of some sort might restore him to his senses before it was too late. If he really had decided to die, however, it was not honourable for her to try to thwart him. That he would eat at all under these circumstances both surprised and encouraged her, so she continued to do what she could, hoping that something would bring about a change.

Meanwhile, the Tower of Demons affair continued to have repercussions. The day after the Feast, representatives of Prince Ozymardien appeared bearing not only ten golden altars in a silken bag as payment for the B'tyrr but also a command that she dance before His Glory again. When it became clear that she would not, agents began to lurk around the inn, apparently looking for a chance to kidnap her. Luckily, none of them ever made the connection between Jame and the Senetha dancer. Surprisingly few people ever did. The B'tyrr did not perform again until the Prince lost interest and recalled his men.

Perfumed notes for the Talisman were delivered every day for a week from the Lady Melissand, whose interest had apparently survived her outwitting.

Less regular and far more irksome were visits from the guards, who searched the inn for the Peacock Gloves several times with a thoroughness that made Jame glad they were no longer in her possession. Afraid they would unearth the knapsack, she moved the Kendar's pallet over to the corner where it was hidden so that no one could get at it without shifting him. Few guards were so intrepid. One, whom Jame suddenly recognised as the man who had nearly caught her behind the Moon, regarded the sleeping Kendar so intently that for a moment she was afraid he would try.

'Doesn't look so good, does he?' he finally said. 'Poor old Marc.'

'You *know* him?'

'Sure – Marcarn of East Kenshold. I met him six, no, seven years ago when he and a bunch of other Kennies were sent to help us during the Lower Town disaster. Didn't recognise him at first in the alley that night, he was looking so patchy. I would have bedded him down in the guards' barracks, but he kept saying that he had to get to this place. So I brought him.'

'That was kind of you. Did you ... tell him why you were chasing me?'

145

'No,' he said, eyeing her speculatively, 'but I will when he wakes up if you don't tell me now where the gloves are.'

'That won't do,' said Jame firmly. 'If he wakes, I'll tell him myself. But you may as well know that they aren't here any more. My word of honour on it.'

'Well, that's something,' he said, looking more cheerful. 'You can't blame an old dog for wanting a bigger bone. After this, Talisman, a proper prize you'll make for the guard who catches you. Keep an old friend in mind if there's a choice, won't you? The name's Sart Nine-toes.' With that, he gave her a clumsy bow and went tramping down the spiral stairs.

Later, Jame dressed for the one of the few new activities that occupied her these days. Once ready, she paused only to check the Kendar's condition (which remained unchanged) and to snatch up an old cloak, then she ran from the inn, bound at full speed for the Temple District.

Because this area was assigned to Penari, Jame had got to know it very well. As the old thief's apprentice, she had the right to steal anything there that she could get away with; but, to the great relief of the priests, she had not as yet exercised this privilege. Most of the local officials had stopped noticing her at all by now. They would have been far less at ease, however, if they had known why she continued to prowl among them day after day; bit by bit, she was beginning to solve the mystery of the gods of Tai-tastigon.

Early in her wanderings through the district, Jame had noticed that the most powerful of these beings were the ones with the most dedicated followers. This suggested to her that, here at least, faith might create reality. It was a beautifully simple solution and quite an appalling one from the standpoint of any Kencyr. After all, if this were true for the Tastigons, might it also be so for one's own people? In effect, had the Three-Faced God created the Kencyrath, or was it the other way around? If the latter, then the Three People had spent the last thirty millennia hag-ridden by a nightmare of their own making. Not only would this invalidate the very principles that justified their existence, but it would mean that they, not some cruel god, were responsible for the mess in which they currently found themselves.

Jame didn't want to believe this. Some instinct told her, however, that she had stumbled on at least one part of the truth, and she felt compelled to dig for the rest. As a result, she had begun a series of experiments in the Temple District on perhaps its more innocuous resident: Gorgo the Lugubrious. It was in front of this god's temple that she found herself some thirty minutes after leaving the inn and up its steps that she rushed, adjusting the hood of her cloak to overshadow her face as she went.

The outer room was empty, as was the tiny courtyard that opened off its far side. Wailed responses sounded dully through the wall to the right. The service was well underway. Jame paused to catch her breath, then slipped through the door into the chapel. This was a small room with a very high ceiling, completely dominated by the towering image of Gorgo set at its front. The god was represented as an obese, crouching figure, with the most sorrow-stricken face imaginable and unusually long legs, the bent knees of which rose a good two feet above its head. A steady stream of water trickled out of tiny holes in the corner of each green glass eye. Loogan the high priest was holding forth in front of it for the benefit of a small, dutiful congregation, all of whom were cloaked and hooded as though in the depths of mourning. Jame settled down unobtrusively on a back bench, mentally breathing a sigh of relief. He had only got to the fourth canticle of the creation ode: she was not too late after all.

The words of the service, uttered in a shrill singsong, scraped about her head. Many of them were pure gibberish, but there was some quite lovely liturgical story-telling scattered throughout, the relic, Jame believed, of an older ritual. There was no doubt that Gorgo was a god of ancient lineage, much come down in the world. Most demeaning was the heirarch, Loogan, whose every gesture and mouthed bit of nonsense seemed like a calculated insult to the dignity of his religion. Still, some vestiges of power remained in this room, enough to convince Jame that Gorgo might serve her purpose. She had already stuck a number of pins into layman and priest alike, hoping to determine exactly what Gorgo was and what relationship faith had to his existence. No pin to date, however, had been as sharp as the one she meant to use tonight.

Ah... Loogan had come to the tenth canticle, a hymn celebrating Gorgo's compassion for the sorrows of mankind. At this point, his assistant, hidden behind the statue, should throw a lever that would open the ducts to a reservoir on the roof and allow water to trickle down on the celebrants. There was a faint,

147

mechanical creak. Loogan looked expectantly at the ceiling, arms raised to call down the benediction of tears. Nothing happened. The congregation stirred uneasily as their priest, his face a picture of anxiety, repeated the signal words. Again, the sound of the lever being thrown; again, no water. Jame stared upward intently. Was there a hint of mist gathering in the upper darkness? She couldn't tell. Damnation.

Loogan wearily dropped his arms and began the whole service over – as he must do until he got the proper results. Jame edged towards the door. The little priest saw her. The surprise mixed with growing anger in his face told her all too clearly that, despite her hood, she had been recognised. Hastily, she slipped out of the room.

Up on the roof, Jame removed the clumps of moss that she had used that afternoon to block the ducts. The pin had been too dull to provoke a miracle after all. Next time, she must try for something more conclusive, more spectacular, but now for some reason the whole business had left a bad taste in her mouth. She climbed down and set off for the Moon to wash it away.

'Have you heard the news?' Raffing shouted over the din as Patches, Scramp's younger sister, made room for Jame at the table. 'Mistress Silver's idiot son has got himself caught for pickpocketing again. That's the third time since last Midsummer's Day.'

'Will the Sirdan ransom him again?' asked the new apprentice.

'Oh, he'll try, if only for his mother's two votes, but the Five may not let him. Rumour has it that one of them – probably Harr sen Tenko – is thoroughly annoyed, and who can blame him? Three times!'

'It'll be the Mercy Seat for sure,' said Hangrell with considerable relish.

'Don't you believe it. I say exile at most. Don't you agree, Darinby?'

'You're probably right,' said Master Galishan's journeyman tranquilly. 'Money has a loud voice in this town. Even so, Carbina of the Silver Court isn't likely to thank Theocandi for anything less than a full pardon. She's never reasonable when that son of hers is involved. No, as long as the Five are adamant, the Sirdan's support in that quarter is at hazard.'

'Does he need it so badly?' Jame asked.

'Every vote will count this time. Let's see. Theocandi can depend on Abbotir of the Gold Court because of Bane, and probably on Master Chardin too. Men-dalis, on the other hand, will undoubtedly get the four Provincial votes. So far, then, it's a tie. Thulican of the Jewel Court will go with whomever looks best, probably at the last minute. Odalian, Master Glass, can be bought and so, I suspect, can the masters' two representatives. That's sixteen votes in all – ten for the five courts, four for the Provincials, two for the masters – and at least six of those will go to the highest bidder, who will use them to win the election. Money will be the key factor this time, make no error about that.'

'Then it will be Theocandi,' said Raffing with disgust. 'He has the whole Guild treasury to drawn on.'

'He is also a miser,' said Darinby flatly. 'He may well be out-bid, especially if Men-dalis's mysterious backer can provide the funds. I wonder if we'll ever find out who he is.'

'One of the Five is already helping Men-dalis by refusing to pardon Mistress Silver's son,' said Patches suddenly.

Jame and Darinby looked at her approvingly, but Hangrell, smothering with jealousy, snorted contemptuously. 'Speak when you're spoken to, girl,' he said. 'Who invited you, anyway?'

'Who, for that matter,' said Jame softly, 'invited *you*?'

Hangrell tried to meet her eyes and failed. Muttering some excuse, he left the table precipitously, pursued by jeers. Never a favourite, the lanky thief had recently lost even more credit through his efforts to worm himself into Bane's favour. He would not be missed at the Moon.

'What an alarming person you are, Talisman,' murmured Darinby. 'Still, it won't help our young friend here if you fight all her battles for her.'

'I don't intend to. The next time someone tackles her, he may be in for a nasty surprise.'

Patches grinned. She was still sore from her last Senethar lesson and looked forward to trying out her developing skills on someone without her instructor's uncanny reflexes.

'Besides,' said Jame, ruffling the girl's sandy hair, 'Half-a-noggin here is too clever not to make her own way once she's got a start, prejudices or no. As for the rest of this lot . . .' her eyes raked over the room, hardening, 'the more afraid of me they are,

149

the better. I'm tired of being underestimated. Now if you gentlemen will excuse me, I have a cat to walk.'

Darinby caught up with her outside. 'I'll go with you for a way,' he said, falling into step beside her.

'What's the matter, afraid of being attacked?'

'No, but you should be. Bortis is back in town.'

'Oh?' said Jame lightly. 'I didn't know he'd been away.'

'You should have. He's a hill brigand, remember. Now that the season is over, he's in Tai-tastigon again, bragging about the massacre under the Blue Pass (for which, it appears, his band was largely responsible), and swearing vengeance on you for the loss of his eye. Oddly enough, it never seems to have occurred to him to blame Bane.'

'Hmmm. Still, boasts break no bones.'

'No,' said Darinby darkly, 'but other things do. You were saying a minute ago that you've had enough of being underestimated, which, I suppose, means of being a target for half the bullies in town. That, admittedly, is a problem, but it's one I expect you'll have all your life. Very few men are ever going to give someone as fragile-looking as you her due in anything. That may be one reason why Bortis can't accept what happened to him: even if you didn't wield the knife that maimed him, you were there, you were the cause. For men like him, Talisman, you're a baited trap. They'll never be warned off because they can't admit to any danger. On the other hand, frightening sprats like the regretable Hangrell isn't going to make you any friends either.'

'You think I need friends like that?'

'No. You've been fortunate in your allies – and in some of your enemies too, come to that. After that run-in with Bane on the Palace steps, half the Guild must have laid bets that you'd be dead within a week. All I'm saying now is that while you may not be able to stop people from underestimating you, you must never underestimate them . . . especially when they've sworn to have your blood. Huh!' he said with a sudden, rueful laugh. 'Harken to the sage. I didn't mean to lecture you, Talisman, only to speak a word of warning in what I'm afraid is still a deaf ear.'

'Sorry, Darinby. If it will make you feel any better, I'll go on from here by the rooftops – where it's safe.'

'You have an odd idea of safety,' said the journeyman, watching her swing easily up onto a portico roof and from there

150

climb to the eaves. 'Watch out for loose slates.'

Jame had, in fact, meant to go aloft as soon as she left the inn. She loved the rooftops late at night, especially when the full moon transformed them as it did now into a wild, mountainous country quite distinct from the world below. Here the wind hunted freely among the gutters and chimney pots, coursing down the sweep of a thatched roof, whistling to itself among the gables. Bits of straw were in the air. Tiles lost their grip and slid, clattering, into the void. A solitary Cloudie crouched on the opposite eave like a lesser gargoyle, fishing for some tidbit below with a grapnel much like the one Jame now always carried dismantled up her sleeve. The streets below glowed with light, with all the pageantry of the late night city. Not one in all that bustling crowd looked up; not one had ever seen the wild, lonely land above, the Kingdom of the Clouds where moon shadows raced.

Jorin was waiting impatiently for her. After checking Marc again, she and the ounce went down the back stairs together, hearing snatches of song from the great hall. They turned right at the old gatehouse into the rim road and followed its curve to the Mountain Gate. Beyond that, the foothills of the Ebonbane rolled on under the full moon.

They had come here every night for the last two weeks. In that time, the summer flowers had bloomed unseen, filling the darkness with their fragrance, while the cloud-of-thorn briers held up their impaled blossoms above tangled shadows. The berries beneath these fragile white flowers already glistened in the moonlight like dark drops of blood. Birds who had eaten them during the day clung to the spiked branches singing ecstatically on and on until their hearts faltered and stopped. Roe deer drawn down from the mountains by the lure of sweet grass drifted over the hills, making Jorin prick his ears and chirp eagerly. There was another presence in the hills that excited him even more, but of that Jame never saw so much as a shadow. She was simply aware on occasion of being watched and remembered the vague stories of a catlike creature, perhaps an Arrin-ken, that was said to live in the mountains above. The first time this happened, she had called to it with her mind as she did to Jorin, trying to reestablish the psychic link. The very quality of the silence that came in response, as though to a child who had spoken out of turn, had so abashed her that she had not tried since.

Instead, she and Jorin had gone on with the business that had brought them here in the first place: learning how to hunt. Night after night, they stalked rabbits, quail, and roebuck. Blind Jorin's ears and nose were keen enough to guide him towards the mark, but the quarry nearly always took fright long before he was in striking range. When it broke, Jame (who had been creeping up on the opposite side) would leap to her feet and try to turn it back towards the cat. They could sometimes keep it boxed between them for several turns, both chirping excitedly, but so far success had always evaded them in the end. Tonight, a doe bolted straight into Jorin, knocking him over, and then streaked off into the darkness with the ounce in wild pursuit. A few minutes later, he came trotting back, panting and obviously pleased with himself. It was all a game as far as he was concerned: the instinct to kill had not yet ripened in him. They drank at a mountain stream, then climbed the highest nearby hill to watch the sun rise over the eastern plain.

The sky had turned the colour of wild honey. Golden light permeated the air, transforming the blades of grass that waved about them into a living bronze relief peopled with small animals and insects stirring after the long night. Far to the south, a grey-prowed rack of clouds sailed through the glowing air. Lightning flashed in its belly and the mutter of distant thunder reached them, but little rain would fall, for Tai-tastigon was experiencing days of growing drought. Below, the city rode at anchor in a sea of mist, pinnacles catching the clear light that was already turning the peaks above to rose.

It was time to be getting home.

They trotted side by side through the grey streets of the waking city. For the ounce, there was only the anticipation of breakfast; for the girl, as always the fear that someone from the nearby catteries would recognise the cub's quality through his stained fur and raise the unanswerable cry of thief. This morning they hardly met anyone, which made the shock all the greater when, turning under the old gatehouse, they found their way blocked by a single burly figure.

Jame had just time to note the eye patch and the broad, cruel grin when a footstep behind her made her whirl. Her raised forearm went numb with the blow but did not fully block it. The iron head of the club glanced off her right temple, seemed to lift her sideways off the ground. She was on the pavement with her back to the inner wall of the arch. There was a great roaring in her head, and blood dripped down on the cobbles by her hand. Jorin crouched before her, terrified. Someone was laughing. A dark form strode forward, bent and caught the cub by the scruff of the neck. Steel glinted. A knife...

Jame screamed and sprang. The old war cry echoed deafeningly off the archway stones. For a moment she saw Bortis's startled expression, and then he was gone. In his place, something cowered against the opposite wall, hands over its face, gurgling.

This time she did not hear the other man approach nor recall his presence until the back of her skull seemed to explode. She found herself lying face down on the cobbles without remembering having fallen. Two boots were very close to her face. He was standing over her, poised for the killing blow.

Rapid, heavy footsteps echoed under the arch, approaching. Something struck her left arm lightly. 'Pardon,' said a deep, preoccupied voice up somewhere near the ceiling, and the boots in front of her both left the ground simultaneously. Overhead, there was the sound of teeth clattering together, with a screech diced fine between clicks. The club fell, narrowly missing her hand. A moment later, some much larger object crashed to earth a good twelve feet away. The shriek, trailing after it, ended abruptly on impact. Large, gentle hands turned her over. The movement unleashed pain and red-shot darkness.

She was being carried... no, she was in the kitchen on the floor. The same hands were taking off her cap, probing carefully at the knot of pain beneath.

'... would have cracked the skull if not for all this hair,' a deep voice said.

Above, a bearded, frowning visage; beyond, other faces, another voice: 'Did you see what that cat did to his face?'

'It wasn't Jorin!' Her own voice, shrill, wild. 'It was...'

The Kendar's palm pressed lightly on her mouth. Over it, she saw Marplet standing at the street door.

'I'm sorry,' he said, quite distinctly.

Darkness closed in again.

'It was the rathorn battle cry that did it,' said Marc, sitting down rather stiffly on the floor so she would not have to look up at him. 'That sound would have raised anyone who ever fought under the Gray Lord up off a pyre, much less out of whatever fog it was that I'd managed to lose myself in.'

'Well, all I can say is that you must have risen – or descended, in this case – pretty fast to have got to the gatehouse so quickly. What did you do, jump out the loft window?'

'No,' said the big Kendar, quite seriously. 'I climbed down two storeys and then, to save time, fell the rest of the way.'

Jame started to laugh, then stopped suddenly, making a grab for her head. This gesture also ended abruptly, with a half-stifled yelp of pain. She hardly knew which hurt more, her head or her arm, which was mottled black and blue from elbow to wrist and should by rights be not only bruised but broken. It was now four days after the attack. She had slept off the worst of its effects and was left only with a raging headache, occasional double vision, and a scar forming just under the hairline of the right temple that would be with her the rest of her life. She had got off far more lightly than she deserved, and she knew it.

'Maybe you should get some more sleep,' said Marc, regarding her critically. 'We can talk later.'

'No, now – if you don't mind. I've too many questions hoarded up, and you know what a rocky pillow those make. Tell me this much at least: where were you going that night I ran into you in the alley?'

'I suppose I was trying to reach the caravan grounds,' he said slowly. 'I was going to take passage across the Ebonbane. Another journey. Sweet Trinity, how many there have been.'

He was silent for a moment, his eyes fixed on memory. Jame, watching him, realised that her question had sent him much farther back in time than she had intended.

'Ah, it's a long road that I've walked,' he said at last, quietly, as if to himself. 'Mile after mile, league upon league. And when I first set out, I thought it would only be for a few days, just a little hunting trip by myself to escape the other boys' teasing. That was nearly eighty years ago. Even then I stood head and shoulders over all of them, too big a target for laughter to miss. It was quiet enough when I came back, though. The gate stood open. The guard lay across the threshold with his throat cut. Inside, dead, all dead, my lord, my family, betrayed by a hall guest who had opened the gate one dark night to tribesmen from the hills. I tracked that man down,' he said, sounding almost surprised by the memory. 'I took my great-grandfather's war axe, which the hall guest had stolen, out of his hand and split his skull with it. His kin hunted me through the mountains half that winter. I killed most of them. Ah, but it was a red, red time. Then I came south into the Riverland and grew to manhood there, searching for a Highborn who would give me hearth space, a new home to replace the one destroyed.'

'Surely someone must have been willing to take you in,' Jame protested. 'After such a loss, it would only be fair.'

Marc shook his head regretfully.

'Fairness isn't a consideration any more,' he said, 'not, at least, for most Kendars. Too many holdings have been lost in recent years, too many lords killed, their people rendered homeless. The surviving Highborn can make their own terms now. The only choice for many of us is to become *yondrigon*, threshold-dwellers, in the house of some lord who often makes us pay our way by leasing us out as warriors, craftsmen, or scholars. Some of us go for years without seeing the threshold we supposedly occupy or gaining any pledge of eventual acceptance there. That was my situation. For thirty-six years, I soldiered from one end of Rathillien to the other as a yondri of the Lord Caineron. Not that I cared much for fighting; that winter in the mountains had taken away my taste for bloodshed. Few care to meet a man my size in battle, though, and it helps to feign an occasional berserker fit. Oh, I was worth something to my lord and hoped finally to win a permanent place in his household. The fall of Ganth Gray Lord changed all that.'

'Ganth of Knorth?' said Jame. 'Dally told me a little about him, but it was pretty garbled. Who was he, anyway?'

'Why, Glendar's heir, Highlord of the Kencyrath. He raised the central houses under the rathorn banner to fight the Seven Kings and would have won too if the border keeps had supported him, his allies had proved true . . . and he hadn't gone mad. Anyway, there was a pitched battle, defeat, and exile for the Gray Lord.

'I didn't fare much better. My Lord Caineron was slain in the fight and I was cast adrift again, no light thing for a man nearing middle-age. No Riverland lord would so much as look at me after that, so I came east. More than thirty years ago, that was. Harth of East Kenshold took me in, one more greying yondri to warm himself by his fire. Ah, he was a fine man, a lord of the old stamp. He only sent his threshold-dwellers out once, when the Five asked for help during the Lower Town crisis. Old Ishtier was high priest then.'

'He still is,' said Jame.

155

Marc stared at her. 'But that was seven years ago, and he'd already been here a good twenty years before that! He must have refused recall again, Trinity only knows why. I shouldn't think that any priest would care to stay in this god-infested place beyond his term. Have they at least sent more acolytes to help him?'

'I don't think so. What happened to the ones he had?'

'All dead, drowned trying to round the Cape of the Lost in storm season, trying to get beyond the Ebonbane. We passed them coming out of the city as we marched in, but not a word did they have for us. I've never seen Kencyrs look so scared.'

'That *is* odd. There's the Lower Town Monster, of course, but if it didn't panic me, why should it them? Do you know of any other reason?'

'None,' he said, shaking his head in bewilderment. 'After that meeting, you may be sure we kept our eyes open; but none of us saw anything but fire and street fighting, the Thieves' Guild having just been set on its ear by the last Council session and the assassination of Master Tane, the Sirdan's chief rival. No, all we got out of that trip were burns and a topic for five years of winter eves.

'Then one night the riders came down on us from the north, yes, out of the Haunted Lands. Three score of them there were, all in black, and they were Kencyr, though I've never seen their like before. Their armour was like something out of an old song, all hardened leather and steel, hacked and dented, and their swords were black with blood. They tore into us without so much as a word. We were fighting for our lives before most of us were fully awake, and a long battle it was, under torch and moon. They were devilish hard to kill. When we did draw blood, it ate into our flesh and pitted our weapons. They penetrated every room in the keep, had a look around, and then fought their way out again. And all that time their leader sat his brute of a horse on the hilltop, watching. Then the cocks began to crow. We saw their banner as they rode away, a black horse on a red field.'

Jame whistled softly. 'The device of Gerridon, Master of Knorth. Do you suppose that's who it really was?'

'If he got the immortality he was after, yes. But he's not had everything his own way for all of that: his left hand was missing.

'At any rate, that's the last action I fought for my Lord Harth. He was a brave old man and stood with us shield to shield all

156

that long night. Their blood was his undoing. I've seen men burned less on their own pyres. The horrible thing was that he lived nearly two years after that, the flesh slowly crumbling away from his living bones. When he finally died, his son told us yondri that we no longer had a place there. Six of us started out for Tai-tastigon. I was the only one who arrived.'

Silence fell between them for a long moment. Marc stared at the floor and Jame at him, not knowing what to say. Then he gave himself a shake like a dog leaving deep water and smiled at her.

'Enough of that. They tell me below that you come from East Kenshold too, though I could have sworn I knew everyone there.'

He undoubtedly had, Jame thought, and was perfectly aware that she had never crossed its threshold. This was simply his way of giving her room to manoeuvre around the truth if she wished to. It took a genuine effort not to do so.

'They say that because it's the only answer that makes any sense to them,' she said. 'In fact, I came down out of the Haunted Lands, from a keep near the Barrier.'

Marc regarded her with amazement. 'But the only thing up there is North Kenshold, and that was abandoned nearly three centuries ago.'

It was Jame's turn to look confused. 'Do you mean to say that my people weren't the original settlers? But then who in all the names of God were they?'

'Perhaps I know,' the big Kendar said after a moment's hard thought. 'You see, when the Gray Lord rode into exile, it was for the Eastern Lands that he was bound. But the report is that he died crossing the Ebonbane. Most of his people turned back then. A few went on, however, passing Tai-tastigon in the dark of the moon and were never heard of again – till now. Those must have been your people.'

'But if that's true,' Jame protested, 'why didn't they tell me about it?'

'Ganth would have wanted it that way. When the Kencyr lords, his own allies, let the Seven Kings strip him of power, he threw down his name as well, in a sense leaving it and his shame with them in the Riverland. His people, including your father, must have honoured his wishes after his death. How many of the household are left?'

'Only myself, and possibly my twin brother Tori. Like you, I came back to a dead keep. Marc, what's a rathorn?'

'Why, it's something like a horse except that it has two horns, scale armour on its chest and belly, and fangs. Some of them also have a taste for man-flesh. Beautiful creatures they are, but nothing more vicious walks the earth – which may be why Glendar adopted one as the family crest when he took over from Gerridon.'

Jame had removed the loose stones in the wall behind her and drawn out the knapsack. Now the small, oblong package was in her hands, and she was gingerly unwrapping it.

'Does it look like this?' she asked, holding out its contents to him on the cloth.

Marc examined the ring with its engraved emerald, which encircled what appeared to be a small bunch of twigs held together with brown parchment. 'Aye, that's the beast,' he said at last, 'and this, I think, is the seal of the Gray Lord himself, lost these many years. But what's stuck through it?'

'A finger,' said Jame, not looking at it. 'My father's. I tried to pull the ring off to take it to my brother. All the fingers on the other hand went as I was prying loose the sword hilt. I looked up into his face, and he was staring down at me – without eyes.' She shuddered. The thing slid off the cloth onto her knee. Marc picked it up quickly and held it cupped in his big hands so that she could not see it.

'By rights, the ring and the sword shard should go to Ganth's son, Torisen Black Lord,' he said thoughtfully. 'Your father must have been greatly trusted to have been given charge of such precious things. I don't really think you have to take the – uh – remains to him as well. A bit of fire would be best for them, and more respectful too. What's that other package you have in there – the big, flat one?'

'Oh, just a book I picked up somewhere. But what's this about a son? You didn't mention one before.'

'I gather he came as a suprise to a lot of people, turning up so long after his sire's death. How he made them believe who he was without seal or sword I don't know, but he did. Now he's the most powerful lord in the Kencyrath. Of course, all we ever heard at East Kenshold were rumours, some of them years old; but from the sound of them, it looks as if he's taken up his father's work. If so, there should be lively times ahead for us all.'

'This Torisen... how old is he?'

'In his mid-thirties, I think,' said Marc. 'Why?'

'Nothing. Just a mad idea.' A flicker of pain crossed her face, and she touched her forehead tentatively.

'That's enough for now,' said Marc firmly, getting up. Something slipped out of his belt and fell to the floor with a clatter.

'Your friend with the incomplete foot must have been here,' said Jame, picking up the guard's truncheon.

'Who... oh, Sart Nine-toes. No,' he said, accepting it back, 'this one is mine.'

'What?'

'Well, it looks as if we're going to be here awhile, so I thought I'd better get a job. Sart suggested the guards.'

'Oh, did he?' said Jame grimly. 'I owe him for that.' And then, much sooner than she intended, she told Marc about Master Penari, Ishtier's judgement, and the Talisman, watching anxiously for his reaction.

'You say a priest approved of this?' he said at last, looking puzzled. 'Odd. Just the same, it could mean trouble. I've made a commitment to the Five that isn't easily broken, and you've probably done the same with your master. If we were sensible people, we would separate and stay out of each other's sight until it's time to leave this city. Are you a sensible person?'

'Hardly.'

'Neither am I,' he said with a slow smile. 'We'll have to work something else out – later, when you've slept and I'm off duty... and by the way, your gloves will wear better if you cut slits in the fingertips. Good night.'

She listened to him clump down the steps, and let out her breath slowly. The moment she had most dreaded was past. He knew the worst about her now, and it didn't seem to bother him at all. Either he was unusually tolerant or maybe, just maybe, it wasn't so terrible to be different after all. She would have to think about that.

The knapsack lay beside her, the small oblong package, rewrapped by Marc, on top of it.

Burn the dead, or join them.

'Father, let go,' she said out loud in a low, exultant voice. 'To ashes with the past.'

9

A Matter of Honour

The Widow Cleppetania was making humble pie. The pastry
shell was ready. The sealed pot of wine, spices, and tripe had
done ten hours worth of simmering in five with the aid of a
simple spell, but the kitchen was wretchedly hot nevertheless.
This was not a dish that she cared to make in midsummer.
Mistress Abernia had specifically requested it, however, and
would shake the rafters if it were not forthcoming.

Once, the widow would have told her to go bark for it.

Now, with the advent of the ambitious Kithra, she found
herself doing all she could to keep Abernia's usual ill-humour
from endangering her hold on Tubain. The possibility of having
to call the new servant girl 'mistress' was more than the widow
could stomach. No, if Kithra must wed, let her have Rothan –
who was already ears deep in love with her – and manage him
until he came into his inheritance. Then Cleppetty and Abernia
would step down, but not before.

'Allied to a figment of someone else's imagination,' said the
widow out loud with a grimace. 'It could only happen here.'

She retrieved the clay cooking pot from the ashes and
transferred the tripe to its pastry shell. Boo lumbered in from
the courtyard, clamouring for the tidbits, which no one was
supposed to give him. Cleppetty surreptitiously put a few choice
pieces down on a saucer for him, turned back towards the south
fireplace, and started violently.

Jame was sitting on the hearth.

'What are you trying to do,' the widow half-screeched at her,
'drive me into conniptions? Why can't you stomp through life
like the rest of us?'

'Sorry, Cleppetty.'

The widow gave her a hard look. 'You're pale. Has your head
started hurting again?'

'No, it's not that. I've just seen Taniscent. In the Lower Town. An old woman crossed the street ahead of me wearing Tanis's favourite shawl – you know, that ghastly orange and purple affair. Then she turned, and I saw that it was Taniscent herself. She looked nearly eighty, all wrinkled and blotchy – half-senile, too, I think – but she knew me. She ran, Cleppetty. She gave a panicky sort of bleat, and she ran.'

'Well, what did you expect?' the widow demanded, floury fists jammed on her sharp hips. 'The sight of anyone from the inn can only remind her of what she's lost. Anyway, even if that beating you gave Niggen did set the whole thing off, you didn't force that overdose of Dragon's Blood down her throat. She was a foolish, vain child and has only herself to blame. Still, she was, and is, one of us. What happened next?'

'I lost her,' said Jame in disgust. 'That district has been so warped by fire and decay that only those born there can master the heart of it now. Patches and her Townie friends have taken up the hunt. If they find Tanis and she isn't ready to come home, Patch says her mother will take care of her until she is. For some reason, that family seems to think it owes me something.'

'That's just as well for Taniscent,' said Cleppetty briskly, turning back to her pie. 'You've done well, child. Now let matters take their course. Sooner or later, she'll come home... and an altered place she'll find it, too, what with Kithra and Marc in residence. Speaking of Marc, how have you and that big Kendar been managing? It can't be easy for a thief and a guard to share the same roof, much less the same room.'

'Oh, it's not all that hard,' said Jame, trying to adjust to this abrupt change of topic. 'I'm only in danger from him when I have stolen property in my possession, so I never bring any back to the loft or into his assigned territory. I think he's even got used to the idea of a Kencyr thief.'

'Well, why not? You've made the profession honourable. The Widow Cibbeth sends her thanks and blessings, by the way. The temple would have repossessed her godson by now if you hadn't retrieved his ransom from that pocket-picking Hangrell.'

'I hate thieves who specialise in robbing old people,' said Jame. 'If nothing else, where's the skill in it? Oh, I know all guildsmen can't be as principled as Darinby, but it's still depressing to come across a specimen like Hangrell, whose highest ambition, apparently, is to become one of Bane's scrap-fed rats.

161

'But if the Talisman doesn't bother Marc, do you know who does? The B'tyrr. Cleppetty, have you noticed that he always leaves the room when I dance? That worries me. His moral sense is very good, far better than mine, and I hate to go against it. But Tubain still needs the B'tyrr, so I guess there's no helping that.'

She was silent for a moment. The widow, watching her askance, saw the haunted look return to her eyes.

'Cleppetty,' she said, raising her head suddenly, 'do you remember what you said to me the day the beam fell, that sooner or later I would destroy someone? Was that someone Tanis, or am I still a danger to you, to Tubain, to everyone I love?'

Kithra's voice cut across the widow's startled response.

'Madam, come quick! It's Marc. I think he's been hurt.'

Jame leapt up and was past Cleppetty out the door before she could move. Heavy feet tramped into the hall. A voice, vaguely groggy, said something about matching scars. The big Kendar was standing in the hall with Sart Nine-toes beside him and a blood-stained cloth wrapped about his greying temples.

'Just the same,' he was saying cheerfully to Jame, 'I bet I've got the bigger headache. After all, mine's the bigger head.'

She brought him into the kitchen, made him sit down on the scullery hearth, and unwrapped the makeshift bandage.

'That's not too bad,' said Cleppetty, looking over her shoulder.

'No,' said Jame with relief. 'More ugly than dangerous, I'd say. Just the same, you're going to be out of it a day or two, my lad.'

They cleaned the wound and dressed it with a poultice of balm leaves steeped in wine. Then Jame took Marc up to the loft. Cleppetty, left alone with Sart, stopped his clumsy advances by stomping on his foot and then, when he opened his mouth to yelp, jamming a wheat cake into it. After several minutes, Jame returned.

'You always seem to be trundling Marc home,' she said to Sart. 'My thanks again. Now, what happened?'

'A trap happened, that's what,' said the guard with a growl. 'We're walking our balliwick, see, when we hear a shout for help. It's coming from a side lane, one of those rotting dead-ends near the Temple District Wall, where the stones crumble if you stare at them too hard. Me, I know the streets well enough to be suspicious, so I hold back, but Marc goes charging straight

in before I can stop him. Then the bricks start to fall. I look up
and see that the whole wall over his head is giving way. So I let
off a bellow. Luckily there's a doorway handy, or he'd have got
more than a broken head. It was no accident, either. I saw the
bastard looking down as the dust settled, the lever still in his
hands, wanting to see most likely if his work was well done.
Well, it wasn't, and now he'll squirm on the Mercy Seat for
injuring a guard – as soon as we can lay hands on him, that is.'

'On whom?'

'Why, didn't I say? On that creep-thief Hangrell. He won't be
easy to find, though, not when it sinks into his tiny little head
that every guard in the city – aye, and half the thieves, too – will
be after him. The gods only know what made him do a damn-
fool thing like that.'

'If they don't,' said Jame grimly, 'I do. Wait here, Sart. No
one knows the hiding holes in this city better than I, except my
master. Be ready to come when I send for you.'

'Now just a minute, Talisman,' he protested, stepping
between her and the street door. 'This man is our meat by law,
and we've got to make an example of him. If we don't, no guard
in Tai-tastigon will ever be safe again, or any thief, come to that,
with the ban against mutual violence broken.'

Cold silver-grey eyes locked with his own. 'I said I would send
for you. Wait.'

He had not meant to step out of her way, much less to stand
staring foolishly after her.

'If I were you,' said Cleppetty drily behind him, 'I would do as
she said ... or do you want her mad at you too?'

Sart Nine-toes closed his mouth with a snap, sat down on the
hearth, and began to wait.

The afternoon light drained away. Dusk glowed and faded into
night. When the message came at last, four guards were waiting
at the inn.

Across the city, in the catacomblike cellars under a gutted
mansion on the edge of the Lower Town, someone else also
waited, nervously, starting at every hollow echo the subterranean spaces threw back. Water dripped, torches splut-
tered, the voices of others in hiding murmured confusedly in the
distance. Thief! Surely someone had called his name. Here I am,
here, here ... no, nothing. Hangrell sat down again on the brick
floor, snivelling a little in the dark.

Again and again, he told himself that here, if nowhere else in the city, he should be safe. Although the hand of every honest thief would be against him now, those who shared this dank, dark refuge were outcasts like himself, breakers of Tastigon or Thieves' Guild law. Both codes forbade the injuring of a guard. Hangrell would not have risked his petty revenge if he hadn't been sure (oh, so mistakenly) that he could get away with it, and that it would be applauded by the one person in Tai-tastigon whom he most wished to impress. Even now, with all plans gone awry, he hoped desperately that the individual would acknowledge the gesture and send help. He must know that it had been done to please him. Oh, why had it all gone wrong? A simple accident – that was what everyone would have called it except for the appreciative few who knew better. If it weren't for that second guard (damn him!) whom he had not seen until far, far too late . . .

Someone was shouting. Voices boomed through the halls. People were running, torches going out. 'The guards!' a boy shrieked in the darkness. 'The guards!'

Hangrell jumped to his feet, heart pounding. They were coming this way. He backed up, stumbling over debris, turned, and fled. Somewhere in this part of the cellar, there was supposed to be a way out. He had searched for it all afternoon in case of just such an emergency and, failing to find it, had hoped more desperately than ever that someone would be sent to show him the way.

Stone grated on stone. Ahead, the shadows on the wall fell away into a widening blackness through which a figure stepped. The thief's welcoming cry died in his throat.

It was the Talisman.

'Well, friend,' she said in a quiet, almost pleasant voice. 'You've really done it this time. If you had dealt with me directly, as Scramp did, we might have come to some understanding; but to injure a guard . . . that wasn't very bright, now was it?'

He backed away from her, panic clawing at him. Say something, anything. 'It wasn't my fault!' he heard himself squeal. 'He made me do it. It's his fault that your friend was hurt!'

'Whose fault, sweetling?'

'Bane's!'

'I . . . see.' Her tone jerked his attention back from the shouts

164

of the approaching guards. 'So. This was how you bought your way into his favour. Cat's paw for a coward. I was going to hold you for the guards and the Mercy Seat, my dear. Instead, I'll give you a choice, a . . . chance. Do you see the stairs behind me? They lead to the sewers, to safety. All you have to do is pass me.'

The shouts were closer, almost at the mouth of the passageway. Hangrell looked wildly behind him, whining, then at the slim, shadowy form that barred the way.

'Come along, little one,' it said, its voice slipping into a deep, full-throated purr. 'I wait – without a knife, without gloves.'

With a choked cry, he spun about and ran straight into Sart's arms.

Judgment Square lay sleek in the moonlight. The stalls that had freckled its surface by midday were gone now and their owners with them, leaving the great, triangular flagstones to wind-whirled debris and the small group gathered in front of the Mercy Seat. The Master of Mercy was arguing with four guardsmen while his assistant crouched behind him, tending a brazier whose coals sparkled fitfully. The wind bore none of his complaint upward. Knowing his reputation as a perfectionist, however, it was easy enough to guess that he was bitterly protesting the conditions under which these hulking guards expected him to work. What did they know of craftsmanship? What did they care? To them, only results mattered, and now they were set on creating an example. At last the Master shrugged and opened his tool case while his assistant took an iron from the fire and spat on it experimentally. The pale, thin form that sprawled on the Seat did not move as the two men bent over it. The drugs had done their work well; once again, the Master had justified his title.

On the south side of the square stood a rich merchant's house with a turret ornamented, in imitation of Edor Thulig, with three huge stone bats in high relief. On the head of the one facing north sat Jame. She was no longer regarding the scene below but her own hands, which rested, still gloveless, on her knees. With an expression of mingled disgust and fascination, she raised one and stared at it, as though it were some wild, unidentified creature that she had found scurrying across the forest floor. The abnormally long fingers flexed and arched. At the tip of each was the nail, razor tipped, fully extended.

Would she really have used them on Hangrell? Yes. Again,

165

she heard her voice dripping black honey, felt the savage, exultant lust for blood. It had taken all her self-control to offer that wretched boy a chance at all, if only of deaths.

Ivory claws, black rage – both were a part of her Shanir nature, that terrible openness to a divine will as ruthless as it often was incomprehensible. But if it was truly another's will, how could she be accountable for its actions? Remember Ishtier, she told herself: he was a Shanir too, as every priest must be; but could she forgive him, even on those grounds, for what he had done to her? No. It was unthinkable. And yet clearly he had no influence over the god's voice when it spoke through him. It simply used him. Was she also being used when these murderous rages fell on her, and if so, to what purpose?

'No,' she said out loud, recoiling from the thought. '*No.* I will *not* be used. Let me be a monster in my own right if I must, but not the puppet of some damned, indifferent god. I will be responsible for my actions, whatever prompts them. I will be free.'

Such freedom would be hard to bear, but she might not have to live with it for long, Jame thought with sudden wryness. Her words in the cellar had been addressed less to Hangrell than to those others hidden in the shadows, and through them to that wretched creature's patron, who would learn soon enough what she had said and done. Defiance, insult, challenge – if she knew him half as well as she thought she did, he would swallow none of them. The uneasy, unaccountable friendship between them was at an end and war declared, her hand against his. She had no illusions concerning her chances for survival.

Meanwhile, there was no point in watching more of the sorry spectacle below. Jame climbed down and set off for home.

The Res aB'tyrr was brightly lit but ominously silent as she crossed the square to it. A sleek young man wearing a d'hen of a rich, dark fabric waited for her in the doorway. He stepped aside as she approached and bowed mockingly. Inside, seven more men leaned against the walls or slouched negligently in the best chairs. Bane sat by himself at the centre table, his long, elegantly booted legs stretched out before him and a small goblet of golden wine at his elbow. He looked up as she entered and said, smiling, 'I got your message.'

Jame had known that this meeting must come, but had somehow never thought of it taking place here, in her home. One of Bane's companions were lounging on the kitchen threshold, another in the room itself by the street door. Cleppetty stood white-faced with anger by the kitchen table, one arm thrown protectively around Kithra's shoulders. A slow, deadly rage swelled up in Jame.

'Get those men out of here,' she said to Bane in a low voice. Her hands had already gone cold, her body slipped to the inner rhythms that precede violence.

'Don't be a fool,' he said sharply, reading her intentions in her stance. 'I would kill you.'

'Get them out or you'll have to. Now.'

He regarded her intently for a moment, then suddenly laughed and dismissed the others with a wave of his hand. Surprise broke the stride of Jame's growing, probably suicidal anger. She had not seriously thought that she could blackmail him with the threat of her own death.

'Sit down, sit down,' he said when they were gone, gesturing to the opposite seat. 'Have some of this excellent wine and do, please, stop glowering at me. For once, I'm not to blame. That imbecile Hangrell was acting on his own against my wishes, whatever he may have thought they were. I would have dealt with him myself if you hadn't got to him first.'

'Why?' said Jame, warily seating herself. 'If you didn't order it, what concern is all this of yours?'

'Do you mean to say,' he said, regarding her with raised eyebrows, 'that you still haven't guessed? Well then, here's a little story for you that may make it clear. About thirty years ago, a group of refugees came over the Ebonbane, fleeing from war and kin-strife, following their mad lord into exile. He died in the mountains. They went on, passing Tai-tastigon in the night, and turning northward into the unnamed lands. Nearly a year later, two of them came crawling back. One, a priest, entered the temple of the Three-Faced God and has not left it since. The other, once mistress to the old lord himself, was taken to wife by a high official of the Thieves' Guild. What no one knew then, or has guessed to this day, is that she crossed his threshold already quick with child. Ah, now you begin to understand.'

'You're telling me that you are also of the Kencyrath,' said Jame slowly; and somehow, she was not really surprised. 'But no Kencyr I've ever known would behave as you do.'

'None?' he said, giving her a sharp look. 'Remember the Mercy Seat. You know as well as I what sort of inner darkness leads to a thing like that. I fought it for years, as you do now. I bound myself in secret to the rituals of our people and dared them to break me. Trinity, but that was hard. Then, seven years ago, my foster-father told me that I must be apprenticed to the Sirdan and become a thief. A thief! Oh, I didn't rush into the arms of the Guild like some others,' he said with a bitter laugh. 'Ishtier pushed me. Honour would be served no other way, he said. I owed it to Abbotir, my benefactor. Neither he nor the priest seemed to understand that if they made me go that far, whether I ever stole or not, nothing would ever hold me back again. It was a nice little paradox, really: how to save one's soul by losing it, and in a sense, that's exactly what I did. I've confused you again, haven't I? Do you like stories? Then here's another one, much older than the first:

'Once long ago, in a time of great danger, a randon warrior went to his lord and said, "Master, our enemies hem us in, we die by the hundreds daily. I can deliver us, but only by such acts as will damn me forever in the eyes of our people and our god. Take thou my soul, so that it at least will be untainted, and loose me on the foe." And so it was done. The Three People were saved, but by deeds so foul that no man would record them. Then, in the great hall, the warrior reclaimed his soul. Its purity consumed him, as if he lay on his pyre alive, and so he died at last with honour... Do you have any idea what I'm talking about?'

'I understand this much at least,' said Jame slowly, regarding his hand and the candlelight that glowed on the polished table top beneath it. 'You cast no shadow. So Ishtier's is double then, but are you sure you can trust that priest to keep it and your soul safe?'

'I have reason to think so. Besides, who else could have done such a thing for me?'

'I could.'

He stared at her, then let his breath out slowly. 'Oh, my lady. Yes, you could, and would – if it weren't already too late. But now you must follow me. Give up the struggle and let go, as I did. What good is honour in life to either of us? The very weight of it twists us. Better to fall. Yes, it's terrifying at first. Life loses all boundaries, then begins to expand, seeking new ones. You never find them. No one can tell you where to stop. Honour no longer matters, no, nor the lack of it. Then, in the end, you take back your soul and let its purity immolate you and your deeds.

An honourable death wipes away all stains. But before that, the *freedom*, lady, to do what you will, be what you are, outside the coils of the law, beyond the touch of man or god – that is the course for you, as for me. As for that hulk of a Kendar or Dallen, that whelp's son, you are ill-matched with both or, if it has come to that, worse mated with either. In the end you will see that and turn to me. Until then, m'lady.'

He sketched a formal salute and was gone, stepping lightly into the night.

Jealousy hung raw on the air behind him. Had Hangrell overheard such remarks as these last and posted eagerly off to his death on their strength? The poor fool, to have measured Bane's pride by his own petty standards.

But she had underestimated Bane too, in more ways than one. No need to have sent a message at all; the deed itself, like the smell of fresh-spilt blood, would have drawn him to her. Marc might be safe, but nothing would ever protect her again, now that Bane's interest had been thoroughly aroused. But perhaps she didn't want protection. Why else offer him the greatest intimacy possible between two Kencyrs ... and since when had she even known that such a thing lay in her power? At every turn, her voice had answered his, darkness speaking to darkness. He might be the dead, consumed with hunger for the living, but it was her own face she had seen staring back at her over the table, monstrously mirrored in those odd, silver-grey eyes.

'Mother of Shadows,' she said out loud to herself. 'What will come of all this?'

'Probably a hall full of angry customers,' said Cleppetty loudly, making her start. The others, who had been locked in the cellar, all came flocking in after her, except for Tubain, who had stayed below on a sudden impulse to inventory the rose wine. 'Those flash-blades have been turning everyone away for the last hour *and* drinking our best wine without so much as a copper put on the boards. I ask you,' the widow concluded, setting loose all her stored wrath at once, 'is this any way to run an inn?'

'No, it's not,' said Jame, 'and I'm at fault. It's time Jorin and I left. He's grown too big, and I too dangerous.'

The junior staff burst into loud protest.

'Bustard balls,' said Cleppetty, cutting across the tumult. 'This is your home. When the time comes to leave Tai-tastigon,

169

you'll leave us too, but not before. You've fought for us in your way; we'll fight for you in ours. Besides, the B'tyrr has promised to dance tonight. After a start like this to the evening, the gods help us if she doesn't.'

Jame at last acquiesced, glad to give in but still uneasy. She was on her way up the stairs when the widow called her back, holding up a folded paper that she had picked up from the central table where Bane had sat.

'Notes, yet,' she said, giving it to Jame, then, more sharply, 'is anything wrong?'

'I – don't know,' Jame said, frowning at the wax seal. 'Probably not.' But to avoid more questions, she turned quickly and ran up the steps with the note still unopened in her hand.

In the loft, the big Kendar lay face up on his pallet, snoring. She knelt to check his condition, then sat back on her heels beside him, broke the seal, and read. A frown gathered on her sharp young face. She sat there for a long moment with the paper in her hands, biting her lower lip, looking down at the guardsman. Left to himself, he would remain deep in *dwar* sleep for another twelve hours. It would be wisest to leave a message with Cleppetty, but something in her balked at the idea. This was Kencyr business, however strange, and not meant for other ears. She bent over the sleeping man and shook him. At last his eyelids slowly peeled back.

'Marc, listen to me,' she said, taking his greying head in her hands. 'I've been summoned to the temple of our god by Ishtier, Trinity only knows why. If I'm not back by the time you wake up again, I suppose you'd better come after me. Do you understand?'

'Issshtier . . . ?' Marc struggled up on one elbow. 'You can't do that . . . he hates you.'

'That's no distinction. He hates everyone. Now go back to sleep.'

'Ha!' said Marc with a cheerful if somewhat blurry grin, climbing unsteadily to his feet. 'You've raised the beast right and proper, and now you'll have to put up with him. I'm going with you.'

Jame swore under her breath. Of course he would say that. It was as natural for him to think of himself as her protector as it was for her to be constantly caught off-guard by the fact. With a sigh, she helped the big guardsman to find his truncheon (which, of course, turned out to be under a cat), and they set off.

*

The two came on the temple of their god from its western approach, with the fire-stricken Lower Town close by to the south. The sounds of the living world followed them through the wasteland of deserted houses, but fell away to the soughing of wind in empty doorways as they emerged on the circle of dust.

'What a mess,' said Marc, staring at the desolation around the temple. 'Folk were beginning to move out when I was last here, but who would have thought that Ishtier would let things go so far?'

Then, absentmindedly, he rapped his companion on the back of the head for luck as though they were shieldmates going into battle together and strode down to meet the enemy. Jame followed, gingerly rubbing her head.

Inside, she took the lead. Even though she knew what to expect this time and had all her mental shields up, the currents of power were so swift that it was hard to walk the halls without reeling. Instinct, not memory, led her forward. There was the door she had crashed into, and beyond it, Ishtier.

The priest stood as before in the shadow of their god, looking as though he had not moved since that distant night. His yellow eyes too were as they had been before, cruel and haughty; but this time Jame met them. So this was the Highborn to whom Bane had entrusted his soul. Was it really safe with him? Bane might think so, but what would he say if she told him that this man had already proved faithless to his own younger brother by abandoning him to madness in the Haunted Lands? After hearing Bane's story, Jame had no further doubts that Ishtier was the priest who had fled the keep before her birth. She would indeed never forgive him for Anar's plight, but since he had not also deserted his lord (who, after all, was dead), his honour was intact as far as she knew.

Therefore she gave him a formal if wary salute and said: 'You wished to see me, my lord?'

'You, yes. Not him.' The words were brusque but power, licking at their edges, blurred them.

Jame tensed. Would he play at singeing her again? She had no time to consider it, for just then Marc, despite a commendably brisk start half an hour before, began to sway. She slipped an arm around his waist to steady him and punched him in the ribs to forestall a rising snore.

'Pardon, my lord,' she said to the priest, getting her shoulder under Marc's armpit and heaving him upright. 'We come as a set. If you try to put him out now, I shall tip him over on you.'

Isthier scowled at the swaying giant for a moment, then, unnervingly, a thin, secret smile flickered across his face.

'I have a mission for you, thief,' he said.

Jame stared at him. 'You want me to steal something? You, who all but spat in my face when I came to ask counsel before joining the Guild? Priest, you have a strange sense of humour.'

'Hunzzaagg,' said Marc.

'What?' snapped Ishtier.

'Never mind him. He thinks he's awake. It's a common delusion.'

'Humph. Listen to me, you insolent, young... guttersnipe. I said nothing of stealing. Look here.' He stepped aside. Behind him stood the small altar on which the temple's copy of the Law usually rested. It was not there now. 'You see? The scroll is gone. Without it, only I, the priest, stand between the people of the Kencyrath and their god, all dread be to him. I want you to retrieve it.'

Jame struggled with an answer. Suddenly, tendrils of power were slipping past her, sliding over her mind, numbing it with their touch. It was the nightmare of that first meeting all over again... but this time it was something else, too. For an instant, she seemed to see the faces of the tavern audience turned up eagerly. A bow, the first step of the dance, and they were hers. Not the mists of desire but tongues of ice and fire licked at her now. Still immobilised by Marc's weight, her mind shied away from them, instinctively tracing the first moves of a wind-blowing kantir. To her amazement, she felt the energy flowing past her, back into its natural channel over the tessellated floor.

The ultimate power, the ultimate dance. She had at last found the true outlet for her strange talent.

The priest was staring at her. 'Shanir,' he said, almost to himself. He must be one himself to wield hieratic power, but there was no dawning welcome in his face. Rather, Jame had the uncomfortable feeling that he was really seeing her for the first time, not just as a plaything or a tool but as an individual dangerously like himself who could only prove a threat.

But there was more at stake here than their mutual hatred. It was neither priest nor god she was asked to serve, but the Law and the code of honour it embodied. Bane's abyss had opened up behind her. If she turned her back on that empty altar, as he

172

undoubtedly hoped she would, it would be beneath her feet.

'Where is the scroll?' she asked in a low voice.

'Look in the temple of Gorgo. Did you think you could trifle with a priest – any priest – and not pay for it? Swear before our god that you will bring me the scroll that lies in the arms of the false idol there. Your word on it, thief.'

'Priest,' Jame said grimly, 'death break me, darkness take me, the scroll will be in your hands tonight. My word on it.'

All the way across town, she tried to talk Marc into turning back. Not only was he hurt, she argued, but unsuited by virtue of sheer size for the job ahead. Moreover, since the guards of Tai-tastigon had no jurisdiction over the city's priests, his official status would be of no use to either of them. Obviously, the only fit place for him was at home in bed, with as few cats asleep on his chest as possible.

Marc only laughed.

This one-sided argument went on street after street, through the twining ribbons of the courtesans' district, over the Tone, past the Tower of Demons, ending only within sight of Gorgo's temple itself, where Jame at last yielded to the inevitable with a sigh.

The sound of ritual mourning rolled down the steps as they paused in the shadows of the opposite building.

'How do we get in?' Marc asked, staring up at the bright entrance.

'The most obvious way,' said Jame. 'Put your hood over your head like a proper worshipper and try to wail a bit.'

They went up the steps together and joined the celebrants within. All were gathered in the outer chamber, waiting for the evening ceremony to begin and working themselves into the approved tearful state. The high priest himself perched precariously on top of a pillar beside the door to the inner chamber with his long silver-grey robe flowing down to the floor on all sides of it. From below, one might have supposed him to be either a very tall man with a very small head or a street performer on stilts. The combination of his loud, simulated grief and the wild circling of his arms every few minutes to maintain balance added considerably to the liveliness of the assembly.

Jame began to edge her way through the crowd with Marc at her heels, trying to make his seven-foot frame as inconspicuous as possible. She had not been in Gorgo's temple since the experiment with the water ducts some time before, which, presumably, had triggered Loogan's vengeance on her now. She wondered why he had waited so long, and where he had found an agent so bold as to plunder the house of her own god, whose very existence he had often so vehemently denied. On the surface, it didn't make much sense, but when had she ever had dealings with any priest that did? Each had his own subtle, tortuous patterns of thought, worn as deep into his mind as riverbeds on the earth's face by the power that flowed through him. Even the clownish Loogan must have his share. As for Ishtier, there was a man so eroded by the force at his command that hardly any of his original nature must be left at all. Small wonder that his code of honour was not her own or that she had so little protection against the wiles that had now manoeuvred her into this nest of enemies. Bodies brushed against her, voices pounded in her ears. Her uneasiness rose as she approached the inner door, remembering suddenly with what ease Loogan had spotted her the last time she had infringed on his hospitality.

The priest had stopped his wailing. Incautiously, Jame glanced up and met his eyes as he crouched on the pillar, staring uncertainly down at her. The little man straightened up with a yelp.

'The blasphemer, the defiler of our temple!' he howled, pointing down at the slender, hated figure. 'Take her, take her! A sacrifice, a sacrifice for the great Gorgo!'

Scores of faces turned towards Jame, contorted in rage. Scores of hands reached out. The mass of humanity in the room seemed to rise about her like the crest of a tidal wave, poised to come crashing down.

'Sweet Trinity,' she heard Marc mutter under his breath, and then his rathorn war cry boomed out almost in her ear.

The human wave froze. Up on his pedestal, Loogan did a passable imitation of an unbalanced statue. The inner chamber door opened and the buck-toothed acolyte, startled by the sudden roar, peered out. Marc reached past Jame with a muttered 'Excuse me,' caught the boy by the front of his robe and threw him over his shoulder. Instantly, the room was bedlam. Loogan pitched head-first off the column with a squeal. Roaring, the crowd of worshippers rushed forward. The big Kendar grabbed his companion by the collar and threw her into the inner room. A stride carried him across the threshold after her. Turning, he pulled the door shut and dropped the bar into place across it.

'Well,' said Jame, picking herself up off the floor, 'here we are.'

The inner sanctum of the temple was just as she remembered it – high, dark, and dank even in this time of drought because of the hand-filled reservoir on the roof. Benches, moss velveted walls, the giant image of Gorgo looking, if anything, more woebegone than usual, and, balanced on its hands over a bed of old ashes, a roll of parchment. Perfect, if one discounted a minor host of enraged celebrants hammering on the door ... or was it? Something about the length of the scroll, the colour of its paper ...

'Marc, see if you can find another way out. I think something is very wrong here.'

While the big guardsman began a slow circuit of the room, Jame took the scroll out of the stone hands and carefully unrolled it. 'EYES THAT READ, BEWARE,' she began out loud, struggling with runes' meaning. 'BE STILL, TONGUE ...'

She recoiled from it, teeth closing with a snap. The words of Forgetting swept through her mind, drowning thought and memory. When she looked at the scroll in her hands again, cautiously this time, not translating, the marks on it were mere lines, their deadly power locked in. She stood there biting her lip for a moment, then looked around for her companion. He was not in sight.

'Marc, where are you?'

There was a scraping sound and a muffled grunt from behind the statue.

'What are you doing?'

'There's a lever back here. Maybe it controls a secret exit. I think I can ...'

There was a sharp crack, then a deep-noted gurgle. Jame sprang back as the glass eyes of the idol flew out of their sockets, closely followed by two thick jets of water.

Marc emerged from the shadows, looking sheepish. He held out a metal bar and said, apologetically, 'It broke off.'

'Never mind that. Look here.' She held out the parchment. He stared at it, making an obvious effort to focus. Like most Kendars with their faith in memory, he had never learned how to read.

'Is that the Law Scroll?'

175

'Not unless they've started writing them in the Master Words of High Runic. No, this is something else, older than any temple copy and far more deadly. See how the figures start out crisp and clear, then here, halfway down, begin to falter? Despite himself, the scribe must have begun to see the words forming under his quill point, and the race began to the end of each line. More speed, less control, ink spattering, lines shaking... and here it simply ends, in midsentence, in midword. Well?'

She glared up at Marc, oblivious both to the water now swirling about their knees and to the irate pounding on the door which had settled down into a steady, bone-jarring blows of some makeshift ram.

'Tell me I've the imagination of a street balladeer. Tell me the annals of the Kencyrath are full of such stories. Tell me this thing isn't Anthrobar's scroll, the only copy, partial as it is, of the Book Bound in Pale Leather. Go on, tell me!'

Marc blinked owlishly at the roll of parchment. 'How did it get here?'

'God knows!' She was beginning to lose patience with him. Here they were, faced with a genuine crisis, and this nodding giant with his bandage slipping down rakishly over one eye was only half-awake. 'We may find out later if – *if*, I say – we ever get out of here, but don't you see what a dilemma we're in now? Short of the Book itself, can you think of any more dangerous document ever entrusted to the Three People? Creation, preservation, destruction – this thing is the key to every power planted in us for good or ill. How many times have our wisest scrollsmen and greatest lords, in the best of faith, nearly destroyed us all by using it? And who wants his talons on it now? Ishtier! Why, the man doesn't even use the power he has properly. Marc, I can't turn it over to him.'

'It isn't the Law Scroll,' said Marc, beginning to sway gently. 'You don't have to.'

'Idiot that I am, I swore to bring him the scroll – *any* scroll – in the arms of the idol. My word binds me.'

Marc shook himself fiercely. 'Aaaugh! But listen: when we thought it was the Law Scroll, freshly stolen, it was all right for you to recover it. Now – how long has this thing been missing? Over two thousand years? – even for something so valuable, the period of jeopardy must have run out centuries ago. Originally Kencyr property or not, under the laws of the city it now belongs to Loogan, and if you steal it, *my* word as a guard binds me to turn you over to the Five...'

'... who will be delighted to dethrone Hangrell in my favour. If you're a thief, as they say, never get too attached to your own skin. Oh, what a trap that priest has sprung on me, and all without telling one direct lie. If I take him the scroll, think of the power he will gain; if I'm killed, he will at least have the satisfaction of my death; if I refuse, I'll be breaking my word to him and he will declare me a renegade, which may be what Bane hoped for when he consented to be Ishtier's messenger. Between them, those two have given me the choice of being dishonourable, irresponsible, or dead. Beautiful! The only consolation is that matters can't possibly get any worse.'

At that moment, three things happened more or less simultaneously: the whole face of the image gave way, releasing a torrent of water into the already half-flooded room; the rings holding the bar across the door, jolted loose, fell away on one side, and Marc suddenly fell asleep, standing up.

Jame looked around the room with raised eyebrows, then back at the scroll in her hand. One complication would have been manageable; two, a calamity; three, ridiculous; but four? It would be an excellent time to burn the manuscript and drown herself, but then there was Marc, who didn't deserve to die alone, much less asleep on his feet. She reached out and rapped the swaying giant on his chest.

'You'd better see to the door,' she said. 'I think we're about to have company.'

'Zaugh... oh!' said Marc, blinking at her. He turned and waded through the water, which now reached almost to his waist, over to the opposite wall. While Jame took refuge on the statue's right kneecap, the big Kendar raised the bar back into place and began to hammer the ring bolts in again with the head of his truncheon. Suddenly he froze, looking startled, then spun about and came splashing back across the room.

'Lass!' he bellowed over the roar of the water. 'I've got it! You can't steal the scroll, but I can!'

Jame saw his hand sweeping up at her out of the corner of her eye. She had been deep in thought and had only half heard what her companion had said. Instinctively, she twisted away from what, from almost anyone but Marc, would have been a threatening gesture. The stone beneath her was slick with spray. Her sudden movement threw her sideways off her perch and down, scroll and all, into the surging water.

177

Marc fished her out and set her sputtering on her feet. She swept a streaming lock of hair out of her eyes, shook herself, then froze.

'*What* did you say?'

He shifted his weight uncomfortably, as if he would have liked to have shuffled his feet if only there hadn't been so much water on them. 'I wouldn't be stealing from a Kencyr, you know,' he said, half pleading. 'I wouldn't be breaking the Law, just – uh – bending it a little. After all, if that wasn't honourable, you wouldn't have been doing it yourself all these weeks.'

Jame's stunned gaze dropped to the soggy piece of parchment in her hand. At the sight of it, she caught her breath, then threw back her head with a shout of laughter. Marc stared at her. She held the scroll out to him. Streaks of ink twisted down it into a muddy lower margin. Not a letter remained legible.

'By Trinity, m'lord Ishtier may be subtle, but he's not omniscient,' she said. 'This is one solution he could never have foreseen. Here, take the damn thing! Just this once, I'll let you steal for me. Now, in all the names of God, let's get out of here.'

'Uh, lass . . . short of staging a massacre, how? I've no taste for these peoples' blood.'

'It needn't come to that. Look here: where there's fire,' she gestured to the wet ashes in the cupped hands, 'there's usually smoke. Where there's smoke, there had better be some sort of ventilation.' Her finger traced a line from the offering bowl to the ceiling far above. There among the shadows was a square of lesser darkness, through which the eyes of the Frog constellation sparkled fitfully.

Her hands had been busy as she spoke, pulling small pieces of metal out of her full sleeve and fitting them into the familiar form of a Cloudie's grapnel. To this she snapped the line that had been wound about her waist. On the third try, the hook shot straight through the hole and caught firmly on something outside on the roof.

Marc went up first, by some miracle not falling asleep halfway to the ceiling, although he had begun to nod again. Jame, following him, heard the door at last give way as the bar dropped off altogether. The shouts of the celebrants changed timbre as the wall of dammed up water came crashing down on them. It was fortunate, she thought, as she scrambled up onto the roof, that they had all come expecting to get wet anyway.

So much for Loogan. Now, to get Marc safely home, and then to settle with m'lord Ishtier.

'Fool, do you know what you've done?'

Jame had come prepared for the priest's anger, but the violence of it drove her back a step, flinching.

'The key to our future was in your hands, and you threw it away. How many ages have you added to our exile? How many eons until night falls at last?'

'Night? Exile?' She had expected his rage to fall on her for denying him (and, unfortunately, the Three People as well) the means for escaping Rathillien to the next threshold world if the barriers here against Perimal Darkling should fall. Why was he looking backward to lands already lost?

At the sound of her voice, the old man stiffened, as though suddenly aware that he had said too much. The shrivelled lips moved again. This time not words but raw power whispered in from the outer corridors, ripping into her, blocking thought, freezing motion. She knew that he meant this to be her death.

'BE STILL, TONGUE THAT SPEAKS ... TO THE CHOSEN LEAVE THE HIDDEN WAYS.'

Afterwards, seated by a sleeping Marc in the loft, Jame touched her sore throat. Yes, she had said that, one hand thrown up to shield her face ... or perhaps, futilely, to seal in the words. But whatever had possessed her to raise it higher, fingers curved, nails unsheathed, beckoning as did the image of Regonereth, That-Which-Destroys, towering over both her and the priest? Sheer defiance, probably. It was dangerous to mimic the god, but well worth it this once to see Ishtier blanch. He had not hindered her leave-taking.

Jorin was pacing from one end of the loft to the other. She needed no mental link to know his thoughts as he turned his blind, moon-opal eyes to her with each pass: *the hills? Now? Now?* Soon, kitten, soon. As she had told Cleppetty earlier, it was clear that he was rapidly outgrowing these cramped quarters and would soon have to be moved elsewhere.

The knapsack lay on her knees. All this time it had been there, and she had been trying to ignore it, as though hoping it would somehow vanish or she would think of an excuse to return it to its hiding place unopened. No such excuse had occured to her. With a sigh, Jame threw back the flap and drew out the large, flat package.

She unwrapped it gingerly, folding back the cloth, layer by layer, to reveal at last what appeared to be simply an old book, remarkable only in the unexpected warmth of its soiled white

179

binding. Fixing in her mind the patterns she hoped to find but not their meaning, Jame opened it. The first page was covered with hieroglyphs of a completely unknown nature. So were the second, third, and fourth, up to the twenty-fifth; and every one of them was written in a different, equally unfamiliar language. The damn thing was playing with her.

'Stop it!' said Jame sharply, rapping it with her knuckles.

The next page was composed of Kencyr Master Words. On it, she found the second set of runes that she had been looking for and, turning back, located the first where before there had only been an unreadable tangle of lines. When she closed the volume, its binding was no longer dingy leather but something finer grained and warmer, with little white hairs and faint blue lines running just under the surface.

So. Now she knew not only why she had been so sure the scroll in Gorgo's temple was Anthrobar's and why its destruction – a potential catastrophe for her people – had not dismayed her, but also why she had been able to quote to Ishtier both a section she had just read and one she had not.

Because the original was in her possession.

Marc's voice sounded again in her mind against the memory of falling water. 'How did it get here?' he was asking. 'How?'

There was only one way. When the elder world fell, the renegade Master of Knorth had kept it with him in the deepening shadows, dedicating it as he did himself and his sister-consort Jamethiel to the service of Perimal Darkling; and there it had stayed for time out of mind, becoming no more than a legend to most of those Kencyrs who had fled. If the Book was in Jame's hands now, it could only mean that she herself had brought it out of darkness. Those lost years, so long a mystery to her, must have been spent in the Master's house, in Perimal Darkling.

'Well?' she said out loud. 'Tell me where else they could have sent you from the middle of the Haunted Lands – south to Rathillien, or north, across the Barrier. Idiot, it's been staring you in the face all this time.'

But she hadn't seen it, had not, perhaps, wanted to see it. There, presumably, they had taught her to dance, fight, read the runes, and Trinity knew what else; yet even now not a memory of it remained. Nor did she know how she had come into possession of the Book. Clearly she was familiar with its contents, had perhaps even used it to flee Perimal Darkling, but once here in Rathillien all recollection of that had faded too . . . until tonight. Now at last the Book Bound in Pale Leather was on its way back to the Kencyrath, in her charge, as the widow would say, for lack of anyone more sensible. Or perhaps not. Such objects of power were said to fulfil their own destinies. If this one had been using her, one might even ask if she had stolen it from the Master's house or it had stolen her. One thing at least was certain: Gerridon of Knorth could not have been pleased to find it missing.

Might he, in fact, have been displeased enough to have come after it?

. . . dead, all dead under the twilight sky, within the broken walls: Anar, her father . . . Marc's demon warriors riding down from the north on East Kenshold, blood already on their armour as though fresh from battle, looking for something – or someone . . .

'Jame!'

She started violently. Ghillie's head had popped into sight around the spiral stair's newel.

'What's the matter with you? Don't you hear them? Aunt Cleppetty says come down quick before they start breaking things, or by all the gods, she'll break *you!*'

She jumped up as the boy disappeared, hearing clearly for the first time the steady, rhythmic pounding below, not hooves on the iron hills but tankards on tabletops, beating an impatient tattoo. A year ago, yet just that evening, she had made a promise; now they were here to see that it was kept. Let the dead wait, she thought, hurriedly returning the Book to its hiding place and stripping off her street clothes. The living would not.

At the stroke of midnight, as Marc lay on his pallet snoring happily and far away the temples of Tai-tastigon heralded the new day with bells, chants, and laughter, the B'tyrr walked down the stairway to be greeted by the waiting crowd with a roar of welcome.

Tubain, who had been considering a hasty retreat down to the wine cellar, beamed at her across the room. Trust a Kencyr always to honour her word.

10

The Feast of Dead Gods

The rabbit's head jerked up, green shoots dangling from its lips. Jame froze. A stealthy movement seen past the quarry's alert ears helped her to spot Jorin, crouching behind a clump of late daisies. It had taken them over an hour of patient stalking to reach their respective positions, all for one stupid rabbit, which, it seemed, was not even going to let them get within striking range. Would it bolt? Yes, dammit, it was – away from them both.

Jame sprang up. The rabbit had broken to the left, but her wild dash set it jinking back towards the daisies. Jorin erupted from the heart of the clump, narrowly missing a perfect pounce. The rabbit was doubling back now towards Jame's original position. She pivoted. Sprinting to turn it, her foot hit something in the grass, and she fell, fingertips almost grazing the white tail as it flashed past.

She was lying flat on the ground with most of the breath knocked out of her when Jorin gave the top of her left ear a tentative lick. 'Has it ever occurred to you,' she said in exasperation, rolling over to look up into his face, 'that you might just once go on without me?'

Apparently, it never had.

The ounce gave a conciliatory little chirp and flopped down beside her. Relenting, Jame ran her hand down the length of his back, feeling muscles flex under the richness of his late summer coat, now tinged with gold where that odious brown dye had worn off. Jorin stretched, purring, and rolled over on his back in a most Boo-like fashion to have his stomach rubbed. Jame sat up with a laugh and obliged. Then she groped back through the grass for the thing that had tripped her.

It was a helmet, rust-pitted, ancient. They had been stumbling over similar armorial remains all afternoon, and once over the top half of a skull in which a family of grass snakes had made their nest. Despite the depredations of scavengers, such things were fairly common here on the Plain of Bones, where the last and most vicious battle of the Skyrr-Metalondrian war had been fought. Jame felt fortunate not to have landed on someone's sword or spiked mace, quietly rusting in the grass. In her opinion, she had tried her luck quite enough for one day. She and the ounce both rose and set off westward into the shadow of the mountains.

It was late afternoon on the last day of summer.

Three nights had passed since they had come up into the hills, escaping the city's heat and bustle. No rain had fallen there all summer to lay the dust or ease the citizens' minds. Here too the land was parched, the leaves brittle on the bough; but a fitful wind off the Ebonbane rustled through the grass, and the evenings were cool. They had set up camp in a shallow cave on the banks of the Tynnet. Despite increasing skill, however, their hunting luck in the foothills had been uniformly bad. So, in the little time left, Jame had decided to see if the game to the east was any better. It wasn't. Now she must take the ounce back to their camp and return to the city, leaving him in the wilds.

This had not been an easy decision to make. She had watched his restless pacing in the loft too long, however, not to realise that he must have more freedom. She would visit him, bringing food, as often as possible, but how much better it would be if he could learn to fend for himself. One kill, just one, might be enough to start him out.

'Well, we'll make do, whatever happens, won't we, kitten?' she said, looking down at the young ounce.

His ears pricked sharply, but not to the sound of her voice. She stopped, surprised, then also listened, wishing for the vanished mind link to let her hear what he heard. Crickets sang in the long grass, a solitary thrush whistled once, and then, from far away to the southeast, came the sound of horns blowing for a hunt gone astray.

The stag seemed to explode over the crest of the next hill, all foam-lathered muzzle and wild eyes. It was in the hollow before it saw them. Jame saw it leap sideways, then stagger as Jorin's weight struck its hindquarters. The needle-pointed tines, the sharp hooves – if the ounce lost his hold . . .

She plunged down the slope after him. Her hands closed on the antlers, and all three – girl, ounce, and deer – fell. God, if she should land on the points ... twisting in midair, Jame saw earth, then sky between the branching horns. For the second time in an hour, the ground slammed into her.

Something cracked loudly.

For a long moment she lay there, afraid to move, and then realised that the stag was also motionless. The angle of its head told the tale.

Jame eased herself out from under the dead beast. By morning, there should be some spectacular bruises from the feel of things, but nothing seemed to be broken. Jorin was crouching over the stag's haunches, looking vaguely amazed at himself and uncertain of what to do next. Then, abruptly, he tensed and began to growl. Jame got quickly to her feet. A moment later the grass on the crest of the opposite hill parted as two hunting leopards slipped through it in quest of their prey. They were magnificent beasts, with sleekly groomed coats and collars that glowed with gold. It did not please them to find others already on the kill.

The horns sounded again, nearer this time.

Jame slipped her knife out of its boot sheath, wondering how much good it would do.

Someone was clambering up the far side of the hill, whistling and calling hoarsely. Then he was on the crest, a thin, harassed-looking man carrying two leashes coiled in one hand and a short whip in the other.

'Away from that stag, you!' he shouted, wrathfully down at Jame. 'This is my lord's land and his kill.'

All four below snarled at him.

A man on a tall grey mare pulled up beside the cathandler. 'What's this?' he demanded, regarding the scene below. The answer was long, impassioned, and apparently reached back to the beginning of the chase hours ago. Meanwhile, another rider appeared on the rise, and another and another until the hollow was ringed with them. Jame, still watching the leopards warily as they circled her, began to feel very conspicuous.

'All right, all right,' said the first horseman suddenly, cutting short the other's tirade. 'I'll grant it wasn't your fault ... this time. You down there, the hunt is yours. Will you be so good as to grant my cats a cup of blood? They'll never settle down without it.'

'My lord,' said Jame, thinking quickly, 'let me present you with the whole deer. I didn't know we were trespassing.'

'Well! That's most kind of you,' said the other. From his tone, which was light and waspish, she couldn't tell if he was being sarcastic or not. 'Such generosity should be rewarded. Come back to my camp and share a cup of wine with me.' Without waiting for an answer, he turned and rode away.

Jame saw that his followers had no intention of letting her decline this invitation. She retrieved her cap, dislodged by her fall, then stripped off her gloves and gathered as much stag's blood as her cupped hands would hold. Jorin lapped it up, rough tongue rasping her fingers clean, while the cathandler sullenly rewarded his own charges nearby. Then one of the riders impatiently gave her a hand up, and they all galloped off after the man on the grey mare.

The camp was small but heavily guarded, blood-feud and kin-strife being the major social conventions in Skyrr. Recent years had seen some lulls in the violence, mostly due to the new Archiem, Arribek sen Tenzi, but things never stayed quiet in the hill cantons for long.

Seated on a low stool in her host's tent, Jame watched the man as he moved restlessly about the room, discoursing on various hunting trophies in it. She wondered who he was. From his clothes, which were of good quality but much patched, she decided that he must be the impoverished head of the local ruling family. His sharp, covert glances were beginning to make her fidget. Obviously she had not been invited – no, ordered – here simply to listen to a monologue on local hunting conditions. The guards had taken her knife at the door. She dropped her hand onto Jorin's head as he leaned against her knee, drawing confidence from his presence.

The man abruptly pivoted to face her. 'Enough of this,' he snapped. 'Confess! It's the link, isn't it?'

Jame stared at him.

'No matter where I go or what I point at, if your eyes follow me, so do your cat's, and any fool can see that he's blind as a brick.'

'Well, I'll be damned,' said Jame, looking down at the ounce in amazement. 'Do you mean to tell me, you young imp, that all this time.... No wonder our hunts have always ended when I've fallen behind! You can't chase what I can't see.'

'One way only, is it?' the man said, at last perching on the stool opposite her. 'That may change. I've heard that these links can take years to form properly, or sometimes only seconds. I envy you the experience. But one thing still puzzles me. Why would anyone stain a Royal Gold that ugly stain of brown? One might almost suppose,' his voice went on, almost purring now, 'that you didn't come by this valuable beast legally.'

Jame swallowed, remembering her promise to the man at the cattery. 'I'm afraid I can't explain, but I didn't steal this cub,' she said carefully. 'I give you my word on that.'

'And if I won't accept it?'

'Then I must defend my honour with my life . . . although I'd just as soon you didn't make it necessary.'

'Indeed,' he said drily. 'The race best known in Rathillien for a certain – ah – inflexibility in matters concerning honour is also the only one that can form mind-links. Check and double-check. Therefore, having established your veracity, tell me how things go in Tai-tastigon, Kencyr.'

This was a formidable request, but Jame did her best, thinking that news must be at a premium here in the hills. In time, her summary came to the doings of the Five. Here as elsewhere, he plied her with shrewd questions, mostly about his countryman, Harr, Thane sen Tenko.

'Would you say,' he asked suddenly, 'that the man is honest?'

Jame hesitated. For all she knew, her host might be related both to Harr and Marplet sen Tenko. 'Well, there are rumours,' she said cautiously, 'I don't know if anything could be proved, though, even in the Skyrrman-Res aB'tyrr clash.'

'Ah, I've heard of that affair,' the lord said, adding pettishly, 'you needn't look so surprised: *some* news filters into this back country, especially when it has to do with our own people. It's an undeclared trade war, from the sound of it. A boy has been beaten and a servant blinded, I understand; also some of the Skyrrman's property has been destroyed – some puncheons of wine contaminated with salt, a pile of bricks smashed, and so forth.'

'Bricks?'

Oh, that must have been when Niggen dropped the beam. Jame described the incident to him, likewise the events that had led up to Niggen's thrashing and the mutilation of Bortis. There was no explanation she could offer, however, for the spoiled wine, which had come to light recently in a rash of petty vandalisms at the rival inn. In connection with these, she could only protest the Res aBy'tyrr's innocence.

'And Harr sen Tenko – according to rumour – has let all this happen? Why?'

'You didn't know, my lord? His brother-in-law is proprietor of the Skyrrman.'

'Ah!' said the other, and promptly changed the topic.

Soon after that, the interview ended. Jame accepted some cuts of venison and set out with Jorin for their own camp to the west. It was early evening when they arrived. She put most of the meat in the cave and slipped away, leaving Jorin to his feast. She tried not to think how he would react when he discovered she was gone.

Tai-tastigon was in a state of subdued bustle. Last minute shopping was being done, children called in from the streets and pets secured within doors. Many houses already presented sealed faces to late passers-by, betraying no glimmer of light in the growing dusk. Silence gathered, flowing down the narrow lanes into the thoroughfares. Summer had ended. Autumn's Eve, that benign and neglected festival, sank under the shadow of the year's darkest night. Soon, soon the Feast of Dead Gods would begin.

Jame found Canden and Dally waiting for her at the inn. While the inn staff scurried around them, preparing for the host of old customers who traditionally spent this night at the Res aB'tyrr, she described her experiences in the hills.

'M'lord Harr seems much in the light these days,' said Dally when she had finished. 'I wonder why your ragged noble was so interested in him.'

'Politics,' said Kithra, sweeping down on them armed with a damp sponge just in time to hear this last remark. 'Up glasses, all. Everyone in the high country knows that if that miserable Harr can buy enough support, he may well become a serious threat to the Archiem. Yes, madam... coming!'

'So it's money he'll be after now,' said Dally thoughtfully as the servant girl darted away. 'At the moment, he has access to the city treasury, but that will end when his appointment does.'

'Mightn't he dip out enough before he leaves to do the job?' Jame asked.

'I expect he'll take all he can without getting caught, but a backer or two later wouldn't hurt him either. Yet, it looks as if he's doing the backing now, while he can,' Dally went on. 'Or at least everyone will think so after the way he embarrassed Theocandi by trying to get Mistress Silver's son executed. I don't think anyone knows how she's going to vote now that the Sirdan has only managed to get the boy exiled, not acquitted.'

'And when Men-dalis is elected and pays Harr back from the Guild treasury seven-fold,' said Canden suddenly, with unusual violence, 'what will happen to Grandfather?'

Jame and Dally looked at each other, startled. They had been playing a political guessing game not unlike a hundred others in the past and had actually forgotten for a moment how personal their own involvement was.

'Why, then he'll be able to retire and live out the rest of his life in peace,' said Dally kindly. 'After all, he's an old man. The Sirdanate must be a terrible strain on him, however much he clings to it.'

'And do you really think he will – live, I mean? They say it isn't like it used to be in the Guild – all the violence, the assassinations, the intrigues – we're more civilised now. But neither you nor your brother were here at the last election. Ask Master Tane's family – what's left of it – about that.'

'My dear Can!' Dally protested. 'Beg pardon, but even if that shadow-thief rot is true, that was when your grandfather won. Things will be very different when it's Men-dalis's turn.' Something in Canden's face made him stop, badly flustered. His idealism had never had to cope with the things that this boy had seen, growing up in the Palace of Thieves' Guild itself. 'At any rate,' he said rather desperately, trying to evoke a lighter mood, 'whatever happens, I'll see that you don't end up bobbing in the Tone – not, at least, without a few more swimming lessons.'

'You might be able to do that,' said Canden miserably. 'But if your brother doesn't win, I won't be able to return the favour. I've no influence in the Palace or the Guild to help friends, family or myself. There'll be nothing I can do... nothing.'

'Well, I'm sure it won't come to that,' said Dally awkwardly, embarrassed by the other's distress. 'Mendy will carry the election, Silver's vote or no, and then everything will be all right. You'll see. In the meantime, it's getting late. C'mon Can; I'll walk you back to the Palace.'

'No... go on, Dally, please. I'd like to talk to Jame for a minute.'

'Oh. Well then, good night, all – Dalis-sar's blessings on you.' And he was gone.

'Would you mind talking on the move?' Jame asked Canden. 'I have an errand across town.'

'Tonight? Is that wise?'

'No, but when has wisdom ever stopped me?'

188

He laughed, and they went out into the night together.

The two walked in silence almost as far as the Tone, their footsteps ringing hollowly in the deserted streets. Though the Feast proper would not begin for another two hours, few residents were taking any chances of being caught out in it. It must have been about this time a year ago when Jame had first stumbled into the city.

Canden cleared his throat, startling her. 'The expedition for Tai-Than leaves in two weeks,' he said. 'Master Quipun has asked me to go with him.'

'Splendid! Have you told your grandfather yet?'

'I tried to. He wouldn't listen. Jame... I-I think I may go anyway.'

For a moment, her step faltered, then she went on without speaking. He was not a Kencyr. He had not been taught how unforgivable it was to desert one's lord in time of peril. On the other hand, supposing Canden stayed and the worst came to pass, what could he do about it? As he himself said, nothing. She had heard stories about the violence, supernatural and otherwise, that followed most Guild Councils, when the loser was no longer protected by Guild law. For the first time, she faced the possibility that if they both stayed in Tai-tastigon through the election, at least one of her friends might very well die.

They neared the Tone. Canden was darting anxious, sidelong looks at her, and Jame suddenly realised, with alarm, that whatever she said next would probably decide the whole matter for him.

How in all the names of God was she, a Kencyr, supposed to solve such a dilemma? Among her own people, the question itself would never have arisen. All such flexibility had very nearly gone out of Kencyrath with the withdrawal of the Arrinken, whose function it had been to unravel such moral conundrums. Yes, and think of the havoc *that* had wrought over the last two millennia in the lives of those, like Bane, who lacked her own dubious talent for finding chinks in the Law. And what was this boy asking for now but a way to adapt his own code of honour to survival, as she had tried to do with hers? It was not simply an escape from death that either of them wanted, but life: she, somehow, among her own people, and he in his chosen work. How her own quest would end, she had no idea, but as for his ...

Canden started as she suddenly turned on him and said, with a vehemence that surprised even her, 'Go! Don't think of your grandfather or the Guild or Tai-tastigon again. I'll take responsibility for the consequences, if there are any. Just get out while you can – and be happy.'

A few minutes later, Jame watched the boy walk briskly away, homeward bound, and wondered what had possessed her to speak as she had. To make oneself accountable for something before the fact was about as intelligent as agreeing to carry an unknown soul, and yet she felt she had done the right thing. He would do well, that boy, if the past would leave him alone. She envied him his future and wondered if she would ever learn what he had done with it.

Meanwhile, it was getting late. She looked once more after Canden's retreating back, noting with satisfaction a lightness in his stride that had not been there before, and then turned and crossed the Tone in pursuit of her own fate, which waited for her in the Temple District.

Soon after their somewhat hectic evening in the house of the lugubrious god, Jame had thought it only fair to tell Marc why Gorgo's high priest had been so eager to see them both dead. It was the first time she had spoken to the big Kendar about either her experiments or her doubts, and it irked her that he listened to the account of both so calmly.

'Don't you see,' she had finally said in exasperation, 'if I'm right about faith creating reality in this city, what is the truth about our own god? Do we believe in him because he's real, or is he real because we believe in him; and what about all the other deities? If even one of them is genuine, then our own holy terror is a fraud, and we as Kencyrs can't honour a lie. How can you be so calm when the foundation of our whole culture may crumble out from under us at any minute? Living here all these months hasn't your faith been shaken even once?'

Marc had considered this for a minute, then said slowly, 'No, I can't say that it has. I never thought we Kencyrs had much choice in the matter, not, at least, since old Three-Face got us by the short hairs. An acolyte did tell me once, though, that some people can decide whether to believe or not. Free will, he called it, and said that faith could be even stronger with it than without, not that I quite see how. You're clever, though; perhaps you understand.'

190

'Clever!'

Moving through the silent streets, Jame remembered her bark of laughter and winced. That afternoon, she had been to the Lower Town to see Taniscent, and the former dancer had hidden from her under the covers, sobbing wildly.

'If I were even halfway intelligent, would I act the way I do? Is there one thing I've done since coming here that hasn't had disastrous consequences? Marc, despite all the time we've spent together, you don't know me. You don't even know my name.'

He had looked at her, perplexed. 'Why, Jame, short for Jameth.'

'No. For Jamethiel.'

'Oh.' For a moment, it was as if he had just eaten something of a suspicious nature and was not sure how it would agree with him. 'Oh!' he said again, stiffening. 'What could your sponsors have been thinking of? Better to curse a child outright at birth than to give it such a name!'

'They may have done that too, for all I know,' Jame had said wryly, beginning to be ashamed of herself for snapping at him. 'Still, there's some distinction of being probably the first to bear that name since Jamethiel of Knorth turned renegade to follow the Master nearly three thousand years ago.'

'Snare-of-Souls, Dream-Weaver, Storm's Eye . . .' he had run through the epithets thoughtfully, checking them off on his fingers. 'Priest's-Bane. The name is an omen in itself. Servants of God, any god, will be bad luck to you, and you to them. I should have as little to do with them as possible, if I were you, especially with such a one as Loogan. He's too vulnerable.'

And she had promised to try.

That had been weeks ago. Now here she was in the Temple District again, preparing for another raid on Gorgo's house. Somewhat reassured by Marc's refusal to be alarmed, she had giving up testing Loogan; but the matter of Anthrobar's Scroll still haunted her. It was perhaps legitimate to say that the copy as well as the original of the Book had, for some obscure reason, been destined for her hands, but that didn't explain the mechanics of the thing. How in all the worlds had that long-lost manuscript come to be in Gorgo's temple? That was the question that drew her back now, on the one night of the year when she thought she could count on a minimum of interference from both god and priest.

However, the District was not as quiet as she had expected it to be. A murmur filled the air, seeming to rise from all directions and none; low, wordless, urgent. Rapid footsteps coming up from behind made her start. A man slipped hurriedly past and in at the door of a humble temple just ahead, letting the sound roll out around him for a second before the portal closed. The faithful held their vigils, praying for the safety of man and god alike, while the dead prowled outside the gate.

Jame had expected none of this. A year ago, she had entered the District later at night and had supposed, incorrectly, that it was deserted. This time she was spared the feverish power that would soon throb through these streets, but could her errand succeed in the face of so much hidden activity?

At any rate, here was Gorgo's temple. She tried the door and found it unlocked. The hinges protested piercingly. She froze, listening. Cool air slid past her face from the dim interior, bearing no sound. Had no one come to keep watch here through the long night? The outer chamber was empty. She crossed it and listened at the inner door. Nothing. Pushing it open a crack, she slipped through into the sanctuary.

It was cool and dark inside, as she remembered it, but no longer with the feeling of a woodland cave. The moss was brittle on the stones and the walls were dry. A fine patina of dust lay on the ranked benches. It had not occurred to her before what a difference the draining of the temple's reservoir would make.

The image of Gorgo loomed at the far end of the chamber, its shoulders hunched against the upper darkness. Some loving but clumsy hand had mortared together the ruined face. One had the impression that if there had been any water, the lopsided mouth would have drooled. Jame approached it, drawn by the sight of something in the idol's hands. It was another scroll. Wondering what on earth she had stumbled on this time, she carefully lifted it out and unrolled it. The writing was Kessic, the substance, a single column of unrelated objects. It appeared to be someone's shopping list.

She was still staring at it when the sanctuary door opened. Loogan stood on the threshold.

The high priest had been in his quarters above the outer chamber, darning his best under-tunic. His acolyte should have tended to it that afternoon but had clearly been too unnerved by the approaching Feast to wield a needle, so Loogan had sent him home. It wasn't likely that there would be work enough to justify keeping him around tonight anyway. There hadn't been, to tell the truth, for several weeks. Soon the boy's father would probably be after him to terminate his son's contract. Well, let him go, let them all go ... no, no, he didn't mean that. What was a priest without his people – and who would follow him now, with his personal demon, that willow of a girl (or was it a boy?) popping up every few days to sow chaos? Dear Lord of Tears, what had he done to deserve such a fate? It was just as the Reader of Bones had prophesied the very day that grey-eyed imp had first come into his life; but even the Reader had not been able to foresee the end of the matter. Would some of the faithful come tonight? They *must*. He wasn't sure that his god could survive the Feast without them.

What was that? The hinges of the front door. Someone had come after all.

Hastily, Loogan snapped short the thread and donned the tunic, then a neck cloth, the alb with its embroidered cuffs (merciful god, would he ever get the thing right-side-out on the first try?), the stole, the wool chasuble with its elevated shoulders and contingent of moths like a fitful nimbus, and finally the whole collection of rings, chains, and clinking amulets to which every one of his hieratic ancestors had made a contribution. Quick now, anything else? Ah yes, the diadem. He snatched it up and hurried down the stairs, threw open the inner chamber door – and found his nemesis standing by the altar.

For a moment, astonishment fixed Loogan to the spot, then rising anger broke the trance. He snatched up the tall candlestand near the door, ignoring the clatter as half the candles fell on the floor, and said, 'Now I've got you, you thieving blasphemer.'

'Why do you always call me that?'

The voice was quiet, even polite. Loogan stopped, blinking. It was his special curse that he could never ignore a question.

'Because you and all your kind profess the Anti-God Heresy.'

'What is that?'

'"The belief that all the beings we know to be divine are in fact but the shadows of some greater power that regards them not,"' he heard himself say, automatically quoting the New Pantheon catechism.

'How do you know that this belief is false?'

'Because the gods *do* exist.'

193

'Prove it.'

The priest stared at her. Then, with an almost convulsive gesture, he threw aside the candelabrum and said shrilly, 'All right, I will!'

Few preparations were needed, and Loogan went about them hurriedly, trying not to think what a rare and dangerous thing it was that he meant to attempt. So the congregation would stay away tonight of all nights, would it, and this artful tempter come in its place? Well, he would show them, he would show them all . . . but merciful god, how long was it since this ritual had last been performed? Not since Hierarach Bilgore's day at least. He lugged the benches aside, too distracted to notice that another pair of hands helped him. The space before the idol was now clear, and the two basins of water set on their tripods on either side. Loogan gave the small area one last, despairing look, then sank to his knees, took a deep breath, and began to chant.

At first, nothing happened. The singsong voice rushed on, gaining speed as it went like that of a reciting child who hurries lest he forget the words. Then bit by bit the air above the right basin and then the left seemed to thicken as a haze formed. Wisps of mist were reaching down from both sides towards each other. They met before the idol, merging into a slow, vapourish swirl. A form was taking shape. It seemed to move fitfully, and more mist wrapped itself around the half-gesture. Loogan chanted on, eyes closed, the sweat running down his plump face. Once he faltered, and the ghostlike thing before him appeared to flinch. Then he was done, suddenly, on a rising note as if he had not realised until the last second that the end was so near. Cautiously, the priest opened his eyes.

The figure that cowered before him at the feet of the great idol was about his own size and just as pale. Elaborate vestments and length after length of neck chain bowed it halfway to the ground. Webbed fingers, their upper joints encrusted with rings, fumbled helplessly at the enormous diadem that had slipped down over one bulging eye and apparently stuck there. Its wide mouth, drooling a bit, opened . . .

'No!' Loogan heard himself shriek. 'No, no, no!'

Gorgo, with a stricken look at his priest, gave a thin, piping wail, sank to the floor, and dissolved.

Loogan was not aware that he had fainted until water from one of the basins hit him in the face. He lashed out wildly at the hand that had thrown it, at the face beyond, drawing blood with one of his heavy rings. Then his wrists were caught and, with difficulty, pinned to the floor. His rage died as suddenly as it had been born.

'I killed him,' he said in bewilderment, looking up into those odd, silver-grey eyes. 'I killed my god.'

'No . . . we did. But don't think about that now. You need a drink, and I'm going to find you one. C'mon.'

Near the Temple District was an inn which, like the Res aB'tyrr, stayed open at least until midnight on Autumn's Eve. Within minutes Jame had secured her charge in a private room with two glasses of neat wine already in him and a third waiting at his elbow.

As the little priest emerged from his daze, he began to talk – rapidly, without a pause, as though afraid of silence. Jame quickly learned that he was not the imbecile she had always taken him for. In fact, there was an excellent brain in that round, balding head; but years of bondage to the often ludicrous rituals of his god had taught him that his only possible dignity lay in unthinking obedience. Now all that effort and self-denial seemed to have been wasted.

'I've let them all down, my god, my ancestors, myself,' he said, and then startled Jame by suddenly shouting, 'Let them go, let them all go!'

'Quiet!' hissed the innkeeper, sticking his head through the curtains. 'D'you want to bring every dead god in town down on us?'

'No, just one of them,' said the priest.

Noting that the hour candle on the table had almost burned down to the twelfth ring, Jame hastily paid the reckoning. Loogan tried to break away from her at the door. He wanted to search the streets for Gorgo. She finally managed to get the priest back to his temple and forcibly put him to bed. He was snoring almost before she turned her back.

The front door snicked shut behind her, locking, and she stood at the head of the stairs, shivering slightly, staring at nothing. Somewhere up in the night above the District's architectural tangle, a bell struck, its single, deep note echoing down the corridors of the sky. Another, farther away, joined it, then another and another until all were in full voice. The boom of their combined tolling made the stones beneath shake. Then

195

the lead bell subsided, its course rung through at last, the others following it as their turn came. At last only a treble was left, its silvery note shivering against the dark, faltering, dying away.

The Feast of Dead Gods had begun.

Jame left the District and took to the rooftops. Dry thunder grumbled in the mountain passes to the west, lightning edged the ragged clouds with tarnished silver as they came scudding over the peaks. The wind hunted where it pleased. Below, indistinct forms were wandering through the streets, sometimes pausing to scratch softly on this door or that, sometimes fumbling at a key hole, whispering in the dry, worm-gnawed voices of the dead. Corpse lights flickered in ghostly procession through the crossroads, over the roofbeams. Wisps of song and lament rose to mingle with the wind's rushing.

Jame went on. Cloudies in hiding who saw her pass thought she must be mad to walk so slowly on such a night. She didn't even bother to take the shortest route home. Once a water pipe down-roof gave way with a screech, as though something too heavy had tried to climb it. Once a great, misshapen shadow swept over the gables after her, barely missing, and a nightbird, caught under it, tumbled down dead at her heels. She paid no attention. It was long past midnight, nearer to dawn, when she at last came to the back roof of the Res aB'tyrr.

As Jame swung a leg over the loft's sill, she happened to look back and saw a muffled figure standing on the roof below her, looking up. Thinking it was some old woman of the Cloud Kingdom who had been caught away from home by nightfall, Jame signalled her to climb up to the dubious safety of the open loft. Then she crossed to her own pallet, sat down, and was quickly lost again in her own dark thoughts.

Sometime later she looked up. The shrouded figure was sitting opposite her. This surprised Jame because she had not heard the other's ascent. Regarding the stranger more closely, she realised with a sudden tightening of stomach muscles that she was not so much looking at her guest as through her. It was the night of dead gods, and death, at her invitation, had just entered the loft.

Seconds passed, then a full minute. The other still had not moved. The face, tilted downward, was hidden in the shadow of the cowl. The shoulders slumped. Even in this short time, the gnarled hands, hanging limply over the peak of shrouded knees, had become thinner and more transparent. Mortar began to rattle down behind the motionless figure. The poor creature was dying even out of death, and she was taking part of the inn with her.

How far would this go? Jame saw faint lines of erosion begin to furrow the opposite wall. She sensed that the stranger hadn't the strength to leave unassisted and knew that she dared not touch her. For a long moment Jame sat there, watching and thoughtfully gnawing her lower lip. Then she rose slowly and edged past her peculiar guest to the head of the spiral stairs.

The guest rooms on the third floor were empty, their lodgers undoubtedly below in the hall with the rest of the company. Jame descended to the second floor and slipped out onto the gallery. From there, she went down by the far stair to the court and crossed it stealthily to the kitchen door. When Cleppetty left the room for a minute, she quickly entered and took what she required. Actually, the widow would have begrudged her none of it, but it seemed best not to let anyone know who was in the loft or what, with luck, was about to be done about it. Clutching the ends of the large napkin in which her booty was wrapped, Jame retreated to the upper regions.

The drooping figure had not moved. The stones behind it were more visible than before, and more decayed. Dry rot was well advanced in the floor boards, with tendrils of it reaching out into the room.

There was no proper fireplace in the loft, so Marc had built a small one out of bricks against the north wall to be used for warmth. Jame soon had a blaze going in it. Then she unwrapped the napkin and began to separate its contents. By the time she was done, lined up in front of her were morsels of raw venison, beef, and pork, brie tart, two oysters, fried artichokes, a pear coffin filled with cooked lentils, spiced capon, marzipan toads, and finally the soggy piece of trencher bread (coloured green with parsley) on which the whole mess had rested. The trick, of course, was to find out if any of these assorted fragments would make an acceptable sacrifice. Jame took the nearest at hand – a ragged chunk of pork – and put it on the grate. Then she withdrew to watch.

The meat began to sizzle over the leaping flames, the odour or its cooking reminding Jame forcefully that she had had nothing but a cup of wine in the hill lord's tent since early that morning. Then it began to burn. The hands of the spectre twitched once, but it made no further move. Several stones fell out of the wall

197

and through the rotting floor. Eventually the bit of pork, reduced to a cinder, fell through the grate and was gone. Jame put the venison in its place.

This process seemed to go on for hours. It must be almost dawn, Jame thought, but she doubted if either the loft or her guest would last that long. The roof groaned and began to sag over the silent, nearly invisible figure. Dust drifted down. The beams overhead had started to disintegrate. Fighting an impulse to bolt below to safety, Jame tried to figure out what she was doing wrong.

'Of course!' she said suddenly. 'You idiot, you've got the whole thing backward.'

True, most of the dead gods craved sacrifices, but it was lack of faith, not food, that had killed them in the first place. Poor Gorgo's sudden demise proved that. Therefore, offerings were valuable to such beings only for the sake of the devotion that prompted them. That was why it did those out prowling the streets tonight so little good to devour whatever they could find or catch, and why her guest did not prosper now.

This presented a new difficulty.

'Goddess,' said Jame to the figure, after a moment's hard thought. 'I think I know now what you need, but not if I can provide it. I'm a Kencyr, a monotheist, it seems, whether I want to be one or not. If that weren't true, I would have been able to accept this city on its own terms long ago. As it is, your kind, living and dead, have been a nightmare to me. I still think that in the end I'll find a way to explain you all away, but not entirely. In some quite alien way, you *do* exist. I believe that now. So, to a certain extent, I suppose I believe in you too, goddess. That's the best I can do. I hope it's good enough.'

And with this, she broke the last of her provisions, the soggy piece of trencher bread, over the fire.

It blazed up in her face. Half-blinded, choking, she threw herself back from it. The loft stank of burned hair. Through the after-image of flames, she saw the shrouded figure bending over the fire. It opened its hood and the smoke billowed up into it. The hands stopped trembling as the veins sank on them and the flesh returned. The outline of the stones beyond showed only faintly through the figure when it at last turned towards Jame. She shrank from it, wondering belatedly if she had outsmarted herself again. But no. It merely sketched what might have been an obeisance and drifted past her. Somewhere beyond the Old

Wall, a cock shut within doors began to crow and was stifled in mid-note. Facing the sun that still swam in seas of mist below the horizon, the goddess raised her hands in welcome to the grey light of dawn and vanished.

Jame sat very still for a long moment, then sprang to her feet and practically threw herself over the north parapet. She could never remember afterwards if she had used the B'tyrr in her descent at all. It was the beginning of a cross-town rooftop sprint that was spoken of with awe for years to come by the few early rising Cloudies who witnessed it. Jame only remembered its start and finish when she fetched up gasping in front of Gorgo's temple, suddenly jarred out of her haze of plans by the solid reality of a locked door.

Fifteen seconds later the lock was picked and she was tearing up the stairs to Loogan's quarters. Here she pounced on the unfortunate priest and began to shake him vigorously.

Loogan woke suddenly with all that had happened the night before clear in his mind, a roaring headache, and someone shouting in his ear, 'Get up, you lie-a-bed. We've work to do!'

'Please stop that,' he said plaintively. 'My head is about to fall off . . . what work?'

'Break out the jubilee wine, old man,' cried Jame, doing a double backward somersault that made him wonder if he was still dreaming. 'We're going to resurrect your god!'

11

The Storm Breaks

'Would you please,' said Loogan, 'go over that again?'

Jame did. It was midmorning by now on the day after the Feast. She was explaining, for the third time, the series of experiments that had led to Gorgo's sudden demise and the theories that had prompted them. Then she told him about her adventures in the loft.

'As soon as I realised that the dead gods weren't beyond help,' she concluded, 'it occurred to me that something similar but more extensive might be done for Gorgo. I think your god can be resurrected if only we can restore his peoples' faith in him.'

'That's all very well,' said Loogan, 'but how do we accomplish that when I wasn't even able to make them keep what little they had left?'

'That *is* a problem,' Jame admitted, 'but I can't help feeling that there's a way. After all, Gorgo must have been a fairly important deity once to have rated even a small temple in the District. Perhaps our answer lies in the past. What was he like in the beginning?'

'Foolish as it sounds, I don't know. Back during the Skyrr-Metalondrian War, Great-great-great-great-great-grandfather Bilgore, who was high priest then, seems to have made some fairly extensive doctrinal changes. Then, to make sure there would be no turning back, he destroyed the early records and forbade the acolytes and celebrants ever to pass on the old ways again.'

'*All* the old documents were destroyed? What about those two I found in the idol's hands?'

'Oh, those,' he said. 'They have nothing to do with Gorgo directly. You've been interested in them from the start, haven't you, or at least since the night the reservoir was drained. They're part of a secret that only the high priest of the order is supposed to know, but it doesn't matter any more, does it? No secrets, no priests, no god. If you really want to know, come with me.' And he led the way down the stairs, a plump, oddly dignified figure in a darned undertunic.

They went across the outer chamber and into the little courtyard beyond, with its now-silent fountain. Cracks of blue sky showed above between the overhanging buildings. In the farthest corner, in the deepest shadows, Loogan bent and slid his fingers under the edge of a large flagstone. Obviously counterweighted, it rose easily, disclosing the first steps of a spiral stair dimly lit with light spheres. They descended.

It was a dizzying way down, farther beneath the streets of Tai-tastigon than Jame had ever imagined that one could go. Plaques set in the outer wall indicated the burial slot of many a hierarch, while squares of rock crystal gave distorted, highly unwelcome glimpses of each occupant. At the bottom, tucked into a widened sweep of the stairs, was a high, conical room lined with shelf after shelf of scrolls, extending up out of sight.

'These,' said Loogan with a gloomy sort of pride, 'are the elder archives of Tai-tastigon. They were hidden here during the last battle of the Skyrr-Metalondrian War when it looked as if the winner, whichever side it was, would celebrate by razing the city. The only ones who knew about the transfer besides the novices who effected it were the Senior Archivist (who was one of us) and Great (times five) Grandfather Bilgore. The novices were given a very handsome wall slot each for their pains. The battle ended quite suddenly when the Archiem of Skyrr and the Metalondrian king decided it would be better to make Tai-tastigon a charter city and have it pay them both for the privilege than for one side to slaughter the other and then destroy the place. The Senior Archivist was brained by a flowerpot upset by a lady on an upper terrace while both were watching events below on the plain.

'That was when my ancestor began to change things. He seems to have had the idea that just in case anyone else did know where the documents were, the alterations would make them that much harder to find. Also, I think, it was an excuse to arrange affairs more to his liking. He got away with it too, on both counts. You're the first outsider to see this room in nearly two hundred years.'

'But if it were such a secret,' said Jame, 'why risk betraying it by taking manuscripts up into the temple?'

'Had to,' said the priest with a shrug, beginning to slide back into the depression from which his bit of story-telling had temporarily roused him. 'They have to be resanctified regularly to stay here ... or did. One a day, twenty-two years to a cycle. If you want to stay, stay. I'm going back to bed.'

He departed. Jame heard his slippers shuffle up the steps and felt the dead, earthen silence close in their wake. She was alone in the midst of one of the richest troves of its kind in all Rathillien.

The shroud-light of dawn lay heavy on the southern plain, giving it the texture of a singularly dull tapestry woven with shadows. Birds flitted over it under a pewter sky. The road to Tai-Abendra, a ribbon of silver in the gloom, stretched away to the south, following the Ebonbane's dark curve. The small caravan was already a long way away. Jame and Dally stood on the battlements of the outer wall, watching it go.

'Do you suppose,' said Dally, 'now that Canden's got safely away, the old man might simply let him go?'

'I doubt it. He'll probably have about two days' grace before his grandfather finds out he's gone, and then maybe two hours more if the Sirdan's spies are slow about picking up his trail.'

'Then we shall have to muddy it a bit for them. There are plenty of people who will be glad to lay some false scents for the Sirdan's hell-hounds. Damn!' he said suddenly, torn between exasperation and amusement. 'All these intrigues, all this deceit. Of course, we'll do away with the lot after the election; but Canden is well out of it for now. I almost wish I were going with him.'

'I wish you were too,' said Jame, 'and myself as well.'

Dally glanced at her sharply, hoping to see one thing, finding another that confused and disconcerted him. What had he said now?

'Well, it's time we were getting back,' said Jame, turning from the parapet. 'After all, if we're going to be dragging bagged foxes around town for the benefit of the pack, it won't do to be seen waving good-bye from up here.'

They crossed over to the inner wall on the same rope walk Jame had used when she plunged to Jorin's rescue. There was the cattery, there the pool, but (thank God) no man carrying a sack from one to the other. Out in the foothills, the ounce would probably be wondering where she was, since this was the time when she normally brought him some food to supplement whatever he might have caught. He would have to wait a little longer.

They were on the Rim now.

'What a night!' said Dally. 'I thought they'd never get everything packed. Canden's going to have a fine time with that lot if they're always so disorganised.'

He found he was talking to himself. As he turned to look for his companion, there was a sudden scuffling sound in an alley that he had just passed and then a loud yelp. Running back, Dally found Jame seated on a small rodent-faced individual whose right arm and wrist had achieved an unusual angle in her grasp.

'Look what I've caught,' she said, adding in a dangerously pleasant tone to her victim: 'Must I promise to nail the ears of every spy who comes crawling after me to the nearest door in order to be left alone?'

The little man made violent signs to the negative. By now, virtually no one in Tai-tastigon took the Kencyr's word lightly.

'But Jame, it's all right,' Dally's protested, approaching them. 'It's only one of the Creeper's men.'

'What?'

The spy, taking advantage of her start, twisted free and sent her tumbling back into the wall as he scrambled to his feet. She was up almost as quickly as he, but ignored him as he scuttled away.

'How long has that creature had people following you?' she demanded. 'Does your brother know?'

'Why, I suppose so,' said Dally. 'It's for my own protection, after all. Mendy worries about me. Stop looking at me like that – it's true. Listen, it's been a long night. Let's go to the Moon and have a drink. Then I can start being devious and you can go on with whatever it is you've been doing in the Temple District this last fortnight. Come on, let's.'

'Let's see,' Raffing was saying owlishly, 'who else will be up for promotion when the Guild Council convenes? You, Darinby, for one. Drink to all candidates for master!'

'Including Bane?' asked Patches mischievously.

'Man's a rogue,' said Raffing, twisting about in his chair and scowling horrifically at the rest of the Moon's common room, which as usual at this early hour was full of thieves relaxing after their night's work. 'A rogue, I say! Bought his commission. Everybody knows it.'

'So they do, old chap,' said Darinby soothingly. 'You needn't shout it at them. I suppose,' he added, trying to return the conversation to its original channel, 'that the Talisman will be on the lists too, for a journeyman.'

'Same difference,' said an apprentice from the Rim. 'Theocandi's pupil uses his father's money; Penari's, his master's secrets. Either way, it isn't fair.'

'Oh, come now. Secrets? What master doesn't pass along his own, if the student is worthy?'

'You know what I mean,' said the other stubbornly. 'Look at the work he's done: the Sky King's britches, the Peacock Gloves, and half a dozen other things that no one else has even been able to touch, much less take. That's not common, honest skill, no, not any more than Penari's theft of the Eye of Abarraden was. There's sorcery in it, or worse.'

'Jealousy too, I should think. It may be only a game to him – I mean to her,' he corrected himself with a grimace, 'but by all the gods she plays it fairly and well.'

'Drink to the Talisman!' roared Raffing, echoed by Patches.

'I still say it's not right,' muttered the Rim apprentice, 'and what's more,' he added, on a surge of false courage, 'if he turns up here tonight, I'll tell him so to his face!'

'Then let us hope "he" doesn't,' said Darinby softly, remembering the death of Scramp. 'For both your sakes.'

'On second thought,' said Jame, 'let's not go to the Moon after all. We're closer to home here anyway. If we ask her nicely, maybe Cleppetty will make us honey cakes for breakfast.'

In a room hung with silver and blue, Men-dalis was pacing back and forth. Wherever he walked, the light went with him, clinging softly to his hair and clothes, the god-glow of Dalis-sar's true son. For the thousandth time, he was counting up the odds.

Masters Gold and Shining were Theocandi's; there was no helping that. Mistress Silver still kept her own council, but was said to be furious with the Sirdan over her son. A pity the boy had only been exiled. The four Provincials were, of course, his. (He would not learn until much too late that one of them was not.) Jewel? The man might jump either way. A show of confidence would have more weight with him than bribes, but not so with Glass or the master thieves' two representatives. There was the crux, for those four votes might well decide the election. Theocandi thought he had bought them. Men-dalis knew that, with the proper backing, the old miser could be outbid; and that backing he would have, although not until the very day of the Council. His supporter had been inflexible about that. His integrity was under suspicion, he had said, and he must establish it at least in the public eye before daring to draw such a sum from the city treasury. Something about dispensing justice in an undeclared trade war on Winter's Eve...

With a start, Men-dalis found that the Creeper had entered the room and was walking with him nearly at his elbow. The thin, scratchy voice began its whispered report. Men-dalis listened to most of it without comment, asked a few questions, then suddenly turned on the master spy and said, quite loudly, 'What?'

The information was repeated. He began to pace again, frowning.

'Well, what of it? If Dally helps that Kencyr hoyden to embarrass Theocandi, all the better. A pity the old man's grandson got away, though; we might have found a use for him later.... Yes, yes, I realise that her master is the Sirdan's elder brother. Those two have been at dagger's point for a dog's age.... You think their rivalry is all a ruse? Yes, if that were true, the Talisman would make a good agent for Theocandi. No one would ever suspect her of it, not with the old men constantly feuding.... Dally? The boy's not very bright, but he can be trusted – I think. Besides, there's been talk of Penari's professional secrets again. If Dally can worm them out of his 'prentice, it will be quite a gem in our crown.... In *love* with her? Well, well, I don't know...'

Back and forth he went, arguing as though with himself while his familiar kept pace one step behind him, its avid face out of his sight. The whispering voice went on and on, and bit by bit the room began to dim.

Jame thought at first that she had begun to hallucinate. In that silent, underground room, time might have stopped for all one could tell. How many hours had it been since she had parted with Jorin on the hillside and Dally (who had gone out with her) at the gate? Two? Ten? And nearly twenty-four awake before that, helping Canden prepare for his flight. No, one didn't begin to imagine things in that length of time. She read the manuscript again, then rolled it up and went quickly out of the room and up the stairs with it in her hand.

Loogan was sitting on the steps to the upper apartment. 'Well, it's happened,' he said gloomily. 'My acolyte's father has got the Priests' Guild to annul his contract to me. I can't say that I blame him.'

'Never mind that now. Listen: *"By day and night, the battle raged, wheels of fire clashing over the seared plain while the heavens burned. Lances of lightning had Heliot and Dalis-sar, the moon for a shield. Their swords were tongues of flame, of woven comet's hair their armour. The earth trembled when they met, and the old gods fled to the deep places thereof to shiver in the dark."'*

'Why read me all this?' said Loogan wearily. 'What difference can it possibly make?'

'Listen, dammit! *"One alone stayed, saw through the green roof of his home the terrible conflict, felt the earth's agony, the forests burning, the waters boiling. And when Dalis-sar had won, Grogiryl came from his sea-deep house to plead for the scorched earth. Taking pity on him and on the blackened land, the new lord of the sun raised him to the heavens so that his tears falling might restore the sunken seas, bring life to the charred fields."*

'Now, is that or is that not, in unscrambled form, part of the ninth canticle of your evening service?'

'Yes,' said the priest, looking puzzled, 'but the name isn't right.'

'That's just the point. It is. Look, I've been going over the religious tracts in your collection this past fortnight, and so far I haven't found one reference to Gorgo, which is ridiculous considering his obvious antiquity. Gorgiryl, however, gets at least a mention from nearly everybody because he was one of the few deities to make the jump from the Old Pantheon to the New essentially unaltered. Then along came your multiple great-grandfather Bilgore. It wasn't just Gorgo's name that he changed, either... you're looking remarkably blank. Am I going too fast for you?'

'N-no. I'm told I always look that way just before the rotten eggs hit.'

'Well, this is more on the order of a spinach custard – just as messy but potentially more nourishing. As I was saying, the old attributes seem to have been kept, but not with the same emphasis ... and that's where things began to go sour for poor old Gorgo – pardon, Gorgiryl. Instead of the tears of life – rain, that is – you have sterile salt water; instead of the world's salvation, endless sorrow. It's the whole myth frozen in the wrong place, with everything distorted to make its lowest point look like its proper end. What easier way to turn a simple, rather dignified religion on its ear? You're still looking blank. Come, I'll show you an example, the best one of all.'

She took him by the arm and led him half against his will to the threshold of the inner chamber. Neither had entered it since the night its occupant had died. The basins were still there, also the short scroll peeking over the idol's webbed fingers, but more vivid than either was the memory of the bowed, bewildered figure in its garish finery that had stood trembling before them for so short a time.

'As the man that Bilgore made him,' said Jame, 'he was ludicrous.' Then she pointed at the statue looking dark and cool in the shadows. 'But as a giant frog ... ?'

It was early evening on a day some three weeks into autumn, and the light was failing rapidly. Marc put down the tiny figure he had been carving. The rough form was there – the cowled head, outstretched arms, even some folds of the enveloping garment – but he didn't trust himself with the finer details at this time of night. Ah, but it felt good to have a bit of work in his hands again. He had almost forgotten the pleasure of making small, cunningly fashioned objects, not to mention his old dream of becoming a master craftsman before necessity and his own remarkable physique had defeated all such gentle ambitions. If he had a hearth of his own, he might have retired to it now to perfect this skill. Instead, all he possessed after a long life of service was his honour – and a few friends to brighten the way.

Still, one might do worse.

A mouse scurried across a beam overhead. Boo was getting lazy, Marc thought, staring up contemplatively at another sample of his handiwork. He and Rothan had had quite a time repairing the loft after its midnight visitor. Matters could easily have been worse, though: without Jame, the top two storeys would probably have collapsed into the hall.

She was clever, that lass, but more than a bit strange. Marc knew how afraid many Kencyrs were of people like her, but he himself had seen too much of life to take fright at something a little odd. He wondered idly how much Highborn blood she had, all Shanirs necessarily possessing at least a trace. A quarter at most, probably. Pure Highborn women and even many half-bloods were strictly sequestered and used by their menfolk to bind together the ruling houses of the Kencyrath. Those with less Highborn blood, especially if it came with Shanir traits, could receive some pretty rough treatment. That might explain Ishtier's initial hostility towards Jame.

Ishtier. Strange things certainly happened to Kencyrs in this city, Marc thought, shaking his head. Here he was carving the image of one dead god for a small household shrine while Jame acted as temporary acolyte to another and their own priest set traps to snare them both. Then there was Bane, who acted like a Shanir, but (as far as Marc could tell) wasn't one, and that old Kencyr, Dalis-sar, deified. No wonder few of the Kencyrath stayed in Tai-tastigon longer than they could help.

So what are you doing here now, old man?

A wail split the air, breaking his line of thought. Someone's baby? No, cats – squaring off in front of the inn directly below. There was a covered chamber pot near at hand. Marc flipped off the lid and tossed the contents over the parapet without bothering to look down.

'Hey!' said a familiar voice below in sharp protest.

Jame had been in the Lower Town that afternoon, checking on Taniscent. Dusk was gathering and the byways were rapidly clearing of their shabby traffic when she left Patches's home. To save time, she turned down a narrow side street, which, according to the patterns of the Maze, should have been a short-cut to the fosse that bounded the area. Several turns in, however, the lane was blocked to shoulder height with the debris of a collapsed wall. Jame climbed the mound and set off along its spine, expecting the way to open up again somewhere beyond. Eventually it did, but only into a wasteland of fire-ravaged buildings and thoroughfares so choked with rubble as to be quite invisible. To her exasperation Jame realised that she was lost. Her knowledge of the city, theoretical and practical, had made her careless, here where the lack of all customary landmarks made caution most necessary. She had forgotten how quickly Tai-tastigon could revenge itself on those who took its mysteries lightly.

It was getting dark. Silence clung batlike to the charred rafters, swelled up out of the shadowed hollows in the heaped debris. A rat scratched and snuffled in the ruins, claws scrabbling briefly on a bone-white board. To go back or forward – return to the heart of the Lower Town or press on towards the deadly circle of her own temple? Night breathed in her ear, waiting to pounce.

'Salutations.'

Jame started violently. A dark, elegant figure had appeared on top of a broken wall above her. 'Well, look who's perching on the battlements,' she heard herself say in a shaky voice. 'Come down, gore-crow.'

'Gladly,' said Bane, and leapt.

Jame sprang backward into a defensive pose. Water flowing met fire leaping, channelled its force aside with a blur of moving bodies once, twice, and again. They broke apart, regarding each other, now that the initial shock was past, with something like satisfaction. Neither had been so well matched in a long, long time. When they met again, it was not in the whirlwind fashion of the first round but with more subtlety of attack and response on both sides. Darkness gathered about them, two lithe, shadowy forms tracing the patterns of ritual combat as old as their ancient race.

Jame could never afterwards say when the fight ended and the dance began. No need to ask then where in the night her partner was, for his movements had become an extension of her own. The kantirs flowed together, water and air mingling with touches of dark fire to smoulder at nerves' end, fingertips tingling with a nearness that never became contact.

Where had she done this before, and with whom?... a vast chamber as dark as this place was now, surrounded by blazing tripods, a canopied bed, a man dancing, his face... no!

Cloth ripped, and Bane sprang back in a startled exclamation. The left sleeve of his d'hen was split from the inner elbow to the wrist. On the forearm beneath, black in the moonlight, was a thickening line of blood. He regarded it with a slow, secret smile. Jame's throat tightened. Without a word, she turned and climbed the wall of jumbled beams. As she set off through the wilderness beyond, Bane was walking by her side.

'The old man knows that you helped his grandson escape,' he

said, as though nothing had passed between them. 'I've never seen him so furious.'

'Damn. That will mean assassins lurking under every flowerpot, I suppose.'

'Oh, he wouldn't be so angry if it were as simple as that. At the moment, he's afraid to interfere with you at all. The bones have warned him. According to them, if he's going to win the election, you'll have something to do with it.'

'What, for God's sake?'

'I shouldn't stop here if I were you,' he said. 'It's following us.'

'It? Oh.' Jame looked back, saw nothing but jagged, darkening shadows and the cusp of the old moon rising. Nevertheless, there was only one thing 'it' could be, here in the Lower Town. 'You don't seem very concerned,' she said, resuming her pace.

'M'lord Ishtier tells me that I shouldn't be,' he said cryptically. 'I'm to trust in him and all will be well. But I don't think it is, even now. If that man has betrayed me, kin or not, the next time he deigns to give me an order, the results may surprise him.'

'Bane, I haven't the faintest idea what you're talking about. Now will you please tell me how I'm supposed to help Theocandi retain his power?'

'If he knew, he would have found a way to get rid of you without endangering his own future long before this, if only to stop the nightmares. Remember the statue at the prow of Ship Island? Every night for the past month, he's dreamed that it had your face and was brandishing his head. Have you noticed,' he said, examining his arm, 'that every time we meet, someone ends up bleeding?'

'I've noticed. Not very auspicious, is it?'

'That depends,' he said, with an ambiguous smile. 'This much at least is clear: If you stay in Tai-tastigon after the election, there'll be trouble – regardless of who wins. Don't trust Mendalis any more than Theocandi, despite that baby brother of his. Something nasty is brewing in that quarter, though no one seems to know exactly what. Beware of the Creeper, and also of m'lord Ishtier. Not only does our esteemed priest hate you, but there are rumours that he had more to do with the Sirdan during the last Council than either cares to admit.'

'Oh? In what way?'

'My spies suggest an exchange of information, probably

arcane. Theocandi is a fair Kencyr scholar, and I know that he has several of our "lost" documents in his library that Ishtier might well have wished to see. Of course, the reverse is true too; remember, this was just before the appearance of the Shadow Thief.

'And now,' he said with a sudden laugh, 'having uttered my share of warning croaks, I'll flap off to the nearest rookery. Your way lies in that direction, over the fosse and home. Our murky friend will follow me, I think; it always does. But there's no point in tempting it.'

On the other side of the little waterway, Jame suddenly turned. 'That statue of yours . . .' she called after him. 'I've just remembered. It carries two heads, not just one. In Theocandi's dream, whose was the other?'

Bane paused, a black silhouette against the sky. 'Oh, didn't I tell you?' he said, the now familiar smile coming back into his voice although the dusk hid his face. 'The other head was mine.'

Kithra sank her jug into the public fountain and heaved it out again, full of water, to balance on the limestone rim. Pretending to check it for cracks, she peered over its round shoulder at the Skyrrman.

What was that man Marplet up to? He had dragged out the construction of his precious inn for nearly two years, and now, suddenly, everything must be finished at once. Even at this time of night, there were craftsmen at work inside, fitting inlaid panels around the walls. What was he readying the inn for? Kithra checked off the major, upcoming public events in her mind; the Thieves' Guild Council, several festivals in the Temple District, the biennial meeting between the Archiem of Skyrr and the Metalondrin king . . . of course, that must be it. Everyone knew that while their heralds exchanged ritual insults, the two rulers usually slipped off to spend Winter's Eve going from one tavern to another. Marplet must be hoping that they would honour him with a visit.

Ah, if she could only get the Archiem's attention for half a minute, what stories she could tell him about his 'honourable' countryman! Gods, what a chance to gut that sleek pig of an innkeeper . . .

Niggen dashed out of a side street with a howl. Although he was feigning terror, Kithra recognised that detestable giggle welling up under all his clamour and wished savagely that the

Talisman could be induced to knock out a few more of his teeth.

And here, as though in answer to her thoughts, was Jame herself, standing hands on hips at the mouth of the street from which Niggen had just bolted. The boy was in front of the Skyrrman now, loudly begging his father's servants for protection and casting looks of mock terror back across the square. The apparent cause of this scene regarded it with raised eyebrows and a look oddly compounded of perplexity, amusement, and distaste on her handsome face. Kithra found herself wishing, not for the first time, that the Talisman really was a boy.

At that moment, two other voices joined the uproar, cutting across it with their undisguised notes of raw hatred. Fang was stalking Boo on the very threshold of the Res aB'tyrr.

'Oh, for pity's sake,' said Jame, and went to the rescue.

At the last moment, something made her look up. She saw what was falling from the loft and, with a shout of protest, leapt for the doorway, snatching up Boo en route. Fang was not so fortunate. Drenched, he backed rapidly away, shaking his head, then turned and dashed off.

'Sorry,' said Marc, looking down.

Jame lugged Boo up to the loft, hoping to keep him out of further mischief. The cat continued to whuffle ferociously at nothing in particular up all three flights of stairs. He gave the impression that when set down he would bounce for some time like a clockwork toy.

When Jame had told Marc about Bane's warnings, the big Kendar said, 'He's right, you know. It isn't safe for you here even now, nor for anyone else, I sometimes think. Too much is coming to a boil too fast. We Kencyrs are used to trouble, but this time most of it isn't even our own; and I'm getting too old to enjoy the thing for its own sake. What are we doing here, lass? We don't belong in this city, however entangled we're become with it. We should be going home.'

Home – the broken walls, the doorways that gaped, the waiting dead – no. The images touched Jame's mind only for a second, then faded away. Home... no longer a place but a people whose face she barely knew but suddenly wished very much to see. The sun on spear points and the moon on shields, the rathorn cry and the charge that makes the earth shake; scrollsmen walking in their cloisters, thirty millennia of knowledge lying cool and deep in their minds; the hearth on a

212

winter's night when friends meet; Tori... a place to belong. It was calling to her here in the dark, stirring her blood as the moon does the sea, and at last – after days, weeks, months of hesitation – she answered its summons.

'Yes,' she said, 'we should go home. Trinity knows what will happen to either of us when we get there, but we should go. Soon.'

'Over the Ebonbane? The passes won't be safe for months.'

'True. How about going south, either cross-country or down the Tone to Endiscar? The storm season will end soon. Then, dead water or not, we can take ship around the Cape of the Lost and reach the Central Lands by the sea route.'

'You don't know what it's like down there,' said Marc, grimacing. 'The land is as rotten as the water, and as haunted as the north in its own way. Still, it may be our best chance at that. When should we leave?'

'Say, as soon after the election as we can manage. I'd like to set something right before I go, and it will probably take me that long at least... if I can bring it off at all,' she added to herself, a worried look settling on her face in the darkness.

The evening service had ended. Jame, by the door, watched the congregation file out, then went down to the front where Loogan was putting his cue cards back in order. Each scrap of paper had part of the revised ritual on it, gleaned from any one of a dozen different sources. With their help, supplemented by some vigorous pantomiming by Jame at the back of the room, he was attempting to replace the old corrupt words – engraved on his memory by thirty years of use – with the new ones.

'That went quite well,' said Jame, coming up to him. 'I'd say that the people were impressed and pleased. They're taking the changes much better than I'd hoped. Gorgo' – they had decided to keep the old name – 'probably hasn't been this popular in years.'

'It helps to be a rain god in the middle of a drought,' said Loogan. 'Up to a certain point. You know, the people of the Far Isles have a priest-king who they believe can summon the rains at will out of his belly. If he fails, they rip him open.'

'In other words, an impressive performance isn't enough. Hasn't it made any difference, getting all these people to come back?'

'None,' said Loogan heavily. 'He's as dead as ever, poor thing, and all that we do in his name is futile. Only a miracle can help him now.'

'Hush.'

A stranger was standing on the threshold, his broad shoulders nearly filled the doorway. 'Are you the high priest?' he demanded.

Loogan drew himself up, some of his old authority returning. 'Yes, I am,' he said. 'How may I serve you?'

'Huh!' said the man, giving the modest interior of the temple a quick, scornful glance. 'I'm part of a delegation of farmers from the Ben-ar Confederation, come up river to petition all the appropriate gods for rain. Damn waste of time, I say, but there you are. We must have it before Winter's Eve or the wheat crop will fail, and that will mean famine throughout the Eastern Lands. I hear that this Gurgle of yours is a rain god. What d'you charge for extra prayers?'

'Sir,' said Loogan stiffly, 'where the good of the community is involved, we charge nothing.'

'I should damn well hope not,' said the other in a tone of satisfaction mixed with a contempt for a fool who drives a poor bargain. 'After all, it may be our wheat, but it's your bread.' And with that he turned on his heel and stomped away. They heard his heavy boots clumping on the tiles, then the slam of the front door.

'What an odious man,' said Loogan with distaste, 'and what an odd sight you make, capering like that. Whatever for?'

'An idea. You wanted a miracle? Well, so did that oaf, and I think I see how we might be able to provide it!'

Three weeks before the Thieves' Guild Council, ninety-nine of the hundred landed masters – one for each district in the city – converged on the Guild Hall to choose their two representatives. Eleven candidates vied for these honoured and potentially lucrative positions, six promising if elected to vote for Mendalis at the general meeting, five for Theocandi. Each needed two-thirds of his colleagues' votes to win and was dropped from the running if his share fell to less than half that. At the end of each round in which no victor was forthcoming, all the ballots were gathered up, wrapped around the shaft of an arrow, and sent – blazing – into the sky as a sign to the rest of the thieves' community of a null vote.

This had been going on since midmorning. By nightfall,

twenty-six such votes had been taken, eight candidates eliminated (one by assassination) and two citizens injured by spent arrows. Nerves were raw, tempers flared. Emotionally as well as physically the city of Tai-tastigon was tinder, waiting for the first careless spark.

Jame had gone up into the hills the night before upon learning that her master really did not intend to join his peers in the Guild Hall. This had come as a jolt to her. She had always assumed that Penari would support the Sirdan in the end, despite the former's professed neutrality. Instead, he stayed home and she fled temporarily into the countryside, not wishing to defend the old man's actions among her fellow apprentices. Her affection for him had not changed, but there was nothing in her nature that helped her to understand, much less explain, the failure of a man to stand by his own brother, however unworthy the latter might be.

Another arrow, a pinprick of light at this distance arcing into the night sky. Even with a glum Cloudie sitting on every roof with a bucket of water, didn't those fools at the Palace realise how easy it would be to set the whole town ablaze?

Here in the parched hills, she would not have dared to start a cooking fire, even if she and Jorin had found any game to prepare on one. Nonetheless, there had been food for both: hers, from the city; his, from a more puzzling source. On arrival the night before, Jame had found the remains of a stag in the back of the cave, a far larger animal than Jorin could ever have pulled down by himself. Besides, it had died with its throat ripped out, an unlikely way for an ounce with its short canines to dispatch its quarry. She could only think that he must have stolen it from a larger predator, but what beast in all the hills was big enough to have left such marks on its prey?

The grass under her hand crackled drily. The hills on all sides lifted seared slopes the colour of Jorin's fur as he lay beside her. When would the rain comes?

'*It must be before Winter's Eve,*' she had told Loogan, '*for the sake of the wheat and, by extension, to serve our own purpose. Remember, you're going to tell the people that if they believe Gorgo can make it rain, he will. The threat of famine should be enough to get them involved. I don't know if the faith-creating-reality aspects of this city will actually work that way, but if it does, or even if the rains simply fall in the course of nature, enough faith may be restored in Gorgo to resurrect him.*'

'*But if it does rain, won't every god in Tai-tastigon claim the credit?*'

'*Let them. Gorgo is still the most likely candidate, since it was just such a miracle that made him a New Pantheon god in the first place. His people will remember that. They must...*'

Hullo, flames – a viper's knot of them growing red and vehement in the darkness. Had those idiots managed to set the city alight after all? If so, they had started with their own house, for surely that fantastic roofline could only belong to the Palace itself. Now there was a sound coming from below, fainter than the crickets that called on all sides but somehow rising above their clamour and growing louder each moment. Shouts, cheering. So the representatives had at last been chosen. Now the real fun would begin.

The Rim apprentice was on his feet, glaring down at Raffing. 'Take that back,' he said through his teeth.

'Why?' said the other, giving him an insolent, somewhat blurry grin. 'Everyone knows it's the truth. Your master may have been chosen as Theocandi's man, but we all know that he'll vote for whoever pays him the most.'

'Liar!' screeched the apprentice, and he leapt forward with steel bright in his hand, as the startled Raffing went over backwards off his bench, feet in the air.

Darinby was between the two. As the Rim thief lunged over the table in front of him, the journeyman caught his knife hand and twisted. Turned over in midair, he crashed down on his back. Tankards flew in all directions. The members of both factions, some with knives already out, froze, staring.

'Let me remind you all of something,' Darinby said quietly in the sudden lull. 'Open conflict between factions can be interpreted as the beginning of an undeclared guild war. If your side starts one, the Five will fine you out of existence. If they can't decide who's to blame, both parties will suffer. If, despite all this, any of you still want a fight, I suggest that you start it with me, for by all the gods I most assuredly will finish it.'

There was an awkward silence. Then, one by one, the thieves sat down again, glaring at Darinby if they had the nerve to face him at all and muttering amongst themselves. The journeyman watched them, casually flipping the Rim thief's knife end over end. When he was sure nothing more would happen for the moment, he tossed the blade back to its owner and said pleasantly, 'If I were you, I should leave. Now.' The apprentice shot one last venomous look at the bemused Raffing and slipped through the crowd towards the door. Darinby resumed his seat, signalling for a new tankard to replace the one now somewhere under the table. Slowly, his heartbeat returned to normal.

In ten other public houses, three younger brothers, two nephews, and five cousins – Guild-men all – waited as he did now, with a timely warning and, if necessary, a ready blade. With luck and considerable impudence, they just might get Tai-tastigon through the night.

Then again, throught Jame, surely there were still a few sane people left in the city. Things would be bad from now until the election, but there would always be those, longer-sighted than the rest, who would try to hold the Guild together despite itself for the future's sake.

Jorin was dozing beside her, his chin on her knee. Suddenly he woke, head jerking up, ears twitching. Jame also tensed. She seemed to smell something, a wild, musky scent not at all unpleasant but oddly stirring. No odour had ever evoked such a response from her before. She wondered briefly if it was reaching her through the filter of Jorin's senses. Then she remembered the stag carcass in the cave and leapt to her feet.

They had been sitting on a slope. The hilltop above them was crowned by a huge thorn bush whose branches spread from a solid black core out to a nimbus of fragile spikes. At its centre were two points of light about five feet off the ground. They moved, detached itself, became a great, shadowy form gliding along the crest. Jorin, with an excited chirp, bounded up the slope to meet it. Gravely, the huge head bent to touch noses with the ounce, then lifted again, turning towards Jame. It winked, and both were gone, leaving the night empty in their wake.

Jame stared after them. 'An Arrin-ken,' she said out loud with awe in her voice. 'I've just seen an Arrin-ken.'

There were isolated clashes in Tai-tastigon that night after word spread that Theocandi's chosen representative had secured one position and Men-dalis's the other, but none of these were witnessed by the guards or resulted in the death of anyone particularly notable.

Patches, on her way home, found Raffing in an alley near the Moon. Only his clothes made identification possible. Of the many knife blows struck, it was to be hoped that the first had brought death.

*

'I'm sorry,' said the secretary, 'but Master Men-dalis doesn't have time to see you today.'

'So you've been telling me for the last week. Are you sure? I'd just like to talk to him for a minute.'

'Sorry,' said the man again, beginning to shuffle through the papers he carried. 'We *are* busy here, you know. The election is only a fortnight away now. Try again tomorrow. Good day.'

Out again on the steps of the New Faction headquarters, Dally paused. Had someone just ducked back out of sight around the corner? Another of the Creeper's agents, probably. *'Watch out for that man,'* Jame had told him. *'I think he wants your brother all to himself, and you're in his way.'* He knew now that he was followed everywhere. Mendy wouldn't tell him if this was by his orders or not. Mendy wouldn't even see him. What had gone wrong between them? When the election was over, perhaps all would be well again. Yes, of course – it was only tension that made his brother act this way.

But if so, why was Dally suddenly so frightened?

Someone was shouting and others rushing about inside the Skyrrman calling to each other in excited voices.

'What now?' Ghillie said to Rothan as they stood at the Res aB'tyrr's front door, listening.

'I smell smoke,' said Rothan suddenly. 'Look. Something is burning, perhaps in the kitchen.'

Behind the front wing of the building, a horse screamed in terror.

'No,' said Ghillie the hostler sharply. 'It's in the stable. Here, you!' he shouted at a servant who had come running out to the public fountain with a bucket. 'D'you need any help?'

'From you?' the man replied with scorn, hurriedly dipping his vessel in the water. 'Think you haven't done enouth already, do you? Well, just wait. You'll pay for this, you'll pay!'

'Pay?' Ghillie repeated in confusion. 'For what?'

'Quiet,' said Cleppetty. She had come up behind them unnoticed and now stood fists jammed on hips, scowling at the activity across the square. 'I don't like this,' she said. 'I don't like this at all.'

And then, at last, it was the dawn of Winter's Eve. Jame was asleep in the loft. The grey morning light touched the sharp line of her cheekbone and jaw, but failed to erase the darkness under her eyes. Over the last few weeks, her triple role of thief, dancer, and acolyte had taken its toll. She had lost weight and slept badly, with the growing foretaste of failure to poison her dreams. The deadline was almost here, and still it had not rained.

She was dreaming now.

Images came and went; faces whirled past like drowned rats in a river. Scramp, Hangrell, and Raffing; Theocandi and Mendalis; Marplet and Tubain; Gorgo and Loogan dancing together, both so horribly alike. They froze, staring at each other, than shrieked and simultaneously melted away. 'The Anti-God Heresy?' croaked the idol. 'Don't know, couldn't care (ribbet) less. Excuse me – my constellation is rising.' And it jumped, up through the smoke hole in the sky. Beams came crashing down, mounds of debris grew. A dark, elegant figure was walking across them under the old moon, an unnaturally swollen shadow at his heels. He turned, and his face was Tori's. 'Shanir!' he cried. 'Priest's-Bane, see what you've done!' A figure crouched before her, rings, chains, and amulets raining down from it; but surely that wasn't Loogan's corpulent form. Bent back, narrow shoulders, hooded visage, and then an altar, tessellated floor, her own ungloved hand raised as though in summons. The figure looked up. Ishtier. Shocked recognition, then hatred and something not unlike fear ripped the remaining shreds of humanity from his skull-like face.

Jame woke with a start, gasping for breath.

What time was it, she wondered confusedly. Ah, dawn . . . but if so, why was the light steadily failing, and what was that distant sound, like rocks cannoning down the mountainside? She threw back her blanket and sprang up. The sun was indeed rising, but towards it rolled such a mighty rack of clouds from over the Ebonbane that it was as if a great shroud were being pulled across the earth. Lightning flickered within the black billows, tingeing them with silver; and the thunder sounded again, closer this time. It was growing steadily darker. As Jame stood by the parapet, the wind came, slipping through the loft, lifting the black wings of her hair, and then the first chill drops of rain struck her face.

At first she could hardly believe what was happening. Then she threw back her head and gave full tongue to the great war cry of victory, waking every sleeper in the house. Before they could even ask themselves what on earth they had heard, she was gone, flying across the rooftops northward towards the Temple District, pulling on her clothes as she went.

The rain was falling harder now. Slates were slick with it, and every gutter held a raging torrent. Soon it was hard to see, even to breathe in the downpour. Jame got as far as the River Tone, then was forced down to street level opposite Edor Thulig. Both arms of the Tynnet were roaring around the island on which the Tower of Demons stood, its upper heights lost in the driving rain. When she came to the first bridge after that, Jame found that the high gates that gave access to the side streets on either side of it were shut. Puzzled, she crossed over to the north bank and loped westward towards the next intersection.

High above, a man struggled with a shutter loosened by the wind. Looking down, he saw the lone figure making its way up an avenue already half awash and shouted at it, 'Get out of the street, you fool! D'you want to drown?' The shutter closed with a bang.

Jame caught her breath, realising at last what she should have guessed immediately. She began to run. At the next bend in the road was another closed gate, but this one had a rickety ladder nailed to it. Jame sprinted for it. Already she could hear the approaching roar. Her foot was on the first rung when a wall of water twenty feet high appeared around the street's next bend. She climbed frantically, hearing it smash into the opposite houses and cannon off them. Her leg was over the top of the gate when the flash flood boomed into it.

Every board shook. A sheet of spray, exploding upward, lifted Jame neatly off her perch. She tumbled down on the far side, more through water than air, to the hard cobbles below.

It was a thoroughly bedraggled, badly limping figure that at last presented itself on the threshold of Gorgo, formerly the lugubrious god. Loogan darted across the outer room, grabbed Jame's hand and half dragged her, hopping on one foot, to the door of the sanctuary. It was raining inside almost as heavily as out, from a private miniature bank of clouds up near the ceiling. A grotesque, indistinct form cavorted about in the middle of the room, bouncing over benches, splashing boisterously in the growing puddles.

'He – ah – isn't very big, is he?' Jame said.

'No,' Loogan agreed, beginning to grin, 'but he's very, very green.'

Solemnly, they drank to the health of the newborn god in rainwater from cupped hands.

12

A Flame Rising

On that day, the whole city rejoiced. The rain ended in the early afternoon, and the sun came out to shine on the remains of a sparkling day. The dust that had lain everywhere was washed away. Gilt towers glowed in the light, and red tile roofs and mosaic prayer walls of turquoise and chalcedony. Bitter enemies met in the streets and went off together laughing; thieves who had not exchanged a word in weeks, except to curse, toasted each other in the taverns. The thoroughfares were full of people walking together, singing, dancing. Whatever tomorrow might bring, today was unanimously declared a high holiday and all set about gathering sweet memories for the troubled times ahead.

Jame and Loogan went out to celebrate with the rest.

In the distance, they could hear the music of trumpets and tabors in Judgment Square where the Archiem of Skyrr and King Sellik XXI of Metalondar were meeting in a blaze of pageantry. Jame wanted to go and see, but her bruised knee hurt too badly. Instead, at Loogan's suggestion, they drifted from tavern to tavern, drinking at each. The afternoon slipped away in a growing vinous haze. At dusk, Jame found herself in the same tavern to which she had taken Loogan on the night that Gorgo had died. The priest had just poured her another cup of wine, spilling half of it on the floor, when Ghillie appeared at her elbow.

'They taunted me about it at the fountain,' he said rapidly, ignoring all offers of wine or a seat. 'They aren't even trying to keep it a secret anymore; they're so confident, and Aunt Cleppetty says they've got reason to be...'

'Ghillie, you're making my head ache. Who are "they" and what is "it"?'

The boy took a deep breath. 'Harr sen Tenko is bringing the

221

Archiem to the Skyrrman tonight, as though by accident,' he said with great care in a brittle voice. 'If the service is good – and the gods know it will be – according to custom, the Archiem will ask Marplet what payment he will take for it. Marplet means to ask for a judgement against the Res aB'tyrr. He'll accuse us of spoiling his wine, terrorising his servants, starting that fire in his stable – in short, of waging an illegal trade war against him. His cellar is full of oiled bales of straw, ready to stack around us and set ablaze. The Archiem needn't hesitate for the city's sake, now that there's been rain. We'll be burned to the ground.

'Please, Jame,' he burst out, all control vanishing. 'Stop gaping at me like that and come. We need you!'

Jame paused in the courtyard of the Res aB'tyrr, drew a bucket of water from the well, and dumped it over her head. Somewhat clearer in mind, she entered the kitchen. Cleppetty turned to stare at her.

'Why is it,' she demanded, 'that every time we have a crisis, you turn up dripping wet?'

'Force of habit, I suppose. What's to be done?'

'Damned if I know,' said the widow in disgust, to the others' horror. 'The way that devil Marplet has arranged things, we might as well all be bound and gagged. Even if we could force our way into that mock court he's setting up over there, who would believe us? It's his game this time, and no mistake . . . if he can really pull it off.'

'Can he?'

'How should I know?' said Cleppetty again, violently. 'Do I look like an oracle? No, no, I haven't given up hope. It's just that I don't know what to hope for. Ghillie has already gone to fetch Marc, and Tubain is up with Abernia. If the worst happens, Jame, you're responsible for getting the two of them out; Rothan, for clearing the stables; Kithra, for seeing that no one is left upstairs. Save whatever else you can, but be sure that you get out yourselves. That's all we can do. Now, out into the hall, all of you, and see that it's in order. Whatever happens, I'll not have this inn go to glory with a dirty face.'

They went. Word of the impending conflagration had apparently spread throughout the neighbourhood, for few of the regular customers had come in that night, despite the prevailing carnival mood in the streets. Jame helped with the table wiping, floor sweeping, and tankard polishing, painfully aware, as the effects of the afternoon's debauch wore off, of her throbbing knee. Then she joined the others at the front door. The Res aB'tyrr waited.

'Does this situation seem at all familiar to any of you?' Kithra asked suddenly.

'Hmmm. Too bad it isn't Marplet's thugs this time. Even given the chance, we couldn't drug two royal courts – or could we?'

'Hush,' said the maid sharply. 'Listen.'

The sounds of the outside world were coming nearer. They heard voices – some laughing, some singing – and saw shadows begin to leap on the house fronts of the square. Torch-bearers were coming down the main avenue from the north. A brilliant crowd followed them. At its centre walked three men, one decked out grandly in scarlet velvet, one wearing the insignia of the Five, one clad in patched jerkin and leather britches.

'Why,' said Jame, 'it's my ragged hill lord.'

Kithra boggled. 'Your *what?* You fool, that's Arribek sen Tenzi himself, the Archiem of Skyrr!'

'Look,' said Rothan, 'they're arguing about something. Harr pointed at the Skyrrman, and the Archiem shook his head. Now what . . . gods preserve us, they're coming here!'

There was a precipitous general retreat from the front door. When the first guest entered, they were all at their posts except Jame, who had been sent tearing across the courtyard and up the stairs to fetch Tubain. Explaining the situation to Abernia through the keyhole took longer than it did for the innkeeper to emerge more or less in his proper attire once he understood what had happened. Jame followed him down the steps, ripping off the random bits of feminine apparel that he had not had time to remove. Luckily, he had on most of his own clothes beneath them, and, due to a wrangle between King Sellik and sen Tenzi over who should enter first, managed to beat both of them into the great hall.

Great confusion followed as the liegemen of both rulers trooped in and settled themselves, shouting orders for everything from honey wine to buttered eggs. Most of them were already in the exhilarated stages of drunkenness, including the monarch of Metalondar, who turned out, at close range, to be a foolish-faced young man with a stammer. Of them all, only the Archiem and Harr, Thane sen Tenko, seemed fairly sober, although each kept urging the other to drink deep. Through their veil of courteous conversation, it was clear that sen Tenko was extremely annoyed about something, and that Arribek enjoyed his rival's discomfort.

Tubain rather timidly entered this poisoned atmosphere to inquire if all was to their satisfaction.

The Archiem's answer, delivered in his clear, sharp voice, easily reached Jame as she stood beside Cleppetty at the kitchen door: 'We have been informed that an exceptional dancer, the B'tyrr by name, is attached to this inn, and I have persuaded my colleagues to enter in hopes that she might be induced to perform for us. Can this be arranged?'

Tubain looked across at Jame, and Jame, in despair, at the widow.

'I know, I know,' the latter said, more gently than usual. 'You're exhausted, your leg is about to buckle under you, and, to tell the truth, you aren't quite sober. Still, will you try? Everything may depend on it.'

Miserably, Jame agreed, and Tubain passed on the good news.

Up in the loft, she combed out her long black hair, now nearly dry, and put on her costume. Then she tentatively tried a few dance steps, stumbled, and banged her sore knee against a stool. Almost in tears with pain and vexation, she sat on the floor hugging it. She would never get drunk again, never, never, never, but remorse wouldn't help her now. She was about to let them all down – Cleppetty, Tubain, Ghillie, all of them – after everything that they had done for her.

The memory of all the times she had danced successfully rose up to haunt her. That first night here at the inn, in Edor Thulig, in the temple of her own god; but that last time it had been different. She hadn't just manipulated a score of half-drunken patrons then but, in some obscure way, the power of the godhead itself. Jamethiel, her namesake, had also danced before their god and before men the night two-thirds of the Kencyrath had fallen. Clearly, hers was a dangerous, easily perverted talent, but it also had surprising potentials. If she could only tap the right one now, darkness damn the consequences.

'Oh, brave, brave thoughts,' she said out loud with a sudden, bitter laugh. 'You fool, you can't even stand up.'

But while she had stood that last time in the temple, she hadn't moved. The Senetha pattern that had channelled the power had been performed only in her mind. Exactly how that could aid her now, she didn't know, but it seemed marginally possible that more of the same mental exercise might help her prepare for the work that she knew she must at least attempt in the hall below. Consequently, she eased herself into the formal kneeling position, closed her eyes, and concentrated.

It was remarkably difficult. Not only to visualise the kantirs but to sense them – the tension of balance, the play of muscle on bone, the rhythm of movement . . . try to encompass them all, and they blurred; focus on one, and awareness of the others began to slip away. For an endless time she struggled with them in the dark, then music came. Behind closed eyes, she seemed to see the spiral stairs, the third floor landing, each step of the way down to the hall just as she had each time in the past, descending to the call of Ghillie's flute. Confidence seeped back as concentration became easier. Now she simply danced, beyond pain, beyond reflection, weaving the ancient tapestry of motion and dream. Then, when the sequence was complete, she bowed, opened her eyes, and found herself on the centre table under the chandelier, with King Sellik, the Archiem, and Harr sen Tenko all staring at her.

There was a moment's silence, then a burst of noise so loud that even when she spun about and saw for herself, she could hardly believe that it was only applause. The performance was over. Her knee felt as if someone had put a live coal under the cap.

'Well!' said the Archiem, his sharp brown eyes regaining their customary glitter. 'I was told to expect something unusual, but *this!* Thana B'tyrr, I had intended to ask this of your master, but in view of the honour shown us tonight, with my colleague's permission' – he glanced at the king, who was still sitting open-mouthed, oblivious to all but memory – 'I'll ask you instead. What pay will you accept for this most exceptional service?'

Jame stared at him. She was still trying to figure out how she had got from the loft to the hall.

'Well?' repeated the Archiem sharply. 'Speak up, girl. What shall I – we give you?'

'Justice,' she said in a whisper.

Harr sen Tenko glared at her. 'What impudence!' he exclaimed angrily. 'My lords, this is an insult to us all. Such a request should be made through the Five. To address it to you personally is to imply that the normal channels of government –

your government, administered by *your* representatives – are not capable of handling it properly.'

'And yet I believe your kinsman wished to ask for something similar,' said Arribek softly. 'Think of the opportunity this gives you to demonstrate your skills as a judge before the most important men of two nations. Come, set up the court. Let the trial begin.'

Harr had been getting steadily redder in the face during this short speech, but now visibly took himself in hand and did as he was ordered. Salt and a fresh loaf of bread were hastily procured from the kitchen and a cockerel from a neighbour's coop. With these, he perfunctorily mimicked a sacrifice to the nameless gods of hill and mountain.

'We are met to determine the culpability in an undeclared trade war,' he announced, holding up the indignant fowl by its feet, not deigning in his own anger to pretend that he knew nothing of the matter at hand. 'Let the accuser speak first.'

Marplet had come quietly into the hall, forewarned, it seemed, of what to expect. Before anyone from the Res aB'tyrr could react, he stepped up to the notables' table, swore by bread and salt to speak the truth, and began to lie most convincingly. After all, he had had weeks to prepare his story. This was not the setting he had envisioned, but what of that? He had the judge of his choice and all his witnesses primed and waiting, including the two stolid guards he had called in when Niggen had been thrashed. One by one he presented them, heard their evidence, and dismissed them with growing satisfaction. He loved a thing well done.

The staff of the Res aB'tyrr listened, dismayed. They had no experience with this sort of smooth mendacity and felt themselves increasingly helpless before such a citadel of lies.

Jame also listened, with a sense of nightmare. In order to give her the justice she had demanded, the Archiem must convince both his followers and Harr's that Marplet, their countryman, was a perjured liar. They would neither like that nor accept it without proof. Arribek was sharp enough to know in what general direction the truth lay, but how could even he find his way through Marplet's wilderness of falsehoods without a guide?

With a jolt, she suddenly realised that all this time, out of the corner of his eye, the Archiem had been watching her. *'Therefore, having established your veracity . . .'* My God, he was taking his cues from her reactions. Once again, as in the hills, her Kencyr honour had become the guarantee of her truthfulness. Gulping, she began to pay closer attention to the proceedings.

Soon after that, Marplet finished and stepped back, a slight, self-satisfied smile on his face.

'Let the accused speak,' intoned Harr sen Tenko.

There were sounds of confusion in the kitchen. The drunken nobles craned, curious to know what was amiss, but Jame could guess easily enough. Tubain had bolted again. Hosting dignitaries was part of his profession, but the crisis he had been asked to face now was so alien to him that it probably had not registered at all. Hence, the inn had lost its rightful spokesman.

'Let the accused speak,' repeated Marplet's brother-in-law impatiently.

Marc came up behind Jame and gave her a light, reassuring rap with his knuckles on the back of her head. The big guardsman took up a position flanking her just as Kithra, unbidden, stepped forward to speak for her adopted home.

It was obvious from the start that the girl had a strong personal grievance against Marplet. Her spitefulness compared unfavourably with his smooth air of injured innocence, and many Skyrr noblemen began to hiss at her. But the Archiem, and now Marplet himself, covertly watched Jame as she winnowed the grains of truth from Kithra's malicious chaff with slight gestures of assent or denial. Despite everything, she found herself trying very hard to be fair to the rival innkeeper.

At last Kithra ended her diatribe and stepped down to drunken catcalls from the audience.

'Well!' said the Archiem lightly. 'There you have it: two totally contradictory sets of facts. Which to believe?'

'Why, surely that's obvious,' said Harr sen Tenko with surprise, real or feigned. 'One believes and supports one's own loyal servants, in this case, the two guards who have testified for our countryman.'

'And what penalty shall the offender pay?'

'Let the victim name it, according to our oldest traditions.'

The Archiem looked at Marplet with raised eyebrows.

'I can ask for the vengeance of fire,' said the innkeeper tranquilly. 'Let this house be burned to the ground.'

Oh God, thought Jame. Was I wrong? Is sen Tenzi going to let them get away with this? She had never supposed that the current dispute mattered to him one jot beyond the chance it gave him to embarrass his political rival, but now realised that whatever his ambitions might be in this respect, he had committed himself – at her request – to achieve them legally. The room was full of supporters with whom he would lose face if he did not.

The Archiem was speaking again. One by one, he listed the major incidents in the conflict between the inns as Kithra had described them, omitting only those with which Jame had disagreed. 'Now,' he said at last, turning suddenly to her, 'do you swear to the truth of these facts?'

'I so swear.'

'So do I,' said Marc unexpectedly, startling everyone.

'Ah, good,' said the Archiem with a thin smile. 'You are a Kencyr too, aren't you? You know, it's an odd thing about these people: they never lie. And they will fight to the death to uphold their word. You there by the door, your guards, can you say the same? Will you do battle for your honour?'

The guards looked at Jame and Marc, then at each other. 'No, sir,' said the bigger of the two flatly. 'We weren't paid enough for that.' And they turned and tramped out of the inn.

'Where is your case now?' said the Archiem to Harr sen Tenko, purring. '"According to our oldest traditions," the judge is responsible for the trustworthiness of the witnesses whose word he decides to accept. You are a false magistrate and a corrupt one as well for letting this situation ever develop. Your position here is forfeit. Now, get out. All honest men are sick of your sight.'

Harr, Thane sen Tenko, did not deign to reply. His group gathered about him as he stalked out into the night, passing his kinsman without a word or glance. There would be war in the hills again over this; but whatever its outcome, his part in the affairs of Tai-tastigon had ended.

'And as for you,' the Archiem said to Marplet, 'let your fate be from your own lips. Someone, bring me fire.'

A torch-bearer stepped forward, offering his still-blazing brand while the retainers drunkenly shouted their approval. Arribek accepted it, beckoned Jame forward, and put it in her hand.

'The hunt is yours – again,' he said in a low voice. 'Now go and draw the blood.'

She walked out into the square. dazed by the uproar, hardly

believing the rapid turn of events. The mixed courts of Metalondar and Skyrr followed her. There stood the doomed inn,
bright, open, and empty. Hearth and candlelight shone on
crystal goblets set out on the tables, the rich gloss of the new
panelling, the beautiful proportions of the great hall. The wind
came, pushing at her back. Overhead, flames leapt hungrily
about the brand, a halo of fire. Surely it was all a dream. No
sound came from behind now, nor from Marplet who had
stepped forward and stood quietly some dozen feet from her.
Their eyes met. She could read nothing in his, nor he, perhaps,
in hers. The fragile bond of understanding they had shared was
gone.

They were still staring at each other when the brand was
snatched from Jame's grasp. Kithra darted forward and thrust
it between the bars of a cellar window. Orange light glowed
behind the grate, then the flames themselves appeared, glowing
brighter as oiled bale after bale of straw, prepared for the Res
aB'tyrr's immolation, caught fire. The dry underpinnings
kindled eagerly while steam began to roll off the damp outer
walls. For a long moment, all was as it had been in the great hall:
then a wilder light than any shed by candle or hearth began to
grow there. The tapestry-hung end walls were in flames.

Marplet watched it all, with a strange little smile. When the
upper storeys began to burn, he turned to Jame, gave her a
slight, mocking salute and walked into the blazing tavern. The
hall beams came down behind him.

The Skyrrman burned most of that night. The next morning,
one of the Creeper's spies thrust a note into Men-dalis's hand as
he was climbing the Guild Hall steps.

*The Talisman, acting for Theocandi, has caused the down
fall of Harr sen Tenko* [it read]. *Ask your brother how she
rewarded him for betraying your secret backer.*

For a long moment, Men-dalis stared to the southwest at the
thin pall of smoke still rising there. Then he turned and entered
the Hall without a word.

Routine business kept the Council occupied all that morning,
afternoon, and well into the evening. Consequently, it was quite
late when the Conclave of Electors finally gathered in an inner
chamber. Odalion and one of the masters' two representatives

entered looking disgruntled: both had hoped to reap greater rewards from this business. Abbotir, Bane's foster-father, came in all his massive dignity; Jewel, in terror lest he choose the losing side; the Provincials, loud-voiced with self-importance and secretly filled with awe. Chardin, unhappily climbing the outer steps, heard that Mistress Silver had not come at all, choosing to abstain rather than vote for or against the man who had secured her son's life but not his freedom.

'Now why didn't I think of that?' said Master Shining to himself, and joyfully returned to his beloved workroom.

The chamber was at last sealed, and the Conclave convened. Half an hour later, it was all over. By a vote of eight to four, Men-dalis had lost to Theocandi on the first ballot.

13

Three Pyres

On the afternoon following the conflagration, Jame went to the Lower Town in response to a message from Patches. She found the area in a state of chaos. Having no intact river gates, it had suffered badly from the flash flood two days back, and so far had made little progress in sorting itself out. All the rickety houses along the Tone had been swept away, while others, seriously undermined, continued to fall with little or no warning. The homeless thronged the streets, terrified at the prospect of another night in the open, but unable to seek shelter elsewhere because of the barricades erected by the remaining four of the Five, who feared riots and looting. Meanwhile, each dawn saw more children ill or dead. The thing that stalked in the dark fed well.

Marc had been in the area since early that morning, alternately helping to keep order and searching through the rubble for the dead. When Jame found him, he put down his crowbar and, with his captain's permission, went with her.

They found Patches's house still standing but befouled inside and out with river silt. Patches herself was there, assisting her mother and siblings to clean away the muck. Though all had been drenched, none were the worse for it except Taniscent, who had developed an inflammation of the lungs. It was for her sake that they had come. At last, the dancer was returning to the Res aB'tyrr.

Marc carried her home wrapped in a blanket while Jame limped along beside him. There, they put her in her old room. She didn't remember anything that had happened to her since the night of the near-riot almost a year before and was very confused. The sight of her own hands, knob-knuckled and blue-veined, upset her badly. She kept asking, in a thin, querulous voice, for a mirror, which no one was so foolish as to give her.

Jame stayed nearby all that long day and well into the night, taking turns with Kithra and Cleppetty at nursing the invalid. Sometime well after midnight, she excused herself from the sickroom and, with a plate of scraps, crossed the square to the fire-gutted Skyrrman in search of Fang.

Someone was huddled on the doorstep. Moonlight shone on Niggen's tear-swollen face as he jerked it up. Misery gave way to terror. He scrambled to his feet, lashing out wildly at the hand that she held out to him. Only after he had lurched past her into the night, fleeing as if for his life, did she realise that he had thought she was about to strike him.

She did not follow him, nor did any ragged feline form slink out of the ruins in answer to her call as it had the previous night. The city had swallowed Marplet's cat as it had his son.

Jame put the plate of scraps on the ground for whomever might claim it and walked back to the Res aB'tyrr. As she reached the front door, someone called her name. Turning, she saw a shadowy figure approaching her across the square. It was Dally.

'Well, it's all over,' he said. 'We lost.'

Almost with a start, she remembered the Guild Election. 'I'm sorry. What happens now?'

'I hardly know,' he said. 'Even now, I can scarcely believe it happened. Mendy's secret backer failed him at the last minute. If it weren't such an odd idea, I'd almost have thought that he blamed you for that. Now ... I just don't know. My brother is used to getting what he wants, usually when he wants it. He might try again in seven years or when Theocandi dies, I suppose, if the Sirdan's assassins don't get him first. Canden was right,' he said with a bitter laugh. 'It isn't easy to stay alive once you've lost. He almost died tonight after the Conclave, coming down the Guild Hall steps.'

'The Sirdan is working fast.'

'Oh, I don't think he ordered this particular attack. It was just some little 'prentice trying to curry favour. I killed him.' An odd look crossed Dally's face. 'I've never killed anyone before,' he said. 'I didn't like it. Anyway, word has gone out that Theocandi has something else in mind, something far surer. There's talk of the Shadow Thief again.'

'Oh?' said Jame. 'The last time that name came up, you weren't even sure that such a thing existed.'

'Nor am I now, but a good many other people are, and some

232

of them – Canden, for instance – are no fools. They say Theocandi's such a traditionalist that he would never have threatened Mendy before the election (candidates being sacred), but now.... Of course, there's still a chance that he could touch off a guild war; but if he were to get Mendy first, my brother's remaining supporters would disband immediately to save themselves, and there'd be no one left to bring charges.'

'Not even you?'

'Who would listen to me?' said Dally bitterly. 'Without Mendy, I'm nothing in this town, not even a practicing thief. I can't help my brother, myself – or you.'

'Me!' said Jame in surprise. 'Why? Do you think I need it?'

'Yes... if what I've heard is true. It's rumoured that the Shadow Thief will have a double assignment this time. You're the second half of it.'

'I'm honoured.'

'Jame, please! Be serious. This is no ordinary assassin. We're talking about a...a "temporarily detached soul of special malignancy and power," or so the Guild archivist tells me, "a psychic vampire that steals the soul and kills simultaneously with the touch of a hand." No one knows who it was seven years ago, but your friend Bane's name has been mentioned, and you've told me yourself that he consigned his soul to Ishtier at about that time. Perhaps the priest loaned it to Theocandi. I've heard rumours too about how cozy he and the Sirdan were during the last Council session. If that was the case then and again now, don't count on Bane's friendship – such as it is – to protect you. The Shadow Thief has no will but his master's, and in this case, that's Theocandi.'

'I'm still honoured. Look, Dally, when Canden left, I told him that I would take full responsibility for any consequences. If they only involve a game of "tag-you're-dead," I'll consider that I've got off lightly. But what about you? What are *your* plans?'

'They hardly matter now, do they?' he said, startling her with his sudden note of hopelessness. 'I'll wait, and see what role Mendy wants me to play.'

'Just the same, it can't be very healthy to be his brother just now. Stay here awhile. The inn is safe enough. Stay with me.'

He gave her a quick glance of surprised gratitude, then looked away again, the light fading from his face. 'I wish I could,' he said dully, 'but I can't desert him, now least of all, when everyone else is. I should be getting back to the party's headquarters in case he needs me for anything tonight.'

'Well, at least take some precautions,' she said, touching the sleeve of his royal blue d'hen. 'You shouldn't go around wearing his colour, tonight of all nights. Change jackets with me. This one should fit you; after all, it used to be yours.'

'N-no.... somehow that would be almost as bad as staying here. I'll be all right. Good-bye, Jame. My father's blessing on you.'

He took her hands and stood looking at her for a moment, then turned and walked away. She watched him go, wondering at her sudden impulse to follow him. Then Kithra called, and she went in to help.

Dally crossed the square, thinking about the boy he had killed. The thin form darting forward, the sudden scuffle on the steps, the boy's astonished face as steel slid home between his ribs ... then Men-dalis looking at him over the still-twitching body, cold, remote. *Do you think this changes anything?*

What had gone wrong?

He turned westward onto a narrow side street, a nameless despair gnawing at his heart, eating it away. The corner light sphere shone down on him, startling a flash of blue from his d'hen as he passed.

Two men muffled in their cloaks watched from the shadow of a doorway. 'Yes, that's him,' said the larger one heavily when the boy had gone by, 'consorting with the chief agent of my enemy, just as you said. I believe it all now.' He stepped out into the street, closely followed by his wizened companion.

Some instinct made Dally turn. He saw the two standing there and recognised both his brother and the Creeper despite their disguises. A sense of unreality and hopelessness deeper than words swept over him. When the others emerged from the shadows all about and closed in on him, he didn't even struggle.

Taniscent lived for two more days. At first, deep in some dream of the past, she called out from time to time for her dancing costume, wine, or Bortis, but then the long silence fell, broken only by the gurgling sound of one who drowns slowly within herself, beyond the help of man.

Patches came to the inn several times during this period, bringing news from the outside world. The Thieves' Guild was not settling down properly after the excitement of the Election.

Usually by this time the loser had either fled or fallen to some assassin's wiles, but Men-dalis refused to do either. He had withdrawn into the fortresslike headquarters of his party and from there held together his followers apparently by the sheer fact of his continued existence. It was almost as if he had not yet given up hope of obtaining the sirdanate, although by what means no one could guess. The entire Guild was on edge, sensing the potential violence that lurked beneath this strange state of affairs.

'One wrong move now and bang!' said Patches at the end of her last visit. 'Guild war. That sort of thing, no one wins.'

'Sounds like a good time to go hide under a haystack. What about Dally? How's he managing?'

'Wouldn't know. No one's seen him since the Election. I expect he's holed up in the fortress with his brother. Oh, before I forget, this is from your master.' She handed James a folded square of paper, begrimed by the dozen or so hands through which it had passed. Naturally, its seal had long since been broken.

'Time I was scooting,' the Townie said, standing up. 'If you do go out tonight, Talisman, walk wary, won't you? You've a lot of enemies out there, the Sirdan not least, just waiting for you to break cover.'

She left. Jame read the note, smiling slightly both at its contents – which, in part, rather surprised her – and at the thought that Patches, illiterate as she was, had still found a way to familiarise herself with the message.

Early that night, Taniscent died. They laid her out in her own room with fire and iron at both door and window and the usual effigy, hastily carved from a bar of soap, in the next room. The Keepers of the Dead would come for her in the morning. Kithra unearthed the dancer's little rosewood box of cosmetics and tried to make her more presentable, but nothing could disguise the network of wrinkles, those sunken eyes with their blue-veined lids or the shrivelled lips. It was very hard to remember just then that Taniscent had only been twenty-five years old.

Jame found that she couldn't face the prospect of an all night wake.

'If you can spare me,' she said to Cleppetty, 'I'm going out. Penari sent me a note this afternoon. It seems that despite everything, I've been promoted to journeyman, and he wants to celebrate.'

'Do you think that's wise?'

'No, but it's the only chance I may get to say a proper farewell to the city. This is Marc's last night on guard duty. In a day or so, as soon as I can find out what's happened to Dally, we'll be off down the Tone, bound for the Eastern Sea.'

'I keep forgetting you two are leaving us so soon. It will seem strange here without you. I've almost forgotten what peace and quiet are like.'

Jame laughed and went.

She found Penari up a spiral stair in the Maze, chucking rare manuscripts over his shoulders onto the floor far below in an irate search for some ancient tract probably devoured by mice a quarter century before. He would never acknowledge the ravages of time, here any more than out in his beloved Tai-tastigon, which made housekeeping rather a problem. In fact, as he came rattling down from the heights, Jame suddenly remembered that the stairway he was on, an infrequently used one, had several broken treads near the top. Before she could shout a warning, however, he was at the spot and past it without missing a step. It must have been the wrong staircase after all, she thought, helping the old man to find his cloak, which Monster had tried to convert into a nest. Then they set off.

Penari had not been out of the Maze since the night he had taken her to be enrolled at the Guild Hall. For the most part, he lived quite comfortably with his memories and the supplies left weekly by arrangement inside one of the Maze entrances, only emerging himself on special occasions, such as the time Monster had chosen the previous Feast of Dead Gods to come down with a sore throat, which required physic. Padding through the streets with him now, Jame wondered if the unspecified tavern of his youth, for which they were bound, was still in existence. It would be just like him to burst into some private home built on its ruins and demand service. Soon, however, she saw that she needn't have worried. Ahead of them loomed the Cross'd Stars, an inn that had stood for better than two hundred years and was good for as many more.

Penari's sudden appearance there caused a considerable stir. He was quickly absorbed at one of the main tables in a babble of greetings, some from friends whom he had apparently not seen in decades.

Jame quietly took a seat a little back from the others. Just as the Moon catered to apprentices, the Stars had masters and high officials of the Guild as its primary clientele. There wasn't another journeyman in the room, and most of the men at the table were arch-partisans of Theocandi, who had probably done everything in his power to prevent her own promotion. Some celebration this was going to be.

She was trying to think of an excuse to slip away when the trouble started.

Someone had congratulated Penari on Theocandi's success, and he was responding in a typically sharp-tongued way when one of the Sirdan's lieutenants slammed down his tankard.

'Thal's balls, man!' he exclaimed thickly. 'What sort of a brother are you not to have helped the Old Man when he needed it? What are a few secrets compared to the sirdanate? "Greatest thief in Tai-tastigon" – ha! If you really had anything worth knowing, it would have come out long before this.'

'Are you trying to say,' said Penari in a dangerous voice, 'that I don't deserve my reputation?'

'D-damn right. Name one thing you've stolen lately, "greatest thief."'

The old man scowled. 'Name one thing – anything – and I *will* steal it. Now. Tonight.'

'Sir, no!' hissed Jame at his back under cover of the commotion that had broken out at the table.

'All right: the other Eye of Abarraden. Steal *that* if you dare.'

'Done!' cried Penari with glee.

'Oh, God,' Jame said, putting a hand over her face.

The argument continued all the way to the Temple District, waxing steadily.

'Look,' said Jame at last, catching the old man's arm and making him stop in the shadow of the gate. 'Even if that man back at the Stars was as drunk as he seemed (which I doubt), look at the situation you've let him manoeuvre you into: no time to scout the land, even less to lay out escape routes, and enough publicity to make an escort of trumpeters superfluous. You think the guards are deaf? One word in the wrong ear and your venerable hide is up for grabs.'

'I tell you, I know what I'm doing,' said Penari petulantly. 'Remember, this isn't the first time I've been on this particular errand. Besides, no one will betray me. Such things simply aren't done.'

'Someone did it to me when I took the Peacock Gloves to the Moon. All right, at the very least, I'm going with you.'

'Huh! You just want to nose out my secrets.'

'If I hear that word one more time, I'm going to take a flying leap at the nearest brick wall. Has it ever occurred to you that I simply don't want that scrawny neck of yours to get broken? Loyalty is the only virtue I happen to possess; kindly stop throwing it back in my face.'

'You mean it, don't you, boy?' he said, peering at her. 'Well, come along, then. I suppose you've earned the right.'

The temple of Abarraden was one of the largest in that part of the District still held by the Old Pantheon. Its front loomed over a small, sun-starved square from which eight minor avenues radiated, two of them sweeping back at an angle along its outer walls to form the boundaries between the old gods and the new. The temple immediately behind it had been burned down the previous year, as the last blow in a temple war dating from the overthrow of Heliot by Dalis-sar nearly two and a half millennia before; many of the huge, decaying temples beyond that were still engaged, however feebly, in similar struggles.

At the height of her power, Abarraden's house had expanded seven times in as many decades, on each occasion gaining a newer, larger, and more shoddily ornate shell. The temple was now like a series of boxes sitting one inside the other with a warren of rooms between each major set of walls.

Once, the whole place must have hummed day and night with activity; now dust muffled Jame's footsteps as she followed Penari through the passageways. Over the weeks since Gorgo's accidental demise, she had become increasingly aware of the gods of Tai-tastigon as a community in their own right, dependent on faith for their creation and specific character-istics, yet often capable of independent thought. And she sensed that they were increasingly aware of her, the god-stalker and theocide, in their midst. It was partly for this reason that she had insisted on accompanying her master, hoping to frighten off Abarraden or at least to divert her divine wrath. It was clear now that that would not be necessary. The goddess slept, her deep breath flowing through the empty halls. Like Taniscent, she would never wake again.

They reached the sanctuary without incident, having seen only a handful of caretaker monks, all easily evaded. This innermost chamber completely occupied the original shell of the temple. It was high, dimly lit with light spheres, and one-third filled by the giant image of Abarraden, once the all-seeing, now the single-eyed. Like most of the Old Pantheon deities, she was a composite of human and animal features – the latter, in this case, predominantly bovine. At her cloven feet lay a broad ring of dark water, the usual barrier against demons. Only bolt holes were left of the spell-shielded bridge that should have spanned it. A constellation of luminious disks floated just under the water's surface. James leaned forward for a closer look, but Penari hastily pulled her back. He took a dusty piece of sausage out of a pocket and tossed it out over the water. A dozen ribbon-thin tentacles whipped up, snatching it out of the air. The eyes blinked once, simultaneously, and waited. Human warders came and went, but the Guardians of the Pool remained.

'This is so ungodly simple,' the old man said in a whisper, 'that I'm almost ashamed to do it. Still, a challenge is a challenge. Go keep watch at the door.'

Jame went. When she looked back, Penari was above the pool with the tentacles snapping futilely up at him, halfway across a bridge that no longer existed.

She was still staring at him, mouth agape, when the sound reached her. Men, a considerable number of them, had entered the temple. She listened a moment longer, hearing the muffled tramp of boots, the low voices arguing which was fastest, then hissed across the room; 'Sir, guards!'

'Damnation,' said Penari irritably. He was standing on one of Abarraden's full breasts with the white eye-gem from her bowed head already in his hands. He pointed to a doorway in the far corner.

'Up the stairs to the roof, quick, but first douse these lights.'

Jame did as she was ordered, extinguishing sphere after sphere with a breathless, 'Blessed-Ardwyn-day-has-come,' all the time hearing the voices draw closer, grow louder. She paused at the last light, waiting until the old man had gained the stairs, then threw the room into darkness just as the first of the guards burst into it. The others piled up behind him, from the sound of it, then came spilling into the room helter-skelter, cursing loudly. At least one fell into the pool.

Good night vision notwithstanding, Jame could see as little in this blackness as any of them, but had the advantage of knowing the room's layout. She had almost reached the stairway when, to her amazement and horror, a strong pair of arms suddenly locked about her. With all her breath, she gave tongue to the rathorn war cry – a shocking thing to do to anyone at close range. The arms released her instantly. Sprinting for the door, she ran head-on into one of its posts, recovered, and scrambled upwards. A spirited free-for-all seemed to be going on below. Then the guards were on the stairs. She half fell out onto the roof, heaved the trap door shut, shot home the bolt, and collapsed on it.

'What kept you?' demanded Penari.

The rooftops of the Temple District stretched out in all directions, a jagged landscape slashed with fissures through which the streetlights far below shone. Penari held up the stolen gem to the moon, turning it over in hands so sensitive that they more than made up for his failing eyesight.

'What a great deal of trouble,' he said with a dry chuckle, 'for a piece of glass.'

'*What?*'

'That's what it was fifty years ago, and it hasn't changed since. I examined both eyes then and took the genuine one. Mind you, that was no such plush job as tonight, but I never have understood why people made such a fuss over it. Fools, the lot of 'em. Why, anyone could have walked out with this bauble anytime since then' – provided they could cross a spell-bridge that was no longer there, Jame thought – 'but the imbeciles managed to convince themselves that it was impossible. This is a city for odd beliefs. Maybe you've noticed.'

'Yes, sir. But how did Abarraden get a glass eye in the first place?'

'Who knows?' he said impatiently. 'Probably some rogue priest made off with the other real one centuries ago. It doesn't look as if the sect survived losing them both.'

The boards of the trap door groaned, one of them beginning to bend under the pressure of a crowbar applied from beneath. Jame shifted her seat hastily. 'Uh, sir, glass or not, these gentlemen are still after our hides. What do you suggest we do about it?'

'Why, leave, of course,' he said, standing up. 'A good thief never overstays his welcome.'

'By what route?' she asked, with a premonition of disaster.

'How many choices d'you think we have up here?' Penari said irritably. 'Across the rooftops, of course.'

He was pointing towards the back of the temple, across the gaping void left by the building that had burned down.

The bridge had been real to him, perhaps those missing steps

240

in the Maze as well, and now – this was hardly the time to shake his self-confidence, but oh lord ...

'Are you – uh – sure it's all right?'

'Of course I'm sure,' he said petulantly, and stepped off into space. He slithered down several feet, regaining his balance with difficulty. 'Reasonably sure, anyway. But what are a few rotten shingles? Come along, boy, and mind the holes.'

She watched him carefully pick his way across the abyss, probing ahead into emptiness with his staff. That solved his problem, at least, provided he didn't slip. But as for her own! She made a rapid circuit of the rooftop, noting the smooth, sheer walls; the opposite buildings, well beyond reach; the distant ground, which a grapnel line would have reached, if she had thought to secure one in her dress d'hen. On the whole, it was not a particularly favourable situation.

'Well, come on,' Penari shouted impatiently from the opposite roof. 'D'you think they'll take all night with that door?'

Patently, they would not. Wood splintered. A hand came through the jagged hole, groping for the bolt. Theoretically, there was no reason why she should run from them at all. Having never touched the stolen object, she was innocent of its theft according to the laws of the city, but something told her that tonight such fine distinctions would do no one any good.

'Well?' shouted Penari, beginning to grow hoarse with exasperation. 'If I can do it, by all the gods, so can you!'

Perhaps he was right. There was no question that he believed what he said; and with this old man, belief was obviously a very potent thing. Jame stood there a moment, ignoring the sounds at the door, Penari capering with impatience on the far roof, forgetting everything except what she had learned over the past year about faith and reality in Tai-tastigon. Then, with eyes tightly shut and infinite caution, she took a step forward, over the edge.

There had to be something there, because her foot slipped on it. Like Penari minutes before, she found herself sliding sideways down what felt like a slick, sharply pitched surface. Eyes still squeezed shut, she checked her descent and began to creep forward along the incline. The surface over which she blindly groped her way had no particular texture at first, and an unnerving tendency to melt away whenever the growing commotion to the rear caused her concentration to waver. She recalled vividly how Penari had so often had her describe a route through or over a house she had never seen – often because it no longer existed – and the kind of imaginative reconstruction necessary for such work. This wasn't all that different, really, discounting the possibility of a hundred-foot plunge. Ah, there *were* shingles. She traced the outline of one, then jerked back her hand with a hiss.

'What's the matter now?' demanded Penari's voice, very near.

'Of all the . . . a splinter, I think. What did you say about . . .'

'Talisman!'

The bellow came from behind, incredulously protesting, and unmistakably from the powerful lungs of Sart Nine-toes. Startled, Jame opened her eyes. There was nothing beneath her, nothing, and she was falling. Her hands flew out wildly as though with a life of their own, and clamped on the edge of the opposite roof.

'I *told* you to watch out for those holes,' said Penari, hauling her up by the scruff of the neck.

After that, Jame insisted on escorting her master out of the district and home, through back alleys, at as fast a pace as the old man could maintain. Although his trophy was only glass, so worthless that by rights the period of jeopardy should have elapsed by the time its length could even be determined, she suspected that there were those who would refuse to treat it as anything less than the genuine article. Someone was out to get Penari, and perhaps herself as well. If it was the Sirdan, he would not hesitate to bend the law as he had already bent the thieves' moral code in betraying them to the guards. Under the circumstances, the best place for Penari was the Maze, and for her, the hills to the northwest of the city, waiting either until things settled down or she and Jorin could rejoin Marc for the trip south. Consequently, she said goodbye to her old master at his front entrance and then set off hurriedly for home by the rooftops, meaning to collect her possessions and get out of town as quickly as possible.

Reaching the Res aB'tyrr, Jame climbed hastily up to the loft and froze, one leg thrown over its parapet. Inside, the floor was strewn with shreds of clothing. The two pallets had also been gutted, and the bricks of the fireplace were scattered everywhere. In the far corner, stones had been pried out of the wall, revealing the dark, secret cavity behind them. The knapsack lay sprawled on the shambles of her bed. The sword shards lay beside it, and the little package that contained the ring was just visible in the folds of the blanket, where it had apparently been overlooked. The Book Bound in Pale Leather, however, was gone.

Jame sat quite still for a moment, taking this all in. Then she swung her other leg over the parapet and went quickly down the inside stairs. Just as she entered the kitchen, Sart Nine-toes appeared at the street door.

'Now wait a minute, Talisman,' he said hastily, seeing that she was about to bolt. 'Believe it or not, it's Marc I'm looking for, not you.'

'Marc?' Sudden alarm sharpened her voice. 'Has something happened to him?'

'That's what I'm trying to find out.'

Cleppetty had come up from the cellar as he spoke and now advanced on them purposefully. Before she could say anything, however, Sart swept her off the ground and clamped his hand over her mouth.

'We're on patrol just outside the Temple District,' he continued, ignoring his squirming captive, 'when the captain comes trotting up with a dozen or so of our lads behind him and says, "Someone is robbing Abarraden. Fall in." So in we fall, and off we go to that puzzle-box of a temple; but someone (in a minute, m'dear) douses the lights just as we come into the idol room. I grab hold of Marc's sleeve, knowing that you Kennies have a way with the dark, and get hauled right across the room. Then someone lets off a godawful yell just about in my ear (wait, love, wait) and the next thing I know, Marc has swung about and is wading into our lads like the last typhoon of summer. I bash a few heads too, just to be companionable, then go pounding up the stairs with the rest and out onto the roof.'

He paused, eyeing her doubtfully.

'You really were standing on air, weren't you? It wasn't just too much ale? Anyway, so I turn to point you out to Marc, and he isn't there. I haven't seen him... ouch!'

Cleppetty, at last losing her patience, had bitten his hand. He dropped her.

'You may not have seen him since, but I have,' she said grimly, smoothing her apron. 'He stopped by about an hour ago. Whatever's going on, I'm afraid it's serious. Jame, he asked me to tell you that "An honorable death wipes away all stains."'

'Oh, God. It's serious, all right. I've got to go after him. Sart,

243

would you mind staying here until I – we get back? I've an odd idea that the inn shouldn't be left short-handed tonight.'

'Glad to,' he said, grinning at Cleppetty. The widow, unaccountably, blushed.

It was obvious what had happened: those had been Marc's arms around her in the dark. By releasing her, a supposed thief, as soon as he had realised who she was, the big Kendar believed that he had broken faith as a guard. For him, that constituted a massive loss of honour, more than any Kencyr would expect him to survive. Consequently, he had gone to restore his good name in the surest way possible, by seeking a death in accordance with the ancient rite at the hands of a Kencyr Highborn. In Tai-tastigon, that could only mean the priest, Ishtier. She must stop Marc before he reached the temple or, somehow, cut short the rites, which could destroy an innocent man as readily as a guilty one.

Once again, the rooftops provided the fastest, safest means of travel. Jame sped over them, following the route that Marc was most likely to have taken, anxiously scanning the streets below. Dally might be somewhere down there too. She would not leave the city until she had seen him, Jame decided, even if it meant invading his brother's fortress; but that must wait until Marc was safe. Nothing else mattered now.

Nothing? Not even the Book? Sweet Trinity, she'd completely forgotten about that. Some guardian you are, she thought, negotiating a treacherous stretch of thatching far too fast.

Her feet shot out from under her. She went cannoning down the slick straw into space, caught someone's laundry line, circled it once, let go and bounced off a shop canopy, somersaulted twice onto the opposite balcony and swarmed up again to the rooftops.

'Next time, bring down a pigeon!' someone shouted from the street below.

It was a night for essentials and establishing priorities. Darkness damn the Book, and her too, if she failed Marc now.

Then she saw him, a tall, unmistakable figure striding along far down the street. He was almost to the circle of decay that surrounded the temple. She swung down to the ground and ran after him, calling. He didn't seem to hear. In another minute, she would be close enough to touch him.

Then, in complete silence, a figure glided out of the shadows to stand between them, one hand raised.

Jame skidded to a stop, staring at it. The night was dark, but even so she should have been able to make out some detail of the stranger's face, or at least of his garments. All were featureless, black, a mere silhouette... no, a shadow – upright, solid, reaching.

So she had not been the second half of Theocandi's assignment at all but the first; and here was his assassin, nameless, faceless, come to execute its commission.

She retreated, shouting again after Marc. His step did not falter. This time he must have heard, but as far as he knew she could say nothing that would redeem his honour or save his life. She must explain the truth to him, she must, but death stood in her way. Too dangerous to try ducking past... she sprang sideways into an alley and ran for both of their lives.

Fleet as her own shadow, it followed. The byways twisted and turned, choked with rubble, treacherous underfoot. It would not let her double back. What obstacle would stop it? Ah, between two sagging walls, the moon-glint of the Lower Town's western fosse. Jame raced for it. One leap and she was across, dashing northward towards the temple. The other kept pace on the far side. They were coming to a bridge, just short of the temple's ring of dust. If it could cross... Jame sprinted. It *had* crossed. She saw its outstretched hand from the corner of her eye and dived forward, out from under it, to roll over and over in the crumbling debris, sending up billows of dust. Coughing, on her knees, she saw that it had stopped, just as that other nightmare had done so long ago, at the edge of the poisoned circle. She rose and ran towards the temple, noting with a little spasm of panic that its door was wide open. Marc had already entered.

She finally caught up with him in the central chamber. He was kneeling before the altar, his big, gnarled hands frozen in a gesture of resignation. To her alarm, he responded neither to voice nor touch.

'You're too late,' said a thin, dry voice. Ishtier stood beside the statue, looking like a pale excrescence on its granite form. 'He is already deep in the death-trance and will sink farther still before the end. Never before have I encountered a man so eager to greet oblivion.'

'But he mustn't! It's a mistake, all of it: he's done nothing to make this necessary.'

'So you say. Nonetheless, I abide by his wish in this matter, not by yours. All your cunning can't save him from himself, anymore than it helped you to retain possession of the Book Bound in Pale Leather. Ah yes, I guessed that you had it,' he said, coming down a step, his face alive with triumph. '"Be still, tongue that speaks... to the chosen leave the hidden ways." You remember that, do you? The first half is indeed from Anthrobar's scroll, which you contrived to destroy, but the second is not. Only someone familiar with the contents of the original would have been able to add that quote. There are a handful of priests and scrollsmen who possess such knowledge – little good it does them without the runes themselves – but none of them have ever been near East Kenshold, your home; and it was to East Kenshold that the Master himself came, looking for something so valuable that he entered the corrupt air of this world in an attempt to reclaim it. A guess, you see, but I was right, wasn't I? Well, it's out of your hands now, and soon to fall into some appropriate ones.'

'Yours, I suppose,' said Jame, trying to conceal her dismay. 'Might I inquire how?'

'You have a friend to thank for that,' he said with malicious relish. 'As soon as Penari's message to you was intercepted, Theocandi laid his plans and I, mine. Bane is responsible for your loss.'

'And perhaps for yours as well,' said Jame, sudden alarm in her voice. 'When I saw him last, he spoke very bitterly of you and said that the next time you gave him an order, the results might surprise you. How long overdue is he?'

'He would never betray me,' Ishtier said, more to himself than to her. 'He couldn't, even if he has been less obedient of late than usual. I have you to thank for that too,' he added, shooting her a venomous glance. 'But this... this would be a betrayal of the whole of our people. No, no, it's unthinkable.'

'To him, *you* are the Kencyrath, and when he spoke of vengeance, it was because he thought that he himself might have been betrayed. You know better than I if you have any reason to fear him now.'

'I deny any reason,' said the priest furiously, 'but I acknowledge my foolishness in trusting someone so unstable. That boy is capable of imagining anything. Assume the worst, then, as he undoubtedly has: what will he do next?'

'In his place,' said Jame slowly, 'I would do the most injurious thing possible. I would give the Book to Theocandi.'

Ishtier drew his breath in with a hiss. 'The man's a savant of sorts, as I have cause to know. And he is ambitious enough to devour the world. If the Book is there, we must get it back. *You* must.'

'I, m'lord? And what of my friend here? If I do this errand for you, do you swear to bring him out of this trance so he can hear the truth and change his mind?'

The priest struggled with this for a moment, then made an ill-tempered gesture of assent.

Jame got as far as the chamber door when a thought struck her. 'Uh, m'lord... a slight problem. The Shadow Thief is waiting out there to kill me. How does one dispose of a demon?'

'Nothing to it,' said Ishtier irritably. 'All you need is its true name and then a great deal of fire or water. That should be easy for you, theocide.'

Water she could provide, Jame thought as she stood just within the temple door, waiting for her chance. As for a name... ah, there the thing went, passing her narrow line of vision through the door's crack as it began another patient circuit of the circle's rim. Wait, wait...*now.* She threw open the door and dashed out, racing for the fosse.

It was marginally faster than she, but with a head start, Jame managed to get to the other side of the little waterway before it closed with her. Almost all the way to the Tone, this slight lead allowed her to shift banks just ahead of her pursuer whenever a bridge gave it access to her side. Then, within sight of the Tone, she stumbled. The assassin cut in front of her. She sprang sideways into a ribbon-bedecked street of the Silken Dark, deserting it as soon as she could for the rooftops of the courtesans' district.

The chase ended on the crest of a house whose upper storeys overhung the swift-flowing Tone. Jame, at bay, turned to see death slipping towards her along the roof's spine. She had one chance now.

'Bane?' she said tentatively.

It rushed at her. She barely had time to block the reaching hand, forearm to forearm, and to get a grip on something that felt like a collar before it was on her. She went over backwards, one foot in its stomach, and threw it over her head. Something hard, swinging down from the shadowy form, hit her in the face. Tears of pain blinded her momentarily. When she could see again, there was only the rooftop, the Tone, and something dark on its surface, being borne swiftly away.

Jame sat on the roof, getting her breath back. On the basis of Dally's description, she had gambled that only the creature's hand was deadly, but as for the name.... Even now, she could hardly believe that she had guessed that correctly, too. As Dally had pointed out, Bane had entrusted his shadow to Ishtier seven years ago, during the priest's 'exchange of information' with Theocandi and just before the Sirdan's erstwhile rival, Master Tane, had fallen prey to the Shadow Thief. If Ishtier (who was supposed to be keeping Bane's soul safe) had lent it then and again tonight for such a foul purpose, he had betrayed his trust indeed. Well, she had put an end to that; but Sweet Trinity, what an end.

The sound of angry voices below broke in on her thoughts. A group of men clad in Men-dalis's royal blue were forcibly restraining one of their number, while Theocandi's supporters jeered at them.

'Quiet, man,' a friend hissed at the angry man. 'D'you want to start a war?'

Jame suddenly realised that the street below was full of thieves – far too many of them. Instead of lying low like their master, the partisans of Men-dalis were out in force, much to the delight of their enemies, who lost no chance to taunt them. If they responded violently, so much the better: an undeclared guild war would bankrupt the side that struck the first blow. But why was the New Faction abroad tonight at all? Its members had the air of waiting for something without knowing exactly...

What was that?

The sound grew, a low, hoarse roar, almost a groan, rising nearby to the north. The thieves below exchanged looks. They began to move, slowly at first then faster and faster, towards the firelight outlining the houses that looked down on Judgement Square.

Puzzled, Jame swung down to the cobbles and joined the flow. Crossing a bridge to the north bank, she saw a familiar figure in a cream velvet d'hen walking blindly towards her.

'Darinby!' she called, fighting her way through the crowd to his side. 'What's happened?'

'Talisman?' He hardly seemed to see her. 'Don't ask. Don't go to look. Just get off the streets. There's nothing anyone can do... nothing.'

She stared after him, shocked, then turned and ran towards the Square.

It was full of men, swarming about the Mercy Seat. Torch flames leaped over their heads, casting a demonic light on the upturned faces, on the back of the Seat where something blue was draped. Jame paused on the edge of the crowd, some touch of prescience sickening her. Then she began to force her way through the press of bodies, pushing and kicking at first, then using her nails with an abandon which would ordinarily have appalled her. Then she was through the front line and saw.

'Oh God... Dally.'

The world narrowed to the two of them, one sprawling negligently on the marble throne, the other on her knees before him, vomiting again and again. The emptiness of her mind ached with the buzz of carrion flies. Slowly, their insectile hum became words, repeated over and over, each time drawing a louder response.

'This is Bane's work!' a man in a blue d'hen was shouting. 'This is war!'

Could the dead do this to the living, she wondered, still half-dazed. But even if she had just destroyed his soul in the Shadow Thief, it couldn't change what had happened here – it might not even change him at once. A slow, withering death, Darinby had once said.

Around her, Theocandi's supporters had drawn back; surprised, frightened by the mob's response. Jame guessed before Men-dalis's rabble-rousers could name it, how this growing sense of outrage and violence would be channelled. The intensity of it almost brought her to her feet, shouting with the rest, but a sudden doubt stopped her. She looked again at what sprawled on the Mercy Seat, taking leave of it, then rose and slipped out through the crowd. At its edge, she began to run, then to climb.

'Why, Talisman!' exclaimed the dark figure that had suddenly appeared at the roof's edge. Its hand, raised to strike, swooped down to help her up. 'What's going on?'

'Sparrow, I haven't time to explain. Any second now, that mob is going to march on the Thieves' Guild Palace, and I've got to get there first. Can you and your people delay them?'

'The Palace? Fleshshambles Street to the river is the best route, with the north bank tangle mazes on either side. Yes, we can do something about that, if you don't mind us maybe dropping four tons of stone bull on a few heads.'

'Smash every one of them, for all I care. Just give me five minutes.'

'You've got them,' said Sparrow, and darted off.

Jame remained a moment, looking down. Below, they were already on the move, torches streaming towards the mouth of the street the Cloudie had indicated. The sound that rose was hoarse, grating, scarcely human. This was what Dally's death had unleashed on the city. Jame stripped off her gloves and let them flutter down into darkness. So be it: nothing hidden, nothing held back.

The roofs of Fleshshambles Street were ornamented with an array of stone animal heads, meant to propitiate the spirits of the beasts sold piecemeal below. One of these, a particularly massive bull on the corner of River Street, already had a dozen Cloudies active at its base, chipping away the few patches of good mortar that held it in place. Jame waited until the mob had nearly reached the Tone, then raced for the corner. The Cloudies shouted a warning as she sprang to the bull's broad head, feeling it bow under her weight, then off again, barely in time, over to the opposite roof. She did not look back either at the sound of that great weight crashing to earth or at the screams that followed it.

Ship Island rode at peace behind its vengeful figurehead.

Jame came into the Guild Hall shouting for Bane and was promptly collared by one of his followers. This man took her back into the Palace and up to the richly furnished apartment from which, so long ago, she had seen the corpse of a boy flung.

Bane turned away from the fireplace into whose flames he had been staring. 'So you've come to me at last,' he said with a smile.

'Never mind that. Did you do it?'

'Let's just say I had it done. Forget the Book, m'lady. It's a filthy thing. You're better off without it.'

'*Damn* the Book! Dally is out there on the Mercy Seat, half flayed in your own favourite pattern, and his brother's men are on their way here now to make you pay for it.'

Bane's henchman swore out loud and hastily left the room to check. His master's smile, however, hardly flickered.

'You have more casual cruelty in you than anyone I've ever met,' said Jame to him fiercely, trying to break through his composure, 'but God's claws, man, you aren't stupid! Whoever did this must have known what would happen. It's the first blow in an undeclared guild war, and right now you look like the instigator. Tell me you haven't been such a fool, especially not for my sake. Tell me!'

Bane's man reappeared at the door. 'The minx told the truth,' he said breathlessly. 'They're coming! What shall we do?'

'Whatever you like. I'm a fool, certainly,' Bane said to Jame, stepping between her and the door, 'but not in this, m'lady.'

'Damn it, then *do* something! I don't want to lose you both in one night . . . oh God,' she said, suddenly paling. 'I'm going to anyway. Bane, I-I think I've just killed you.'

'What on earth do you mean?' he said, looking amused. She explained. To her amazement, he burst out laughing. 'Indeed, you've out-guessed yourself this time. No, look farther away and yet near at hand for your thief of souls, m'lady.'

'What do you mean . . . and why do you keep calling me that?'

'You'll have to get used to it, you know. After all, it's probably the least of your titles.'

'*What?*'

'Do you mean to say that you didn't know?' he said, surprised at last. 'No one ever told you? How very odd.'

'Wait a minute,' Jame protested. 'How do *you* know all this? Have I got a sign on my back that says, "Kick me, I'm Highborn?"'

'Go around offering to carry other peoples' souls, and you might as well have. All Shanirs must possess at least a touch of the Highborn strain, but soul-carriers like you and Ishtier need blood as pure as it comes. Besides, how many Kencyrs are there, even among the Highborn, with your talents or training? For such a clever person, you really are remarkably ignorant. What a pity I shall never have the chance to educate you.'

Below, the Guild Hall door crashed down. Someone screamed. Now many feet were thundering through the passageways, many voices howling on the trail of blood.

'You know,' said Bane, turning back to her with a smile, 'this may not be quite how I envisioned our last meeting, but you must admit that for us, it *is* at least in character. Farewell, my lady. Remember me.'

His hand slid up to the back of her neck and he kissed her, fiercely. Through sudden pain, she heard a sharp click behind her, then staggered backwards as he pushed her away. The wall beside the fireplace was not where it had been. As she came up hard against some further surface, the panel swung shut again, sealing her in.

From the chamber beyond came the screech of wood as its outer door gave way.

Jame tore at the panel with her nails, raking up splinters,

251

knowing all the time that it was hopeless. A spot of light touched her hand. Hurriedly she knelt and peered through the spy hole.

They were in the room, a semi-circle of them almost facing her, with more pressing in behind, all held at bay. Even now, with their overwhelming numbers, their prey terrified them. In that brief, petrified silence, Jame heard him quite clearly no more than inches away on the other side of the wall, laughing quietly as though at some private joke. Then they closed in on him.

He fought with the knife and the Senethar, with consummate skill and savage joy. Within a minute, the dead lay thick at his feet and the living drew back, appalled at the carnage. Jame heard his quiet laugh again.

'Dogs,' he said softly, advancing on them, drawing their eyes from the secret panel. 'Is death sweet? Jackals, come and lick the blood.'

There was a movement on the floor behind him. Jame saw the hand of a fallen thief stealthily close on a dead neighbour's knife. She cried out, but too late. The man sprang up. He caught Bane around the throat with an arm and plunged the knife up under his ribs. Bane shook himself free. With a movement too fast even for Jame to follow, he broke his assailant's neck. Then, almost contemptuously, he jerked out the knife. Blood poured down. Something like a sigh went through the room. They were waiting for him to fall. Instead, he advanced on them again, one step, two, and then he went down on one knee, a hand pressed to his side. He looked up at the spy hole and smiled. Then they descended on him.

Not a man there struck less than once, and some many, many times, but Jame could hear Bane's ragged breath as clearly as her own long after it should have ceased. He was still breathing when they took him away. A man who has lost his soul dies very, very hard; and a Kencyr hardest of all.

Jame found herself sitting on the floor, leaning against the panel. Pain had roused her. In a half-dazed fashion, she raised a hand to her face, then held it up to the arrow of light from the peephole. The fingertips glistened darkly. Bane had bitten nearly through her lower lip.

She was still staring at her raised hand when something came between it and her face. Jame threw herself sideways with a cry of horror. The other's fingers almost brushed her cheek. No amount of river water would suffice if the name was wrong, she thought wildly, springing to her feet. It had tracked her down again; she was alone with the Shadow Thief in the dark.

She ran. The secret passageways formed a maze within a maze, twisting past all the Palace's major rooms. Shafts of light from many spyholes pierced them. Jame raced on, seeing little ahead and nothing behind but the swift, silent darkness that broke each beam of light as it passed. This was not the Tower of Demons nor was the thing that pursued stupid Thulig-sa, whom this obscurity would have baffled. Despite its name, it meant to touch her, not her shadow, and was perilously close to doing so. Desperately, she put on a fresh burst of speed, rounded a corner, and ran head on into a wall.

Half-stunned, she saw the dark form bending over her, haloed by the furtive light of the peepholes.

Then, far away, someone screamed.

The Shadow Thief froze, its hand inches from Jame's face, then incredibly, it whirled and was gone. She marked its rapid progress down the corridor. Some instinct brought her unsteadily to her feet, sent her after it, stumbling at first, then moving more swiftly and surely. The hunter became the hunted, both now racing in the direction of that terrible, unfaltering cry. God, how could anyone sustain such a ghastly sound so long without once pausing for breath?

Ahead, the end of the corridor was rimmed with light, momentarily obscured as the other passed through it. The scream, very close now, sank to a hideous gurgle. Jame, skidding to avoid another collision, came up against a soft, yielding surface, the back of a wall tapestry. She swept it aside, and stepped into Theocandi's private study.

The Sirdan himself sat at his desk, his gnarled hands gripping its edge. His head was thrown back, his eyes wide, wide, open. Eyes? He had none, just dark holes punched out under the bristling brows, opening into greater darkness. A thin, hissing noise still escaped between his clenched teeth. Under its heavy chain of office, the frail chest continued to contract until the ribs themselves collapsed with a flesh-muffled crunch. And all this time, the Sirdan's returning shadow grew darker on the pages of the Book Bound in Pale Leather, spread out open on the table before him.

'A savant of sorts,' Ishtier had called this man. Clearly, he had been enough of one to summon the Shadow Thief and to unlock the runes, but the latter had proved beyond his control. Anthrobar must have looked much like this when the Book had finished with him.

'It is a filthy thing, isn't it?' Jame said to the motionless figure. 'For what it's worth, I'm sorry that this happened.'

She closed the Book and gingerly rewrapped it in its old linen cloth, shuddering at its obscene warmth. Then she slipped out into the main corridor with it in her arms.

The hallways of the Palace seethed with people, each one intent on saving himself from the coming holocaust. No one paid any attention to the slight figure clutching a flat white parcel, who joined the general flight out into the cool night air. Frantic as they were now, how much greater the rout would be when word of the Sirdan's death spread among them.

At the prow of the island, the figurehead brandished its grisly trophies over the swift water, the sky turning red with flames behind it.

14

The Untempling of the Gods

In the quiet of the temple, Jame hesitated, looking at Marc's motionless form. Then she put the Book Bound in Pale Leather in Ishtier's hands.

'Now,' she said, 'keep your word. Wake him.'

But the priest seemed to have forgotten both her and his victim. With trembling fingers, he unwrapped the Book and cradled it awkwardly in one arm, his free hand turning the heavy pages slowly as he gloated over each one.

'At last I have it,' he murmured, with barely suppressed excitement. 'The power, the power to set things right, to bring down the Barriers and restore my people to their rightful lord under shadow's eve. I have it, I have it, I...'

'What in Perimal's name are you talking about? Will you rouse him or not?'

'Rouse him?' The priest drew himself up, staring coldly down at her. 'You petty-minded little fool, what does that matter now? You don't understand what has happened, do you? Then I will explain it – in Perimal's name – if you think your weak wits can stand it. After all, you still believe that the Kencyrath is the chosen champion of God against the ancient enemy, Perimal Darkling, Devourer of Worlds. Like the rest, you spit on the name of Gerridon, Master of Knorth, whom most call renegade and traitor because he withdrew his loyalty from your divine monstrosity and gave it instead to the Lord of Shadows. But he was right to do so. I went into exile with the Gray Lord. I saw the face of darkness and know that in all the Chain of Creation there is nothing to equal it.'

'Wait a minute... are you saying that the Gray Lord survived the crossing of the Ebonbane?'

Ishtier flinched away from the question. 'Nothing to equal it, I say!' he repeated, his thin voice becoming noticeably shriller.

Jame sensed a change in the flow of power around them, a

growing element of instability. The priest's control had begun to slip.

'M'lord . . .' she said sharply.

'Then I came to Tai-tastigon,' the priest continued, overriding her, rushing on. 'Gods everywhere, hundreds, thousands of them, when we are taught that there is but one. But you think, you presumptuous guttersnipe, that you were the first to ask questions, to experiment with the fabric of reality in this wretched town? Before you were born, I was here, wrestling with the enigma. Seven years ago, the answer was mine at last.'

Again, he drew himself up, and an ominous tremor passed through the room. Out in the hallways of the temple, a low moaning began.

'The force embodied in the Three-Faced God, which we are taught to fear and obey, which has controlled the fate of our people these last thirty millennia under the pretence of being the sole source of divinity in all the worlds, this force, I say, is not unique! For three hundred centuries, it has used us, deluded us, kept us from the truth. All this I have proved,' he said with a wild laugh. 'I! Of what worth is the Kencyrath if it continues to serve such a fraud? What price is godhood itself when any man can create it?'

The chamber door groaned softly. At its foot, the tiles had begun to ripple.

Jame stared at the priest. So his doubts had paralleled her own, but how had he come to such a conclusion? Then, almost against her will, she understood.

'Oh, God. So the Townies were right to blame us for their misery. While Theocandi was calling forth the Shadow Thief, you used the same knowledge to create the Lower Town Monster. But Ishtier, it's a demon, not a god! It lives off the life-force of children and as for its soul . . . Trinity! No wonder it always followed Bane like a shadow: that's exactly what it was. The timing is right, the characteristics . . .'

Butcher of children, are you thinking of me?

The image of a marble seat, dark with blood, crawling with flies, suddenly filled her mind. Once again, perhaps for the last time, her thoughts had crossed his.

'Theocandi couldn't die until his shadow returned to him,' she said with rising horror, 'and neither can Bane. Ishtier, we've got to help him! He's still alive, and they're taking him to the Mercy Seat.'

'Serves him right,' said the priest with a malicious snicker. 'He should never have betrayed me.'

'You betrayed him first, by agreeing to carry his soul and then by using it in such a damnable manner,' Jame cried, unconsciously shifting into High Kens as shock changed to fury. Cat's paws of power rippled through the room. The patterns on the floor changed at their touch. 'He trusted you because you brought his mother, once the Gray Lord's mistress, down out of the Haunted Lands, because he thought – and you let him think – that you were his father. But Ganth Gray Lord was alive when you deserted him, wasn't he? You've betrayed not only Bane and Anar, your younger brother, but your liege-lord as well. I brand you coward and lack-faith for what you did then, and renegade now for trying to pull down the Kencyrath so that you might hide your shame in its ruins!'

'Who are you,' he almost shrieked, spittle flying from his lips, 'to pronounce sentence on me? A petty thief and a tavern whore, an outcast from East Kenshold!'

'I am not from the east,' she cried, enraged beyond all control. 'Like you, I came from the north, and from the same place. The lord you betrayed was my father, the man consigned by you to torture on the Mercy Seat, perhaps my half-brother, and I – I am Jamethiel Priest's-Bane ...'

'... *who shall yet be thy doom.*'

With a look of horror, Ishtier dropped the Book, hands flying to his mouth as though to seal in the words he had just spoken. The god-voice flowed unimpeded, uncontrollable, through his spider-thin fingers, booming prophecy to the far corners of the room.

Jame scarcely heard him. She had suddenly become aware of the changed atmosphere of the room, the growing fury set loose. A demonic howling had begun, the sound of trapped energy moving faster and faster. The walls groaned. Cracks began to lace their smooth surfaces. The three Kencyrs were in the eye of the storm here, protected only by one slowly disintegrating door. Already power flowed around its edges. The floor mosaic shifted again, throwing Jame off her feet. Triangles of green serpentine, lapis-lazuli, and ivory moved under her hand.

'... *who may yet save the chain of creation or destroy it ...*' Ishtier's altered voice was crying, each word like some great weight crashing down. The priest was on his knees now, hands scrabbling at his face, staring wildly at nothing. The power that

257

he had scorned had him by the throat. No help would come from him now.

Through all of this, Marc had not stirred. Jame staggered to her feet, clinging to him as to a rock in storm-maddened seas. His broad shoulders were warm and steady to the touch. Her dazed mind slowly cleared, then began to focus on what she must do next. When her self-control had fully returned, she carefully stepped away from him, bowed to the towering image of her god, and began to dance.

It was like weaving through fire. The dark joy she had felt in moulding the dreams of men turned to agony, a flaying of body and soul. This was the maelstrom where god and man met. The god-head itself was flowing through her, consuming what it touched. She struggled to control it, grimly desperately.

'... *champion, fratricide, tyr-ridan*...'

Tyr-ridan?

No, ignore it, concentrate, concentrate.... So much power and no place to channel it. Had the floor begun to shake? They would all die unless she found an outlet here, beyond... yes, there was a place, many of them, waiting, filling the night with their hunger. No time to ask what they were, no time for anything but to send the power spiralling out to them through the movements of the dance.

'... *Torrigion*...'

That-Which-Creates. (A roaring noise...)

'... *Argentiel*...'

That-Which-Preserves. (Quickly now, increasing, louder...)

'... *Regonereth*.'

That-Which-Destroys. (Done.)

Ishtier, in his own voice, began to scream. The sound pursued her, ringing down the halls of her failing consciousness until at last the final echo died away. Then all was still.

Marc heard the scream too. It seemed to come from a great distance at first, weaving through his trance-numbed mind, growing rapidly louder. Then he forgot it as memory returned. Was he dead and his pyre somehow neglected? While the body remained, so did the shadow, a soul trapped by death, held naked in the presence of the hated Three-Faced God – or so Marc had been taught. Cautiously, fearfully, he opened his eyes.

A book lay before him, its pallid cover uppermost. The

mosaic of ivory and semi-precious stone beneath it had been shaken loose from its pattern. Vaguely, he remembered some upheaval. That must have been when the animal got in, for assuredly there was one somewhere in the room now, its voice raised in a yammering frenzy, broken at intervals by a slobbering sound. He turned stiffly to look for it.

What first met his gaze, however, was a crumpled figure several yards away, lying at the centre of a large, well-defined spiral, which certainly had not been there before. Recognition and alarm cleared his wits instantly. He rose painfully, cursing his cramped legs, limped over and knelt beside the still figure. A moment later, Jame's eyes fluttered open.

'Are you all right?' he asked, helping her to sit up. 'You look a proper mess.'

'I'll bet I do,' she said with a shaky laugh, wiping blood off her face. 'Like something the cat threw up, probably. I ought to be dead.'

'So should I.'

Jame gave him a startled, remembering look, then launched into a rapid explanation of the night's misadventures. 'And now that that's been cleared up,' she said at last, 'what in Trinity's name is making that uproar? It scarcely sounds human.'

They went to look, and found Ishtier crouching on the far side of the altar, quite mad, trying to gnaw off the hand that had touched the pages of the Book Bound in Pale Leather.

'What do we do about him?' Marc asked, eyeing the priest doubtfully.

'Nothing.' The cold hatred in her voice surprised him. He had not, after all, been there to hear her speak to Hangrell in just such a tone. 'He brought this on himself and more besides. Let's just get out before something else happens.'

She picked up the Book, grimacing at the feel of it and at the darkening patch on the binding where it had hit the floor. 'One man dead because of this, another insane, and all it has are bruises,' she said with disgust, much to Marc's confusion. 'I've a mind to throw it into the first fire we come to, but I won't. Guardians never get off that easily. Besides, the damn thing would probably find some way to come crawling back.'

They went out through the ruins of the door, which crumbled to dust at a touch. The outer halls were quiet. Though the directing influence of the priest was gone, it would be weeks before the power here built up again to a dangerous level. By that time, Jame hoped, help would have been sent out by those sensitives in the Kencyrath who, however distant, could scarcely have failed to note the chaos unleashed in Tai-tastigon that night.

She and Marc began to get some idea of it as they stepped out of the temple.

'Something's wrong with the skyline,' said Marc, pausing uncertainly on the threshold. 'We should be able to see the Tower of Bats near Judgement Square from here, and Fumble's Folly, and look: Edor Thulig is gone.'

There were in fact many unfamiliar gaps in the city's skyline, especially near at hand, where whole rows of deserted houses had tumbled down, greatly increasing the circle of ruin about the temple. Beyond, most structures except a few of the tallest still stood – or at least leaned – though over all hung such an unearthly air that it was hard to think of the whole as Tai-tastigon at all. Odd lights played out across the sky, blooming silently from the labyrinth of streets and quickly fading back into it. Hollow, booming sounds were heard in the distance, almost but not quite resolving themselves into words. The odours of incense, burning, and death rode the cross-winds.

The two Kencyrs looked at each other, baffled, then back at the strangely altered city. Marc gave a sudden exclamation. A light was coming towards them, growing steadily brighter. Within seconds, they could distinguish over the intervening rooftops the sparks that flew upwards from it and the tower of smoke that rose at its heels. Jame gripped her friend's arm.

'Dalis-sar!' she said.

Before he could react, she had thrust the wrapped Book into his arms and was gone, racing off through the mounds of dust towards the approaching blaze. He followed as quickly as he could, with a curse at his still-cramped legs. Jame disappeared around a corner at the circle's rim. When Marc caught sight of her again, she was at the far end of the street, silhouetted against an inferno whose brilliance made him look quickly away, seeing nothing but gigantic wheels of fire rolling slowly on, hearing only the roar of the flames and Jame's voice shouting over and over:

'Bane! Its name is Bane!'

Then the greater light was gone, southward bound. In its wake, everything burned – houses, rubble, even the slight, dark figure that had thrown itself face down on the ground, arms wrapped about its head.

Marc was hobbling to the rescue when something else came down the street. It was about half the size of the first apparition and appeared at first to be nothing more or less than a small ambulatory storm cloud, complete with fitful flickers of lightning and sharp little thunderclaps. The rain it let fall extinguished most of the flames its predecessor had left behind. When Marc came up to Jame, she was on her feet, slapping at the patches of her soaked jacket that still smouldered. Staring down the street after this strange procession, Marc saw that there was something in the heart of the retreating cloud, something that hopped along jauntily in time to its own warlike music and seemed, by what light there was, to be a particularly vivid shade of green.

'Gorgo?' he said incredulously. 'But how? What in all the names of God is going on?'

'They're on their way to the Lower Town to destroy its monster,' said Jame, still slapping at her clothes. 'Armed with fire, water, and its true name, they ought to succeed. Dalis-sar has waited a long time for this. I suspect he sensed from the start that it was a Kencyr affair, but there was nothing he could do about it as long as he remained securely templed. As for Bane, now at last he can die. I suppose in a way it will even be an honourable death, what with Ishtier, Dalis-sar, and myself all contributing to it. Perhaps that was all he ever really wanted from me. Now I will never know.'

Marc was still staring after the two gods.

'How did they come untempled?' he asked, bewildered. 'I've heard tell of one god breaking loose before, but two at once?'

'I think I know,' said Jame, 'but let's go home. If I'm right, we'll find out soon enough.'

At the first step, she stumbled. Marc, hastily catching her arm, realised then that the light of Dalis-sar's war chariot, so painful even to him at a distance, had temporarily blinded her. Well, if she didn't want to speak of it, they wouldn't, nor of her torn lip, which was clearly the work of someone else's teeth. All in good time. They set out for the Res aB'tyrr with his hand on her shoulder.

The streets of Tai-tastigon presented a curious spectacle. At first, much of the damage there suggested natural causes: an earthquake, perhaps, that had left downed buildings, fissured roadways, and fires casually gutting homes from which all occupants had fled. But there was more to it than that.

Vast, shadowless forms prowled the thoroughfares. Some

pulsed with light; others seemed like holes cut out of the fabric of space; many were so nebulous that nothing could be said of them at all except that they moved and, somehow, lived. Whole blocks crumbled with their passage, if they did not turn from stone to crystal, sprout flowers from every cranny, or perform some other unnerving if temporary transformation. Voices boomed in the distance. Overhead, an enormous, grotesque creature scuttled along the walls, leaving a phosphorescent trail and, at intervals, triumphant proclamations in schoolboy Kessic that 'Edolph the Bat-Wing was here . . . and here . . . and here.'

More often, however, the two Kencyrs came across scenes of consternation. One indistinct form raced wildly around block after block, cutting through the corner houses to the great dismay of their occupants; another frantically tried to creep into a lay-temple half its size; a third simply huddled at the end of a blind alley, whimpering. What had happened was now clear enough, at least in general terms: *All* the gods had come untempled, and most were finding the experience profoundly unsettling.

'"All the beings we know to be divine are in fact but the shadows of some greater power that regards them not,"' said Jame suddenly as they neared the inn, interrupting Marc's description of a shimmering form that he had just seen flutter past the end of the street, closely pursued by a priest brandishing what appeared to be a giant butterfly net.

'It's the Anti-God Heresy in action,' she explained. 'When I channelled energy out of the temple tonight, it entered the so-called gods of Tai-tastigon. They must live on it. In fact, I'll bet that they were created out of it in the first place, with their worshippers' faith to give them form and life. Why, they're nothing but parasites, so insignificant that their host doesn't give a damn if they exist or not! The senior priests must have discovered that and called it a heresy to keep their power intact. I don't think the gods themselves knew the truth until tonight, when they suddenly got more power than they could comfortably swallow. Poor things, no wonder they're so upset.'

'Look,' said Marc abruptly.

They had come to the edge of the Res aB'tyrr's little square, and he was pointing across it at the inn. Jame, whose sight had by now returned, stared in disbelief. Golden light streamed out of every window and up like a beacon from its courtyard into the night sky.

Everyone was in the kitchen, clustered around the open courtyard door, staring out of it incredulously. Cleppetty swung around sharply as they entered the room.

'Bloody, singed, *and* dripping wet,' she said, regarding Jame with fists jammed on bony hips. 'Now I know we've got a crisis.'

Jame ducked under Sart's arm, around Rothan, and between Kithra and Ghillie, who made room for her without once taking their eyes from the scene outside. A familiar figure was walking back and forth over the flagstones. The black, hooded robe had not changed, but through it shone a golden light, outlining the lithe body within and playing about the beautiful hands as they traced wide circles in the air, as though ecstatically embracing all before them. There was still no face within the hood, only light and more light. When it touched the B'tyrr figures on the wall, they wriggled with joy, stone lips parting in silent laughter, ivy-bound hands flexing, bursting their green bonds.

'I've just one question for you, missy,' said the widow's voice belligerently at Jame's elbow. 'The last time we had that lady for a guest, the roof almost fell in. So now when does it catch fire?'

'After this,' said Jame slowly, 'probably never. She's returning your hospitality. I think you've just acquired a resident goddess.'

'Look!' said Ghillie suddenly. 'She's disappearing!'

They watched as the light slowly faded, the moving figure becoming less distinct. The same thing was probably happening all over the city, to everyone's great relief. It was to be hoped that the other deities would withdraw to their own temples now that they had expended enough energy to fit into them; but the Res aB'tyrr's still nameless guest had no place else to go. Indeed, even when her form had vanished entirely, it was clear that she remained because the walls of the inner court continued to glow, and would, as it turned out, for years to come.

While the others exploded into a babble of excited conversation, Jame tried to explain to the widow what had happened.

'Well,' said Cleppetty at last, 'with Theocandi out of the way, at least you won't have to go rushing off. A few days' rest will do you good after a night like this.'

'I expect it would, but it isn't that simple. Too many people know I was in the Palace trying to get something back from the Sirdan just before he died. No, I've got to leave now, tonight, before the Guild gets its breath back.'

'The Talisman is right,' said Sart. 'If Men-dalis takes power now, he'll need something to get folks' minds off that odd business with his poor brother. A hunt for the murderer of a sirdan should suit him just fine, especially since he seems to hate you anyway. Off-hand, I can't think of anything that would pull the Guild together faster. What I don't see,' he said, scratching an ear, 'is how you're going to get far enough away fast enough. Come the dawn, they'll be down the Tone after you like a wolf pack.'

'Then I won't go that way. There are still the mountains.'

'In the middle of the storm season? You haven't a hope of a guide,' said the widow, sounding outraged. 'And as for proper clothing...!'

'There's an outfitter's shop near the Mountain Gate. I'll raid that. As for a guide, one of my own people, an Arrin-ken, lives up there. He may help... if I can find him.'

'If we can, you mean,' said Marc.

She gave him a searching, hesitant look. 'You're sure?'

'I never try to commit suicide twice in one night,' he said with a slow smile. 'We'll get through all right. Anyway, I'll not have it said in the houses of the Kencyrath that you shook me off so easily.'

Two hours later, he was still smiling slightly as they left the Vale of Tone and began to climb up into the lower reaches of the Ebonbane. Decked out in a preposterously small mountaineer's jacket (the largest, nonetheless, that the outfitter's shop could provide), he might well have been quietly laughing at himself or at Jame, who, by contrast, looked as if she had been swallowed alive by her new, oversized clothes. The little mound of coins they had left on the counter was probably too large for such dubious comfort, but Jame had been determined that, as a parting gesture, it should be large enough. She never meant to steal again.

Still, awkward fit or not, it was a pity nothing similar could be done for Jorin. He was trotting beside her now, as he had been ever since her silent, anxious call had drawn him to her down from the foothills to the north. She slid a gloved hand over his winter coat, noting its richness. Perhaps, after all, he was better prepared than either of them.

Already the air was much colder.

Jame turned on the slope, looked down through the valley of the Tone for the last time at the city below. At the world and the people she had known, Penari, to whom she had not even said good-bye. Though perhaps he, of all people, would best understand why she left. Every detail of the Res aB'tyrr's warm kitchen came back to her, every word spoken in those last hurried moments; but most of all, she remembered Cleppetty's sudden, almost defiant announcement that since it was a night for surprises, she would contribute one of her own: during the course of their long vigil that evening, Sart Nine-toes had proposed to her and she had accepted. What was more, she believed that Rothan and Kithra had come to a similar understanding.

One leave-taking, two engagements and three – no, four pyres. Jame hardly knew whether to laugh or cry.

She had said good-bye to Tubain through the locked door of his 'wife's' apartment. To her astonishment, the inn-keeper and Abernia had both answered from inside, speaking simultaneously. Taniscent, of course, had had nothing to say at all. Standing at the door, Jame had taken a last, silent farewell, seeing on that narrow cot the symbol of all the lives lost – friends' and foes' – since she had first slipped through the Warrior Gate on that night so many, many days ago.

A very different emotion went through her now as she regarded not memory but Tai-tastigon itself, that marvellous city, flayed with fire and prostrate with terror. A great fissure had split Judgement Square in half, swallowing whole the Mercy Seat and whoever had occupied it, Dally or Bane, in those last minutes when the mob still ruled. She was tired of feeling responsible for things beyond her control, and angry at those whose schemes had unleashed the chaos below, especially at that one who, if her instincts and Sart's were correct, was getting away with murder. But not forever. There would be an accounting for that someday, if she lived to bring it about.

This certainty remained as all else began to slip away, an entire way of life flowing back into the darkness. Was the Gray Lord really her father and she Highborn? In the temple, the thought had seemed almost inspired, but here the possible reality of it was harder to grasp. If it was true, then in Torisen Black Lord, leader of the Kencyrath, she might find her long lost twin brother Tori – miraculously ten years older than herself. Well, stranger things had happened, even within the last hour. Perhaps time moved at a different pace beyond the Barrier, or even near it. Perhaps she had even first fled Perimal

Darkling to some place other than Rathillien: after all, the Master had come searching for his precious book a good two years before her own arrival with it in this world.

Questions, always questions. Still, some answers were at last beginning to emerge. Soon she would know them all, and no longer be a stranger to herself.

Marc was calling her from farther up the path. She took one last look at the city, settled her pack, and turned to follow him. A sudden feeling of happiness lightened her step. Despite the uncertainty that awaited them both, despite fire, ruin, and the snow that had begun to fall, they were going home at last.

Dark of the Moon

15

Fire and Ice
The Ebonbane: 7th of Winter

Tai-tastigon burned.

'Wake, wake!' shouted city guards under windows barred for the night. Fists pounded on doors. Bells began to shrill. From the roof of the Council Hall came the sudden boom of the warning horn, all five of its mouthpieces manned at once.

The citizens woke. They tumbled bleary-eyed into the streets to find the sky alight overhead. From the north came shrieks and the crash of falling buildings. An unearthly wail rose from the Temple District as the gods, bound in their sanctuaries, felt the stones heat around them. Fiery motes danced in the air. What they touched, burned: roofs, clothes, flesh. Panic spread. Now people were running, some already on fire, down through the twisting streets, towards where the River Tone ran between dark buildings. Quick, the water. The swift, cold current bore them downstream under the soaring bridges to smash against the prow of Ship Island or drown in the white water along its sheer sides.

On the island itself, in the Palace of the Thieves' Guild, an old man sat in a tapestry-hung room. On his lap lay a book bound in white leather with the texture of an infant's skin. His head tilted back. Gaping mouth and empty eye sockets opened only into darkness.

The chamber room door burst open. A man clad in royal blue stood on the threshold, his golden hair shining softly in the gloom. He stared at the old man. An unpleasant smile twisted his handsome features, but when he turned to the dark figures crowding the corridor behind him, they saw only anger and grief in his face.

'The Talisman has done this,' he said to them. 'Get her.'

A low growl answered him. The hallway emptied. Moments

later, shadowy forms slipped through the streets, oblivious to fire and ruin, growling still. Swift as they were, rumour outpaced them:

The Lord of the Thieves' Guild is dead, is dead. The Talisman has slain him. Brother thieves, the hunt is up!

The Talisman ran for her life, ran for home. One corner more, and there was the inn, the Res aB'tyrr, blazing. Dark figures came at her, silhouetted by the glare.

'The fire might have spared it, Talisman. We didn't.'

They closed in on her. Someone inside the inn began to scream. She fought her captors' sooty hands, shouting the names of her friends: Cleppetty, Ghillie, Taniscent.... But here was Tanis now, clinging to her arm.

'A party, Talisman, a lovely party, and you're the guest of honour! See, here's a friend to escort us.'

The brigand Bortis shambled out of the darkness, grinning. The blood streaming from the red ruin of his eyes looked black in the light of the burning inn. He took her arm. The streets were lined with silent people, staring at her: Hangrell, Raffing, Scramp with the rope still around his neck, Marplet . . . dead, all dead. Judgement Square. The Mercy Seat.

Dally was sitting on the stone chair. He looked up, smiling, and courteously rose to make room for her. His skin hung in tatters about him.

'I loved you, Talisman. See what your love did to me.'

Still smiling, he bound her to the chair with strips of his own skin.

They were all coming for her. Firelight flashed off knives, off short, flaying blades, their edges white hot. She huddled back in the Mercy Seat, but they kept coming, coming...

'No!'

Jame woke to her own cry of horror. Stone pressed against her back, but where were the knives? The air here was cold, so cold that it seared her lungs as she drew a deep, shuddering gulp of it. Where was she? The wind keened and snow stung her face, numbing it. No, not in Tai-tastigon at all, but high above it in the storm-locked passes of the Ebonbane. She had fled the city before the thieves could catch her. Now a blizzard had her instead, and she was lost in it. But why was it so dark? She drew back against the rock that sheltered her, fighting the first feather touch of panic.

'Marc, where are you?'

Jorin whimpered in her arms. Blind from birth, the ounce cub saw through her eyes – when she could see anything at all.

'Marc?' Fear sharpened her voice, making her sound even younger than her nineteen-odd years. 'Why is it so dark? Did you let me sleep past moonfall? Marc?'

Feet crunched on the snow. 'Lass? Softly, softly. Let me look.'

She felt the Kendar's big hands gently touch her face.

'H-have I gone snow blind?'

'Ah, no such thing. Your eyelids are only frozen shut.'

Tears? thought Jame. *But I never cry.* Then she remembered the inn.

'They all burned to death,' she said unsteadily. 'Cleppetty, Tubain, everyone at the Res aB'tyrr except Taniscent, and she was dead already.'

'Well now, I suppose it could happen,' said Marc slowly. 'A good bit of the city was burning when we left, but that was three days ago, after the worst of it, and the inn was safe enough then. Now, if you were a farseer –'

'But I've been spared that at least, haven't I?' Jame's voice sounded strange even to her, as if it belonged to someone else, locked away in the dark, gripped by nightmares and memories. 'You needn't remind me that I'm Shanir. The old blood, the old powers – god-spawn, unclean, unclean...'

Marc shook her. Gentle as he was, the tremendous strength in his hands shocked her away from the memory of her father shouting those words after her as he had driven her from the keep that had been her home, into the Haunted Lands. But that had been long ago, before the years in Perimal Darkling, which she could no longer remember, before she had returned to Rathillien to lead her double life as the Talisman, apprentice to the greatest thief in Tai-tastigon; and as the B'tyrr, tavern and temple dancer.

Jorin anxiously touched noses with her. Then she felt the rasp of his tongue on her frozen eyelids. There in the dark, still closer to dreams than reality, she tried to sort one from the other.

'So the Res aB'tyrr is probably safe, but Dally and Bane.... Is Dally really dead?'

'Yes. Very.'

Jame shivered. 'And Bane? Is he dead too?'

'We can only hope so.'

So, in the end, it came to that. Bane, Dally, Tanis,

Scramp. . . . She gave a bitter laugh. 'It occurs to me, somewhat belatedly, that I'm rather hard on my friends.'

At that moment, the ice sealing her eyelids at last melted away. Jorin rubbed his soft cheek against hers, purring. His whiskers tickled. Marc had let her sleep almost until morning, Jame saw, but in that time the storm had eased. Now more snow seemed to be blowing than falling, and the full moon low in the sky glowed through a thinning cloud cover.

By its light, Jame regarded her friend with concern. The biggest mountaineer's jacket they had been able to find barely fit across his broad shoulders, much less down those powerful arms. The exposed wrists looked blanched. His beard was white too, both with frost and years. At ninety-four, late middle age for a Kendar, surely he was too old for such a desperate adventure.

'Why did you ever let me talk you into this?' she demanded.

'As I recall,' he said mildly, 'it was more a case of not being able to talk me out of it. We'd pretty well decided even before the uproar that it was time to leave. You have that twin brother of yours to find – name of Tori, wasn't it? – and I've an itch to see old friends in the Riverland. We're going home, you and I. This is just the shortest route.'

'Right. Just as jumping out a third storey window is the fastest way to the ground.'

'Oh, I've tried that too,' said the big man placidly.

Jame started to laugh, then drew in her breath sharply. Simultaneously, Jorin's head snapped up. The ounce might see quite well through her eyes, but she had only recently gained a limited use of his nose and ears. Now she heard what he heard, distorted at first, then all too clearly.

'Wolves,' she said, and scrambled to her feet.

Marc rose almost as quickly, but his stiffened knees betrayed him and he lurched against a rock. 'No, no,' he said absently, pushing Jame aside as she reached out to steady him. 'Always stand clear or some day I really will fall and smash you flat.' He drew himself up to his full seven-foot height, towering over her. 'Wolves you say? If we're lucky.'

'Trinity. And if we aren't?'

The howling began again, closer, unexpectedly shrill.

'Wyrsan,' said Marc. 'An entire ravening of them, from the sound of it, and headed this way. They may be smaller than wolves, but they're faster and fiercer. These rocks won't protect us for long if they catch our scent. There may be better cover up near the Blue Pass.'

He stepped out into the open. Leaning into the wind, he trudged stolidly up the nearly invisible path between snowdrifts, his bulk breaking both the ice crust and the wind's force for Jame as she struggled after him with Jorin bounding along behind her in their footsteps. The worst of the storm might be over, but the wind was still savage and the driven snow blinding. Jame could see nothing of Mounts Timor and Tinnibin, which must be looming over them now, or of the Blue Pass, which cut between them, straddling the spine of the Ebonbane.

The situation was bad enough without wyrsan on their trail. Not much was known about these beasts because they usually kept to the deep snow of the heights during the brief travel season when the passes opened. Superstition claimed that they were possessed by the souls of the unavenged dead. Rumour had it, perhaps more accurately, that they were prone to killing frenzies and could tunnel nearly as fast under the ice crust as they could run on top of it.

The two Kencyr had risked this winter crossing largely because they had hoped to find quite a different sort of creature here among the jagged peaks. Long ago – nearly two thousand years, in fact – the first of the Three People had grown disgusted with the rest of the Kencyrath and retreated to the wilds of Rathillien to think things over. They were still at it. One of these catlike, almost immortal Arrin-ken made his home here in the Ebonbane, but Jame had been mentally calling to him for three days now without success. It looked as if she and Marc were on their own.

Abruptly, the Kendar stopped and Jame ran into him. He shouted something, then turned and climbed the snowbank to the right. Jame scrambled after him. A sloping snowfield stretched out before them, wind rilled, sheltered by the flank of Mount Timor. Snow blew over their heads off the mountain's spine. The ice crust here was thick enough first to bear Jame and Jorin's weight, then Marc's.

Jame drew level with him. 'What did you say?'

'I thought we might find something useful up here. The top of that mound up ahead might be our best bet for a stand.'

Not far away, Jame saw a rectangular pile of rocks about ten feet high with sloping sides and a flattened top. Suddenly, she knew exactly where they were. This was the field where Bortis

273

and his band of brigands had slaughtered last season's first caravan, the one Jame herself would have joined if it hadn't been for Marc's unexpected arrival in Tai-tastigon. That thing ahead was the burial cairn of the victims.

The wind moaned about it, raising ghosts of snow around its black flanks. Subsequent caravans had not only raised this monument, but, to conciliate the dead, had built into its outer walls whatever personal possessions the brigands had over-looked. Here a bride's broken mirror gave back a splintered reflection of the moon, there a wooden doll thrust a stiff arm out between the stone blocks. Jame slowed, staring. Her own people believe that while even a single bone remained unburned, the soul was trapped, but here were hundreds, thousands of bones.

Marc had reached the cairn. 'Come on, lass,' he said, holding out his hand. 'You first. We only have to hold on until dawn.'

Jame still hesitated. This was ridiculous. She had dealt with bones before, and with the dead themselves, if it came to that. They simply obeyed their own rules. Once you found those out, you could usually cope, however messy things got. Besides, in a sense, she and Bane had already avenged these poor folk in that before the massacre, he had put out one of Bortis's eyes protecting her; and after it, she had got the other one defending Jorin. No one had seen Bortis in Tai-tastigon since. She wondered fleetingly what had become of him, then put him out of her mind and began resolutely to climb the cairn's sloping side.

The stones were slick with ice under her hands. She thought she felt a vibration deep inside the cairn. Then, suddenly, a stone gave way under her weight and her right leg plunged into the mound up to the knee. Something inside grabbed her foot. Her startled yelp turned into a grunt as Marc's arm shot around her waist and jerked her back. Something white furred and slobbering was wrapped around her foot. It let go, plopping back into the hole. Marc swung her down to the base of the cairn where she collapsed breathless in the snow. Her boot hung in shreds.

'What in Perimal's name was that?' she gasped.

'A wyrsan kitling. It looks as if they've converted the entire mound into a ravery.'

'But wouldn't it have been pretty solid?'

'Not after they'd eaten the bodies out of it. Jorin!'

The ounce had been warily sniffing the edge of the hole. He jumped back as a shrill, yammering cry came out of the mound, immediately echoed by other voices down wind.

'That's done it,' said Marc. 'The adults will be all over us in minutes. Run.'

They ran. Some distance ahead, the field ended in a steep, rocky slope that, if they were lucky, the wyrsan would not be able to climb. Suddenly Marc floundered. Jame grabbed his arm as the white expanse before them split open, great chunks of it thundering down into darkness. They stared in dismay at the gaping crevasse. Behind, the yipping grew rapidly nearer.

'Now what?' said Jame.

'Too late to turn back. I might be able to catapult you across.'

'And leave you here to have all the fun? Forget it.'

'As you wish. But for future use, let's make a pact: Whatever you can't outwit, I hit. That should take care of most contingencies.'

'It's nice to know you think we still have a future,' said Jame, watching as he dropped his pack and unslung his double edged war-axe. 'Just the same, I'm more likely to start hitting things than you are.'

'Not wyrsan,' said the big man firmly.

The howling began again, much closer this time. It was a sound that slid the thin knife edge of panic between thought and action. Hearing it, one only wanted to run and run. Then, in the midst of that shrill chorus, one voice wavered and broke into hysterical laughter.

'That was no wyrsa,' said Jame.

'A haunt?'

'This far south of the Barrier? Well, maybe, but I've never met one yet who thought that being dead was funny.'

'It's not,' said Marc. 'Stand behind me.'

Jame stepped back nearer to the crevasse and reached for the knife usually sheathed in her right boot. She touched only shredded leather. Damn. The blade must have fallen out during the kitling's attack. She stripped off the remains of the boot so as not to trip over them and stood stocking footed in the snow. Her toes began to ache with the cold.

The outline of the cairn moved as the wyrsan swarmed over it. Then clouds swept over the moon, bringing a fresh flurry of snow, and Jame could no longer see the mound. Jorin pressed against her knee, protesting the loss of their shared sight.

275

'Too bad there's nothing here to burn,' said Marc, peering into the darkness. 'A bit of fire, now, that would be useful.'

Jame stood still a moment. Then she dropped to her knees and began to rummage frantically through both their packs. In her own, she touched a broken sword with a defaced hilt emblem, a ring, and something warm, but bypassed them all for things more suited to their present need.

'My spare pants weren't exactly what I had in mind,' said the Kendar, sceptically regarding the clothes she was hastily laying out in a semicircle around them. 'That lot won't burn very long.'

'What we need are some ashes. I'm going to try a kindling spell.'

'Careful. Remember what happened the last time you tried a piece of Tastigon magic.'

Jame grimaced. Early in her stay at the Res aB'tyrr, Cleppetty had tested her culinary skills by presenting her with a lump of unleavened dough and the household book of spells. She had indeed got the loaf to rise, but when Cleppetty had sliced into it, they had discovered that its expansion had been due to the growth of rudimentary internal organs. After that, Jame had left Tastigon magic alone. Now, with some trepidation, she called to mind the spell Cleppetty used every morning to start a new kitchen fire from the ashes of the old.

'Listen,' said Marc suddenly.

'I don't hear anything.'

'They're running silent. It's now or not at all, lass.'

Jame hastily set fire to the semicircle with steel and flint. The clothes burned grudgingly. Wondering if she wasn't about to do something profoundly stupid, she recited the charm.

Instantly, a great cloud of fire-shot smoke billowed up around them. Choking, half-blind, Jame heard Marc's shout, then a meaty thunk. A wyrsa shot out of the darkness to land heavily at her feet. Snarling, it gathered its stocky body to spring at her, but then the terrible wound left by Marc's axe opened, spilling blood and bowels into the snow. She stared at the creature. The coarse white fur down its back was smouldering.

Now the smoke seemed full of hurtling bodies. The war-axe sang somewhere ahead of her, parrying what looked like flung torches. The spell circle was apparently kindling anything that passed over it. Jame sidestepped a blazing wyrsa. Were these creatures really so singleminded that they didn't realise they were on fire?

The snow crust in front of her erupted. For half a heartbeat, Jame stared down the throat of the beast springing up at her. Then Jorin met it in midair. Ounce and wyrsa disappeared into the smoke, snapping at each other, rolling over and over. Jame ran after them.

'Down!' roared Marc's voice almost in her ear. She fell flat. Axe and wyrsa met over her head with a crunch and a spray of blood.

'That's nineteen,' said the Kendar, scooping her up. 'Stand clear.' And he pushed her to one side out of his weapon's reach.

She could hear Jorin and the wyrsa still thrashing about somewhere nearby but couldn't find them. The ounce would be fighting blind without her eyes to guide him, but then, despite her excellent Kencyr night vision, she herself could barely see anything in this chaos of smoke, snow, and darkness. Where was the crevasse? Sweet Trinity, to step over the edge of *that* in the dark . . .

A wyrsa charged her, all the fur down its back ablaze. No time for evasion. She went down backward, caught the beast in mid-spring with her foot and flipped it over her head. Its wailing cry faded in the distance before ending abruptly. So that's where the crevasse was.

Jame was just thinking that for a street fighter she wasn't doing too badly when the snow beside her exploded. She barely saw the wyrsa before it landed on her. Its weight drove her head and shoulders through the weakened ice crust. The powdery snow beneath filled her eyes and mouth. Bent over backward with fifty pounds of maddened wyrsa on her chest, tearing at the heavily padded arm, which she had thrown up to protect her throat, she fought back in mindless terror, slashing, clawing. The night was red, red, and stank of blood.

Only exhaustion finally made her stop. The wyrsa sprawled on top of her, its teeth still locked in the reinforced sleeve of her knife-fighter's *d'hen*, its face a gory, eyeless mask. It was quite dead. For a moment she lay there gasping, then, with difficulty, heaved the beast off and sat up. Her gloves hung in blood-soaked rags. She stared numbly at her hands, at the fingernails, razor-tipped and edged, still fully extended. Oh God, she had used them again.

No one at her old home in the Haunted Lands had realised what she was until her seventh year. They had thought it odd that she had no fingernails, but no one had been prepared for the retractile claws that suddenly one day had broken through the skin on her fingertips. Then her father had known what to call her when he drove her out:

Shanir, god-spawn, unclean, unclean...

There was blood under the nails. She plunged her hands into the snow again and again until common sense stopped her. She could never wash away the taint in her blood that made her what she was.

Something breathed in her ear. Jame started, then turned and threw her arms around Jorin. The ounce nuzzled her face as she ran anxious hands over him, looking for serious wounds, finding none. Ancestors be praised for that, at least.

Then, for the first time, she noticed how quiet everything was. The semicircle still smouldered, but most of the smoke had blown away to reveal a battlefield lit by the burning carcasses of some thirty wyrsan, all in various stages of dismemberment. Marc might hate killing, but if need be, he was certainly good at it. But where was he?

She scrambled to her feet, cold with sudden fear. Only his footprints remained in the trampled, bloody snow, indicating that he had been driven backward several paces by the fury of his assailants. The trail ended at the edge of the crevasse.

Jame threw herself down on the snow and peered into the abyss. It was too dark for her to see more than a few feet, and her voice woke only echoes, cracking off icy walls farther and farther down. Sweet Trinity, if he had fallen all the way to the bottom...

Behind her, beyond the firelight, someone chuckled softly. 'Jamethiel!' called a husky, sweet voice from the darkness. 'Child, I've come for you.'

Jorin backed into Jame, the fur down his spine rising. She felt her own scalp prickle. Whatever was out there, it knew her real name, and she almost felt she knew what to call it, too. When had she heard that loathsomely familiar voice before? Not in Tai-tastigon, not at the keep...

'Dream-Weaver, Snare-of-Souls, Priest's-Bane...'

The voice chanted the epithets softly, mockingly. Only the last was one that Jame had ever used. The rest belonged to the first Jamethiel, her namesake, who some three thousand years before had danced out the souls of two-thirds of the Kencyr Host at the bidding of her brother and consort, Gerridon, Master of Knorth.

'Soon the spell-circle will weaken. See, already the fire is dying. Do you remember the Master's House, burning, burning, the night he called you to his bed?'

... she was climbing the twisted stair, naked under a cloak of serpent skins sewn together with silver thread. The snake heads thumped on each step at her heels. A man was waiting in an alcove... who? His face was like a refleshed skull, his fingers cold, so cold, as he slipped a knife into her hand, and she was climbing, towards a door barred with red ribbons, towards the darkness beyond...

Jame flinched away from that splinter of memory, all that was left of so many lost years. The Master's bed? But it was the first Jamethiel who had been and, for all she knew, still was the arch-traitor's consort. What on earth did all this have to do with her?

But you were in Perimal Darkling yourself. The thought breathed cold on her. She wanted to deny it but *You have the Book Bound in Pale Leather, kept in darkness by Gerridon when he fell. There isn't any place you could have got it but in his House, under shadow's eaves.*

Damn. The spell-circle *was* weakening. Eyes gleamed across the dying flames, and that soft, gloating chuckle came again. 'Soon, Jamethiel, soon.'

It was as if her entire lost past waited there in the darkness ready to pounce. What would hold it back? All Jame could think of was fire... and the Book. Trinity, that was it. She scrambled for her knapsack and dug into it. Her cold hands closed on something warm. She drew out a package and hastily unwrapped it to reveal the Book Bound in Pale Leather. It throbbed in her grasp as if shaken by a slow heartbeat. Then it seemed to shiver. Goose bumps rose on the soft skin of its binding as the cold air hit it.

There was a sudden movement beyond the still smouldering semicircle. Something pale and curiously lopsided shambled forward, its exact shape hidden by the thickening snow.

'What are you doing?' it demanded, its voice rising sharply. 'You little fool, stop!'

Jame wrenched her eyes back to the Book. On the page before her was the rune she wanted. She stared at it with horrified fascination as its power began to unfold in her mind. Lines of vermilion, lines of gold.... Heat grew, and with it, pain. Jame slammed shut the Book, but the rune seemed etched on the inside of her eyelids. The images began to blur, to expand, going out of control. Jame grimly forced the power generated by the rune back into its proper shape. Then, when it felt as if the top of her head was about to blow off, in the language of the Rune-Masters, she said:

'BURN.'

The word seared her throat. She fell to her knees, gagging, as waves of heat rolled over her. Looking up, half dazed, she saw a wall of roaring flame just beyond the ash circle, rising, spreading backward. Fiery motes stung her upturned face. The very sky seemed to be burning. For a moment, Jame believed she had fallen back into her nightmare, but then...

Ancestors preserve me, she thought. *I've set fire to the blizzard!*

Out in the heart of the flames, something screamed. A burning shape hurtled over the now defunct spell-ring. It somersaulted once in the melting snow to extinguish the flames, then came bounding forward. Jorin leaped to meet it. The creature sent him flying with a blow and came on. It looked like some warped parody of a wyrsa, but much larger and furred only in singed patches. Its fire-cast shadow, monstrously distorted, sprang on before it.

Jame leaped to her feet, then went over backward as the thing crashed into her. She found herself sprawling on her back, staring up into a face that seemed to be all eyes, muzzle, and teeth. It was a changer out of Perimal Darkling, she realised, horrified, one of the Master's fallen Kencyr servants. Once this creature must have been as recognisably human as Jame herself, but that had been long, long ago.

It grinned down at her. 'Just like old times, eh? I always said Tirandys was a spoilsport for teaching you how to fight back.'

'What are you talking about?' She hardly recognised her own voice, breathless, cracking with near panic. 'What do you want?'

He laughed again, a half-mad sound. 'Want? I? It's our master who wants, and what he wants is you. Naughty girl, to have run away from his house like that, after all the pains we took with you. But it's been a long, lean time up in these mountains, waiting for you to leave that god-ridden city. Master Gerridon can wait. My turn comes now.'

She had her hands braced against his shoulders, but that gloating face oozed down the length of her arms, changing shape as it came. Shreds of rotting meat were caught between his teeth. His breath stank.

Then, abruptly, something blotted out the fiery sky behind him. The changer was wrenched away. Jame heard the crunch of bones as he landed a dozen feet away. She saw a huge, dark shape crouching over the changer and smelled the tang of wild musk. The Arrin-ken had arrived at last.

So, Keral, well met again, purred a deep voice in Jame's mind. *It's been a long time.*

'Not long enough,' snarled the changer. 'I think you've broken my legs.'

Have I? The Arrin-ken patted one of the creature's twisted limbs experimentally. The changer screamed. *So I have. How clumsy of me. I meant to break your back.*

'You wouldn't dare! I am a favourite of the Master himself! Harm me, and he'll nail your mangy hide to his trophy wall with you still in it!'

Foolish boy. I've already harmed you. The flesh of your kind heals quickly, but what a pity that bones take so much longer.

The purr deepened. Through it ran changing depths, and a sudden sense of many voices plaited together like the currents of the sea.

As for that wall, we remember it well, and the bloody hall where so many of our kind were slain the night Gerridon betrayed us all to Perimal Darkling and shadows swallowed the moon. We even remember how many Arrin-ken you blinded with live coals before your half-brother Tirandys stopped the fun. Indeed, Keral, we have looked forward to this meeting for a long time.

The changer had begun to shake. 'You think you're so noble, so wise,' he spat. 'So I'm the fool, am I, for having chosen the winning side and won immortality? You could rot for all your precious god cares, but I tell you my lord values me, as the Darkness does him, and both will avenge me!'

The Devourer of Worlds values nothing that has outlived its usefulness, and as for your master, we suspect that he too will be glad to see the last of you. Look at yourself, Keral.

The great cat opened wide his luminous eyes. In their depths, the changer saw himself, and flinched.

Mirrors aren't to your liking any more, are they? We remember when they were, but that was millennia ago. Since then, you say, you have become immortal. The Mistress reaped souls to keep Gerridon of Knorth young; but you have gained your 'immortality' by coupling with the foulest shadows that creep in the farthest rooms of the Master's House, across the thresholds of a hundred fallen worlds. Now you crawl back to them whenever lust or severe injury drives you and find renewal in their arms. But they warp you, Keral, body and soul, more and more each time. Even now you can no longer hold any true shape. Soon you will crawl on your belly like some pallid slug until your very bones liquify. What price immortality then? It would be more merciful to give you back to these flames, to a quick death.

The changer gave a bleat of terror and tried to drag himself away, but the Arrin-ken pinned him, almost absentmindedly, with one great paw.

Ah, yes, but are we inclined to be merciful? No, we think not. Good-bye, Keral. May you live a long, long time.

With that, the huge beast reared up, black against the flames. As a cat might a mouse, he hooked the changer into the air and batted him into the chasm. Keral's scream faded into the distance, ending suddenly. Then the great cat turned to the fire and, in that silent voice woven of many voices, spoke a word. The flames died. Most of the storm had been consumed, leaving a night sky scattered with stars and lit by a full moon now just peering over the shoulder of Mount Timor. It shone on a mountainous landscape reduced almost to its underlying rocks. Water cascaded down them. Here and there, steam hissed up from heated stones. The Arrin-ken turned back to Jame.

And now, as our friend said, 'Your turn, Jamethiel.'

Jame tried to speak, but only managed to croak.

Think it, child, said a cool, deep voice in her head. This time it spoke alone. Under it ran the detached murmur of those other voices which, Jame suddenly realised, must belong to the other Arrin-ken in their distant retreats. One had a rustle in it as if of dried leaves, another sparkled with the bright sound of a mountain stream, a third echoed to the sea's boom, and so on and on. They all seemed to be discussing her.

W-we met once, in the hills above Tai-tastigon, she said silently to the great beast before her. *You taught Jorin how to hunt and... and you at least weren't hostile to me. But now, somehow, I don't think I've been rescued.*

Not necessarily. Then, you see, I didn't know your name.

'I'm not –' she began, then stopped, choking. *I'm not Jamethiel Dream-Weaver. It may be my misfortune to be named after her, but surely it isn't my fault.*

Perhaps. So, not the Mistress, but in possession of the

Master's property, or so he would claim, just as he claims the Ivory Knife and the Serpent-Skin Cloak, all kept by him in Perimal Darkling when the elder world fell. And yet here the Book is now. Are you a runaway Darkling?

Jame stared up at him. *I have been beyond the Barrier, yes, but I'm not a Darkling. Sweet Trinity, can't you tell?*

Not easily. You have more than a touch of the Darkling glamour. Did you steal the Book?

This brought Jame up short. The Master certainly hadn't given it to her. In fact, she suspected that everyone at her old home keep had been killed by Gerridon of Knorth when he had come there searching for both it and her. She had been a 'prentice thief in Tai-tastigon with the priest Ishtier's grudging permission, provided she never stole from one of her own kind. Her honour had depended on that. But had she already forfeited it by stealing from the Master? The past was an abyss into which only the faintest rays of light fell. What *had* she done in Perimal Darkling, and what had been done to her?

The moon had slipped behind the Pass now. Fingers of shadow from the Ebonbane's ragged spine scrawled over what was left of the snowfield. The Arrin-ken sat watching Jame, his luminous, unblinking eyes a good three feet above her own. His outline had vanished altogether in the sudden gloom of moonfall, but she felt his presence as one does that of some huge, immovable object in the dark.

I'm on trial, she thought suddenly, with an involuntary shiver, *and this is my judge.*

Yes, she must have stolen the book – but was the Master really of the Three People any more? If he was, he was also still the rightful Highlord of the Kencyrath. But the Arrin-ken had stripped him of that title and given it to Glendar, his younger half-brother, who had then led the flight to Rathillien. So Gerridon of Knorth had indeed been judged a traitor, bereft of rights, and she hadn't stolen the Book at all but only retrieved it.

Agreed.

The silent word made Jame start. The Arrin-ken must have been following her thoughts as easily as if she had shouted them. Anger touched a spark to her already frayed nerves.

If you already knew, why did you ask? Damnit, stop playing games!

Amusement cool as a wind off the heights answered her. *Ah, no. I may tease, but I also test. For those ignorant of the Law, some allowances are made. You are not ignorant, therefore you are responsible.*

Trinity! *For what?*

Perhaps for everything.

Abruptly, Jame felt another mind enter her own. Even though it was shielding itself, she felt as if the entire Ebonbane had just unfolded in her consciousness. Something stalked her through it on velvet paws. It followed the scent of certain memories and tracked them down...

She was dancing at the Res aB'tyrr. Her career as the B'tyrr had begun when a rival innkeeper had sent ruffians to destroy the inn that had become her adopted home. To gain time, Cleppetty had told her to dance for the mob. She had, with great trepidation, not even sure that she knew how. But she did. Where had she learned this strange, intoxicating dance that somehow fed on those who watched it? What was it doing to them? To her? That worried her sometimes, but not now as she danced. Now there was only exultation, and growing hunger.

She stood in the temple of her god. The priest Ishtier, possessed, was booming obscure prophecies while in the outer corridors uncontrolled power ran mad. She must dance it down or they would all die, and she did.

She knelt in the snows of the Ebonbane with the Book open on her knees and said, 'BURN.'

'No!' Jame gasped, and wrenched her mind and memory free. It was the present again.

The Arrin-ken's silent voice broke over her, implacable as the cold that shatters trees in winter, woven with the sounds of sea, desert, and forest. *Child, you have perverted the Great Dance as your namesake did before you. You have also usurped a priest's authority and misused a Master Rune. We conclude that you are indeed a Darkling, in training if not in blood. On the whole, your intentions have been good, but your behaviour has been reckless to the point of madness and your nascent powers barely under control. Three days ago, you nearly destroyed a city. Now, shall we let such a one as you loose on our poor, battered people? Answer, child.*

Jame stared at the great cat. She must say something – yes, no – but her mind had gone completely blank.

Then there was a sound behind her. A hand came up over the edge of the crevasse and fumbled for a hold. Before the other one could appear, clutching the double headed war-axe, Jame was on her knees grabbing for Marc's sleeve.

'Sorry it took me so long,' he said apologetically, hauling himself up. 'I heard you call, but I'd just landed on a scrap of a ledge down there and had the breath knocked out of me. Then it rained fire. Then a wyrsa fell on me – or at least I think it was a wyrsa. But what's happened here?'

'Company,' Jame croaked, indicating the huge, silent cat.

Marc regarded the Arrin-ken with awe. Like most Kencyr, he had never seen one before. 'My lord, your servant,' he said formally. 'So, everything has come out all right at last.'

'Not quite,' said Jame, struggling to bring out the words. 'I think . . . that he . . . means to kill me.'

'Kill you? But why?'

'Because . . . of what I am.'

The big Kendar gave her a perplexed look. If he wondered what she meant, however, he didn't ask. Instead, almost absentmindedly, he picked up his weapon.

'Lord or no, I don't see how I can permit that.'

Jame was appalled. It might be pleasant on a winter's night to sit around the hearth discussing what chance a three hundred and fifty pound, ninety-four year old axe-man would have against a six hundred pound, nearly immortal cat, but she had no desire to see it put to the test.

'You idiot!' she croaked, stepping between them. 'Before I'd . . . let you do that, I'd . . . chuck myself into . . . that damn crevasse.'

In an instant, impossibly, she was falling. The reeling darkness closed about her. No sky, no walls of rock, no ledge either. She had missed it. But she didn't miss the steep, rock studded slope below that broke both her fall and several ribs as she tumbled down it. A moment more in the air, and then a smashing blow. She was lying on the floor of the crevasse, face down in half-melted snow. Blood bubbled in her throat. When she tried to move and couldn't, she realised that her back was broken.

Nearby, something stirred. Rocks shifted, grating, as a heavy body dragged itself painfully over them towards her. She couldn't even turn her head. The sound of hoarse breathing echoed off the chasm walls, nearer, nearer, and then came a low, ragged laugh.

'My turn . . . again, Jamethiel.'

'That's enough,' said a familiar voice sharply, as from a distance. 'Stop it.'

She found herself huddled at the lip of the crevasse with Marc kneeling beside her, his big hands on her shoulders.

'Did you hear me?' he said again, speaking over her head in an angrier tone than she had ever heard him use before. 'I said, "Stop it!"'

The Arrin-ken sat like a boulder, watching them. This time, she realised, he had drawn not on her memories but on foreknowledge. That was exactly what it would be like to jump, to die down there in the dark, helpless at that creature's mercy.

Your choice, Jamethiel.

Suddenly, Jame was very, very angry. She shook off the Kendar's hands and rose. The mountain air still vibrated with the power set loose by the Master Rune, which the countersign had not wholly dispersed. With a sweeping defiant gesture of the dark dance, she gathered in the errant force to tingle down exhausted nerves like strong wine on an empty stomach.

'My choice.' Her voice, stronger now, caught the same purring note as the Arrin-ken's but with an even colder undernote. 'My choice! So I can jump or see you fight and probably kill my friend. But what if there's a third alternative? You like games, cat, don't you? Well, perhaps it's your turn to play "Mouse."'

'Lass, don't...'

Marc touched her arm, then recoiled with a sharp exclamation. His hand shook as if with sudden palsy. Jame hardly noticed. With the abrupt influx of power, the night had seemed to unfold around her. She felt the patterns of force that wove through it: the vipers' knot of energy to the east that was Tai-tastigon, still seething after three days; the changer's hectic heartbeat as he lay in the cold, open grave of the crevasse; but before her sat the Arrin-ken, like some great rock around which all currents must flow. When she probed for the patterns that made up his life, her mind slid off them as if off rimed marble. His aloofness provoked her. She would weave the dance around him. She would lure him out of his inner citadel and ... and ... what?

Strange thoughts stirred in the depths of Jame's mind, and a stranger hunger that she remembered as if from some half-forgotten dream. It would be sweet to reap the soul of an Arrin-ken.

But what was that? The very night seemed to shift, as though shockwaves rippled through it. The Arrin-ken's massive head lifted. He had felt it, too. The mountains to the north blotted

286

out much of the sky, but behind their peaks a light grew. It became brighter, brighter, and then its source shot into view, blazing like a comet. Jame thought she saw a figure at its heart, dancing down through the night. She found the Arrin-ken standing at her side.

I was wrong. The Master wants his pet changer back after all. Beware her touch.

Her?

The light shot overhead. It circled the field and came flashing back. For a moment, it hovered over the crevasse, then Jame felt its attention shift. It landed. Gliding towards her like a sleepwalker was the most beautiful woman she had ever seen, and one whom, surely, she had seen somewhere before. But her mind didn't seem to be working properly. She couldn't think, couldn't even move as the other reached out to her. A slim, ivory hand touched her cheek. The woman was smiling dreamily at her, murmuring... something, but all Jame heard was a great buzzing in her ears. Her borrowed power flowed from her like blood from a gaping wound. She felt as if her very soul was about to be ripped away. The woman's eyes were a cool, almost inhuman silver, but their pupils plunged down, down beneath the dreaming face. In their depths, on the edge of black chaos, a white figure danced on and on desperately, as if afraid to stop. Jame plummeted towards her. The woman raised her head...

... and abruptly Jame found herself on the ground with the Arrin-ken crouching between her and the shining woman.

Mistress, take what you came for and go. Nothing else here belongs to you – yet.

The woman's smile shivered, as though about to crack, then froze again. She bowed and, like a falling star, plunged into the crevasse, only to shoot out a moment later with the changer's broken body dark in her arms. He was shrieking, in far more pain that ever the fall had caused him. Scream and light faded into the distance until the darkness of the north swallowed both.

Jame struggled up on one elbow, feeling drained. If not for the buffer of extra power, that woman would have drunk her soul to the very lees with her cold touch, not because she wanted to, but because it was her nature. But what had the Arrin-ken called her?

The great cat sat as before, his unblinking eyes on her.

Yes, that was the Dream-Weaver, although nightmares are more her lot now.

'Trinity,' said Jame out loud, almost reverently. *But why was she so interested in me?*

You don't spend much time in front of a mirror, do you?

With this face? Of course not. But what...

A sound interrupted her. Jorin was stumbling towards her, even his blind, moon-opal eyes managing to look unfocused. Jame hugged him joyfully. Marc knelt beside them. His face was pale, but the arms he put around them both were as steady as ever.

'So, everything has worked out after all.'

Jame looked at the Arrin-ken. *Has it?*

That depends. Do you still want to play cat and mouse?

'Oh, hell.' Jame felt her face redden. What in Perimal's name had she been thinking of? *Of course I won't fight you, lord, and neither will my friend, even if I still have to throw myself over the edge to prevent it.* She swallowed, remembering the cold, lonely death that awaited her there below. At least the changer wouldn't be on hand to enliven things.

That is still your choice, as it always was. All the voices were back, purring together. *You judged yourself, child. You chose the pit. We expected your power and recklessness, but not that. It seems that you are willing to take what responsibility you can for your actions. An unfallen darkling. We would not have believed that possible. Clearly, there are forces at work here beyond even our understanding.*

Marc nudged Jame. 'What is Lord Cat saying? All I hear is a rumble.'

'I'm not sure, but I think I've just been given a reprieve.'

Yes. Only the silent voice of the big cat before them answered. *The best part of wisdom is knowing when not to meddle. Besides, someone has to take that accursed Book back to the Kencyrath, and it seems to have chosen you.*

For lack of anyone more sensible. Jame thought.

Perhaps. Its tastes were always... eccentric, but I gave up quarrelling with both them and it millennia ago. The great objects of power choose their own paths, and this one is returning home none too soon. A storm is brewing over the Riverland, over all Rathillien, north and south. I hear thunder, and horns blowing. And I see darkness across your path, child. Tai-tastigon was a sheltered place. Others besides Keral may be waiting for you to break cover. Beware of them, but even more, beware of yourself.

'I don't understand.'

No? Then look.

The big cat opened wide his luminous eyes. Jame stared at herself reflected in them, at the high cheekbones, the sharp lines of nose and chin, the large, silver-grey eyes that stared back at her. She looked in mirrors so seldom that her own face was almost that of a stranger to her, but this time it was familiar in an unexpected way. This time, from certain angles, she might almost have thought that the Mistress looked back at her.

'I-I still don't understand.'

Then you truly are an innocent . . . but innocence and even good intentions are sometimes poor protection. Take a lesson from your namesake. Jamethiel Dream-Weaver didn't understand the evil that Gerridon asked her to commit until it was too late. She never really consented to it. Nonetheless, her abuse of power opened the deepest reaches of her soul to the void beyond the Chain of Creation where Perimal Darkling itself was spawned. At first, that breech was small, manageable, but over the past few decades it has gaped wider and wider. Now souls fall into it through her as if into a vortex, and she must dance on and on at its brink or be consumed by it herself.

'B-but just now, she smiled at me . . .'

You were probably like a dream to her. All the external world must be, now. Mind and soul, she dances and dares not stop while her body drifts on at her Master's will. Be warned, child. That could happen to you, or worse. The Dream-Weaver acted in ignorance and so bears only partial responsibility for her actions. You may still be innocent, but not ignorant – and you have already played at the very game that doomed the first Jamethiel. If you do eventually fall, it will be as the Master fell, knowing the evil you do, welcoming it. The abuse of power will push you in that direction. On the other hand, its mere use may drive you the other way, towards our god. That is what it means to be a Shanir, to walk the knife's edge.

Jame shuddered. 'But I don't want to fall either way!'

A rich, rumbling chuckle answered her. *Which one of us does? For us, alas, good is no less terrible than evil. We can only trust our honour and try to keep our balance. I commend you to both. Now I will escort you over the pass and as far down the other side as Peshtar. There you can refit and, who knows, perhaps find a new pair of boots.*

'Boots?' repeated Marc, apparently catching this last word if nothing else. For the first time, he noticed that Jame was only half shod. 'Here now, how long ago did that happen? You could easily lose a foot to frostbite up here.'

Jame wriggled her toes inside the wet sock. 'That's odd. They aren't even cold. Are you?'

'No.'

Overhead loomed Mount Timor, stripped now of snow but ice-sheathed after the fire-storm thaw. Although a bitter wind blew off it, only traces of it reached the field below. Jame and Marc looked at each other, then at the Arrin-ken. Jorin had tottered over to the big cat and was leaning against him, eyes closed in bliss, as the great beast bent down to lick his head. At their feet, glowing faintly in the first light of dawn, lay a white carpet of star-shaped spring flowers.

16

The Hell Hunt
Tagmeth and Kithorn: 6th-7th of Winter

The hanging man moved restlessly in the breeze under his oak bough, his feet barely clearing the tall weeds sprung up between the River Road's paving stones. His body had been encased in boiled leather, moulded to his limbs and sealed with wax. Only his gaping mouth and distended nostrils remained open to the cold night air. He faced northward towards the mountains of his people. Then the wind caught him and he turned east, then south to stare with leather-blinded eyes down the road into the curving valley of the Riverland.

The two men on horseback looked at him.

'A watch-weirdling,' said the younger, slighter of the two. 'So this is why we had to leave our weapons at Tagmeth. What kind of a noise does this thing make when it smells Kencyr steel?'

'You wouldn't want to hear it.' The burly Kendar scowled mistrustfully at the tangled shadows lining the road before them. 'This is the edge of our territory, lord. The Riverland may belong to the Kencyrath, but these hills haven't been ours since Kithorn fell to the Merikit nearly eighty years ago. Another step and that thing will scent the iron in our horse gear. Turn back, Lord Torisen. Please.'

'Please?' The Highlord looked at him, a glint of amusement in his tired, silver-grey eyes. 'You haven't used that word on me since Urakarn. Where would you be now if I'd listened to you then?' He dismounted and tethered Storm, his black quarter-blood Whinno-hir, to a bush. The stallion snorted, his breath white plumes in the sharp air, and tried to back away from the hanging corpse as the wind turned it creaking to face him. Torisen quieted him.

'You forget,' he said in the same soothing tone, looking up at Burr. 'I'm on an inspection tour of the northern keeps, and

Kithorn is the northernmost of the lot, except for a few like my old home up near the Barrier. Stay with the horses, if you like. I shouldn't be long.'

He turned and walked up the overgrown road.

Burr shook his head. '"Stay," he says. Huh!' He tied his grey horse next to Torisen's black and followed his lord.

Dry leaves crackled underfoot, cold stone rang. This was the grey margin between autumn and winter, with bare branches stark against a full moon and fat snowflakes drifting down from a nearly cloudless sky. In the distance, a fox barked. It was almost midnight, and bitterly cold.

Back at Tagmeth, watchfires would be burning in the ruined courtyard while Torisen's Kendar retainers lay rolled in their blankets beside them. Burr remembered the cheerful glow fading behind them as they had slipped out into the night like a pair of thieves. He wondered if Torisen – always so quick to chill – was warm enough now, but knew better than to ask. He himself missed his short sword more than the fire's warmth. If the Highlord should be attacked here, so far from help...

Tagmeth, from which the two had come, had been empty for a long time. Like all the paired keeps that faced each other across the Silver at twenty to twenty-five mile intervals down the length of the Riverland, it had been built nearly a thousand years before to guard the northern frontier between the ancient kingdoms of Bashti and Hathir. Both the Riverland and the keeps had eventually been ceded to the Kencyrath so that it might serve as a buffer state here in the far north. Tagmeth had been claimed once, then abandoned as blood feuds and foreign wars thinned the ranks of the Highborn and the great houses began to gather their strength in keeps farther south. Now frost-blackened brier roses scrambled in and out of Tagmeth's shattered walls and owls roosted in what was left of its rafters.

Its semi-ruined state had intrigued the Highborn boys who had come there with Torisen. They had clambered all over it at the risk of their necks, hunting relics of its past life, disturbing bats and foxes. Then, that evening they had sat around the fire in its solar above the hall, under the open sky, sipping hot mulled wine and trying to sound like seasoned warriors on campaign. They had quite forgotten that the Highlord of the Kencyrath was in the same room. Torisen had withdrawn to a window ledge just beyond the light, where he quietly sat, warming his hands on his wine cup, watching the boys' flushed faces.

Every six months, he summoned nine different Highborn youngsters from various houses of the Kencyrath to serve him. Some, one day, might become the heads of their respective families; others might die in the vicious blood feuds that still wracked the Highborn even after three years of relative calm under Torisen's rule. He wanted these boys to know him, and each other. If the Houses ever became as linked by friendship as they were by blood, perhaps at last the killing would stop. But that was years in the future.

Still, he reminded himself, when this lot first assembled at Gothregor a month ago, he had thought it might take decades, if not centuries. These boys were the Highborn in microcosm. Four came from major houses, five from minor ones; most were only distant or bone kin to each other except for Morien and Brishney, half-brothers; and nearly all had some blood feud festering at home. There was even one of Lord Caineron's numerous grandsons here: Donkerri, a timid, palefaced boy who had clearly been reared to think of Torisen as Grandpa's greatest enemy, which he probably was. The Highlord had brought the whole troop on this inspection tour largely to keep them from each other's throats. And it had worked. The leisurely two-week trip up the Silver, with its hunting and camping – not to mention visits to all the keeps north of Gothregor – had brough most of them closer than he had dared hope, even if they were still a bit shy of him. Now as they sat around the fire sipping wine and talking, he regarded them one by one, remembering all the good men lost to blood feuds over the years, wondering how long these boys would honour their campfire fellowship.

Their voices began to blur. Torisen jerked his head up, shying away from the ambush of sleep. Burr was watching him. He forced himself to concentrate on the boys' chatter.

'We're close to Kithorn here,' Morien was saying. 'Brishney, remember when we went bone hunting on a winter's night like this four years ago and nearly got caught by a Merikit hunting party?'

Brickeny laughed. 'I remember. It's a good thing we brought back that tibula for the pyre or Father would have finished the Merikits' work for them.'

Torisen raised his eyebrows. 'Explain,' he said quietly to Burr as the Kendar refilled his cup.

The boys started at the sound of his voice and exchanged glances. Burr shook his head.

'He wouldn't know about it, lord,' said Brishney. 'It's ... well, it's a kind of open secret among us boys. You see, Kithorn fell through treachery. One night, a Merikit hall-guest opened the gate to his kinsmen, and every Kencyr there, Highborn and Kendar alike, was slaughtered.'

'Surely that's no secret.'

'No, m'lord, of course not. You've probably heard that most of the bodies were recovered the next spring when word of the massacre filtered south. But some couldn't be found. Boys started slipping into the hills on bone hunts. Our grandfathers started it, and our fathers went, too. Now we go, although there's precious little left to find, and we get beaten at home if we're caught at it; but, well, it's become a sort of ritual, and Trinity help the boy who doesn't visit Kithorn at least once before he turns fifteen.'

They began to compare notes. All had their own stories of search if not success and, often, of narrow escape, for the hills were well guarded. Only Donkerri was silent. When at last someone asked him what his luck had been, instead of answering he turned suddenly towards the shadowy figure seated on the window ledge.

'How old were you, Highlord, when you went up into the hills?' he demanded.

The others stared at Donkerri.

'Donkey, you ass...' hissed Brishney urgently.

'How old?'

At fifteen, half a lifetime ago, escaping the nightmare of his father's keep, the terrible trip south through the Haunted Lands, Ardeth's Riverland keep... 'Sir, I am Ganth Gray Lord's son.' 'If you stay here, boy, the other Highborn will kill you. Join the Southern Host under my name. They'll think you're some bastard son of mine I'm trying to get rid of, but never mind. Here's your commission, and a servant, Burr.' At fifteen, learning to fight, to command and, at the red ruin of Urakarn, to survive.

The boys were staring at him, Caineron's grandson white-faced his hands clenched together as though to hold him in his seat.

'I didn't grow up in the Riverland,' Torisen said quietly. 'Your grandfather must have told you that.' *Children,* he thought, looking at them. *They're all children. You can't make them stay up all night just because you're afraid to sleep.* He rose and stretched. 'That's enough for now. Yes, I know it's still fairly early, but remember that we start back tomorrow at daybreak. Now go to bed.'

They filed out, still subdued. Burr collected the wine cups.

'You should send that brat home,' he said over his shoulder.

'Donkerri? The boy just didn't want to admit that he'd never been to Kithorn.'

The Kendar snorted. 'His grandfather's keep is close enough. You could ride from Restormir to Kithorn in four hours.'

'Let it rest, Burr.' Torisen rubbed his stinging eyes. 'We all find our own rites of passage.'

'*You* should rest. It's been four nights now.'

'So you've kept count.'

Burr froze, his hand inches from a cup.

'And to whom will you pass that information now that Ardeth is no longer your master? Poor Burr, after all those years of spying on me and now no one to accept his reports. Oh hell,' said Torisen abruptly, in quite a different tone. 'Sorry. Get some sleep yourself. I still have work to do.'

The Kendar bowed silently and left the room.

Torisen sat down by the firepit. When he held his cold, scarred hands out to the flames, they shook. *You're weak, boy,* his father's voice jeered at him out of the past. *As weak as your sister.* But Jame had never been weak, even as a child. *They won't teach me how to fight, Tori, but you will. I'll make you.* And she had tried, pouncing on him when he least expected it, learning snatches of the Senethar from his counter moves. Trinity, but he had been furious. How long ago that had been... and why was he thinking of it now? *Forget the past,* he told himself. *You have no time for the dead. Now, to work.*

He drew a sheaf of papers from his saddlebag. The first was a formal note from Prince Odalian of Karkinor, an ancient princedom far to the south near the Cataracts. The Prince congratulated the Highlord on his third year of successful rule. Torisen snorted. Successful, perhaps, in that he hadn't yet managed to get himself assassinated. But Odalian didn't mean that. His family, the Agontiri, had always had close ties to the Kencyrath because their capital city – in fact, their very palace – was built around a Kencyr temple.

Odd how other people so often seemed drawn to those nine houses on Rathillien of the Three-Faced God. Kencyr preferred to avoid them, partly because they shunned everything connected with their hated god, partly because no one, not even the priests, fully understood the temples. Kencyr hands hadn't even built them. Every time the Three People had been forced to retreat to a new threshold world, the temples had simply been there, waiting for them. Because all the temples on all the worlds bore the same architectural signature, as it were, scrollsmen suggested that their god had bound or at least commissioned a fourth people and sent them ahead to prepare the way. For lack of a proper name, these hypothetical folk were simply called the Builders. Their work was certainly impressive, but also unnerving, at least to Kencyr.

Those Kencyr priests obliged to serve at the Karkinaroth temple were the honoured guests of the Agontiri. Odalian had recently gone one step beyond his status as host, though, by marrying the only Highborn lady even permitted to form an alliance outside the Kencryrath. Torisen suspected that the Prince would gladly become a Kencyr himself if that were possible. Well, there was no accounting for taste. He would answer the letter when he got back to Gothregor.

Next came a bundle of documents, claim and counter-claim. This was more serious business. Lord Coman of Kraggen Keep had recently died without designating a successor. It was customary in such instances as this for the oldest son to become the new head of the household. This would have suited Torisen well enough in one sense because Demoth, the son in question, was half an Ardeth and had virtually promised to follow his lead in all High Council votes. But he had his doubts about Demoth's ability to command. So, apparently, did most of the elders of Demoth's own family, who supported a younger son named Korey. Unfortunately, Korey's mother was a Caineron, and to give that family any more influence could prove fatal to the Highlord's own power.

The whole business made Torisen's head ache. How was he supposed to make a fair choice between the Coman's interests and his own, which might be considered those of the Kencyrath as a whole? This was the sort of problem that really needed the impartial judgement of the Arrin-ken; but in the great cats' absence, the other Highborn had accepted him as Highlord so that he might judge such cases and stave off the cataclysmic civil war that had seemed only one more blood feud away. Caineron must really have been desperate to have accepted such a check to his ambition, or maybe he had thought that he could easily dispose of Torisen when the time was right. All the lords must have felt equally endangered to have accepted on his word alone, without ring or sword, that he was Ganth Gray Lord's son. Even Ardeth must have had his doubts at first. Of course, he had wanted reports while Torisen fought under his standard with the Southern Host, and Burr had had to supply them. It was unfair, almost irrational, to hold that against Burr, but he still did.

Torisen recoiled from the thought. That was how it began, the slow slide down into madness. It ran in the Knorth blood. Ganth had died insane, screaming curses at the silent warriors out of Perimal Darkling who had broken into his keep, ravaging, slaughtering. Torisen had gone more than two weeks without a normal night's sleep trying to stave off the horrible dream that had shown him his father's death. That had been just after he came of age three years ago and couldn't decide whether or not to claim the Highlord's seat. His intolerable restlessness had finally driven him from the Southern Host and into the Wastes, where he had taken refuge in one of the vast, ruined cities whose bones littered the desert. But the nightmare had come anyway. They always did. Did he believe them? No, of course not. To far-see, even in dreams, was a Shanir trait and he – ancestors be praised – was no Shanir. But he had believed that dream enough to claim his father's power, and the other Highborn had given it to him.

The flames ran together before his eyes, close, much too close. The papers had caught fire. He threw them into the pit, cursing. Obviously he wasn't going to stay awake if he just sat here thinking. *Dwar* sleep? Six hours of its healing oblivion would certainly help, but what if this time the dreams followed him even there? To be trapped, unable to awake... He rose and began to pace restlessly about the room.

Burr had stretched out on the landing in front of the upper chamber's door. He woke abruptly as someone stepped over him and, without thinking, grabbed the other's foot.

'Now, Burr,' said Torisen's voice softly above him the darkness. 'D'you really want me to fall down these stairs head first?'

Burr let go and sprang up. 'My lord, where are you going?'

'Out.'

Burr swore under his breath. He knew only too well Torisen's habit of wandering about at night unescorted when he didn't want to sleep. In fact, that was why Burr was here now. 'Those wretched boys and their bone-hunting stories...'

'Kithorn? Now there's an idea. Much obliged to you, Burr. Now go back to sleep.'

'No. I can't stop you, my lord, but if I raise my voice, others will.'

'And you will no longer be in my service – which, on the whole, would be a pity. All right, we compromise. How do you fancy a moonlight ride to Kithorn, Burr?'

The Kendar sighed. 'I'll get the horses, my lord.'

And now they were almost there. Above them on its bluff, the fortress hunched sullenly against the mountains' darkness. Its outer ward was surrounded by overgrown cloud-of-thorn bushes whose berries hung like drops of dark blood in a lacework of three-inch spikes. Burr noticed something black on one of the bushes. It was a bat, upside down with its wings spread, impaled on a thorn. There was another on the next bush, and another and another, all with charm beads hung around their necks, all in various stages of decomposition. Burr slowed instinctively, feeling his scalp prickle. What were they doing here? This land no longer belonged to the Kencyrath – if, indeed, it ever really had. It didn't want them here now.

But what was that? He stopped short, straining to hear. Drums? The nearest Merikit village was only half a mile upstream. Then the wind veered, taking the distant throb with it.

If Torisen had also heard, he gave no sign. Burr hurried after him. They had come now to the ruined gatehouse, covered with vines. Wild grape leaves rattled down on them as they passed under its shadow and began to climb the steep road to the outer shell of the keep.

Inside, all was ruin.

They stood in the middle of the inner courtyard beside the well, looking about. The tumbled ruins of the armoury, bakehouse, and granary lined the inner wall. Ahead loomed the tower keep. This has been the stronghold of a very old but minor house, already well on its way to extinction when the Merikit had wiped it out.

Torisen could see it all too clearly; the hall-guest creeping out in the dead of night, cutting the guard's throat, opening the main gate, the silent tribesmen pouring into the courtyard.... A spark of fire, and there went the halls' thatch, roaring up into the night. The Kendar tried to get out, but the doors were blocked. They threw wet blankets over their children and started to hack at the walls. Some cut their way out, only to die in the open, fighting, with shrieks from the tower echoing around them...

Now leafless vines hung over the walls, and saplings grew in the blackened ruins. Torisen shook his head to clear it. For a moment, he had almost plunged into the dream-memory of his own home's fall, had almost thought he heard small bare feet running, running, with fire and death behind them. Jame? No, of course not. She had been driven out of their father's keep long before the end; he should have left too, before the old man's madness had reached out for him.

'So they all died,' he said, and hardly knew which keep he meant.

'Not quite all, lord. There was one survivor, a Kendar boy named Marcarn, who was out hunting by himself when all this happened. Afterward, he hunted the Merikit and killed one for each member of his lord's family and his own to pay the blood price. Of course, he only did what he had to, but because of him, the hills have been closed to us ever since.'

'He must have been a great warrior,' said Torisen rather absently.

'Oh yes, and a thumping big man too, when he was full grown. Like a siege tower walking. But for all that, I don't think he was very fond of bloodshed.' Burr smiled. 'He used to feign berserker fits in battle to scare off the enemy. It worked so well that some of our own lads went straight up the nearest tree the first time they saw it. I nearly did myself. But that was thirty years ago and more. Good old Marc. I wonder where he is now.'

Torisen was no longer listening. He had crossed over to the far wall to look at something. Behind the vines was the crude image of a face, gap-mouthed and eyeless, drawn in dark lines on the pale stone. Beside it was another and another, all down the length of the wall. They were *imus*, symbols of a power so ancient that all but the name had been lost – or so most civilised men believed. Torisen touched one of the lines. It came away in brown flakes on his fingertips.

'Dried blood,' he said, sniffing it. 'Human, I think. Burr, you were right: we don't belong here.' Suddenly he stiffened. 'There, again!'

'Lord?'

'Don't you hear it? The patter of small feet running, running... I didn't imagine it!'

Burr wasn't so sure. His own senses weren't as keen as Torisen's, but then sleep-starved men often heard and saw things that weren't there. Then Burr did hear something, all too clearly.

'Drums,' he said.

Torisen was already halfway up the crumbling stair that led to the battlement. Moonlight gleamed on the river as it twisted northward through the dark hills into the darker mountains. About half a mile up stream in the Merikit village, a great fire burned. Figures shuffled around it to the beat of a drum, while their chanting, borne southward by a freshening wind, grew louder and louder. Burr leaned forward over the parapet, straining to hear.

'"Come, Burnt Man. Come, Burning Ones,"' he translated. '"We mark him and cast him out, now hunt, hunt..." Trinity!'

A scream had cut across the chant, shrill as a woman in pain, but from no woman's throat. A dead silence followed. Then, from far up in the hills, came the booming answer, hoarse, wordless, inhuman. The men around the fire scattered. The flames flared up once, then sank, dying away altogether within seconds. In the darkness that followed, a distant yelping began, far, far away, but getting rapidly nearer.

'I take it we picked a bad night to visit.'

Burr grunted. 'You might say that, lord. The Merikit have driven out a kin-killer – probably a parricide – and called the damned down out of the hills to claim him, if he doesn't outrun them to the border.'

'That, I suppose, puts us directly in his path, and theirs. Time to make for home, old friend.'

They descended to the inner courtyard. At the foot of the stair, Torisen suddenly caught Burr's arm. 'There!' he said. 'Running, running... look!'

Burr saw the shadow sweep across the flagstones towards the keep and glanced upward for the night-bird that must have cast it. There was none. When he looked back, Torisen was halfway across the courtyard, darting after the shadow. Burr ran after him, shouting.

'Lord, the keep floor is rotten! Don't go –'

But the Highlord had already raced up the steps and through the keep's door. There was a splintering crash. Burr paused on the threshold, blinded by the darkness within.

'Oh God. Tori...'

'Mind your step,' said Torisen's voice, apparently from under the earth.

Steel struck flint, and a flicker of firelight outlined the jagged hole in the floor from underneath.

'Burr, you'd better come down here. I've found her.'

Her?

The Kendar edged cautiously up to the hole, hearing timbers groan underfoot, then jumped down into the keep's still room. The chamber was surprisingly undisturbed, considering the destruction above. Jars of preserves lined the walls, the seals still intact on those that hadn't long since exploded. Under them were jugs, their remaining contents unrecognisable under a five inch fur of dust. The corners of the room were buried as deep.

Torisen had set fire to a heap of wooden utensils on a side table and now crouched by the still's boiler, looking at something on the floor behind it. As Burr peered over his shoulder, he carefully folded back the tattered blanket. Under it was a huddled pile of bones, pathetically small and defenceless without even a scrap of cloth or flesh to cover them.

'There are no bloodstains on this,' Burr said, examining the blanket.

'No. She must have fled here on the night of the massacre and died of shock and starvation, in the midst of all these provisions. A child's soul, trapped in these ruins for eighty years.... Burr, we've got to take her home.'

The Kendar grunted, almost with amusement. 'What else? But quickly, my lord. The hell hunt will be snapping at our heels as it is.'

Torisen spread the blanket on the floor and hastily piled the bones on it while Burr held up a burning wooden spoon to light the work. Then the Highborn ran his fingers through the dust in a final check, knotted together the corners of the blanket, and rose. By now, the side table was also on fire. The preserves behind it began to explode with the heat.

'Right,' said Torisen, ducking a spray of sticky glass. 'Now we leave at a dead run before the wine cellar below this goes. Oh lord,' he said, seeing Burr's expression. 'You mean there actually is one? Climb, man. You first.'

301

The Kendar scrambled up out of the hole, getting splinters under his nails, and turned barely in time to catch the blanket bundle as Torisen tossed it up to him. The Highlord swung himself up. At the keep door, however, he stopped suddenly, a hand thrown back in warning.

A man had come staggering into the courtyard through the main gate. He was dressed in the usual Merikit leathers and furs. His coarse black hair should have been braided, one plait on the right side for each son sired, one on the left for each man killed, but the right hand braids had been hacked off and the ones on the left apparently burned away. He looked wildly about, panting, then lurched towards the tower keep.

'Take the child and run,' said Torisen without looking around. 'Use the back way.' He stepped forward over the threshold.

The Merikit stopped by the well, staring at him. Then he came on, his hands held out as if in supplication, making formless sounds. Torisen saw that his tongue had been cut out.

'Parricide,' he said softly.

The yelping was very close now, just beyond the gatehouse. 'Wha? Wha? Wha?' belled the pursuers. *Where? Where? Where? Here!* They were coming up the road to the main gate.

The Merikit turned at bay.

The hunting cry died as the Burning Ones swarmed into the courtyard. They were men, or once had been. Now they ran on all fours, or on wrist bones and knees for those whose hands or feet had dropped off. As they moved, their charred skin cracked open in fissures ember red and glowing like those on a half-burnt log. With them came the stench of burning flesh and a continual sizzling.

They played the Merikit back and forth across the courtyard as he bolted in yammering panic first one way and then another. Where they touched him, his clothes smouldered. Then he tripped. Hissing, they swarmed over his thrashing body and began to feed.

Burr pulled Torisen back inside the tower and slammed the door. 'Those are only the hounds. D'you want to meet the Hunt-Master?'

'I told you to leave by the back way.'

'There isn't one.'

At that moment, the fire at last reached the wine cellar and a pillar of spirit-fed flame came roaring up through the hole in the floor. The two Kencyr backed away, scorched by the heat.

'Climb!' Torisen shouted over the uproar, pointing to a mural stair. They scrambled up to the second level. Even there, the air was rapidly growing hot and a lurid glare came up between the cracks in the floor boards. Torisen went to a south window.

'Too far to jump,' he said, eyeing the shell's curtain wall some twenty feet away. 'Pry up a plank.'

They freed one of the long floor boards, its underside already smouldering, and shoved it out the window. It barely reached to the wall-walk.

Burr regarded it apprehensively. 'You first, lord. I weigh half again as much as you do.'

'And would rather burn than walk it. I remember how you are about heights. No, you first, Burr, if you don't want me to roast up here, too.'

The Kendar swallowed. The very thought of putting a foot on that board made him feel sick. 'Some people would be ashamed to take advantage of a man's weakness,' he muttered, and stepped up. Eyes screwed shut, he began to edge out over the void.

'After nearly fifteen years, you should know me better than that,' said Torisen's voice behind him. 'Nothing is sacred but honour. Anyway, why so glum? I got you out of Urakarn. Trinity willing, I'll get you clear of this, too.'

'Me glum? You're the one who's only happy when someone's trying to kill you.'

The board groaned and sagged under his feet. He froze, gasping.

'In three seconds, I'm coming out there,' said Torisen behind him. 'One, two . . .'

The Kendar bolted forward, eyes still closed, and almost went over the battlement between two merlons. Behind him, he heard the board crack. Spinning around, he made a wild grab, caught Torisen's arm, and pulled him up onto the wall-walk. The other was still clutching the blanket full of bones.

'So far, so good,' he said, rather breathlessly. 'Now, how to get down?'

Close by, a black walnut grew just outside the wall, with its branches scraping against the stone. Torisen persuaded Burr to descend by the simple expediency of pushing him through a crenel into its boughs. When the Kendar reached the ground, swearing and sweating, his lord tossed the bundle of bones to him. But then, instead of climbing down, Torisen hesitated. He turned back to the courtyard.

'What *is* it?' Burr hissed up at him, fairly dancing with impatience.

'The Burnt Man is coming.'

Hoofbeats crashed in the hollow shell of the keep, followed by a hoarse, wordless shout and the crack of a whip. A fierce wind sprang up in the enclosed space. Blazing leaves whirled skyward, mixed with flakes of burnt skin like black moths. Torisen stood looking down. Wind lifted his dark hair. Fire haloed him.

'Lord!' Burr shouted, trying to break the spell. Then he spun around, listening. From the south came a thin, high wail. Even at this distance, it scraped on the nerves, like some small insect trapped in the inner ear.

Torisen had also heard. He vaulted over the parapet and swung down through the bare branches, dropping the last ten feet.

'The watch-weirdling?'

'Yes. Someone has crossed the border carrying weapons. Your guard from Tagmeth, perhaps?'

'If we're lucky. If not, we'd better get out of here before someone cuts us off. This way.'

There was a postern in the wall not far away and the vestiges of a path leading down the steep, southern slope from it to the outer ward. They plunged down, first through rocks, then through a dark spinney of pines, into the overgrown meadow. Long, dead grass clutched at their legs as they ran. Behind them, the harsh roar in the courtyard grew. The tower keep roof burst into flames. Firelight sent their shadows leaping before them. The cloud-of-thorn hedges narrowed on either side as they neared the lower end of the ward. Ahead was the barbican, and Torisen's black horse plunging out of its shadow towards them. Burr's grey ran at Storm's heels, both his reins and the black's still tangled in the bush, which they had pulled out by the roots and were dragging after them.

'You have more sense than I do, Storm,' Torisen said to his stallion, disentangling the reins and springing up into the saddle. 'Here.' He reached down for the blanket bundle, which Burr handed up to him.

Storm leaped forward, only to skid to a prancing halt a moment later as Torisen pulled him up sharply. Two riders on heavily lathered horses had emerged from the barbican. Burr's grey drew up level with the black. 'Caldane, Lord Caineron,' the Kendar said under his breath to Torisen.

'And Donkerri's father, Nusair. But who...'

A third horseman rode out of the shadows. Moonlight gleamed on his prematurely white hair.

Torisen stiffened. 'Kindrie, Caineron's tame Shanir.' He forced himself to relax, although Storm continued to dance nervously. 'All right. Easy does it.' He rode at a crab-step towards the gate. Burr, following him, saw that the archway behind the three Highborn was full of the lord's Kendar retainers.

'My dear Knorth,' said Caineron genially. 'What a delightful evening for a ride.'

'My dear Caineron. Yes, isn't it, although I'm a bit surprised to see you so far north.'

'Oh, I was at a hunting camp just south of Tagmeth when I heard about your little expedition. News travels quickly, even in the wilderness, if one has sharp eyes and ears.'

Meaning that he had had spies watching Tagmeth. Damn. Torisen hadn't anticipated that, but then he hadn't thought that Caineron was ready to move against him either. Even if he really wasn't, this situation must be tempting the man to the far edge of his caution.

Behind them, the upper story of the tower caved in. Flames leaped up into the night.

'Ah,' said Caineron, watching them. 'Nusair tells me that one can always tell where you are by the sound of falling buildings.'

'He should know. The last one he pulled down on me himself, oh, purely by accident, of course. At Tiglon, wasn't it?'

Nusair glowered at him.

'Or was it at Mensar? No. That was where that adder somehow got into my boot. I limped for a week, but the poor snake died.'

'Accidents will happen,' said Caineron blandly. 'Especially if people are careless. It strikes me, Knorth, that it wasn't too clever of you to come up here alone on such a night. The Merikit aren't gentle with trespassers. How unfortunate if they should catch you here, so far from all assistance, and you without a single blood kinsman to make them pay the price. Now, if you had given my granddaughter the baby she wanted... but we won't dwell on such blighted hopes.'

Burr tried to quiet his horse, knowing that it was only reacting to his own tension. Torisen wasn't handling this situation all that well; but then the presence of a Shanir always put him badly off stride, as Caineron well knew. What the rival lord apparently didn't know was that a Merikit hell hunt was about to ride down his throat.

A hollow boom sounded in the keep. The wind shifted, pushing against Burr's back.

'. . . and all for nothing,' Caineron was saying. 'Anyone could have told you that all the Highborn remains were retrieved years ago.'

'I see. Then the Kendar don't matter.'

A shadow of vexation crossed Caineron's broad face. He wanted the Kendar and Shanir to think of him as their champion, but they were just fools enough to take such a slip to heart.

'Of coure they matter,' he snapped. 'But it's hardly likely that –'

'My lord!' Kindrie suddenly rode forward, pointing. 'Look!'

They all looked. There on the ground before Torisen was his shadow, Storm's, and that of a child sitting in front of him on the saddle. His arm tightened involuntarily around the blanket full of bones. On the ground, the shadow child turned to look questioningly up at the shadow lord. *Trinity,* he thought numbly. *Sweet, sweet Trinity.*

'*Wha?*' came the yelping cry from Kithorn. '*Wha? Wha? Tha!*'

Dark figures spilled out of the postern, their black skins laced with a glowing fretwork of lines. They disappeared under the pines, reemerged at the top of the ward. There was one more of them than before. They ran shambling on all fours, fire-mouthed, baying, and the dry grass burned in their wake.

'Oh my God,' said Caineron, staring.

Torisen gathered Storm, holding him just barely in check.

'Gentlemen,' he said, 'I'm taking this child back to Tagmeth. I suggest you all follow me. In case you hadn't noticed, Burr and I aren't the only ones on Merikit land.'

As Storm sprang forward, Kindrie's mount jumped sideways with a squeal, straight into both the Caineron. While the three horses were still entangled, Torisen and Burr swept past them under the barbican. The Kendar opened a path. In a moment, they were back on the River Road, their horses' steel-shod hooves striking sparks from the ancient stones. The hanged man's shrill wail grew closer, louder. There he was, hovering ghostlike directly in their path. His voice buzzed in their ears, in their heads, like a swarm of trapped mosquitoes. Storm's stride faltered. He started to shy, shaking his head at the maddening sound, then steadied. In a moment they were past the weirdling. It turned with them, but its voice was already fading. The sound died away completely as the last rider crossed the border.

Torisen fought Storm down to a canter. This could still turn nasty if Caineron thought he was running away. Would the man try something anyway? He must be tempted, and they were still at least twenty miles from Tagmeth. But suddenly, around a turn in the road, came more riders thundering northward. It was Torisen's guard, charging to the rescue at last. Caineron gave an ironic salute and fell back. Too late, my dear Caldane, too late... this time, at least.

'God's claws, but those Caineron are a public menace!'

Torisen was again pacing the upper chamber. He had been seething ever since his return half an hour before, but as usual had kept himself well in check while others were present. Now, with only Burr as a witness, it all boiled over.

'Of all the half-witted ambushes.... Caineron is the brightest of the lot, and even he can't see beyond his own petty schemes.'

'Not so petty,' said Burr to the cup he was filling.

'Not really so stupid either. He nearly got me. I'm the one with mashed turnips for brains.'

Burr advanced on him. Not liking to be touched, Torisen backed away, straight into the chair that the Kendar had positioned behind him. Burr shoved the cup into his hand.

'Drink, lord, and rest. Names of God, I've seen men three days dead that looked better than you do now.'

Torisen sipped the wine, grimacing. 'If you want a pretty face, court Nusair.'

'Huh! You should challenge that smug toad. How many times has he tried to kill you?'

'Who counts? Most campaigns are too dull anyway. And if I did challenge him, then what? Nusair won't lie, because that would cost him his honour, but Caineron isn't likely to sanction a duel, thereby forfeiting his right to a blood feud if I should win. At any rate, I'm no longer a mere commander of the Southern Host, able to fight as I please, nor am I all that secure as Highlord. It all comes to this: I can't afford to dignify

Nusair's bungling with any attention at all, much less pick a fight with his father that, at present, I can't possibly win.' He put down the empty cup and rubbed his eyes. 'Odd that a Highborn can stab a man in the dark and keep his good name if only he doesn't disown the deed. I used to think that honour meant so much more.'

Burr refilled the cup. He didn't know if he could get Torisen drunk, even in his present condition, but it was worth a try. Anything to make him sleep, and dreams be damned. After fifteen years, Burr knew at least in general terms what Torisen was trying to avoid and had little sympathy with the evasion. After all, dreams never hurt anyone, did they?

Turning to put down the ewer, Burr saw first the parcel of bones resting on the edge of the fire pit and then, with a start, the shadow on the wall of a small figure holding out spider thin hands to the blaze. He hadn't meant to say anything more, but this startled him into speech.

'Lord, you should give that child to the pyre as soon as possible, here, near her home. Look. She's reaching out to the flames.'

'She's only cold. All those years alone, shivering in the dust. . . . My sister wasn't much older when . . .'

'My lord?'

Torisen shook his head, irritated at the slip. 'Never mind. Anyway, we can't raise a pyre without a priest to speak the pyric rune.'

'Kindrie was in training for the priesthood before he rebelled. Lord Randir disowned him for that.'

'He's Caineron's man now.'

'After tonight? Probably not for long. I think he deliberately rammed Caineron's horse to let us pass – why, God knows. Ask him for the rune, lord.'

Torisen didn't reply.

Burr opened his mouth to argue, then closed it again. The other's head had begun to droop. *About time, too,* thought Burr, and retrieved the full wine cup before Torisen could drop it. The child would have to wait. It shocked his blunt nature to think of her soul trapped between death and oblivion a moment longer than necessary, but after eighty years, a few hours more would hardly matter. He put another log on the fire and carefully draped a coat over the young man's shoulders, then sat down opposite him. His own bones suddenly began to ache with weariness. Keeping up with Torisen Black Lord was no easy job at the best of times, but it was his job. He looked across at the dark, bowed head, at the touches of white among the black, and remembered the day that Torisen had put aside his commander's collar.

'Well, Burr, that's the end of that. From now on, I will go under my own name and claim my own power. But what about you? What will you do now?'

Burr had swallowed, dry-throated. Here it came at last. *'Lord, I had hoped to serve you at Gothregor.'*

'Indeed? And does my lord Ardeth still need someone to spy on me?'

'Lord, I broke with Ardeth this morning.'

A long moment of silence had followed. Burr could still recall vividly how sick and empty he had felt, masterless for the first time in his life.

'I see,' Torisen had finally said, in a gentler tone. *'You never were much good at planning for retreats, were you? Well then, I suppose you had better swear to me.'* And he had held out his beautiful, scarred hands.

The fire in the pit had sunk to embers. Burr groaned and straightened out his stiffened joints, surprised to find that he had slept. It must be almost dawn. But something had awakened him. What? Hoofbeats, down in the courtyard. Burr rose as quietly as he could and went to the window. Below, one of Torisen's Kendars held the reins of a post horse. Steam rose from its flanks. The rider must have already entered the main hall below. Yes, he could hear hushed, urgent voices. Burr slipped past the still sleeping Highlord and went quickly down the stairs.

A few minutes later he came back, making no effort this time to move quietly.

'My lord, wake up! There's news ...'

The dark head moved. 'Burning,' murmured Torisen, in a voice Burr had never heard him use before, higher pitched and somehow younger than his own. 'Burning, burning ...' He was still asleep.

A cold wind seemed to blow through the Kendar's heart. He remembered the last time he had heard Torisen speak with a voice not his own, in a bone-white room, in a bleached city, in the heart of the Southern Wastes. He and Harn Grip-Hard, Torisen's randon commander, had tracked Torisen there after his sudden disappearance from the Southern Host. Three years ago, that had been, just before he had claimed the Highlord's power. They had found him raving in a deep, hoarse voice that sounded so like Ganth's and had thought that he was delirious or, worse, mad.

'He has no eyes,' said that strange voice, through the flash of Torisen's clenched teeth. 'That damned book killed him. They're after me. Run, run, run...'

He half rose, would have pitched forward into the glowing embers, if Burr hadn't forced him back into the chair.

'Blood and flies, crawling, crawling.... His skin is a tattered cloak... rope... tied down. C-can't move.'

His head whipped back against the chair. The eyes, half open, showed only white.

Burr shook him, now thoroughly alarmed. 'My lord!'

'Knives. They have knives... no!'

The Kendar seized the wine ewer and dashed its contents into his lord's face. Sputtering, Torisen fought his way out of sleep.

'Blind...' he said, almost in his own voice, covering his eyes. Then he forced his hands to drop and stared down at them, blinking. His pupils reappeared. He slumped back in the chair. 'A dream, a stupid dream.... Why are you staring at me like that? Everyone has them.'

'Yes, lord.'

Torisen wiped sweat and wine from his face with a shaking hand. 'You could at least have used water. Trinity, what a mess. Wait a minute. You said something about news.'

'Yes, lord. A post-rider has just arrived from Gothregor...'

'Well?'

'The Horde has stopped circling and is moving northward.'

'Oh my God. All three million of it?'

'Apparently. The Southern Host has marched out to meet it.'

'That damn fool Pereden. What does he think fifteen thousand can do against three million? But then King Krothen probably didn't give him any choice. Where's that messenger now?'

'Below, lord.'

'Well, fetch him, man. Hurry.'

Burr bowed and left the room.

Torisen found a bucket of water in a corner and plunged his hands into it. Wine stained the water like blood. He washed the stickiness from his face and hair, scrubbing long after both were clean, as though trying to rinse away the last traces of nightmare. But if one bad dream had ended, another was about to begin. He thought of Krothen, King of Kothifir, gross and greedy, but oh so rich. Kencyr troops were hired out all over Rathillien. Only Krothen, however, could afford so many of them that the resulting force could properly be called a host. The Southern Host was his elite guard and the Kencyrath's major source of income, as well as its field training ground for young officers and troops. Krothen had used the Host at Urakarn to lead a hopeless assault against his enemies, but would even he pit it, apparently unsupported, against such an overwhelming foe as the Horde? And what about young Pereden, Ardeth's son, who had taken command after Torisen had left to become Highlord? Why had he consented to such a suicidal use of his troops?

Torisen sighed. The first major threat since he had become Highlord, and it had to be this.

He dried his face and hands on a cloak. Ready? No. The parcel of bones still sat beside the fire. On the wall, shadow lord and shadow child confronted each other. Torisen stood there a moment, biting his lip, then picked up the bones. On the wall, the child put her arms trustingly around the lord's neck. He carried the bones to his pallet and covered them with his cloak.

Footsteps echoed on the stair. Torisen, Lord Knorth, sat down again by the fire and waited.

17

Old Friends, Old Enemies
Peshtar: 7th-8th of Winter

The travellers reached the timberline on the western slope of the Ebonbane around noon of the seventh of Winter. There they paused to eat some of the provisions that Cleppetty had hastily shoved into their packs, which, up until now, had been frozen solid. The Arrin-ken's influence still shielded them from the worst of the mountains' chill.

Coming down through snow and rock, they could see the Central Lands spread out before them, still splashed here and there with autumn colour. Jame thought once that she even glimpsed a flash of the great River Silver a hundred leagues away. She rode the Arrin-ken, her unshod, stockinged foot thrust into one of Marc's mittens, while the Kendar walked beside them and Jorin bounded on ahead. They came down among the pine and ironwood of the upper slopes. Scarlet birds flashed against the dark green needles, making Jorin bleat with excitement whenever Jame spotted one.

For the most part, though, she didn't notice. Her thoughts kept going back to that strange series of predawn encounters, and especially to the changer Keral. He had spoken as if he knew her, as if he had played his cruel games with her before. Then, according to him, his half-brother Tirandys had interfered by teaching her how to fight back.

Jame shook her head in wonder. It was like falling into some old, half-forgotten song. Both Keral and Tirandys were of the Master's own generation, which should have passed into history millennia ago and would have if it weren't for the Fall. At the heart of the Master's treachery had been four blood-kin Highborn. From the Knorth had come Gerridon himself and his sister-consort, Jamethiel Dream-Weaver; from the Randir, Gerridon's maternal half-brother Tirandys and Tirandys's

312

paternal half-brother, Keral. The Knorth had also produced Glendar, who had led the remains of the Kencyr Host to Rathillien. Jame vaguely remembered that Tirandys had had a full brother – a twin, in fact – named Terribend, who had tried to oppose Gerridon but failed. No one knew what had become of him afterward.

But if Terribend was an obscure figure, Tirandys certainly was not. He had been obsessed with honour. The keystone of any Kencyr's honour is his fealty to his lord. Tirandys was torn between loyalty to the then-Lord Randir – a third or bone cousin – and Gerridon Highlord, his blood-kin half-brother. Blood told. When Gerridon fell, Tirandys felt honour-bound to follow, even though he knew it would lead to his own damnation. Many others followed his example, including Keral. The story of that bitter choice was told in an ancient lay called 'Honor's Paradox'. Other songs, equally old, hinted that Tirandys was also influenced by his love for his half-sister, Jamethiel Dream-Weaver.

And this was the man who, Keral had suggested, was Jame's instructor or Senethari. If so, she must have known him quite well, but now his name only set up a kind of hollow ringing inside her and a vague sense of loss.

At that moment, the Arrin-ken abruptly sat down, and Jame, caught unprepared, slid off rump first into the melting snow. It was dusk now. Below lay the mountain town of Peshtar.

Here I leave you.

'You really won't come to the Riverland with us?' Jame coughed, one hand on her sore throat. She tried again. 'All these years up here alone.... Don't you ever get lonely, ever feel the pull to return?'

The great cat sat like a stone, staring past her into space. *In the depths of winter, I hear the distant thoughts of my own people ringing like crystal in my mind. There are so few of us left, so very few. Yes, I feel the pull, but our time has not yet come. Someday, someone will call us.* His massive head swung back to Jame, eyes amber pools of light in the dusk. *It might even be you. My name is Immilai, the Silent One. Yours, I already know. Fare you well, my children.*

He turned and melted into the shadow of the trees, taking the last of the day's warmth with him. Jame shivered, wishing that she hadn't abandoned her mountaineer's jacket, stiff with dried wyrsan blood though it had been.

313

'Now what?' she demanded.

'New boots,' said Marc firmly, 'and supper and a real bed. You'll like Peshtar, I think. It's a friendly town.'

They went down the slope towards the city gate. Peshtar was surrounded by a high palisade with sturdy wooden bastions at each corner. Its walls formed a rectangle about two hundred yards wide, the sides angling sharply down the mountain. Inside, a jumble of one- and two-storey buildings raised sharp rooflines against the sunset. The gate was closed. Marc pounded on it until a small panel opened and a man peered out.

'Here, now, what do you want? It's past sundown.'

'Not quite, surely. We're travellers from Tai-tastigon in search of lodgings for the night.'

The man turned his head and spat. 'You think I'm soft-headed? No one crosses the Ebonbane at this time of year. This is the Black Band's night in town, and their full quota came in hours ago. Whose man are you?'

'My own, unfortunately. But I'm not...'

'A wolf-head, by god, and his fancy boy.' Jame gave him a baleful glare. 'Well, now, by rights I'm not supposed to let folk like you in at all, but for a small sum, say, ten golden altars...'

'Talk sense, man. That's the price of a good horse.'

'Well, then, sleep in the snow for all I care.' The panel closed with a bang.

'Friendly, huh?' said Jame, through teeth that had begun to rattle together with the cold.

'Ah well, never mind. There are other ways to convince the man.' Marc unslung his war-axe. He braced himself and took a good swing at the gate. It boomed, but didn't even score.

Inside, they could hear the man laughing. 'That's ironwood, you fool,' he called.

'Indeed?' said Marc placidly. 'And this is Kencyr steel.' He swung again, this time leaving a dent along the grain. 'Did I ever tell you, lass, how we used to lumber ironwood in the forests near my old home?' *Crash!* 'A fair-sized tree would take a week to cut with the lot of us working in shifts.' *Crash!* 'Then we would trim it, drill a hole in its bore, drop live coals into it until it kindled –' *Crash!* '... which usually took several months – and haul it down to one of the great Riverland keeps to set up as a fire timber in their subterranean halls.' *Crash!* 'A prime piece of ironwood will burn for generations, and rare good warmth it gives on cold nights like these.' *Crack!* The axe wedged in the board. Marc carefully worked it out, raising splinters around the gouge. The panel popped open again.

'What the hell . . . ouch!'

In trying to see the damage, the gatekeeper had incautiously stuck his nose out between the bars, and Jame had seized it.

'"Boy", huh? Marc, what's the usual gate-fee?'

'It used to be a silver crown.'

'Right. Here's one. Now, friend, it's up to you where I put it.'

Inside, the bar dropped, and the gate opened. The gate-keeper stared at the axe gouge, rubbing his nose. 'Who's going to pay for *that?*'

'You, probably, unless you want to explain your special rates to the City Council. Come along, lass.'

They entered the town.

Peshtar smelled overwhelmingly of resin and rot. Everything there seemed to be made of wood: the houses with their ornate carved façades, the steps, even the narrow streets, whose grooved boards zigzagged through the city down the steep incline of the mountain. Marc led the way between two buildings, down a precipitous staircase with moss-slick treads. The noise of the main thoroughfare rose to meet them.

'What was all that about Black Bands and wolf-heads?' Jame asked.

'During the summer, Peshtar caters to the caravan trade,' Marc said over his shoulder. 'In the winter, though, the brigands come in from their camps for a bit of fun, one band at a time. The City Council insists on that, and on a reasonable degree of order. The merchants and innkeepers here are very proud of their independence, although I doubt if they'd like to see it put to too severe a test.'

They emerged on the main street. After the silence of the Ebonbane, the uproar made Jame flinch. The narrow way seemed packed with burly, raucous men. Inside the low-beamed taverns that lined the street, brigands drank and gambled while dancers undulated on tabletops and occasionally fell off. The noise and stench were terrible. Jorin pressed against Jame's knee, nose wrinkled, ears back. All that he heard and smelled flooded her senses, crashing in on top of her own impressions.

'This is orderly?' she shouted up at Marc over the din.

'More or less, for this part of town.'

Just then, a man blundered drunkenly into the big Kendar and drew a knife, muttering something about Marc's recent

315

ancestry. Marc knocked the blade out of the brigand's hand, picked him up by the slack of his filthy jacket, and began to shake him. Nearby ruffians started to clap as if beating time for a dance. The faster they clapped, the faster Marc shook, until he had shaken the man half out of his clothes and several teeth entirely out of his head. Then he deposited his dazed, erstwhile assailant in a convenient rainbarrel. The other brigands cheered.

'You enjoyed that, didn't you?' Jame demanded as they went on.

'Oh, moderately. At least it was one way to deal with the man without having his friends turn on us. We masterless wolf-heads have to be careful.'

His voice dropped as he spoke, and Jame silently cursed the gatekeeper for having reminded her friend of his status. He had been a *yondri-gon,* a threshold dweller, at East Kenshold, until the old lord died and his son turned all the aging *yondri* out. Damn their god anyway for having made the once independent Kendar so dependent on the Highborn, and double damn the Highborn for taking such ruthless advantage of the fact. She wondered, not for the first time, how Marc would react when he learned that she herself was a pure Highborn and not the quarter-blood Shanir bastard that he assumed.

He looked down at her, a twinkle lightening his momentary depression. 'That explains one term, at least. Now, as for "fancy boy"...'

'That part I got.'

He chuckled. 'Yes. Well, right now "odd" would be a better word for you than "fancy". In case you've forgotten, you're still wearing my mitten on your foot.'

Throwing back her head to laugh, Jame saw a man in a second-storey window staring down at her. Or at least she thought he was. A black hood concealed his face, but his head turned as she passed. His right hand rested on the window sill. The thumb was on the wrong side. Then the two Kencyr turned the corner, and the man was hidden from view.

They found a cobbler's shop on one of the stairways. The little craftsman turned out to be a Tastigon, which was fortunate, because none of his ready-made boots were anywhere near the right size. Jame put on a pair of fine black leather. Her feet felt lost in them. The cobbler stroked the boots with a tiny image of his patron deity, trying to invoke the god's power all the way from his temple in Tai-tastigon. Jame considered helping, but then remembered the kindling spell; with her luck, she would probably shrink her feet instead of the boots. The craftsman's charm finally worked, however, leaving him exhausted and Jame shod. She gladly paid him twice what he asked.

Then they found an inn several streets below the main thoroughfare and bespoke supper and a room.

Jame looked around the common room after they had been served. Of the handful of customers there, most were townsmen, stolidly eating their suppers. How different it all was from the habitual uproar of Res aB'tyrr. Jame sighed and reached for the bustard wing that she had saved for last. It was gone. From under the table came the sound of Jorin cracking bones.

Marc had been staring into space with an absent frown. 'I've been thinking about Lord Cat,' he said in answer to Jame's questioning look. 'He said that there was trouble brewing in the Riverland. It would be best to find out what, if we can. I've a mind to make some inquiries.'

'Now?'

He smiled. 'No, firebrand, in the morning. Maybe you can go at a dead run from now until the coming of the Tyr-ridan, but this old man is tired.' He rose and stretched, all his joints creaking. 'I'm for bed.'

Their room was at the back of the inn. Asleep that night on a goosedown pallet, Jame dreamed that she was trying to explain her bloodlines to Marc. He listened, his expression unreadable.

'So you think your father was the exiled Ganth of Knorth, not just one of his retainers. And your mother?'

'I don't know. One day our father brought her back out of the Haunted Lands. After Tori and I were born, she simply walked away, back into the hills. No one at the keep ever saw her again.'

'And you think that Torisen Black Lord, a man at least ten years older than you, is your lost twin brother Tori?'

'Yes. Time apparently moves more slowly in Perimal Darkling than in Rathillien. . . . Marc, Father taught my brother to hate the Shanir. Tori didn't raise a hand to help me when Ganth drove me out of the keep, and now I feel myself being drawn back to my brother. Marc, I'm frightened. What will happen to me in the Riverland, among my own people? What will I do if you drive me out too? I can't help it if I'm a Highborn, Marc. Promise me it won't matter, please.'

317

'*Yes, my lady.*' He was drawing back, expressionless. She tried to reach out to him, but her rich, heavy garments anchored her to the ground. '*No, my lady. Of course, my lady...*'

Jame woke to the Kendar's gentle snore. Jorin stirred in her arms, then nestled his head under her chin and, with a sigh, slept again. Below in the street, a man passed by, drunkenly singing a love song. His voice seemed to go on and on, growing ever fainter and more off-key.

On the edge again of sleep, Jame thought that someone sat beside her bed, just out of sight.

'*What is love, Jamie? What is honour?*'

She tried to turn towards that quiet, sad voice, but her head wouldn't move. '*Who are you?*'

'*Someone best forgotten.*'

With a sudden effort, she broke the bonds of sleep and turned, but, of course, no one was there. Jorin protested her abrupt movement. She lay back and stroked his golden fur until his sleepy purr faded into a faint snore. Damnit, she *knew* that dream voice just as she had known Keral's. While the changer's accents had stirred a sense of loathing, however, this voice suggested a feeling of precarious security. Someone best forgotten? No. Someone who had comforted her once and now sounded in need of comfort himself. Someone who had called her 'Jamie'.

She stirred uneasily, stopping herself before she woke Jorin again. Her encounter in the Ebonbane with Keral had apparently cracked the wall that sealed off her lost years. A few good memories might seep through, but how many more there must be that were best left in darkness.

She lay awake a long time, thinking, and then slipped unaware back into a light, dreamless sleep that lasted until dawn.

In the morning on the eighth of Winter, Marc set out before breakfast to ask his questions. Jame went with him, hoping that the crisp mountain air would clear her mind. She remembered the previous night's second dream, but little of the first, except that her mother had been in it. That was strange in itself. She hardly ever thought about her mother, perhaps because there was so little to remember. Her clearest memories were of the stories her mother had told her, although Jame must have heard them at a very early age. Old songs, bits of history, descriptions, especially one of a vast, picture-lined hall with a big fireplace and rich fur rugs spread on the cold, dark hearthstones....

Jame remembered that hall as if she had actually seen it. Odd, the things that stick in a child's memory.

Then she noticed that they had turned westward towards the quiet lower end of town.

'Who down here would know anything about the Riverland?' she asked as they clambered down yet another alley stair. 'Anyway, it's just occurred to me that even if whatever it was the Arrin-ken foresaw has already happened, surely the news wouldn't reach Peshtar this quickly.'

'By ordinary means, no; but the last time I was in town, some thirty years ago, a remarkable old woman lived here. Ah, there's her lodge now.'

Before them across the street was a building so low that it seemed half sunken into the ground. The door posts and lintel were carved in high relief with intricate, serpentine forms. On the walls in either direction were painted a series of ovals with circles in them, rather like a multitude of crude faces with gaping mouths.

'Thirty years is a long time. Suppose she's dead?'

'Women like Mother Ragga are like oak roots: the older, the tougher.' He knocked on the door. It opened a crack. Bright, feral eyes peered out at them from about the height of the Kendar's waist. 'May we see the Earth Wife?' he asked. 'I've brought her a present.'

The door flew open. A ragged, skinny girl stood frozen in the doorway for a second before bolting sideways out of sight. Behind her, the darkness moved.

'Present!' croaked a hoarse, eager voice. An incredibly dirty hand thrust out of the shadows, age-swollen fingers crooked. 'Gimme!'

Marc detached a small leather sack from his belt. It was snatched from his grasp, and the lump of darkness retreated with it at a fast waddle. Ducking under the lintel, Marc followed with Jame and Jorin at his heels.

Inside, several steps led down to the dirt floor of a large, low-beamed room. The air was thick with dust and the smoke of three ill-tended fireplaces. As her eyes adjusted to the murky light, Jame saw that the room's sparse furnishings were all pushed up against the walls. Perhaps the irregularities of the floor explained that. There were long earthen ridges running across it, hollows where water had collected, and even untidy piles of rocks.

Mother Ragga had stepped out into this confusion of earth

319

and rock, clutching Marc's present. Seen by firelight, she looked rather like an abandoned jackdaw's nest, all layered scraps of clothing held together with gewgaws, twigs, and what looked like dried mud. She also had the filthiest ears Jame had ever seen. For a moment, the Earth Wife stood there, irresolutely plucking at her lower lip. Then with a crow of triumph she scuttled to the northeast corner where she opened the sack, dumped its contents (which turned out to be dirt) on the ground, flopped down, and put her ear to it.

'Hoofbeats,' she said after a moment's scowling concentration. 'Fast. One leg lame. Ha! Someone's gone tail over spout. My, what language!'

'That's probably young Lord Harth, trying to ride Nathwyr again,' said Marc bleakly. 'Nath was old Harth's mount, a full-blooded Whinno-hir. We older *yondri* tried to tell the boy that no Whinno-hir can be ridden without its full consent, but he wouldn't listen. We insisted, and he ordered us to leave.'

Jame was startled. 'You lost your place at East Kenshold because of a horse?'

'Because of a Whinno-hir, one of the breed who have been with the Kencyrath almost from the beginning. Because of a friend.'

'Sorry,' said Jame, chastened. She thought of those six aging Kendar driven out, beginning what for five of them had been a death march to Tai-tastigon, and all because of one arrogant Highborn, one of her own race. 'But how did Mother Ragga know?'

'Ha!' The Earth Wife glared at Jame around the patchwork bulk of her own broad behind. She scrambled to her feet, dusting off her hands. 'Stepmother to you, girl, if even that. This isn't your world. But you, Kendar, you're a good boy. Now what?'

'The Riverland?'

'Done!'

She waddled back across the room, stepping over one earthen ridge, then another before flopping down again.

'Why, that's a map!'

'Yes, of course,' said Marc, 'with the appropriate earth from each part of Rathillien. That's why she was so delighted to get a sample of genuine East Kenshold loam.'

He turned back to watch the old woman as she worked her way inches at a time up the trough that represented the

Riverland. Jorin began to dig in a corner, but Jame quickly called him to heel.

'Wait until we get outside,' she said.

Just then, someone kicked her in the leg. She spun around to find the ragged girl behind her, holding up an intricate cat's cradle. Without thinking, Jame raised her own gloved hands and the string web was deftly transferred to them. The girl shifted a loop here, another there, and suddenly Jame couldn't breathe.

Binding magic! she thought, choking down panic. She had heard of such things, but had never had to cope with them before, much less while rapidly suffocating. The girl had stepped back and was smirking at her. *Why, the dirty, little brat . . .*

Jame had a sudden, vivid image of herself, hands still trapped but nails out, lunging at the girl's throat.

'No!' she gasped, recoiling.

When she looked down at her hands, almost expecting to see blood on them, she found that she had in fact untangled the string without thinking.

The girl was staring at her, thunderstruck. She thrust out her grubby hands, and Jame transferred the cradle back to them. Again, the girl wound up the charm and this time struggled with it herself. Jame watched without really seeing. What had possessed her even to dream of using her nails so freely, so wantonly?

Torrigion, Argentiel, Regonereth – the three faces of our God. That-Which-Creates and That-Which-Preserves are terrible enough, but ah, Jamie, those Shanir with claws have an affinity to That-Which-Destroys, the most terrifying of all our God's aspects. Use yours as little as possible.

That voice again, in memory this time, and ringing with authority.

Yes, Senethari, I hear you, she thought automatically, then did a sort of mental stumble. Senethari? Was it Tirandys she had begun to remember?

The girl's face was starting to turn blue. Jame hastily untangled the string for her and then did it again more slowly so that the other could see how it was done.

'Present,' she said, with a rather shaky smile.

'Hooves,' said the Earth Wife, settling back on her hams with a grunt. She pointed to the extremes of the Riverland, then brought her plump hands together near the lower end of the valley. 'Many hooves, many more feet, coming south, coming north, coming here.'

'Gothregor,' breathed Marc. 'Lord Cat was right: The Host is gathering. But why? What could be important enough... Ragga, where is the Southern Host?'

The old woman scurried on all fours down the furrow that represented the Silver and plopped down again to the left of its base. Here she listened one place, then another. 'Moving south from Kothifir.'

'South? But the only thing in that direction –'

'Is the Horde.' On hands and knees, she scuttled a few more feet, then again put her ear to the ground, only to jerk back a moment later with a sharp hiss. 'Yes. Moving northeast.'

'Oh my God,' said Marc. 'It's happened at last.'

'What has?' demanded Jame. 'The Horde – isn't that that mass of people down in the Southern Waste who've been chasing their own tails for the past few hundred years?'

'In a way. I think it all began when one desert tribe drove another from its water hole. The displaced people moved into their neighbours' territory and uprooted them in turn. And so it went, one tribe dislodging another, until eventually scores of thousands of square miles had been set in motion. That was nearly three centuries ago, and it hasn't stopped since. Now there are some three million people down there caught up in it, circling, circling...'

'Here,' said the Earth Wife, stabbing a finger at the map. 'And there.' She spat on the ground beyond its edge.

'Yes, that's the most worrying part of it. As their numbers have grown, the circle has expanded until part of it lies across the Barrier in Perimal Darkling. There are rumours that the Wasters have mixed their blood with what crawls there in the shadows until many of them are barely human themselves. Certainly, they've come to live on whomever they can catch. Their drink is the blood of men and beasts and their way is obscured by a perpetual cloud of powdered human bones. It's very windy down there, you see. The part of the Wastes that they circle has become a continual maelstrom. I've even heard stories that they throw the most deformed of their babies into it and that whatever lives in the heart of the storm feeds on them. When I was with the Southern Host, we used to wonder what would happen if the Horde ever stopped circling. Now it looks as if we're going to find out.'

'And you think the Riverland Host will march south to help?'

'If the Highlord can mobilise it in time. The other Highborn may resist. One way or another, we've picked quite a time for a homecoming. Home –' He hesitated, then drew a second leather pouch out of his shirt. 'One final listening, Ragga. Please.'

The Earth Wife gave him a shrewd, not unsympathetic look. 'Same as last time, eh? Of course.' She took the sack and trotted back to the top of the Riverland, where she placed it on the ground unopened and put her ear to it.

'Quiet,' she said. 'Very quiet. Leaves blowing, thorns rattling, dry grass singing...'

'The cloud-of-thorn berries would be ripe now,' said Marc as though to himself. 'So would the chestnuts. We used to roast them on cold autumn nights and Willow would usually burn her fingers.'

Scowling with sudden concentration, the Earth Wife pressed one ear harder against the sack and stuck her finger in the other. 'Small bare feet, running, running...' she said. Marc stiffened. 'Other footsteps, booted, heavier, and someone else running, pursued. Fire, hoofbeats, howls. Fading now... gone.'

'The earth has a long memory,' said Marc heavily. 'That must have been nearly eighty years ago, the night the keep fell.'

'No, not years. The earth warms, cools, warms... two days ago.'

'And now? The running child?'

Ragga listened for a moment, then sat back on her heels, shaking her head. 'Gone.'

'Willow,' said Marc, looking stunned. 'My little sister. I recovered the rest of my family for the pyre, but not her. I searched the ruins for her body more times than I can remember, that red winter when I hunted the Merikit and they hunted me. In the end, I thought she must either have escaped or been carried off, alive or dead, by the hillmen or a wild animal. And all of this time she's been there, up until two days ago.'

'*Some* child was there, anyway, but how can you be so sure it was your sister? It could have been anyone.'

'Not quite,' said Mother Ragga, peering up at them through her stringy grey hair. 'This one had footsteps and a shadow, but no weight. This one was dead.' She returned the leather sack to Marc. 'Here, Kendar. No other earth on this world will ever be so nearly yours.'

Turning to go, Jame nearly collided with the ragged girl, who thrust something into her hand.

'Present,' she said, with a gap-toothed grin, and bolted back into the shadows.

Out in the morning light of the street, Jame saw that her gift was a clay medallion with a crude, eyeless face printed on it. It made her gloved hand tingle in a not altogether pleasant way.

They walked back up through the town with Marc deep in sombre thought and Jame not liking to intrude. Jorin found a tub of earth and dead petunias in which he was happily industrious while Jame mounted guard. Back at the inn, the Kendar roused himself and ordered breakfast. Then he asked to see the medallion.

'Careful,' Jame said sharply, but he had already picked it up.

'Why?'

'Somehow, I had the feeling that it might not be safe to touch bare-handed. Don't you feel anything?'

'Some warmth and maybe a slight vibration, but nothing else.'

'Well, Mother Ragga liked you. Maybe this thing does, too. But what is it?'

'An *imu*, I think. I've run into them all over the more primitive parts of Rathillien. Many people carry them as charms.'

Rather gingerly, Jame took back the medallion. 'There's certainly *some* kind of power bound up in this thing, and in Mother Ragga's earth magic too. Now, where have I come across something like it before? Ah, in the Temple District of Tai-tastigon among the Old Pantheon gods, I think. This seems different, though, as if the only force invoked is that of the earth itself.'

'The power of the earth,' said Marc thoughtfully. 'We had a priest at Kithorn who used to talk about that. He claimed that there are thick and thin areas in Rathillien. The thin spots are like the Haunted Lands, with Perimal Darkling just under the surface; thick areas are more like the hills above Kithorn and down by the Cataracts where Rathillien is most itself and least susceptible to any encroachment. The thickest spot of all is supposed to be the Anarchies, in the western foothills of the Ebonbane. We'll be skirting it on our way to the Riverland.'

'Marc, will we get there before the Host marches?'

'Possibly, if the Highlord is delayed that long. It could be disastrous if he is, though. I don't know where the Horde is bound or what it thinks it's up to – assuming it thinks at all – but the longer we put off meeting it, the worse things will be.'

'Maybe the Southern Host can deal with it without help.'

'Outnumbered two hundred to one?' He laughed, a bit ruefully. 'We're good fighters, the best in Rathillien, but not that good. At best, the Southern Host can only hope to delay the Horde, unless King Krothen demands a pitched battle. He could. After all, despite its Highborn officers, the Host is his élite guard, made up of *yondri* from nearly every house in the Kencyrath.'

'Whose pay goes to enrich some lord snug at home in the Riverland,' said Jame bitterly. It made her furious to think that a displaced Kendar like Marc could spend most of his life as a *yondri,* only to be cast off by his sometime lord when he grew too old for active service. 'How can the Highlord permit such a thing?'

'He isn't omnipotent,' Marc said mildly. 'It's a pity, of course, that anyone has to be a *yondri,* but it's been a long time since there have been enough lords to give all the Kendar real homes. Then not all lords are all that rich. The Riverland may be nearly two hundred and fifty miles long, but it's only about ten miles wide, and very little of that is fit to grow crops or even graze cattle. We have to buy most of our food, and sometimes the *yondri* pay for it with their blood. Perhaps that isn't fair, but it's the way things are.'

Jorin had stretched out on the bench beside Jame with his chin on her knee. Suddenly he raised his head and began to growl. Now what? Out in the street, the patter of swift, stealthy feet. . . . The handful of patrons in the hall exchanged quick glances, then rose and hurriedly left – all but two. There at a table in the far shadows by the kitchen door sat the hooded man whom Jame had seen watching her the previous night from a second-storey window. Beside him lounged a big man in brigand garb with a strip of black cloth knotted over his eyes. Jame put her hand on Marc's arm. Following her eyes, he tensed.

'Bortis.'

The innkeeper emerged from the kitchen, staggering under the weight of a tray piled with brie tart, shortbread, and an enormous humble pie. He plumped down his burden before the two Kencyr.

'There, masters! Now, can I get you anything else?'

'Yes. My war-axe.'

The innkeeper stared for a moment, then began to chuckle. 'Ah, the wit of an empty stomach. You know perfectly well, sir, that this is a restricted area. No unsheathed weapons here, if you please.'

'Don't tell me,' said Marc, getting slowly to his feet. 'Tell them.'

Thirteen big men, all armed with the distinctive curved knife of the brigand, had entered by the street door. They ranged themselves in an arc across the room facing the two Kencyr, blocking the windows and door. Bortis and the hooded man rose.

'By the Dog,' the innkeeper said, staring. 'Black Band himself and his pet necromancer.' He made a dive for the kitchen, only to run head-on into several more brigands who had entered by the back way. They let him pass. A moment later, the rear door slammed.

'Well, now, Talisman, isn't this nice.' said Bortis, grinning. Once he had been handsome in a coarse way. Now he was only coarse, with a bulging stomach, greasy hair, and an unwashed smell that reached Jame across the room through Jorin's senses. 'I was just getting the lads ready for a visit to Tai-tastigon come spring to see you again, and here you turn up on my doorstep. Now, I call that accommodating.'

'Hello, Bortis. If you'd visited the Res aB'tyrr a few days ago, you would have been in time for Taniscent's funeral.'

'So the old girl finally keeled over. Good. That's one less senile slut to soil the world's sheets.'

'That "slut" loved you, and died of old age at twenty-four because you gave her an overdose of Dragon's Blood.'

'My, my, you do keep score, don't you? Well, so do I. You owe me for a pair of eyes, Talisman. I'm here to collect.'

'I wouldn't advise it,' said Marc quietly.

The brigand cocked his bandaged head at the sound of a new voice. His grin deepened. 'So now we find out how many men a Kendar is really worth. Not to fret, though, Talisman. There'll still be enough of us to make things interesting for you, and more in the hills afterward. All right,' he said to his men, his voice suddenly hoarse with a gloating eagerness. 'Take them.'

Marc pushed Jame back against the wall behind him. 'Stay out of this as long as you can,' he said over his shoulder. 'This isn't your kind of fight.'

Jame eyed the advancing mob. 'Is it yours?'

The biggest of the brigands rushed forward with a roar. There was a sharp crack, and he staggered back, hands to his face, blood streaming between his fingers from a shattered jaw. Marc stood there gently rubbing his knuckles.

'Next,' he said.

They all rushed him at once. He shrugged off one attacker, floored another, and then went down under a welter of bodies.

Jame circled the heaving mass in an agony of helplessness. Marc had been right: This wasn't her sort of combat at all. Her friend might be killed if she didn't help, but what could she do? Dance. Yes, that was it, but not as she had at the Res aB'tyrr. Paralyze these bastards. Strip away their souls, shred by shred...

A hand closed on her arm and wrenched it up behind her back. Pain shattered her thoughts.

'Well, well,' Bortis' voice wheezed in her ear. His breath stank. 'So you couldn't stay away from me even this long.' He twisted her arm harder, making her gasp with pain. 'Patience, pretty eyes. Watch for both of us.'

The mass split open, and Marc struggled halfway to his feet, dragging men up with him. A brigand rose, clutching a short-handled mace. He brought it down hard on the Kendar's head. Marc collapsed. Two brigands caught him by the arms and held him up. A third jerked his head back by the greying hair and put a knife against his throat. Its edge drew blood.

'Now, chief?'

'Now,' said Bortis hungrily.

Suddenly he gave a yelp of pain. Jame twisted out of his grasp as he went down with Jorin's teeth sunk in his leg. The brigands were staring at them, caught off guard. When Jame darted at them, two of the hulking men actually flinched away as if from some small creature with bared teeth and sharp claws. Jame somersaulted over one of them, using his broad shoulders as a springboard. Her foot caught the man with the knife in the face. He dropped. The others were too tightly packed to defend themselves properly. She stepped on shoulders and heads, lashing out at everyone within reach. They surged back. Marc's would-be killer was groping in a dazed way for his knife. As his hand closed on it, Jame landed on his back. Her long fingers slid around his muscular neck. He fell forward, gurgling. She crouched over the Kendar's body, claws fully extended and dripping.

'Next.'

There was a moment's startled silence, and then a commotion began near the door. More men were crowding into the room. If these were more brigands... but no. Here came the innkeeper, triumphantly leading the city guard. As a fine battle took shape around them, Jame bent anxiously over her friend. Blood was pooling under his head from a torn scalp, but his skull seemed intact and his breathing was regular. Ancestors be praised for a good, hard head.

She was dragging him out from under the combatants' feet when someone grabbed her. Jame twisted around in her attacker's grasp and a pair of strong hands closed on her throat. The hooded man bent over her. She grabbed his little fingers, remembering in time that he had two left hands, and jerked them back to break his hold. They shifted disconcertingly in her grasp. He laughed down at her. Gasping, she struck up at him, and his hood fell back. Instead of breaking his nose, her blow had only shoved it up between his eyes. Even now it was settling back more or less in place. He grinned. His mouth angled across his face, splitting it open like a rotten fruit. He was another changer.

'Well met, Jamethiel. Like our boarish friend, I thought I would have to use the Black Band to get you out of Tai-tastigon, but here you are.'

Jame clawed desperately at his hands. When her nails broke the skin, his blood seared her. He tightened his grip.

'Naughty, naughty. Be grateful when someone does you a favour, or would you rather be a guest in Bortis's camp? At least this way you can die knowing that your death will lead to the eventual downfall of the Master himself. Good-bye, Jamethiel.'

Through the roar of blood in her ears. Jame heard a crash behind her as the table that she and Marc had been sitting at overturned. The humble pie landed beside her, miraculously right side up. Simultaneously, a small object shot past her, hitting her assailant in the face. It was the clay medallion. The changer let go of her throat and clawed at it as it sank into his flesh with a muffled hiss. Wailing, he staggered towards the door, crashing into furniture and men. Brigands and guards alike scrambled out of his way. On the threshold, he got his nails hooked under the clay disc and tore it away with a wet, ripping sound. He lurched out into the street, hands over his mutilated face. The *imu* medallion lay on the doorstep, the changer's

328

blood slowly eating away the stone under it.

Jame sat up gasping, one hand on her bruised throat. Sore again, damnit. This was getting monotonous. Jorin slipped up to her out of the corner, chirping anxiously. He wasn't really used to people, much less to tavern brawls, and this one looked as if it could still turn into a massacre. The guards were clearly getting the worst of it. Despite the advantage of numbers, they were up against tougher men and dirtier fighters. Marc groaned. Jame helped him to sit up, anxiously noting his glazed eyes and dazed expression. They might still have to fight or run at any moment.

Their movement had been noted. 'They're getting away!' a brigand shouted across the room to Bortis.

'Stop them, damn you!' bellowed the robber chief. 'A hundred gold altars to the man who brings me their heads!'

Four brigands advanced on them. Jame felt Marc tense. He came off the floor with a howl, sending three attackers flying. The fourth he grabbed and jammed up the chimney. The rest backed away from his wild eyes and bristling hair. He tore apart a bench with his nails and teeth and charged at them, brandishing a six-foot plank. Foam and blood flecked his grey beard. One brigand jumped out a window, and then another. Suddenly there was a struggling knot of them at the doors, all fighting to get out. Two of Bortis's lieutenants grabbed him and hauled him with them, kicking and swearing. On the threshold, he fought free and spun around.

'I'll be back, do you hear? I'll rally every brigand in the five bands and come ba—umph!'

The humble pie hit him squarely in the face. His men dragged him out as the Kendar charged them again, howling like a wolf. All four disappeared down the street. A few minutes later, Marc came back, wiping his beard and laughing. He found an unspilt tankard of ale on the mantelpiece, drained it, and looked around.

'Hello, where is everybody?'

One of the innkeeper's slippers landed on the floor in front of him. Looking up, he saw the innkeeper himself and half the guard clinging to the rafters, staring down at him. The rest peered warily out of the kitchen and Jame and Jorin from around the edge of the overturned table.

'Oh, come out,' he said, grinning at them. 'I won't eat you.'

'Is that a promise?'

It took awhile to retrieve everyone and even longer for them all to recover. The innkeeper helped with plenty of free ale. Soon a festive mood set in, compounded as much of relief and exultation as of alcohol. They had actually beaten the Black Band, or at least part of it. Never in the history of Peshtar had there been so great a victory for the rule of order. They celebrated by sending down to the cellar for more ale and by putting matches to the feet of the brigand still jammed up the chimney. Meanwhile, Jame bandaged Marc's head.

'That's exactly where I got hit the last time Bortis and I tangled,' she said, examining the wound. 'The man is at least consistent.' She daubed at the torn skin with a wine-soaked cloth. Marc yelped. 'Serves you right. You nearly scared the boots off me, pulling a stunt like that.'

'The splinters are a nuisance, but on the whole I'd rather break furniture than heads. Too bad I didn't remember that before my own got broken. I did tell you that I used to feign berserker fits in battle, didn't I?'

'Oh yes,' said Jame, winding a strip of cloth around his head, 'but that was hardly adequate warning. I did get a bit suspicious, though, when you threw that pie. Bortis should wear tripe more often. It suits him. There.' She secured the end of the bandage, a troubled frown clouding her face. 'I wish I knew what's going on, though. It's natural enough that Bortis should come after me, but why the changers? That's two of them in a week, the first for the Master, the second against, if that's possible. Then too, why in all the names of God should my death mean Gerridon's ultimate ruin? It's like a puzzle with half the pieces missing.'

Just then, the innkeeper came bustling up with an ewer of wine. 'What, my masters, not drinking? Here, the best in the house!' He refilled their cups to overflowing. 'Drink to the rout of the Black Band and of Bortis, the worst bully on the western slopes!'

'Doesn't it worry you that he's promised to return?'

'If he does, we'll lick 'em again,' said the innkeeper with relish. 'But, just among the three of us, why should he? After all, in the final reckoning it was just a tavern quarrel, spectacular, I grant you, but nothing all that serious.'

Marc looked up at Jame. 'You'd better tell him.'

Jame nodded. 'I'm afraid it was and still is serious enough.' she said to the innkeeper. 'You see, I'm the one who cost him his eyes.'

The little man stared at her. His mouth opened, closed, opened again. 'Excuse me.' He put the ewer down on the table with a thump and scuttled over to the carousing guards. They listened to his urgent whisper, laughing at first, but not for long.

'I take it the party is over,' Jame said to Marc.

The captain of the guard stalked over to the table. 'What's all this nonsense?' he demanded, giving Jame a scornful look. 'As if a famine's filly like this was worth any man's eyes.'

Jame glared at him. Not having seen her fight, he apparently assumed that Bortis had been blinded fighting over her – which, she suddenly realised, was partly true.

'Gently, gently,' said Marc in Kens, chuckling. 'At least he knows you're a girl. That's an improvement over last night. How many men can Bortis actually rally?' he asked the captain.

'Not the five bands, perhaps, but certainly the rest of his own, and there are four times as many of them as we let into Peshtar yesterday. That means we could be under siege by some four hundred brigands by nightfall. You had better be gone by then.'

'So much for the celebrated rule of order,' said Jame.

The captain turned dusky with anger, but his men shuffled their feet, embarrassed. He was a mercenary brought in from the Central Lands, but they were townsmen, and they had their pride.

'Now, lass, don't taunt them,' said Marc softly. 'There's a delicate balance here between rule and chaos. We don't want to be besieged anyway.'

'No, of course not. But if they want to keep their civic pride at our expense, let them pay for it. We can't leave until we're refitted,' she said to the townsmen. 'Most of our clothes were burned in the mountains, and if we're going to be on the run, we won't have time to hunt for food. We'll need supplies for at least two weeks.'

'No problem there,' said one of the guards eagerly, disregarding his captain's sour look. 'We'll collect what you need. I'm sure the Council will even be glad to foot the bill.'

'And we need a pack pony.'

There was a moment's disconcerted silence.

'Yes, of course,' said the little innkeeper, glaring at the others. 'I'll pay for that myself, if necessary. It's the least we can do. Thank you, my dear. Now, make out your list and these chaps will attend to it while I fix you both another breakfast. And will someone please get that man out of my chimney?'

By the time the Kencyr had eaten, their supplies were ready and packed on a shaggy little beast with shrewd eyes. Someone had even found Jame a new pair of gloves. As she put them on, she remembered the brigand whose throat she had slashed and was uneasy for a moment. Of course, it was wrong to use her claws so freely... but the man had deserved it, and that was that.

At the gate, Marc fished something out of his pocket. 'I almost forgot to give you this,' he said. 'It was still lying on the doorstep.'

She took the medallion gingerly. The clay face was softened by a mask of moulded leather, which Jame suddenly realised must be skin from the changer's face. Only the mouth remained uncovered, with a trace of dried blood on the lips. Its power seemed muted, or perhaps just temporarily sated.

'I'm beginning to wonder just what sort of a present this was meant to be,' she said. 'Amazing that that stampede of brigands didn't smash it to a powder, but then, like the Book, perhaps it can take care of itself.' She slipped it into her pocket. 'Ready?'

Marc hesitated. 'There's one more thing. Mind you, I think we can outrun this wolf pack, but if Bortis should catch up with us, he had better not take you alive. Agreed?'

Jame swallowed, her throat suddenly dry. 'Agreed.'

They went out Peshtar's western gate and started down the caravan road. The Central Lands spread out before them, shining in the morning light.

18

First Blood
Tentir: 7th-8th of Winter

By dawn on the seventh, Tagmeth seethed with life. Everyone
had heard the news of the Horde's march. The packing was
already done and the cook fires ready to douse. Torisen had
listened to the messenger's full report and sent him down to
snatch half an hour's sleep in a corner of the main hall. Now
while Brishney tore a spare shirt into squares, Torisen rolled up
his sleeve, and Burr carefully nicked his arm. Morien caught the
Highlord's blood in a silver bowl. Donkerri, watching, turned a
dirty shade of white. He got up, trying to appear unconcerned,
and nearly walked into the fire pit before Rion caught him.

'Blood-blind,' said Morien scornfully. He began to dip the
corner of each cloth square into the bowl.

Torisen regarded Donkerri. When Caineron had spoken of
having eyes and ears at Tagmeth, had he meant his grandson? It
would be like Caldane to use his own blood-kin, and a child at
that, as a spy. Torisen decided that he didn't like spies, whatever
their age.

Donkerri huddled by the fire, feeling sick and miserable as he
always did at the sight of blood. He felt the Highlord's cold,
considering eyes on him and turned paler still.

Torisen's herald entered the room. He gave her the scraps of
cloth. 'Pass the word down the river to every keep that there will
be a High Council meeting at Gothregor on the ninth and a
general gathering of the Host no later than the tenth. Give each
lord one of these squares and say to him: "The blood calls.
Answer or be foresworn".'

She bowed and left.

'That should make them jump,' said Torisen to Burr. 'By
tomorrow night, every Highborn in the valley is probably going
to wish I'd never been born, if they don't already – and what are

you staring at? Is my face still dirty?'

'No, lord.' Burr gave him a critical look. 'That bit of sleep did you some good. Now you only look as if you've been dead one day instead of three.'

'It's nice to know that I improve with age,' said the Highborn tartly. 'Hello, what's that?'

From the north came a distant rumble. Black clouds were beginning to pile up beyond the white peaks, towering higher and higher.

'A storm is brewing up near the Barrier,' said Burr, looking out.

'Yes. With our luck, it will probably chase us all the way to Gothregor. We aren't leaving the north a moment too soon.'

They rode out of Tagmeth within the hour, the light already dimming around them and an unseasonably warm wind pushing fitfully at their backs. It was fifty leagues to Gothregor, past five pairs of keeps. Lord Caineron and Nusair joined the cavalcade as it passed Restormir, leaving Sheth Sharp-Tongue, their randon commander, to bring the troops after them. Caldane chatted cosily with Torisen for a way about their lucky escape the night before and then dropped back to ride with his own retinue. The blood summons bound him as it did every other lord in the Riverland; if he had any new schemes in mind, he would probably wait until the Council session to spring them.

At Mount Alban, the scrollsmen's keep, a cheerful historian and a grey-haired singer joined them, one to record the facts of the coming campaign (assuming there was one), and the other to immortalise it in song, using the singer's cherished prerogative of the Lawful Lie.

All day, the storm clouds built up, growing blacker, towering higher, but they didn't burst until dusk. The wind, fitful until now, began to rush past the riders, driving dead leaves with it. Thunder boomed in the near distance. Caineron spurred his mount up to Torisen's.

'This looks bad,' he said, uneasily regarding the lightning-shot darkness now roiling down on them. 'We had better turn back.'

'Tentir isn't much farther away than Mount Alban. Surely you aren't afraid of a little rain, my lord.'

'Of course not,' said Caineron with a bland, superior smile, buttoning up the collar of his red velvet coat against the blast.

'It's simply that no well-bred Highborn rides in all weather like a leather-shirt trooper if he can help it.'

Torisen suppressed a smile. In his serviceable riding leathers, allowing for his slighter build, he could easily have passed for one of his own Kendar retainers.

'As you please, my lord. We're going to make a run for Tentir, where supper should be waiting for us. You're more likely to get wet going back anyway.'

Storm sprang forward. Torisen heard one of the boys give a whoop and reined in until Morien drew up level with him. Brishney and the others weren't far behind. Then he let Storm go again. The black stretched out in a full gallop, his ears back as he listened to the other horses thundering after him. Lightning was striking the peaks above them now. Its glare briefly gilded bare branches bent in the wind and the ruffled surface of the River Silver running swift beside the road. The boys were shouting, their voices shrill against the tempest's oncoming roar. Torisen laughed. As if they had a chance of catching a quarter-blood Whinno-hir like Storm. There was a blinding flash, a boom like the sundering of worlds, and a forty-foot pine crashed down ahead of them, its tip across the path. Storm shied, then steadied. He took the jump gallantly, his hooves barely skimming the fallen tree's needles. The saddlebag containing the bones thumped against his side as he landed.

'Hold on tight!' Torisen shouted over his shoulder.

Then, there across the river, was Tentir, the randon college, black against the mountains. Lights shone in the guest quarter windows. Torisen galloped across the bridge, up between the training fields, and through the gate house. Raindrops stung his face. The door swung open, and he rode full tilt into the main hall of the old keep. Storm skidded to a halt on the age-slick flagstones. The boys clattered in after him, shouting friendly insults at each other. Burr and the others followed, with Caineron's group last of all. By now, it was pouring outside. Nusair rode in looking like a half-drowned cat, and Caineron, as proud as ever, but with his fancy red coat bleeding dye over his hands.

'He'll find some way to make you pay for this,' Burr said in an undertone as a servant led their horses down the corner ramp to the subterranean stables.

'He can try,' said Torisen placidly. 'Even if he succeeds, it was worth it.'

Behind them, the guards struggled against the blast to close the hall's massive oak doors. One of them, glancing up as lightning struck the mountain side, thought he saw something large and white soaring down the wind towards the keep. Then the darkness closed in again with a shout of thunder, and it was gone.

Torisen and Burr went up to the quarters on the second floor of the old keep that were kept in permanent readiness for the Highlord's infrequent visits. A fire blazing in the grate and open ducts to the fire timber hall three levels below heated the three-room suite. Torisen put his saddlebag on the huge bed and crossed over to the fireplace. Perhaps for the first time since coming north, he would actually get warm. Burr's movements caught his attention.

'What have you got there?'

The Kendar had been unpacking a bag. Now he carefully unfolded something dark and lustrous, with flashes of silver at the throat and wrists.

'You brought one of my court coats on a hunting trip?'

'Well, you never know, do you?' said Burr with a touch of guilty belligerence. 'And it has come in handy, hasn't it?'

The Highborn smiled at him. 'Poor Burr. Caineron caught you on the raw with his talk of leather-shirt troopers, didn't he? Very well. You can dress me to the teeth tonight, and we'll see if I can dazzle him.'

Burr held the velvet coat so that his lord could slip into it. 'It would be easier if you didn't always wear black and go armed.' He transferred Torisen's two throwing knives to their sheaths in the collar of the dress coat.

There was a scratch on the door. A Knorth cadet entered.

'My lord Caineron's compliments,' he said, nearly squeaking with nervousness but gamely coming out with his message. 'Since he has learned that only his people and yours are still at Tentir, he has arranged for everyone to eat in his hall, as – as his guests.'

Burr glowered at the boy, putting the seal on his confusion. 'That man... as if *he* were master here!'

'Never mind. It's just his revenge... and I still say it was worth it. Ready?'

Burr eyed him critically, then nodded in grudging approval. They left the room.

*

High above the keep, something balanced awkwardly on the wind on pale skin stretched taut between its body and extenuated limbs. It was naked except for a grey, undulating mass wrapped around its neck. Above that was a face very nearly human, though pinched by the cold and concentration. The creature hovered unsteadily, white hair whipping in the wind, then swooped down towards an open second-storey window in Tentir's north wing. At the last moment, a violent down draft caught it. It veered wildly, first towards stone, then into and through the closed shutters of a lower window. A cot broke its fall; likewise, it broke the cot, and ended up tangled in blankets, thrashing about and swearing on the dormitory floor. Suddenly it stopped struggling, one web-fingered hand leaping to its bare throat.

'Beauty?' It called in a husky, distorted voice. 'Where are you?'

From under a nearby cot crawled a grey, segmented wyrm, about as thick around as a man's upper arm. Its antennae felt delicately ahead of it, while behind it left a trail of slime. The changer picked it up and stroked it.

'Are you all right, girl? Well, I'm not. I can't ... change ... back ...'

He began to shake with the effort. The webbed skin of one hand subsided into wrinkles like an overstretched glove, but that was all. The changer stopped, panting and sweating.

'It's no use, girl. I need blood, lots of blood ...'

Out in the hallway, there was the sound of approaching voices.

Torisen and Burr followed their young guide down to the first floor and into the new section of Tentir. Barracks and training halls had been built onto the ancient keep, forming a large, hollow square around an inner ward, which cadets claimed was always solid mud. Although the young Kendar men and women trained together, they slept and ate with others from their home keeps. Caineron's hall was in the north wing. Walking down the long corridor towards it, Torisen heard the heavy floor planks groan as the wind struck the outer wall. The air in the hallway shifted, making their guide's torch flare uncertainly and shadows leap ahead of them.

'So everyone else has gone home,' he said.

337

'Yes, lord, as soon as your message arrived. Lord, will we be fighting soon?'

Torisen smiled at the boy's eagerness. 'I'm afraid so. There must be about fifty Knorth cadets here now. How many has Lord Caineron?'

'One hundred and thirty-five, lord.'

Torisen was momentarily startled, but then remembered that while his fifty were sworn to him personally, many of Caineron's must in fact belong to his seven established sons.

'And Harn? Will he be joining us?'

'No, lord. Old Grip-Hard... I beg your pardon, sir! Keep Commandant Harn never dines in public.'

Burr and Torisen exchanged glances. 'Doesn't he, by God!' murmured the latter. 'That's something new.' He stopped suddenly. 'I thought you said everyone was gone. Who's that, then, breaking up furniture?'

The cadet stopped too, listening. 'These are the Coman's dormitories, lord. No one should be here. I think it's coming from that one down the hall.'

By the time they reached the room, all was quiet inside. The cadet threw open the door.

'There,' he said, holding up his torch. 'The wind must have slammed open that shutter and broken it.' He went over to secure what was left of the window's covering.

'Did the wind break that cot, too?' muttered Burr. He drew his short sword, relieved the surprised boy of his torch, and began a methodical search of the room, poking into corners, peering under beds.

Torisen stood in the doorway. He too felt a touch of whatever-it-was that had made Burr instinctively bristle, but he couldn't identify it. The Kendar finished his search.

'Nothing,' he said, sounding faintly puzzled.

The Highlord shook himself. They were acting like a pair of Shanir, starting at shadows. 'Come along, then,' he said, waving the other two out of the room and firmly closing the door after them.

As their footsteps receded down the hall, the changer dropped from the ceiling with the wyrm clinging to his neck.

'Two too many for us, Beauty, but did you see who the third was, there, by the door? We're close, very close...'

He slipped out of the room and scuttled silently after the three Kencyr, an avid light in his pale, half-mad eyes.

*

Torisen, Burr, and their escort came at last to Caineron's hall, only to find the door firmly shut against them.

'Full formalities, I see,' said Torisen, amused. 'This is known as "Putting the upstart in his place". You had better announce me.'

Burr pushed the cadet aside and struck the door three measured blows that made its panels shake.

'Who knocks?' demanded a voice inside.

'Torisen, Lord Knorth, Highlord of the Kencyrath,' roared Burr at the closed door. It swung open.

'Welcome, my lord, to my lord Caineron's hall,' said the seneschal, bowing and stepping aside.

The cadets and their few remaining instructors came smoothly to their feet. Caldane at the high table rose in a more leisurely fashion, the torchlight striking sparks of gold and scarlet off his ornate court coat.

'All gates and hands are open to you,' he said in formal Kens.

Torisen, in the doorway, gave a half bow. 'Honour be to you and to your hall.'

Standing there with candlelight on the fine bones of his face and hands, he looked as austere and elegant as heirloom steel in a velvet sheath. Caineron, in contrast, suddenly appeared both overdressed and overweight.

Torisen went up to the high table. Nusair was also there, as well as the two Kendar scrollsmen and Kindrie. The Highlord faltered a second when he saw the Shanir, then steadied and mounted the dais. He and Caineron exchanged another ironic half bow and sat down simultaneously. The cadets resumed their seats. Bowls of thick soup were passed around to the lower tables while Torisen's nine boys waited on the Highborn and their two Kendar guests.

Dust floated down into one cadet's soup. She looked up and thought for a moment that she saw something white move among the high rafters. When it didn't reappear, she shrugged and began to eat, keeping a surreptitious watch, like everyone else in the room, on the high table.

'A pity our host couldn't join us,' said Caineron. 'I gather he's become something of a recluse, but then considering the circumstances under which he left the Southern Host a year ago, that's hardly surprising. An... impetuous man, our Harn, but remarkably good at training randons. He used to be a friend of yours, I believe.'

Torisen sipped his wine. So that was how it was going to be. 'Harn was second-in-command when I led the Southern Host,' he said levelly. 'Years before that, he was my immediate superior, when I was a one-hundred captain at the battle of Urakarn. Your eldest son Genjar was in charge then, I believe.'

Nusair bristled. He had apparently been drinking since his arrival at Tentir. 'What about Genjar, my lord?'

'Oh, nothing. It's – ah – unfortunate, though, that the only time a Caineron ever led the Southern Host, his commission ended with the decimation of his forces. The Karnides are religious fanatics, you know. Those of us they captured, they tried to convert by torture – as if our own damned god had given us any choice in matters of faith.'

'Is that what happened to you, my lord?' asked the historian.

Torisen looked down at his hands cupping the wine goblet, at the filigree of fine white scars crisscrossing them, and thought of other scars less visible. 'It was a long time ago,' he said, suddenly weary. 'Perhaps the whole thing is best forgotten.'

'As you say, my lord,' said Caineron smoothly, overriding his son. 'Instead, why don't you tell us about the cause of this remarkable general muster? All I've heard is that the Horde is on the move, although why that should concern us I can't imagine. After all, it's nearly two thousand miles away.'

'But apt to get a great deal closer. The Horde isn't striking out at random; our spies report that it's headed straight for the Silver, and that, eventually, will put it on our doorstep here in the Riverland unless we stop it.'

'But why should it come after us specifically?' asked the historian. 'There are no historical accounts that I know of, or songs,' he added, with a nod to his colleague, 'that record any previous contact with these folk. Why should they be after our blood now?'

'Perhaps because theirs demands it. Remember, because their endless line of march lies partly beyond the Southern Barrier, everyone of these people has spent part of his life in Perimal Darkling. Many of them must be at least half-blood Darklings by now. Then too, consider that the Horde is really a mixture of tribes, most of whom are blood enemies. Yet now something apparently has united them, causing them, or at least their vanguard, to break out of a pattern centuries old. What could that be but a Darkling influence; and given that, where could they be going but after us, the Shadows' greatest enemy on Rathillien?'

'That makes a certain amount of sense – superficially,' said Caineron, playing with his cup. 'But can you prove any of this?'

Torisen shook his head, frustrated. How could he explain his desperate sense of urgency to someone who had never even seen the Horde? Instinct, not logic, would tell anyone who had ever served with the Southern Host where the danger lay, but not this arrogantly ignorant Riverland lord.

'You see, my boy, it's not enough to cry "Darkling" and expect people to jump,' said Caineron in a patronising tone. 'We aren't even really sure any more what the term means, what with the historic and poetic records getting so jumbled during the flight to this world. The more enlightened of us now believe that much we once accepted as fact – changers and so forth – is actually some ancient singer's rather – shall we say – fanciful invention. Wouldn't you scholars agree?'

The young historian looked embarrassed, but the singer, a former randon named Ashe, raised her grizzled head with the light of battle in her eyes. 'My lord, it's true that we don't know if some of the old records are history or song, but only a fool underestimates Perimal Darkling.'

Caineron gave her a long look. Then he turned back to Torisen exactly as if the woman had never spoken.

'It isn't as if we had had any recent contact with anything from beyond the Barrier, you know. We've been left virtually undisturbed since we came to Rathillien over three thousand years ago. No, my lord, it's going to take more than fanciful supposition to convince me that we're about to be attacked now, and you do remember, I hope, that this time a single vote will be enough to keep the Host from marching.'

'You're going to look a proper fool,' said Nusair, and snickered drunkenly.

Torisen gave him a cold stare. 'You know, Nusair, it really is time things were settled between us. Genjar bought his honour back after Urakarn by using a White Knife.' He drew a coin from his pocket, deliberately choosing a valuable gold one, and tossed it across the table. 'Buy whatever you need and meet me openly. I'm tired of looking for you behind every door.'

Nusair picked up the coin. For a moment, he stared at it blankly, and then rising anger drove the wine-flush from his face.

'Why, you... you imposter, you changeling! Showing up here without ring or sword and maligning a real lord like my brother...'

'Gently, gently,' said Torisen. 'You're frightening the children.'

Nusair gasped, as if the wind had been knocked out of him. Then he felt the weight of eyes and turned to find all the cadets staring at him. He made a choking noise and hastily left the hall.

Torisen sipped his wine. 'That boy should be trained or put on a leash. Changeling, eh?'

'"That boy" is older than you are,' said Caineron more stiffly than usual. 'You'll have to excuse him, though. He was very fond of his brother. So was I.'

The meal ended soon after that, to everyone's relief.

Burr had eaten at one of the lower tables. By the time he reached the head of the room, moving against the flow of dismissed cadets, Torisen had disappeared. The Kendar felt a sharp stab of alarm. He thought he knew where his lord was bound; but even so, this was no night for anyone to be wandering around alone. Despite that empty dormitory, Burr felt instinctively that something unnatural was loose in Tentir. He would follow Torisen and... what?

Poor Burr, after all those years of spying on me and now no one to accept your report...

Burr flinched at the remembered tone. No, he would not follow. Torisen had a right to some privacy and was usually quite capable of looking after himself.

'Burr.' Kindrie suddenly appeared at his elbow. 'Please light me to my lord's chambers.'

'Yes, Highborn.'

Why ask him rather than one of Caineron's people, Burr wondered as they walked in silence back towards Old Tentir. He glanced curiously at the young Highborn. Kindrie had Torisen's slight build, but not the Highlord's nervous strength or grace. Stripped, he must be more bone than flesh and nearly as fragile as an old man, an impression heightened by his fine white hair.

'Burr,' he said abruptly as they neared Caineron's quarters, 'why does Torisen hate the Shanir so much?'

Burr gave him a sharp look. Caineron was quite capable of sending a Highborn to ferret information out of a Kendar, but was it like Kindrie to play such a game, even under orders? Somehow, he didn't think so.

'Sir, I think it's less a hatred than a... an involuntary repulsion. He tries to control it.'

Not with much success. Burr remembered Torisen once

saying bitterly that it was his only legacy from his father – that, and nightmares.

Kindrie walked on in silence for a moment. 'Knorth was a great Shanir house once,' he said, almost to himself. 'Many of us still have a touch of Knorth blood. I do myself and... and I would like to come home. You might tell him that, Burr, if he ever seems inclined to listen.'

He turned down the hall without another word and entered Caineron's quarters.

As the cadets dispersed to their dormitories, Torisen slipped out of the hall by a side door into the arcade that skirted the muddy ward. Rain mixed with hail thundered on the roof, sweeping in under it in gusts whenever the wind veered. Thoroughly damp and chilled, he reached the east end of the arcade and gratefully entered the relative warmth of the old keep's main hall. Three cadet guards huddled around a small blaze in the enormous fireplace. Unnoticed, Torisen slipped by them and up the stairs, past his own rooms, and up again. He remembered Tentir fairly well from his last visit nearly two years ago, but how different its halls seemed now, darkened and echoing, stripped of life. More than once, he thought he heard footsteps behind him, but saw no one. Then, ahead, there was a blazing wall torch beside the door to the northeast tower. Under it stood a cadet on guard. She swung nervously around as Torisen emerged from the shadows and found herself holding the Highlord of the Kencyrath at spear-point.

'Gently, gently,' said Torisen, moving the point aside. 'If you ruin this coat, Burr will never forgive either of us.'

'M-my lord! I beg your pardon. It's this damned storm.' She started as hail struck a nearby shuttered window like a volley of flung stones. 'I come from one of your border keeps. When the wind blows across the Barrier like this up there... well, there's no telling what might come with it.'

'You don't have to tell me,' said Torisen wryly. 'I grew up near the Barrier myself, which is a great cure for scepticism. A pity Lord Caineron can't say the same. Is Commandant Harn in his quarters?'

'Yes, Highlord. Shall I announce you?'

'No. Let's not frighten the poor man more than necessary.'

He entered and climbed the spiral stair to the first of two levels. This had originally been a watchtower, but Harn had

343

commandeered it, apparently in another effort to separate himself from his garrison, as if prolonged contact with him might contaminate it. The furnishings were as sparse as those in Torisen's own apartments at Gothregor, but he could never have lived in such a muddle of weapons, discarded clothes, and scattered papers. There was, at least, a roaring fire and, on a table near it, an untouched meal. Torisen sat down, suddenly very hungry. He had barely eaten a mouthful in the hall below and had drunk more than he cared to on an empty stomach. He picked up a bustard wing and began to gnaw on it.

'That's my supper,' growled a voice behind him.

'If you mean to eat all this,' said Torisen, taking another bite, 'you've got too large an appetite anyway.'

'Blackie!' Harn sat down abruptly opposite him, a huge, shaggy Kendar in his late sixties, untidily dressed. 'I thought you were that scamp of a guard, sneaking in again for a bite. Border brats are all alike: too independent by half.'

'So you always told me. I'm glad to hear that someone can still approach you, even if you habitually bite her. Why didn't you eat with the rest of us?'

'With Caineron there? Besides,' he said, looking away, 'I thought you might prefer not to see me.'

'What, not even to compliment you on this year's randons? Even Caineron says that they're good.'

'Oh aye, they're all fine youngsters. I should be glad to have accomplished something, I suppose, and it is worthwhile work, but sometimes I can't seem to breathe here. Tentir is a world in itself... a small world. I feel... caged.'

And indeed he looked it in this cluttered room, sitting hunched in his chair like something wild confined in too small a lair. Torisen regarded him with concern.

'I said I would take responsibility for what happened, and I have. The price is paid, Harn. You're free.'

The Kendar shook his head like a baited bear. 'Not from myself.'

'Harn, it's not all that rare a problem. One out of every few hundred Kendar must have a touch of the berserker.'

'They aren't high-ranking randon; and with me, it's more than a touch. You weren't there when I killed that boy. I don't even remember it myself; only him on one side of the room and me on the other, still holding his arm. Caineron's cousin...'

'About seven times removed. Just be glad it wasn't that idiot

344

son of his or we really would have been done for.'

'The blood price must still have been ruinous.'

'Oh, it would have been if I had paid in gold –' Torisen stopped short, silently cursing himself.

Harn looked up sharply. 'In what, then?'

'Have a wing,' said the Highborn, taking another one himself. 'Do you realise that this bird has three?'

'In what, my lord?'

'I gave my word that the next time the Host gathered, the entire High Council would have to consent before it could march out of the Riverland.'

'You *what?*' Harn's chair crashed over as he surged to his feet. 'You young idiot!' he roared, looming ominously over Torisen.

'It was either that or order you to use the White Knife instead of forbidding it.'

'By God, you should have let me kill myself! Now look at the mess we're in. You think Caineron is tamely going to let you lead out the Host?' Harn bellowed down at him. 'Once you've assumed that much real power, he might as well dig a hole for his ambitions and bury them before they begin to stink! And now with the Horde on its way... sweet Trinity, this could be the end of us all!'

'I made my choice, and I stand by it,' said Torisen quietly, looking up at him. 'The Host will march, one way or another. When it does, will you come with me, as my second-in-command?'

Harn stared at him. Just then, the wind worked loose a shutter behind him. He turned mechanically and reached out for it, but then, instead of closing it, stood there blindly staring out into the storm as rain began to darken his broad shoulders.

Caldane, Lord Caineron, returned to his guest quarters after dinner to find Nusair there before him, drinking again. He ignored the young man as servants carefully stripped off his scarlet coat and brought him a white satin dressing gown with jewelled studs. Three full-length mirrors gave back his reflection. He regarded it with less approbation than usual, noting the thinning hair and thickset figure, which no amount of sartorial splendour could entirely disguise. It was exasperating that Torisen with his slim, unconscious elegance should look so thoroughly like one of the Highborn on an ancient death banner, especially when Caineron was trying to start a rumour that the Highlord was actually the result of some long-forgotten indiscretion between Lord Ardeth and one of his Kendar.

His eyes met Nusair's in the mirror.

'That was actually quite an acceptable meal, considering its source,' he said, waving the servants out of the room. 'However, it amazes me that anyone could swallow so large an insult without choking on it.'

Nusair flushed. 'What choice did I have? You won't sanction a duel –'

'And you, apparently, can't rid yourself of an enemy in any less public way.'

'I'm not the only one,' said Nusair sullenly, refilling his cup. 'You haven't done so well yourself.'

'My dear boy, when I eliminate a rival, I hardly need do it by dropping a building on him. Ah, what have we here?'

Small, bright eyes peered at him around the corner of the mantelpiece. He picked a crumb, which his servants had overlooked, from the sleeve of his scarlet-coat and held it out on his palm.

'So far, I've merely played with this little upstart lord – and he is an upstart, you know, even if he really is a Knorth: the strength of that line was broken forever when we exiled Ganth.'

The mouse timidly emerged, nose twitching. Half-tamed by some cadet, hunger made it even less cautious. It inched into Caineron's hand.

'My father was his father's dupe and paid for it with his life in the White Hills. For that, I destroyed Ganth Gray Lord. My son, my Genjar, died after Urakarn, his name fouled by Knorth lies. For that, I will destroy Ganth's son.'

His fist closed. There was a shrill squeak and the muffled crunch of small bones breaking.

'... but in my own time, dear boy, and, preferably, in a way so subtle that he won't know he's dead until decomposition begins. To break him over the Council vote is almost too easy, too... crude. I would prefer a more lingering end, but fate may have taken that choice out of my hands.'

'Just so you get him,' said Nusair vehemently.

Caineron tossed what was left of the mouse into the fireplace and turned back to his son with a bland smile.

'And you think that that will increase *your* worth? Dear boy, what use have you ever been to me? You haven't the courage to fight or the intelligence to intrigue. Since Donkerri's mother died bearing him, to both his discredit and yours, you can't even add to my stock of grandchildren. On the whole, the most constructive thing you could do, short of killing Torisen, would be to let him kill you. Ah, now that would be really useful.'

Nusair slammed down his cup, white-faced. 'A choice, is it, father? Well, then, I'd better go shove that damn coin down his throat, hadn't I?' He seized a torch and left the room, slamming the door behind him.

Caldane picked up the cup and raised it in a mocking salute. 'My blessings, dear boy. Either way.'

The Caineron quarters were on the third level of the old keep's south side. Nusair expected to reach Knorth's rooms within minutes. Instead, he got lost. Two-thirds drunk as he was, it took him awhile to realise this. Half the time, he scarcely seemed to be in Tentir at all. At first, he put this down to the wine, but as his anger cooled and his senses cleared to some extent, he grew uneasy.

Then the footsteps began behind him. Nusair nearly turned back in hopes of finding a guide, but the scuffling, scraping quality of the sound made him hesitate. It was as if he was being followed by someone who couldn't walk properly. He went on, more and more quickly. The footsteps followed. It seemed to his befuddled senses that sometimes they came from behind, sometimes from a hallway he had just meant to turn down, sometimes from all directions at once, but always they came closer. They were herding him, he thought, beginning to panic. He tried to think where he was, which hall would take him back to the hated but safe presence of his father. His mind wouldn't work. Here was a short corridor and, at its end, a single door. The shuffling sound filled all the empty space behind him, seemed to push him down the hall to the door. He opened it and slipped inside, closing it quietly behind him. It had no lock. Outside, the footsteps were coming closer, closer. He backed away from the door, bumping into dusty furniture, until his foot unexpectedly came down on something soft.

It moved.

Nusair went over backward with a yelp. The torch, flying out of his hand, landed still alight in the far corner. He tried to get up, but couldn't. Something grey and slimy was wrapped around his leg. Even as he started to gag, it bit him. and the world seemed to crumble. He couldn't remember where he was or why he was on the floor. The room swung dizzily around him, filled with leaping shadows.

The door slowly opened. Something white crouched on the threshold. Nusair cast wildly about for a way to make sense of this apparition and could only remember Caineron's satin dressing gown.

'Father?'

The figure shuffled forward, seeming to grow. Nusair could almost make out the rippling cloth and the familiar bland smile.

'Dear boy,' it said, so nearly in Caineron's voice. 'I had to follow you. I have suddenly realised how badly I have undervalued you all these years. Of all my sons, only you are fit to be my heir. I will announce it when we reach Gothregor and bind myself to it here in private, by blood rite. Dear boy, give me your knife.'

It was all wrong. Nusair understood that at some deep, instinctive level, no matter what his poisoned senses told him, but he wanted desperately to believe. After a lifetime of rejection and revilement, to hear this, the ultimate acceptance...

'Yes,' he said, breathlessly, drawing his knife and holding it out hilt first. 'Oh, yes.'

It was taken from his grasp and his hand gripped. He braced himself for pain, but it came like a coldness against the skin – too high. Looking down, he saw not the usual palm cut but spurting blood.

'M-my wrist!' he stammered. 'You've cut my wrist!'

'It doesn't hurt.' The pale eyes held his own brown ones, taking away the pain. 'Do you still want this honour?'

'Y-yes...'

The changer bent and drank greedily. Nusair felt life flowing out of his veins. It was wrong, all wrong...

'No!' he gasped, trying weakly to draw his hand out of the iron grip.

The changer shuddered. The very bones of his bowed shoulders shifted, and muscles crawled under the skin now glistening with sweat. Then he gave a long sigh and raised his head. Nusair found himself looking into his own face, crowned by wild, white hair, framing pale, triumphant eyes.

'Too late, fool. You have given freely, and I have taken what I need. Now I will give you what you want most: a chance to be really useful.'

He shoved Nusair back on the floor and opened the young man's coat. Ignoring the feeble attempts to push him away, he carefully positioned the knife and drove it up under Nusair's ribs. When the body had stopped twitching, he stripped it and put on its clothes. In one pocket he found Torisen's coin. The changer put it in Nusair's mouth against the teeth so that its golden glint showed between the bloodless lips.

'There, little Highlord,' he said with satisfaction. 'Explain that. Now go down to the fire-timber hall, Beauty, and wait until I bring our real quarry to you.'

He left the room with a light stride, rejoicing in the strength and suppleness of his stolen form. Behind him, firelight set shadows leaping in a mockery of life around the still, white body on the floor.

The storm raged on. Blasts of wind and rain buffeted Tentir, shaking the windows, making fires dance and smoke in their grates. The cadets tried to sleep. Caineron paced his quarters, composing a speech for the High Council designed (oh, so gracefully) to flay the Highlord alive. Meanwhile, Torisen sat by the fire in the northeast tower, patiently waiting for Harn's answer.

Someone hammered on the door below. Harn swung away from the window, rain dripping unnoticed off the crags of his face. Hasty footsteps sounded on the stair and the guard burst into the room.

'Sir! One of the guard cadets from the main hall wants to see you.'

'At this hour? Why?'

'I-I can't make that out, sir. He's nearly in shock. Please, sir...'

Harn brushed past her and ran down the steps with the guard and Torisen on his heels. The cadet huddled under the torch. As the commandant appeared, he raised a stricken face and held out his hands. They were covered with blood.

'D-dead,' he stammered. 'Dead, dead, dead...'

Harn shook him. The cadet stopped with a hiccup and began to cry, clinging to the big randon's arm. Harn held him for a moment, then gently pried loose his hands.

'Stay with him,' he said tersely to his own guard, and set off at a run down the hall. For so large a man, he moved very quickly. Torisen barely kept up. Then they were on the stair leading down to the main hall with a clear view across it.

The other two cadet guards lay on the flagstones before the meagre fire. At first glance, they seemed impossibly close to each other, as if caught in some guilty embrace that had gone much, much too far. Then Torisen saw that they had in fact been smashed together face to face so violently that their very bones interlocked. Blood formed a widening black pool on the floor. Harn knelt in it, trying to disentangle the bodies without causing more damage. He must have realised that it would do no good, but he didn't seem able to stop himself.

Torisen sensed someone behind him. He turned and found Nusair watching him from the shadows.

'We have unfinished business, Highlord.'

Torisen heard voices. No alarm had yet been given, but other cadets were coming, drawn perhaps by that special sense that so often alerted them to danger. He also noted that Nusair was wearing one of the dead boy's caps pulled down over his hair. A thrill of warning went through him.

'We can't settle anything here,' he said.

The other chuckled. 'Now, is that discretion or fear? Follow, and prove which.'

The stair leading down to the subterranean levels was behind him. He turned and descended without looking back. Torisen saw that the back of the dead cadet's cap glistened as the pavement had around the two broken bodies. He followed.

Donkerri saw them go through a thinning haze of blood-blindness. Had his father actually worked up the courage to challenge the Highlord? Sick as he still felt after his glimpse of what laid on the flagstones, he must not lose Torisen now or Grandfather would make him feel infinitely worse later. Swallowing his nausea, he rose and again followed.

Meanwhile, Caineron had finished polishing his speech and was ready to retire when he suddenly realised that Nusair had not yet returned. How like the wretched boy to get lost and require a search party. It would serve him right to be left wandering until dawn, thought Caineron, getting into bed – but what if he had simply fallen down drunk in some corner? A fine sight that would be to greet the morning's first passerby, and what great credit it would reflect on the family. No, damnit, the imbecile would have to be found. He shouted for Kindrie.

A Kendar servant entered instead. 'My lord, there's a

disturbance of some sort in the main hall. The Highborn has gone down to investigate,'

'Has he indeed?' murmured Caineron.

Kindrie's post was his lord's outer chamber, and there he should have stayed, come what may. That Shanir was getting above himself and had been for some time. Caineron even suspected that Kindrie had deliberately rammed his horse at Kithorn to let Torisen pass. The Shanir would be made to confess that, as soon as Caineron felt secure enough to use the means that suited him best. He licked his lips at the thought.

The Kendar was watching him uneasily. Smoothing out his expression, Caineron sent him to find his son. The man returned almost immediately, white-faced.

'My lord, I-I found him...'

Caineron rose at once. The moment he stepped out into the hall, he smelled something burning, and followed his nose as much as his servant around the corner to a small storage room at the end of a short corridor. While the Kendar put out the fire that the dropped torch had started, Caineron stood looking down at his son. Torisen must have gone mad, he thought, to flaunt his kill so brazenly, and what an odd kill it was, too. Why the cut wrist when the heart-strike would do, and why in Perimal's name strip the body afterward? But then madness ran in the Knorth blood. Everyone knew that. The important thing now was to remind the High Council of it before Torisen could tell his side of the story, assuming he was still rational enough to do so. In fact, it might be arranged so that the Highlord wouldn't even have the chance.

Caineron was halfway out the door before he remembered his son's body. 'Do something about that,' he told his servant, and walked on, considering what one should wear when arresting one's liege lord.

The stable lay immediately below the main hall. Only a few horses occupied the maze of wooden partitions now, and they moved uneasily in their boxes as the two passed. Torisen wondered who or what he was following. The other certainly looked like Nusair, but he was behaving entirely out of character. Then too there was the murdered boy's bloody cap on his head and his shadow, dancing behind him as they approached a wall torch. Torisen had never seen one more warped. If it was truly the soul that cast the shadow and not the body, how hideously deformed the creature that he followed must be. He must get it as far from the cadets as possible, Torisen decided, and then deal with it as best he could. Neither of them realised that they were again being followed.

Another stairway led down to the brick floor of the fire-timber hall some fifty feet below. Tentir had fifteen upright ironwood timbers, more than half of which were prime with fire glowing in the deep cracks of their bark. Of the rest, six were still too green to burn properly for another century or so and two, kindled soon after the keep's founding, had at last been reduced to heaps of embers in their deep firebeds. A dusky orange light permeated the chamber. It was stiflingly hot. Torisen faced his guide across one of the glowing pits.

'Who are you?' he demanded. '*What* are you?'

The other chuckled, his voice a deep, viscous gurgle. 'Why, who or what should I be but Caineron's idiot son?'

'I don't know, unless . . .' His eyes widened as the pieces of the puzzle began to fall into place. 'You're a darkling, a changer. One of the fallen.'

'The more enlightened of us now believe that changers and what not are only some ancient singer's invention,' said the other mockingly, paraphrasing Caineron. It began to circle the pit. Torisen kept on the opposite side, out of that terrible grasp.

'I'm a border brat. I believe all sorts of unlikely things.' Even this, that a creature out of legend should be stalking him in the orange glow of Tentir's fire-hall? 'But your kind left us alone for so long,' he protested, raising one last barrier against belief. 'Why has the Master sent you among us now?'

'The Master!'

The other spat into the embers. Its saliva burst into flames on contact. It sprang across the pit. Torisen slipped out of its way in a wind blowing move and threw a knife into its back before it could turn. The knife hilt clattered to the brick floor, its blade burned away by the other's blood. The changer turned, chuckling. Torisen backed into an open space between the timbers, the second knife poised to throw.

'Afraid, little man?'

'Of you? Moderately.'

'Now, what would really frighten you, I wonder. Shall we find out? Beauty, now!'

Out of the corner of his eye, Torisen saw something grey near his feet. His knife hand whipped down. The blade buried itself in the wyrm's head just as it fastened on his leg. Someone screamed. The chamber seemed to tilt, throwing Torisen to the floor. The wyrm's venom tugged at his senses. Random nightmare images flickered through his mind, going faster and faster. It was like falling down a steep slope, clutching at things too loathsome to touch. Then for a moment he felt the rough bricks of the floor under his hands and clung to them grimly.

Someone was crying. Torisen thought it might be himself, but then as he fought back to consciousness, he saw the changer kneeling not far away, cradling the wyrm's twitching body in his arms. His cap had fallen off. Wild white hair tumbled over his eyes.

'Shanir!' Torisen gasped. 'Y-you were bound to that thing...'

The changer's head snapped up, its face grotesquely twisted with grief and rage. It lunged at Torisen. He felt its hands close on his shoulders, felt the terrible strength in them. His velvet coat ripped down the back, the prelude to tearing muscles, splintering bones...

Pain came and then, incredibly, faded. He was on the floor again, with Burr bending over him.

'I've ruined my coat,' he said to the Kendar.

'*Damn* your coat.'

Beyond them, Harn and the changer reeled back and forth on the lip of the pit, gripping each other in deadly silence. Their shadows grappled on the floor. Then Harn caught the other's arm and twisted. There was a wet, ripping sound and a terrible wailing cry. The changer staggered away. Harn stared at its arm still in his hands, his face white.

'Oh my God, not again, not again...'

Kindrie caught his hands and wiped off the changer's blood before it could burn too deeply. There wasn't much of it; the ghastly wound had sealed itself almost immediately. Crouching in the shadow under the stair, Donkerri thought he saw more blood, much, much more – waves, oceans of it, roaring over him. He sank to the floor in a dead faint. Above him, feet pounded on the stairs. There were a dozen Kendar in the chamber now – cadets, instructors, even Ashe, the grey-haired, lame singer – holding the changer at bay with its back to the pit. It looked more like a wild animal now than anything human, all resemblance to Nusair gone.

'Careful,' said the singer sharply. 'If this is what I think it is, steel won't help.'

Burr was still on his knees, holding Torisen. He didn't know what had happened to the Highlord, but the changer's attack alone would hardly account for the young man's clammy skin or a heartbeat so fast that it seemed to shake his entire body. Torisen gripped his arm with surprising strength.

'Slipping...' he muttered hoarsely. 'Slipping...'

The changer heard. Its lips curled back over sharp white teeth, the entire jawline shifting.

'Highlord!' Its voice was a guttural bark. 'Hellspawn! Blood will have blood...'

It charged. The cadet directly in its path grounded his spear and caught it full in the chest. It fought its way down the splintering, burning shaft, and took off half the cadet's face with a single blow. The others threw themselves on it.

Torisen half rose. 'Child of Darkness!' he cried in a harsh voice not his own. 'Where is my sword? Where are my – FATHER!' He crumpled to the floor and lay there without moving.

The changer fought free. In the moment before it could gather itself to charge again, the singer's staff caught it with a jolting chin-strike. It stumbled backward. She limped after it, coolly striking again and again, keeping it off balance. The others scrambled out of the way except for one cadet, either slower or cleverer than the rest, who was still on hands and knees at the edge of the pit when the changer reached him. The singer slipped under a vicious swing and pushed the changer backward over the cadet. It fell into the pit. Sparks swirled up from the disturbed embers, lodging in its stolen clothes, igniting them. It tried to climb out, but Kendars now ringed the pit. Its skin began to char.

'Don't think you've won!' it howled from the depths. 'We know now what frightens you, little lord, we knoooo...!'

The flame had laid bare that searing blood and now kindled it, wrapping the creature in veins of fire. It flailed about, shrieking, as the fire worked inward. Flames burst from every orifice. Then with a roar, it exploded, spraying the pit walls with burning blood and bits of charred flesh. A charnal cloud of greasy black smoke shot with red rolled up towards the ceiling.

Everyone recoiled. Soot settled on their clothing and a foul taste lingered in their mouths, but it was over. The cadets began to pull their shaken wits back together. For most of them, this had been their first serious fight, their blooding, but for none more so than the boy who had stopped the changer's initial charge. Locked in a nightmare of pain, his face ruined, all he wanted was release, the White Knife. Kindrie knelt beside him. Instead of drawing steel, however, the Shanir cupped his hands over the cadet's ravaged face. His own pale features went taut with concentration. After a long moment, the boy slipped from pain's grasp into the healing oblivion of *dwar* sleep. Then Kindrie turned to the Highlord.

Torisen hadn't moved. Even in the ruddy light of the fire-timbers, he looked grey with shock and scarcely seemed to be breathing. Burr had put his coat over him. Kindrie reached out hesitantly to touch his face, then stopped abruptly.

Caineron and his guards came down the stairs, weapons drawn.

Images came and went in Torisen's mind, swirling, melting into each other:

> *The dungeons at Urakarn: 'Do you recant... do you profess...' no, no, no (the dead, rotting in piles – don't look) 'Then we must convince you, for your own good.' ... gloves of red-hot wire... oh God my hands!*
> *Burning, burning, the towers of Tai-tastigon, the Res aB'tyrr*
> *(What? Where?)*
> *... trapped, they're all trapped, burning alive... Dead. The Southern Wastes black with corpses... Squat figures moving among the slain, taking a leg here, a head there... meat, fresh meat... Fifteen thousand against three million? Oh, Pereden, you fool, you god-cursed, jealous fool...*

Burr was bending over him with a worried frown. 'My lord? Tori? Hold on to me, just hold on...'

... slipping...

> *The tower keep's inner door groaned, then burst open, and black-clad warriors swarmed into the great hall, voiceless, shadowless. The defenders fell back before the silent fury of their onslaught. Tables crashed over. Benches splintered against the wall. The captain of the guard grabbed his arm.*
> *'My lord, we can't hold these lower rooms!'*
> *'Betrayed!' The word burst from him in a hoarse bray, and the defenders faltered. 'You've all betrayed me again and again and – Can't hold, you say? Then climb, man, all of you, climb!*

.Make the bastards pay for every step.'

And here the Darklings came, silent still, their eyes like those of the dead weary for sleep. For every one of them that fell, two more took his place, and there were so few defenders left. Up the spiral stair, through the second storey maze of living quarters, leaving fallen comrades behind in every room, up again to the battlements.

The crystal dome over the solar glowed like a second moon within the hollow crown of the parapet. Dark figures swarmed over it and it cracked. He was driven back against the door of the northeast turret. There the captain fell, fighting at his side, and suddenly he was alone, ringed by still, white faces.

'You're all dead wood!' he shouted at them. 'Give me something living to hew!'

'Will I do, Gray Lord?'

A man stepped forward, also black-clad but wearing the rhisar and steel armour of a Highborn. He grinned. His face involuntarily shifted into a wolf's leering mask.

'Keral. Oh yes, you'll do nicely.'

He brought Kin-Slayer whistling down. The changer tried to counter the blow, but it shattered his blade and drove him down to one knee. Ganth's sword sheered through armour into the changer's flesh. The wound closed around the blade and blood burned it away, Keral rose, laughing.

'Poor Ganth. Can't trust anything, can you?'

The Gray Lord stared at what was left of Kin-Slayer. Then, in a burst of blind rage, he swung up the hilt-shard to strike again. An arrow caught him in the shoulder. He staggered back against the turret door.

'The Master has a question for you, Gray Lord. Answer, and he may spare your life, if not your soul. Now, where is your daughter?'

'I have none!'

Two more arrows jolted him back, nailing him to the door.

'Wrong answer. We'll look for ourselves, if you don't mind.'

He bowed mockingly and left. The others followed.

The arrows wouldn't let Ganth fall. He was trapped with the agony that each breath cost him and the ever greater pain of a life finally and utterly come to ruin. They had all betrayed him, again and again and again: his people, his consort, even his son. Pain and light faded together, but into the long darkness of the unburnt dead he took his hatred and spent his last breath whispering it:

'Damn you, boy, for deserting me. Faithless, honourless ... I curse you and cast you out. Blood and bone, you are no child of mine ...'

No!

Torisen thought he had shouted the word, but it woke neither echoes off the stone walls nor Burr, dozing uneasily in a chair beside the bed. He was in his own chamber, he saw, lying on the bed under every blanket Burr had apparently been able to find. A fire roared in the gate, branches (fingers?) snapping, black tunnels in the red, twisting, turning, lost ...

Torisen fought the slow drift back into nightmare. He remembered all too vividly what came next: flight through the labyrinth, sleeping city; Ganth's iron boots crashing in pursuit; *'Child of Darkness! Where is my sword? Where are my ...'*

What?

His heart pounded with the dream memory of that chase, but what had it all meant? The nightmare of his father's death was the one he had fled into the Southern Wastes three years ago, the one that had caught him in that ruined city. As far as dreams go, it had made some kind of sense. But as for the other, which had first come nearly two years later ... a child of darkness was a Shanir, and as for Kin-Slayer, he only wished he did have it, however fickle the luck it was said to bring. In fact, the second dream hardly seemed to be his at all, any more than the one at Tagmeth had. But he didn't want to think about them, and he wouldn't. Ultimately, none of them meant anything anyway.

Somewhere in the far recesses of the apartment, stone grated on stone. Burr snapped awake and jumped up, his hand automatically going for his short sword. The sheath was empty. He stepped between the noise and his lord, poised to fight. Then abruptly his whole stance changed.

'Sir!'

'Give me a hand with this,' said Harn's voice, oddly stifled.

Burr left Torisen's line of sight. He heard the randon grunt, and then the grate of stone.

'Damn near got stuck for good,' said Harn's voice. 'Blackie was right: I eat too much. How is he?'

Their voices sank.

'If you're discussing me,' Torisen called with a touch of petulance, 'talk louder.'

When Harn and Burr reached the bed, he had pushed back the mound of blankets and was swinging his feet to the floor. The room faded as a wave of dizziness rolled over him. When it came back into focus, Harn was holding his shoulders, apparently to keep him from pitching forward headfirst.

'... sure you're all right?'

'Well enough, considering. That damned wyrm.'

'Wyrm?' The two Kendar exchanged glances. 'What wyrm?'

'You didn't see it?' Torisen felt suddenly cold. 'It must have crawled away. Damn. I thought I'd killed it.'

'There's a darkling crawler loose in Tentir?' Harn straightened. 'My cadets...'

'They'll all leave tomorrow, and it should have been too badly hurt to attack anyone else tonight.'

'So that's what happened to you. We weren't sure.'

'Sweet Trinity. You didn't think I threw a fit like that out of sheer boredom, did you?'

'Caineron said you'd gone mad.'

The word hung in the air like an obscenity.

'And you weren't sure,' said Torisen softly. 'Like father, like son, eh?'

Burr flinched.

'Don't be daft,' Harn said impatiently, with no apparent sense of incongruity. 'You've got trouble enough without trying to tear strips off us. Nusair is dead, and his father is going to accuse you of his murder. That means a blood feud, you against the entire house of Caineron, unless the High Council takes pity and declares you insane. Either way, we won't march against the Horde, and that, ultimately, may mean the end of us all.'

'But, sir, will the Council really take Caineron's word against the Highlord's?' Burr asked.

Torisen gave a bitter laugh. 'Most of them will probably be delighted to. When they acknowledged my claim three years ago, they said they wanted a leader, an impartial judge, but every one of them – yes, even Ardeth – thought that justice meant having things his own way. Now Caineron will promise them everything, or seem to. What's the alternative? A mad lord from a mad line who has only kept the peace and satisfied no one.'

'So what do we do?'

'If Caineron tells his story first, with me shut up here unable to refute it, my power will be broken forever. Caineron knows that. So I've got to reach Gothregor before he does.'

'Ride? Tonight? Are you strong enough?'

Torisen stood up, slowly, carefully, fighting down a fresh

surge of dizziness. His face was bleak, as if stripped to the iron core of his will.

'I can do anything I have to.'

The randon gave him a hard look, then nodded. 'Yes. You always could.'

Burr brought his lord's riding coat and the saddlebag full of bones. At the back of the apartment was a counterweighted stone wall through which Harn had squeezed with great difficulty. It was still open only a crack. Torisen stopped short, his hand on it. Somewhere in the passageways beyond the guarded door, a voice had cried out in pain.

'Who . . .?'

'Kindrie, I think,' said the randon. His expression hardened. 'Caineron said something in the fire-timber hall about giving him his back pay tonight.'

'He pays a Highborn wages?' said Burr, blankly.

'For Kithorn, yes.'

The cry came again, wilder, bitten off in midnote.

Burr took an involuntary step towards the door, but Harn caught his arm. 'We can't help him now. Besides, he's buying us time, and I think he knows it.'

Old Tentir was riddled with secret passageways. Caineron's spies had apparently never discovered this, but Harn had made himself master of their hidden ways within weeks of his arrival. The stone stairway plunged down between dank walls in steps so narrow that they barely offered a foothold. Harn went first, a torch in his hand, his bulk nearly filling the passageway. Some thirty feet down, he put his shoulder to the wall, forced open another concealed panel, and squeezed through. The other two followed him out into the subterranean stable.

Feet rustled on straw, and seven of Caineron's retainers surrounded them, steel drawn.

'We're sorry, my lord,' the eldest of them said apologetically, 'but our lord insists that you stay.'

The shadows moved behind him. Something clipped the man on the side of the head. He dropped without a sound. The others turned, startled, and another one of them went down with a grunt before the singer's iron-shod staff.

'Ashe!' exclaimed Harn, and sprang forward to help.

He nearly collided with a cadet vaulting over one of the wooden partitions. Four more followed, all Knorths, all survivors of the timber hall fight. Torisen sat down on a bale of hay to watch. Let someone else do the fighting for a change, especially since he was in no shape to help.

'Don't let me hinder you,' he said politely to Burr.

The Kendar only grunted. Clearly, the cadets didn't need the help of the veteran randon. Harn had indeed trained them well. The battle was over before any of Caineron's people had even thought to give the alarm.

'I'm glad to see you finally remember who I am,' said the singer to Harn as they bound and gagged the fallen Kendar. 'After that blank stare you gave me in the fire-timber hall, I thought your wits had finally gone missing.'

'No, just on a long hike. Ashe and I were cadets and one-hundred captains together with the Southern Host long before you were born,' he said to Torisen. 'She gave up her commission after an axe blow nearly took off her leg, although I still say a good healer could have lessened the damage. The fool would never see one.'

The Highlord rose and gave the scrollswoman a full ceremonial bow. 'Fool or not, singer, I'm still in your debt. How may I repay you?'

'My lord, I don't know what's going on, but there must be a song in it somewhere. I'll ride with you, if you're willing.'

'May we too, my lord?' asked a cadet eagerly.

Torisen glanced at the bound Kendar. 'After this, you had better.'

'Right,' said Harn briskly. 'Saddle up, then, and two of you go see if you can get the main gate open before we run into it nose first.'

'You never answered the question I asked you in the tower,' Torisen reminded him.

'Eh? Oh.' Harn went down clumsily on one knee in the straw. 'I will serve you, my lord, in any way that you require. Now and forever.' He looked up under bristling bows. 'Besides, any fool who takes on a changer single-handed needs all the friends he can get.'

'I reconfirm our bond and seal it with blood,' said Torisen formally, repeating the ancient formula. He gave the randon his hands. In the days long before Rathillien, when the Highlord had often been not only a Shanir but a blood-binder, his palms would have been cut across for the full blood rite, which would have bound his liegeman to him body and soul until death, and possibly beyond. 'Now, be a good chap and do something really useful, like saddling my horse for me.'

Within minutes, they were all ready, with two mounts to spare for the cadets who had gone ahead. Torisen pulled himself up onto Storm.

'Ready? Then come on!'

Storm thundered up the ramp. As he burst into the main hall, Torisen saw first the main gate, still firmly closed, and then a dozen of Caineron's guards running towards him. At least half of them were cadets.

Torisen reined in abruptly, the other horses crashing into him from behind. *I can't fight these children,* he thought in dismay . . . *but can they fight me?*

He spurred Storm, giving the rathorn war-cry as the stallion sprang forward. The scream echoed deafeningly off the stone walls. Cadets and veteran retainers alike faltered. Their primary allegiance was to Caineron, but through him they were also bound to his overlord, Torisen. The war-cry reminded them. Their hesitation only lasted a moment, but in that time the horses had swept past them.

Shadows moved by the main gate. The two Knorth cadets darted out of hiding to lift the cross bar and shoulder open the door. The wind whirled wet, dead leaves in around their knees. Then Torisen was past them, plunging out into the night, into the blinding rain.

19

Under Green Leaves
The Anarchies: 8th-11th of Winter

The trade road from Peshtar wound westward down through
the mountains, following a boisterous stream called the Ever-
quick. During the caravan season, this route was well travelled,
but now Jame, Marc, and Jorin had it to themselves.
Wilderness surrounded them. To the north, the Ebonbane
merged with the even higher Snowthorns, which also flanked
the Riverland. Some seventy leagues ahead, where the road
dipped southward to meet the Silver, lay the Oseen Hills. To the
south, across the Ever-quick, was the fringe of the Anarchies.

On that first day, there was no sign of pursuit, unless one
counted the shadow. It swept over the travellers not long after
they left Peshtar, and looking up, they saw something large and
pale high in the sky, gliding in a southwesterly direction towards
the Oseen Hills.

'What in Perimal's name was that?' Jame asked.

'Trinity knows.' Marc watched it vanish into the distance. 'A
snow eagle, maybe, but the shape didn't seem right. It looked
more like some huge albino bat with short wings. Anyway, it's
nothing to do with us – I hope.'

They went on, forcing the pace as much as their somewhat
recalcitrant pack pony would allow. By dusk of the first day,
Marc estimated that they were a good forty miles and, he hoped,
eight hours ahead of Bortis's brigands, who would only now be
rallying at Peshtar. When it became too dark to travel, the two
Kencyr pitched camp under a stand of pine trees beside the
stream. While Marc built a small fire, Jame unloaded a pannier
and found that, again, the Peshtan innkeeper had been more
than generous.

'As far as I'm concerned,' said Marc, lying back contentedly
when they had finished eating, 'the honour of Peshtar has been
more than restored.'

Jame was staring into the darkness across the Ever-quick. The land beyond, invisible as it now was, drew her thoughts as it had off and on all day.

'Marc, tell me about the Anarchies.'

The big Kendar gave her a look of mild surprise. 'Well now, there's not much I can say. The hill tribes call them "The Place Where No Man Rules," which translates rather inaccurately as the Anarchies. I've never been in them nor has anyone I know, but there are rumours. As I said before, the old priest at Kithorn claimed that they were the "thickest" area in Rathillien – that is, the most truly native, with the greatest natural resistance to Perimal Darkling. They've had a reputation for strangeness as far back as anyone can remember, and only the rathorns move freely there, to mate and to die.'

'Once in Tai-tastigon I saw a cuirass made of rathorn ivory. It was beautiful, and worth any two districts in the city. Surely, if rathorns go into the Anarchies to die, men follow them.'

'Oh yes. As you say, but those few hunters who do manage to penetrate the Anarchies tend never to come out again. The land itself is said to be treacherous, and then too, most rathorns are man-eaters, given the chance. Also, they're "beasts of madness," or so our old priest used to say. I've heard of seasoned war horses running themselves to death out of sheer terror after simply catching a rathorn's scent.'

'Trinity. Imagine riding one into battle.'

Marc chuckled. 'Oh, the effect would be devastating, I should think, for all concerned. I wonder if that was in Glendar's mind when he adopted the beast as the Knorth emblem to replace the Master's dishonoured black horse crest. Some say that it was an unlucky choice, since about at that time madness first entered the Knorth bloodline.'

'But the present Lord Knorth, this Torisen Black Lord,' said Jame rather sharply. 'Surely he's sane enough.'

'Why, yes, as far as I know. At any rate, he should be glad to get that ring and sword you've got in your knapsack. They should easily earn you a place in his service, if you want it.'

She almost told him then that in Torisen she hoped to find, not a lord, but a brother, but the words wouldn't come. A silence fell between them. After a bit, Marc rose to build up the fire for the night, and they lay down on opposite sides of it to sleep.

Rolled up in her blanket with Jorin snuggled against her,

Jame listened to the crackle of burning pine needles and the gregarious voice of the stream. She felt suspended between two worlds. Behind her lay Tai-tastigon, where she had made a life for herself – an odd one perhaps by Kencyr standards, but very much her own. Ahead lay the Riverland and a brother whom she no longer knew, but under whose shadow she was about to come. She had never really thought about what Torisen would do with her, or she with him. At any rate, she would see that Marc was rewarded properly. Tori would owe her that much at least.

At daybreak they went on. Across the river, beyond a narrow meadow sprinkled with white flowers, the forest of the Anarchies stood veiled in mist. Rain-coloured birds rose, circled above the trees, and plunged silently back into them.

The north bank began with a fringe of trees, but on the other side of the trade road the land sloped up to the lower reaches of the Snowthorns in a series of bare hills. This was tribal territory. A dozen clans vied for hunting space here, marking their boundaries with *malirs*, the skull of their totem animal mounted on a pole with its bones hanging below from a cross piece. Sometimes the headless and not very fresh corpse of a trespasser was lashed to the pole. When the wind blew, the clatter of bones filled every hollow.

'I begin to see why westward bound caravans don't disband at Peshtar,' said Jame. 'This is not what I would call hospitable country.'

'Just be glad that at this season most of the tribesmen are off hunting deer and each other on the lower slopes of the Snowthorns. Every year the game gets scarcer and the clans more savage. Before long, they'll be reduced to cannibalism, like the Horde.'

'But if the hunting is so bad here, why don't any of the tribes claim lands across the Ever-quick? Those woods must be seething with game.'

'All the clans consider the south bank to be sacred ground. As I understand it, some three thousand years ago, not long before our kind came to Rathillien, someone or something suddenly barred them from the Anarchies. Before that, they believed that their dead crossed the river to a new life, and that the soul of the tribe itself had its roots on the far bank. Their shamen still take turns crossing the Ever-quick to perform secret rites on the far side, which they hope will eventually get them back into the

Anarchies. They can have them too, for all I care.'

'Oh, I don't know,' said Jame, looking across the river. 'The place might be worth a visit, and those rites could be very interesting indeed.'

Marc gave her a worried, sidelong glance. He knew how intrigued Jame was by other people's religions, but he had never before heard quite that note in her voice, as if she were imagining with some relish ceremonies of a particularly gruesome nature. In fact, he had been uneasy about Jame since Peshtar, where she had so casually slashed that brigand's throat. Like most Kendar, Marc was not particularly bothered by the Shanir, perhaps because one had to have at least a touch of Highborn blood in order to be one. He had always assumed that Jame was at most a quarter Highborn because not even a half-blood would have been allowed to run as wild all her life as Jame obviously had. He had known about her claws almost from the start, and they too had never disturbed him in themselves. He also knew, however, how reluctant Jame ordinarily was to use them. Had something changed? He didn't know and didn't like to ask.

That second day and the third they made slower time because of the pony, which apparently had gone lame. Jame suspected it of malingering and proved her point by setting Jorin on it. After its initial fright, however, it limped as badly as before and was harder to scare. Marc kept a wary eye on the hills. He had by no means told Jame all that he knew about the hill tribes' less endearing customs.

The third night, they camped in a stand of poplars on a cliff above the river. In the morning, Jame shook down her long black hair and ran her fingers through it.

'Filthy,' she said with a grimace, and went down to the river with Jorin trotting beside her.

Again, the Kendar said nothing, despite his misgivings. If he had stopped to think about it, he might have wondered why in spite of his seven decades' seniority he had never felt easy giving Jame orders. Now Marc tried to forget his uneasiness and set about preparing their breakfast. He had just rekindled the fire and was reaching for the food pouch when a foot came down on it. A hillman stood beside him. Marc reached for his axe, but froze as steel pricked his broad back. Two more men had silently come up behind him, armed with hunting spears.

'Who are you?' he demanded loudly, hoping that Jame would

hear and take warning. 'What do you want?'

Ignoring him, the first man began to rifle through Jame's knapsack. He pulled out the sword, but threw it aside when he saw that it was broken. Next he found Ganth's ring, still on the Gray Lord's withered finger. He threw the finger into the flames and put on the ring. The man had just burrowed down to the Book Bound in Pale Leather when one of his comrades gave a startled exclamation and pointed.

Jame stood in the shade of the poplars. Slender and still with sunlight dappling her bare limbs, she looked like some spirit of the grove in human form. There are still such wild things in the wild corners of the earth. Even Marc, seeing her, felt a touch of near primordial dread.

The first hillman rose and backed towards the Kendar, his eyes still on Jame. Then, almost experimentally, as if to see how this strange apparition would react, he turned and struck Marc a heavy blow on the head with his fist. The Kendar swayed, half stunned. He thought for one numb moment that he had gone blind, but then realised that it was only blood, running down from a forehead cut made by Ganth's ring.

As his vision cleared, he saw the silver sheen in Jame's eyes and her slow, chilling smile. Jorin cowered away from her. Now she was gliding, almost dancing, through the woods towards them, and the morning light seemed to darken around her. Marc had seen Jame dance at the B'tyrr back in Tai-tastigon, and had been disturbed by it. Now he sensed that this was the true dance of the Dream-Weaver, of which the B'tyrr's had been only the shadow.

The hillmen were staring open-mouthed, caught in the dark web of the dance. Jamethiel glided up to the one who had struck Marc. With deft touches, she brought his soul trembling to the edge of his being, ripe for reaping. Then she put her arms around him. Marc saw her draw the backs of her unsheathed nails slowly, sensuously, along the sides of his neck across the pulsing arteries. They poised for the forward sweep.

'No!' he cried.

Jame blinked. What the hell...?

She brought her knee up sharply into the hillman's groin and again with a crack into his chin as he doubled over.

Marc threw himself backward, twisting sideways. One spear point passed under his arm. The other tangled in his jacket. He snapped the first one's shaft by catching it between his body and arm and turning sharply the other way. The other spearman was trying to free his weapon. Marc grabbed it. He jerked its head forward through his jacket and the man into his fist. By the time he had freed himself from the spear shaft, the other hillman had fled. He and Jame stared at each other over the bodies of the two fallen men. She looked very young, and very frightened.

The big Kendar shook his head as if to clear it. Jame could almost see memory fading from his eyes.

'That man hit me and then... and then... ah, no matter.' He wiped the blood off his face. 'Your throat and my head certainly have taken a beating lately. Here.' He bent and pulled Ganth's ring off the hillman's hand. 'I'm afraid the finger that wore this is gone, but then I always did think it should be given to the pyre. You'd better wear this now for safe-keeping.'

Jame took the ring. She was suddenly very cold, both from the Ever-quick's icy waters and from delayed shock. She dressed hastily, with shaking hands. Yes, Marc had really forgotten. One mystery of the B'tyrr's dance had always been that no one could recall its exact details afterward, not even the dancer – not until now. This time Jame did remember. Sweet Trinity, she had nearly taken both that man's life and his soul. And before that? The impulse to use her claws on the Earth Wife's imp and to dance at the Peshtar inn; had her encounter with Keral triggered all this, or had she always been so reckless? The Arrin-ken had spoken of honour and balance. How far could one go in either direction without falling? Where did innocence end?

Girl, you don't want to find out, she told herself. *Be very, very careful, because it would be so easy to let go.*

Jame put on her father's ring. Even on her thumb it was too big, but her glove kept it in place. Its cold touch steadied her. She held this and the sword in trust for her brother, and they must go to him. That was her primary responsibility now. She picked up Kin-Slayer and nearly dropped it again. An odd tingle had shot through her hand. There were many strange stories about this sword, including a tradition that it enhanced the strength of its rightful wielder; but Jame had handled it before without noticing anything unusual. Of course, she had never worn the ring before either. The sensation faded. Jame shrugged and returned the sword shard to her knapsack.

Marc had bound both captives with their own belts and was now questioning the one whom Jame had stunned.

367

'We have a problem,' he said quietly to Jame in Kens. 'This is a Grindark, all the way up from the Oseen Hills. He says he and his brothers were hunting nearby – poaching, really – when a man swooped down on them out of the sky.'

'A man?'

'Well, for lack of a better name. He was naked and seemed to be gliding on skin stretched between his limbs and torso, rather like that white thing we saw yesterday. Also, he had the image of an *imu* burned into his face.'

'Trinity! That must have been the changer from Peshtar.'

'That's likely, especially since he said he was an emissary from the Black Band. It seems that Bortis has a pact with Grisharki, the Grindark warlord, who used to be one of his brigands. The upshot is that these hunters were sent on ahead to waylay us while the changer went to summon more Grindarks from Wyrden, Grisharki's stronghold. They must be well on their way by now.'

'So we've got Grindarks coming at us from one direction and brigands from the other. Lovely. Now what?'

'We could angle northwestward and try to outflank the Grindarks... but no. We would only run into more hunting parties. So it looks as if you'll get your wish, lass: the Anarchies it is.'

Four large stepping stones led across the Ever-quick, each one carved with an *imu* face. On the far bank were two *malirs.* Surmounting each was the skull mask of a rathorn, a stallion on the right with both the nasal tusk and the ivory horn curving back from between wide-set eye sockets, a mare on the left with only the nasal tusk. The bones hanging beneath each chimed together in the wind. A road paved with white cobbles stretched back between the *malirs* into the meadow, towards the trees.

'That's the hill tribes' spell-path,' said Marc. 'Their shamen won't enter the Anarchies by any other route and no ordinary hillman is likely to at all. So here we give the slip to the Grindarks and perhaps to any brigand with hill-blood.'

'But not to Bortis?'

'I doubt it. He isn't likely to honour the taboo, but with luck we can still evade him without going too far into the Anarchies. Ready?'

Jame settled her pack more comfortably. In it, besides the sword and Book, was a portion of their food and spare clothing.

The pony stood nearby, looking bewildered to find itself both unloaded and free.

'Ready,' she said.

'You first, lass, and mind your step.'

Jame backed up a few paces, then took a running leap at the first stone some six feet from the shore. The water rushing past it was both very swift and surprisingly deep, and the stone itself slick with moss. She bounded from one to the next across the stream, seeing the green faces flash past under her feet. On the far side, she turned so that Jorin could use her eyes to cross. Marc followed the ounce.

They went up the spell-path of white cobbles through the meadow. Ahead, the road ended untidily under the shadow of the trees. Some of the cobbles there seemed to be covered with moss of different colours, which birds were carrying strand by strand up into the trees. No, not moss. Suddenly Jame knew what the shamen's rites were, and what use the hillmen found for the heads of their enemies.

From behind came the sound of voices. Drifting mist momentarily obscured the meadow, and under its cover, the two Kencyr gained the trees. Looking back, they saw snatches of the far bank, then the entire length of the river with some thirty men on the other side. One of them was all too familiar.

'Damn,' said Jame in a low voice. 'Bortis. He must have been one step behind us all the way. But how?'

'Maybe he didn't go back into the Ebonbane to rally his men after all. Maybe he just came after us with as many as he could find of the ones who had been on leave in Peshtar.'

'He's got one of the Grindark spearmen. Now what... Trinity!'

A shriek cut across the Ever-quick's loud gurgle. The hillman was cowering at Bortis's feet, one of his forebraids, roughly severed, dangling from the brigand chief's hand.

'Come on,' said Marc. 'We'll have to go farther in than I expected.' He turned and set off with a long stride towards the deeper woods. Jame and Jorin trotted beside him.

'But why? What's happened?'

'I underestimated Bortis's cunning and cruelty. The Grindarks believe that the roots of their manhood lie in those braids. That hillman will lead Bortis anywhere rather than lose both of them, and his sense of smell is nearly as keen as a wolf's.'

They went southward through the trees, through a patch of a

weed called 'deadman's breath,' whose stench should stun the tracker's nose temporarily at least. Beyond was a brook running down to the Ever-quick. This they followed for some distance, wading upstream in the shallows, before turning southward again. Winter apparently came late in this corner of the world. Few leaves had as yet even changed, and the air was almost warm. A deep silence lay over the land. Dense as these trees had seemed from the other side of the stream, Jame now saw that the real forest still lay ahead, on the other side of a large clearing. They passed under the shade of a solitary red maple, nearing the line of darker trees. Mist blew across the meadow, and abruptly they were back beside the maple.

Jame stopped short, gaping. 'What in Perimal's name? Marc, am I losing my few remaining wits or did we just jump backward about fifty yards?'

'So we did. How very odd.' The Kendar walked on over the ground they had already covered once, Jame and Jorin followed. 'Now, how far had we...'

He vanished.

'...got?' said his voice behind Jame. She spun about and saw him loping towards her, away from the maple. 'Just about to here,' he said, stopping beside her, pointing to the ground a few feet ahead. 'This, I would guess, is how the Anarchies were closed to the hill folk.'

'And to us?'

'Maybe, maybe not. After all, a few hunters have got in, although they keep the way a secret.' He stroked his beard thoughtfully. 'Have you ever heard of step-back and -forward stones?'

'Of course,' said Jame impatiently, her mind on brigands and weed patches. 'Certain rocks are supposed to be so closely linked to where they developed geologically that if you move them, they somehow exist simultaneously in both the old and new sites – that is, if you know how to set them properly. Songs say that the Builders played all sorts of tricks with them. Ah,' she said as Marc dropped to a knee and began to cut out a square of sod. 'I see what you mean. If some of those special rocks are buried here under the grass...'

'Then stepping on them automatically transports us to their original location, back under that maple.' He lifted out the sod. At the bottom of the hole were stones, smoothly fitted together, carved with intricate figures.

'Those are Builders' runes,' said Jame, peering down at them. 'A ring of step-back stones? That would certainly close the Anarchies, but why should the Builders want to do that, assuming this really is their work?'

'I have no idea. No one knows much for sure about those folk. We'd be safer if we could cross this barrier, but off-hand, I don't see how.'

'One possibility does occur.'

Jame let her pack drop. She backed up several yards, then ran towards the exposed stones. Just short of them, she leapt head first over the barrier, rolled – and came up back under the maple. Damn. Marc was just turning. She sprinted towards him through the clinging grass. Her foot came down in his cupped hands and they launched her with all Marc's tremendous strength added to her own. She left his hands as a stone does a sling. The ground passed in a blur twelve feet beneath – no, less: in fact, here it came. She rolled over and over, finally coming to a breathless stop – almost under the dark trees.

'Are you all right?' Marc called after her.

'Fine, fine,' said Jame, gingerly picking herself up. 'Just send my stomach along by the next post rider. Now, where's the edge of this thing... ah.' Her probing knife struck stone under the sod. 'Twenty feet wide.'

'Here.' Marc picked up Jorin, and hurled the surprised ounce across the hidden stones. Then he threw Jame's pack after her.

'Now you.'

The big Kendar shook his head regretfully. 'There's no way I can jump that far. You go on, lass. I'll cover your retreat.'

Jame stared at him, appalled, as he unslung his war-axe and turned to wait for the Black Band. She had never stopped to consider how he would cross. It was unthinkable to leave him and yet... and yet... no. There had to be another way across those damned stones.

Stones.

Jame turned and began to hunt feverishly through the grass for some of the rocks she had just rolled over. Finding one, she pried it out of the ground. Marc looked back, puzzled, as the stone thudded to earth some eight feet behind him. Jame had already pried another, even bigger rock and was staggering back with it.

'You were trying, maybe, to get my attention? No games now, lass. Run while you can.'

'Don't be...' she heaved the second stone, only managing a few feet's distance with it '... stupid. Look, the earth that's accumulated over the step-back stones obviously doesn't hinder them much, but then it belongs where it is. But the two stones I've just thrown are displaced. They come from ahead. I haven't the skill or knowledge to build a "step-forward" with them, assuming they've even the right kind of rocks, but just maybe they can counteract the old rune-ring enough to act as stepping stones.'

Marc looked dubiously at the two rocks, now almost invisible in the grass, and again shook his head. 'It's too chancy.' He stiffened. 'Here they come. Go now, quickly.'

'Listen, you idiot,' Jame hissed at him. 'Either you come over here, or I'm going over there. My word of honour on it!'

Marc gave her a quick look, then shrugged. He went back a pace, then leapt for the first stone, the second, the far side. Jame caught his arm.

'Well, I'll be damned,' he said. 'It worked. Look out!'

He knocked Jame backward, away from the first wave of bandits. They rushed onto the hidden stones, shouting, and suddenly found themselves back level with the maple. The slower brigands turned, thinking they were under attack from behind. As a lively – if confused – free-for-all began, the fugitives took cover in the trees. A shadow swept over the clearing.

'Damn,' said Jame. 'It's the changer. If he saw how we crossed, he'll tell the others. Now what?'

'We go farther in.'

Jame looked back into the shadow of the trees. A vast silence waited there, and a lurking presence of leaf and blade, bough and branch that numbed her mind. But what choice did she have?

'Yes, we go on. We have to.'

They slipped back into the trees, and the shadows swallowed them.

Boughs arched against the sky like the ribs of some great cathedral roofed with leaves. Green light filtered down from above. Grey birds glided between the trees, the underside of each wing marked by a single, almost human eye picked out in subtly shaded feathers. Below, mist drifted around ferns, between the silver-grey trunks. Everything was hazy and dreamlike, a quality enhanced by the great silence of the place. What sounds there were carried with unnerving clarity and seemed to come from all directions at once. Jame and Marc moved as quietly as they could, listening for their pursuers. They heard nothing, but that might only mean that Bortis had had the sense to keep his men quiet once past the step-back stones. Meanwhile, the roof of leaves and mist hid them from the changer, if he were still looking for them. Maybe they really had shaken off pursuit. Marc thought their best plan would be to cut back across the rune-ring as soon as possible and continue down the Ever-quick on its deserted south bank. He didn't tell Jame that he was no longer sure exactly where the stream lay.

Jame was equally confused. Not only had she no idea in which direction they were going, but also her senses felt oddly muted. These woods reminded her of the Earth Wife's lodge in Peshtar, except that here one sank into the strangeness of the place as if into deep leaf mould. She *had* felt a faint murmur of this among the decaying temples of Tai-tastigon's elder gods. There was something so strange about them and this place, something so... alien. But then she and Marc were the aliens here, as the Earth Wife had said. This wasn't even their world. What if there was a native force on Rathillien that had nothing to do with their god? What would that do to the Kencyrath's monotheism, to its entire self-conception?

Damn. These were the same doubts that had seized her the first time she had stumbled into the Temple District. Well, this time she wouldn't panic, at least not before she had good cause. But sweet Trinity, she thought, looking uneasily around, how strange it all was.

There! A flicker, seen out of the corner of her eye, gone when she spun around to face it.

'What is it?' Marc asked.

'I... don't know. Something short and grey. It was watching us. Jorin?'

The ounce stirred uneasily. He had clearly caught her visual flash, but had no sensory impressions of his own to add. Whoever... *what*ever the watcher had been, it had left neither scent nor sound. Suddenly the cat's ears pricked. A hoarse, coughing cry welled up around them, as if out of the very earth. Leaves shivered on nearby trees.

'What...?'

'Hush.' Marc pivoted, but mist and undergrowth cut visibility

373

to a few yards in each direction. The sound could have come from anywhere. 'That was a hunting cry. There are rathorn about.'

'Wonderful. Why do we always get a choice of disasters?'

'Virtue has to have some reward, I suppose.'

Jame snorted. 'Just once, I wish it would pick on someone else... hey!'

At that moment, her foot had suddenly broken through the leaf mould into the tangled roots of a dead sapling. They closed on her ankle. She tried to pull it free, without success.

'What in Perimal's name – Marc, these roots – they don't want to let me go!'

The tree groaned and began to topple, straight towards her. Marc pushed it aside. It hit the ground with a crash that echoed on all sides, bounding off one tree after another, until it at last faded away into the distance. The roots twisted as the tree fell, clamping even tighter on Jame's foot. She gave a hiss of pain.

'Use your axe... ah! It's crushing my ankle.'

Marc stripped away mould and earth, exposing the fibrous network beneath. He thrust his big hands down into it. 'The shamen never even bring edged tools here, must less weapons. We mustn't use them either, if we can help it.' He gripped the roots on either side of Jame's ankle. The muscles on his arms bulged, wood creaked, and the foot suddenly came free. Jame rubbed her sore ankle gingerly. Ancestors be praised for a stout boot. But had that been a freak accident or a deliberate attack? Just how strange *was* this place?

Then both her head and Marc's snapped up. Somewhere in the woods, somebody had uttered a loud yelp of surprise and pain. A babble of voices followed, quickly hushed.

'Maybe someone else put his foot in it,' suggested Marc in an undertone, without much humour.

Clearly, the Black Band *had* crossed over the step-back stones. The hunt was on again. Marc gave Jame a hand up, and they went on, as quickly and quietly as they could.

The day stretched on and on in green twilight. They heard little of their pursuers and less of any wildlife except for the grey birds, which continued to swoop low over them, coming much closer than wild birds normally do. They were probably only curious, Jame thought. Humans must be a rarity here. One landed on a nearby branch and flexed its wings so that the feathered eyes seemed to blink at the intruders. Jame noted that these were the only eyes the bird had. Somewhere in the distance, a rathorn coughed and then was silent. They still couldn't tell if it was hunting them, the brigands, or neither.

Most of the time, Jorin trotted at Jame's side, ears pricked, sniffing, but only a few of his impressions reached her now. Either her still tentative link with him had begun to fade again, or this place was starting to come between them. Then he chose a tree and began happily to dig among its roots. It let all its leaves fall on him at once. The cat erupted from the leaf mound with an affronted squawk and raced back to Jame's side where he plumped himself down and began to wash as if nothing had happened.

'*Now* what?' said Jame, eyeing the suddenly denuded tree warily.

Marc chuckled. 'Oh, that's only a *dorith*. They're fairly common down the length of the Silver.' He stepped up to another tree covered with what looked like a myriad of small cocoons. 'Here's something rarer, though. It's called a "host." Watch.'

He rapped its trunk lightly.

All the cocoons burst open. A flurry of pale green new leaves leapt into the air and vanished, golden veins flashing, into the upper mist.

'But when will they fall?' asked Jame, staring after them.

'Not until they reach their winter host tree far to the south. They'll come back in the spring...'

It was beginning to get dark. Mist and shadows grew under the trees, taking on the hint of ghostly shapes, dissolving again as a breath of wind rustled the leaves above. Below, the ferns whispered together.

'We'll have to stop soon,' said Marc. 'This is no place for anything human after dark. We'd better not risk a fire, though. For one thing, Bortis's men might see it; for another, I have a feeling that we should do as little damage as possible here.'

Jame caught his arm. 'Look.'

Ahead, a light glowed between the trees. They approached warily, thinking they might have circled around on the brigands' camp by accident. Instead, in the middle of a glade they found a fragmentary ring of standing stones. Actually, only one still stood. The others tilted drunkenly or lay in the long grass, and most had left behind nothing but empty, over-grown sockets in the earth. All the stones that remained were composed of some cloudy crystalline substance. All glowed softly in the gathering dusk.

'Diamantine,' said Marc. 'I've seen small chunks of it before, but never a complete lithon. We could make our fortune with one of these, lass – if we could get it out of here. This stuff is almost as hard as diamond and it retains sunlight.'

His voice set off a faint echo in the glade that seemed to come from the stones themselves. Jame put her gloved hand tentatively on one. It was vibrating slightly. Regarded more closely, its internal cloudiness seemed to suggest some definite but rudimentary shape that she couldn't quite make out. Her fingers brushed against gouges scarring the stone's side.

'I thought you said no one brought edged tools into the Anarchies.'

'Let's see. Ah. Rathorns did that. They must spend about a quarter of their lives hacking at stones like these or at anything hard they can find. Apparently a rathorn's ivory goes on growing throughout its life. It can't do much about the chest and belly plates or the greaves, but unless that big horn is constantly honed down, it eventually curves around so far that it comes through the back of the rathorn's skull. Some scrollsmen even claim that the beast would be immortal if its own armour didn't eventually kill it.'

'Marc, let's stay here for the night.'

'Well now, there's a fresh spoor in the grass. We may have unwelcome company before dawn.'

'At least we can see them coming.'

The big Kendar glanced at the shadows gathering around them. Very soon, it would be very dark out there indeed. 'I take your point.'

They ate a frugal supper, then lay down beside the standing stone. Jorin stretched out between them, yawned, and almost immediately fell asleep. So did Marc, although he had intended to keep the first watch.

Jame lay awake watching darkness gather beyond the diamantine's glow. It seemed to her that the woods were full of shadowy forms, drifting, standing, watching. She could almost hear them whisper in voices like the rustle of dried leaves. They wanted to tell her something, to warn her, but the gentle snores of her comrades drowned them out. Now the stones around her began to echo the sound until she seemed to be surrounded by sleepers, human, feline, and lithic. The somnolent hum pulled at her, drew her bit by bit down into sleep.

20

The High Council
Gothregor: 8th-10th of Winter

Gothregor was nearly as far from Tentir as the randon college was from Tagmeth. Of those seventy-odd miles, the first twenty-five were by far the worst, with the trailing edge of the storm pouring down rain occasionally mixed with hail and the River Road nearly washed out. The nine riders were soaked and all of their mounts spent except Torisen's black and Burr's grey when some three hours later they reached Wilden and Shadow Rock Keeps, facing each other across the Silver. Lords Randir and Danior had both already left with their troops, stripping both keeps' stables but luckily not their riverside posting station.

By now, it was about midmorning. The thunderheads rolled on before them, leaving the brilliant but cool sunlight of an autumn day. Wet leaves lay in drifts of crimson and gold across the road. On bare branches above, raindrops hung like sparkling buds.

Harn twisted to look back up the road. 'Odd. I thought Caineron would be snapping at our heels by now. We didn't exactly slip out of Tentir unnoticed.'

'No well-bred Highborn rides in all weathers like a leather-shirt trooper if he can help it.' Torisen quoted. 'Now that I've slipped out of his grasp, I suppose Caineron will wait for his troops and descend on Gothregor sometime tomorrow with all their weight behind him.'

'Besiege it, d'you mean?'

'Trinity, no, not with all the other lords there, too. The man's not that big an idiot. He will simply want to impress the rest of the Council. A Knorth defeat there will serve him much better than a quiet assassination here on the road. He must be very sure of himself. Knowing Caldane, he's probably convinced himself by now that you carted me off a raving maniac, tied to Storm hand and foot.'

'That could still be arranged. You must have got that crawler before it could really get you; but just the same, let me know if you decide to fall off.'

'I'm resisting the temptation.'

Harn looked at him askance, clearly unsure how serious he was. Torisen grinned.

'Now, Harn. I've kept you guessing for the better part of fifteen years. Is this any time to stop?'

The burly randon only growled.

They took the next two stages at an easier pace, changing mounts again at Falkirr, and came within sight of Gothregor in the late afternoon. The fortress was set on the plateau of a mountain spur that jutted out into the Riverland some one hundred and fifty feet above the valley floor. The outer ward and the fields beyond seethed with troops. As the riders approached, they saw the wolf standard of Hollens, Lord Danior, flying from the branch of an apple tree in the orchard just outside the northern barbican. Danior's people, some one thousand of them, were camped under the trees among the windfalls. Torisen reined in.

'Lord Danior... Cousin Holly!'

A young man in hunting leathers seated by a campfire turned his head sharply. He rose and came towards them, smiling. 'Torisen! You made good time. We weren't expecting you until tomorrow.'

'I had some help. Announce me, will you?'

'With pleasure!' He went off shouting for his horse.

'Is this really necessary?' demanded Harn.

'After last night? Yes.'

Holly came back riding a skittish bay mare. He galloped up to the barbican and gave a loud blast on his hunting horn. The mare nearly threw him.

'A Knorth entering!' he shouted up at the guard.

'The gate's already open, you fool!' shouted back the Kendar, who apparently had neither understood what Holly had said nor recognised a Highborn in such rustic clothing.

'A *Knorth!*' bellowed Lord Danior.

'Sweet Trinity,' said Torisen in an undertone. 'D'you think it's too late to sneak in quietly after all?'

Just then, the guard saw him.

'M-my lord! Gothregor!' he turned and shouted across the inner ward. *'Gothregor!'*

378

Danior rode through the outwork with Torisen behind him. The others ranged themselves in the Highlord's wake. The broad outer ward seemed to sway up and towards them as the Kendar came to their feet. There was the leaping flame standard of Brandan and the stooping hawk of Edirr, Jaran's stricken tree, and the Coman's double-edged sword flying over a token force: the rest would be waiting down river at Kraggen Keep, as would be Ardeth's at Omiroth and the Edirr twins' at Kestrie. Even so, counting Torisen's people, there were nearly ten thousand Kencyr here.

'Knorth!' one shouted, and the rest took up the chant:

'K-*north!* K-*north!* K-*north*...!'

'Who's trying to impress whom?' muttered Harn under cover of the roar.

'*Trying*, sir?' said Burr.

The randon nodded to the west, across the river. 'There's one lot who aren't buying.'

Over the ruins of Chantrie, Gothregor's sister keep, flew the standard of Kenan, Lord Randir: a gauntleted fist grasping the sun. Kenan had brought nearly eight thousand five hundred troops to the gathering of the Host, and of those, watching from the overgrown wards and crumbling battlements, not one raised a cheer for the Highlord's homecoming.

Torisen rode through the roaring crowd to the causeway that led up to the gatehouse. The section passing through the middle ward was so steep that steps had been cut out of the underlying rock. Ahead, the rounded twin fronts of the gate-house loomed dizzyingly up against the sky. Torisen's own Kendar leaned over the battlements, shouting. Inside was the inner ward, broad, green, surrounded by barracks, armouries, and domestic offices, all stacked three storeys high and built into the outer wall's thickness.

Torisen swung down, wincing. The leg that the wyrm had bitten had stiffened during the long ride. He hung onto Storm for a moment, feeling lightheaded, cursing softly, then let go as Rowan, his steward, limped across the grass to meet him. She too had been at Urakarn and bore the name-rune of the Karnid god burned into her forehead.

'My lord! We weren't expecting you so soon.'

'So I gather. Is everything ready for the Council tomorrow?'

'Yes, lord. Everyone is here except Lord Caineron.'

Torisen reclaimed his saddlebag, and grooms led the horses

away. Gothregor's subterranean stables were four times the size of Tentir's, but, until winter, the garrison's mounts were stabled in converted ground-level barracks. The Kendar certainly didn't need them all. Torisen and his two thousand retainers rattled around in this huge fortress like dried peas in a helmet even when all of them were home. Now as usual, about five hundred were off serving with the Southern Host and elsewhere, a duty that they all took by rotation to earn Gothregor the money it needed to keep going. He could easily have fielded four times as many *yondri-gon* and filled Chantrie with men and women willing to rebuild it with their bare hands for half a promise of eventual acceptance among his regular troops. Caineron and his sons had built up their own huge army that way. Ardeth kept urging him to accept *yondri;* but how could he make promises he might not be able to keep? Even at two thousand, he felt the strain. It was as if every time he bound a Kendar to him, he gave that man or woman a piece of himself. There was simply no more to spare.

'Lord Jaran has been asking for you, my lord,' said Rowan as they approached the keep. 'Or rather he keeps asking for Ganth Gray Lord.'

'He's gone soft?'

'As a rotten peach.'

Damnation. At one hundred and sixty, Jaran had been overripe for years, but he had picked an awkward time to go off altogether, as he must well know. If he couldn't hold himself together through tomorrow to support the Highlord, his great-great-grandson would take over, and the boy was half a Randir.

'Poor old Jaran. Make him comfortable, but see that he's kept as far from Lord Ardeth as possible. Adric thinks that senility is contagious.'

Rowan gave him a startled look. 'Isn't it?'

'Who knows? Just be grateful that a full-blooded Kendar like you never catches it.'

'Yes, lord – and by the way, have I begun to lurch more than usual or are you limping, too?'

'The latter. You wouldn't believe how big the vermin are at Tentir this fall. But speaking of Lord Ardeth, where is he?'

'In your quarters, lord, making himself at home as usual. He asked that you attend him as soon as you arrive – his words, you understand,' she added sourly, 'not mine.'

'Indeed. Then I had better go see him at once, hadn't I?'

Rowan and Burr exchanged glances.

'My lord, won't you have some supper first?'

'Burr can bring it up to my quarters.' He had already set off with a fast if uneven stride towards the keep, still carrying the saddlebag.

'Me and my big mouth,' said Rowan ruefully.

The keep had the same general outline as the larger fortress – rectangular with a drum tower at each corner. Its first floor was windowless and dark. Here the lord of Knorth dispensed domestic justice under flaring torches and the stern death banners of his family. The second floor – brighter, more richly appointed – also was a hall of judgement, but for disputes between other houses. The third floor, as usual, took Torisen's breath away as he stepped out of the spiral stair in the corner. All four walls between their stone arches were stained glass. Here the High Council met, under the emblems of all nine major houses blazing with light, three by three by three. On the fourth wall facing east was a map of Rathillien in coloured glass, all Kendar work, of course: the Highborn were about as artistically inept as an intelligent race could be.

Torisen stood gazing at the map for several moments as he got his breath back. Then he turned. On the western wall, catching the last of the day's light, was his own rathorn crest, flanked by Ardeth's full moon and Jaran's stricken tree. They were the two oldest supporters of his house, in more ways than one. If he was about to lose Jaran, it would be suicidal to quarrel with Ardeth, whatever the provocation.

He entered the stair and climbed more slowly, favouring his leg, to the room at the top of the northwest drum tower, which served as his study.

Adric, Lord Ardeth, sat by the fire in the room's only comfortable chair, reading a book. He looked up with a smile as Torisen entered.

'My dear boy, how delightful to see you again.'

'And you, my lord.'

It *was* a pleasure, despite everything, made all the more piquant by the old undercurrent of resentment. Then he saw that the book in the old lord's hand was his journal. Ardeth noted his change of expression.

'Memory is safer,' he said placidly. 'I never could understand the compulsion to write everything down.'

Torisen put the saddlebag on the table and lifted the book out of Ardeth's hands. 'Hardly everything.'

'Oh come. Surely after all these years we two have no secrets from each other.'

None, at least, that you haven't tried to sniff out, you old ferret, thought Torisen. 'You shouldn't begrudge me some poor scraps of privacy,' he said lightly.

'My dear boy, when have I ever begrudged you anything?'

Torisen was startled into a laugh. 'I've just realised where Caineron gets those... er... remarkable manners of his,' he said in answer to Ardeth's look of inquiry. 'He's trying to imitate you.'

An expression of extreme distaste crossed the old lord's face. 'Oh really! Caineron....' He became thoughtful. 'That man is apt to cause trouble.'

'You agree, then, that the Host must march?'

'Of course. You forget that I also served with the Southern Host, back when Krothen's great-grandfather paid its hire, and that my son Pereden commands it now. We have seen the Horde. A pity that Caineron hasn't, and that you gave him that idiotic promise. I said at the time that it was a mistake.'

'Perhaps. But if I hadn't, Harn Grip-Hard wouldn't be here now to act as my second-in-command.'

'You reinstated him? But the man is a berserker, unreliable on his own in a battle.'

'I rely on him.'

'Well, you know best. Still, this will stick in Caineron's throat if nothing else does. He sold his consent for a promise once, though; perhaps, for the right price, he will again.'

The young man snorted. 'And what can I offer him this time, short of the Highlord's seat itself?'

'A grandchild?'

Torisen made an impatient gesture. 'We've been through all this before. On your advice, I took Caineron's daughter as a limited term consort, and that did keep her father off my back for nearly a year. Kallystine was sure I would extend the contract to include children. She still is. But if Caineron ever gets his hands on a legitimate Knorth grandchild, I may as well cut my own throat to save him the trouble. Trinity knows, after a night with Kallystine I've often considered doing it on general principles.'

'And yet I'm told that she *is* very beautiful.'

'So is a gilded sand viper.'

'Yes, well, just the same, you should be forming some permanent alliances. Look at Caineron. He has children and grandchildren with mothers from nearly every house in the Kencyrath.'

Torisen gave a snort of laughter. 'Don't I know it. That man is prolific enough to sire offspring on a mule.'

'I daresay. Caldane's fancy has been known to wander. I could tell you tales of his exploits in Karkinaroth some twenty years ago . . . but never mind. The point is that the bloodlines of his legitimate children form a net of power, one that Caldane may eventually use to entangle and destroy you. Now, if you were to contract to one of my great-granddaughters and I had the right to avenge you if necessary, that might make him hesitate.'

'Perhaps,' said Torisen dryly, 'but it will hardly make him let the Host march the day after tomorrow.'

'True,' said Ardeth.

He steepled his long, elegant fingers and gazed thoughtfully at them. Firelight woke a spark in the depths of his sapphire signet ring and another in his hooded blue eyes, still keen after nearly fifteen decades.

'I will have to pull a few bloodlines myself. Now, if Caineron should cast the sole dissenting vote, he might be pressured into changing it. He cares what others think of him, or at least will until what they think no longer matters. Randir will be the most difficult. Between them, he and Caineron command more than a third of the Riverland Host. Danior and Jaran are yours as, of course, am I. The Edirr twins will be swayed by their whimsy, and Brandan by his sense of responsibility. As for the Coman, there should be no problem once you've confirmed Demoth as lord.'

'I haven't decided about that yet,' said Torisen.

Ardeth stared at him. 'Of course you will confirm Demoth. His mother was one of my great-granddaughters.'

'And for that I should give the Coman a lord who is quite possibly an idiot?'

'An idiot, perhaps, but one who supports you and is of my blood. In case you'd forgotten, the alternative is Korey, whose mother is a Caineron. That would be quite unacceptable. But enough of this useless debate,' he said, rising. 'The matter is settled. Tomorrow at the Council session you will declare for Demoth.'

'No,' said Torisen.

It was the first time since becoming Highlord that his instincts had led him flatly to refuse one of Ardeth's more serious 'requests.' He had expected the old resentment to come boiling up. Instead, all he felt was exhaustion and a dull ache in his leg. He leaned against the mantelpiece, looking down into the flames, feeling the bite of Ardeth's cold eyes.

'I'm Highlord now, Adric, not your field commander,' he said, not looking up. 'I have to do what I think is right for the Kencyrath, whatever your wishes, whatever mine. The best I can do is promise to protect your interests whenever I can. I owe you that much at least. As for the Coman, I simply don't know Demoth and Korey well enough yet to choose between them.'

'You young fool. How much time do you think you have?'

A footstep on the spiral stair made both men turn sharply. Burr stepped into the room, carrying a covered tray.

'Supper, my lord.'

'Oh hell,' said Ardeth, in quite a different voice, and sat down again abruptly, putting his hands over his face.

'Adric?' Torisen bent over him. 'Are you all right?'

'What we don't have time for,' said Ardeth in a muffled voice, 'is a stupid quarrel.' He let his hands drop. Every one of his one hundred and forty nine years seemed etched deep in his face. 'Especially not when the Southern Host has already marched. Do you really think Pereden was ready to take command?'

'I hope so,' said Torisen carefully. 'He did have nearly a year's training as my second-in-command.' *With Harn doing all the actual work.*

Ardeth leaned back in the chair for a moment, his eyes closed. 'He is the child of my old age, my last son. All the others died in the White Hills, fighting for your father. Sometimes I wish I had died with them.' He stood up again, more carefully this time. 'Think about the Coman. Of course, whichever one you chose, the other is apt to come after you with a knife, but you'll find in the end that I'm right – as usual.'

He glanced at the far wall and blinked, a startled expression flickering across his face.

'Adric?'

'Nothing, nothing.' Ardeth shook his white head as if to clear it. 'Just eat something and get some sleep. You don't look as if your northern trip was all that restful.' He paused at the top of the stairs. 'Pereden thinks very highly of you, you know, but no less than I do.'

'"Highly" my left boot,' muttered Burr as the Highborn disappeared down the steps. 'That spoiled brat would spit on your shadow if he dared.'

Torisen sighed. 'I know. See that Ardeth gets safely back to his quarters, won't you?'

'Yes, lord.... You didn't tell him what happened at Tentir?'

'Trinity! No, not a word.'

Burr grunted. 'He'll hear about it soon enough anyway.' He went down the stair, shutting the door behind him.

Now why hadn't he said anything about Tentir? It hadn't been a conscious decision at all, more like an instinctive reluctance to tell Ardeth any more than he had to. Torisen picked up the journal and leafed through it. Names, dates, events... Anar, his old tutor, had kept a book like this when he had felt his mind beginning to go. Anar, the keep, Ganth... Ardeth believed that the Gray Lord had died before his son's departure. That he hadn't was one secret that the lord of Omiroth must never even be allowed to suspect.

'Memory is safer,' murmured Torisen, and threw the journal into the fire.

As the pages burst into flames, he turned and saw the child's shadow on the wall, sitting on the shadow table, swinging her legs back and forth. So that was what had given Ardeth such a start. What was he going to do about her? What was he doing with her in the first place? The answer lay just beneath the surface of his mind, but he flinched away from laying it bare. Things were complicated enough already. Just this once, he would do as he pleased and ask himself no questions. He picked up the saddlebag and sat down before the fire holding it.

'So what do I do about Caineron?' he asked the air.

No answer. He was too tired to think of anything but grandchildren. Yes, he could promise Caldane one, as a last resort. That would at least launch the Host and – who knows? – he might die fighting the Horde anyway. If he didn't and Kallystine bore his child, Caineron would certainly move against him in the child's name. He might still control events but, if not, he could at least prevent a civil war by killing himself. Then Caineron would be Highlord in all but name and soon, probably, even in that.

'He cares what others think of him, or at least will until what they think no longer matters.'

Torisen remembered Kindrie's cry of pain. Was that the sort of cruelty the Three People had in store? Could it possibly be what the Kencyrath's cold, enigmatic deity wanted for them?

Torisen sat staring into the flames, following the same thoughts around and around, until the distant blare of a horn broke the circle. He woke suddenly beside the dead fire, surprised to find that he had been asleep. Who in Perimal's name could be blowing a challenge this late at night? He rose and threw open a shutter. From this height, the outer ward seemed starred with campfires, but they were nothing compared to the river of torches flowing down from the north, grouped in battle formation. The horn sound again, imperious.

'Restormir!' came the guard's hail from the barbican. 'Restormir!'

So Caineron had arrived, twelve thousand strong and apparently ready for a fight. It must have surprised him to find the outworks open and the walls unmanned. Would he be stupid enough to rush in on the sleeping camp anyway? Torisen wished he would, since that would turn the other lords against him with a vengeance.

Here came torches under the gate: two, six, twelve; a delegation, then, riding up to Gothregor.

Torisen put on his coat. Carrying the saddlebag, he opened the southern door and stepped out of the tower. Beyond was a narrow platform, then a catwalk suspended between the keep's two front towers. It swayed underfoot as the wind caught it.

Below, Caineron rode up through the gatehouse into the inner ward. Three of his established sons were with him, as well as a small, miserable figure who could only be Donkerri. The herald blew another blast, waking a volley of echoes off the stone walls.

'Quiet!' Torisen shouted down at him. 'People are trying to sleep!'

Caineron looked up, and flinched. Torisen remembered with sudden amusement that the lord of Restormir was nearly as squeamish about heights as Burr. He unobtrusively shifted his weight to increase the catwalk's sway.

'Highlord!' Caineron shouted up at him. 'My son's blood is on your hands. I will have justice!'

'So will I!' Torisen shouted back. 'But in the morning.'

The walk swayed back and forth, twenty feet down to the flat roof of the keep, seventy to the flagstones before the door.

'Your rank will not protect you from the consequences of this foul deed!' bellowed Caineron, rather desperately launching into a formal challenge, which he had not expected to deliver at the top of his voice, much less to a moving target. 'If you deny your guilt, I say that you lie and ... and ... *will you stop that?*'

'Stop what?' Torisen shouted back. The walk swung him up towards the stars and back again with the wind whipping his black hair in his face. 'Caldane, go to bed! Your quarters are ready, and I've moved the Council meeting up to nine tomorrow morning. If you're too excited to sleep, have pity on those of us who aren't. Good night!'

Caineron seemed inclined to argue but, from what Torisen could make out at this distance, he was also beginning to look distinctly unwell. He let his sons persuade him to go inside.

Torisen waited for the walk's swing to slow and then went on to the southwest tower, which housed his sleeping quarters. Good. Someone, probably Burr, had started a large blaze in the fireplace. He stripped by its light and lay down before it. Tomorrow no longer worried him. Caineron had tripped over his own feet before, rushing in for the kill, and somehow, he was about to do it again. Their god might favour a cruel man, but never a fool. He fell asleep almost at once, and dreamed that he was a child again, pushing his sister in a swing back and forth over the edge of a precipice.

The trumpets sounded, high and sweet. Another procession was coming in under the gatehouse. The morning sunlight blazed on crimson velvet and white fur, on steel and ivory. Brandan's flame banner cracked over his head, its flying shadow throwing the deep lines of his face into even deeper relief. The retinues of the lesser houses – Danir, Edirr, Coman, and Jaran – waiting in the inner ward raised their war-cries in welcome, to be answered by Brandan's troops. Following Brandan would be Randir, Ardeth, and Caineron, in ascending order of importance.

'I still say you should bring up the rear,' muttered Burr, giving Torisen's boots a final buff before handing them to his lord.

'You mean sneak out the postern at dawn and come back in by the front door, banging a drum? No, thank you. Let them come to me.' He pulled on the boots, trying not to wince as the top of the right one came up over his calf.

'Still sore, eh?'

Torisen gave the Kendar a dirty look. 'Nothing to complain about.' In fact, the wyrm's bite only looked like a ring of fading bruises this morning.

Burr held out his black dress coat with its full sleeves, and he slipped into it. The high collar felt odd without the throwing knives sheathed in it, but even if they had survived the fight with the changer, it wouldn't have been proper to carry them on such an occasion. A pity that the armourer probably wouldn't be able to replace them before the march south, assuming there was one. There. That was it, except for one item.

'I hope you haven't forgotten the Kenthiar,' he said to Burr.

Burr snorted. 'I hoped that you had. Here it is.'

He opened an iron box. Inside lay a narrow silver collar, ornately inscribed with runes of forgotten meaning, set with a gem of shifting hue. It had been found in the unfinished temple at Kothifir when the Kencyrath first came to Rathillien. Some claimed that it was a parting gift from the mysterious Builders; others, that it had simply been left there by accident. At any rate, in those times of self-doubt just after the Master's fall, the Kenthiar had become both the emblem and test of authority, for supposedly only the true Highlord could wear it in safety. Many questioned that belief now, but admired the nerve of anyone willing to put the thing on.

Burr gingerly lifted it out of its box. Those who carelessly touched the collar's inner surface were apt to lose their fingers, or worse. After Ganth had surrendered it and the title, it had lain on his chair for twenty years, a challenge and a taunt to all would-be successors. Then a drunken Highborn had put it on during a dinner party as a joke. The next minute, his neatly severed head had fallen onto the table and bounced into a soup tureen. No one else had even dared touch the thing until Ganth's son came to claim it ten years later.

Personally, Torisen didn't trust the Kenthiar at all. During its long history, it had also decapitated three Highlords whose claims to power, as far as anyone could tell, had been perfectly legitimate. No wonder so few in recent centuries had been willing to take the risk. If Caineron were to snatch power, he probably could get out of wearing it altogether; but Torisen, coming to claim his father's place with neither Ganth's ring nor sword, had felt that he must make some gesture to prove himself. Now he was about to make it again.

'Ready, lord.'

'You're sure you want to risk another good coat? All right, all right . . . go ahead.'

Burr put the silver collar around his lord's neck. The hinges on either side of the gem straightened, and the catch closed with a vicious snap. Torisen caught his breath. Nothing.

'All serene,' he said to Burr with a smile. 'No spilt soup today... and just in time.'

Up the spiral stair came confused sounds from the Council Chamber below.

The lords of the Kencyrath turned and fell silent as the Highlord entered. They were clustered at the far end of the room, under the map of Rathillien now ablaze with morning light. Torisen thought for a moment that they were all avoiding him, but then he caught a whiff of something rotten nearby. The bundle of furs in the chair to the left of his own raised its head. It was Jedrak, Lord Jaran. Green light from the window mottled his bald pate like mould. His nearly toothless mouth stretched in a lopsided, welcoming smile.

'Ganth!'

Torisen went forward immediately and took the clawlike hands which the old lord held out to him. Someone on the far side of the room gasped.

'No, not Ganth,' he said gently. 'Torisen. Remember?'

A look of confusion and near-panic flickered through Jaran's cloudy eyes. 'Torisen?' His expression sharpened. 'Tori! Yes, of course. Stupid of me. My great-great-grandchild, Kirien.'

A soberly dressed young man who Torisen hadn't even noticed stepped forward and gave the Highlord a half bow. His features were unusually delicate and his expression quite unreadable. Torisen returned the bow, then turned to the others. Here it came.

'I expect you all know by now that Nusair was killed the night before last at Tentir, and that my lord Caineron thinks I did it.'

Caineron snorted loudly. 'Thinks!'

'He has probably also suggested to you that I have finally succumbed to the madness that runs in the Knorth blood.'

Ardeth made a small, distressed sound. Madness, like senility, was considered not only hereditary but contagious and unsafe even to mention.

'Obviously, this matter will have to be settled before we can discuss anything more important. To save time, we'll consider the challenge already issued. As for the answer, no, I did not kill Nusair. That leaves it up to you, my lord Caineron: prove me a liar – if you can.'

He sat down at the head of the table, folded his hands, and waited.

For a moment, the assembled lords stared at him. By now,

they all probably knew something about what had happened at Tentir; but none, least of all Caineron, had expected the Highlord to tackle it so directly. Ardeth took his seat at Torisen's right, casting a look of barely concealed horror across the table at Jaran. Danior also sat down, with an air of defiance; and Demoth of the Coman, hastily; and Brandan, because it was only proper. The Edirr twins exchanged questioning glances and a sudden grin. One sat, one stood, cancelling out each other. That left Caineron with the elegant Randir and Korey of the Coman, glowering from a corner.

'Well, my lord?' Torisen prompted.

Caineron gave him a sour look. He had really convinced himself that the Highlord had gone over the edge and was affronted to find him so calm, so... rational. But then even madness had its cunning, and so did he. He began to pace back and forth, hastily reshaping his argument.

'This murder was the culmination of an old quarrel and not altogether unexpected. Lord Knorth never liked my son.'

'Who did?' muttered Danior, and was hushed by Ardeth.

'He has even hinted that Nusair tried to assassinate him, once with a snake and once (Ancestors preserve us) with a wall.'

'So that was what happened at Tiglon,' said Essien, the seated twin, with a solemnity undercut by a flash of pure mischief.

'We always wondered,' said the standing Essiar, in the same tone.

Caineron gave them both a furious glare. Then, forcibly composing himself, he went on to describe the argument at Tentir, and the subsequent finding of Nusair's naked, mutilated body with the gold coin jammed into his mouth.

'That certainly sounds like the work of a madman,' said Brandan thoughtfully, 'or of someone feigning madness to implicate the Highlord – your pardon, Torisen – but in itself it hardly proves anything one way or the other.'

'And so perishes your case, my lord,' said Danior with a laugh.

'Not yet, not quite yet. I have one final proof, and rather a convincing one at that. You shouldn't have been so quick to stake your honour, my dear Knorth, for now you are foresworn and dishonoured. Not only did you slay my son, *but you were seen doing it*. Ha! Now I've shaken you at last, haven't I?'

'Bewildered is more the word for it. How could anyone see me do something I never did?'

'Seen by whom, Caldane?' interposed Randir. 'If not by you, you can only repeat what you are told, not vouch for the truth of it. You had better bring forward your witness.'

Caineron demurred at first, then let himself be persuaded. Watching him, Torisen thought: *He and Randir have rehearsed this. Whatever Caineron's nasty surprise is, he can hardly wait to spring it.*

'Very well,' said the lord of Restormir at last, with obviously feigned reluctance. 'It would have been kinder to spare the boy, but apparently I can't. Donkerri, come here!'

Donkerri slunk out of the shadows, looking utterly miserable.

'Knorth, I take it you don't question my grandson's truthfulness?'

'I never have had cause to – before.'

'Very well, then. Boy, tell them what you saw.'

Donkerri gulped. 'I-I saw . . .'

'Louder, boy, louder.'

'I s-saw Torisen, Lord Knorth, kill my father.'

Even Ardeth looked shocked. They all had an instinct for the truth, and this boy seemed to be telling it.

Torisen leaned forward. 'Donkerri, how did I kill him?'

'With a knife in the back . . .'

Caineron looked up, startled.

'And then Commandant Harn tore his arm off, a-and then I-I fainted.'

'This is very odd,' said Brandan. 'Caldane showed me Nusair's body this morning. I didn't see his back, but the poor lad certainly had both arms.'

Torisen fought a terrible desire to burst out laughing. 'Caineron, d-do you mean that you set this boy to spy on me and then didn't even listen to his full report?'

Caldane shook his head as if to drive off some buzzing insect. 'This is nonsense. The fool is thinking of his cousin. Surely that damned berserker hasn't taken up dismembering Cainerons for a hobby.'

'He hasn't.'

The voice came from behind Torisen. Kindrie stood in the shadows by the spiral stair, a long slender bundle in his arms.

'What are you doing here?' Caineron barked at him. 'I told you to stay at Tentir!'

'The bond between us broke the night before last,' said the

young Sharnir in a completely colourless voice. 'You know that.'

He came forward into the jewelled light of the windows, moving as if no part of him wanted to bend. As he leaned forward stiffly to put his burden on the table, both Torisen and Ardeth saw lines of blood suddenly appear on the back of his white shirt. Ardeth unwrapped the bundle.

'Is this the limb that you saw torn off?' he asked Donkerri.

'Yes!' said the boy. A look of great uneasiness flickered across his face. 'Yes...'

Essien, ever curious, lifted the arm at the wrist. It dangled bonelessly in his grasp like a dead snake. He dropped it hastily.

'My God! What *is* this thing?'

'That, my lords of the Council, is the arm of a changer,' said Torisen. 'Rather more substantial than the stuff of songs, isn't it, Caldane? I suspect that this is the hand that killed your son. It certainly is the one that I fought in the fire-timber hall at Tentir where the creature lured me in your son's likeness and where Harn ripped its arm off. That must have been the battle that your grandson witnessed. I took part in no other.'

'I don't believe –' Caineron burst out angrily, but managed to stop himself just short of offering the Highlord a mortal insult. 'Damnit, why didn't you tell me any of this before?'

'When did you give any of us a chance?' Kindrie answered in that same dead voice.

'A changer,' said Danior wonderingly. 'After all these years. But why? What was it after?'

Torisen stepped away from the table, away from the living Shanir and the arm of the dead one. 'It meant to kill me,' he said, 'or, failing that, to entangle me in a blood feud with Caineron as his son's supposed murderer.'

'But again, why?' said Brandan, picking up the question. 'And why now?'

'I can only think of one reason: to keep the Host from marching. Laugh if you wish, my lord Caineron, but consider this: For the first time in centuries, the Horde moves north; simultaneously, a changer tries to kill or discredit the one man who can rally the Host to march south. Now, maybe this really is a coincidence. Maybe something else is brewing that we know nothing about...' He thought of the changer spitting at the Master's name. '.... but can we take the chance? Caldane, you asked me at Tentir if I had anything to substantiate my fears.

Well, now I've got that.' He pointed at the arm.

'And we mustn't forget the Southern Host,' said Ardeth, leaning forward with a new ring of urgency in his voice. 'It would be madness for King Krothen to order a pitched battle, but he might. We must support our own people, even if – Ancestors forbid – that only means gathering their bones for the pyre.'

'Then too,' said Randir, examining his nails, 'I understand that Prince Odalian of Karkinaroth has asked for help.'

Torisen looked at him sharply, surprised. 'Not from me he hasn't. Caldane?'

'Yes, yes,' said Caineron, giving his sometime ally a nasty look. 'A messenger arrived late last night. Odalian asked me as the father of his consort to present his request to the High Council. He says that he's calling in all his troop levies and asks that the Host meet him at Hurlen just above the Cataracts.'

'Well, surely that settles it,' said Ardeth. 'You can't refuse to help your own son-in-law.'

'Oh yes, I can,' said Caineron, looking mulish. 'There was no mutual defence clause in the marriage contract. I told him it wasn't necessary.'

'Names of God,' Torisen said, disgusted. 'To get the best bargain by sleight-of-mouth – is that all honour means now?'

Caineron drew himself up sharply, his lip curling with scorn. 'Another lecture, my young lord? You always seem to be telling me where my duty lies, you who weren't even born when I took over my house after your father had reduced it to bloody shambles in the White Hills. You can trust me to safeguard my own honour –'

'And to pay your servants their back wages.'

Caineron started at the sound of Kindrie's inflectionless voice. 'You damned spook!' he burst out. 'Will you get out of here?'

'Perhaps you should leave, Kindrie,' said Ardeth in a silken tone. 'My lord Caineron seems to find your presence disturbing... for some reason.' His sharp blue eyes met the Shanir's faded ones. Kindrie gave a ghost of a nod and began to turn, giving Caineron his first glimpse of the Shanir's back.

'Now, now, let's not be hasty,' he said with considerable haste. 'Stay, man, stay. A broken bond shouldn't break friendship as well.' *What about a broken skin*, wondered Torisen. If the others saw that bloodstained shirt, Caineron would be explaining his honourable system of 'back wages' from now until the coming of the Tyr-ridan.

'My lords,' he said, 'it seems that you have a choice of three reasons to let the Host march. First, to support the Southern Host. As my lord Ardeth says, these are our people; we can't simply abandon them. Second, to support Prince Odalian who is, after all, the closest thing to an ally that the Kencyrath has left on Rathillien. And third, to support your poor, lunatic of a Highlord, who still believes that the Horde is about to march down our collective throats. Take your choice of reason, but in all the names of God, let's not waste any more time. Now, do we march or don't we? Ardeth?'

'*Yes.*'

'Randir?'

'Yes, regrettably.'

'Brandan? Edirr? Danior?'

'Yes.'

'Yes.'

'Yes.'

'Coman . . . damn, I forgot. Demoth, the Coman is yours, for the time being at least. I'll make a final determination later.'

'Yes, lord,' said Demoth, sulkily. He had expected full confirmation.

'Jaran?'

A rasping snore answered him.

'Jedrak?' The old lord's great-great-grandson shook him gently, without result. 'I'm sorry, my lord. When he drifts off like this, he may be gone for hours or even days.' Caineron gave a crack of laughter. 'However,' said the young man calmly, ignoring the interruption, 'I am authorised to speak for him.'

'And?'

'I vote "yes." What else?'

'Well, Caldane,' said Ardeth, 'it seems you decide the matter after all; your vote against our eight. What do you say?'

Caineron glowered at him. His plans all awry, he looked ready to bid defiance to them all out of sheer ill-humour. At that moment, Burr entered the hall. Caineron turned on him, snarling, but the Kendar's expression made him hesitate.

'Burr, what is it?' Torisen demanded.

'News, my lord. The Southern Host has engaged the vanguard of the Horde.'

'Oh my God. With what result?'

'None as yet, when the messenger was sent out. But he says it looked bad, very bad.'

'Pereden,' said Ardeth under his breath, almost in a moan. 'Damn you, Krothen, God curse and damn you...' The next moment he was on his feet, confronting Caineron as fierce and bright as drawn steel. 'You will vote now, my lord, and you will vote "yes," or it will be war indeed, your house against mine. Well?'

'Yes,' said Caineron, going back a step. 'Yes, of course. This news changes everything. But sweet Trinity, there are barely fifty thousand of us here ready to march. Even if Odalian sends the troops he has promised, what can we do against an enemy three million strong?'

'There is one place where we can hold them.' Torisen went to the far end of the room where the stained-glass map of Rathillien blazed in green and blue and gold. He traced the southward twisting path of the Silver, from the Riverland to a spot where the craftsman had frosted the glass to indicate billowing clouds of spray. 'There. The Cataracts. Odalian has the right idea. If the Horde keeps to its present course, it must pass here, up the narrow Mendelin Steps to the top of the falls. There we stop it, or not at all.'

'So it's a race to the Cataracts,' said Brandan, regarding the map with a practiced eye. 'Roughly two thousand miles for us, and about a fourth that for the Horde, which luckily travels at a near crawl. Just the same, this is going to be very close. When do we start?'

'Just as soon as we've given Nusair to the pyre. The marching order to Omiroth will be according to whoever is ready first. We'll sort things out there. Any questions? Then let's get at it.'

The lords dispersed, except for Ardeth. Donkerri tried to slip out in his grandfather's shadow, but Caineron turned on him, all his frustrations spilling over.

'You ill-omened brat, get out of my sight! I never want to see you again!'

'Grandfather, please...'

Caineron drew himself up to his full height. 'I cast you out!' he roared. 'Blood and bone, you are no kin of mine.' He jerked the hem of his coat out of Donkerri's grasp and stalked away, leaving the boy standing white-faced, staring after him.

'.... *damn you, boy, for deserting me. I curse you and cast you out. Blood and bone, you are no kin of mine....*'

Torisen flinched at the memory. If a father's dying curse held any power, he was as disowned as Donkerri, or as Kindrie, for that matter. But that had only been a dream. This was real.

'Burr, take the boy up to my quarters and then fetch a doctor. We've got a casualty up here.'

'Yes, lord.' He dropped his voice. 'Lord, there was a second message, this one from Randon Larch.'

'My old five-thousand commander. Yes?'

'She says that King Krothen didn't order the attack. He didn't even order the Southern Host to march out. The whole thing was Pereden's idea.'

... squat figures moving among the slain ... oh, Pereden, you fool, you god-cursed, jealous fool ...

'Ardeth isn't to know, not if we can keep it from him. Understood?'

Burr nodded and left the chamber, taking the stunned boy with him.

Ardeth had made Kindrie sit in his chair. The Shanir had his head down on the table and seemed to have fainted, for he didn't even twitch as the lord cut away his ruined shirt.

'I've sent for a physician,' said Torisen, coming up to them.

'That won't be necessary. Look.'

Ardeth had carefully uncovered the Shanir's back. Kindrie was painfully thin, almost emaciated. His ribs showed quite clearly under white, nearly translucent skin, crisscrossed now with the marks of a Karnid corrector's scourge. But even as the two Highborn watched, the bruises seemed to be fading. Then the more serious cuts, which had broken open when Kindrie bent to put down the changer's arm, suddenly closed, the raw edges knitting together into cicatrices.

Torisen turned abruptly away, feeling sick.

'Wonderful!' Ardeth said behind him. 'A pity we can't all do that, eh? But then it's rare, even for a Shanir. You know, my boy, you owe this young man a great deal. How fortunate that he is no longer bound to Caineron. Now you can repay him properly by taking him into your service.'

Bind himself to a Shanir? He did owe it to Kindrie, and it would be a shameful thing to refuse, but ... but.... He remembered the changer's arm, still lying on the table behind him. Its fingers had seemed to reach out towards Kindrie, as if to touch his white hair. Another Shanir ...

'I'm sorry, Adric,' he said without turning. 'I-I can't. I just can't.'

'Very well,' said Ardeth coldly. 'Then I will, until you can bring yourself to do your duty.'

Torisen left the hall without a word, without looking back. At Tentir, he had said to Harn, 'I can do anything I have to,' and that had always been his creed. Now, for the first time, he had failed.

Nusair's pyre was set in Gothregor's inner ward, with four priests officiating. Several days before, two other of their number had set off for Tai-tastigon to cope with trouble in the temple there, and a seventh had left even more recently with three acolytes for Karkinaroth on a similar mission. No one knew what was wrong at either temple, only that the balance of power in each had shifted, suddenly, dangerously. But that was priests' business, and no one else paid much attention to it. What they did notice was that at least one of the priests at Gothregor wasn't very adept with the pyric rune because, when it was spoken, not only Nusair burst into flames but also about four hundred chickens being prepared for lunch in the fortress's kitchen. Otherwise, it was a very successful cremation.

By dint of practically getting behind his troops and pushing, Lord Danior got them into second place behind the rathorn banner. He and his guard rode ahead with Torisen. Ardeth's full moon followed Danior's wolf standard, but Adric stayed with his people, Kindrie riding pale and silent beside him. The token forces from Kraggen and Kestrie followed, then Jaran, Randir, Brandan, and finally Caineron. Caldane's troops had already marched nearly one hundred and twenty-five miles over the past forty-eight hours and had arrived the night before in a state of collapse. Several hours of *dwar* sleep had nearly repaired the damage, but not quite. That night at Omiroth, every one slept deep, and in the morning the order of march was confirmed. That day the Edirr and Coman forces joined the column. Early that afternoon, on the tenth of Winter, the Host marched out of the Riverland, nearly fifty thousand strong.

21

A Rage of Rathorns
The Anarchies: 11th-12th of Winter

The Black Band crossed the step-back stones into the Anarchies after a brief but confused battle that left several men injured and one dead. The half-dozen brigands originally from the hunting clans refused to cross at all. The rest had caught the scent of blood, however, and pressed on, all the more eagerly because of the reward that Bortis had first offered in Peshtar. The blind bandit chief himself led the way with his Grindark tracker. When he thought about what he would do to the fugitives, especially to Jame, he drooled a bit and lashed at the bound, hobbled Grindark to make him go faster.

The woods took the brigands by surprise. They were used to the evergreen forests of the Ebonbane, but the expanse and quality of the silence under these green leaves awed them. Bortis didn't have to tell them to move quietly. Only once was the silence broken, when they heard the crash of a tree falling somewhere in the distance.

'It's them!' exclaimed one man excitedly, and the next moment went down with a grunt under Bortis's hammerlike fist.

'Quiet, you half-wit. D'you think they've taken up lumbering to pass the time?'

They continued, foraging as they went. One man handy with a sling had already brought down a number of grey birds. Now another bandit saw what appeared to be a giant puff-ball mushroom, but when he reached for it, the fungus cap turned itself inside out around his hand. His cry of surprise turned to one of pain. The others cut it away to reveal a hand covered with small punctures like wasp stings, but ringed with orange-tinged flesh. The fingers had already begun to swell.

By dusk, it was fairly clear to everyone but Bortis that they were lost. Their only hope lay in the tracker, who still seemed to have some intermittent idea of where he was going. At nightfall, they built a large fire and roasted the birds on spits. Then they tore down boughs and uprooted ferns from a nearby hillock to make their beds.

All slept deep that night, including those assigned to keep guard. Through all their dreams ran the steady sound of munching.

In the morning, several men could not be awakened, and the four who had lain down against the denuded hillock were simply gone. That reduced the Black Band to fourteen men, including the one who had been attacked by the puff-ball. The others found him already awake, staring with rapt, almost greedy attention at his hand. The fingers now were so swollen that they seemed to merge. The skin was puffy and orange. He backed away from the other brigands, holding his bloated hand against his chest.

'You can't have it! I found it. It's mine, mine!'

He sank his teeth into the spongy mass and tore off a strip.

'It's mine!' he muttered again, chewing furiously. 'Find your own!' With that, he darted off into the woods with his prize. The others didn't follow.

'Up!' said Bortis harshly to the Grindark, jerking him to his feet.

'But what about them?' protested one man, indicating the half-dozen brigands who slept on as if drugged.

'Leave them. They're no good to me like that.'

'Yeah?' said another brigand. 'And what good will that reward of yours be to any of us if we never get out of here to claim it? I say turn back, and if you won't,' he finished, belligerently, glancing at the others, 'we will.'

'Oh, will you?' Bortis gave a nasty laugh. 'Then go. I can't stop you. I can't even see you. But you know who can, and what he'll do to you if you break faith with me.'

To a man, the bandits glanced up with apprehension at the canopy of leaves that hid the sky. They hadn't seen the changer since the previous day, but not one of them doubted that he was up there somewhere or that he would deal with them as viciously as he had with others in the past who had challenged Bortis's orders.

The brigand chief waited, a growing sneer on his lips. 'What, no more debate? Then come on, you gallows-bait. Just think how rich you'll be when we catch that Kencyr brat, and how well entertained.'

*

After a night of dark dreams, Jame woke to find the woods swept clean of shadows, aglow with golden light. It must be near dawn. Marc and Jorin slept on, both snoring faintly. The ounce lay stretched out on his back, head cushioned on the Kendar's arm, paws curled over his chest. When Jame put her hand on the warm cream-coloured fur of his stomach, his respiration changed into a sleepy purr, but he didn't wake. She lay back, wondering at her own uneasiness. It seemed to her that in her dreams she had been warned, but by whom and against what? Here with Marc, she felt quite safe, but then he often had that effect on her, as if there was some innate quality in the big man that shielded him from evil. Even the Earth Wife had sensed it. But she couldn't spend her life in his shadow. Even now, thirst made her slip away from him and rise. Now, where was that brook?

She followed its sound, moving in quite a different direction from the previous night. Then too, it was – or seemed – farther away. Perhaps she was simply approaching it at a different point. She scrambled down to it through the bushes and knelt on the grassy bank about a foot above the water. As she leaned over to scoop up a handful, the ground suddenly gave way under her.

Jame surfaced, sputtering. The water was only chest deep, but shockingly cold, and the current made it hard to stand. Of all the clumsy, fumble-footed accidents. . . . She clutched at the bank. It crumbled away. Downstream a few steps, a bush overhung the water. Jame let herself be carried down to it and grabbed a branch, only to let go immediately with a startled exclamation. Blood from a deep puncture stained the thumb of her glove. She saw then that each branch ended in a blunt, blind head, green barked, with thorns instead of fangs. Every head was turned towards her. Downstream, similar bushes on both banks closed over the water . . . and upstream, too. Surely those hadn't been there before, not the ones surrounding her now. She felt a chill that had nothing to do with the icy waters. They were closing in.

Jame backed into midstream, bracing herself against the current.

'Marc!' The name came out in a croak, but loud enough, surely, to wake the Kendar. *'Marc!'* No answer. Then she remembered his deep, slow breathing. Somehow, *dwar* sleep or something very similar had claimed him. He would not hear her now, even if she screamed.

The branches were closer now, rustling. They would arch over her, press down. She would tear her hands to bloody rags on them, then drown beneath their slight weight.

A grey bird landed on a nearby tree branch and spread its wings. The two feathered eyes regarded her unblinkingly, as if the entire forest were watching. The Anarchies had tried and condemned her, Jame thought wildly. But why? She had played by the rules, harming nothing. It could only be because she really was a darkling, as the Arrin-ken had said, and the Anarchies hated anything with the darkling taint. Marc couldn't help her now. Her own god wouldn't even if, as she half doubted, his power did extend to this strange place. But did that deprive her all protection?

Slowly she reached underwater and drew the *imu* medallion out of her pocket. She held it up to the feathered eyes of the grey bird.

'I-I have the Earth Wife's favour.'

The wings beat once, eyes blinking, then again and again. The bird soared off between the trees. The bush's nearest blind head took the medallion from Jame's hand. It was passed back through the bush from mouth to mouth, and the branches withdrew in its wake. She scrambled back onto the bank. On the far side, a green head offered the medallion back to her. She took it. There was blood on the *imu's* lips again – her blood this time from her thorn-stabbed finger. She collapsed on the grass, shaking first with cold and then with helpless laughter. Saved by a pun! She wondered what the Earth Wife had done to her imp when she discovered that the medallion was missing. Finally getting a grip on herself, she rose and went back to the ring of diamantine stones.

Marc and Jorin still slept. Jame changed into dry clothes, then paused, looking down at them. Perhaps the Kendar had somehow fallen into *dwar* sleep, but the ounce, too? Frightened now, she shook them and called their names. They woke, slowly, reluctantly. Marc stretched.

'Ah, lass, you should have got me up sooner. We had better eat our breakfast on the move.' He rose and looked about, in a puzzled way. 'That's odd. I could have sworn that group of trees was over there. Everything seems to be turned around. Hello, what's that?' He turned sharply, then shook his head, even more perplexed. 'Gone.'

'What is?'

'Something grey. I only saw it out of the corner of my eye. A

401

bird, maybe. Now, which way did we come?'

They couldn't tell. Nothing seemed to be where it had been the night before, and the mist so diffused the morning light that they couldn't even be sure in which direction the sun rose. Jorin was confused, too. Jame circled the clearing with him, and as far as the ounce's keen nose could tell, they had never entered the ring of stones at all.

'So much for Bortis's tracker too, I hope,' she said, then turned abruptly. 'There, again, by that larch! No, it's gone.' Or was it? When she looked directly at the tree, nothing was there, but at the edge of her field of vision she saw... what?

'A figure, wearing a grey hooded cloak,' said Marc. He had caught the trick, too. 'Why, it's no bigger than a child.'

'And it's beckoning to us. I think it wants us to follow. Should we?'

Marc considered this briefly, then nodded. 'Maybe it can lead us out of here. It's worth a try, anyway.'

They collected their gear and followed, with no idea if their spectral guide was conducting them out of the Anarchies or farther in. It wasn't even easy to keep that grey figure in sight.

'I've lost him again,' said Jame, for the third time in half an hour. 'This undergrowth is too dense.'

In fact, they had got into a real thicket now, flourishing under the arched boughs of the trees. Dark leaves surrounded them, edged here and there with the rose and hectic red of autumn, hung with berries bright as drops of blood. A breeze rustled through the dense foliage. Like all sounds in this strange place, it seemed to come from every direction at once in a flurry of crosscurrents. Jorin stiffened, his nose twitching. The fur down his back slowly rose. Then Jame caught a sharp, tangy scent that made her own nose itch and startled a host of fragmentary, fleeting images.

'What is it?' Marc asked in a low voice.

'I... don't know. Something very close, very wild...'

She slipped away through the bushes without waiting for an answer, hardly knowing if she fled this unknown thing or sought it. Branches closed about her. The breeze made them dip and sway, surrounding her with shifting planes of green. For a moment Jame hesitated, completely disoriented. The wind died. She forged ahead, suddenly emerging on the edge of a small glade. Across it, beside a small hillock from which most of the greenery had been stripped, stood a rathorn.

Jame's first impression was of a black stallion wearing elaborate ivory armour, and then of some fantastic cross between a horse and a dragon. The creature was tall and finely made, with slender legs and a broad chest tapering back to powerful hindquarters. His arched, almost serpentine neck supported a small head encased in an ivory mask, out of which grew the nasal tusk and curved horn of a rathorn stallion. Ivory plates curved around his neck, chest, and abdomen. More ivory sheathed his forelegs like a pair of greaves. His white mane and tail hung against his ebony coat like falls of heavy silk. He stood absolutely motionless, staring at her. She stared back, only dimly aware that the four mares of his rage were behind him with their heads up, also watching her. A man lay in the grass at one of the mare's feet. His belly had been ripped open. In all that glade, the only movement was of his blood slowly spiralling down the mare's tusk.

The rathorn scent hung heavy as incense in the still air, numbing the mind, making the senses hum. It drew Jame forward one halting step, then another. Under its hypnotic lure, she felt a hunger for young meat, fresh meat, that was not her own.

Then, from everywhere and nowhere, came a moaning cry. It rose, faltered, sank into a series of deep sobs. A shriller voice echoed it, note for despairing note.

The rathorns' armoured heads turned as one. Between one blink and the next, the mares had disappeared in a blur of ivory and ebony. The stallion backed away, ears flat in their mask grooves, then pivoted in one supple, flowing motion and sprang after his rage.

'That was close,' said Marc's voice behind her.

Jame drew a deep, shaky breath. The world seemed to redefine itself around her. 'Yes. But what on earth would frighten a rathorn like that? Marc, there's a body in the grass. Several of them.' She started forward, but he caught her arm.

'Wait a minute.'

They waited. When the terrible cry wasn't repeated, they went cautiously out into the clearing.

'Why, these are some of Bortis's brigands,' said Jame, crouching beside one while Jorin sniffed at him warily. 'This man seems to be asleep.'

'These, too.' Marc shook one bandit, then another and another, without result. Jame remembered how deep in sleep she had found her friend earlier and shuddered.

'There must be something in the air.'

'Phew!' said the Kendar, straightening. 'There certainly is. What's that stink?'

They circled the hillock. On the far side were three skeletons jumbled together, covered with green slimy mould. The hill made a sound that was half rumble, half gurgle, and excreted a fourth skeleton from a foul-smelling hole hidden under a fringe of its few remaining ferns. Jame backed away, holding her nose.

'What a charming place. D'you suppose our friend in grey brought us here on purpose?'

'A trap, you mean? It could be and yet, somehow, I don't think so. Do you?'

'Somehow, no. Trinity!'

The cry had come again, closer, double-noted. It wasn't a sound so much to inspire fear, Jame decided, as utter, hopeless misery. The wretchedness of it was almost contagious. For a moment, curiosity tugged at her, but then that terrible moan sounded a third time, almost in her ear, and nearby leaves began to wither on the bough.

'I have an idea,' she said to Marc. 'Let's go someplace else.'

Since their grey guide was still nowhere in sight, they followed the path beaten through the thicket by the rathorns. They had just got clear of the bushes when the sound of other cries and then of screams reached them, apparently from ahead.

'Trouble,' said the big Kendar tersely. He unslung his war-axe and loped off between the trees towards the source of the commotion. Jame and Jorin ran after him.

'Marc, wait! What if it's the Black Band?'

It was the Band, but by the time the two Kencyr reached it, none of its members was in a position to do them any harm. The slashed, trampled bodies lay on ground soggy with blood, among white flowers slowly turning pink, then red. The rathorns' trail led through this carnage and beyond.

'So much for that,' said Jame.

Marc looked slightly surprised at hearing her dismiss a dozen lives so casually. All he said, though, was, 'Not necessarily. Bortis isn't here, and neither is the Grindark.'

'Perhaps they didn't make it this far.'

'Perhaps. But then there's still the changer, and our mist cover is beginning to wear thin in patches.'

As if on cue, sunlight brightened around them, startling a

flash of white beyond the nearby trees.

'That looks like a building,' said Jame. 'What on earth is one doing here?'

Marc shook his head. 'I can't imagine.'

They went towards it through the trees, still following the rathorns' trampled path. More white showed through the leaves, resolving itself into a low, vine-draped wall, which stretched about one hundred yards in either direction. Beyond, rose a jumble of white buildings, the tallest of them barely over fifteen feet high. The rathorns had apparently leapt the wall. Jame, Marc, and Jorin followed until they came to a postern so low and narrow that the Kendar almost got stuck as he squeezed through it.

Inside, an equally narrow lane zigzagged back between the buildings. Crosswalks spanned it here and there, connecting second or third storeys. Only Jorin could walk under the former without ducking. Overhead, circular windows glazed with crystal and rimmed with decorative motifs faced each other across the way.

They soon came to what appeared to be the main thoroughfare. Like the other streets, it was very narrow. Unlike them, no walkways spanned it, and it was paved with the cross-sections of diamantine lithons quarried, perhaps, from the broken ring where they had spent the previous night. The glowing stones were worn down to a groove as if by the passage of many feet, or hooves. The smell of rathorn clung to the walls. At a guess, the rage had also come this way, still in full flight. The two Kencyr followed warily.

They began to pass doorways opening into rooms lit by diamantine blocks set in the walls. The lighted, empty interiors gave Jame the uncanny feeling that at any moment some diminutive householder might lean over his door jamb to invite them in. The sense of arrested life was strong in this place, but so was the feeling that everything had stopped here long, long ago.

Marc had also been looking about. 'Now, that's odd,' he said. 'See that decorative band up there, the one with alternating rathorn skull-masks and *imu* faces? The faces parody the masks. I've seen lots of *imus* in my time, but never before one that was used to make a joke. Who could have built this, anyway?'

'Apparently someone who knew how to make a step-back ring. Why seal off the Anarchies unless to protect this place?'

The Kendar shook his head in wonder. 'They had more than their share of nerve, then. Imagine laying a claim here. But what could have happened to them?'

'Look!' said Jame sharply, catching his arm.

In the far corner of a lighted entry hall hung something grey.

'Oh,' she said disappointed. 'I thought for a moment that it was our guide. That does look like his cloak, though.'

'Maybe he got home before us,' said Marc, half joking.

'I wonder.'

She ducked under the low lintel. White stone dust rattled down on her head and shoulders. The interior walls, she saw, were shot with deep cracks, radiating out from the diamantine blocks.

'Careful,' said Marc, bending to peer in after her.

'I think it must be safe enough or Jorin wouldn't have come in here with me.'

She crossed to the grey object. It looked exactly like their erstwhile guide's hooded cape, but when she touched it, it crumbled to dust. Beside the hook where it had hung was a narrow hallway that had been quite invisible from the door. It led back into the house. Jame wrestled briefly with temptation and lost.

'Marc, I'm going to do a fast bit of exploring.'

'If you like. I'll wait out here and spare my old back the stooping. Be quick, though.'

Jame stepped into the hall. As in the first room, the ceiling was barely five feet high, forcing her to keep her head well down. The corridor seemed to extend quite a preposterous distance, one hundred yards at least, when the entire house could hardly be more than forty feet square. Her first step took her a good fifty feet down the passageway. So, whoever had built this place liked to play with spatial distortions.

A few more steps, and here was a doorway opening into a fair-sized room with a ceiling at least twice as high as the corridor's. The only piece of furniture was a long marble table about two feet high, apparently standing on the left hand wall. Jame stared at it. Could something so massive be bolted to the wall? The threshold was at a forty-five degree angle, but it felt level as she stepped on it. So did the floor ... but it wasn't the floor, or at least it hadn't been a moment ago. Set in the far wall was a large oval window. The right half of it was dark with the trees of the Anarchies, all horizontal. The bright left half was the misty sky. Jame shut her eyes hastily. The sense of vertigo disappeared at once. Yes, she was standing on the wall beside the table, and it felt perfectly natural.

'What a place for a party!' she said out loud.

In fact, it looked as if there had been one, Trinity only knew how many years, or centuries, or millennia ago. At one end of the table was a litter of small bottles. One of them still contained some clear liquid, which instantly broke down into crystals when Jame touched the glass. On impulse, she emptied the bottle's dehydrated contents into an inner pocket lined with waterproof silk. Who knew, someday she might find someone she disliked enough to test the stuff on.

She left the room, stepping down to the hall floor, and went on up the passageway. Within a few steps, the corridor turned. Although it still looked perfectly flat, Jame felt a strain in her leg muscles as she went on and wasn't surprised, when she came to a window, to find herself on the second floor.

Here there were several rooms that once might have been living quarters; but a window had broken, and the wind, blowing through, had long since reduced everything to dust.

At the end of the corridor was one last door, made of ironwood, with three massive locks. It stood ajar. Jame pushed it open cautiously and paused on the threshold, startled. The rest of the house had been bright with sunlight and diamantine reflecting off white walls. This last room seemed to be hewn out of a dark, half-familiar stone shot with luminous green veins. The moss covering the floor also glowed faintly. What little other light there was came from a large oval window set in the far wall. Like those below, it was sealed with rock crystal; unlike them, heavy bars also crossed it. Beyond was a sullen sky, the colour of a bruised plum, and a deep valley overgrown with luminous vegetation. The ruins of a white walled city lay in the valley's folds. Vines had almost consumed it, but enough remained to show its resemblance to the miniature city of which this house was part.

But those ruins clearly weren't in the Anarchies, or even anywhere in Rathillien. This entire room must be made of step-back stones, stepped all the way back to some fallen world far down the Chain of Creation, deep within the coils of Perimal Darkling. Why cling to such a desolate view? Why, unless that distant, lost world was somehow precious. Unless, perhaps, it was home.

Some pieces of the puzzle began to click together. The Anarchies had been sealed off some three thousand years ago by people who knew how to use step-back stones and who quite possibly weren't native to Rathillien. Neither were the mysterious and elusive Builders, who at approximately the same time had been erecting the Kencyr temples using a host of architectural tricks including both step-back and -forward stones. It seemed very likely, then, that this city too was Builders' work. It might even have been their headquarters on Rathillien, despite its distance from all of their building projects. The seclusion of the Anarchies would certainly have appealed to them, and they might well have believed themselves more than a match for the land's strangeness.

But if so, what had happened to them? When their work on Rathillien was complete, had they simply moved on to the next threshold world as they had done so often before? That was possible, but it hardly explained the odd atmosphere of this city, as if life here had stopped suddenly, unexpectedly.

Jame shrugged. The puzzle still lacked too many pieces, and perhaps always would. She turned to go, and stopped short. In the corner, in the door's shadow, lay a pile of bones. They looked nearly human. The skull wasn't quite the right shape, though, and the entire skeleton reassembled would barely have come to her waist. So. Wherever the rest of the city's diminutive occupants had gone, here was one at least who hadn't got very far.

Jame knelt by the bones, feeling awed. Could this possibly have been a Builder? In all the long history of her people, no Kencyr had ever even seen one before, much less come so close. The dark behind those large eye sockets was like the darkness of this room, as if it held the secret of an entire race, obscured now forever.

Looking closer, she saw that most of the bones were shot with hairline cracks like those that fissured the walls. She touched the skull tentatively. It fell into fragments. The rest of the skeleton followed, crumbling bone by bone. Jorin sneezed, and bone dust filled the air. Jame sat back on her heels, rueful. She'd done it again, destroying where she had only meant to investigate. But then among the ruins she spotted one bone that hadn't disintegrated. It was a third phalange, the tip of a finger, twice as long as her own. She picked it up gingerly, marvelling at its delicate structure. Here was something, at least, saved for the pyre. She carefully wrapped it in a handkerchief and slipped it into her pocket. Now to rejoin Marc, who probably thought she and Jorin had fallen down a hole somewhere.

But down in the narrow street, there was no sign of her friend.
'Marc!'

Echoes answered her, and wisps of mist drifting around the next corner. The silence rang. Jorin pressed against her knee, uneasy. Other doorways opened off the street, their interiors glowing softly, invitingly, but with no sign of life.

'Marc!'

This time she thought she heard an answer, towards the heart of the city. She followed it, calling again, hearing the same faint, distorted reply. The mist grew denser with each turn. Jame ran one hand along the nearest wall while keeping the other on Jorin's head to guide him. Suddenly he slipped away. She called after him with voice and mind, but neither brought a response. Damn their mind-link anyway for being so unreliable. But a moment later there he was again, chirping anxiously, running nose first into her knee. She took a firm grip on his golden ruff.

'Hush, kitten. Listen.'

That voice called again, closer now. It did sound like Marc, but there was something odd about it, something almost mocking.

Jame felt Jorin's fur bristle under her hand. He knew that voice, and suddenly so did she. Bortis. They went on, stalking more than seeking now, but still blind in the swirling mist. The glow of the diamantine pavement faded away underfoot, and then Jame's hand lost contact with the wall. She groped for it, without success. The city must be built around some kind of open space. A half-dozen more blind steps and her foot struck something a ringing blow. Someone nearby chuckled.

'Brave Talisman, pretty eyes,' crooned that hated voice, making no effort now to disguise itself. 'How does it feel to be lost and blind?'

The sound seemed to come from everywhere and nowhere. Jame felt her sense of direction slip away. She heard stealthy movements in the mist, growing louder, nearer, seeming to surround her. She crouched, arms around Jorin. The cat's ears pricked, but he clearly had no idea which way to turn. Hopefully, neither did Bortis, but if he still had the Grindark tracker and they were approaching from down wind...

A low, wailing cry cut through the opaque air, its shrill double note echoing sharply back as though from close-set walls. The nameless thing that had put to flight an entire rage of rathorns was in the city, drawing closer. Someone almost at Jame's elbow gave a hoarse exclamation. Two pairs of footsteps crashed away, apparently in all directions at once. She and Jorin must flee too, but which way? A black despair, not her own, gnawed at the edges of her mind. The closer that thing came, the more likely that they would run straight into it. What to do? The cry came again, closer, paralyzing in its misery. In a moment of near panic, Jame felt again how out of place she was here, how unable even to understand this land's threats, much less to cope with them. But she still had the *imu*, whose power was somehow linked to this strange place. She drew the medallion out with unsteady fingers.

'Help us,' she whispered to it.

Nothing happened. Had it lost its potency or had she forgotten something? Yes, damnit: the thing had to be fed. She thrust the edge of her hand against the *imu*'s mouth. A sharp pain made her gasp and she jerked her hand away. A small crescent had been bitten out of it right through the leather glove. For one startled moment, she watched blood well out of the tiny wound before wondering why she could see it so clearly. The mist swirled as densely as before around them, but not in front of the *imu*. She turned the medallion's face outward. A path opened before her as if a beam of light had transfixed the mist and burned it off, but there was neither light nor heat, only a shaft of clear air lit through the mist by the morning sun riding high above.

At Jame's feet lay the skeleton of a rathorn. She had accidentally kicked one of its ivory belly plates, which still curved around emptiness to meet the cage of overlapping ribs. The skull mask was twisted towards her, the impotence of death rendering its frozen fury all the more savage. Its massive horn had curved all the way around the beast's head and split its skull open from behind. There was another skeleton beyond it, and another and another, a fortune in ivory, a wilderness of death.

Jame picked her way through them, her hand again on Jorin's head. She saw a glow in the mist before her, and a few moments later came up to a pair of diamantine stones each a good nine feet tall. Stepping between them, she found herself in a circle some fifty feet across, ringed with standing stones. No mist came here. It formed a shining roof over the circle and walled it, but Jame could clearly see the huge, gape-mouthed *imu* faces on the far side, thrusting out of the diamantine lithons. Each stone's internal cloudiness had been freed by nature to take its natural form so that she seemed to stand in a ring of tall, narrow heads, their chins sunk in the ground. Only two were different. One had a sort of leathery caul on top of it. The other's mouth had been hollowed out so deeply that darkness gathered in the heart of the shining stone.

Something moved in the shadowy maw of the second stone. Bortis and the Grindark emerged. The latter crouched like some hunted thing brought to bay at last. Bortis stood beside him, keeping a cruelly tight grip on the hillman's surviving forebraid. The blind brigand chief was grinning. Saliva ran down from one corner of his mouth to hang in a glistening thread from his chin.

Jame approached him slowly, moving on the balls of her feet. 'What have you done to Marc?'

Bortis leered crookedly. 'So you miss that decrepit boyfriend of yours already, do you? You had young suitors – Bane, that fool Dally – and you killed them. You killed me. Why, Talisman? Are you that afraid of a real man?'

They were circling each other now. The Grindark scuttled sideways, retreating from Jame, but kept in the ring of stone by the bandit's ruthless grasp. The hillman's teeth had begun to rattle together. He could both see and sense what Bortis could not: the inhuman, silver sheen growing in their opponent's eyes, the darkness gathering around her.

'I never went out of my way to hurt you, Bortis.' The voice was low, almost purring. 'You attacked me. Three times. Does it threaten your manhood that your prey fought back and won? That wasn't supposed to happen, was it? Oh no, not to the great bandit chief. Well, I blinded you once, and by God, I can do it again.'

She sprang at them. The tracker recoiled, jerking his captor off balance. Jame caught the brigand's thumb and wrenched it away from the Grindark's hair. Bortis howled. He made a wild grab for her, but she tripped him, and he fell sprawling. The Grindark scrambled clear. Clutching his remaining braid with both hands, he scuttled out into the mist.

Jame circled the fallen brigand. 'Now, what have you done to my friend?'

Bortis lay face down on the ground. His shoulders began to shake. He was laughing.

'Oh, it was funny! H-he thought you were calling him. "Marc, oh Marcarn. . . ."' He gave a fair imitation of Jame's voice, spoiled by an attack of giggles. 'I lured him into that doll's house and – and pushed a wall over on him. The floor gave way too.

411

He fell down, then sideways – if that whoreson Grindark wan't lying – straight through another farking wall!' The brigand jerked up his head, wet mouth rimmed with dirt. 'You've killed another one!' he crowed. 'Get yourself a new lover, Talisman. The old one's worm-bait!'

Something colder even than her building rage chilled Jame. A trick step-back room. Even she wouldn't trust her reflexes, falling into something so unexpected. And Marc, as Bortis kept saying, was no longer young.

Jorin had cowered away from her to the edge of the circle. She remembered how he had darted off minutes before, and felt suddenly sure that it had been because he had caught the Kendar's scent. She had called him off then. Not now.

'Find him,' she said to the ounce. 'Bring him here... if you can.'

Blind Jorin gave her a wide moon-opal stare. Then he was gone in a flash of gold.

Jame circled Bortis again, feeling the cold berserker rage rise, savouring it.

'Dear Bortis. *Who's* worm-bait?'

Someone on the edge of the ring laughed softly.

Jame spun around, Bortis temporarily forgotten. The caul on top of the first stone had raised its head. Diamantine light cast into even greater relief the angry scars that formed the shape of an inverted *imu* burned into its face. The eyes on either side of it glittered, and the misshapen mouth lifted in a smile.

'Ah, child, how you love your work. What a reaper of souls you will make someday.'

Jame recoiled a step. Then she quickly drew out the medallion covered in the changer's skin and held it up as if it were a protective charm.

'You came back, maybe, for your face? Here it is.'

'So I see. And you've been feeding it, too. How... considerate.'

The changer gathered himself as if to spring, then collapsed, panting. His face was grey with exhaustion. Jame slowly lowered the *imu*. The changer's smile twisted, distorting his warped face even more.

'Quite right. Even if this accursed place wasn't killing me by inches, after two days aloft with barely a breeze for support, I'm in no shape to harm you.'

'Why did you want to in the first place? Back in Peshtar, you said that my death would mean the Master's eventual downfall. Sweet Trinity, how?'

'Now, child, no games.'

'Damnit, it's true. I don't remember – if I ever knew at all.'

'Indeed?' Malice lit his pale eyes. 'Now, would it be more amusing to tell you or not? I think not.'

His gaze suddenly shifted. Jame heard boot leather scrape on stone behind her and turned, just as Bortis charged at the sound of her voice. He knocked her flat. His weight, crashing down full on top of her, drove the air from her lungs. He had her hands pinned above her head before she recovered. His heavy body shook on top of her as he began to giggle uncontrollably.

'And now,' said the changer's cool, malicious voice, 'I think that friend Bortis will also amuse himself.'

A moaning cry welled up around them, echoed not by walls this time but, it seemed, by the very earth. Bortis started. Jame got free an arm and struck him sharply in the nose with the heel of her hand. His head snapped back. She shoved him off and rolled backward into a fighter's crouch, nails out, ready to defend herself.

'Take her, damn you!' the changer was screaming. 'She's right in front of you!'

Bortis ignored them both. He was listening, mouth agape, blood dripping unnoticed onto his chin. The cry came again, all around them. Its desolation seemed to jar something loose in the man's broken mind. He bolted, sobbing, between the lithons, out into the mist.

Some hunter's instinct almost sent Jame after him, but then she shrank back. Two figures had come into the circle. For a moment, Jame had the half-dazed impression that they were human: a woman bent with age and grief, a slender, white-haired child with fierce red eyes. Then she saw that they were both rathorns.

The mare was indeed old. Her coat, nearly hidden by encroaching plates, had faded from black to silver grey. Her slim legs trembled under the ivory's weight, while a massive skull mask bent her head almost to the ground. She breathed in great gasps between bared fangs because the mask's nasal pits had grown shut. So had one eye socket. She was slowly being buried alive in the ivory tomb of her own armour.

Snatches of her scent and the colt's reached Jame, even though this time they weren't directed at her. With each breath

413

she drew, memories not her own swirled around her: the smell of dawn on the wind, the touch of a snowflake on the tongue, the sound of rathorn stallions belling in an autumn wood. Each memory flashed and died, leaving only a sense of infinite loss. The mare was destroying them one by one, ripping apart the vivid tapestry of her past, unmaking herself a bit at a time because she knew of no other way to die.

Jame fought the swift current of the other's memories, but every breath she took plunged her back into it. She began to sense the mare's underlying emotions like great jagged rocks in the riverbed of the rathorn's consciousness: despair, that so long a life had left so many memories to be destroyed; rage, that her own traitor body had made such a destruction necessary; grief, that bit by bit she was losing all the bright, fierce days, all the glowing nights. But most of all she grieved for the colt at her side, her last foal with his white coat and his red, red eyes. Her coming end had put its mark on him even before his birth. Now, the longer she took to die, the longer he was bound to her and her self-destructive agony, the more warped he would become. She foresaw that already no rage would ever accept him. He would grow up bitter and alone, a rogue, a death's-head, her child. She moaned again, and the colt echoed her, furious in his denial:

No, you're not going to die! No, no...

'No...' breathed Jame, and then with a gasp wrenched her mind away from theirs. If she stayed, the rathorn's despair would suck her down as it nearly had the colt. If she ran away... but that was unthinkable. Stupid as it probably was, she could no more turn her back on this mare than on one of her own people in agony, pleading for the White Knife. She drew her own blade.

'Don't!' hissed the changer. His voice rose. 'You fool, don't...!'

Jame sprang forward on the mare's blind side. She caught the tusk and jerked the rathorn's ivory encrusted head around. Like water deep in a well, the mare's sunken eye caught and held a warped reflection of Jame's face. The mirrored lips moved.

If you kill me, said a cold, precise voice in her head, *my child will kill you. Kill me.*

The eye closed. It was her choice, then, with full knowledge of the consequences. So be it. She drew back her knife to strike.

The colt's furious charge sent her sprawling. He had no tusk as yet and his horn was only a bump, but those small ivory hooves splintered rock beside her head. She rolled clear. He came at her again, bounding on his hind legs with fangs bared and forehooves slashing. His scent, rank with rage, sent a scream lancing through her head:

No, no, no, no . . . !

Jame slipped aside and spun. Her kick caught him just behind the ear between the undeveloped skull mask and the throat plates. He crashed down, stunned. Jame stood over him, panting. She could kill him now. She should, or he would never stop until he had killed her, if not today, then tomorrow, or next week, or next year. Think of him full grown, a rogue, a death's-head, coming to claim the debt of blood . . .

She heard a sharp hiss behind her, almost in her ear. The rathorn's head was poised above her, that ponderous weight of ivory balanced on the serpentine neck, ready to smash downward, to pulp flesh and splinter bone. Jame drew a deep shaky breath.

'All right, I won't hurt him. But if you kill me, I can't help you. Do you still want help?'

For a moment, the rathorn didn't move. Then, with a sigh, she lowered her head until her chin came to rest on Jame's shoulder. Jame had to brace herself as the weight settled. Hesitantly, wonderingly, she ran her fingers along the mare's mark, along the cool ivory. All this beauty and strength, all this proud spirit about to vanish forever. But everything, eventually, comes to an end, and destruction is only one more face of God. Jame took a firmer grip on her knife. Then, with all her strength, she drove the blade through the mare's eye deep into her brain.

The beast screamed. Jame staggered back, hands over her ears. That terrible piercing cry went on and on as the rathorn slowly collapsed. Her very soul seemed to be tearing its way to freedom, and the diamantine *imus* gave back the murderous echo. The changer had curled himself up like a spider on top of his stone, but now he plummeted to the ground, shrieking. Blood and grey matter ran out of his ears. He convulsed once, horribly, and lay still. The stones under him began to crack.

Jame took a step towards the edge of the circle and fell, half paralysed by the noise. The rathorn's scream was bad enough, but the stones' echo was raw power, enough easily to kill.

But what was that? A shadow sped past her across the stones, cast by no seen form. It darted to the hollowed-out *imu* and back again, away and back. No more grey cloak, because the cape in the entry hall had disintegrated at her touch. No more child-sized figure seen from the corner of the eye, because all his bones but one had turned to dust. But their mysterious guide would still lead her to safety if only she could follow him – but Jame ... couldn't ... move ...

Running footsteps. Someone snatched her up, and she found herself hurling towards the darkness inside the shining stone. The *imu*'s mouth swallowed both her and her rescuer. Inside, the diamantine boomed with the rathorn's scream. Her rescuer stumbled and dropped her. She rolled down steep stairs between booming walls, down into silence.

No, not quite silence. The ringing went on and on, only now it was only in her ears. She was lying on stone pavement. More stone seemed to be heaped on her chest, making it hard to breathe. The weight shifted, and a wet nose anxiously touched hers. She threw her arms around Jorin and hugged him as he burst into a thunderous purr.

A dying murmur from above still echoed in the stairwell. Then, as it faded entirely away, a terrible shriek rose in its place, full of despair, wild for revenge.

Jorin went straight up into the air and came down with all his fur on end. Jame scrambled to her feet. She heard hooves thundering down the stair. Oh God, the colt. She must bar his way, but how? There, folded back against the wall on either side of the stairwell: doors. Their stiffened hinges resisted her at first, but with a final, frantic effort she managed to slam them shut in the colt's very face. A lock clicked. Almost simultaneously, the young rathorn hit the other side with a boom. Jame felt the door shudder. She heard sharp ivory hooves tear at it, but its panels were made of ironwood and they held. One last scream sounded on the other side and then there was silence. Jame leaned against the wood. She knew as surely as if he had shouted it in her ear what that last cry had meant:

If not today, then tomorrow, or next week, or next year. Wait.

Trinity. She had daydreamed about riding a rathorn into battle, but here she was instead, launched into a blood feud with one. Just the same, it would probably be years before the colt was old enough to come after her, and, at this rate, she would be lucky to get as far as tomorrow. *Let's just take one crisis at a time*, Jame thought, and, for the first time, looked about her.

She was in fair-sized subterranean chamber lined with close-fitted masonry, dimly lit by patches of luminous moss dotting the floor. It was ringed by open doorways, ten in all. Shining runes marked their lintels. Beside one of them, someone quite large was raising himself on an elbow.

'Marc!' Jame cried, and threw herself into the Kendar's arms. Jorin pounced on both of them. 'But how did you get out of Bortis's trap, or cross that killing circle up there, or –'

'Just a minute, lass.' The Kendar stuck a finger in first one ear and then the other, dislodging what looked like mud. Jame saw that the little sack of earth from Kithorn was hanging outside his shirt, empty.

'Oh, Marc, your home-soil!'

He shrugged. 'I thought it might protect me. Luckily, it did. A good thing I hung on to it these sixty odd years, eh? As for Bortis's trap, a funny business that was, falling first one direction and then the other. But, you know, those cracked walls practically powdered when I hit them. There was no real impact to speak of at all. It took me awhile to climb out; but when I did, there was Jorin, waiting to guide me here.'

'Cracked...' Jame thought of those shattered walls, the stones breaking under the changer, the fissured bones. The ghost of an idea began to form in her mind, but before it could take on substance, she started violently. Out of one of the doorways, as if from a great distance, had come a voice:

'Hello? Is anyone there?'

Jame sprang to her feet. She had not heard that voice for years, except in dreams, but she had no doubt who was calling to her now.

'Tori! My God, where are you? Answer me!'

She plunged through the nearest doorway into the tunnel beyond, still calling her brother's name. Moss formed a luminous carpet for the first few yards, then broke down into clumps, more and more widely spaced. Beyond lay utter darkness. Jame called again. Only echoes replied. Could she have chosen the wrong door? Yes, easily. She must try again.

Jame turned quickly to retrace her footsteps, and again found nothing but darkness before her. Where was the luminous moss? She could only have come a few yards beyond it, yet now it was nowhere in sight. Marc's voice called her name. How impossibly far away he sounded. She took a hesitant step towards him, and in the distance saw a faint green glow. Of course: the tunnel must be paved with step-forward stones. Another stride or two and...

Her foot came down on emptiness.

She pitched forward, twisted, clawed at stone, hung there in space by her fingertips, heart pounding. A rock, dislodged, plummeted away. It never seemed to hit the bottom. Instead, from below came a scuffling, scratching sound, oddly furtive. An exhalation of air cold with earth and deep stone breathed up around her.

Then Jame almost lost her grip as something touched her hand. It was Jorin. A moment later, Marc caught her wrists and pulled her back up onto the path.

'What in Perimal's name is down there?' she demanded.

Steel struck flint. A spark flashed blindingly in the dark and grew as dead moss kindled. Marc rose and kicked the blazing clump over the edge. It fell, revealing a deep, narrow crevasse running parallel to the trail. The chasm's lower reaches were studded with rocks, each one about the size of a clenched fist. A hundred points of light glowed briefly like small feral eyes in their craggy folds, then all blinked out at once. In the utter darkness that followed, the stealthy scratch of claw on stone began again.

'Trocks,' said Marc's voice in the dark. 'The Builders brought them to Rathillien. Their digestive juices dissolve stone, you see, so they were useful in temple masonry and, I suppose, in hollowing out tunnels like this. We had better go back to that underground chamber. At least there was some light there. . . . Wait.'

They listened.

'They're between us and the chamber,' said Jame. 'Now what – try to make friends?'

'No. These may have been the Builders' pets once, but they've run wild for many a long year now. I shouldn't think even a Builder would care to deal with them now.'

'But if they're stone-eaters, surely they won't hurt us.'

'Oh, they eat other things as well: lichen, boots, feet. . . . Krothen had an infestation of them in his dungeon at Kothifir once that cleaned out every prisoner he had, not to mention quite a few guards. Most areas around our temples have a problem with them, off and on. They don't like light, though.'

Again the click of steel and flint; again a spark. As moss caught fire, Marc tore up a clump and threw it down the passageway. The path was thick was small grey rocks that certainly hadn't been there before. They covered the moss. As it caught fire under them, the spreading flames kindled the glow of many eyes, and a piping wail arose. Then the fire came leaping back up the tunnel towards Jame and Marc.

They retreated. The walls of the step-forward passage blurred as if they were moving impossibly fast, but the flames followed faster over the carpet of dead moss. Jame and Marc plunged into a side tunnel with Jorin on their heels just as the fire roared past. The dry moss burned fiercely, but not for long, leaving a path strewn with rapidly dying embers. Darkness closed in again.

'We aren't having much luck with fire on this trip,' said Jame in a rather shaken voice. 'At least I don't hear any more scratching. Marc?' The darkness pressed in around her, more absolute than anything she had ever known. 'Where are you?'

'Here.' His voice came from somewhere to her right. 'We seem to have got off the step-forward stones. They probably only line the main passageway.'

'But why? Where does it go?'

'Trinity knows. More to the point, where do *we* go from here? Some light should help.'

She heard him draw out his fire making tools again, then give a disgusted grunt. 'Dropped them.' Joints creaking audibly, he knelt to search the floor.

'Don't bother,' said Jame. 'I still have mine.' She groped in a pocket and pulled them out. The handkerchief-wrapped bone came too and fell before she could catch it. She didn't hear it hit the floor. The next moment, the flint and steel were snatched from her grasp. 'Hey! Give me a chance.'

'What?' said Marc's voice, still down by the floor.

Jame stood very still. She heard nothing, and yet. . . . 'Marc, I don't think we're alone down here.'

He rose. 'Where are you?'

'Here.' She reached out. A hand closed on hers – slim, long fingered, very, very cold. She dropped it with a gasp and sprang back, only to trip over Jorin. That cold grip caught her flailing hand and steadied her.

'What on earth are you doing?' said Marc's voice behind her.

She gulped. 'Making someone's acquaintance, I think, someone who apparently doesn't want to be seen and who isn't very tall.'

'Our friend in grey?'

'Maybe.' That unearthly hand still lay in her grasp. Now its cold fingers tightened and tugged at her. 'I think he wants us to go with him. Should we?'

A moment's silence, then: 'Yes,' said Marc. 'After all, we've been following him since this morning. Here.' His own hand, huge and warm, closed over hers. 'Lead on.'

The darkness confused Jame's sense of direction, but she was fairly sure that their guide was taking them back to the main corridor. In confirmation the burnt smell grew and then charred moss crunched underfoot. They turned left, away from the subterranean chamber. Jame went on, one hand gripping the cold fingers that led her, the other engulfed in Marc's warm grasp as he followed in her wake. Only the sound of her boots and his echoed off the walls, sometimes close by, sometimes far off, as if the path momentarily skirted the edge of some vast cavern. There were depths too, or so the faint echoes hinted, occasionally on both sides of the trail at once.

How long had they been walking? Time seemed to slow, almost to stop under the weight of darkness. Where were they going? If the stones underfoot still stepped forward, they must have already come a considerable distance.

Jame's thoughts spun in circles, snatching at answers that the darkness denied her. She remembered how frightened she had been as a child during the dark of the moon. Perimal Darkling gripped that part of Rathillien that overlapped the next threshold world, the one that had fallen with the Master, but the shadows always sought to expand. Someday they might reach from the planet's surface up into the orbit of its single moon. If that happened, Perimal Darkling would swallow the moon and soon after both the sun and stars; that had happened before on other threshold worlds where the Kencyrath had fought and lost. If ever Rathillien's moon disappeared, the Three People would know that they had lost again. But, in the meantime, for five nights out of every forty-day lunar cycle, the moon was dark, and those below waited anxiously for its reappearance, afraid that the end had come with no one the wiser until too late. But even during 'the Dark,' there was some light. Not so here.

This wouldn't do, Jame told herself firmly. If she kept thinking about the darkness, it would consume her. To steady herself, she turned her mind back to the mystery of the cracks, and soon came up with some guesses that made her even more uneasy.

'Marc...' she said. 'Suppose the Builders did try to claim the Anarchies. Then suppose the rathorns came back, maybe through these tunnels, and ... and used the *imus* to scream the city to pieces, with the Builders still in it. I found a skeleton in that house I explored. It wasn't human. There could have been more there, hidden in corners and holes all over the city, where they crawled trying to escape. Perhaps all the Builders are dead, and if they are –'

'There'll be no more temples,' Marc finished, his voice echoing hollowly in the darkness. 'If we have to retreat to the next threshold world, we'll be completely cut off from our god. Oh, I don't like the old grump any more than you do, but without him . . .'

'Or her, or it.'

'. . . we're helpless.'

'So, if the Builders are dead, this is it: Rathillien, the Kencyrath's last battlefield. But if that's true, just who or what is holding onto my hand?'

She didn't get an answer. Jorin had been walking beside her, his shoulder brushing her leg. Suddenly she felt him stop. His keen ears had caught a faint, distant sound. Jame heard it too, somewhat distorted, through his senses: many claws on stone, rapidly getting closer. The cat began to growl.

'Lass?'

'Company, and no more fire to make them welcome.'

'Then let's not be at home when they get here.'

Their guide seemed to agree for that cold hand tugged impatiently at Jame. They ran, tripping, stumbling in the dark. Behind them, the scratching sound grew closer, louder, and a thin, excited whistling filled the air.

Then between one step and the next, light exploded around them. Half-blinded, Jame skidded to a stop, with Jorin tumbling over her heels. She turned in bewilderment and saw Marc standing behind her, rubbing his eyes. There was a wall close behind him – so close, in fact, that his pack seemed to be embedded in it. Then he gave a startled grunt and rocked back on his heels, as if something had given him a sharp pull from behind. The next moment, he surged away from the wall and hastily shrugged off what was left of his pack. It had been ripped open and its contents half dissolved by a slimy grey substance through which white larvae wriggled.

'It must be the breeding season,' said Marc grimly, and kicked the pack back through the apparently solid wall. 'I've heard old songs about gateway barriers like this. Ancestors be praised the songs were right. Now, where's our guide? We apparently owe him more than we realised.'

But the small grey figure from the Anarchies was nowhere in

sight. Then Jame realised that she was still holding something. She opened her hand. In it lay the long, slim finger bone from the Builder's house. It crumbled into dust.

'Good-bye, friend.' She let it sift through her fingers. 'Now, where on earth are we?'

They were standing on the edge of a large, nine-sided chamber. Its walls were painted in a continuous sylvan mural, and rib girders rose from each angle like tree trunks to meet overhead in a tangle of painted leaves, branches, and sky. From the apex of the ceiling hung a light sphere. Jame had seen others like it in Tai-tastigon, but this one was much larger and dimmer. The blinding glare was actually no more than a twilight glow now that her eyes had adjusted to it, and apparently hadn't been more than that for some time, for the real grass carpeting the room had had begun to die. But what really astonished her was the white, windowless structure standing in the middle of the floor.

'Why, it looks just like a model of our god's temple in Tai-tastigon!' she exclaimed.

'That's no model,' said Marc. He looked around in amazement. 'I've heard of this room. We're in Karkinaroth, Prince Odalian's palace. But how? That's three hundred leagues south of the Anarchies.'

'The step-forward stones! I thought we'd probably gone quite a distance, but this...!' She stopped, struck by a thought. 'Marc, there are supposed to be nine Kencyr temples on Rathillien, aren't there?'

'Why, yes.'

'There were ten doors in that underground chamber.'

'Well, there's Wyrden in the Oseen Hills. That's Builders' work, too. Grindark hillmen live there now, but there's a tradition that their ancestors were the Builders' craftsmen.'

'So they would have to get to the building sites, too, maybe by a step forward tunnel to that room under the Anarchies and then on by one of the other nine doors. Well, it's a thought, anyway. It would at least explain how we got here.' She approached the miniature temple cautiously, wary as always in the presence of her god. 'But are you sure this thing is real? It's so small.'

'Only on the outside. The Builders could be very playful about space. Three priests and nine acolytes are supposed to serve here.'

'It doesn't look as if anyone has for some time. Why, the door is even bolted shut.' She put her hands on it, then jerked them away with a startled exclamation. 'There's power in there. Too much of it, barely under control. Where are the priests? Trinity, don't they know how dangerous this could be? Tai-tastigon nearly got ripped apart when the temple there was mismanaged.'

'I think I hear someone in there.'

They leant as close to the door as they could without touching it. From inside came a whisper of a voice crying over and over in Kens:

'Let me out! Oh God, let me out, let me out...'

Marc pushed Jame aside. He gripped the rod bolted across the door and pitted the whole of his great strength against it. Muscles bulged, bones creaked, but the rod didn't move. He let go and looked rather blankly at his hands, blistered by the power from within the temple.

'This calls for a lever,' he said. He unsheathed his war-axe and regarded its wooden shaft critically. 'It might hold up against that rod, but then again...'

At that moment, three guards wearing the Prince's buff and gold livery entered the room. They carried steel-shafted spears.

'Now, one of those will do nicely,' said the big Kendar and stepped forward. 'Here, friend, lend me your weapon. Someone is trapped inside...'

The guard reversed his spear and struck with its iron shod butt. By skill or luck, he clipped Marc on the head just where Bortis's brigand had hit him four days earlier. The big man crumpled without a sound. Jame found herself facing two poised spears.

'What about the cat?' one man asked another.

'We have no orders about that. Kill it.'

'Jorin, run!' Jame cried, and threw herself forward, twisting. One spear point passed under her arm and the other clashed against it as the second guard tried too late to block her. She dropped the first man with an elbow to the throat. The man who had struck Marc tripped her with his spear shaft. She came up rolling and saw Jorin disappear in a golden streak out the door. The next moment, the back of her head seemed to explode.

But these people are supposed to be our allies, she thought with amazement, and then thought nothing more at all.

22

Interlude with Jewel-Jaws
Wyrden: 12th of Winter

Two days after leaving the Riverland, the Host of the Kencyrath
seemed to have left behind impending winter. While Kithorn
had been cold and stark, here in the Oseen Hills some three
hundred and fifty miles to the south, maples and sumac still
blazed red and gold on the slopes and migrating birds flew
overhead. Holly, Lord Danior, still rode beside Torisen, shying
stones at every *dorith* tree he saw. Whenever he hit one at just
the right moment, in just the right way, all of its leaves fell off at
once with a most satisfying 'whoosh.' Torisen finally sent the
young lord and his riders on ahead to scout the next stretch of
road.

'Running you ragged, is he?' said Harn with a chuckle, pulling
up beside the Highlord. 'Now you know how I felt when I was
your commander.'

'At least I never tried to bury you in *dorith* leaves. How are
things down the line?'

'Just stay away from the Coman. Demoth and Korey are
ready to cut each other's throats or, preferably, yours. Which
reminds me. Although you've sent your regular guard back to
their respective commands, you haven't picked your war-guard
yet. Now, I've got my eye on a score or so of your randons
who –'

'Harn, no. We won't reach the Cataracts for nearly three
weeks. Let it wait.'

Harn bristled. 'You think nothing can happen before then?
You've got more enemies than just the Coman, boy, and you're
too valuable to risk. You need protection.'

'Harn, I'm not going to spend the rest of this march tripping
over a parcel of well-meaning bodyguards. I just don't like to be
followed about. You know that.'

'In case you hadn't noticed, you're being followed by the entire Kencyr Host.'

'That isn't quite the same thing. Drop it for now, Harn. I promise, I'll be as sensible as you like – when we get to the Cataracts. Now, how are the foot soldiers holding up?'

'Well enough,' said Harn grudgingly, 'as long as they get at least one night of *dwar* sleep out of three. We must be covering a good sixteen leagues a day. Not bad. But to have our strength cut by a third every night when we're this spread out ... d'you realise that the line of march stretches back nearly ten miles?'

'We'll be out of these mountains in two or three days.'

'Aye, and on the edge of the White Hills. What d'you think of Caineron's suggestion that we cut through them instead of following the River Road? It would save us nearly three hundred miles.'

Torisen snorted. 'That wasn't why he suggested it. My lord Caineron simply wanted to remind everyone of what happened there and whose fault it was.'

The White Hills – white with the ashes of the dead after Ganth's defeat ... no Kencyr had walked there since, and Torisen didn't want to be the first. Who knew what might wait in a place like that?

'Harn,' he said abruptly, changing the topic. 'You served with Pereden for a year after I left. How has he shaped up?'

The randon scratched an unshaven chin, his nail rasping on stubble. 'Well now, that's not so easily answered. It was a quiet year, without much to test the boy's mettle. I would say, though, that Pereden wanted to be a great leader without having to work for it. He seemed to think that command of the Southern Host was only his due.'

'So it would have been from the start, if Ardeth hadn't given it to me. You know the tradition: where there's no Knorth heir, the heir of Ardeth commands in the field – except when Caineron got his finger in the pie just long enough to pull out Urakarn.'

'But you were the Knorth heir.'

'Yes, but Pereden didn't know that. No one did but Ardeth until I came of age. You thought I was delirious when I told you in that ruined desert city where you and Burr tracked me down.'

'Oh aye. And stayed drunk for a week along with half your staff when we heard you'd actually made the other lords accept you.'

Torisen laughed, then caught his breath sharply. Flashing across the road scarcely a dozen paces away was a rage of five rathorns. The lead stallion spun around to face the Host, fangs bared. Sunlight fell into the blackness of his coat, blazed off his two horns and wealth of ivory. Every war horse in the vanguard rocked back on its heels, wild-eyed. Not one would have stood its ground if the great beast had charged. Instead, he gave a scornful snort and bounded over the Silver after his rage. A moment later, all five had vanished as if the hills had swallowed them whole.

'Trinity!' breathed Harn, soothing his frightened mount. 'That was quite an omen.'

'Of what? I think the emblem of my house just laughed in my face. But where on earth did they come from?'

He dismounted and followed the rathorns' path, clearly marked by trampled grass. Ahead there seemed to be nothing but a vine-covered cliff face. As he drew nearer, however, Torisen saw darkness behind the leaves. He pushed the vines aside. Behind them was the mouth of a tunnel, high vaulted, lined with smooth, expertly fitted stones. The shaft seemed to go back a long, long way. Its cold breath, heavy with the smells of earth and rathorn, breathed in his face. A faint, confused murmur arose from the black distance, almost like the sound of voices.

'Hello? Is anyone there?'

His voice echoed back harshly again and again and again. He caught his breath, feeling as if he had shouted down into a place better left undisturbed. Then, somewhere, far, far away, someone called his name.

The unburnt dead come for you out of darkness, calling, calling, and if you answer, you are lost.

But that was only how he and Jame used to frighten each other as children. It was just a silly game born out of a stupid superstition... about as stupid as believing that someone down there in the dark actually knew his name.

Harn called to him from the road. 'Blackie! Here comes Ardeth.'

The Lord of Omiroth was riding up towards the vanguard on his grey Whinno-hir mare Brithany, a matriarch of the herd and Storm's granddam. Kindrie, the two Kendar scrollsmen, and Ardeth's war-guard followed him at a distance.

Harn grunted. 'Confrontation time, huh? I'd better take myself off, then.' He cantered back towards the main body of the Host, saluting Ardeth as he passed.

Torisen swung back up onto Storm and waited, not without some trepidation. He and Ardeth had not spoken since Gothregor when the older man had dressed him down for not honouring his obligation to Kindrie.

'My lord, my lady.' He included both Highborn and horse in a wary salute. Ardeth, to his surprise, looked almost embarrassed.

'My boy, it seems I owe you an apology. I didn't know that the changer who attacked you at Tentir was a Shanir, much less that he was bound to a darkling wyrm.'

'Kindrie saw the wyrm? Good. I was beginning to think that I'd imagined it. But he waited this long to tell you?'

'You never told me at all,' said Ardeth, a trifle sharply. 'Still, what cursed luck that it was a Shanir. The Old Blood can be dangerous. It opens us up to godborn powers few of us still know how to control. But is it necessarily so foul a thing, say, to share senses with an animal? Now, if it were Brithany here instead of some crawling thing, wouldn't that at least tempt you?'

'*No*,' said Torisen, and gave a startled yelp as the mare nipped his leg. 'Sorry, my lady. Forgive me?' He held out his hand to her. She made as if to snap at his fingers, but only grazed them with a velvet lip.

'You always were one of her favourites,' said Ardeth, smiling. 'That was in part why I took a chance on you in the first place.'

'So that's why you introduced us that first night. The lord of Omiroth, taking advice from a grey mare. Hey!'

Storm, growing jealous, had turned to snap at Ardeth's foot. Brithany put back her ears. Her grand-colt subsided, chastened and a bit sulky.

'The idiot child,' said Ardeth, regarding him coolly. 'Why don't you look for a full-blooded Whinno-hir? I know of at least one three-year-old in the herd who would be honoured to bear you.'

'Even a half-blood wouldn't have the weight to carry me into battle. Storm does. Besides, he'll take me straight through a stone wall if I ask him to, without an argument.'

'As I said, an idiot. Look!'

Across the river, a flight of azure-winged butterflies rose from the tall grass at the sound of the horses' hooves, then settled back again out of sight.

'Jewel-jaws,' said Torisen absently. 'There must be something dead in the grass.' He peered ahead down the road. 'Holly's been gone a long time. I sent him ahead to check out the next post station.'

'You expect trouble?'

'I don't really know. We should have had news from the south before now, unless the post-rider has been waylaid somewhere along the line.'

'Or no one escaped to send word,' Ardeth concluded bleakly. He turned to watch two more swarms of butterflies dancing above the grass, them gave himself a shake. 'Your pardon, my boy. It's an old man's weakness to think too much of death. This post system of yours is really remarkable. Imagine, news from the far side of Rathillien in only ten days. Of course, if you put the Shanir to work on it, they might come up with something even faster...'

'No.'

'Ah well. Have it your way. It must be quite a job, though, protecting stations in this wilderness.'

'I have an arrangement with the local warlord, one Grisharki. If he were a Grindark like his followers, I would trust him more, but he comes from the Ebonbane and boasts that he was the lieutenant of some famous brigand there named Bortis.'

'Grindark,' Ardeth repeated thoughtfully. 'An odd people, that, with an even odder connection to us.'

'Because they're supposed to have been the Builders' workmen?' Torisen asked.

'Oh, there's no doubt that they were, my lord,' said the young historian eagerly, spurring up level with them. 'They were my speciality, you know, when I qualified for the scrollsman's robe. I know all about them.'

Ashe, riding a length behind him, cast up her eyes, but the two Highborn smiled at his enthusiasm. Ardeth gave him a half bow.

'Well, scholar, will you share your learning or leave us in outer darkness?'

The historian blushed – with embarrassment, gratification, or both. 'It seems that once the Grindarks were like any other hill tribe, if poorer than most,' he said. 'Then the Builders came. They offered the Grindarks rewards and secret knowledge if they would work for them. Of course, the Grindarks agreed, especially since their first job was to seal off the Anarchies from the other rival tribes.'

'How?' Torisen asked.

'I can't explain, lord, and neither can they. They've also forgotten how they built a city in the Anarchies, and the temples themselves. Oh yes, they also built Wyrden, just for themselves.'

'And I'll bet they don't remember how they did that either,' Ashe muttered. 'Forgetful bunch of buggers.'

The historian laughed. 'Not as forgetful as the Chief Builder, though. He had something – a talisman, a device, I don't know what – that was supposed to protect him and his people from the Anarchies. When the temples were done and the Builders moved on, the Grindarks were to have it and the city in the Anarchies. Considering how all the hill tribes feel about that place – sacred ground and all that – you can imagine what a prize it was. So the Grindarks worked like madmen putting up eight of the temples around Rathillien and most of the ninth in Kothifir. Then one morning not a single Builder was waiting to direct them. Instead, they found this talisman, this *Men-thari* as they call it, just lying where the Chief Builder had apparently forgotten it the night before. Why finish the temple at all, the Grindarks asked themselves. Why not just grab this thing they'd been slaving to win and run with it?'

'The Builders might have had something to say about that,' Ardeth said.

'Ah, but you see, lord, the Grindarks had convinced themselves that this thing, whatever it was, was the source of the Builders' power. They thought if they had it, they could do anything. But when one of them put it on, it quite neatly cut his head off.'

Torisen had been watching the scavenger jewel-jaws on the far shore. How many there were, five more flights at least, each one dancing over something hidden in the tall grass. Holly had been gone such a long time...

Then the historian's words penetrated his abstraction and he started, one hand going to the silver collar of the Kenthiar, which he wore again. Ardeth noticed the gesture.

'And that wasn't all, either,' the young scrollsman was saying with relish. 'They suddenly noticed that they were starting to lose their memories as well. Oh, not all of them, just those connected with things the Builders had taught them, like how to set step-back stones, or read the Builders' runes. It was the Builders' revenge, they thought, for their treacherous intentions. They panicked and bolted, all the way back to Wyrden.

And there they've been ever since, dwindling in number, periodically under siege by the other tribes, who suspect they had something to do with closing the Anarchies.'

'That's quite a remarkable story,' said Ardeth. 'I commend your research. Now, about this *Men-thari*...'

Torisen stiffened in the saddle. 'Hoofbeats,' he said tersely.

Brithany tossed her head, nostrils flaring. 'And smoke,' said Ardeth.

Lord Danior and his war-guard careened around a curve in the road, nearly barrelling into the vanguard. 'Tori, trouble...'

Torisen spurred past him. The road twisted back and forth, hugging the curve of the river, past larch and maple. He could smell smoke now too, a stale, wet stink. He rounded a clump of red sumac and there were the ruins of the station, still smouldering. Four figures in hieratic robes waited motionless in the middle of the road. As Torisen rode up, he saw that each one was fixed on a sharpened stake driven up through the body. Each face under its hood wore a seething mask of blue butterflies. He brushed the insects away from one. Behind him, Donkerri leaned over his horse's neck, retching.

'Does anyone know this man?'

'He was the priest in charge of the mission to Karkinaroth,' said Kindrie. Gingerly, he brushed clear the other faces. 'These were his acolytes. I trained with them.'

Torisen glanced at him, then abruptly away. 'Friends?'

'No. When a Shanir has no liking for the priesthood, the other initiates consider it their duty to break him to it. But none of them deserved this.'

Torisen wheeled Storm away.

'Holly, get these men down and ready for the pyre. Check the ruins for more bodies, and also the far bank of the river. Follow the jewel-jaws. Donkerri... get control of yourself, boy. All right? Then ride back for Harn. Tell him what's happened and where we've gone. Also tell him to keep the column moving on the main road. Kindrie, you'd better go with Donkerri.'

Because he still couldn't bring himself to look at the Shanir, Torisen didn't see the surprise and then the hurt in the young man's faded eyes.

'Y-yes, my lord,' Donkerri was stammering, 'but where *are* you going?'

'Why, to Wyrden, Grisharki's stronghold. Where else?'

*

430

The warlord's fortress was barely five minutes' fast ride back into the Oseen Hills. Torisen caught a glimpse of its square white towers as Storm burst from a defile into the narrow valley that housed it. Ardeth and Burr rode at his stirrups with the former's war-guard thundering after them.

Behind, someone shouted.

Torisen twisted around to see the first of Ardeth's guard crash down, entangled in a net thrown from above. Thrashing horses blocked the mouth of the defile.

''Ware attackers!' Burr shouted, and the next moment toppled from his horse with a grunt as a rock hit him.

Grindarks rushed in on them down the steep slopes. Ardeth was thrown as Brithany sprang nimbly away from her assailants. A body crashed into Torisen. He fell, locked in powerful arms, but twisted in midair to land on top. A bearded face snarled up at him. He smashed the man's larynx with a fire-leaping strike and sprang clear, drawing his short sword. A stone hit his elbow, numbing it. The sword dropped from the nerveless fingers. He made a grab for it with his other hand, but at that moment his arms were seized from behind and wrenched back. A Grindark picked up the fallen blade. Torisen stared at him.

My God! he thought with blank amazement. *I'm going to die!*

The man drew back his arm to strike. Then his eyes fell, widening, on Torisen's throat, laid bare in the struggle. The Kenthiar gleamed coolly against the tanned skin. The Grindark fell back a step, then another, whining. He dropped the sword. For a moment, it looked as if he might bolt, but then he flopped down suddenly and lay grovelling in the dirt.

Torisen's arms were released. He turned sharply, ready to strike, but this assailant too stood staring as if thunderstruck. Then his eyes rolled up and he tumbled down in a dead faint.

'*Men-thari*,' another Grindark breathed, and dropped to his knees.

'*Men-thari, Men-thari...*'

The word went through the hillmen's ranks like the breath of terror, and they went down, one way or another. The smell of voided bowels arose. Torisen was left standing in their midst, rubbing his bruised arm and looking rather bemused. Then he saw Burr nearby and went quickly to him, stepping over prostrate bodies.

'Are you all right?'

'Yes, lord.' The Kendar rose unsteadily, wiping blood from a cut on his forehead. 'They were only after you.'

'Brithany, back, lady. Careful...' The mare had been standing over Ardeth protectively. Now she stepped back, placing her delicate hooves as if among unbroken eggshells. The Highborn stirred, groaning. Torisen helped him up. 'My lord?'

'All right, my boy, all right. What happened?'

'I guessed correctly about the Kenthiar and so, I think, did you.'

Meanwhile, Ardeth's guard had disentangled itself and came galloping down to secure the unresisting prisoners. The trap could only have held them a few minutes in any event, but if its sole purpose had been to kill the Highlord, a few minutes were all the attackers would have needed.

'Now what, my lord?'

'We pay our little visit to Grisharki.'

They rode down the valley to Wyrden, taking their prisoners with them. Grisharki's stronghold was partway up the far slope with steep cliffs behind it. It was square, with a tower at each corner and a crenellated battlement lined with the decaying heads of tribesmen from farther back in the hills, with whom the Grindarks waged continual war. Brown stains ran down from the crenels. The whole fortress was not very large, but its white walls gave the impression of great strength.

Torisen rode within hailing distance of the closed gate. 'Announce me,' he said to Burr.

The Kendar took a deep breath. 'Torisen, Lord Knorth, Highlord of the Kencyrath, summons Grisharki, Warlord of the Grindarks!' he roared.

An arrow struck the ground between Storm's forefeet, making him dance backward. Laughter sounded.

'You fool!' It was Grisharki himself, leaning out between two merlons, the wind in his black bush of a beard. 'You escape one trap and walk straight into another! I can shoot you down from where I stand, and you and every half-wit with you!'

'Do that, and you'll bring the entire Host down on you!' Burr shouted back.

Grisharki spat. 'That, for your Host! Run away while you can, little lord. You can't take this place by storm and you haven't time for a siege.'

'He was willing to risk both before when he ambushed us,' said Ardeth. 'Why settle for a warning now?'

'I expect friend Grisharki has had second thoughts. Who

knows what the Host might do with sufficient provocation?'

'Hmmm. Just the same, he's right: we can't waste any more time here.'

'Waste?' Torisen gave him a sharp look. 'With the priests' blood price still unpaid? Yes, damnit, we haven't the time, *but how does he know?*'

'Sir, can you read the runes over the door?' Burr asked the historian in an undertone.

'No, unfortunately. If I could, we could order the gate to open and it would, whatever bars Grisharki has put on it.'

Torisen overheard. 'Perhaps we still can. You.' He gestured imperatively to the captured Grindarks. They shuffled forward apprehensively, so close together for mutual support that they practically trod on each other's toes. 'Do you believe that this collar is the *Men-thari?*'

Twenty dark heads nodded in unison.

'Do you still believe that the wearer of the *Men-thari* can do anything – even destroy Wyrden?'

'Y-yes.'

'Then go and tell your brothers that.'

They gawked at him for a moment, then turned and bolted for Wyrden in a compact knot, tripping over each other's heels. The main gate opened a crack and they piled in. It shut again with a a clang. Up on the battlements, Grisharki crowed with triumph.

'It occurs to me, somewhat belatedly, that you could have taken the priests' blood price from that poor rabble,' said Ardeth. 'After all, they're the ones who attacked us.'

'Only under orders, I suspect. No, I want the man who swore to protect the post station and then broke his word. I want Grisharki.'

Ardeth gave him a sidelong look. 'You know, my boy, sometimes I find you almost alarming – just like your father.'

Torisen stiffened. Then one corner of his mouth relaxed into a wry, twisted smile. 'If you're going to insult me, I'm leaving.'

'My dear boy, where?'

Torisen stripped off his heavy black coat and handed it to Burr. 'Guess.'

'Here now,' said Ashe sharply, spurring her horse in front of Storm. 'You aren't thinking straight. They're all back inside Wyrden now, behind virtually impregnable walls. D'you think they're still going to fall flat at a word from you?'

'After having been scared literally shitless? It wouldn't

surprise me. Move, Ashe, please.'

She did, reluctantly, and he rode forward, sunlight glinting on the Kenthiar.

'Grindarks!' His voice rang from Wyrden's wall. 'Open your gate for the *Men-thari!*'

Grisharki jeered down at him from the battlements, his voice sounding strangely far away. When Torisen glanced up, he saw that the walls rose higher and higher as he approached them, looming fifty feet, seventy-five, one hundred. No wonder besieging forces down through the millennia had lost heart before this place, even if much of that height was probably an illusion.

'Stop right there!' Grisharki shouted down at him in a voice rapidly growing fainter with distance. 'All right, damn you, you've been warned. Archers!'

He should never have left his coat behind, Torisen thought. Its braided inserts of *rhi-sar* leather would have turned aside any shaft. Giving the Grindarks another clear glimpse of the dreaded collar was hardly worth being turned into a pincushion by their arrows. The shadow of Wyrden fell across him, striking cold through his thin shirt. Storm crab-stepped nervously towards the gate – fifty feet, thirty, twenty, and still no arrow fell.

'*Archers?*' The warlord's voice barely reached Torisen now. 'Where the hell . . . ?'

Inside the fortress, there were sounds of confusion. Fifteen feet to the gate, five, and it swung open before him. The inner courtyard was full of kneeling Grindarks.

Ardeth, Burr, and the others charged in through the gate after him, swords drawn, and had to pull up sharply to keep from ploughing into the crowd.

'Well, I'll be damned,' said Ardeth, staring about him.

Torisen had also been scanning the bowed heads. No black bushy beard, and fewer Grindarks than he had expected.

'Where are the rest of you?' he demanded.

'Sent east on the road to Peshtar, one, two, three days ago,' answered a grizzled hillman. 'I swear it.' He touched his forehead, which was scored by a band of scars very similar in shape to the runes on the Kenthiar.

'Our priests bound for Tai-tastigon must be halfway to Peshtar by now,' said Ashe.

'See that a one-hundred command is sent after them to provide protection,' Torisen said to Burr. 'If they've been molested too, I want the head of every Grindark responsible. Now, bring me Grisharki and his first lieutenant.'

He dismounted and walked into the main hall. Outside, it didn't look very large, but inside it was enormous. Flagstones stretched nearly out of sight in both directions, a vast, stone-laid field under the smoke blackened sky of a roof so far up that it could barely be seen. Here the Grindarks camped, their habitual squalor scarcely noticeable in such immense surroundings.

The Grindarks shoved a narrow-faced man into the hall – Grisharki's second-in-command, apparently. And the warlord himself? The hillmen shook their heads. He wasn't outside, and as for the hall, well, my lord could see for himself.

Torisen looked down to find a small, incredibly grubby child tugging at his sleeve. It pointed to the huge fireplace. Clinkers of corroded soot were rattling down onto the hearth.

'Build me a fire,' Torisen said.

Ardeth's riders piled filthy straw bedding in the grate and kindled it while the children all gathered around, delighted. Flames and black smoke roared up the chimney. Inside, there was a muffled howl. A man tumbled out onto the hearth, smeared with soot, his clothes smouldering. The children cheered. Ardeth's riders seized him.

'Well, Grisharki,' said Torisen, 'what have you to say for yourself?'

The warlord drew himself up to his full, not inconsiderable, height and glared down through the singed remains of his beard. 'This is the way you honour our contract? What's the matter with you, man? Can't you take a little joke between friends?'

'A joke. I swore to deal with you as you dealt with me, Grisharki, and I always keep my word. Someone, prepare a sharpened stake.'

Grisharki crumpled as if the bones had melted in his legs. 'No, lord, no!' he babbled. 'I was against that, but he made me do it. He said it would bring you running, and then . . . and then . . . Lord, he bewitched me into it!'

'Who, Grisharki?'

'T-the stranger with the *imu* burned into his face – a demon, I swear! All his features kept shifting. Why, he couldn't even keep his nose on straight!'

'Another changer,' said Ardeth.

A guard approached and saluted. 'Lord, the stake is ready.'

'Take him to it.'

Grisharki pitched forward with a howl and grovelled at the Highlord's feet. Torisen regarded him dispassionately.

'I always honour my word, Grisharki, but there is some room for mercy. Kill him first,' he said to the guards. They dragged the man away.

His lieutenant watched, rigid and silent. His eyes snapped to Torisen's face as the Highlord turned to him.

'Now, what am I going to do with you? Grisharki is a poor enough blood price, and yet. . . . As his successor, will you take the oath that he took, to protect my post station and never raise your hand against my people?'

The man's head jerked in a nod.

'And you really believe you can trust him?' demanded Ardeth.

'I think I can, if he swears on this.'

Torisen took off the Kenthiar and held it out by the edges. The man stared at it, wild-eyed, then reached out desperately and gripped it.

'I swear . . . ah!'

His fingers fell to the floor, neatly severed, the wounds instantly cauterised.

'That was a false oath. Swear again, with your other hand. It's that or the stake, man,' he added in a lower voice. 'Swear.'

The Grindark swore and sat down abruptly on the hearth, white-faced but with one hand intact at least. Torisen started to put the Kenthiar back on. Ardeth stopped him.

'Let the wretched thing settle down a bit first.' He glanced at the fingers still lying on the floor. 'The longer, the better, eh?'

Ashe had been looking through a pile of gear halfway down the hall. Now she raised her voice in a hail: 'My lord!'

Just then, there was a commotion outside, and Harn stormed in. 'You young idiot!' he roared, startling bats off the high rafters. 'What d'you think you're playing at, charging off like that and nearly getting yourself killed? *I'm* the berserker, I'll have you know, not you!'

'Why isn't anyone ever pleased to see me?' said Torisen rather plaintively, and went to see what Ashe had found, leaving Harn open-mouthed.

Ashe handed him a post-rider's pouch, its seal broken. The dispatch was still inside. Torisen drew it out and read, his expression becoming grim.

'So this was how Grisharki knew we had no time for a siege. Adric?'

He turned to find the lord of Omiroth already there, reaching for the dispatch. Ardeth read. A stricken look came into his eyes.

'We must make haste. Now, Tori, now.'

'Yes, now.'

He took the old man's hands and held them for a moment. Then he was off down the hall, shouting for Harn.

They rode out minutes later, past the rigid figure of Grisharki mounting silent guard at his own door, down the valley, out through the defile. The stench of burning flesh met them. The souls of the priests and their escorts had been freed by fire, never again to walk in the shadow of their dread god. The main body of the column was just coming up the road. Torisen called over the randon captain in charge of the first Knorth one hundred.

'There's been a massacre,' he told him. 'The Southern Host has been virtually wiped out except for a handful of survivors who are withdrawing towards the Cataracts. We've got to get there as quickly as possible to cover their retreat. That means a faster pace with one night's *dwar* sleep out of two, and a route that lies through the White Hills. You've got all that?'

'Yes, lord,' said the captain.

Lord Danior had ridden over to listen. 'The White Hills, eh?' he said, rather uneasily. 'Do you think that's wise?'

'Probably not, but what choice do we have?'

Behind them, the captain was repeating the Highlord's words verbatim to his command and to the next captain down the line. As the news spread from group to group, a murmur rose among the ranks, then died into grim silence. Many of these Kendar had once served in the Southern Host; nearly all had friends or kin there who might well be feeding vultures or worse now on that distant battlefield. This was their fight now, even more than their lords'.

The one-hundred captain raised his hand. When all eyes were on him, he dropped it, and his command rocked forward as one into the loping stride that eats up nearly seventy miles a day as steadily and inexorably as the sun falls. Sunlight glinted on shield and helm, on sword hilt and spear point. Torisen reined aside to watch them pass, line after line, proud, fierce, determined. Then he cantered forward to take his place in the vanguard. Behind him, the captains called the running chant, their seconds on the far wing taking every other line. Two days' march ahead lay the White Hills.

23

The Haunted Palace
Karkinaroth: 14th of Winter

Jame dreamed that she sat on a fur rug beside a cold hearth. A vast hall stretched out before her, paved with dark green-veined stone, lined with death banners. Someone leant against the mantelpiece behind her. She couldn't turn to see who it was but his presence warmed her as the fireplace never could.

'Who *are* you?' she demanded.

The voice answered in a fading whisper. 'Ah, Jamie. Someone best forgotten.'

Now she could turn and did, crying, 'Tirandys, Senethari!' But no one was there.

The hearth was cold, and the skin beneath her that of an Arrin-ken. The nails of its flayed paws flexed on stone.

Scee, sceee, sceeeee . . .

Jame woke with a gasp and sat up – too fast. A lightning stab of pain shot through her head, then slowly faded to a dull ache. She touched the back of her head gingerly and felt a considerable lump. *Why, someone hit me,* she thought dizzily, then remembered who and under what circumstances. The grogginess was largely the aftermath of *dwar* sleep. Sweet Trinity, how long had she been unconscious? She raised her head and looked about. No windows. No way even to tell if it was day or night.

But if the room lacked a view, it had just about everything else, including nine sides. The canopied bed in which she sat was against one of them. Across a white marble floor was a small fireplace with a gracefully carved stone mantel and embers still tinkling cheerfully in the grate. If her greeting from Karkinaroth had been rude, Jame thought, looking around her, at least someone was trying to make her stay comfortable. Best of all, on a slender-legged table by the bed was a plate neatly piled with

438

fruit and honey cakes. Beside it stood a flagon of cool white wine.

Jame's last meal had been in the Anarchies – days ago, if her hunger was any indication. She ate and drank ravenously, getting crumbs everywhere. The wine had a curious after-taste, but she ignored it. Who knew what spices the southern vintners might use?

Then she dusted off her hands and rose to inspect the room. The marble floor felt cool on her bare feet, but her boots were nowhere in sight. For that matter, neither were her clothes. Jame shook down her long black hair for warmth and padded over to the fireplace. She didn't see any sign of her knapsack on the floor or under the bed. Damn. The Book Bound in Pale Leather could usually take care of itself, but Ganth's ring and sword were her responsibility. She began to look behind the tapestries on the walls for any kind of alcove where her gear might have been stored. Behind five of the seven hangings and the bed, she found only blank walls. The sixth swung aside to reveal another smaller room, lined with tiles and fitted with a sunken bath as well as with other essentials. The seventh tapestry, opposite it, concealed a locked door.

Someone apparently thought that that and the lack of clothing could keep her a prisoner here. Someone was about to get a surprise.

Jame knelt by the door, extended a nail, and began to pick the lock. She *had* to get out. There was the knapsack to find, of course, but most of all she was worried about Marc. The Kendar had also been hurt, perhaps badly. She must find him and Jorin too, who was (she hoped) still free, even though he would be having to cope in strange territory without the use of her eyes. She called to him by the mind link, but got no answer. Damn and blast. If only her head ached less and her thoughts were clearer! But why had they been attacked in the first place? Prince Odalian was supposed to be an ally of the Kencyrath. None of this made any sense.

There was a sharp click inside the lock. Jame opened the door a crack and peered out. No guards. She stepped cautiously into the hall and turned to shut the door after her.

Its outer surface was scored with deep, raw scratches that formed the crude outline of a dagger.

Jame stared at them, teased by some half memory but unable to grasp it. She shrugged and turned away. The hall curved off in both directions, silent and empty. Which way to go? In the absence of all information, it hardly mattered. She went left.

Other rooms opened off the corridor, all of them lit. They seemed to be guest quarters, each one more opulent than the last. Some gave the impression of having recently been occupied, but no one was in any of them now. Then came a sweeping staircase leading down into a suite of larger public rooms. She drifted on from room to room like a ghost, looking for some sign of life or even for a window that might give her a glimpse of the outside world. There was none. The palace seemed completely shut in on itself, locked in some indolent dream of sweet-scented wood and marble and tapestried princes riding forever under cloudless skies.

But at last she came upon a new current moving through the heavy perfumed air. It brought with it a different odour, one that refused quite to define itself but that seemed as disturbingly out of place as a whiff of decay in a king's bower. Jame followed it out of the suite to the head of another staircase, again sweeping downward. She descended. A broad corridor stretched away before her at its foot. Ahead, the light spheres glowed more dimly. An almost tangible darkness hung in the air, shrouding the details of the hallway beyond. As Jame warily approached, she saw with amazement that the corridor itself seemed to fade in the distance. Some of its lines remained but were suspended ghostlike in midair. Beyond, space seemed to open out into a much larger hallway. A cold wind breathed out of that farther hall, lifting Jame's hair in black, fluttering wings about her face. With it came that odour, stronger now, like the breath of ancient sickness. Jame shivered. She *knew* that smell, but what was it? If only her mind were clearer! Just the same, in another moment surely she could identify it.

A hand closed on her bare shoulder.

Without thinking, she caught it and spun around. The man thumped down on a knee, his arm stretched stiffly up, immobilised by a Senethar wrist lock.

'You're hurting me,' he said through his teeth, in Kens. Jame let go, astonished. 'Who are you?'

The man still cringed at her bare feet – or was he a boy? With such sharp, thin features, his age was hard to guess. He showed his teeth again. 'My lady calls me Gricki.'

Jame repeated the name with distaste. It was uncomfortably close to the Easternese word for excrement. 'I can't call you that.'

'As you wish, lady.'

He wasn't about to tell her his real name, Jame realised. After all, that was hardly a safe gift to make to any stranger. 'Well, I can't put a wrist lock on you every time I want to get your attention. I'll call you Graykin.'

The moment the word was out, she could have bitten her tongue. Graykin was the name of a mongrel dog in one of the old songs; but he had been a faithful brute and, in his own way, something of a hero. The young man shot her a startled, not displeased look, instantly suppressed.

'Graykin, where is everybody?'

'Gone... lady.' He gave the title with a kind of cringing sneer, as if daring her to take offence.

'Yes, but where, and why?'

He clearly didn't want to tell her, but the direct question forced a direct answer from him. 'Fifteen days ago, Prince Odalian learned that the Horde was on the move, coming this way. He immediately sent out messengers to summon the Karkinoran troop levies and to request help from the Kencyr Highlord. That night, he had a visitor. Don't ask me who,' he added defensively, as if this ignorance diminished his credit. 'I don't know. The next day, with no explanation whatsoever, he ordered everyone out of the palace. There are only three guards here now, and the Prince and his lady (who refused to go), and the spook.'

'The what?'

'Spook. I don't know where he came from, but I think the Prince and his guards stayed to hunt him. Odd-looking man. Face like a year-old corpse. D'you know him?'

'No.'

'That's strange,' he gave her a sly, sidelong look. 'He seems to know you. At least, I caught him scratching on your door.'

A man waited in the shadow of the stair, his face a death's head. He slipped a white-hilted knife into her hand. She went on climbing, climbing, towards a doorway barred with red ribbons, towards the darkness beyond...

Jame shivered. *That* was the memory that the scratched drawing of the dagger had half awakened; but the stair, the knife, and the skull-faced man had all been in Perimal Darkling years ago. Even now, she didn't remember enough to know what that fragment of a memory meant. Anyway, there were more important things to think about now.

'Graykin, you only mentioned six people, seven, counting

441

yourself. I'm looking for my friends – a big man with greying hair and a golden ounce. They must be here somewhere, too.'

'Not in the palace,' he said emphatically. 'I know every room here, yes, and every cell in all seven dungeons, too.'

'What do you know about that?' Jame pointed down the corridor into the darkness.

This time Graykin shivered. 'That isn't part of Karkinaroth. I don't know what it is or where it came from. Since the stranger's visit, it's simply been there, getting more visible all the time, taking over.'

'Graykin, who is your lady?'

'Why, Lyra, my prince's consort, my lord Caineron's daughter.'

'I had better meet her.'

'Yes . . . yes, of course.' This time he really cringed, as if a whip had been raised against him. 'This way, lady.'

He led her back up into the palace, away from the phantom corridor. Jame followed, glancing at him curiously. He had called her 'lady'. Was that just his cringing way, or had he actually sensed that she was pure Highborn? Marc never had. Perhaps some Kencyr were quicker to make the distinction than others – but was Graykin a Kencyr? Her own impression of him was curiously mixed.

They had come through quite a tangle of hallways when the young man stopped and scratched tentatively on a door. No answer. He opened it anyway and slipped furtively inside. Jame followed. She found herself in a lavish suite of rooms, all red and gold, plush and velvet. Rich carpets covered the floor; richer hangings, every inch of the walls. All showed exquisite craftsmanship except one, a stitchery portrait of a young, fair-haired, brown-eyed man, so clumsily done that it could only be the work of a Highborn. Under it, flames leaped in an ornate fireplace. The suite was hot and airless. There were, of course, no windows.

Graykin was hastily fishing bruised apples and battered cakes out of his pockets and piling them on a table. Jame wondered if he had provided the food in her room, too. Somehow, she didn't think so.

'Odalian?'

Graykin dropped an apple and bolted for the door. Too late. A girl stood silhouetted on the threshold of an inner room.

'Oh,' she said, scornfully. 'It's just you. Oh!' – in a different tone – 'Food!'

She came quickly into the light, her long crimson skirt swirling. Above that was a broad gold belt, an embroidered bodice that looked painfully tight, full sleeves, gloves, and a mask. From her voice and the way she moved, Jame guessed that she was about fourteen. Then she saw Jame and stopped short.

'Oh! But you're dressed... I mean undressed... I mean... wait!'

Lyra darted back into the inner room and out again clutching a scrap of cloth that she thrust into Jame's hand. Jame stared at it, then shrugged and put it on. It was a mask.

'I would be honoured if you would share bread with me,' Lyra said formally.

It would have been impolite to demand her guest's name, and the Prince's consort clearly meant to be very correct indeed, despite her hunger. She cut an apple into precise pieces and offered each section to Jame first before wolfing it down, bruises and all.

'Really, it's so awkward,' she said. 'Odalian should at least have remembered to keep a few servants and a cook on hand, but then he's so impetuous.'

'Why did he order everyone to leave in the first place?'

Under her mask, Lyra seemed to frown. Direct questions apparently were impolite too, at least by Southron standards, but it wouldn't do to remind a guest of that. 'I suppose he wants to lead out as large an army a possible when he goes to meet the Kencyr Host,' she said rather vaguely.

Even palace maids and pastry cooks? 'When does the army march?'

'Oh, I never bother with details. Gricki?'

'In six days, on the twentieth of Winter,' the young man said from the shadows by the door where he had retreated, apparently in hopes of being overlooked. 'Both the Host and the Horde are expected to reach Hurlen above the Cataracts around the thirtieth.'

'Clever Gricki.' Lyra smiled, with a touch of malice. 'He always knows the details – about everyone and everything. Don't you, Gricki?'

Jame hastily interrupted. 'Lady, would it be possible to pay my respects to the Prince?'

Lyra glanced up at the portrait over the fireplace. 'If you can find him. Oh!' She rose abruptly, flustered. 'That is, he's been so busy lately. Duties here and there... I hardly ever see him myself. But it's all quite normal, you know.' She gave Jame an anxious look. 'There certainly haven't been any violations of the contract.'

'Contract?'

'*You* know,' said Lyra as if to a simpleton. 'The *marriage* contract. It comes up for review at Midwinter. My father, Lord Caineron, won't renew it if anything is, well, not quite right. Then I would have to leave. But if the Prince helps Father win at the Cataracts, maybe he will even extend the contract to include children. Oh, I would love that!'

Jame stared at her. 'Don't you have anything to say about it?'

Lyra stared back. 'Of course not! Lord Caineron is the head of my family. Naturally, I have to do what he tells me.'

'Naturally,' Jame echoed, looking peculiar.

'But then you won't tell my lord father anything about this because you're a woman like me,' said Lyra with an abrupt, sunny smile. It fell away as she turned on the young man in the shadows. 'And you won't because there's nothing to tell! Do you promise?'

'Lady,' said Graykin miserably, 'you know I can't.'

She made a little angry dart at him, small fists clenched. 'You *will* promise, Gricki, or ... or I'll tell this lady some details I do know about *you*. Think, Gricki.'

From the way she spat out the nickname, Jame knew that it meant the same thing in Southron as in Easternese. The young man cringed.

'Lady, please...'

'"Lady, lady,"' she mimicked him, then spun around, skirt belling, to face Jame. 'Do you like riddles? Here's one: What do you call a half-Kencyr-half-Southron bastard? Answer: Anything you want.'

Graykin abruptly left the room, not quite slamming the door. Jame stared after him.

'I didn't know that sort of a blood-cross was possible. Who made the experiment?'

Lyra shrugged, already losing interest. 'Oh, a kitchen wench and someone in my father's retinue, apparently. He visited Karkinaroth about twenty years ago when Odalian's father was prince. Will you find Odalian for me?' She caught Jame's hands and spoke in a breathless whisper. 'Oh, please do! I couldn't say it in front of that ... that sneak, but things have been so strange here, and I've been so frightened. Will you?'

'I'll try, lady,' said Jame, and made her escape.

Out in the hall, she leaned against the door and took a deep breath. Those awful, airless rooms! Was that how a Highborn woman lived, bound in a stifling world of convention and obedience? Would Tori try to make her into another Lyra? To be a pawn sent here or there as politics demanded, to warm this man's bed or bear that one's children, to live in stuffy halls for the rest of her life? Jame shivered. But a great deal could happen before then. She might even manage to get herself killed. Somewhat cheered, she turned and saw Graykin sitting on the floor against the wall, sharp chin on sharp knees.

'You knew she would tell me, didn't you?'

'She tells everyone when she remembers,' he said in a muffled voice. 'She remembers when she sees me.'

'Look, Graykin...'

'Don't you mean Gricki?'

'No, I do not. You're no more responsible for your blood-lines than ... than I am for mine. Look, running around like this may be good for the circulation, but I'm starting to get cold. Can you find me some clothes?'

He gave her a sharp look. 'Some of Lyra's, d'you mean?'

'Trinity, no.' She took off the mask and dropped it on the floor. 'Some of yours will do.'

Graykin started to laugh, then saw that she was serious. 'Wait here.' He jumped up and disappeared down the hall. In a few minutes he was back with an armful of clothing, including one undergarment for which Jame had no use whatsoever.

'Very funny,' she said, handing it back to him.

She put on the rest: soft black boots cross gartered from instep to knee; black pants; broad black belt; loose black shirt; even a pair of black gloves.

'There,' said Graykin, surveying her. 'The perfect outfit – for a sneak.'

Jame raised an eyebrow at him. 'As you say. Perfect. Graykin, will you take me to the temple?'

'As you say ... lady.'

He led her there by a tortuous route, full of unexpected twists and turns. Jame smiled. Clearly, he didn't want her to master the intricacies of the palace anymore than she would have welcomed a rival in the Maze back in Tai-tastigon. She fixed each turn in her well-trained memory.

Then Graykin cautiously opened a door, and there stood the

temple in its nine-sided chamber. Jame estimated that it was at least forty-eight hours since she had last been here. In that time, the light sphere suspended from the ceiling had grown dimmer and the patches of dead grass larger. Worse, a continuous ripple of power warped the air like heat over a sun-baked rock. Graykin stopped at the door. Jame went slowly up the temple as though making her way through treacherous currents. She called, but this time no voice answered from inside. The bar was still in place. If only it had been a lock, she could have mastered it, but this required at least Marc's great strength. Dangerous, dangerous... She backed to the door.

'Graykin, you'd better keep an eye on this place in case I don't get back. At some point, the temple door will start to disintegrate. Then you and Lyra had better get out of the palace fast before it comes down on top of you.'

'Yes, lady.' Graykin sounded impressed despite himself. 'But where are you going?'

'You said my friends aren't in the palace. Could they have been taken out to where the army is gathering?'

'No. The Prince has bolted shut all the doors but one, and I've been keeping an eye on that.'

'Damn. As far as I know, then, that only leaves one place they could be: in the shadows.'

They had left the temple room and were walking back into the heart of the palace. Suddenly Graykin caught Jame's arm. Before them, the hallway dimmed and distorted, shadowy depth within depth.

'That wasn't here before,' said Graykin in a low voice. 'The darkness is spreading. And you want to go into it?'

Jame wrapped her arms about her, shivering. 'No. I don't want to at all.' *In fact*, a small, cold voice seemed to whisper in her mind, *it could be a terrible mistake.* 'But what choice do I have?'

Graykin regarded her with astonishment. 'Why, you really don't know what you're doing, do you?'

'Very seldom,' Jame admitted with a sudden wry grin. 'If I did, I probably wouldn't be doing it, but as far as I can see, the alternative is to spend the rest of my life standing in a corner with a sack over my head. I'm serious about Lyra, by the way. Watch out for her. She may be a cruel, stupid child, but she's one of us. See you later – I hope.'

She walked into the shadows.

24

The Lurking Past
The White Hills: 14th-16th of Winter

At dusk on the fourteenth of Winter, the Kencyr Host came to the place where the road bends nearly due east following the curve of the river. That night, it camped beside the ancient paved way. At dawn on the fifteenth, it forded the Silver and marched south through the untrodden grass into the rolling, forbidden land.

At this season, the hills were green and yellow rather than white, and the sky was a clear, eye-aching blue. Tall, coarse grass waved on the summits. Below, the hollows bristled with a kind of brier that grows tinder dry in the fall but no less sharp of thorn. Laced through the barbed branches were white flowers, which looked quite pretty from a distance, but, at closer range, resembled tiny, deformed skulls. At dusk, a billion crickets sang and mist gathered in the hollows.

The first night passed without incident.

The second day they pushed on as quickly as the terrain permitted, but at sundown still found themselves uncomfortably close to the old battlefield. All day, they had been stumbling across bones in the high grass, missed by those who had searched the hills immediately after the fight. These they gathered in case any of them were Kencyr, for a later pyre. That night, some told stories around the watchfires of the unburnt dead while others remembered the grief and shame of Ganth Gray Lord's fall. Many of the older Kendar were survivors of that last bloody battle. All felt uneasy and unwilling to sleep, despite their exhaustion.

Donkerri did sleep, but poorly. He dreamed that he again stood shivering by the fire in the Highlord's tower quarters after his grandfather had disowned him. *'I'm not good at forgiving those who spy on me,'* said Torisen. *'Ask Burr. But I will try if you promise never to do it again.' 'But you never went bone hunting at Kithorn,'* the other boys jeered at him. *'Baby, baby, blood-blind, blood-blind, blood-blind...'*

Donkerri woke with a gasp to the sound of the taunting chorus. But no, it was only the crickets. He *hadn't* been cast out, not utterly. Torisen *had* taken him in, and here he was now, safe in the Highlord's tent. He still belonged somewhere and, somehow, he would still find a way to prove himself. Donkerri wrapped that thought around him and slept again, comforted.

In his own tent, Lord Caineron was commiserating with would-be-lord Korey. No, it wasn't right that the Highlord had put that blockhead Demoth in charge of the Coman. Once the family would never have accepted so deliberate an insult. Wasn't it sad how the standards of honour had fallen.

Randir looked across at Caineron's lit pavilion and wondered with scorn what stupidity the man was up to now. All that power, in the hands of a fool.

Brandan walked among his own people, exchanging a quiet word here, a tired smile there. For perhaps the hundredth time, he wondered what he was getting them all into, following this young, possibly mad Highlord of a broken house.

The Edirr twins sat beside a brazier in their tent, discussing women and, as usual in private, finishing each other's sentences.

In his own richly appointed tent, Ardeth pored over his maps as if counting the leagues to the Cataracts over and over would somehow lessen the distance.

Holly, Lord Danior, slept.

To Torisen, restlessly walking the northern perimeter alone, came the boy Rion, almost in tears.

'Lord, lord, come quick! Great-great-grandpa Jedrak wants to see you. I-I think he's dying.'

The Jaran standard had been raised on a hilltop some distance away, almost outside the eastern perimeter. Everyone had instinctively chosen the summits and upper slopes, leaving the lower reaches to the remount herd so that it might drift from slope to slope, grazing under the watchful eyes of the dozen or so Whinno-hir who had accompanied the Host. Torisen passed rapidly below the herd with Rion trotting beside him. Above, fires dotted the hillsides. Below, mist swelled up in the hollows. Then they were climbing again towards the watchfires through the silent, waiting ranks of the Jaran's people. Torisen noted that many of them were rather old for military service, and then remembered that most of these Kendar, even the former randons, were scrollsmen and scrollswomen first, and warriors second.

Kirien emerged from the main tent carrying a fine linen cloth, which he carefully spread on the ground under the Stricken Tree banner. A long sigh rose from the darkness. He drew a knife, nicked his thumb, and let a drop of blood fall on the centre of the cloth. Then he handed the knife to Rion. The boy jabbed vehemently at his hand, producing a spray of blood, most of which he managed to get on the cloth's centre. He gave the blade to the nearest Kendar and burst into tears.

'I'm sorry,' Torisen said to Kirien. 'I came as quickly as I could.'

He followed the young man into the large tent's innermost chamber. Jedrak lay on his pallet, his sharp profile visible through the cloth laid over his face.

'Poor old man. He should never have come on an expedition like this.'

'So we all told him.' Kirien covered the brazier near the old lord's bed, letting the shadows enfold him. 'He would have his way, though, always – except this one last time.'

'Rion said he wanted to talk to me. Do you know what about?'

'Two things. First, he didn't want to mix his ashes with those already thick on these accursed hills.'

'That's easily arranged. We'll be clear of these lands by the day after tomorrow at the latest. His pyre can wait until then.'

'Good. Second... hush, Rion. What would Grandpa think of you, making a noise like that? Here, lie down and try to sleep. There's a good lad.'

He came back into the light, leaving the boy curled up on his pallet in a corner, choking down sobs. Torisen stared at him. Something about his face, about the way he moved...

'Have I finally lost my few remaining wits or are you a woman?'

Kirien smiled. 'Not quite. I don't come of age for a few more years.'

'Well, I'll be damned. But how on earth have you kept it a secret all this time?'

'Who said it was a secret? The Jaran have always known. As for the other houses, my mother died giving birth to me, you see. That made both me and my father suspect as breeding stock, so

449

no one outside our own house has paid much attention to either of us ever since, rather to our relief. Not that Jaran Highborn have ever been considered very good matches. Too eccentric, you know. Lord Randir condescended mightily in letting his niece contract to my father. Then she died. I could have been born a three-legged hermaphrodite for all my esteemed grand-uncle Randir knew or cared.'

'And now?'

She smiled. 'I still could be, but since Jedrak declared me his heir . . .'

'Randir assumes you're male.' He gave her a sharp look. 'Was I supposed to confirm you, making the same assumption?'

'Of course not. Jedrak was going to tell you tonight. He wanted your promise before he died that you would support my claim. That was his second request.'

Torisen turned away, running a hand distractedly through his hair. 'Of all the crack-brained, senile whims, but even if I were to sanction such a thing . . . surely the Law wouldn't. Jedrak must have known that.'

Kirien gave him a cool, almost scornful look. 'We are a house of scholars. Give us credit at least for having done our research. There's nothing in the Law that prohibits a lady from heading a family instead of a lord. In the case of fraternal twins like the Master and the Mistress, the power even used to be shared. It's only since Jamethiel Dream-Weaver fell that so many restrictions have been put on Highborn women, and most of them are pure Custom, not Law.'

'But surely the male Highborn in your house will challenge your claim.'

She snorted. 'Which one of them would want to? As I said, we're scholars, each one of us wrapped up in his or her own work. My own speciality is the Fall. You might say that the entire house of Jaran flipped a coin for the post of administrator, and I lost. Great-Uncle Kedan will officiate until I come of age, but short of violence you couldn't get him to stay on any longer. The question is: Will you confirm me when the time comes?'

Torisen considered this rather blankly. 'I hardly know. The idea will take some getting used to, and then things will depend a good deal on how much power I have when you finally come of age. The High Council is sure to raise a howl audible from here to the Cataracts.' He smiled suddenly. 'It would almost be worth sponsoring you just to see the others' faces. Trust the Jaran to come up with something so unconventional.'

'Unconventional.' Kirien glanced back into the shadows towards the bed. When she looked back at Torisen, a tear glinted in her eye. 'Jedrak always said that was what he liked best about you, too.'

Torisen paused in the tent's entrance to turn up his collar against the night's chill. The Kendar were still silently paying their respects, a drop of blood each. The border of the mourning cloth was stained nearly black by now. Before the blood dried, the cloth would be folded and placed on Jedrak's chest, to go with him into the flames. In the old days, the blood-bound followers of a Shanir lord would have slain themselves on his pyre. The rite might now be purely symbolic, but it was still a private ceremony in which the Highlord had no part. Torisen withdrew.

The Jaran's main tent was practically at the easternmost point of the camp. Beyond were a few watchfires on the hilltop, then only the moonlit slopes rolling towards the distant Silver, towards the much nearer battlefield. Torisen walked out beyond the perimeter and sat down on the hillside, looking eastward over the diminishing swell of the hills.

He thought about Kirien. The idea of a lady holding the power of a house still left him thoroughly nonplussed, but then he knew so little about Highborn women in general. Most were kept strictly sequestered and their contracts arranged solely on political lines. He hadn't even met Kallystine before his agreement with her father had been sealed. Ah, Kallystine, so beautiful, so vicious. Would his lost twin sister have grown up into a woman like that? He couldn't imagine. All his life, he had felt haunted by Jame, but in a curiously abstract way, as if by a ghost without a face, without a voice. Only over the past year and a half had his sense of her presence sharpened, especially just before or after a nightmare, so that now sometimes he almost felt as if she were standing behind him. But who or what would he turn to find? The wind teased his hair, breathed down his neck.

Tori, I've come back. I'm coming to find you. Torieeeee...
He started violently, waking from a half-doze. This would never do. Last night, he had told himself that it was better to stay awake because any dream here would be particularly vile;

but now he suddenly wondered if another of those special nightmares like the one at Tagmeth was creeping up on him. Usually, he had more warning – days or even weeks, depending on the severity of the dream. Surely it was too soon for another one. No, he must only be disturbed because of Jedrak's death and because of where he was. Time to move on.

As Torisen rose, however, his eyes stayed on the rolling land to the east, and he hesitated, puzzled. The shape of those distant hills looked so familiar, but how could that be? He had never been here before. That hill there to the left, nearly out of sight ... beyond it should be one almost with a peak and beyond that another shaped like a barrow and beyond that ...

Bemused, Torisen walked down the slope away from camp, limping slightly, towards the beckoning land.

Kindrie had been offered space in one of the large inner chambers of Ardeth's tent where the lord's Highborn kinsmen slept, but instead he had chosen a tiny room on the edge of the pavilion. It was barely large enough for his pallet and had only one opening with an inner gauze flap for good weather and an outer one of canvas for bad, but it was all his. After years in the acolytes' dormitory, such privacy filled him with incredulous delight. On the first days of the march, he often lay awake far into the night just to savour it. When the Host's pace quickened, however, sleep became more precious. Then, in the White Hills, it became almost impossible.

On the second night, Kindrie was dozing uneasily in his canvas-walled cell. He wasn't used to so much riding, and his bones ached with fatigue. Even half an hour of *dwar* sleep would have given his healer's body a chance to recover itself, but everytime he slid down towards it, confused dreams woke him again with a start. Now it seemed to him that the hills had begun to swell beneath the tent, like the restless billows of the sea. Up, down, up ... no, it wasn't the canvas floor that rocked him, but hands, bone white, bone thin, tugging, tugging.

Wake up, wake up! he thought he heard the faintest thread of a voice cry. *Oh please, wake up! He needs you!*

'Who?' Kindrie said out loud, half waking. 'Who needs me?'

A watchfire had been kindled outside, and golden flickering light flooded into the cubicle through the gauze doorway. Shadows moved on the outer wall. Voices murmured in the night, but none spoke to him. He was alone ... or was he? On the rear wall of his tiny room was a shadow that hadn't been there before, bending over the shadow of his own recumbent form. Kindrie regarded it bemusedly, convinced he was still asleep. It was very small and painfully thin. Ah, it must belong to the dead child whose bones the Highlord had taken from Kithorn and still carried with him in his saddlebag. Now, what could she want with him, even in a dream? She tugged and tugged. His shadow started to get up.

Kindrie threw back his blanket and hastily rose. Dream or not, he had no intention of letting his shadow go anywhere without him. He rapidly pulled on some clothes and followed it out of the tent. It and the smaller, moon-cast shadow of the dead girl led him through the camp towards the eastern perimeter, keeping to the lower reaches of the slopes. Beyond the Jaran's camp, he followed the shadows up to a hilltop. The hills rolled on eastward before him under a quarter moon, and up one of their slopes went something dark. Another shadow? No. Someone clad all in black. Someone who limped slightly. Torisen.

Kindrie caught his breath. His first, almost unconscious act of healing as a child had been the repair of his own weak eyes, but somehow the improved vision had never carried over into dreams. He could see the hills, the moon, that dark, receding figure all too clearly. This was no dream. He was awake, and that was the Highlord of the Kencyrath going alone, unprotected, towards the field of slaughter that had been his father's ruin, towards the unburnt and possibly vengeful dead.

Torisen *knew* these hills. Their curves, the texture of their grass and stones, everything spoke to him of a place and time he had thought safely behind him forever. Ahead, darkness rose like a wall, black on black, blotting out the stars. As a child, he had sometimes lain awake at night staring out the window at it, hardly daring to breathe lest it topple, crushing the keep, the Haunted Lands, all of Rathillien. Now here it was again: the Barrier, with Perimal Darkling pressing against its far side. One more rise and there, impossibly, was the keep itself, his old home, nine hundred miles away from the White Hills.

He walked down the slope towards it in a kind of horror-struck daze. Here was the stone bridge that spanned the encircling ditch, here the main gate, hanging askew. Beyond the gatehouse lay the courtyard, surrounded by the stone barracks, granary, and other domestic offices, tight against the outer wall with the battlements running along their roofs. Ahead rose the squat tower keep. He walked slowly towards it, still numb with disbelief. Grass grew between the flagstones, catching at his feet. Leech vines hung down over the walls. How quiet everything was, how... dead.

Before the tower door was a black, tangled mass – the remains, apparently, of a bonfire. Now who would set one there? Father would raise three kinds of hell when he... no, not charred branches, but arms, and legs, and faces...

Torisen recognised everyone that flame and sword had left recognisable: Lon, who had taught him how to ride; Merri, the cook; Tig, with all his battle scars scorched away.... He had dreamed of their deaths in that final assault over and over, but never of this.

It's still a dream, he thought, feeling the cold paralysis of nightmare creep over him. *I fell asleep on the hillside, and I'm trapped. I'll never wake up again.*

'My lord!'

Footsteps sounded behind him. Hands turned him around. He looked dully into Kindrie's face, barely focusing on it.

'Go away. You don't belong in this dream.'

'Dream? No, lord, listen to me: *This is real.*'

'Real?' Torisen blinked at him. 'How can it be? This is the keep where I grew up, where my father died cursing me. These are the Haunted Lands.'

The Shanir looked about, shivering. 'Somehow, I didn't think we were still in the White Hills – although if we were, we'd be just about in the middle of the old battlefield now. Correspondences.' He shot Torisen a look. 'Why, don't you see, the White Hills must have gone soft. Perimal Darkling is just under the surface there, as it obviously is here too, and when two contaminated areas are so similar in geography, architecture or – or whatever, sometimes in a sense they overlap, as if one were laid on top of the other. That must be how we got from there to here.'

'"We"?' Torisen turned on him, beginning to rouse. 'Why did you follow me? What do you want?'

Kindrie fell back a step, flinching. He'd forgotten how much Torisen hated to be followed or spied on. 'T-The child brought me, lord. See, here she is now. I-I think this place scares her.'

The child's shadow had moved between them on the moon-washed stones when the Highlord had turned. Now it came quickly to his side, so close that he unthinkingly reached down to touch the head that wasn't there. Yes, she was frightened. This place must seem very like Kithorn to her ... assuming both she and it weren't simply fancies of his sleep-locked mind.

Abruptly, he dropped to one knee and slammed his fist into the pavement. Blood speckled the stones.

'It's *not* a dream,' he said, rising, looking in wonder at his broken knuckles. 'It *is* real. Good. Then I can cope. Now, what in all the names of God happened here?'

Kindrie looked at him, surprised. 'Why, I understood that darklings attacked here some fifteen years ago and killed everyone but you. You escaped and came to the Riverland, where you took service in disguise under Lord Ardeth. At least, that's the story people tell.'

But then why had Ganth died cursing his son, the Shanir wondered suddenly.

'That's what people say,' Torisen agreed, not meeting Kindrie's perturbed look. Of course, he had heard the story often enough before and never contradicted it. It was probably even true, except that the massacre had happened only a few years ago, long after he had fled. If anyone ever learned that he had left while Ganth was still alive, without his permission, the repercussions could be severe. 'At any rate, this happened later.' He indicated the bodies piled before the door. 'Someone has been here since I left.'

'It looks like an attempt at a pyre,' Kindrie said. 'These people were dragged here and set alight by someone – a Kencyr, I would say – who meant well but didn't know the proper pyric rune. Odd.' He peered more closely at the charred bodies, curiosity getting the better of repulsion. 'They hardly look as if they've been dead fifteen years. My God!' He sprang backward, his face turning as white as his hair. 'That woman's hand ... it moved!'

Torisen also backed away. 'Haunts ... they're all becoming haunts. Nothing stays dead forever in this foul place, not unless it's reduced to ashes and blown away. The fire only set them back. But if they're still here, maybe he is, too.'

'My lord?'

'Stay here with the child. I'll be back in a minute.'

Torisen edged around the failed pyre and ran up the steps to the keep's first-storey entrance. Both sets of doors had been smashed open. He paused just inside the inner one, waiting for his eyes to adjust to the faint light that came in through two deeply recessed windows. Before him lay the circular great hall where the garrison had met to eat and hear justice dispensed – or what had passed for justice in those last days before his flight fifteen years ago.

'Traitors!'

Memory caught the echo of that shrieked word, saw the Kendar freeze, faces turned to the lord's table.

'You eat my bread and yet you conspire to betray me! You, and you, and you –'

'Father, no! These men are my friends and loyal to our house. Everyone here is.'

'To my house, perhaps, but to me? No, no, they deceive you, boy, as they did me. But never again! You three, in your hands are knives to cut your meat. Turn them on me, or on yourselves.'

'Child, come away. You can't help them.'

It was Anar, the scrollsman, tugging at his sleeve, pulling him out of the hall into the private dining chamber on the other side of the open hearth. From behind came the sound of something heavy falling, again and again. The Kendar had made the only choice that honour permitted. Anar quietly closed the door.

'You're father's quite mad, you know,' he whispered, and choked down a giggle. *'Oh yes, so am I – sometimes. It's this place, this foul, accursed place... You've got to get away, child, before he gets tired of killing your friends and turns on you. Oh yes, he will: The thought is already half in his mind. Who else can take away what little power he has left?'*

'But Anar, Ganth isn't just my father: he's Lord Knorth, the head of our house. He'll never let me go, and if I leave without his permission, desert him, that will be the death of my honour.'

Anar shot a scared look at the door, then leaned close. *'Child, there is a way...'*

And he told him. If every Kendar in the house gave his or her consent, their will overbalanced that of their lord. Anar's brother Ishtier had tried to gain his release this way, but the Kendar hadn't consented. After all, he was their priest. They needed him. But Ishtier had left anyway, honourless, for the safety and comfort of Tai-tastigon far to the south. But the Kendar could see what was happening now. They would let Tori go, with their blessings.

'But Anar, how can anything outweigh a lord's authority?'

456

'*Child, this can ... I think.*' He gulped. '*And if it can't, I-I take responsibility for whatever you decide, on my honour.*'

The door to the hall crashed open. Ganth loomed black on the threshold. '*And what's this, then? Talking behind my back, conspiring ...*'

Torisen faced him. '*Sir, we were only discussing honour – and options.*'

Now the hall lay silent and empty before him, lit only by moonlight streaming in between the bars of the two windows. Something rustled furtively in the shadows by the door. Torisen didn't investigate. Quickly crossing the hall to the spiral stair just off the private dining room, he climbed in utter darkness to the second floor, his feet remembering the height of each irregular step.

Here were the family's living quarters, a maze of interconnected rooms circling the lord's solar over the great hall. Some moonlight filtered into the outer rooms through slit windows. The inner ones lay buried in shadows too deep even for a Kencyr's keen night vision, and not all of them were vacant. These Torisen passed through quickly, seeing nothing, hearing nothing, but knowing that he was not alone. Beyond, the stair in the northwest turret began its spiral upward.

After the darkness below, the battlements seemed dazzlingly bright. The cracked crystal dome over the solar shone like a second moon, and the white gravel roof gave back its glow. In the shadow of the northeast turret, Ganth Gray Lord waited.

Torisen stopped, catching his breath.

'Father?'

No answer. How still that grim figure stood, the dead piled high about him like half-burnt kindling. Torisen slowly crossed the roof towards him, poised to fight or run, he hardly knew which. Those shadows on Ganth's chest. ... He was nailed upright to the turret door by three arrows. The ring finger on the right hand had been snapped off. Of the left hand, which had wielded Kin-Slayer, not one finger was left. Both ring and sword were gone. The corner of something white protruded from the grey coat just above the singe-line of the pyre's flames. Torisen stepped gingerly in among the dead and reached for it. His father's head moved. He snatched the folded cloth and leapt backward. Something grabbed his foot. He fell, rolling, breaking the grip, and fetched up against the crystal dome. Ganth was staring down at him, without eyes.

457

'*Child of darkness...*' The words were harsh, croaking, spoken in a voice that both was and was not his father's. '*Where is my sword? Where are my fingers?*'

Torisen bolted towards the northwest turret. Behind him, the dead around Ganth's feet were moving, slowly, unsteadily, disentangling charred arms and legs. He nearly fell down the spiral stair. At its foot, rustling, scraping sounds came to him from the darkness ahead. All the dead were awakening.

A *trap*, he thought wildly, *I've walked into a trap... Steady, boy, steady. One, two...* 'three!'

He sprinted through the second-storey rooms, twisting, turning, into moonlight, into darkness. Here was the stair. He half-threw himself down it and raced across the great hall.

A dark shape lurched into his path from the shadow of the door. Torisen tried to dodge past, but tripped over a shattered bench and fell heavily. Someone bent over him.

'... wrong...' croaked a familiar voice. 'I was wrong... Nothing outweighs a lord's authority. Take back the responsibility, child. It burns me... it burns...'

Torisen stared up horrified into Anar's face. The failed pyre had seared it hideously, laying bare cheekbones and patches of skull. He gave an inarticulate cry, shoved the haunt aside, scrambled to his feet, and bolted out the door. The other's broken voice pursued him:

'Child, set me free... free us all...'

Kindrie had backed into the middle of the inner ward, away from the pyre, away from the stone barracks now alive with furtive sounds. Torisen grabbed him.

'The rune, man, the pyric rune... can you say it?'

The Shanir stared at him, terrified. 'I-I don't know...'

He stopped with a gasp. The pile of half-burned bodies by the door had begun to seethe sluggishly. Torisen shook him.

'Say it, damn you! Set them free!'

The pale young man gulped and shut his eyes. Torisen very nearly slapped him, thinking he was about to faint, but instead Kindrie took a deep breath and spoke the rune. It fought its way out of his throat like a living thing, and he fell, gagging. Torisen caught him. The mound of twitching bodies burst into flames. Sudden firelight lit the inside of the barracks, and the keep's great hall, roared up above the tower's battlements. Torisen half dragged Kindrie out under the gate-house and across the stone bridge. On the hillside, he finally let the exhausted Shanir sink down into the tall grass, while he himself stood, breathing hard, watching his old home go up in flames.

Fifteen years ago, he had paused on this same hillside to look back before slipping away southward into the night. If he hadn't left, Ganth would surely have killed him sooner or later. Then the Three People would be without him now, when they needed him the most. But he had left poor Anar to bear his guilt, and that was a shameful thing, however good his reasons. Perhaps his honour was safe in the letter of the Law, but he felt compromised in its spirit and sick at heart.

Torisen shook himself. These thoughts did no one any good except, perhaps, his enemies. Surely, this whole thing had been a trap, but set by whom and, ultimately, for whom? Only the changers, with their affinity to Perimal Darkling and their determination to stop him, could be responsible. First, there had been the Shanir's attack at Tentir, then Grisharki's crude but nearly lethal ambush, then the carefully preserved, barely hidden post pouch. Any Kencyr would know what effect that desperate message would have. Of course, the Host would make for the Cataracts at top speed, by the most direct route. Then came an element of chance. The Highlord might not even notice how like the Haunted Lands those distant White Hills had suddenly become, much less go out to investigate. But he had, and there had been the keep waiting for him, a festering sore ready to burst. Perhaps his very presence had triggered that eruption. Perhaps the changers had counted on that.

Below, red light spilled out of the tower's door and down the steps onto the courtyard. More light and the flames poured out of the south window between the bars. The hall must be an inferno by now. The pyric rune only affected dead flesh, but flesh in turn could kindle wood. How many dead there must have been.

Flames, fire, fire-timbers, Tentir...

'Now, what would really frighten you, I wonder? Shall we find out?'

'Child of Darkness! Where is my sword? Where are my...'

Yes, he had been frightened to hear that dead mouth repeat the words of his nightmare, but not half as scared as the real thief of the sword and ring would have been. But who could have taken them?

Then he remembered the cloth that he had snatched from inside Ganth's door. It was still in his hand. He unfolded it. It wasn't a proper mourning cloth at all, just a square of fabric ripped out of someone's shirt. In the exact centre was one dark stain, the mark of blood kinship. But he was the only surviving member of Ganth's immediate family unless... unless...

Jame, the Shanir, the Child of Darkness, his sister – she *had* returned. For a moment, all Torisen felt was numb shock. Then he abruptly sat down on the hillside and began to laugh, helplessly, almost hysterically.

'My lord?' It was Kindrie, sounding scared.

'No, no, I haven't lost my wits – I hope. The fools! All that work, and they set their trap for the wrong twin!' He choked down his laughter. 'We've got to get back to camp or I really will come unstuck. But how?'

'Walk, I suppose.'

'More than three hundred leagues?'

'Less, I hope,' said Kindrie hastily, as if afraid Torisen would start laughing again. 'After all, the child couldn't get that far from her physical remains. We've got to follow her back and keep exactly to the path she marks, or I'm afraid it will be a very long walk indeed.'

'Yes... yes, of course.'

Torisen rose and followed the child's shadow as it danced ahead of them. He was still struggling to regain his mental balance and, he suspected, not doing a very good job of it. He knew he had frighted the Shanir badly. Kindrie was still keeping his distance from him, as if from something dangerous and unpredictable, which was just how Torisen felt. He turned suddenly on the young man, who shied violently away.

'Just now, you sounded rather strange. Are you all right?'

'Y-yes, lord. It's just the rune burned my tongue a bit. I'll heal.'

'You always do, don't you?' Even to Torisen, that sounded like a sneer. Trinity, what was wrong with him?

Kindrie took the question seriously. 'So far, lord, yes. I may not be strong, but I'm apparently tougher than I look – a family trait. My grandmother was a Knorth, you know.' He shot a sidelong look at Torisen. 'I know that that doesn't give me much claim on the house of Knorth, but some pride does go with it. You shouldn't have sent me away with Donkerri at Wyrden.'

'God's teeth and toenails! I saw what Caineron did to you back at Tentir because of me. D'you think I wanted to put you in danger again? But now I have anyway, and you've put me under a deeper obligation than ever.'

He spoke with such bitterness that Kindrie flinched. 'Oh, please! Don't think of it that way. It's true that you are my natural lord. I can't help that; you can't change it. But if you don't want to acknowledge my claim, I-I'd rather that it was forgotten.'

'Very noble, but that hardly discharges the obligation, does it? For someone who says he only wants what I can freely give, you certainly keep finding ways to put me in your debt.'

He turned on his heel and went on after the child's shadow, limping a bit more than before, leaving Kindrie to flounder after him. Damn and blast. For years, he had avoided the Shanir and lulled himself into thinking that he had got over his irrational aversion to them. Now here he was, deeply obligated to one and paying him back with words savage enough to have come from his mad father. Ganth was glowing ashes behind him. Why in Perimal's name did his shadow still fall across his son's life?

Kindrie gave a sharp cry. Torisen spun around to find the Shanir sprawling on the ground behind him at the edge of a mist-filled hollow. In trying to catch up, he had cut too close to the hidden ground and apparently tripped on something. Mist swelled up around his legs. He couldn't seem to rise.

'Oh, for God's sake,' Torisen said in disgust and went back to help.

'My foot!' the young man gasped as Torisen grabbed his arms. 'Something has a hold on my foot... ah!'

He was jerked back, almost out of the Highlord's grip. Torisen braced himself and heaved, nearly freeing the Shanir. A hand rose out of the mist. Its skin hung about it like a tattered glove, exposing white sinews and a flash of whiter bone. It was clutching Kindrie's ankle. Kindrie gave a bleat of terror. Then both Kencyr fell, as the hand suddenly released its grip and a dark figure surged up out of the mist.

Kindrie sprawled across Torisen's legs. He thrust the Shanir aside, out of the way, barely in time. The thing from the mist blotted out the stars. It fell on him, its cruel fingers fumbling for his eyes, his throat. It stank of death. Somehow he managed to brace his foot against it and flip it over his head. It landed heavily. He went after it before it could recover, caught it in a headlock and, with a quick, lateral twist, broke its neck. It convulsed, throwing him. He rolled nearly into the mist before coming up short in a fighter's crouch. Clearly, however, the brief battle was over.

'That should at least slow it down some,' he said unsteadily, and drew a sleeve across his face. The cloth stank from the creature's touch.

Kindrie stared at the twitching body. 'B-but it's still alive!'

'Moving, yes; alive, no. You can't kill something that's already dead.'

'It's another haunt?'

'Yes. These hills are rotten with them. I used to hunt them occasionally when I was a boy. More often, they hunted me.' His head snapped up. 'Listen!'

Far away over the hills, a horn sounded, and another and another.

Torisen sprang up. 'The camp – it's under attack!'

He raced off towards the sound with Kindrie stumbling after him. Ahead, clouds rolling out of the west cloaked the sky, and distant thunder rumbled. Mist was swelling up even more thickly in the hollows, sending tendrils snaking up the lower slopes. The hills were becoming islands in a dim white sea. The fires of the Jaran's camp crowned the next rise. Torisen scrambled up the steep slope towards them. Suddenly, dark shapes emerged from the grass all around, ringing him with spearpoints.

'Here now, watch that!' he snapped, pulling up short.

'This one talks,' said a voice from the shadows. 'Maybe it will tell us what it is.'

'Gladly! I'm Torisen Black Lord.'

'There certainly is a resemblance,' said another voice. 'Perhaps it's a changer, or maybe an 'uman. Remember, there's a reference in the fourth canto of the Randirean saga to one who changed into a bat.'

'No, no – that was only in the aberrant version...'

'Kirien, help!'

'What in Perimal's name...' said Kirien's voice from above. 'Luran, why are you holding the Highlord at spear point?'

'Oh. Sorry, my lord.'

The spears swung around to cover Kindrie as he staggered up the slope. Torisen knocked them down. 'Sorry. That's not an 'uman either – whatever that is. I've never been the subject of an academic debate before,' he said to Kirien as he joined her on the hilltop. 'It's a singularly unnerving experience. Now, what in all the names of God is going on?'

'Confusion, primarily.'

'That I can see. What are these horses doing up here? You

must be playing host to at least a quarter of the remount herd.'

'Under the circumstances, we can hardly begrudge them the room. About ten minutes ago, the lot came stampeding up the hill. Then our guards on the lower slopes shouted up that they were under attack. They were gone by the time we got there – yes, completely. Then these... these *things* started coming up out of the mist. There! Do you see that?'

It was hard to see anything below now that clouds had swallowed the moon. Beyond the circle of fires, beyond the Kendars' double shield-wall, Torisen could just make out a horde of dark figures swarming up the lower slopes. They coalesced into a silent wave that beat and tore at the wall of shields with voracious hands that ignored the bite of spear and sword. The wall swayed but held. As the moon broke free for a moment from the advancing stormclouds, the wave receded as silently as it had come, leaving behind nothing but mist.

From off to the south came a battle cry, rising, falling.

'That's the Coman,' said Torisen sharply. 'What's that idiot Demoth up to now?'

'Whatever it is, he tried it after the first assault, too.'

'Ho, Kirien!' The shout came from the next hilltop, which the Jaran also held. 'Are you still there?'

'That's my great-uncle. Ho, Kedan! Where else would I be? Your shield-wall held?'

'Of course. But damnit, how can we fight what we can't even name? "War with the What's-it" – ha!'

'Not "ha",' Torisen shouted across at him. 'Haunts!'

'Ancestors preserve us,' said Kirien softly. 'Our own unburnt dead from the White Hills...'

'Perhaps, perhaps not.' Someday, he might tell her about the Haunted Lands, the other possibility, but not tonight.

'But if they're haunts, we can't kill them, we can't even wear them down. Have we lost already?'

'No.'

There *had* to be a way. The pyric rune would ignite every piece of carrion within half a mile, but Kindrie clearly hadn't the strength to speak it again, and the idea apparently hadn't even occurred to the other priests, wherever they were. But did they really need the rune?

'Fire,' he said to Kirien. 'Get torches.'

Below, the double row of Jaran Kendar waited. Singer Ashe limped restlessly back and forth behind the second line. By rights, she shouldn't have been even that close because of her maimed leg, but the battle horns had reminded her that before an axe cut her military career short, she had been a randon, one of the élite. She wondered where Harn was. In their days together, first as cadets and then as one-hundred commanders, she had always covered his back, knowing that he forgot it when the berserker rage seized him. The best way to manage Harn Grip-Hard, she had always maintained, was to give him a good clout on the head before any major battle. Anything to slow the man down a bit.

Then the moon again disappeared, this time for good. The shadow of the storm rack rolled eastward over the hills, dipping, swelling over hollow and crest. Darkness came in its wake, and the nearing rumbles of thunder. The front line tensed.

'Here they come again!'

The wall closed, shields locking with a crash. The Kendar leaned into them against the mute fury of the assault. Nails scraped on steel. Hands groped over the top of the shield-wall, clutching at heads and hair. The second line of Kendar opened ranks to slash at them. Their shields were still down when a wave of haunts broke over the first line, swarming on top of each other, rolling over the Kendar. Ashe saw them coming.

''Ware their teeth!' she cried, and limped back a pace to gain room for her staff.

A haunt crashed into her. The impact knocked the staff from her hands and her off her feet. Bodies piled on top of her. Their stench, their loathsome touch – it was like being at the bottom of a mass grave, but all the corpses moved. Sharp nails tore at her clothes. Teeth locked on her arm, which she had thrown up to protect her throat. They were all fighting to get at her.

Then light exploded between the chinks of bodies. A great hissing arose, and the limbs about her thrashed wildly, trying to disentangle themselves. She caught a knee in the stomach and was still doubled up, gasping for breath, when the mound of haunts above her broke apart.

'Harry them home, but stay out of the mist!' shouted a familiar voice over Ashe's head. Hands pulled her up. 'Well, singer, how goes the song?'

'Highlord?'

She blinked at him with fire dazzled eyes. His face seemed to float ghostlike before her, black clothing and hair melting back into the night. Torches blazed everywhere, and everywhere the haunts were in retreat.

'The song?' Ashe repeated. 'At least this time it won't be a dirge.'

'Oh well. The night isn't over yet. You stay clear from now on, though, and have a physician look at that arm. Remember, you're the one who's going to immortalise us all.'

'Lord!' The hail came from downhill. 'My lord, the mist!'

Torisen spun around and plunged off down the slope.

Ashe sat down heavily. 'My arm...?' She looked in dull wonder at the shredded, bloody sleeve.

Below, Kendars ringed the hollow, staring at it. They made way for Torisen. Ground fog still seethed in the depression, but now it seemed to be lit from within, its shifting surface fitfully aglow.

'Lord, is it on fire?'

'I don't think so. No, look. It's the brambles.'

Now they could all trace the arabesque of stem and skull-shaped flower etched in fire under the white surface of the mist. The mist began to melt away in the growing heat, leaving behind only ashes and hard-packed earth. The door between the White Hills and the Haunted Lands had closed. In a nearby camp, a horn sounded, then another and another, signalling the end of battle. Now it was time to count the cost.

Torisen walked alone through the camp, hollow by hollow. Either his cry for torches had carried or others had come up with the same solution, for every depression had recently been fired, and some were still smouldering. Apparently no encampment had been overrun. Most were now clearing the hilltops and taking down any standards that might attract the lightning flickering closer and closer in the black bellies of the stormclouds. As he passed under Lord Danior's camp, Holly came down to meet him.

'Only three guards killed and two missing,' he said proudly. 'That's not bad for my first battle, is it? Lots of people got a bit mauled, though.'

'Keep an eye on them. Haunt bites infect easily and make haunts of their victims after death. There's the Coman standard, still up. Now what... oh my God.'

Ahead lay another smoking hollow, surrounded this time by a four-foot bank. In its midst, rising out of the very earth as if to clutch brambles now reduced to ashes, was a hand.

'Why, someone's been buried alive!' Holly exclaimed.

He jumped down into the hollow before Torisen could stop him and grabbed the hand. It came away in his grasp. There was no arm attached to it, no sign of a body on or beneath the ashes. The earth itself seemed to have sheared it off.

On the lower slopes were many more bodies, some still twitching, others all too still. Many had been gnawed almost beyond recognition. Korey stood among them, rigid with fury, facing Demoth. The upper slopes were dark with silent, watching Kencyr.

'You have no right!' That was Demoth, nearly shrieking. '*I* lead the Coman! *I* order attack or retreat, or anything else I damn well please! You're nothing, do you understand? Nothing!'

'What's happened here?'

They both spun at the sound of Torisen's voice.

'He ordered my people back!' raged Demoth. 'He fired the hollow, against my express orders!'

'And he sent Kendar down into the mist to fight. Three times.'

'Sweet Trinity. How many lost?'

'Over a hundred, and as many killed on the slopes,' Korey said angrily. 'This is as much your doing as his, Highlord. You insulted the honour of the Coman by appointing this... this bungler. You insulted me.'

He drew a knife.

Torisen had turned to Demoth. 'I was wrong, and your kinsmen were right: You aren't fit to lead.'

He turned back and saw first the knife, then Korey's thunderstruck expression. He put his hands on the young man's shoulders. The knife point pricked him through his coat, just under the ribs.

'Korey, you idiot, put that away. I've just given you the Coman.'

'Blackie!'

Torisen heard Harn's shout and saw Korey's bewildered gaze shift to something behind him. A footstep, the hiss of descending steel, and Korey shoved him aside. His sore leg failed him. He was already falling when knife and sword met with a crash, inches from his face. The violence of his swing had unbalanced Demoth. He stumbled into Korey, and both fell, catching up Torisen as they rolled down the slope. For a moment, all three were over the bank, in midair. Then they crashed to the floor of the depression, with Torisen underneath. He landed on a rather large rock. Demoth lurched to his feet, still gripping his sword.

'The Coman is mine! You can't take it away from me! I'll kill you first, I'll kill...'

He took a shambling step and pitched forward at Torisen's feet. Korey's knife jutted out of his back.

Harn skidded down the bank. 'Blackie, are you all right? From where I stood, it looked as if that bastard nearly took your head off!'

He helped the Highlord sit up. Torisen was breathing in great, painful gasps.

'Grindarks... haunts... homicidal Highborn... and I do myself in... on a damned rock!'

'Ho, that's it, is it? Serves you right if you've broken half your ribs. Of all stupidities, to turn your back on an angry Coman. Trinity! Here comes Ardeth.'

'Ardeth...' Torisen dragged himself to his feet, hanging on to Harn. 'I've just killed your cousin, or maybe Korey has. As maternal blood-kin, what blood price do you demand?'

Ardeth stood on the edge of the bank, looking down. Torchlight turned his white hair into a glowing nimbus, but left his face in shadow. 'What price?' he repeated numbly, then straightened. 'Why, none, my boy. I saw everything. It probably was an accident.'

'And you?' Torisen turned to Demoth's paternal kinsmen on the slope.

'None, my lord.'

'Ancestors be praised. A simple solution for once. All right, everyone settle in for what's left of the night and sleep if you can. The hills should be quiet enough for the time being. By tomorrow night we'll be out of them and able to honour our dead fittingly. None are to stay here. Understood? Then pass the word.'

He turned and found himself face to face with a truculent Korey.

'You haven't bought me, you know. I'll never crawl for you the way that worm Demoth would have.'

'I wasn't expecting it. Just act for the good of your house; and as for owing me anything, who just prevented whose decapitation? My lord Caineron is going to be furious with you.'

'So "Blackie's luck" is still a proverb,' said Harn as he,

Torisen, and Ardeth walked back towards the Knorth encampment with several members of Ardeth's war-guard following at a tactful distance. 'I always thought you were too lucky for your own good.'

'Never mind him,' said Torisen to Ardeth. 'Eventually, he'll forgive me for not having got myself killed. Just the same, Ashe was wrong: The song *was* a dirge.'

Harn snorted. 'There could be sadder ones... your pardon, my lord.'

'No, no,' said Ardeth absently. 'You're perfectly right. Demoth turned out to be somewhat less than satisfactory. Now, if I can just arrange a contract between Korey and one of my great-grandnieces...'

At his own campsite, the old Highborn left them.

Torisen looked after him with a wry smile. 'I'm beginning to think that Ardeth can survive anything if only there's a deal to be made out of it.'

'And when he finds out about Pereden's role in the Southern Host's destruction?'

'I don't know. The best we can hope, I suppose, is that the wretched boy dies honourably. We've got to salvage Pereden's reputation if we can, for his father's sake.'

Harn stopped short. 'Not if it means maligning his officers.'

The Highlord turned and stared at him. 'Sweet Trinity. Those Kendar were my officers too once, and the only family I knew for nearly half my life. D'you really think I would turn on them now?'

The stiffness went slowly out of Harn's shoulders. 'Well, no – of course not. Damn stupid thing to say, really...'

'And if you say anything more, it will be even stupider. What the –'

A small figure hurled down the hill from the Knorth camp and threw its arms around Torisen. He recoiled with a hiss of pain.

'All right, Donkerri, all right. I'm glad to see you, too. Just mind the ribs.'

Burr came down the slope at a more sedate pace. 'We just heard about the fight and Lord Coman's death. Are you all right, my lord?'

'Ribs,' Harn repeated sharply. 'Here now, why didn't you say you'd really been hurt?'

'Oh, I don't think anything's broken. Cracked a bit, maybe...'

With that they closed in on Torisen and bore him off, a protesting captive, to his own tent.

The rains came, pelting the hills, running down in rivulets between the tents, pooling in the hollows. Lightning ripped, thunder boomed. Torisen lay on his pallet listening to the storm, watching the tent's framework stand out in black relief around him with each flash of light. Although his leg felt sore and cramped, he resisted the temptation to stretch it because he didn't want to disturb either Burr or the parcel of bones nestled in the curve of his arm. His side ached too, but he was fairly sure now that it was only bruised. As Harn would say, Blackie's luck still held ... but for how long? What if, as he half suspected, his sister Jame really was on her way to him?

With the emblems of my power in her hands, boy.

Yes. Torisen was virtually certain that she had taken Ganth's ring and sword. But what of that? She couldn't wield them. She was only a girl.

So is Kirien. 'Nothing in the Law prohibits a lady from heading a family instead of a lord.' And she has power of her own, boy. Why do you think I named her 'Jamethiel'?

But she was his sister.

And your Shanir twin, your darker half. Why do you think I drove her out, boy? Now she returns, to rival, to destroy you.

But h-he loved her. He always had.

Therein lies your damnation.

The storm grumbled off into the distance unnoticed. Torisen lay in the dark, listening to the hoarse, mad voice that was both his dead father's and, somehow, his own, muttering on and on long after he had run out of ways to answer it.

25

Into Shadows
Perimal Darkling: 14th-21st of Winter

Jame entered the shadows of Karkinaroth warily. At first, though, that was all they seemed to be, just an obscurity lying over the rich features of the palace, dulling the crimson carpet, turning the purple and gold hangings grey. The light spheres burned more and more dimly. Between them, the details of the palace seemed to fade, or rather almost to melt. New depths opened up in the shadows, reaching back to distant walls. Between the circles of light, the coldness of the floor struck through Jame's thin boots. Here was pavement that had never known the touch of a carpet. Now the light spheres were only faint glows bobbing in midair. A few hints of the palace's architecture hung ghostlike about them, but that was all. Karkinaroth had disappeared.

But where was she now?

Jame went on, shivering slightly in this colder air. Outside windowless Karkinaroth there had been the warm, southern land of Kinkinor. What lay beyond these walls . . . and what was that smell? It surrounded her now, vaguely sweet, vaguely rotten, like the faded perfume of decay. The very walls seemed to exude it. How frighteningly familiar it was, and how dull of her not to recognise it.

A doorway opened between the phantom light of two spheres. Jame almost went past it, thinking it was some strange tapestry woven of shadows, but a breath of air came out of it. She entered. Her memory told her that if she had continued down the hallway in Karkinaroth and turned at this door, she would have found herself in the palace's main ballroom. This too was a room, but an even more enormous one. Jame walked out into it. Her soft boots made no sound on the dark, green-shot floor, woke no echoes in the impossibly high vault of its ceiling. Around its walls hung rank upon rank of memorial banners. In a normal Kencyr hall, these traditionally were tapestry portraits of the Highborn dead, woven of threads taken from the clothes in which each man or woman had died. Usually, the faces were calm and the hands held low and open, crossed at the wrists in benediction. But the faces on these banners grimaced hideously. Their hands clutched tattered clothing. Dark stains as if of dried blood streaked the walls beneath.

Jame looked about with growing horror. Surely this was the big picture-lined hall that her mother had described to her all those years ago; but the pictures were portraits of the dead, and they all looked so starved because . . . because the souls had been eaten out of them. But how could she know that? Then, too, there were so many of them. Too many? Why in Perimal's name should she think that? She had never actually been in this hall before – or had she?

At the far end of the hall was a huge fireplace, the trunks of several trees piled in it. Fur rugs covered the cold hearth. More complete rugs with snarling masks, were nailed to the wall above. They were all pelts of Arrin-ken.

Her mother hadn't told her that, but she had remembered it in the dream that had first awakened her in Karkinaroth. Surely, she knew more about this place than any story could have told her. She had stood there before in her dreams, in the flesh. This was the great hall of the Master's House, where her father's cruelty had driven her so many years ago, where she had spent her forgotten childhood. She was in Perimal Darkling.

Jame turned to bolt, but the door by which she had entered was gone. She was trapped.

Jame stood in the middle of that vast hall under the eyes of the dead and began to shake. Far too many memories were pressing against that wall in her mind. If they all broke through at once, if suddenly she remembered everything . . .

No, she told herself. *Keep control. Let through only what will help. You've bumbled through most of your life in stark, staring ignorance. Don't stop now.* She took a deep breath and let it out slowly. *All right. Now stop shaking and go find your friends.*

. . . and the sword and the ring and the Book and the Prince . . .

Trinity, was everyone and everything lost but her, or was she the most lost of them all? *Don't answer that. Just go.*

Jame went – across the hall, through an archway, into the depths of the House. As the Talisman, she had learned how to move like a shadow among shadows, and so she did now, every sense alert, every nerve taut. Everything was so big, so empty. High-vaulted passageways, broad stone stairs spiralling up or down, more corridors, more halls. Everywhere, cold stone and colder shadows. But where was everyone?

Dead, said a familiar voice as if in her ear. *They're all dead.*

'Marc?' She spun about. Nothing. No one. It must have been her imagination. Forget it.

Now, where might a prisoner be held? Not one of the archways she had passed so far had even been hung with a door. A cold, thin wind breathed unhindered through the twisting ways. Something kept Jame from calling. The place seemed deserted, but who (or what) might hear?

Jame went on. There was a sort of horrible fascination about this, as if at any minute her forgotten past might spring at her from some dark corner. A terrified, outcast child had come to this place and emerged the person she was now. Someone had taught her the meaning of honour; someone had taught her how to reap souls. Thanks to those lost years, she was a paradox, a creature of both light and darkness.

And Master Gerridon, what of him? Before his fall, the long retreat from Perimal Darkling had been bitter, but at least endurable for it had been done with honour. After, even the descendants of those who had fled his evil felt tainted by it. And that evil still existed... didn't it? Marc had seen at least three score of the Master's folk three years ago when they had swept down on East Kenshold from the smoking ruins of her own old home, still looking for her and the Book. In fact, Marc had even seen Gerridon himself, sitting his black horse on a hilltop, watching East Kenshold's sack.

His face would have been in shadows, Jame thought, and his upright form shrouded in a patchwork cloak of stolen souls. One gauntleted hand, the right, would have gripped the reins while the other, mere emptiness in a silver glove, rested on the stallion's ebony neck.

That left hand when it was still flesh and blood, reaching out to her between the red ribbons of a curtained bed... 'So you've lost a father, child,' *a soft voice said.* 'I will be another one to you and much, much more.' *The hand closed on her wrist. In a blind panic, she slashed at it again and again until...*

472

No. Jame leaned against a wall, shaking. She wouldn't remember that. She wouldn't.

But what if the only way to find Marc and Jorin was to open her mind fully to the past? She might once have known where prisoners were held. Did she dare take the risk? And why was she so sure that it *was* a risk? Something here was already tugging at her. She didn't feel as frightened as she had at first, or as repulsed. Even that pervasive smell of decay was losing its disagreeable tang. Once this place had been home. Once she had been accepted here as, perhaps, she never would be anywhere else. But it could never be home again.

Remember that, she told herself with sudden anger. *And remember what terrible things have happened here. Remember where you are.*

Prisoners... something about a cage without bars, but what had that been, and where? Perhaps something farther along would give her a hint. She pushed herself away from the wall and went on, deeper into the House.

All her senses, all her thoughts began to lose their edges. She drifted, feeling half asleep, dimly wishing after a time that she could sleep or at least find something to drink. Her mouth felt full of dust. How long had she been walking anyway? It felt like days. She began to have a vague feeling that the rooms through which she wandered weren't entirely unoccupied after all. Dim light and shadow became silent figures standing ghostlike in this corner or that. Their empty eyes followed her. Perhaps to them she was the ghost.

The wind blew in her face. She had been following it for some time without realising it, but now its strength and the curious smell borne on it half roused her. She was facing an archway, its upper curve shaped like a mouth. Once it had been walled up. Now massive blocks lay tumbled about it like broken teeth, and the wind blew through them. The smell was... unearthly. Something dead, something alive, many things in between... The light in the room beyond was strange too, a sort of shifting green. Jame stepped between the blocks, through the archway. The light came from a window, the first she had seen in this place. The window was barred. Vines curtained it with leaves and white flowers, shaped like bloodless, pouting lips, with glimpses between them of a sickly yellow sky.

Barred windows, unearthly landscapes... this was like that step-back room in the Anarchies.

Jame hugged herself, shivering. Old songs claimed that the

Master's House stretched back down the Chain of Creation from threshold world to world. Until Gerridon's fall, the Kencyrath had even used the House itself as an escape route during their long retreat, sealing off each section, each world, behind them when they could no longer hold it. Nothing could have shattered those seals from the far side. Nothing had. It had taken a Kencyr's treachery to break down the barriers between the worlds, to open the farthest, long-abandoned rooms of the House where shadows crawled and changers were made.

This was clearly not a good place to be. Jame backed towards the archway.

From the window came a low sigh, as if from many throats. Something white shot past Jame's face, trailing green. The vine wrapped itself around her neck. Another caught her arm, and another and another. They jerked her a step back toward the window. She clawed at those around her neck, but they only tightened. The white flower lips sighed in her ear, nuzzled against her throat. They began to turn pink, then red. Blood thundered in her ears. Vaguely, she felt the iron bars press against her back, felt the strength go out of her legs.

Then someone was beside her. A knife flashed – it was all white, hilt and blade, she noted in a dazed way – and the red lips fell away with a whispered shriek. Leaves rained down, already withered. She was on the floor now, and someone was bending over her: a man with a face as emaciated as any on the death banners in the Master's hall.

Shouts. The man jumped up and darted away, deeper into the House.

'Terribend, you fool, wait! You three guards, after him!'

Retreating footsteps, running.

Someone else bent over her now. Fair hair, a young face, silver-grey eyes...

'Prince Odalian?'

He smiled. 'Close enough. You had got yourself into a mess, hadn't you? Some things never seem to change. Let's see.' He tilted her chin one way, then the other. 'Not much damage, luckily, although you've probably lost a fair amount of blood. Can you stand?'

She tried and lurched into his arms. 'Damn.'

'Never mind.' He picked her up. She was surprised at such strength in one so slight.

'Size isn't everything,' he said, just as if she had spoken.

'Neither is strength. But then you should know that. Hang on.'

He carried her through the archway back into the grey halls. From his swift, sure stride, it was clear that he knew exactly where he was going.

'Prince, what did you call that man?'

He went on a few paces without answering. Then, 'Bender is one of his names. It will do.'

She could have sworn that Odalian had called the fugitive Terribend, but that was the name of Tirandys's brother, the one who had disappeared from song and history at the time of the Fall. Bender? That sounded familiar too, but she couldn't quite place it. If only her head would stop spinning...

The Prince put her down on a bed. She looked around in amazement at the apartment's rich furnishings. Had he taken her back into the palace, or was this some oasis among the House's bleak rooms? She guessed the latter. White wine splashed into a crystal cup. Odalian stood for a moment by the fire, frowning at the glass. Then he brought it over to the bed and thrust it almost roughly into Jame's hands.

'Here.'

She drank thirstily, noting without really paying attention that it had the same unfamiliar aftertaste as the wine she had drunk earlier, only this time the tang was much sharper. Her head swam alarmingly.

'Wine on an empty stomach,' he said, sitting down on the edge of the bed and taking the cup from her. 'I don't suppose you remembered to pack any provisions for this mad expedition of yours. No, of course not. You never did take a sensible interest in food.'

She stared at him. The way he spoke, the way he moved, both were so very familiar and yet surely she had never met the Prince before. She had only known what he looked like because of Lyra's clumsy portrait, and that had barely suggested anything beyond his general coloration. Wait a minute...

'Odalian's eyes are brown,' she said, drawing herself back in the bed away from him. 'Yours are grey, like mine. *Who are you?*'

Those steady grey eyes regarded her as if through a mask that was Odalian's face. 'You don't remember me. Good. But you've probably at least guessed what I am.'

She nodded, her throat suddenly dry despite the wine. 'You're another changer. What have you done with the Prince?'

'I?' He gave a sudden harsh laugh. 'Personally, very little. I came to see him the night he sent his message to the Kencyr High Council asking for help. He thought I was Torisen. We can approximate virtually any form, you know, until the shadows get too much of a grip on us, as they have in Keral, whose acquaintance I believe you renewed in the Ebonbane. At any rate, I told the Prince that I had decided to confirm him as a full ally of the Kencyrath before our forces met. He was pleased, especially when I offered to seal myself first to the pact by blood rites. Once I had tasted his blood willingly given, I was able to take his form.'

'But not exactly.'

'No, not quite. The eyes have always given me trouble. It takes many rebirths in the farthest rooms of the House to make one . . . er . . . malleable enough to get all the details correct, even with the full blood rites.'

'But too many rebirths result in something like Keral, who can no longer hold any true shape,' said Jame, trying to sound defiant. 'It seems to me that you changers have a pretty limited usefulness.'

'Oh, yes. Our prime only lasts a millennia or so, by Rathillien standards. Good endures, I'm told. Well, perhaps. But I know from experience that evil eventually decays, as my lord Gerridon is beginning to learn. But we were discussing Prince Odalian. He was understandably surprised to find himself face to face with even a flawed copy of himself, and even more amazed when a moment later he was taken in charge by three of his own suborned guards. Then I opened the barriers between Karkinaroth and the Master's House, and they took him into the farthest rooms. There they left him, chained.'

Jame shuddered. 'My God, what a vicious thing to do!'

'Yes, wasn't it? But my lord Gerridon insisted. "So the little prince wants to be a Kencyr – like you. Very well. Grant him his wish." So I did. My lord has . . . strange whims sometimes.'

Jame stared at him, struck by his tone. 'Why, you hate this, don't you? You loathe what you've done. But why do it at all? Why is it so important that you take the Prince's place?'

'Poor Jamie. No one ever explains anything to you, do they? If Gerridon had the last time, you might not have panicked, and he would still have both hands. I won't make that mistake. You see, there's been a revolt among the changers. Some of them have taken over the Waster Horde and are leading it against the

Kencyrath. Others of their number have tried several times now to kill both you and your brother: you, because of the blow your death would deal to the Master; your brother, because at present he alone seems to be holding the Kencyrath together. If the rebel changers should finally succeed in eliminating him, before or even during the final battle, the Horde will surely defeat the Host.'

'But wouldn't that please the Master?'

'In itself, yes, but then the rebels plan to use the Wasters to take over all of Rathillien to serve as a base against their former master. That prospect does not please my lord at all. He intends to pit his two enemies – the Kencyrath and the rebel changers – against each other. Whoever loses, Gerridon wins. But at the moment he's far angrier at the renegades than at the Highlord, so I have been ordered to sacrifice every man in the Prince's army if necessary to support the Host against the Horde.'

'B-but the real prince would have done that, too.'

'Oh yes, but consider the aftermath. If by some miracle the Host actually wins, there Prince Odalian is, ready to claim subject ally status. Torisen is a fair man. He won't refuse after all those Karkinorans have died fighting by his side. And when I have tasted his blood, why, I can replace him. Then, through me, Gerridon of Knorth will again be Highlord of the Kencyrath.'

She recoiled from him. 'And when you and your precious Master have accomplished all this, what happens to Tori? Will you chain him up in the shadows, too?'

'No. My lord may wish it, but I would never do such a thing to one of my lady's children. Of course,' he went on thoughtfully, 'if these were the full ally rites in which both sides drink, my blood would probably kill him on the spot, just as it would have Odalian if he had drunk first. Considering that changers' blood is corrosive enough to eat through tempered steel, it would be an excruciating way to die. The only worse fate I can think of would be that of a changer tricked into the rites with a Shanir blood-binder. The contest between the two bloods in his system would probably tear the changer to pieces, but I have no idea if even that would kill him.

'But as for your brother, I promise: no chains in the dark, no death agonies. You see, all parts of a changer are virulent to some degree. My saliva in Torisen's palm cuts will give me at least enough control over him to make his assassination relatively easy. He will die quickly, painlessly, probably within an hour of the rites. My word of honour on it.'

'Honour!' She almost spat the word back at him. 'Do you still have any?'

A stillness came into that stolen face. The eyes took on a silver, inhuman sheen. Jame drew back, suddenly reminded that she was in very close quarters with something very dangerous. Then the changer rose and backed stiffly away until the shadows of a corner obscured his face.

'Honour,' he repeated, in a voice clearly not the Prince's. 'Define it.'

Jame was shaken. This was all so familiar, but her head was spinning worse now than ever, and she couldn't quite grasp the memory. 'W-we've discussed this before, haven't we?'

'Many times. But you were a child then. Perhaps, since then, you've learned something.'

Jame found herself stammering something about always keeping one's word, standing by friends, protecting the weak . . . It all sounded perfectly idiotic blurted out like that, but she couldn't seem to focus her thoughts.

'Honour,' said the changer again in his dark corner. 'I used to be as sure as you that I knew what it was. One kept one's word. One obeyed one's lord. But then my lord ordered me to do what was dishonourable. I decided the shame was his alone and did as he commanded. I was wrong. But that was my choice, and I must stand by it. That is my honour now, for as long as I live. May I die soon.'

'B-but that's "Honour's Paradox"!' Jame stammered. 'Tirandys, Senethari . . . c-can you die?'

'Fire will kill me, if it kindles my blood.' He gave a self-mocking laugh. 'We changers scorned death, and now each one of us is his own pyre, waiting for the first spark. I have often thought about that.' He went over to the fireplace, bent, and picked up a glowing ember in his bare hand. 'I could hold this until it eats through the skin —'

'Don't!'

'No.' He tossed the ember back into the flames. 'Not yet, while I still have a role to play, and not here. If I ever do fall, let it be far from this foul house. If only there were someplace so far away that my lady Jamethiel would not be sent to bring me back; but she will be, even if I should fall at the worlds' end. My lord Gerridon can't allow any of his loyal changers the luxury of death. He has too few of us left.'

'Too few... is everyone else dead or... or has the House always been this empty?'

'For you, very nearly. You have always been confined to the House's decayed present. The rest of us whom the Master favours can move through layers of its fallen past, not that that does us much good. Nothing ever changes. We tried to teach you the trick, but you were too young.'

'Yes, yes...' Oh, if her head would only stop spinning... 'I almost remember. B-but all those death banners... Tirandys, what's been happening here? Why did the changers revolt?'

'Why, quite simply the Master has very nearly devoured all the Highborn souls that the Mistress reaped for him on the night so many of us fell. That puts my lord Gerridon in rather an uncomfortable position. If immortality alone would satisfy him, he could accept the tainted souls which Perimal Darkling offers as gifts– or rather as bait. The shadows wish to enfold my lord, to... to possess him. He served them best as Highlord when he betrayed his people and opened up the fallen worlds. Now they would have him serve them as their creature, their voice. It would be only justice for him to lose the humanity which he has bartered away in his followers, but he is far too clever a man to make so great an error – I think. If he wishes to remain both immortal and human, he must have more of his own kind to feed on, or he can turn on the Kendar and changers.'

'Y-you still have your soul, Senethari?'

'Yes, however warped. All of us to who willingly took part in the Master's treachery. That was to be our reward. The changers who have rebelled did so because they were afraid that as my lord's hunger grew he would go back on his word and find a way to feed on them, too. As for those whose souls the Dream-Weaver did reap, most have become unfallen sacrifices to buy Gerridon his immortality. My brother Terribend is one. Poor Bender. He weakened for a moment, and his soul was stripped from him. Ever since, he has fought to regain it and to bring Gerridon to ruin; but the Master is stronger than he and keeps his soul hostage. He won't believe that he and I have the same goals. In a sense, the Dream-Weaver herself is another one of Gerridon's victims. She was only his tool and may yet save her compromised honour by choosing to disobey him. I would gladly give what remains of both my honour and soul to see that.'

'I-I don't understand,' said Jame, through teeth that had

begun to rattle together as if from the cold. 'The Master has nearly run through his stolen Highborn souls. He needs more. Why can't he go back into the House's past for them or – or have the Mistress reap more for him in the present?'

'He can't go back for more because the past doesn't work that way. We can go through the same motions over and over, but they only really happened once, and nothing can change them, not even our foreknowledge of their consequences. The past *is* past, even when we move freely in it. As for the Dream-Weaver, she has lived almost entirely in the House's former days since she came back from the Haunted Lands. My poor lady may not have consented to the Master's evil, but it was still too great to leave her unmarked. Now when she comes forward to the present, it can only be as the fell creature she has become, which reaps souls with a touch whether she wants to or not, and she can neither give them back nor pass them on. The Master can only use her to bring home his injured changers, most of whose souls, like Keral's and mine, are so deformed by now that they resist even her touch. Gerridon foresaw long ago that this would eventually happen. When he found that opening the House to its fallen past didn't help, he sent Jamethiel Dream-Weaver across the Barrier to Ganth Gray Lord. You were the child that he wanted. Your brother came as an unwelcome surprise, just as, I gather, you did to Ganth. Twins have too much potential of their own. They don't lend themselves well to other people's schemes. Gerridon found that out when he tried to force you prematurely to become the new Mistress. You hadn't fallen then. You haven't yet... quite. Perhaps now, you never will.'

His words seemed to break over Jame in waves – swelling, crashing down, receding. She knew she wasn't taking them all in. Only once before had she been drunk, and it hadn't felt anything like this. This felt more like... dying?

You fool, do you always drink everything anyone hands you?

She tried to rise and fell, an interminable distance, it seemed. Now she was half on the bed, half in the changer's arms. She looked up at him, astonished.

'Senethari, y-you've poisoned me.'

'Yes. With wyrm's venom in the wine. You drank some seven days ago when you first woke in Karkinaroth, and a great deal more just now.'

'B-but why?'

'My lord commanded that you be drugged. He wants to take

no chances with you this time, you see. It occurred to me, though, that you would be much better off dead, especially since that would end the horror for all of us, too. Oh, not immediately – the Master still has a few souls left to munch on – but soon, unless he's fool enough to take what the shadows offer him. Then too, this is a game that should be played out among my lord Gerridon's own generation, which he betrayed and damned for his own selfish ends. You should never have been brought into it, Jamie. Strictly speaking, you should never ever have been born. This is the next best solution. Large doses of wyrm's venom have unpredictable results, however. I don't know if I've killed you or not. You do understand, though, that I've tried to act in your own best interests, don't you?'

She was still staring up at him with wide grey eyes, but all understanding had left them. The lids fluttered and closed. He held her for a long minute, looking down at her face, then carefully picked her up and put her back on the bed.

'If the worst happens, child, if you do survive, at least I've taught you the Senethar by my example and honour by my mistakes.' He kissed her lightly on the lips. 'Welcome home, Jamie.'

26

Night Pieces
The River Road: 17th-24th of Winter

The Kencyr Host reached the far side of the White Hills well after dark on the seventeenth, after a forced march of nearly eighty miles. That same night, pyres were raised for those who had died in the hills and the pyric runes spoken. Then virtually everyone lay down around the dying flames and slept as if they themselves were the dead. Torisen spent the night wandering restlessly among them. Ashe watched the Highlord pass. Just so, forty years ago, Ganth had stalked among the dead on the slopes of the White Hills, and she had lain there, too weak from loss of blood to call out, watching him pass. Tonight she was silent again, for almost the same reason. Her mangled arm ached dully. She had not shown it to a physician.

Early the next day, the Host again struck the River Road, which had shifted to the west bank back at the confluence of the Silver and the Ever-quick. The Kendar moved well after their night of *dwar* sleep. From now on, they would have its benefit every other night, and need it after the forty to fifty leagues they would cover every two days. It was a ruthless pace, but given the foot soldiers' remarkable constitutions, the horses would probably wear out first.

They were passing between the Elder Kingdoms now, with Bashti on the west bank and Hathir on the east. Thousands of years before, these two colossi had controlled most of the Central Lands; but Hathir had long since disintegrated, and decaying Bashti was a power now in name only. Consequently, the Host overtook very little traffic on the road and almost none on the river.

The only time the Host met opposition was on the twenty-first when Torisen again led it off the winding River Road to take a shortcut across a corner of the vast forest known as the

Weald. Even at the height of its power, Bashti had never succeeded in imposing its rule here, except around the edges. The wood had swallowed armies whole in its time. Huntsmen sometimes did better, but only one in a generation penetrated to the black oaks of the forest's heart and returned alive to report that they were still there. In times of famine, the Weald might have been said to rule Bashti, when red-eyed wolves emerged from its tangled shadows to ravage the countryside and even to stalk the streets of Bashti's proudest cities. But when the wolves came to town, they came as men, still red-eyed, but with fingers cunning enough to pick any lock and a hunger for women not always confined to the stomach.

The corner that the Host cut was called the Grimly Holt. It was hardly as intimidating as the deep woods would have been, but the Kencyr still looked askance at its dense undergrowth and the green shadows of its maple and birch. The shattered remains of an old road led through it. Even when the road was new, though, it had never been well travelled for the Holt had its own denizens, and they objected to traffic.

All day, the vanguard of the Host saw quick flickers of movement in the undergrowth, and their horses danced nervously. Harn would have sent scouts out to investigate, but Torisen sharply forbade it. Harn and Burr exchanged glances. The Highlord had scarcely spoken to anyone in days and often moved as if in a waking dream. He barely slept at all since the White Hills. Burr noted that when not riding, Torisen limped more than ever. Harn wondered if the judgement of a sleep-starved man, even this one, could be fully trusted. Both remembered the White Hills and what had happened the last time Torisen had led them off the road. Dusk fell, and a murmur as of wind passed under the leaves. But none of them moved.

Abruptly, a stone whizzed out of the twilight and struck Burr on the shoulder, almost unhorsing him. In a moment, the air was full of flying objects, some rocks, some softer, but no less objectionable. From the undergrowth came an excited yapping. Torisen spurred Storm off the road into a small glade.

'Hoy, Grimly!' he shouted at the surrounding forest. 'Stop that!'

The hail of stones ceased instantly. Again the murmur of rapid question and answer, and then a sudden, joyful yelp:

'Hoy, Tori!'

A shaggy figure erupted from the undergrowth. Torisen

dismounted. By the time Ardeth and his warguard came charging into the clearing, the Highlord was trying to disengage himself from the glad embrace of a young man wearing a wolf's pelt – or was it his own? All around them, other hairy figures had emerged from the forest to watch.

'Lord Ardeth, my friend the Wolver Grimly, luckily at home. He spends part of the year at King Krothen's court, playing the wild man and studying *rendish* poetry.'

The Wolver grinned. All his teeth came to very sharp points.

That night, he and his people set a feast for all of the High Council who would come to the ruined keep that served as their lair. They ate by torchlight, sitting on mossy blocks beside a brook that gurgled down the length of what had once been the keep's main hall; and forest folk passed among them, shy, wild eyes glowing red in the firelight, filling horns with honey mead. Out in the Holt, the rest of the pack sang in yelps and long, crooning wails which took on the rhythms of some complex poetry.

'You know,' said Lord Danior to Torisen in a low voice, 'these wolves aren't anything like what I expected. All those horror stories must be pretty exaggerated, huh?'

'That depends. Grimly's people live according to their own system of esthetics, and on the whole are less prone to violence than the average human. But the farther into the Weald you go, the wilder things get. The wolvers of the deep-wood Holts are as bad as you can imagine, if not a good deal worse.'

'Yes, but how did any of them end up in King Krothen's court? I mean, they're hardly my idea . . .'

'Of courtiers?' The Wolver popped up beside him with a toothy grin. 'Now, that's a word to spit at. I'm a poet, friend. A poet!'

'Grimly,' said Torisen, 'stop making faces and tell him the story. Once upon a time, when you were just a cub . . .'.

'There was a king who loved to hunt. His name was Kruin of Kothifir, and he was King Krothen's father. Now, Kruin had gone after all sorts of game: rhisar in the Southern Wastes, rathorn, once even an Arrin-ken – the last without success, I'm glad to say. Then some fool told him about the Weald. The next thing we knew, he had arrived on our doorstep with a hunting party the size of a young army. He took over this keep as his base camp. We hid, of course, and when he went into the deep-wood, some of us followed.'

'Why?' Danior demanded.

'Curiosity, mainly. Then too, we don't often see our wilder cousins of the deep-woods – or want to, for that matter – but here was a chance to go visiting with what amounted to an armed escort. Well, the escort didn't last long. There are more ways to get yourself killed in the deep Weald than you can imagine. Within a day, Kruin was down to a handful of men, long before he'd got far enough to meet even the least... uh... impetuous of our cousins. And he was lost too, just for good measure. Well, by this time we'd got tired of watching men die in singularly unesthetic ways, so we led the survivors out.'

'I trust Kruin was suitably grateful,' said Ardeth.

The Wolver grinned. 'He accused us of ruining the best hunt he'd been on in years. He'd come to the Weald to get a wolver pelt for his trophy wall, he said; but he was a fair man. If any of us cared to go back to Kothifir with him, he would find us an appropriate place in his court. The place that immediately occurred to us was that trophy wall, so we said we'd think about it. Well, I thought about it for some fifteen years until I came of age. Then I went south to Kothifir.'

'By then, Krothen was on the throne,' said Torisen. 'Luckily, Krothen doesn't hunt...'

'Most days, he doesn't even move,' the Wolver interposed.

'... and he hated his father. So the trophy wall had long since been torn down, and Grimly became a poet instead of a pelt. The work he does in his own language is quite good – the pack is performing some of it now – but when he recites his poetry in *rendish*, it's the audience that usually howls.'

After that, the talk became general. Ashe arrived at the feast late and ate nothing. She left, unnoticed, before Harn came in from checking down the line of camps. Soon after that, most of the other Kencyr left to rejoin their people and get some much needed sleep. Torisen stayed. So did Burr, determined not to let the Highlord out of his sight. He settled down in the shadows of the ruined hall to wait, but soon began to feel the effect of the holt-dwellers' potent mead. His lord's face, pale and fine-drawn, floated before him in midair. Opposite it, the Wolver's white teeth and red eyes gleamed in the firelight. Their talk ran together, merging with the brook's burble.

Then something fell with a crash. Burr started up blurry eyed, and saw that Torisen's mead horn had slipped out of his hand.

The Wolver caught the Highlord as he started to topple forward.

'Venom in the wine,' they both heard him say indistinctly.

'Wine?' Burr repeated, confused. *'Venom?'*

'Here.' The Wolver thrust Torisen into the Kendar's steadying arms and dropped to all fours beside the puddle of spilt mead. He sniffed at it, then took a cautious lap.

Torisen shuddered violently, breaking out of the light doze into which he had fallen. He saw the Wolver still crouching at his feet and gave a shaky laugh. 'There's nothing in your good mead but an uncommon amount of alcohol, Grimly. I must be more tired than I thought. No.' A bewildered, almost frightened look flickered across his face. 'There was more to it than that. I was almost asleep when something down in the dark caught and tugged at me. Hard. And then I began to slip away from the light.'

'Tentir,' muttered Burr.

'Yes, like that.' Torisen absentmindedly rubbed his leg where the wyrm had bitten it. 'Something has happened; what, I don't know. Damnit, I don't *want* to know! Things are complicated enough as it is. Grimly, Burr – just humour me and help me stay awake tonight, as if my soul depended on it.' He shivered. 'Who knows? It might.'

It was a long night. When dawn came at last, Burr was left with the feeling that they had merely postponed the danger, whatever it was. At the breakfast council, Caineron gave Torisen such a look, half speculation, half smug satisfaction, that Burr longed to shove the Highborn's fat face into the nearest pile of manure. He took some pleasure, though, in Caineron's thunderstruck expression a little later when Torisen rode up to the vanguard with a huge grey wolf trotting at his stirrup.

By noon on the twenty-second of Winter, they were back on the River Road.

Two nights later, Ardeth sat in the reception chamber of his tent, sipping pale blue wine. Outside, the night cry passed from sentry to sentry while more than half the camp lay in the healing grip of *dwar* sleep. A mild breeze blew through the gauze tent flaps. It was very late on the twenty-fourth with some three hundred miles left to go. In five days, the Host should reach the Cataracts where, they hoped, Prince Odalian's forces would be waiting. And the Horde? Ardeth glanced at the map spread out on the camp table before him. There had been no word from the Southern Wastes since that message at Wyrden; but if the Horde was moving at its usual fifteen miles a day crawl, it was probably well within one hundred miles of the Cataracts. As Brandan had said back at Gothregor, this was going to be close.

Ardeth sipped more wine. Its bouquet hid the disagreeable smell of the hemlock, but didn't mask the juice's bitter taste. Still, he had developed a liking for the stuff during his career as a diplomat nearly a century ago, and it did help to calm him. He needed to be calm now.

On the table beside the map lay the coded report of his agent in Kothifir. It had arrived just that evening. The news was nearly a month old, but the agent hadn't been able to get his report out sooner because Krothen had put every Kencyr left in the city under house arrest. He was furious because Pereden had marched out the Southern Host to meet the Horde against his orders.

Pereden.

Ardeth sipped more wine.

Of course, the boy might have had information that made it essential for him to lead out his forces immediately. At the very least, his suicidal attack on the Horde had bought the Northern Host time that it desperately needed. But at what cost? The worst military débâcle since Urakran...

Calmly, old man, calmly, he told himself. *You don't know that for certain yet.*

In fact, what if the message at Wyrden announcing the massacre had been a fraud? Torisen had seemed to trust it, but for all his cleverness the Highlord wasn't infallible. Perhaps instead of the reported pitched battle, Pereden had simply used his forces to harry the enemy. Perhaps he would emerge as a hero after all. Yes, perhaps; but Ardeth couldn't forget the petulant tone of Pereden's dispatches ever since he had joined the Southern Host, complaining first because Ardeth had given command to Torisen and later because (he claimed) his officers weren't giving him adequate support.

Ardeth wondered if Torisen knew that Pereden had led out the Southern Host against orders. Thinking back to what the Highlord had said at various times, and more importantly, to what he hadn't, Ardeth concluded that he had indeed known for quite some time. Probably one of his former officers with the

Southern Host had passed on the news. Then why hadn't he shared it with the man whom it most concerned? Could the Highlord be playing a game of his own? It seemed unlikely, but Ardeth still knew far less about Torisen than he liked, despite all the years the young man had served him. Then too, it was becoming increasingly difficult to control a game in which one's principal player continually made unexpected, even erratic moves. Damn. He had to find out what was going on before Caineron made some half-witted play of his own that finished them all.

Voices spoke softly out by the watchfire. Ardeth recognised one of them. Ah, now here was someone who might tell him something, if properly asked. He beckoned to his servant and murmured an instruction. The man went out. A moment later, Kindrie appeared at the tent flap and stood there blinking in the light. The breeze ruffled his white hair.

'You wished to see me, my lord?'

'Come in, come in.' Ardeth gestured graciously to a camp chair that his servant had just unfolded and set next to the table. 'Sit down and share a cup of wine with me. It's just occurred to me that we haven't had a really good talk since– when?'

'Before the White Hills, my lord.' Kindrie sat down and accepted a glass of pale blue wine. He seemed ill at ease.

'Ah, yes.' Ardeth smiled benignly at him. 'And how have my folk been treating you? No complaints, I hope?'

'None, my lord.' Kindrie swallowed some wine and almost made a face at its bitter taste. He rested the glass on his knee, both hands cupped around it. 'They've treated me remarkably well considering –' He stopped short.

'Yes?'

'Considering that I'm a Shanir.'

'I hadn't forgotten,' said Ardeth dryly. 'Actually, quite a few Shanir serve me. My other people have, I hope, learned to treat them with respect. After all, once all our greatest lords were acknowledged Shanir and many of them blood-binders at that.'

'That was a long time ago,' Kindrie muttered into his glass. He took another cautious sip.

'Times change, and change again,' said Ardeth enigmatically. He eyed Kindrie's glass. 'My dear boy, you should have said that you disliked hemlock. I could have offered you something else. But I see that you've already dealt with the problem.'

Kindrie blushed. With an abrupt gesture almost of defiance,

he put his glass on the table. His wine had entirely lost its poisonous blue colour.

'Very impressive,' murmured Ardeth. 'The priesthood lost a powerful healer in you, didn't it?'

'Only a half-trained one, my lord. I left before my final initiation.'

'Ah, yes. We must discuss the reason for that sometime. Just at present, though, it would interest me even more to hear something about your adventures in the White Hills with Torisen.'

'Please, my lord. I can't discuss that.'

'Has he bound you to silence?'

'N-no. That wasn't necessary. Oh, you don't understand. You can't!'

Ardeth leaned back and steepled his long white fingers. 'I think I can... in part. Torisen is more your natural lord than I am. He is also, despite his antipathy to the Shanir, a very attractive man.'

Kindrie rose abruptly. 'My lord, I am grateful for the protection you have extended to me these past few days and sorry to give you such a poor return for it. I will remain in your camp tonight if I may and look for a new place tomorrow.'

Ardeth sighed. 'My, how stiff and stilted. Wait a moment, dear boy, please. This is too serious a matter to bury under a cartload of compliments. Something happened to Torisen in the White Hills. As far as I can determine, he's barely slept since, and not at all since the Grimly Holt. Now we're only five days away from the Cataracts. If I don't know what happened to him, I can't help him; and I think he does need help. Desperately.'

Kindrie wavered. Then, 'I'm sorry,' he said. 'It would be too much like betraying a confidence, and we Shanir can keep faith, whatever some people might think.'

Ardeth's bland expression didn't change, but something flashed in the depths of his blue eyes that made the young man go back a step. 'I never doubted it. You know, dear boy, it's a pity you were born into a Shanir-hating house like Randir's, especially with that white hair. Other Shanir traits are so much less noticeable; but then in some houses the hair wouldn't present much of a problem either. Mine was stained a fairly handsome shade of brown from the day it first grew until my ninetieth birthday.'

Kindrie stared at him. He stepped back to the table and sat down as if someone had hit him behind the knees. 'I should have known. Back in the Oseen Hills, where your mare smelled the burning post station and you knew what she'd smelled long before any of us possibly could have, I should have known.'

'That was a slip,' said Ardeth tranquilly, sipping his wine. 'Luckily, only you seem to have caught it. Yes, I am indeed mind-bound to Brithany, my Whinno-hir. That and my hair seem to be my only Shanir traits, except, of course, for the ability to bind men to me.'

'But every Highborn can do that... can't he?'

'No. Actually only a few can. The lords must, of course, or they wouldn't be lords. What do you think holds the Kencyrath together?'

'I-I assumed it was the will of our god, although I remember that some Highborn used the blood-bond once.'

'That was long ago, in a more trusting time. The blood-bond gave a Shanir lord almost complete control over his followers, body and soul. Usually, only Highborn were bound that way and then only under special circumstances. Then came the Fall. As far as I know, the Master wasn't a blood-binder; but he did abuse what Shanir power he had so spectacularly that afterward we of the Old Blood were made the scapegoats for all of our people's sins. But I hardly have to tell you that. As you well know, all the Shanir talents came under suspicion, even the beneficial ones. As for the blood-bond, no one would even have dared to mention it. So our ancestors fell back on the milder psychic bond that had always been used to bind the Kendar. What they don't seem to have realised is that even that bond can only be made by a Highborn with at least some trace of the Old Blood – in other words, by a Shanir.'

'Why, the hypocrites.' Kindrie thought of Randir and Caineron, of all the Highborn who had made his life miserable by sneering at his Shanir blood. 'The lying hypocrites...'

Lying? That word brought him up short.

'No,' said Ardeth gently. 'The other lords simply don't understand. If you asked any of them if they were Shanir, they would thunder back, "No!" And as far as they know, they'd be telling the truth. Ignorance goes a long way towards protecting honour.'

'B-but who else knows about this? My God, what a thing to have kept secret all these years!'

'Oh, the Shanir of my house have always known. We do love a good secret. I remember my great-grandfather chortling over this one while the rest of us tried to imagine the most devastating circumstances under which to spring it on the other houses. Now I sometimes wonder if we've waited too long. But all of this, in a roundabout way, brings me back to my immediate concern. If all the other lords are Shanir...'

'Then so is the Highlord.' Kindrie sat back limply, taking in the implications. 'Sweet Trinity. Torisen is not going to like this.'

'That,' said Ardeth, 'is putting it mildly. That is also why I sincerely hope he doesn't find out, at least not before he can bear the truth.'

'And yet you've just shared it with me.' Kindrie leant forward. 'My lord, why?'

'Because I think that, despite everything, you love Torisen. Because I hope that that love will make you want to help me protect him from himself.'

'I ... don't understand.'

This time Ardeth leant forward and spoke with unusual intensity. 'Listen, my boy. We're not talking here about someone with only a trace of the Old Blood. Consider all the people who are bound to Torisen personally, far more than to any other single lord. Oh, his two thousand Kendar don't look like much compared to Caineron's twelve thousand or even to my ninety-five hundred, but Caldane and I have dozens of blood-kin adding their people to ours. Torisen stands absolutely alone. All right so far. But a Shanir that powerful usually has other traits, too. What Torisen has, if nothing else, are dreams.'

'My lord?'

'Apparently he senses when one is coming and stays awake nights, even weeks, attempting to stave it off, as he's apparently doing now. That suggests a kind of Shanir foreseeing at the very least. But the dreams themselves are the mystery. I've never been able to determine what they mean; they're obviously pretty shattering. Just before he claimed his father's powers, he had one that first drove him out into the Southern Wastes and then nearly killed him. Burr reported that when he and Harn found him, Torisen was raving about silent warriors, massacre, and a son's betrayal. You spoke?'

'I ... no.'

'To continue, then, I don't know if these dreams are dangerous in themselves or only in his violent reaction to them. It certainly doesn't help that he wastes half his strength in trying to avoid them. One way or the other, they've begun to threaten his health and possibly his sanity. You've seen what he's been like since the Grimly Holt. So has Caineron. If I knew what these dreams meant, perhaps I could help him deal with them. That's why I need every scrap of information about Torisen that I can get. Burr used to gather them for me, but he isn't my man any more. Neither are you, of course, but you've been closer to the Highlord recently than anyone else, especially in the White Hills. Perhaps what happened there will finally tell me what I need to know. Perhaps you can show me how to save Torisen from himself.'

Kindrie hesitated, feeling torn. Of course he wanted to help Torisen, but would he do that best by speaking or keeping quiet? Ardeth was the Highlord's oldest friend. Surely he could be trusted; but why was there even a question of trust? What he had seen corroborated the common story about Ganth's death, except that Torisen had let slip that his father had died cursing him, and now Ardeth had mentioned a son's betrayal. There was some mystery about all this, but Kindrie had no key to it. Perhaps Ardeth did. But would it help or hurt Torisen to have the puzzle solved, and would he ever forgive Kindrie for having in effect become another one of Ardeth's spies?

Ardeth toyed with his cup, covertly watching the Shanir's obvious indecision. There *was* a secret here. He might be getting on a bit in years, Ardeth told himself, but his instinct for such things was as keen as ever. He also sensed, though, that if Kindrie didn't tell him now, quite possibly he never would.

Suddenly a figure appeared in the tent opening. It was Burr. Of all times for anyone to interrupt...

'Well, man?' Ardeth demanded, with a shade less than his usual coolness. 'What is it?'

'Lord, just now my lord Torisen was walking the perimeter, and I was following him. Then he stopped to look up at the stars. The next thing I knew, he'd just folded up in a heap on the ground, fast asleep. I got him back to his tent.'

'Well, surely that's a good thing,' said Ardeth, impatient for the Kendar to leave. 'Trinity knows, the man needs some rest.'

Burr stood there, wooden-faced, rigid with distress. 'You don't understand, lord. He's begun to dream again and ... and I can't wake him up.'

27

Converging Paths
The River Road, Perimal Darkling,
Karkinaroth: 24th-26th of Winter

They wanted her to wake up. Jame could hear them whispering around the bed. Her eyelids felt as if they were glued shut, and her head was pounding. Oh, why didn't they let her sleep? Nimble fingers plucked at her clothes.

Get up, up, up, Chosen of our Lord! Get undressed and dressed. Tonight is the night!

'Oh, go away,' she groaned. 'I'm sick, I'm... what night?'

Giggles answered her. She forced open her eyes. They were crouching all around the bed, peering at her over the counterpane with golden, gleeful eyes. Long fingers like shadows in the coverlet's creases poked at her. Except for their eyes, their bodies seemed no more substantial than those shadows. She struggled up on one elbow, fighting down a wave of dizziness.

'Who *are* you?'

Forgotten us so soon? Shame, shame, shame! Our lord sent for us, called us from our dim world into his dim rooms, up from the depths of the House. Said, 'Teach this child the Great Dance, as you taught the other one. One name will do for both.' And so we taught you, the new Dream-Weaver. Years, it's been, all to be consummated tonight. Now get up, up, up... or shall we get into bed with you?

'No!'

Jame swung her feet down to the floor and nearly pitched head first out of the bed. How groggy she felt. Some of it might be due to *dwar* sleep, but as for the rest... This was like one of those leaden nightmares in which one couldn't rouse oneself enough to fend off some ill-defined threat even as it crept closer, closer...

The shadowy forms crouched about her feet, staring avidly

up at her. She clawed her way up the bedpost and stood, clutching it, swaying.

Ahhhh...! sighed the shadows. They rose about her, tall and lithe, no more distinct than before. Their eyes shone. *Now undress and dress, Chosen One. Quick, quick, quick... or shall we help you?*

Jame fumbled at her clothes, all the Talisman's deftness gone. It was becoming harder and harder to remember that such a person had ever existed. The fire had long since died, and the air was chill on her bare skin. How cold the House always was. She remembered... remembered... what? Her head seemed full of dustballs. They were offering her something. A garment. It seemed to be nothing but spun shadows, weightless in her hands, but she thought she remembered how to put it on. There. Except for its full sleeves, it clung to her like a shadow, at the same time leaving bare much skin in unexpected places. Wonderingly, she ran her hands down the length of her body.

Ahhhh...!

Someone had worn a costume like this before, someone called... the B'tyrr? But who had that been? Her head spun again, and she barely kept her balance. Time seemed to be collapsing in on itself, past and present merging, the past swallowing the present. Sweet Trinity, to be a child again, here! To be forced to live through all those lonely, frightening years again... They tugged at her with the quicksand grip of nightmares half remembered. She fought them desperately, swaying on her feet, but the poison in her blood pulled, too. The past few years faded away. Tai-tastigon was gone, and the Anarchies and Karkinaroth. This was the Master's House. She was the Chosen, and this was her night. Shadowy hands combed out her long black hair, caressed her, plucked impatiently at her sleeves.

Ah, don't keep him waiting. Come with us, come! Quick, quick, quick!

She went.

Burr led Ardeth and Kindrie through the sleeping camp. The Host was strung out nearly two miles in the long strip of meadow that ran at this point between the River Road and the banks of the Silver. Down by the river, witch-weed cast its red glow over the rippling water. In the meadow between the watch fires, fireflies danced. The deep, slow breathing of nearly twenty-five thousand Kendar in *dwar* sleep made it seem as if the night itself slept. But there would still be watchers and little chance of concealing everything from anyone who really wanted to find out.

'Still, let's not make Caineron a present of any more than we have to,' murmured Ardeth, putting a hand on Burr's shoulder. 'Walk slower, my friend. Now, who saw you helping the Highlord back to his tent?'

'Luckily, it happened just beyond the Knorth encampment. Only his own people saw, and not all that many of them.'

'There, you see? Things aren't so bad. Now *slow down.*'

The Knorth camp was at the far southern end of the camp, and the Highlord's tent was very nearly at the southern perimeter. Sentries patrolled beyond it. Beyond them, a thin crescent moon rode over dark meadows and the silken sheen of the river. Everything seemed peaceful, until a shaggy form rose up in the tent's shadow, growling softly.

'Be quiet, Grimly,' Burr hissed. 'How is he?'

The Wolver straightened up and stepped out into the firelight. Somehow, he looked less hairy than he had a moment before.

'Worse. We had to gag him.'

He held open the flap and they all went in. Torisen's tent was much simpler than those of the other lords; it consisted of only three chambers, one inside the other. Donkerri jumped up as they entered the innermost room. He was clutching a piece of firewood and looked terrified but ready to do battle. When he saw who they were, however, he dropped the wood and burst into tears. Burr took him in charge.

Torisen lay on his cot. His arms had been tied down and a piece of cloth forced between his teeth. His pale face was wet, and the bedding beneath soaked. Apparently Burr had come closer to drowning his lord than waking him with a bucket of water. The Highlord was twisting slowly in his bonds. His eyes, open only a slit, showed nothing but white.

Ardeth sat down beside him and gently pushed the damp hair off his forehead. 'My poor boy. Was he this bad, Burr, when you and Harn tracked him down to that city in the Southern Wastes?'

'No, lord,' said Burr. 'This is much worse: like what happened then combined with Tentir, nightmare on top of poison.'

'Before we gagged him, he was raving about shadows with

golden eyes,' said the Wolver, 'and he mentioned venom again. Venom in the wine. Burr has told me about Tentir. Could this have something to do with the wyrm's attack there?'

'It's possible. The old songs say some odd things about the effects of wyrm's venom. Of course, there are some poisons available even here on Rathillien that can tie a Highlord into fancy knots, especially if administered in wine over a sufficient period of time. How long have you been the Highlord's cupbearer, boy?'

Donkerri backed away, blinking, stammering. 'I-I didn't do anything, lord. I wouldn't! I *belong* here.'

Ardeth regarded him coolly. 'It was just a question. Don't take everything so personally, boy.'

Torisen made a stifled noise. His teeth ground into the cloth, and his head began to rock back and forth.

'It's starting again,' said Burr hoarsely.

Ardeth steadied the young man's head. He hesitated. Then obviously consumed with curiosity, he cautiously loosened the gag. Everyone braced himself, hardly knowing what to expect. Torisen surprised them all. In a low, rapid voice, he was muttering one word over and over again:

'. . . don't, don't, don't . . .'

The cold, grey halls – no longer entirely empty. Indistinct figures stood in obscure corners, sat in mouldering chairs. They were all so terribly thin. Only their eyes moved, following Jame as she passed with her escort of shadows. She stared back at them. Surely she had seen many of their starved faces on death banners in the Master's Great Hall. Then the faint breeze changed, and they all vanished.

Now hangings rippled against the wall, so threadbare that the stones beneath showed plainly through them. The faded carpets, too, scarcely hid the pavement they covered. Jame's feet rang on them as if on naked stone. It seemed to her dazed senses that shapes flitted about her now, casting no shadows on the cold floor. A hiss rose, faint but vehement:

The Dream-Weaver, the Soul-Reaver! Traitor, cursed be . . .

Tattered clothes, haggard faces – they were less distinct even than the motionless figures had been; but Jame could see now that they were the same folk, only younger and less emaciated. Their bone-thin hands were making the ancient Darkwyr sign – against her.

'No!' she cried, trying to clutch at them. 'That wasn't me! I never hurt you, I never hurt...' but the breeze changed again, and they melted out of her grasp like mist unravelling.

Shadowy figures pulled at her. Golden eyes gleamed. *Why are you dawdling, naughty child? The dead are dead. Come, come, come!*

She went, stumbling a bit with shock. The venom in her blood must have opened the abyss of the past to her, to see if not to touch. If so, she was the only true phantom here, a ghost from the future, drifting through the murky shadows of what had been.

More halls, more rooms. They passed a large chamber in which the floor fell sharply away around the walls, leaving a small central island. Something moved sluggishly in the pit. A loathsome stench arose and a sound like the monotonous muttering of curses. Jame hesitated, troubled. She vaguely remembered something about a cage without bars, but was that the bare island or the malodorous pit that surrounded it – and the cage of whom? Her guides plucked impatiently at her again, and she went on.

More rooms, more halls. As the fitful breeze blew, flickers of ghostly life came and went.

They passed another chamber, deep, high-vaulted. At its far end loomed an enormous iron face with flames in its mouth. Firelight glowed red off the ranked weapons that lined the walls. A breath of air, and the armaments were mounds of dust on the floor, the face a noseless, rusting hulk; but on an anvil before its ash-filled mouth lay a sword. The air about it wavered with heat, making the serpentine patterns on its newly reforged blade seem to quicken with uneasy life.

Then they were beyond the room, going down a corridor, around a corner and down a stair into the Great Hall of the Master's House.

Jame hesitated on the threshold. Surely she had just heard a faint thread of music. There it was again, the merest whisper. Wisps of colour moved around the edges of the vast dark hall, and something white shimmered in the centre of the floor. A woman, dancing? Patterns of force wove about her, reached out, fed. The music faltered, and the bright colours faded.

Then Jame understood. Of all the memories that the House held, this was the oldest, the darkest. 'Don't!' she cried, and darted forward to grab the Dream-Weaver's arm. For a moment, she thought her hands had actually closed on something. The faintest glimmer of a face turned towards her, then dissolved in the breeze she herself had brought with her rush across the floor.

'The past cannot be changed.'

Jame spun around towards the faint but distinct voice. Someone stood on the stairway. She could see the steps through him, and yet felt his presence more vividly than that of any other object in all that vast hall. He looked very tall and lordly, clad in the splendour of elder days; but shadows fell across him, and she couldn't see his face.

'I go ahead to prepare the way,' he said. 'Follow soon.'

He turned and went up the stairs. With each step, Jame saw his retreating form more clearly, as if he were climbing out of the well of the past, drawing closer to her even as he moved away. The silver glove on his left hand flashed, then the lintel of the doorway hid him. The sound of his footsteps, still climbing, echoed in her head.

Sweet Trinity, Gerridon.

Jame turned to bolt and stumbled into the arms of her golden-eyed guides. They dropped a cloak on her shoulders.

Here, here! A present, child, an heirloom full of life!

It was made of black serpent skins sewn together down two thirds of their length with silver thread. The snakes' tails, coiled together in a knot beneath her chin, twitched. The sense of nightmare rose again, overwhelming her. Surely this had all happened before. They would lead her to the stair, and she would climb after the Master up, up towards red ribbons, beyond...

There was another ghost in the hall. Jame saw it indistinctly by the far wall, standing in shadow. It seemed different from the others she had encountered, but her scattered wits couldn't quite grasp in what way. The others had seen it, too. They whispered together with a sound like the wind singing through river reeds. Then a silver ripple of laughter moved among them.

See, child, see, a gift for your betrothed! Now dance with us, dance for us, and gather this wilted flower for your lord!

She didn't want to. It was wrong, wrong, but now one of them had slipped off the cloak again, and the rest were darting around her with avid golden eyes, their shadowy fingers barely touching her skin in phantom caresses. She didn't want that, and yet she did. Her skin glowed. Almost despite herself, she began to move, tracing the first *kantirs* of a dance that she had never brought to consummation. Its power unfolded in her. To shape the dance, to *be* the dance! At first shadows glided with her, touching and touched, but then she moved alone, reshaping the very air with her passage.

On the edge of the dance was a presence. The ghost. The dance reached out to him, tantalising, seducing. It sensed what he wanted most – to belong, finally to have both a place and name of his own. The dance gave no promises, but oh, what hints it made. Sway, turn, the hands moving just so. He couldn't conceive of how thoroughly he could belong. The soul was a small price to pay for such utter acceptance, such intimate satisfaction. What good was a soul anyway? It only weighed one down. She could take it oh, so easily. She hungered for it. But ... but ... but it was wrong.

The unbound energies of the dance spun outward to dissipate in the hall. Tapestried faces crumbled at their touch. Jame came back to her senses with a gasp to find Graykin lying in her arms, pale, ready. She dropped him.

'Ancestors preserve me. What did I almost do? Graykin, are you all right? Graykin?'

He blinked up at her for a moment, and then burst into tears.

Jame felt like crying herself. 'Oh, hell. I'm sorry. I'm so sorry.' She sat down with a thump beside him, suddenly too dizzy to stand. The immediate past was rushing back in on her, jumbled up with scraps of those now-not-entirely-lost years that she had spent in Perimal Darkling ... spent *here*. The nightmare hadn't let go yet. She felt its cruel pull and tried desperately to anchor herself to the present with questions.

'Graykin, what are you doing here? Has something happened?'

'Happened?' He sat up and glared at her. 'Why, what could happen except that the prince has bolted shut the last palace door on the outside and the whole temple has started to disintegrate, and now there's some farking giant of a man I've never ever *seen* before sneaking around with an overgrown cat while the place begins to collapse around our ears – and what are you laughing at?'

'It's Marc and Jorin. It has to be. Graykin, men his size don't sneak. They aren't physically equipped for it. So at least he and Jorin are free. Ancestors be praised for that. But you said the palace was sealed off now from the outside. So the Prince has left it. When does his army march to join the Host?'

'Four days ago. It's the twenty-fourth of Winter, you skinny twit. You've been cavorting around in here – wherever "here" is – for ten days.'

Ten days. Was it possible? Between *dwar* sleep and the slower passage of time here, yes, damnit, it was. And Tirandys, impersonating Prince Odalian, had already marched off to meet her unsuspecting brother. She must warn Tori. She must... must...

'Hey, stop that!'

'Stop... what?'

'Fading, damnit!' Now Graykin looked indignant and more than a bit frightened. He was also beginning to take on some aspects of a rather dirty window.

'You're fading too, Graykin.'

Trinity, what was happening? Jame had assumed that whatever images of the past she saw, she herself was still in the House's dusty present as she apparently had been all the years she had been growing up here. But she had been here ten days longer than Graykin this time. Had her present become subtly dislocated from his? Or had she finally learned how to move in the past? Or...

The wyrm's venom wrenched at her mind. She couldn't tell any more what made sense and what didn't. Under her panicky efforts to think, the fear grew that she would never leave this place again. Just the same, Tori had to be warned.

'Graykin, listen.'

Rapidly, she told him about the changer, Odalian, and the trap set for the Kencyr Highlord. He listened, his sharp features becoming less and less distinct, his expression less readable.

'And that,' she concluded breathlessly, 'is why you have to carry word of all this to Torisen. Find that giant and tell him what I've told you. He can break you out of the palace if it's humanly possible and help you and Lyra to reach the Host. Well?'

He hesitated. 'Are you sure about all this?' His voice sounded thin and distant. 'I mean, if you've really been poisoned, you might have dreamed a lot of it. It all sounds so fantastic.'

'Sweet Trinity. Is it any more fantastic than this?' She jabbed a finger at his now almost transparent chest. It sank in up to the first joint without hurting either of them. Graykin drew back with a gasp.

'All right, all right, I believe you! But will the Highlord believe me?'

She hadn't thought of that. 'Proof. He's got to have proof. But what ... Graykin, up those stairs over there, left around the corner and down the hall, there is a room with a furnace in the shape of a huge iron face. On an anvil in front of it is Kin-Slayer, the Knorth heirloom sword, reforged. Take that to the Highlord and ... and tell him his sister Jame sends it. Then he'll believe you.'

Graykin stared at her. From his standpoint, it was as if a ghost had spoken those incredible words in a voice as faint as a whisper from the tomb. He could hardly see her at all now.

'Promise me you'll warn my brother, Graykin,' she was saying in a desperate tone, holding out phantom hands pleading to him. 'Promise...' And she was gone.

Graykin jumped up. He didn't like this place. There were things here he could never understand, could never control. That strange girl had promised him... what? Something he would almost have given his soul to possess. Almost? But what she *had* given him was information, and that was power.

All right, my lad, he told himself. *Let's not falter now. One, two, three...!*

He dashed across the hall, up the marble stairs, around the corner, down the hall, and fetched up gasping on the threshold of a room. There was the rusting, iron face and there lay the sword. Even with its hilt emblem smashed, it was beautiful. He touched it almost reverently and snatched back his hand with a gasp. The blade might still be hot, but the hilt was so cold that it almost burned his hand. He dropped his handkerchief over it and picked it up. The pride of the Kencyrath, in a half-breed's hand. He would show them. Oh yes, he would show them all. Now, one, two, three...!

He dashed back the way he had come. On the second flight of stairs, he almost thought that he passed someone. A coldness went past, and a glimmer of something white like the profile of a blanched face. Graykin almost followed before he checked himself. No one had ever stood by him. Why should he stand by anyone else? But she had refused to call him by that hated name and had trusted him with her own. Yes, but again, there was no way he could help her now, even if he wanted to.

He ran down the stairs and across the hall. At the far side was the door that opened into the palace's corridor. You couldn't see it from this side, but it was there. He had checked. Graykin paused on the threshold, looking back at the hall. He still didn't know where he had been, but he did know what he had gained: the Highlord's sister had put Kin-Slayer in his hands, and he hadn't given her his promise.

Jame climbed the stairs. They seemed to rise forever, twisting this way and that. Sometimes the uneven stone treads ran up between narrow walls, sometimes one side or the other opened up into echoing depths. A cold wind blew down from above. The serpent skin cloak lay dank and heavy on her shoulders. Everytime its trailing heads bumped up another step at her heels, the tails, coiled together under her chin, twitched in protest.

She tried to think what she should do. Was everything going to happen just as it had the first time; or by some cruel twist was *this* the first time, different only in her foreknowledge of it? Ancestors preserve her, to be trapped in the same round of events, years' worth of them, happening over and over...

An alcove by the stair and in it, waiting, the man who had scratched on her door in the palace and later rescued her from the leech vines, whose ravaged face had haunted her dreams for years.

'Bender? Terribend? What's going to happen? What should I do? Please tell me!'

He pressed something cold into her hand. A knife. It was all white and all of a piece, hilt and blade, as if hewn from a single bone. Its pommel was carved with the faces of three women, or perhaps of one woman at three different ages: maiden, lady, hag. It didn't warm to Jame's touch. When she looked up again, the skull-faced man was gone.

She began to climb again, knife in hand, moving slower and slower with each step.

At the top of the stair was a doorway opening into darkness. Red ribbons tumbled about it, plaiting and replaiting in the wind that blew through from the other side. Jame stopped, just out of their reach. Oh God, now what? Was he waiting, just beyond the light, waiting for her to cross his threshold? She had once before, armed as she was now, intent on... on... what?

Jame sat down abruptly on the steps, on the cloak. The serpent heads rose hissing in protest, but she ignored them. Earlier she had felt this memory rising and in near panic had thrust it back into darkness. Now it lurched to the surface despite her.

The last time she had come here and the Master had reached out from the beribboned bed, had started to draw her in, she had slashed wildly at him, not because she feared him but because she was afraid of herself. She had wanted to go to him. He would have given her power, security, love – all the things she had never had before. Priest, father, lover. There was no wish, no desire he could not have fulfilled, or so it had seemed.

Even now, the lure drew her. Her desire to belong was at least as strong as Graykin's, and her chances of acceptance among her own people perhaps just as slight. They would shun her, she thought, for the very things that the Master would prize: her darkling training, her Shanir blood, herself. What chance did she have among her own people? What chance had they ever given her? But here she was offered acceptance, power, yes, even a red ribboned bed, velvet shadows, the touch of a hand in the dark...

She put her own hand to her cheek and felt its flushed warmth even through gloved fingertips. Lost, lost... but not perhaps quite yet. This was the way the first Dream-Weaver had gone, taking the pleasure, never counting the cost – to herself or to anyone else. This was the end of innocence, of honour, and perhaps, finally, of the Kencyrath itself. Nothing was worth that.

All right, then, she thought, trying to force her chaotic thoughts into cool, logical patterns. *If you're not going to let yourself be seduced, then what?*

First option: kill the bastard.

She had tried that before, without success. Could she trust herself to strike the man now, to *kill* him? No. Not with a mere knife. Especially not with this damn poison slowing her reflexes, muddling her thoughts, yes, perhaps even her loyalties.

Second option: run away.

That too she had tried and bought herself several years of freedom before coming back full circle to this threshold. This time, however, the venom in her blood trapped her in this place, at this time.

Third option:...

Her mind scrambled for it, stumbling over half-formed ideas, groping for a solution that refused to take shape. Only one thought remained brutally clear: If she went through those ribbons now, she would be lost forever, knowing the evil she did, welcoming it.

Damnit, it wasn't fair! She hadn't asked to be dealt into this game, much less born into it. Think of all the lives it had shattered over the past three millennia, all the honour and joy lost; and if the Master finally won, so did Perimal Darkling. How did the old song go? *Alas for the greed of a man and the deceit of a woman, what we should come to this!* Gerridon's greed, the Dream-Weaver's deceit, or rather her willful ignorance that had brought her to such shame. And she was Jame's mother? She thought Tirandys had said so, but that wasn't an idea she felt strong enough to cope with just now. No, better to think of her only as someone else whom Gerridon had used, just as he wanted to use her now. Well, she wouldn't let him, not while a single option remained. But what options were left? Sit here until she turned blue? Find a good book to read? Take up knitting snake cozies?

'Oh hell,' said Jame, and put her head in her hands.

The poison's grip was tightening. Soon there wouldn't be a coherent thought in her mind, probably just about the time the Master got tired of waiting and came to look for her. A fine mess she had made of everything, as usual. Tirandys was right: She should never have been born. But perhaps he was also right about the next best solution.

A stillness came over Jame, as if for a moment her heart forgot to beat. Yes, of course. The final option. It had been there all the time, waiting for her to recognise it.

Your choice, Jamethiel.

In Tai-tastigon, she had chosen to take responsibility for her own actions, whatever the cost. In the Ebonbane she had chosen the pit rather than see Marc fight an Arrin-ken in her defence. Perhaps it wasn't her fault that she had originally been given a role in Gerridon's game; but if she went on, she might soon become responsible for deeds so terrible that nothing would atone for them. Best not to take the chance.

She leant back against the wall. Poison might flow in her veins, but it was life pounding there that she felt now. How much she had wanted to accomplish with it. So much to do, so much to see; yes, and so many mistakes yet to make – great, thumping big ones, if the past was any guide. Oh well. One couldn't have everything. She didn't have a mountain crevasse or another cup of venom, but what she did have was even better.

Jame looked at the white knife. Her fingers were numb from

504

gripping it, and her hand had begun to shake. But it was very sharp. It would do. She raised it and laid its keen edge carefully against her bare throat.

'I don't like the looks of this,' said Ardeth.

He gently wiped Torisen's forehead with a piece of silk scarcely whiter than the Highlord's face. Torisen lay motionless. One had to look carefully to see that he still breathed at all.

'For a moment, I thought he would wake up,' said Burr in a husky voice.

'He came close,' growled the Wolver. He padded over and sniffed at his friend. 'Now, this is bad, very bad.'

'I think,' said Ardeth, 'that you might try your hand at this, Kindrie. After all, you *are* a healer.'

The Shanir had withdrawn to the far corner of the tent out of the light, out of the circle of friends around the cot. 'You need a fully trained healer for this,' he said in a stifled voice. 'I'm not qualified.'

Burr turned on him. 'You helped that boy in the fire-timber hall at Tentir.'

'That was only first-aid.'

'You drew hemlock out of that glass of wine,' murmured Ardeth.

'That was only wine. My God! You don't know what's involved in deep healing. You have no idea how far into his very soul I might have to go and, more to the point, neither do I. My lord, listen! He can't even stand the sight of me! What if I get lost in there? What if his being and mine become so intertwined that we can never be separated? What will *that* do to his sanity?'

'Lord, I could go for another healer,' said Burr. 'Lord Brandan has one who could be trusted...'

'That would be too late.' Ardeth's tone, quiet as it was, made them all turn sharply towards him. 'I really think, Kindrie, that you should try something. We're losing him.'

The Shanir stood stock still for a moment, then thrust both hands into his white hair. 'All right,' he said through the bars of his thin forearms. 'All right.' He stood there a moment more, collecting himself, then dropped his hands. 'Where is the child?'

The others looked in surprise at white faced Donkerri, but Burr immediately went to a pile of clothing and drew out from under it the saddlebag full of bones. He put it on the table. Ardeth started when he saw the child's shadow cast on the tent beside the shadow of Torisen's head. The Wolver growled.

'You bring death to the dying, healer?'

'I'll do whatever I think will help,' snapped Kindrie, pushing the shaggy man aside and taking Ardeth's place on the edge of the cot. 'She helped me find him once. Perhaps she will again.'

There. Everything was set. Kindrie reached out to touch the Highlord's face, and hesitated.

For each act of deep healing, the healer had to reach down to the very roots of his patient's being. At that level, it was possible to do much good, but even greater harm. The safest way was to discover what metaphor each patient was currently using, consciously or unconsciously, for his own soul. For those concerned with growing things, for example, the botanical image of root and branch often worked very well. On the other hand, scrollsmen could often be reached through the metaphor of a book, which must first be unlocked and then deciphered. Hunts, battles, and riddles were other common metaphors. Once the healer sensed which one to use, he could deal with his patient's illness or injury through it in a way that was at least compatible with the other's basic nature. Kindrie had only done this before in practice. He had the innate power – almost too much of it, one instructor had sourly remarked after Kindrie had accidentally almost reanimated the man's sheepskin coat – but the thought of dealing so intimately with Torisen almost paralysed him.

'Well?' said Ardeth, with an undernote of growing urgency.

Kindrie took a deep breath. *Relax*, he told himself. *Torisen can't hate you any more than he already does*. He rested the tips of his long sensitive fingers on the Highlord's eyelids.

A blurred image began to form in his mind: black hills, a sullen sky veined with green lightning. Wind blew, carrying a faint, sweet smell, as if of something long dead. Weeds rattled. Something dark loomed over him. More lightning, briefly illuminating the windowless façade of an enormous house. An archway opened into the dark interior.

Was this a soul-metaphor, or something else? Kindrie had never used one like it before, and somehow it didn't feel right for the Highlord either. Then too, everything was so indistinct. He had probably wandered into the hinterlands of Torisen's nightmare. Damn. Dreams were tricky things, far less stable than some metaphor under the healer's control. Standing on the threshold peering in, Kindrie was haunted by the feeling that this bleak, blasted dwelling had no roots even in Torisen's

506

dream consciousness. It was as if they both had simply stumbled on this nightmare place, here, in the dark of the Highlord's sleep.

Kindrie hesitated. It could be dangerous to meddle at all with something like this. On the other hand, how much worse could things get? More lightning, and a small shadow slipped past him into the house. Well, that settled it. He followed.

Inside, dim corridors, cavernous rooms, decay. Whenever Kindrie tried to focus on anything, it immediately blurred almost out of recognition. It wasn't just his poor dream-vision this time either: he felt subtly out of phase with all his surroundings, as if he didn't quite share the same plain of reality with them. Ancestors be praised that he could still see the child's shadow, however faintly... and now he had something else to guide him as well. It registered on his half-trained senses as both a smell and a taste, sharp and metallic. So there was poison here after all. He sensed it faintly all around him, but the farther in he got, the stronger his impression of it became, until he felt as if he were sucking on a copper coin crusted with verdigris. Down interminable corridors, across a great hall lined with what looked like the blur of many faces, up a stair.

An indistinct figure sat on the steps above him on what appeared to be a knot of writhing shadows. It held something white. He had a strong sense that, like the house, it had another existence elsewhere. Everything here, in fact, seemed to be only the shadow of some other reality cast on Torisen's sleeping mind – but if so, that shadow was killing him, for here was the poison's primary source.

Now, what on earth could he do about it?

Kindrie crouched before the ghostlike figure. He didn't think it could see him at all. He could see that it was raising that white object, very, very slowly. Dark hair, grey eyes with a silver sheen – it might almost have been Torisen himself seen through a heavy mist, but with some indefinable difference. The white object was almost at its throat now. The eyes closed. On impulse, Kindrie reached out and touched the shadowy lids...

... and again saw a mental image of the House. This time it was a true soul-metaphor, but not Torisen's. Kindrie's next move should have been to repair whatever damage this architectural soul image had sustained, but he could barely focus on it because of the shifting levels of dream and reality that separated him from it.

Kindrie felt panic rise in him. Ardeth had been wrong to insist that he try this. He *wasn't* qualified, and despite the slower temporal flow on this level, time was running out. He could feel it. Torisen would die unless he did something quickly, but what? There was the trick he had used to draw the poison out of Ardeth's wine, but that technique was intended only for use on inanimate objects with neither life nor sanity to lose. No matter. He simply couldn't think of anything else.

But it didn't work quite as Kindrie had intended. When he extended his power to exclude the venom from its victim's blood, the venom resisted. When he tried even harder, it struck back. Too late, Kindrie realised he was dealing with a parasitic poison whose active principle was psychic rather than physical; it took a dim view of being forcibly evicted just when it was getting comfortable. But it would move if necessary, especially when another host so conveniently offered itself.

Kindrie felt the venom surge into him through his fingertips. Too late to raise any barriers. Too late even to draw his hands away. Numbness spread up his arms. He should have been thinking of a way to counteract this latest disaster, but all that ran through his mind like some idiot's chant was

Never say things can't get worse
Never say things can't get worse...

Then he saw that the serpentine shadows upon which the other sat had reared up to twine themselves about his arms. Kindrie didn't like snakes. These, however, he could barely see and could not feel at all, at first. Then the numbness began to recede, leaving in its wake sharp, stinging pain. His arms felt as if they had been stuck full of needles. In fact, the snakes had sunk their fangs into them. Just as he came to this not altogether welcome conclusion, the shadowy forms uncoiled themselves and tumbled back to the floor. Kindrie sprang backward. His arms were covered with punctures just beginning to bleed, but the venom was gone. The snakes had sucked it all up. The coppery taste in his mouth faded. By God, he had drawn the poison to a reachable level, and they had got rid of it entirely.

But now everything was beginning to fade. Of course. With the venom gone, Torisen was beginning to wake up, and here Kindrie was, still fathoms deep in the other's mind.

Never say things can't get worse
Never say...

He could see through the steps underfoot. Somewhere, the real stairs were probably still solid enough; this was only their dream image, and the dream was dissolving. The house began to open up beneath him, walls and ceilings fading like mist in the sun. Beside him was the child's shadow. It darted down the stairs and back, down and back. He could almost feel small, phantom hands tugging at him.

You big dummy, run, run!

He ran. Down the steps, across the great hall, into the labyrinth corridors. The shadow cut through dissolving walls now, and he followed, almost seeing the slight Kendar child who ran ahead of him. The dead know so much, and they never tire. Kindrie was very tired. He had never been strong in anything but his half-controlled healing powers, and now even they were too spent to help him. His breath burned in his chest. Sweat half blinded him. He couldn't see the child's shadow now at all, but a small hand gripped his, urging him on. A dark opening ahead. The front door. He pitched through it headfirst...

... onto the floor of the tent.

Someone was holding him. Strong, steady hands. Burr, probably. Voices ran together around him.

'... all right!'

'Trinity, look at his arms.'

'Tori, my boy, wake up, wake up...'

That last was Ardeth. Kindrie tried to focus on the cot and saw the old lord bending over Torisen. The Highlord's eyes flickered open.

'Dreams,' he said indistinctly. 'Everyone has them.' Then, more clearly, 'Adric, you look awful. Get some rest.' His voice faded again, and his eyes closed. He began to breathe with the deep, slow respiration of *dwar* sleep. Ardeth pulled the blanket up and sat back with a weary sigh.

'Lord, is he all right?' Burr asked anxiously.

'Yes, now.'

'Good,' said Kindrie, and fainted.

Jame woke on the stair, dazed. Overhead was naked sky seen through charred roof-beams. Sullen clouds scudded across it. Lightning flashed in the belly of one, tinging it with sulphurous green. Thunder snarled. Of course, Jame thought numbly. The last time she had been here, years ago, she had left the place in flames, hence no roof. But what was she doing here now? She groped for the memory and caught scraps of it. God's teeth and toenails, what a nightmare. Why, she had been about to... to...

The white knife was still in her hand, numbing her fingers. She dropped it with a gasp. The snakes dodged the falling blade and hissed at it as it vibrated on the step beside her, its point wedged in a crack. Sweet Trinity.

More of the poison nightmare came back to her, and then, with a rush, all of it – but it had been no dream. What in Perimal's name had happened? She should be dead or dying now with these wretched snakes lapping up her blood. Instead, here she was, not only alive but apparently healthy. And the Master?

At the head of the stairs was the doorway, its post and lintel scorched. Two or three singed ribbons fluttered from it. They might have been red as tradition decreed, but in this light they looked black. And beyond? She rose and climbed warily. Another lightning flash, and she saw the room. Its far wall still stood – tall broken windows looking out into darkness – but both the roof and the floor were gone except for the stub of a ledge just beyond the door and a few scorched beams groping out over the void.

Footprints disturbed the ashes on the ledge. Someone *had* stood just beyond the ribbons, waiting. Gerridon. It had to be. *Nothing new ever happens in the past*, Jame remembered, staring at those prints. He had come forward in time to get at her, whatever her poisoned senses had told her. If she had crossed the threshold this time, with her mind and motives as confused by the drug as they had been, she would indeed have been lost. Instead, she had chosen the knife; and suddenly, miraculously, been cured. For a moment, she was almost tempted to think that the second aspect of her despised god – Argentiel, That-Which-Preserves – had finally deigned to show his hand, but that hardly seemed likely. In her experience, the best one could hope for from the Three-Faced God was to be left alone.

At least Perimal Darkling in the form of Gerridon had also left her. As lightning flickered again, she saw faint ashy traces of his footsteps going down the stair from the door, fading away before they came to the step where she had sat. Thwarted, he had gone back into the fabric of the House, into the blighted past, which was preferable to its desolate present. Tirandys had said that he still had a few souls left to gnaw on, probably including Bender's. How long before he ran out, before hunger drove him either to try for her again or to accept the tainted gifts that would cost him his remaining humanity? She had no idea. Gerridon had made his pact with darkness and was living to learn its price. He had bred her to serve his need, but found that while he could tempt, only she could damn herself. Very well. That was the game, and those were the rules. They would see who won in the end.

But in the meantime, Gerridon had made his next move by withdrawing. How should she respond to that? Follow? Trinity, no, not even if she could. She had no idea what Shanir powers he still possessed, and no desire to find out. Retreat to Karkinaroth? Fine, if she could find the way and if it hadn't tumbled down yet. Graykin and Marc should already have left to warn her brother about the changer Tirandys, taking Kin-Slayer, Lyra, and Jorin with them. The ring and the Book Bound in Pale Leather were still here in Perimal Darkling. She hated to abandon either, but had no idea where to look for them – or did she? For the ring, no, but the Book...

Jame snatched up the knife and ran down the steps. The stairway spiralled down through a series of chambers, all once part of the Master's living quarters. She had barely noticed any of them on the way up. Here, however, was one that she remembered well from former days. She entered.

Shelves stretched up almost out of sight on all sides and wandered off into the murky distance. Books lined them, some charred, some half-devoured with luminous mildew, all crumbling. The smell made Jame sneeze.

This was where someone (Bender?) had taught her in secret how to read the runes, both common and Master. Knowledge is power. Gerridon would not have approved if he had known. This was also where she had first encountered the Book Bound in Pale Leather, and here she had fled in search of it while the flames from the brazier she had accidentally upset spread through the upper chambers. The Book had helped her to escape by ripping a hole through to the next threshold world. As far as Jame could remember, she had had to jump out the window to take advantage of that dimensional portal, or perhaps she had simply fallen through it. The latter seemed more in character. Also, she was pretty sure that she had landed on her head.

One more turn, and there was the window through which she

had tumbled, still broken. Black hills rolled away beyond it under a lightning veined sky. Before it on a table, as she had half expected, lay something pale. It was the Book. Ganth's ring lay on it, and beneath the table in a dark huddle was her knapsack.

Kin-Slayer had been left in the armoury where it had been reforged. What better place to put the Book Bound in Pale Leather than back in the library? Jame thought she saw Tirandys's hand in this. The Master had undoubtedly told him to secure both objects, and after doing so, the changer had simply put each where it belonged. Who found them first, Gerridon or Jame, was another matter. The fact that the ring and knapsack were here too made her suspect that Tirandys had also wanted her to have them back if she survived to come looking for them. At any rate, they were in her hands now, and Gerridon was out of luck again.

So, of all the various lost items she had come in search of here, that left only the Prince. Poor Odalian, chained in the back rooms of the House among all the horrors of the Kencyrath's fallen past.

She knelt and began to rummage determinedly through her knapsack. Oh, good. Here were all her surviving Tastigon clothes, the Peshtar boots, and even the *imu* medallion. At least she wouldn't arrive back on Rathillien dressed like something out of a travelling show. She let the serpent-skin cloak slip to the floor, then hesitated. It wasn't often that she thought of mirrors, but for a moment she did wish she could see herself. This shadow dancer's costume made her feel so . . . so . . . no, forget it. That belonged to another life. She hastily stripped off and picked up the familiar street fighter's *d'hen*.

Dally's *d'hen*. Jame stood there for a moment looking at the jacket, remembering the dead friend who had given it to her. He had been in love with the Kencyr glamour too, perhaps fatally so.

She put on the coat, then her pants and boots, fumbling a bit because her right hand was still rather numb. Odd that the knife should have had such an effect, especially since she didn't remember gripping it all that tightly. Jame disliked knives in general and this one more than most, but at least it was a weapon. She slipped it into her boot sheath. Now, twist her hair up under her cap, pack up the Book, put on the ring with a glove over it to keep it in place, pocket the medallion and . . . where was that blasted cloak? Halfway out the door, bent on a slithery escape. Jame caught it and put it on again, with some distaste, over the pack. Reduced to a set of matched snakes for company. Oh well. At least they were alive, and she felt in need of companionship where she was bound now.

Perhaps it was because she hadn't been able to save Dally; perhaps, because the shadows still drew her more than she cared to admit; but Jame found she had no intention of leaving this place without Odalian.

The trip back through the House to where Tirandys had found her seemed both long and short. Back in Rathillien, who knew how many days had passed by now? Perhaps her brother's fate had long since been decided. Perhaps Rathillien itself had fallen into the dark of the moon – some twelve nights distant when she had gone into the shadows of Karkinaroth – and had never emerged from it again. The Kencyrath's millennia-long battle might have been lost while she stumbled on here in ignorance. She certainly felt ignorant. The more she learned about herself, about the nature of things in general, the less she seemed to know. 'Honour,' Tirandys had said. 'I used to be as sure as you that I knew what it was.' Now Jame wondered if, in fact, she had ever known. The concept was too big, too abstract, like 'good' and 'evil.' Perhaps all one could do was stumble on in ignorance, in shadows, making one decision at a time in the best faith one could manage, hoping for the best.

Jame certainly hoped for the best now. Before her was the archway shaped like a' mouth, and beyond, the shifting green light. She took a deep breath and crossed the threshold, keeping a wary eye on the window. The vines outside rustled, and the pale, lip-shaped flowers kissed the bars, but when she edged into the room, the serpent heads rose with a hiss, and the flowers retreated, pouting. Jame went on.

Since her goal was the farthest rooms down the Chain of Creation, she tried to follow the outer wall of the House. It wouldn't do to wander off and lose herself in any of the threshold worlds that the House spanned. But the outer wall hardly ran straight and was frequently windowless. She could often only tell that she was making progress by the changing character of the rooms through which she passed.

Then too, the changes were often subtle. Jame realised this when she came across one of the three Karkinoran guards Tirandys had sent in after Bender. The man had apparently got this far back and then made the mistake of sitting down to rest.

He seemed oddly sunken into the chair. It was, in fact, consuming him. He watched Jame edge past with glazed eyes in which no humanity remained.

Then came a series of moss-mottled floors, treacherous under foot. The paving stones here felt not only slippery but unstable, as if they might suddenly tip like blocks on an ice floe.

Beyond were walls covered with what looked like murals. In one of them, the second guard fled from something with many eyes across a darkling plain. On closer examination, the picture broke down into different colours of lichen on the stone wall; but when Jame looked back at it from the doorway, the gap between pursued and pursuer had narrowed.

There were occasional windows, some barred, others not. Each one looked out on another threshold world deeper inside the coils of Perimal Darkling, worlds on which the Kencyrath had once lived and fought. The scrollsmen had songs about all of them, from green Lury to golden Krakilleth, and Ch'un, where the very stones sang; but not one world was recognisable now. All lay under shadow's eaves. All had begun the slide towards the ultimate interpenetration of animate and inanimate, of life and death, that was the essence of Perimal Darkling. Nonetheless, many of these worlds still seemed to be inhibited. Jame caught glimpses out of windows of strange figures moving across distant landscapes or wheeling against alien skies. Nearer at hand, jewel winged insects the size of her fist crawled on a window ledge and raised tiny, shrivelled faces to stare as she passed. One of them had features strangely like the third guard's. It flew after her, crying something in a piping thread of a voice, but the snakes snapped it out of the air and tore it to pieces at her heels. The farther in she went, the stranger and more terrible the 'life' forms became, but not all of them were limited to one world or one suite of rooms. By breaking down the barriers, Gerridon had laid the Chain of Creation open practically from one end to the other.

All that remained was to break down the final barrier between Perimal Darkling and Rathillien. Soft areas like the Haunted Lands might serve, but how much more devastating it would be if the Master could create a breech linked directly with the House and this corridor opening into all the fallen worlds – Trinity, just as Tirandys had done in the palace of Karkinaroth. The priests should have prevented that. Gerridon must have ordered the changer to confine them to their temple so that they could still manage it but not interfere with his plans.

But the priests weren't managing. They were apparently dead or dying, and the temple in consequence was rapidly going out of control.

'Of course!' said Jame out loud and hit the ledge of the window out of which she had been blindly staring.

If the temple went, so would both the palace and Gerridon's primary beachhead on Rathillien. Tirandys must know that. In fact, he had probably arranged it by sealing the priests in without adequate provisions. Such an act might well come within the scope of his orders if Gerridon hadn't been any more explicit than when he had told the changer to put venom in Jame's wine. So Tirandys had again honoured his bitter code of obedience and at the same time had done what he could to bring about the downfall of the lord who had betrayed him. Oh, Senethari, clever, unhappy man. Who would ever have dreamed that the paradox of honour could have so many sides?

But if the temple destroyed itself and the palace while she was still here in the shadows, she might never get back to Rathillien. Time to move on. Outside lay a dark, glistening landscape that looked and smelled like raw, spoilt liver. The window ledge had begun to bleed where she had hit it. Clearly, she must be very far into Perimal Darkling. God help her if she had to go much farther.

Somewhere nearby, someone moaned.

Jame moved towards the sound. It came again – low, hoarse, urgent. Something crawled on the floor in the shadows ahead. There seemed to be a tangle of half-seen shapes there, slowly writhing.

'Ahhh...!' sighed an all too familiar voice in the darkness. Feral eyes gleamed. 'Your... turn... Jamethiel?'

Jame went back a step, throat suddenly dry. 'No, Keral. Not yet. Where is Odalian?'

'The little prince? Stopped crying, has he? Heh! Mother's boy. Doesn't know how to... enjoy... ah! ah! ah!' Pain and pleasure wove through the changer's panting voice. The shadowy mound heaved. 'Ooohhh...! And again, and again, and again... You're still there? Come here or go away.'

'The Prince?'

'Oh, that way.' She could barely see the doorway he indicated. As she passed hastily through it, his voice came after her. 'I'll have my turn with you eventually, Jamethiel. We all will.'

The room beyond was even darker. A pale form lay

spreadeagled on the floor, surrounded by tittering shadows that poked teasingly at it. It stirred and groaned. Jame drove back the shadows and knelt beside it. Fair hair matted with sweat, a blanched young face, puffy with tears . . .

'Odalian? Your Highness?'

His brown eyes opened, glazed at first, then widening with horror as he focused on her. 'No.' He tried to twist away, but his bonds held him. 'No, no, no . . .!'

What in Perimal's name! Ah, Tirandys had tricked the young man into the blood rites while wearing her twin brother's face.

'Hush.' She tried to touch his cheek, but couldn't feel anything there. Trinity, now what? 'Hush,' she said again as he still flinched away. 'I'm not Torisen or the changer. I'm a friend. I've come to take you home.'

He repeated the word silently, first in disbelief, then again in wonder, and burst into tears.

She could just barely see him in the gloom, but as far as her sense of touch went, he wasn't there at all, just as with Graykin earlier. Ah. She had been in Perimal Darkling ten days longer than Graykin, but the Prince had been a prisoner here at least sixteen days longer than she, and in farther rooms. She reached for the chains that held him down and touched cold metal. Good. They at least were within her grasp.

Around them, shadows rustled, crept forward. Jame felt the cloak move on her shoulders. Then snakes fanned themselves out over both her and the supine prince. Their heads rose in a weaving, hissing fence that struck at every shadowy form that edged too close. Under their cover, Jame picked the locks that held Odalian down.

When she helped him to rise, she found to her surprise that now she could almost feel something. He seemed to be taking on a shaky solidity that grew as she concentrated on it. Was she bringing him forward in time or going back to meet him? Tirandys hadn't said what the trick of time travel was here in the House, only that she had been too young before to learn it. Well, maybe now she was old enough, if just barely.

Complicating matters in escaping was the House itself, which apparently didn't want to let them go. They were followed from room to room by creeping forms and booming inhuman voices calling urgently to each other in remote chambers. The snakes hissed and snapped. Their knotted tails tightened uncomfortably around Jame's neck. They crossed the slippery stones with difficulty and bypassed an empty, inviting chair. Here was the barred window, beyond, the arch. Then through the outer rooms of the House back to the Great Hall.

Jame had long since figured out that it had been stupid of her not to check the door into the palace from this side. Such portals might not be visible from all angles, but they didn't usually just disappear, lock, stock and keyhole. Luckily, this one hadn't either. She and the Prince stumbled through into the palace hall beyond.

Things obviously were not well in Karkinaroth. Tremors ran continually through the floor, and cracks climbed the walls. At the end of the hall, a chandelier swung uneasily, tinkling. Fragments of crystal rained down through a cloud of plaster dust.

Abruptly, the serpent tails relaxed their hold, and the cloak tumbled to the floor with a meaty thump. The snakes hastily sorted themselves out and whipped back into the shadowy corridor, heads stretched out with urgency, long black bodies all moving with the same undulant ripple. Jame started to go after them, but just as they whisked back through the door into the Master's Great Hall, the floor shook again, and the door vanished along with all other shadowy traces of Perimal Darkling. So much for Master Gerridon's new beachhead on Rathillien.

Odalian gave a cry. Chunks of plaster fell around them, and then the roof beams came down with a crash. For a moment, Jame couldn't see anything. Since she couldn't feel anything either, she rather assumed she was dead; but then the dust began to clear. They were standing up to their waists in a pile of rubble. The debris had fallen straight through them as if they weren't there.

Wonderful, thought Jame. *More complications.*

She hauled the Prince clear, feeling the wreckage drag at them more with each step. At least they seemed to be readjusting. The next piece of plaster to fall hit her shoulder with a painful thump, fair warning not to stand under any more collapsing architecture. She was also beginning to get a more secure grip on Odalian. The chill of his flesh stuck her even through her thick *d'hen*. She stripped off the jacket and draped it over his bare, trembling shoulders, despite his feeble protests.

'Look,' she said impatiently, 'when I want you to die on my hands, I'll let you know.'

He gave her a shy, sidelong look. 'You're very strong, aren't you?'

That startled her. 'Trinity, no, I'm just too stupid to give up.'

He shook his head, haunted eyes focused on something far away or deep inside. 'I've never been strong.'

'Oh, be quiet. You've done all right so far.'

They stumbled on through the quaking palace. Plaster powdered their shoulders and made them sneeze. Hangings rippled on the walls, tapestried princes trying to ride to safety. In distant rooms, mirrors shattered. Jame didn't know which door Marc had (she hoped) broken open to let everyone out. The best she could do, she decided, was to get Odalian to Lyra's quarters and hope the roof didn't fall in on them again on the way.

Rather to her surprise, it didn't, but she was even more amazed when Lyra herself came running out of the inner room to meet them as they staggered into the suite. They put Odalian on a couch and piled every blanket they could find on top of him as well as half the wall hangings. Then Jame turned on the young Highborn.

'Why in Perimal's name are you still here? Didn't Graykin – er, Gricki – tell you to get out?'

'Oh, yes.' Lyra fussed around the couch. 'But I couldn't leave without my prince, could I? Anyway, that huge Kendar said if Odalian could be found at all, you'd probably be too stubborn to come back without him.'

'Marc?' He's been here?'

At that moment, the hall door opened and a golden streak shot across the room. Jame went over backward with a grunt as Jorin barrelled into her and then pranced up the length of her fallen body in an ecstasy of excitement. She sat up and hugged the ounce while he rubbed his cheek against hers, purring thunderously.

'I'd say offhand that he missed you,' said Marc from the doorway.

Jame sprang up and hugged him too. The big Kendar started to respond, then checked himself. His restraint surprised Jame. She tried to ignore it.

'But where were you two?' she demanded. 'I've been looking in the most ungodly places for you!'

'Oh, we've been in some strange parts, too, but I'll tell you about that later. We've just been scouting the area around the temple. The walls are starting to collapse down there, and the destruction is spreading. I'd suggest, my lord and ladies, that we leave.'

518

Ladies. Jame felt the word go through her like a cold wind. 'Graykin did find you,' she said numbly. 'He told you who I am.'

Marc gave her a sober look. 'Yes... my lady.'

Just then, Odalian began to laugh. It was a terrible sound, edged with jagged hysteria.

'Don't!' Lyra was saying. 'Oh, please, don't, don't...!'

The Prince had seized one of his own fingers and was tugging at it. It stretched, long and thin as a worm. 'Just like pulling taffy! Just like...' He burst into another horrible laugh.

Oh God, Jame thought. She hadn't got to him in time. The shadows of the House were in his blood and soul now. He had become a changer.

Odalian began to thrash about on the couch, getting more and more tangled up in the blankets. Jame darted over to help Lyra hold him down. He seized the knife from her boot. The next moment, Marc had swept both girls aside and was kneeling by the couch with the Prince half off it, holding the young man's wrists in a gentle, unbreakable grip.

'There, my lad, softly, softly...'

Odalian stopped struggling and dropped the knife. It scratched his arm as it fell. His face turned white.

'Sorry,' he whispered. 'I never was very strong.'

Then he shuddered violently and went limp.

Lyra gave a shriek. 'He's dead! Oh, I know he's dead!'

'Fainted, more likely.' Marc lifted Odalian back onto the couch. 'A good thing too, poor boy.'

But Lyra was right.

'I don't understand it.' The Kendar stopped trying to find a pulse and sat back, bewildered. 'Trinity knows, I've seen more than a few people die in my time, and in some pretty strange ways, but never quite like this. I'd say that peculiar knife was to blame, but it barely touched him.'

Jame had scooped up the white knife and was staring at it. She began to swear softly, passionately. All her life, she had known about the three great objects of power lost when Gerridon fell. One of them – the Book Bound in Pale Leather – had actually been in her possession for at least two years now. You'd think that that would have made her realise these objects weren't purely mythical. But up to an hour ago, she had been wearing the Serpent-Skin Coat, giver of life, without once recognising it for what it was; and now here was the Ivory Knife, the very tooth of death and the original of every white-hilted suicide knife in the Kencyrath, whose slightest scratch was fatal.

She hadn't had it when she climbed to the Master's bed and ended up cutting off his hand. This time Bender had taken no chances. This time, she could have had Gerridon's life.

While all this was going through Jame's mind, Marc was looking from her to Lyra and back again, somewhat at a loss. Here was Caineron's daughter, settling down to serious hysterics, and the Highlord's sister, quietly exercising a vocabulary the scope of which amazed him. But he also heard something else: a series of rumbling crashes, coming closer. The floor trembled underfoot.

Jame had heard it too and broke off in mid-curse. 'Old lad, you were right: time to scamper.'

'Just a minute.' The Kendar composed Odalian's body and drew a gold-figured hanging over it. Then he took several brands from the fire and thrust them under the couch. Flames began to lick at the bullion fringe. 'Now we're ready.'

Out in the hall, they could see the walls farther down caving in. The palace was collapsing in on itself. The power set loose by the crumbling temple spread both outward like ripples and inward, drawing everything to it. It made Jame's scalp prickle and Jorin's fur stand on end. She had prevented something like this at her god's temple in Tai-tastigon by dancing the rampant power into new channels, but it was too late for that here. Walls sagged and beams crashed down. Plaster dust choked and blinded them. Marc went first, carrying Lyra. Jame followed, hanging onto his jacket with one hand and Jorin with the other.

Here at last was a door, its bolt lock shattered. The big Kendar thrust it open, and they staggered out into a warm, starlit night. Below lay the city of Karkinaroth, sparkling with lights, and beyond that, the midnight plain, now empty, where the army had gathered. There was no sign of the moon. The Dark had fallen.

Behind them, the palace groaned. Deepening cracks laced its high, outer walls. They began to collapse inward slowly, as if in a dream. Towers tumbled. Pinnacles broke and fell, streaming golden banners. The whole vast structure seemed to crouch, lower, lower, drawing in on itself, filling every internal space with rubble and shattered treasures. The rumble went on and on, in the air, in the ground, in one's bones, until at last it slowly died out of each in turn.

Silence.

Then below in the city, shouting began and the howl of dogs.

28

Gathering Forces
Hurlen: 29th of Winter

The Host came within sight of Hurlen on the twenty-ninth in the early afternoon. Torisen reined in. The River Road dipped sharply here. To the left was the Silver; to the right, a series of natural stone ledges called the Upper Hurdles, which cut across the top of the Upper Meadow to the woods some two miles beyond. The citizens of Hurlen usually grazed their sheep here, but not one white back broke the green expanse now. Cloud shadows chased sunlight over the sward down to Hurlen, perched on its cluster of islands where the River Tardy rushed into the Silver. On Grand Hurlen, the nearest island, stone spires showed white, then grey under the shifting light. Opposite it on the far bank rose another, much larger city, this time of brightly hued tents.

'So the Prince made it after all,' Torisen said to Harn. 'How many troops, d'you think?'

Harn peered down the slope, shading his eyes. 'Nine, maybe ten thousand. Not bad considering Karkinor has no standing army. Still, we'll see how long this lot stands when thing get lively. Amateurs. Huh.'

They rode on with the Host behind them. Here the river bent sharply to the east and swerved back a mile later to rejoin the road. Downstream, where the Silver narrowed slightly, ferries waited on either bank, linked by cables to huge winches. Powerful draft horses also waited in harness, swishing at flies, to set the winches in motion. Hurlen derived its modest prosperity as a sort of dispatching centre for goods coming down the Tardy from Karkinor bound either north or south on the River Road. Soon, the ferrymen would be busy carrying the Karkinoran army fifty at a time over to the west bank battlefield and undoubtedly making more money in a day than they usually did in half a year. War was proving good business for Hurlen.

Just beyond the ferries, where the Silver met the Tardy, the water broadened almost into a lake studded with about thirty islands, ranging in size from Grand Hurlen to rocks barely ten feet across. All of them had been hollowed out millennia ago, perhaps to serve as dwellings for some long-forgotten religious order. The work was far cruder than that of the Builders, and much older. Later generations had built up the walls, first with stone blocks, then with wood. Stone bridges connected the lower stories. Two of them also extended to about fifty feet of each bank, ending in wooden drawbridges. The wooden spires rising above the islands' masonry were laced together with catwalks. Laundry fluttered like bright banners from them.

The Host pitched camp in the Upper Meadow opposite the city. The Highlord's tent was barely up before Burr began pressing Torisen to rest. For this solicitude, he got a ringing snub. It was five days since the near-fatal crisis, not that Torisen realised (on a conscious level, at least) that it had been so serious. In fact, he remembered very little of it and, for once, virtually nothing about his dreams. Mostly, he tried to forget the whole thing. It was enough for him that his leg no longer hurt and that he felt blessedly sane again, if physically a bit fragile.

Because he wanted to forget, it irritated him that Burr, Ardeth, and the Wolver had all been watching him so closely these past few days. Even Kindrie had been hovering just on the edge of his notice, looking so washed-out that on a sudden impulse Torisen had ridden over to demand if *he* felt all right. That, to a Shanir. It was all very strange.

Here was Burr again, mulishly offering a posset.

'You know I hate that stuff,' Torisen snapped.

'Just the same, my lord.'

Torisen looked at the cup of wine-curdled milk, at his servant's scarcely sweeter expression, and suddenly laughed. 'All right, Burr, all right. I've been rude enough for one day.'

Just then, a guard appeared at the inner door to announce the approach of Prince Odalian. Torisen went to the outer most chamber of his tent to greet the Karkinoran ruler, reaching it just as Odalian entered. The Prince paused briefly in the shadow of the tent flap. Torisen also hesitated, suddenly tense without quite knowing why, but then forced himself to relax as the other stepped forward. Whatever impression he had received in that brief moment when shadow lay across Odalian's face, it didn't fit this slim young man with his diffident manner. They greeted each other formally and made polite conversation while messengers went to summon the rest of the High Council. The Prince congratulated Torisen again on his third year as Highlord. Torisen, rather cautiously, felicitated the Prince on gaining Caineron's daughter as a consort.

'If it's done anything to bring the Kencyrath and Karkinor closer together,' said Odalian, 'I'm glad. It has occurred to me, though, that a stronger connection might be even more beneficial to us both.'

Torisen agreed in principle, thinking that the Prince was probably just finding out how slight a claim he actually had on Caineron. 'What do you have in mind, Highness?'

'Well, my lord,' said the young man diffidently, 'I was rather thinking of subject ally status for my country.'

'But that would make you practically our vassal,' said Torisen, surprised.

'Would the council approve Karkinor as a full ally?'

'No. We've had rather bad luck with both subject and full allies. Some people blame my father's defeat in the White Hills on their treachery.' As he spoke, Torisen realised he wasn't too eager for any such connection himself, but that might just be Ganth's savage bitterness speaking. He made an effort to be open-minded.

Odalian had been thoughtfully sipping his wine. Now he looked up again as if just struck by an idea. 'What if the potential ally was to accept blood-binding?'

This time Torisen was really startled. 'Highness, that's a rite hardly ever practised these days even within the Kencyrath. Anyway, you need a Shanir blood-binder to do it properly. Otherwise, it's just a symbolic act. But if you were willing to undergo it,' he added, trying to be fair, 'it *might* impress the more traditional members of the High Council. Trinity knows what your own people would think of it, though. We'll wait and see. There's one great-granddad of a battle to win first.'

At that point, the rest of the Council began to arrive. Only Caineron had met the Prince before. He greeted him now with all the jovial condescension of a father-in-law, but as he stepped back, he looked momentarily puzzled. Something about Odalian's face, the colour of his eyes . . . no. Of course they had always been grey. Caineron prided himself on his good memory.

Burr was serving wine and cakes when Lord Danior burst

into the tent. The messenger hadn't found him in his camp because he had ridden ahead some three miles to the edge of the escarpment.

'The Horde is in sight!' he exclaimed. 'It's like . . . like a black carpet covering the plain, and the sky is black above it!'

Caineron started, spilling his wine. 'We must arm the camp!'

Danior gave him a scornful look. 'Oh, it probably won't get here until sometime tomorrow. Plenty of time – but oh, Tori, you should see it!'

Torisen had put down his posset, still untasted. 'I think we all should,' he said grimly.

It was a fair-sized group that rode out some ten minutes later. Each lord has his full war-guard with him now, ranging from Danior's ten to Caineron's fifty. Odalian's retinue had also joined the cavalcade, as well as twenty of Torisen's randons, all trying to look inconspicuous. Harn had apparently impressed on them that they were not to get in the Highlord's way for fear that even at this late date he would dismiss them out of hand.

The road ran along the river at the head of the Mendelin Steps, but they all rode down through the meadows. Torisen had come this way fairly often, travelling between the Southern Host and the Riverland, but he had never regarded this terrain before as a possible battlefield. Now he felt as if he were seeing it for the first time. Between the upper and middle meadows was another set of stone steps called, predictably, the Lower Hurdles. The lowest step was quite steep in some places, constituting nearly a six-foot drop. The middle field narrowed to a bottleneck at its southern end, hemmed in by the river and by woods.

The woods struck Torisen as rather odd. For one thing, even as they approached, the individual trees were hard to distinguish, as if mist obscured them. Also, rabbits startled by the horses jumped towards their cover only to stop at the last moment, as if they had run into a wall.

Beyond the bottleneck was a small lower meadow that ran almost to the stony edge of the escarpment. The Mendelin Steps began here, level with Eldest Island, which split the river into two channels. The much narrower western channel descended in two falls, the first about one hundred feet high. The second, at the edge of the escarpment, plummeted twice that far into a cauldron of seething water at the Cataracts' foot. The stairs followed in two steep flights, separated by a level stretch at the foot of the first cataract. The entire gorge was about one hundred and fifty feet wide, and the steps forty. Tears-of-Silver trees overhung it on both sides.

Beyond the trees, beyond even the second, higher falls, the escarpment jutted out in a stony promontory over the plain. The Wolver crouched at its edge, the wind ruffling his fur. Torisen dismounted and went out on the bare cliff head to stand beside him. The others followed.

The great southern plain spread out nearly three hundred feet beneath them. Close to the curving cliff wall to the left, where the Silver bent southeastward in its course, grass and trees were green. Farther out to the south, the yellow marks of drought began. Farther still, and yet frighteningly close, the ground turned black. The blackness was moving. It crept forward ever so slowly, like a stain, sometimes breaking into individual dots but mostly coming in a solid mass that was miles wide and stretched back out of sight. Storm clouds followed it. All the sky to the far southwest was as black as night but shot with sudden forked tongues of lightning. Back under the shadow of the storm, the darkness on the ground sparkled with a million torches. The faintest growl of thunder, like a muttered threat, reached them there on the cliff despite the Cataracts' roar.

'Now that,' said Brandan, 'is moderately impressive. So what do we do about it?'

'Go home?' the Wolver suggested, without looking up.

'Tempting, but not practical. I think you were right, Torisen: that lot out there is a knife levelled at our throats. Best to meet it here.'

'Yes, but what can we do?' Caineron sounded almost peevish. 'A fine thing to drag us all this far and then shove *that* in our faces.'

'As I see it,' said Torisen slowly, 'we have three chances to hold them...'

'On the stair,' said Danior.

'In the lower meadow,' said Korey of the Coman.

'At the first set of hurdles,' said Essien and Essiar together.

Torisen smiled at this eager chorus. 'Yes. If they get into the upper meadow, we'll probably be overrun. That, on the whole, would be unfortunate. Stepped, rubble-work barriers at the foot of each flight of stairs should help.'

'I'll see to it,' said Harn, and went off to do so.

Kirien had been staring out over the plain, frowning slightly.

'Yes, but how long can we hold them in any event? There are so many. Of course, none of this falls within the scope of my studies, but it seems to me that if they simply keep coming, in the end we're all the dog's dinner.'

'It would perhaps be better,' murmured Randir, without looking at her, 'if those without experience held their peace.'

Oho, thought Torisen, glancing at them sideways. *She's already got under her great-uncle's elegant skin, and he hasn't even realised yet that she isn't his grand-nephew.*

Ardeth had also been gazing out over the plain, wrapped in his own bleak thoughts. Now he turned to Randir. 'My dear Kenan, surely you would make some allowance for an intelligent comment even from a novice – or was it the intelligence of this one that upset you? The lad is quite right: we can only hold them so long. Our sole hope, it seems to me, is somehow to turn them back or even aside. This escarpment runs a good five hundred miles in either direction. If they turn west, that puts them on Krothen's doorstep or, even better, on the Karnides'; if southeast, there's Nekrien. Even if I were three million strong, I wouldn't care to tackle the Witch-King in his own mountains – or anywhere else, for that matter. But the big question remains; how do we turn them?'

'Kill so many that they give up,' said Danior.

'I doubt if the death of even a million would discourage them much,' said Torisen. 'Remember, the Horde is really a vast collection of tribes that have never done much before but chase and eat each other. If we knew what united them now, we could strike at that. I only hope we learn while fighting them, and learn in time.'

Odalian had half-started at these words, and Torisen caught the sudden movement. When he turned, however, the Prince only gave him a bland smile. 'These abstractions are rather beyond me. Perhaps, though, you would like to continue this discussion in the hospitality of my camp?'

'Go on ahead,' Torisen said to the others. 'I'll follow.'

They went, leaving the Highlord and the Wolver in silence on the windy cliff, looking out over the plain, while Torisen's war-guard waited at a tactful distance.

'You've never commanded a really big battle before, have you?' the Wolver said at last.

'One this big? Nobody has. But, of course, you're right. I was only a one-hundred commander at Urakarn. After that, things

526

were lively enough in the Southern Host, but we didn't tend towards pitched battles.' He sighed. 'It feels like a lifetime since we last sat in Krothen's guardroom, discussing the ethics of love and war.'

'This is different,' said the Wolver, still staring out. 'This is real.'

Torisen snorted. 'You're telling me.'

He half turned to leave, then paused, looking across at the island that split the Silver. The larger, higher cataract was beyond, filling the air with mist and thunder. The projecting cliff where he stood gave a glimpse of it, but even a better one of the island's head. Untold millennia ago, unknown hands had carved a giant face there. Its smooth forehead rose almost to the island's shaggy crown of trees. Its chin disappeared into the boiling cauldron of spray below. In all, it was more than three hundred feet high. Some claimed that the founders of Hurlen had been responsible for this too, that, in fact, it was the reason for Hurlen. Perhaps they had meant it to honour a king, perhaps a god. Ages of wind and water had left it characterless, ageless.

'Grimly, long ago, when we were talking about the Cataracts, you said that if we ever came this way together, you would show me something very old, very special.'

The Wolver growled. 'I must have been drunk.'

'You were. Very. I wouldn't remind you now except – well, you can see what we're up against. If there's anything about this terrain that will give us the slightest edge, I want to know about it.'

'I don't see how it can help.' He rose and shook himself. 'But all right.'

They went back the way they had come, with the Wolver trotting beside Storm and the war-guard trailing along behind. Torisen wasn't really surprised when he saw that they were headed for the woods. Storm went about a hundred feet under the overlocking boughs before halting, stiff-legged. The Wolver seized his bridle. He drew his thumb slowly down the length of the stallion's face, turning the sharp nail inward at the last minute to draw a drop of blood, which he flicked to the ground. Storm tossed his head, snorting with indignation.

'Do you have to do that to me, too?' Torisen asked.

'And send you into battle tomorrow with a bandaged nose? Burr would never forgive me.'

'You had better wait here,' Torisen said to his guard.

They looked perturbed.

'My lord,' said the oldest of them, 'if we let you out of our sight, Harn Grip-Hard will nail our ears to the nearest tree.'

'I think, on the whole, you had better wait.'

'Yes, my lord,' said the guard unhappily.

Torisen and the Wolver went farther in. It was an eerie place, full of leaf-filtered light and mist drifting between grey-trunked trees. Close as the Cataracts were, no sound of them penetrated here. Ferns dripped. Storm's hooves thudded on deep leaf mould. The bluff loomed ahead of them. Occasionally breaks in the leaf cover gave glimpses of its wooded heights. Ahead stood a bare Host tree. As they approached, a swarm of pale green leaves fluttered down through the mist, golden veins flashing, and settled on its naked boughs. Beyond, the bluff scooped inward, whether by art or nature it was hard to tell. The resulting hollow was about one hundred feet across at its lower end and somewhat deeper than that. It had rather the shape of an egg with the opening at its smaller upper end. Ferns covered its floor. Mist roofed it.

The Wolver stopped, almost cowering, at the hollow's threshold. 'This is the heart of the woods,' he said. 'This is sacred ground.'

His voice woke the ghost of an echo in the hollow, as if other voices had caught his words and were whispering them from wall to wall.

'Strange, definitely strange,' said Torisen. 'But sacred to whom?'

'To the people of rock and stone, who built Hurlen and carved Eldest Island, who were masters here millennia before your ancestors came, before mine learned to walk like men. There's a legend that they used to bring their enemies here and ... and shout them to death.'

'How?'

'I have no idea. It's just an old story. There are a lot of stories about this place, some pretty grisly. There were terrible forces awake in Rathillien once – gods, demons, I don't know. None of our words seem to fit them. They still sleep in places like this.' He crept backward, shivering. 'Let's go, Tori. We don't belong here. No one does, now.'

Torisen sighed. 'I suppose not. Too bad. I'd hoped we could make some use of this place.' He began to turn away, then suddenly spun back. 'BOO!' he shouted at the top of his voice, into the hollow.

'Yawp!' squawked the Wolver, and shot five feet straight up into the air, coming down again in his complete furs.

The echoes of both their cries boomed from cliff wall to cliff wall, multiplying into a wild cacophony of shouts, fading again into silence one by one.

The Wolver cowered wild-eyed under the ferns, all his fur on end. 'Gods, Tori, don't *do* that!'

'Sorry. Just testing.'

'For *what*?'

'I don't know. Anything. But you were right: There's nothing for us here. Come on, let's go partake of Prince Odalian's hospitality. Maybe he can cheer us up some.'

They went, but the last faint echo of their voices remained, murmuring from cliff to cliff, and some dirt dislodged from half-obscured carvings on their heights came rattling down.

'Do you realise,' said Jame, shifting to a more comfortable position on her sack of potatoes, 'that it's only been about twenty-six days since we left Tai-tastigon? That was the third of Winter. We were in Peshtar on the seventh and eighth, in the Anarchies by the eleventh, and in Karkinaroth by the twelfth or thirteenth. That means we spent about fourteen days in the palace. Amazing. You still haven't told me how you passed the time.'

Marc glanced up at her from the bales of fodder on which he was stretched full length, with Jorin curled up asleep beside him. For a moment, Jame was afraid he would point out that she hadn't told him much either.

At first, there hadn't been an opportunity. People last out of a palace that has just collapsed for no discernible reason are apt to be asked questions. Since neither Jame nor Marc had cared to answer and Lyra was in no shape to do so, they had hidden in the ornamental garden on the slope while citizens swarmed up to gape at the destruction. When the crowd was large enough, the four fugitives had quietly descended to the city under its cover and found a pleasant inn that would put them up for the rest of the night.

In the morning, Lyra talked incessantly; but the other two found that an odd reticence had seized them both, at least about their new relationship as Highborn and Kendar. They could discuss their current situation, however, and did. It seemed to both of them that they had better get to the Cataracts as quickly as possible. The best solution was a supply barge bound down the Tardy to Hurlen. Since the island city was stocking up for a possible siege if the Horde broke through, barges were leaving Karkinaroth's wharf every other hour. The three Kencyr had bought passage on one of these and were nearing the end of their journey now.

It had been a pleasant two days in some respects. The barge surged along, first through green fields, then between canyon walls, towed by its draft horses. Three were harnessed to it by cables on either side, massive, placid beasts trotting heavily along worn paths on either bank. The faster the river ran, the more vital they became as brakes. At regular intervals, they were changed – one at a time, still going at a trot – by relief riders from post stations. Roughly every two hours, the travellers met an empty barge being towed back upriver. When one came in sight, they could see the other bargemen scrambling to reach the nearest stanchion so that they could moor their tow cables high enough not to foul the descending horses.

Lyra had enjoyed every minute of the journey. She had recovered so quickly from Odalian's death that Jame at first wondered if the girl was half-witted. On consideration, though, she decided that Lyra had simply never been taught to think seriously about anything except, perhaps, marriage contracts. For the past two days, the girl had been running all over the barge like a flame in her tattered red shirt, getting into more trouble than seemed possible in such a confined space. The crew plainly couldn't decide whether to laugh or throw her overboard. At the moment, she was up in the bow, shying apples at the horses.

Jame wished she had Lyra's lightheartedness although not her terrible aim. The voyage was almost over. Soon she and Marc would probably be back in the thick of things with little opportunity to talk – and there were things they did need to discuss.

Now or never, she thought, and, as casually as she could, asked Marc about his stay in the palace.

'Fourteen days?' he repeated. 'Odd. I was going to say that it felt like less than that, but thinking back, it felt like more too. Well, my lady, it was like this: I woke up in a peculiar room. Its floor didn't reach to the wall, and there was something down there in the pit that made an ungodly noise, like an idiot trying to curse.'

The cage without bars, Jame thought, but didn't interrupt. Maybe, as he went on with his story, he would forget that he spoke to a Highborn.

'I don't know how long I was there,' he said thoughtfully. 'Time doesn't seem to behave properly without a sun or moon. All I know is that I got very hungry and thirsty. Jorin had tracked me there. The poor kitten sat in the doorway and cried until he could only squeak. I thought I would sleep a bit to scrape together some strength and then try to jump across to him, but when I woke up, he was curled up beside me. Someone had shoved a plank across the pit.'

Bender, thought Jame, *or perhaps even Tirandys.* But still she said nothing.

'So we crossed. I shoved the plank into the pit out of sight just to give whoever put me there something to wonder about. Then we wandered around a good bit, don't ask me where. It was all so grey, so... dead. Eventually we got back into the palace and went looking for the temple. When we found it, I broke in.' He hesitated, remembering. 'All the priests and acolytes were there.'

'You said, "Dead, they're all dead",' Jame burst out.

He stared at her. 'Yes, I did, but how...'

'I heard you, or rather I heard what Jorin heard. Interesting.' She bent over to stroke the ounce, who stretched luxuriously without opening his eyes. 'I didn't realise the link could work that way. And were they?'

'Dead? Yes. Very. I'd say at a guess that they were shut in without food or water and, as they weakened, the power of the temple started to work on them. There wasn't much left by the time I got there. When I gave them the fire rites, they went up like dry straw. After that, the kitten and I wandered around some more, trying to pick up your scent. I think we crossed it a few times, but that damned house kept shifting. It was all very confusing. We did find the kitchens, though, and Lady Lyra. Eventually, that boy you call Graykin found us.'

He fell silent. Jame looked down at her black gloved hands, gripped tightly together on her knees.

'It's never going to be the same again between us, is it?'

'No, lass. How could it?' Suddenly he rolled over and put his hand over hers. 'Now, now, cheer up. It's just that we've got to strike a new balance – and we will, eventually. Just give it time.'

Jame looked up with a tentative, almost shy smile.

Just then, Lyra darted back towards them, pointing to the north shore and crying out excitedly. The bank they had been running along beside dipped like a curtain falling away. Beyond was a meadow covered with bright tents, bustling with soldiers. The biggest tent of all, set in the midst of the others like a young palace all of gaudy silk, flew Prince Odalian's colours

Now the two horses were bracing themselves against the barge's pull. Water peeled in sheets off the sharp curve of the stern. Hurlen appeared ahead, its easternmost island set almost squarely at the mouth of the Tardy. Men waited on its wharf. The horses on either bank had reached the end of their paths, which ran down to the edge of the Silver. All six of them were practically sitting on their haunches, braced, while their rider played out the ropes. Heavy as it was, the barge lurched in the current. If a rope snapped or a horse lost its footing, the craft might smash into the island or be carried past it down the Silver towards the Cataracts. They were fairly close to the island now. Bargees threw ropes attached to heavier mooring cables across to the wharf. The wharfsmen reeled them in against the currents. A thud, a shout, and the voyage was over.

They arrived about midafternoon. Marc and Lyra had assumed that they would go straight on to the Host's camp, but Jame hesitated. From what she heard on the wharf, she knew that Tirandys was still impersonating the Prince, with no one apparently the wiser. In fact, he was entertaining the Kencyr lords in his camp at this minute. Had Graykin betrayed her? She had been uneasy about him from the start, but had assumed that because he had told Marc and Lyra about Odalian, he would also tell her brother. It occurred to her now, though, that Graykin had had to give Marc some explanation or the Kendar would never have let him leave the palace with Kin-Slayer. What explanation would have been better than the truth? But while Graykin had told Marc that she had asked him to warn the Highlord, he hadn't said that he would do it, just as he hadn't promised her.

On the other hand, though, even if Graykin had passed on both the news and the sword to her brother, Torisen probably wouldn't move against the changer until after the battle when he no longer needed the Karkinoran army. In that case, her sudden appearance might disrupt his plans, perhaps fatally. That was too big a risk to take. She suggested that they find lodgings in Hurlen for the night.

This proved rather difficult. Hurlen was generally considered impregnable once its bridges were up, and everyone within twenty miles had flocked there for sanctuary. The travellers did eventually find a room in the southernmost island's single tower. It was about large enough to swing Jorin in, if anyone had wanted to do such a thing, and was well above the masonry level. When the wind caught it right, the tower creaked in all its wooden joints and swayed a bit. One night's lodgings cost them all the money they had left as well as half the pearls off Lyra's bodice.

Several more gems bought them supper: bowls of almond fish stew, luce wafers, and salmon tart, washed down with a flask of river water guaranteed to have come from well upstream. Marc ate in the room itself while Jame and Lyra risked sitting crosslegged on the rickety balcony thirty feet above the Silver. Downriver about a quarter of a mile the rapids began. Just before them, the water rose in a gleaming ridge over the top of the boat-guard, a massive cable stretched across the Silver to stop the occasional runaway barge.

It was dusk by now. Watchfires sparkled on the west bank where the Host camped. Stars began to come out.

'It's still the dark of the moon,' said Jame, looking up. 'When Tori and I were children, we use to stay awake whole nights sometimes watching for the crescent to reappear. Our old tutor Anar told us that if ever it didn't, that would mean Perimal Darkling had swallowed the moon and all the stars would follow one by one.'

'Soldiers say the same, with reason,' said Marc. 'It's happened before on other worlds, just before we lost them.' He snorted. 'A cheerful thought for the eve of battle.'

'I'm tired,' said Lyra. 'Who gets the bed?'

There was only one, a straw pallet in the corner.

Jame laughed. 'I'm going out to look around, so you two can fight for it. Just save a corner for Jorin.'

Normally, the city raised its two drawbridges at dusk, but tonight both were still down as Hurlen offered to serve either camp in any way it could, for one last grab at the soldiers' gold. Very few came from the west shore, but the narrow, lower walks and bridges swarmed with Karkinorans.

Torches flared over rushing water. Bursts of raucous laughter

533

erupted from small, crowded rooms and occasional sharp cries from dark corners. The smells of roast mutton and ale filled the air, but under these was another tang, sharp as sweat, heady as wine. So this was what it felt like, Jame thought, to go among men who knew that by tomorrow night they might be dead.

She and Jorin kept to the upper catwalks. Even up there, a few soldiers did accost them in Southron, which Jame barely understood, with intentions all too clear; but it was still early, and no one pressed the issue. For the most part, they were left alone, suspended above firelight and laughter like spectators at a play.

The stone walkways that connected the two mainland bridges were the closest thing that Hurlen had to a street. Jame and Jorin crossed it. The farther north they went, the richer and quieter Hurlen became. At its northernmost point was the island of Grand Hurlen where the city's upper class lived in a hive of rooms, towers, and twisting passageways so narrow that one practically had to turn sideways to get through. All the doors were shut now and the windows barred, although light shone through the cracks. Jame and Jorin threaded past them towards Grand Hurlen's centre, where the island opened out into an earth-filled hollow about two hundred feet across. Grass grew there, and flowering shrubs and dwarf fruit trees, not that much could be seen of them now for the park was currently full of sheep, waiting to play their part in case of a siege.

Jame leaned against the stone rail. Above, stars shone brightly, but the absent moon seemed to say, *You may already have lost more than you know.*

Could she lose what she had never really had: her people, her place, her brother? What if Tirandys won? He would still have to follow Master Gerridon's orders, but in his own devious way as he strove for his lord's ultimate downfall. She knew the quality of his mind and the strength of his will. Despite his handicaps, he would put up a good fight, better, perhaps, even than Torisen could, considering the enemy. Maybe it would be a good thing if he won, if she let him win . . . but no, of course not. That was only the darkness calling to her again, whispering that Tirandys already thought better of her than perhaps Torisen ever would. She wanted to belong, but certainly not at the cost of her brother's life. Anyway, if Tirandys did win and she fell into his hands again, he would probably either send her back to the Master or kill her; the latter, preferably.

Below, the flock had caught Jorin's scent and was milling about restlessly. Sheep, sheep... goat.

She didn't see how she could find out if Graykin had betrayed her short of asking Tori himself, but that wouldn't do. He would be surrounded by people now, including the false prince, and probably in no position to explain the sudden acquisition of a sister, much less one possessing such dangerous information. Assuming Graykin had reached him, though, there was no need for her to try until much later. But if he hadn't, what then? The principal thing was that the Highlord learn about Tirandys before the blood rites, assuming he and the changer got that far. If Graykin had betrayed her, it was to someone who now presumably knew this, too. Would any Kencyr stand by and watch Torisen doom himself in such a way? That should be unthinkable, and yet... and yet...

Lyra had been talking incessantly for two days. What she said usually had no more substance than puff-pastry, but a rather muddled version of Riverland politics had emerged. It was clear that, as far as Lyra was concerned, Daddy's enemy at the Cataracts wasn't the Horde but Torisen. Forgetting to whom she spoke (if, in fact, she had ever know), she gave Jame a highly partisan account of all Caineron's clashes with the upstart Highlord. My lord Caineron, Jame decided, sounded like a thoroughly nasty piece of work. Yes, but surely even he...

Around and around her thoughts went.

'Damn,' she said suddenly, cutting them short. It wasn't just all the unknown factors that were muddling her. Running under everything like a scarlet thread was fear. One way or the other, soon she would see her brother again, after all these years, and the thought filled her with near panic.

Jorin had been standing on his hind legs, forepaws and chin on the rail beside her hand, his nose twitching at the smell of the livestock below. Now he raised his blind moon-opal eyes and gave a questioning chirp.

'All right, child, all right.' She scratched him behind the ear. 'I'm just being silly. Let's go get some sleep.'

By now, the number of Karkinorans in Hurlen had grown, and so had the uproar. Men began to shout in the distance. As Jame and Jorin neared the crooked main street, the noise settled into a chant, one Southron word repeated over and over. Jame recognised it from its Easternese cognate.

'Highness!' the soldiers were shouting. 'Highness!'

535

Down the street came the false Prince Odalian. Torisen was walking beside him.

Jame recoiled into the shadow of a tower. She had only seen her brother for a moment, but she remembered every detail. His dark hair, the set of his shoulders, the way he moved... it was all utterly strange, utterly familiar, like catching an unexpected glimpse of oneself in a mirror. Even that wry smile he shot at Odalian...

Torisen would never had given that look if Graykin had told him who and what his companion was. He didn't know. *He didn't know.*

Others followed the Prince and the Highlord, some Karkinoran nobles, some Kencyr Highborn. One of the latter caught Jame's eye because he was so much more richly dressed than the other lords and wore his finery so poorly. A thin figure darted out to him from the crowd, spoke a hasty word in his ear, and faded back among his retinue. It was Graykin. His restless eyes swept the street, the bridges, the catwalks, and met Jame's. For a moment, they stared at each other. Then he ducked away and disappeared down the street with the others.

Jame stood very still long enough to draw four or five deep breaths. She didn't know which Highborn Graykin had approached, but his intention had been obvious. And now he knew she was in Hurlen.

'Just once, why can't we have a simple crisis?' she murmured to Jorin. 'Stay close.' They set off at a run for their lodgings.

Graykin had been in Hurlen for several days, waiting for the Host and wrestling with his conscience. His life had always had a single goal: to gain a real place in the Kencyrath. His Kencyr blood was responsible for that craving. His Southron mother, however, made it very unlikely that he would ever succeed. He knew that perfectly well, but hope refused to die. He had always scrambled for every crumb of encouragement his lord had let fall and probably always would, hating himself more and more.

That was a bitter thought, especially now. For the first time, someone had actually trusted him. Perhaps she had had very little choice, but she had still done it, and refused to call him that hated name. No one had ever offered him those scraps of self-respect before. He found himself savouring them again and again, before he remembered what must follow.

But it wasn't betrayal, he reminded himself fiercely. He

hadn't given his word, so he owed her nothing. Graykin knew the forms of honour. In a sense, he owed his lord nothing either because 'his lord' had never given Graykin the right to call him any such thing. Even a *yondri* would have had a better chance of eventual acceptance.

But perhaps things would change now. Torisen's sister had given him information that could give his patron great power, perhaps even make him Highlord. Surely that was worth something. Perhaps, finally, Graykin would be acknowledged.

So he waited his chance, spoke his word in Caineron's ear, and then saw Jame up on the catwalk.

Caineron's tent was close to the bridge that connected Hurlen with the west bank of the Silver. It was a huge affair with many internal compartments, rather like a canvas maze. Caineron led the way to his own quarters, poured himself some wine (without offering Graykin any), and sat down.

'This had better be good,' he said, leaning back in his chair.

Graykin took a deep breath. *Too late to back out now*, he thought miserably, and told Caineron what had happened at Karkinaroth. When he finished, Caineron grunted.

'That's quite a story.'

Graykin felt his pale face redden. 'My lord, I'm not lying.'

'To me? Not even you would be that big a fool.' He considered, heavy eyelids lowered. 'So, the little prince is an imposter, a changer, no less, and out for our fine Highlord's blood. All right. Let him have it. Then we'll see who pulls the strings, Gerridon or me. But a sister, now, that's very interesting. She could be extremely useful ... in the right hands.'

He considered this for a moment in silence, the corners of his thick lips slowly lifting. Graykin followed his thoughts without difficulty. What Caineron needed more than anything else was some blood claim on the Highlord's seat. This unknown Knorth girl mated to one of his sons could give him the grandchild he needed ... or perhaps even a son.

Graykin had reasoned all this out long ago, much faster than Caineron, but he tried not to think about it. This was no time for qualms, not at these stakes. Graykin swallowed.

'Lord,' he said, 'if you want this girl, I can give her to you. She's here, in the city. I saw her not twenty minutes ago.'

'Well, now.' Caineron's eyes widened. '*Well*, now.' He rose. 'Then I had better go make her acquaintance. The sooner the better, eh? Meanwhile, you fetch that sword. Oh, and here.' He threw a handful of coins on the table – barely enough, Graykin saw, to get him back to Karkinaroth. 'You're worth every bit of it, Gricki.'

'Please . . . don't call me that.'

Caineron gave him a blank stare. 'Why not? It's your name, isn't it?' He disappeared into the recesses of the tent without waiting for an answer.

Graykin stood there, swaying slightly, until a servant came in.

'You were thinking of spending the night? Out, you, and take your pay with you.'

Blindly, Graykin scooped up the coins and left the tent. He couldn't seem to catch his breath. Caineron would never acknowledge him. He had let himself be used for years for no more reward than this, and he would never be offered a greater one.

He stood by the river in the dark, his quick mind sorting out new possibilities, killing old hopes. Then, because his wits and will were both stronger than his stomach, he hastily found a fair-sized bush and was violently ill behind it.

Four Kendar and a shorter man, muffled in a cloak, went past. Graykin easily recognised Caineron despite his disguise. As the five started across the bridge to Hurlen, Graykin slipped out of the shadows and followed them.

It took Jame and Jorin nearly twenty minutes to get back to the room. Even the catwalks were crowded now. It began to remind Jame of Tai-tastigon during the Feast of Fools when all gods are mocked and nothing is counted a sin. Citizens were starting to shut and bar their doors. Many were probably beginning to regret that the bridges had been left down so late tonight.

Jame found Marc calmly polishing his war-axe by the light of a candle while Lyra slept on the pallet across from him.

'It's getting lively out there,' he said tranquilly. 'Not much discipline, these foreigners.'

'Things may get worse fast. Listen, Marc: I want you to take Lyra to the Host's camp, to my brother. Now. Tell him about Odalian. Then you can return Lyra to her father, but not before.'

'Oh, I doubt if any of the soldiers will bother us up here.'

'It isn't the Karkinorans who worry me.'

She told him about Graykin. He listened soberly, then sheathed his axe and rose.

538

'We'll go immediately. And you?'

'I'll be all right. Anyway, we have a better chance of warning Tori if we separate. And Marc, you'd better take Jorin.'

He gave her a hard look this time, then shrugged and bent to wake Lyra. Long before Karkinaroth, he had realised that there were things in his friend's life that he couldn't understand and from which he couldn't protect her. Lyra woke and was herded, sleepily protesting, out the door. Marc paused on the threshold holding Jorin, who also didn't want to leave and was saying so, loudly.

'Lass, be careful.'

'Aren't I always?'

He laughed and went out.

The room seemed suddenly very quiet, very empty, leaving Jame to wonder at the strong impulse that had made her send them all away. She could feel her blood stir as if before a fight; but if one came, it was hers, not Marc's or Jorin's. The fewer encumbrances now, the better. That included the Book. She had nearly lost it in Karkinaroth and didn't care to risk it again now. Best to hide it. She used the Ivory Knife to pry up some floorboards in the dark corner by the pallet. They came easily, their edges crumbling at the blade's cold touch. She put the knapsack into the hollow and fitted the boards back over it. There. The damned thing would take care of itself for a while. She slipped the Ivory Knife into her boot, hating its touch, but unwilling to give up so lethal a weapon. Hopefully, this crisis would be over before it ate through either the leather sheath or her leg.

Someone was climbing the stair. Several people. The only other way out was the door opening onto the decrepit balcony. Jame backed towards it, out of the candle's feeble sphere of light. Perhaps the soldiers had run out of sport on the lower stories. Perhaps ...

A man stood in the doorway. He was muffled in a cloak, but something about his swaggering stance reminded Jame forcibly of the Highborn whom Graykin had approached in the street. She knew instinctively that this was an enemy.

'My lady of Knorth.'

'My lord Caineron.' It was a guess, but apparently the right one. 'I wasn't expecting you quite so soon, much less in person.'

'Now, would it have been courteous to send a servant for such a distinguished guest? As for finding you so quickly, I had a stroke of luck there. You see, I met my daughter Lyra and her escort on the bridge. You sent them right out into my arms, my dear. Lyra told me where to find you.'

Jame hid her dismay. Damned if she would give this smug toad any more satisfaction than she had to. 'A family reunion. How nice. And the escort?'

'Safe enough, although perhaps not very comfortable at the moment. One of my guards had to give him a clip on the head to make him more... cooperative.'

Poor Marc. That was the fourth time he'd managed to get himself hit since they had left Tai-tastigon, 'And the ounce?'

'Oh, I would never harm a royal gold, even a blind one. He will make an excellent addition to my cattery as breeding stock.' Caineron stepped forward. Candlelight caught the gloat in his narrowed eyes.

Jame had involuntarily gone back a step, onto the balcony. Caineron stopped short in the middle of the room.

'Don't move, girl.'

Now, what did the fool think she...

The balcony sagged. Nails screeched in wood. For a moment, Jame balanced precariously, feeling her heart pound. Someone in the nearest tower cried out. It sounded like Graykin. Then one end of the structure tore loose, and she fell, thirty feet down into the river. The impact knocked the breath out of her. When she surfaced, grasping, Hurlen was already fifty feet away and rapidly receding. The swift current had her. From ahead came the sullen roar of the rapids, and beyond that, the Cataracts' boom.

29

The Killing Ground
The Cataracts: 30th of Winter

The first skirmish came shortly after midnight on the thirtieth when a dozen Waster scouts from the Horde ran into a Kencyr ten-command on wide patrol about a mile from the foot of the Mendelin Steps. The result was eleven dead scouts and one prisoner.

News from this encounter spread through the Host in quiet ripples from camp to camp. Because the Horde itself wasn't expected until midmorning, however, no one leapt to arms. The older veterans, in fact, went back to sleep. For a good many, though, this was their first major battle, and they began quietly to prepare for it.

Harn walked up through that subdued stir, bringing the prisoner under guard to the Highlord's tent.

Burr barred his way at the outer door. 'Sir, I've finally managed to clear out all those Karkinoran nobles and to get my lord to lie down. He's asleep.'

'No, I'm not,' Torisen called from the inner room. Harn entered to find the Highlord stretched out on his cot, fully clothed, hands behind his head. He opened his eyes. 'What is it?'

Harn told him about the clash beyond the stairs. Torisen immediately rose and went with him back through the war-guard's quarters to the outer chamber where the Wastelander was being held. They all regarded the prisoner curiously. He was clad in a patchwork of poorly cured hides, some still tufted with mangy fur, others that looked human. Charms made of teeth and hair hung about his neck. Around his waist was a belt studded with nipples.

'B-but what's wrong with his face?' Donkerri blurted out, staring.

The man seemed to have two of them, one inside the other.

541

The outer skin was wrinkled and translucent. It looked dead. Other features moved ghostlike beneath it. Harn reached out. The man tried to lurch back, but the guards held him. The outer skin came off in Harn's hand, and the scalp with it. Underneath was a smooth face and shaved head. The Waster glared at them with yellow eyes slit-pupiled as a cat's, while Harn held his trophy at arm's length.

'What *is* this thing?'

Torisen took it from him and spread it out to show the Wolver who had just come in. Grimly nodded.

'It's a death mask,' said Torisen. 'Surely you've heard stories about them, Harn, even if you've never seen one before in the ... er ... flesh. The Wasters believe that a man's strength passes to whoever wears the flayed mask of his face. Each elder is supposed to wear the face of his tribe's founder. If that's true, some of these masks must be centuries old.'

The prisoner suddenly exploded into vehement speech that sounded like the yowl of a cat fight. He ended with a burst of scornful laughter, baring filed teeth.

'*Ka'sa* dialect, I think,' said Torisen. 'That's one of Ashe's specialities. Where is she?'

'I sent a messenger,' said Harn, 'but he apparently hasn't found her. Come to think of it, I haven't seen her either since the White Hills. As near as I can make out, though, this chap says we're all going into his tribe's cookpot now that – someone – has come back to lead them.'

'Who?'

Harn scratched his scraggy head. 'Well, I think he said the tribe's forefather, but that hardly seems likely.'

'I wonder. Have all the founders come back?'

Harn laboriously translated this question into dialect and got another spat of snarling syllables in reply. 'He says the Horse-head and the Goat-eye tribes have, as well as several others. They all follow his people in the circling and apparently are allies of a sort. The other tribes are *fed-chi* ... dog's pus. So are we, by the way, and then some.'

'By which I gather that news still only passes among one's immediate connections, unless the elders are better informed,' said Torisen. 'Interesting.'

He fell silent, pursuing his own thoughts, while Harn made another halting attempt to question the scout and in return got what sounded like a ritual chant extolling the great strength and vast appetite of his tribe's founder. The uproar stopped

542

abruptly when Harn, in disgust, rapped the Wastelander on the head with his knuckles. The guards took the man out, reeling between them. Harn threw the death mask after them, then turned on the Highlord.

'*What's* interesting?' he demanded.

'Why, that the Horde hasn't suddenly become one big, happy tribe, all bones buried and never mind who ate whose grandfather. It isn't primarily a question, then, of unification but of motivation. The Horde is marching against us because its founding fathers have returned and told it to. It needn't even be all of the founders, either. If any sufficiently large clump of tribes broke the circle and set off on a tangent, the others would probably follow out of sheer habit.'

'That's right,' said the Wolver excitedly. 'They've been like dogs sniffing after each other for so long that it's probably second nature now. In that case, if you somehow manage to turn the ones under orders, the rest will follow.'

'Yes, but under whose orders?' Harn growled. 'Who are these so-called founders when they're at home? Are we up against three-hundred-year-old ghosts now?'

'After the past few weeks,' said Torisen dryly, 'it wouldn't surprise me. But I'll give you a more likely name: changers.'

'Eh?'

'Well, consider: We already know from Tentir that at least one of them is mixed up in all this. What if there are more, masquerading as the tribal forefathers? The death masks would give them faces of a sort to copy. You know that I've always thought some darkling influence was at work in the Horde. This isn't quite what I had in mind, but it would still explain a good many things.'

Harn snorted. 'Yes, everything except how to fight them, unless you mean to dig firepits all over the landscape and shove them in. Hello, what do you want?'

A breathless messenger had appeared in the tent opening. 'Sir, our wide patrols have apparently run into the vanguard of the Horde... less than two miles from the Steps.'

'What!' Harn sprang up. 'Why didn't the lookout on the escarpment spot them?'

'Sir, they're coming on without torches. We think they must have started a forced march just after dark. The main body of the Horde is still apparently hours away.'

'Ancestors be praised for that at least. Off you go, then, and sound the alert. If you're right,' he said to Torisen as the messenger darted off, 'this vanguard is the lot under orders. Nice to know who one's enemies are, isn't it?' He bared his teeth in a fierce grin and left the tent.

Just outside, the Knorth warhorn sounded. Like the rathorn battle cry, it began with a shriek, then abruptly deepened into a roar that made cups on a nearby table rattle. Before it hit the second, deeper note, it was joined by the howl of Danior's horn and a moment later by those of the other seven houses as the alarm spread. The Host awoke with a shout.

'So now it starts,' Torisen said quietly to the Wolver.

As the wild cacophony of the horns died, thunder could be heard growling in the south, and stars began to wink out one by one before the coming storm.

'Do you mean to say,' said Danior, shouting to make himself heard, 'that it's always like this in the heart of the Wastes?'

'Worse, my boy,' Ardeth shouted back. 'Much worse. The Horde circles a perpetual maelstrom. Be glad they only brought a touch of it with them.'

'Hold on,' said Torisen sharply.

Another blast of wind hit, making Brithany stagger and the two heavier war horses brace themselves, ears flat. They were on top of the escarpment. The leading edge of the storm had reached them, bringing strong, shifting winds and a darkness hard even for Kencyr eyes to penetrate. Far back in the plain's gloom, the Horde's torches sparkled fitfully like stars fallen to earth. From below came the confused sounds of battle. Then lightning split the sky almost overhead with a crash that made the horses jump. In the darkness that rushed in again, the image remained of a seething mass extending from the foot of the steps almost a mile back onto the plain. The full body of the vanguard had arrived.

'Now that, as Lord Brandan said, is moderately impressive.'

No one had noticed Prince Odalian ride up. His voice, speaking in a lull, made them all start.

'I've been settling my people in at the second barricade, relieving yours, Lord Danior, according to plan,' he said. 'Lord Ardeth, your people seem to have the first barricade well under control, although I think they're getting tired. One hour is too long a stint, considering the opposition.'

'Still bad, eh?'

'Worse than ever. They just keep coming, and the bodies are

starting to pile up. That lower barricade may have a twelve-foot drop on the far side, but if this keeps up, they'll be able to climb over it soon using their own dead as a ramp.'

'Nasty,' said Torisen.

'And then some.'

'I wish we could see what's going on,' Danior complained. He had ridden over the edge of the escarpment and was trying to peer back up the gorge. 'These damned trees ... wait a minute.' The tenor of the shouting below had changed. A rising gust of wind brought a cacophony of *Ka'sa* war cries – the names of tribal founders, mostly – shrill with blood-lust and triumph.

'Something has happened,' Torisen said sharply.

He wheeled Storm and set off at a gallop northward towards the head of the stairs with the others riding after him. Half-way there, a messenger met them.

'My lord! The first barricade has fallen, and I don't think the Karkinorans will hold the second!'

'Oh, won't they, by God,' said the Prince through his teeth. 'We'll see.' He spurred on with his retinue scrambling to catch up.

'What happened?' Torisen demanded.

'Lord, t-they say that Pereden came to the barrier and ordered his father's men to withdraw. They hesitated, and – and were overrun ... Lord Ardeth!'

Torisen turned quickly to find Ardeth bent forward over Brithany's neck. He caught the old man's arm to steady him.

'Adric, listen! I told you about our suspicions that changers are leading the Horde. Well, this proves it. That wasn't your son Pereden. Do you understand? *Do you?*'

Ardeth drew himself upright with an effort and nodded. His face was haggard.

'Good. I thought you were going to have a heart attack.'

'I ... was seriously considering it.'

'Listen!' said Danior.

The uproar in the gorge was getting louder. Then it swept northward. About a quarter of a mile ahead, dark figures began to spill off the steps into the lower meadow. There were hundreds, thousands of them. Shrill *Ka'sa* war cries rose in a continuous chorus.

'They're between us and the main body of the Host,' said Torisen. 'Damn.'

'Shall we fight our way through?' Danior asked eagerly.

'With a combined war-guard of only about a hundred riders?' Then too, there was Ardeth, who still looked shaken and wasn't even wearing full armour since he hadn't expected to take any part in the fighting. This upset had caught them all badly off-balance. Still, 'Harn is with the Host. He'll see that the contingency plans go into action. We'll get back as fast as we can, the long way: through the woods.'

The Kendar of his war-guard exchanged glances. On the whole, they would rather have gone straight through the Horde.

The surviving defenders of the steps fell back to the bottle-neck between the middle and lower meadows where they met the Kencyr reserve coming down to reinforce them. About four-fifths of the Host was engaged now and most of the Karkinoran army, spread across the quarter-mile gap between the river and the woods. No one – Host, Horde, or army – went in among the trees.

Harn met Odalian and the tattered remains of his retinue just behind the front line shield-wall.

'How long can we hold here?' the Prince asked, shouting over the uproar.

'Trinity knows. They just keep coming. We need Caineron's people. But he hasn't brought them down yet from the camp. Damn that man. If he's forgotten his part in the plan. I'll – I'll have Ashe put him in a song he'll never live down... heads up!'

A screaming wave of Wastelanders had charged in among the levelled spears and hit the shield-wall. They swarmed up over it. The first across died on the defenders' swords, entangling them, and the next wave crashed down alive on the far side. Harn swept the Prince behind him. His own shield was only a small buckler strapped to his forearm, but it served to turn aside the Wasters' weapons of stone and bone while his own war axe cleared a bloody arc before him.

He felt the red tide of berserker rage rise in him. The night narrowed to the flash of steel, the spray of blood, the crunch of axe on bone, again and again and again. How simple everything suddenly was. One knew one's enemies, and one killed them. Vaguely, he heard the shout of the one-hundred command that swept in to the rescue, heard the crash of the shield wall closing again against the continuing onslaught from the south. Still deep in the blood-lust, Harn only knew that he was running out of enemies to kill. He turned, questing. Ah, here was one more, the last, the greatest enemy of all. Others tried to stop him. He swept them aside, raised his axe to strike at the slight figure of his foe. It slipped away from his blow. The rage gave him speed and strength, but the other still outmatched him. He struck again, missed again, and in the moment before he could regain his balance, the other caught him. Harn fell. He struggled but was held fast. Someone was shouting in his ear:

'Harn! Commandant! Get control of yourself, man!'

The rage receded. Harn found himself on the ground, caught in an earth-moving grip that completely immobilised him. The voice in his ear was that of the Prince.

'Highness! W-what happened?'

'Well, so far you've slaughtered about thirty Wasters, terrorised your own people, and very nearly massacred what was left of mine. You also seemed pretty determined to make mincemeat of me. Are you still so inclined, or can I let go?'

Harn tested the other's grip again and found it unshakeable. He relaxed with a grunt. 'You know a thing or two about the Senethar, don't you, Highness?'

The Prince released him. 'I like to think so. Now what?'

The tenor of the shouting had changed to the east.

'Can you hold here?' Harn demanded.

'We can try.'

'Good enough.'

Harn loped off eastward through the one-hundred command which had helped to close the breach. The Kendar hastily made way for him. Beyond their torchs, chaos reigned. To Harn's right was the shield wall with a second and sometimes a third line of defenders behind it. It surged back and forth, roaring, a solid mass of blackness except where torchlight fell on strained faces and the flash of swords. Harn went on behind it, tripping over bodies, slithering on grass wet with blood. Damn this darkness anyway. Deeper patches of it moved across the meadow like cloud shadows, obscuring everything. This was like the fall of worlds after moon-dark, when all things come unmade and the void gapes.

Harn scarcely felt more settled in his own spirit. He had just tried to kill Prince Odalian. One of the few good things about his past berserker rages was that even in the deepest blood-lust, he had always instinctively known friend from foe. Now, for the first time, he had deliberately gone after an ally. He felt as if he were beginning to lose control – of the battle, of himself. Where the hell was Blackie? Harn knew that Torisen was still alive, as did every Kendar bound to the Highlord, but he needed him here, now. Somehow, Torisen's mere presence always helped. Harn had been all right with the Southern Host until the boy had left to become Highlord. If he were starting to lose his grip for good now as aging berserkers often did, it was high time that he turned to the White Knife. But not just yet. Blackie was depending on him to keep his head, to keep control, and so he would, by God – if only he didn't lose his temper. Damn and blast this darkness!

Someone ran into him. 'Sir!' It was one of his randon cadets, an Ardeth, almost in tears. 'Sir, the line has broken! We couldn't hold. I'm sorry, sir...'

Horns in the darkness, signalling three, four, five breaks in the line.

At this point, he should signal plan four – all houses to close the line except Caineron's, which was to deal with those Wasters who had broken through. But as far as he could tell, Caineron was still no place on the field. Damn and blast.

'Signal four and find me a horse,' he snapped at the cadet. 'Quick, boy!'

The horns belled behind him as he galloped up through the middle field. The night was full of dark, running figures. How could so many have broken through? Suddenly his horse ploughed into a knot of them and almost floundered. Hands clutched at him. *Ka'sa* cries rose in a venomous, suppressed hiss as if he had stumbled into a nest of vipers. His horse gave a shriek and bolted free.

The Host's encampment was a good two miles farther on. Horse and rider scrambled up the Lower Hurdles at a point where the lowest step was only about three feet high and galloped on among the watchfires into Caineron's camp. All the lord's troops were still there. Harn's mount skidded to a stop in front of the tent of Sheth Sharp-Tongue, Caineron's randon commander. The Kendar who ran forward to hold his horse gave the beast a startled look. Harn saw that the animal's flanks and legs were covered with bleeding bites.

He stormed into the tent, sweeping aside Sheth's aide. The commander himself sat at a small table, reading something. Candlelight brought out the hint of Highborn blood in the sharp lines of his face. It said a good deal for the strength of his nerves that he didn't flinch as Harn loomed over him.

'Why in Perimal's name aren't you at your post?' Harn bellowed down at him. 'The line was broken, and I've signalled four. Trinity only knows how many Wasters are halfway here now!'

Sheth closed his book and rose. He was thinner than Harn but a good head taller, which gave him the impression of stooping over the burly Kendar. His acrimonious manner, feared throughout the Kencyrath, for once wasn't in evidence.

'Gently, Harn, gently. My lord Caineron ordered that we wait for him to lead us into position. I think,' he said, as if the words gave him some difficulty, 'that he wants to lead a charge. He's never done that before.'

'Well, now's his big chance. So where in all the names of God is he?'

'Gone.'

'*What?*'

'He came back from Hurlen earlier this evening in foul temper. Whatever upset him, I think he was still brooding about it even after the alert sounded around one o'clock this morning. At any rate, his servant tells me that he suddenly acted as if he'd got a brilliant idea and went rushing out again with a few of his most trusted war-guard. That was about an hour ago, just before we heard that the barricades had fallen. I have no idea where he is now.'

'And you can't move until he gets back.'

'No.'

'Yes, you can,' said a voice at the tent entrance.

The two randon turned sharply to find Donkerri standing there with Kindrie and Burr behind him.

'We came to find out if there was any news of the Highlord,' said Kindrie hastily.

'None,' said Harn. 'Highborn... Doni... what do you mean?'

'Grandfather told me that if he wasn't here, I had the authority to order his troops to their posts,' said Donkerri in a high, defiant voice.

Harn and Sheth looked at each other. They both knew that Donkerri had been disowned and was almost certainly lying. Kindrie knew, too.

'Don't!' he said sharply to the boy. 'Think what you're saying.'

'I have thought. I owe Torisen a debt. Now I'm paying it.'

549

'Do I understand,' said Sheth carefully, 'that you are taking responsibility for this, on your honour?'

Donkerri took a deep breath. He was very pale. 'Yes.'

'Then we can move.' Halfway out of the tent, Sheth turned. 'Thank you,' he said to Donkerri, and was gone. They heard him outside shouting orders.

'Y-you'll tell the Highlord?' Donkerri asked Harn in an unsteady voice. 'Try to explain...'

'He'll understand, and be very proud of you. Now you'd better come with us.'

'Sir, there's no time for the proper rites,' Burr protested.

'The essentials won't be up to us anyway, thank God. Just find him a sword.'

'And armour?'

'No.'

Kindrie caught Harn's arm. 'You can't take him into battle. My God, he's only a boy!'

'"We all find our own rites of passage",' said Burr unexpectedly. 'It was something my lord said at Tagmeth,' he explained.

'This rite may have saved us all, but through a lie that's cost Doni his honour,' said Harn. 'The only way that honour can be restored is through an honourable death. You know that, Highborn.'

Kindrie let his hand drop. 'Yes,' he said numbly. 'I know that. Good-bye, Donkerri.'

When they were gone, Kindrie stood for a long moment in the empty tent. Outside, horses neighing, shouts, receding hoof-beats. Caineron's troops had been ready to move at a minute's notice for hours and now did so. When the Shanir emerged, all twelve thousand of them were gone, with dust still swirling in the light of abandoned watchfires. Far downfield, horns were sounding the news of a line utterly broken. Then came the Cainerons' eldritch war cry, faint in the distance, and the crash of horses clearing the Lower Hurdles. The wind veered, taking the sounds of battle with it. Upfield, a sheep overlooked by its shepherd was bleating disconsolately.

Kindrie went through the empty camp. No, not quite empty. Ahead was a large tent full of light and activity, guarded by Jaran and Coman one-hundred commands. Inside, bandages were being folded, poultices and potions prepared.

'Yes, Highborn?' A red smocked surgeon bustled up, brisk, impatient. 'Can we help you?'

Kindrie gulped. 'Perhaps I can help you,' he said diffidently. 'You see, I'm a ... a healer, of sorts.'

The cable stretched to infinity. Gleaming water surged over it, under it, pulling, pulling. Her arms ached from fighting the strain. Hemp fibres lodged under her nails like splinters. Every time she released one grip to take another inches farther on, the current tried to sweep her over or under the cable, down towards the rapids. Trinity, what a relief it would be to let go, to rest until she hit the white water and then to die. Drowning was supposed to be an easy death. But her hands went on, grip by painful grip, as if they had determined on their own not to let go of life.

... too stupid to give up, too stupid to give up ...

Jame blinked. She still heard the rapid's almost deafening roar, but what she saw were flames. A small bonfire, with her *d'hen* and boots drying beside it. A sharp face across the flames turned towards her.

'Hello,' said Graykin.

'Hello.' She had to raise her voice almost to a shout to make it carry over the water's noise. 'I assume I didn't drown.'

'Not quite. You got nearly to shore before passing out, and fetched up on some rocks a few yards downstream. We're about a hundred feet farther down the gorge now, about level with the Lower Hurdles. The River Road is on top of that cliff behind us, which you can't see because it's about as light down here as the inside of a boot. So much for the geography lesson. How do you feel?'

'As if drowning might have been a good idea.'

She pushed back the blanket and sat up. Her arms felt as if every muscle in them had been pulled. She looked at her hands, at ruined gloves and nails scarcely in better shape. She wouldn't be using them again soon. At least by some miracle Ganth's ring hadn't fallen off. She considered pocketing it, then on impulse stripped off what was left of her gloves, wrapped a bit of fabric around the ring and put it back on.

'Let's see. So far tonight I've fallen out of a tower, almost drowned, nearly been declawed, and now I'm apt to lose my voice from shouting. Once, just once, I'd like to spend a quiet evening at home – wherever that is. So when does your lord Caineron arrive to collect me?'

Graykin spat into the shadows. 'He's not "my lord" any more.

Mind you, he still would be – as much as he ever was – if he had given me what the news of your arrival was worth.'

'And he didn't, huh?'

Graykin drew a handful of coins out of his pocket and let them spill, flashing, onto the ground. 'What do you think?'

'That Caineron is a fool. Also that you're being very... blunt.'

He shot her a look across the flames. 'I'm no more apt to lie than you are, but there are a hundred ways to hide the truth. I'll never use any of them with you, ever. That's a promise.'

She stared at him, wondering if she had heard correctly. 'Graykin, that's one hell of a concession. Why? Guilt?'

'No. I simply follow my own interests. Listen: People in power need sneaks like me to be their eyes, to keep their hands clean. I've been Caineron's sneak most of my life – not bound to him, you understand, just letting him use me. Well, that's over now. He'll never give me what I want, but perhaps some day you can. You'll need someone like me when you have power. Oh yes, you'll get it. Nothing stops you. When that day comes, I want to be your sneak – if you're half-witted enough to want me.'

Jame shook her head. 'Graykin, this is one of the strangest conversations I've ever had, which is saying something. Even if you're right about the power, which I doubt...'

'Why should you trust me? A good question. The best I can do is offer two tokens of my good faith. First, this.' He picked up a long bundle and handed it to her across the flames. 'It's your brother's sword. Caineron wanted it, but he'll have to do without. Second, when we last met, you trusted me with your name. Unfortunately, my Southron mother didn't live long enough to give me one. All my life, I've answered to whatever people chose to call me. But I can tell you who my father is: Caineron.'

'Sweet Trinity. Does he know?'

'Oh yes,' said Graykin with great bitterness. 'He thinks it means that he owns me. I thought that if I served him well, perhaps some day he would acknowledge me as his son. Yes, yes, I was stupid. Just wait until you want something that badly, though, and see how wise you are.'

Jame tensed. 'Do you hear something?'

They listened. It was so dark that the world might have ended at the edge of the firelight. Beyond that, the river's roar and its echo off the cliff face hemmed them in with walls of sound. They had been exchanging confidences almost at a shout. Now Graykin dropped his voice so that Jame could barely hear it.

'I think something has been going on downstream for some time now. Down here, it's hard to tell, though. There!' He sprang to his feet. 'Voices... upstream. I'll check. You had better dress.'

Jame was pulling on her boots when he came back.

'It's Caineron, searching the shore,' he said, kicking apart the fire and stomping on the embers. 'He must have remembered the boat cable – a mere five hours after the event. You'd better run for it.'

'Where?'

'Up the cliff – there's a path of sorts – and across the road. I left a horse on the far side, tied up behind some bushes.'

'Such foresight.'

'A sneak's virtue. Here's the sword.'

She had to grope for it.

'Here's the path.'

She paused in the pitch blackness and caught the hand with which he had been guiding her. 'Graykin, I'm going to trust you again. Go to the room where I was staying in Hurlen on the southernmost island. Under a loose board in the corner, you'll find a knapsack. Hang onto it for me. If I manage to get myself killed, let my brother take his turn being responsible for the nasty thing. Promise?'

'Yes... my lady.'

He spoke with a sort of wonder, as if the title had been surprised out of him. As for Jame, for a moment she couldn't tell where her hand ended and his began. Then torches appeared upstream. She had scrambled nearly to the top of the gorge when the thought struck her.

Sweet Trinity, I think I've just bound that man to me.

Up on the road, the light was better, but just barely. Jame paused, her ears still ringing from the echo chamber of the gorge. What a difference it made to be out of it. To the south she heard shouting, a continuous, distant roar. Graykin had been right: something *was* going on downstream. And behind? No sound came out of that well of noise except the water's roar, but lights were winding back and forth up the cliff face. Damn. Caineron had found the path.

Jame quickly crossed the road and scrambled down among the bushes on the far side. There was a horse, a white, battle-

553

scarred trooper, straining at his tether. Jame untied him and mounted awkwardly. Whatever else she had learned in Perimal Darkling, apparently no one had taught her horsemanship. The lowest step of the Lower Hurdles stretched out before her like a white chalk wall. She rode westward along it.

Downfield, the shouting got louder. Now horns were blowing, Jame reined in. Thunder came from the north, a continuous, rumbling roll of it. She rose in the stirrups, trying to see over the step, but the tall fringe of meadow grass on top of it blocked her view. The stone of the step face vibrated under her hand. The rumbling grew louder. Her mount snorted and turned to face southward. She could feel him collect himself. Now what on earth...

Lightning split open the sky. In that brief, lurid glare, the middle and lower meadows leapt into sight, black with figures running towards her. The rumble grew, thunder crashed, and Caineron's riders came over the lowest step, over her head, in a screaming wave.

Jame nearly fell off as her mount bolted. He hit his stride just as the other war horses recovered from their plunge. She found herself galloping between two riders, one apparently raving mad, the other little more than a boy. The latter stared at her with his mouth open. Jame clung to her horse and to the sword, sure that at any moment she would lose one or both of them. Her feet had already slipped out of the stirrups. The Kencyr line crashed into and through the first wave of Wasters, then the second and third, riding them down. Jame's horse stumbled on bodies, recovered, then put his foot in a rabbit hole and somersaulted. Jame found herself in midair, still clutching the sword. She had just time and wits enough to wrap herself around it before she crashed into the ground. For a moment, the night went very dark indeed.

Some light returned to her stunned senses and sound: a shrill yelling, very close. The boy was standing over her, facing a huge Waster, shouting defiance in a cracked voice. The Waster laughed. His teeth were filed and very white. He scooped the boy up and broke him over his knee like a dry stick. Then he lowered his head to bite.

Jame lurched to her feet with the rathorn war cry of her house. She swung the sword. The blade sheered through its wrappings, through the Waster's boiled leather armour, halfway through his body. He dropped the boy with a grunt of amazement, took a step, and pitched forward on top of her. Jame dragged herself clear. Her right hand, wearing the ring, gripping the sword, tingled as if it had been asleep. So at least one of the stories about Kin-Slayer was true. She drove the blade into the earth and knelt beside her would-be rescuer. With horror, she saw that the boy was still alive.

He stared up at her with blank amazement. 'Why, it doesn't hurt at all. I can't feel a thing. Did I do well, Highlord?'

'But I'm n...' She swallowed. 'Yes. You did very well.'

'Good,' he said, and died.

'Tori!' The shout, almost a bay, rose from somewhere close by out of the battle's uproar. 'Tori, I heard your war cry. Where are you?' A shaggy figure burst out of the seething darkness and stopped short, red eyes glowing. Its pointed ears flattened and it crouched. 'You aren't Tori. Changer!'

It sprang. Jame lunged for the sword, but was knocked away from it. The wolf was on top of her, snapping at her throat. She jammed her left forearm, protected by the *d'hen*'s reinforced sleeve, between its jaws and tried to reach the Ivory Knife in its boot sheath. Her fingers brushed, then grasped it. She was poised to strike when the wolf gave a sudden yelp of astonishment and sprang back, regaining his human aspect in midair.

'You aren't a man!'

'I'm not a changer either,' she snapped. 'Where's the Highlord?'

'I don't know!' the other wailed. 'I leave him on his own just for a minute, and *this* happens!' He spread his arms to include the entire battlefield with perhaps two hundred thousand warriors locked in bloody combat on it. 'Anyway, who in seven hells are you?'

Before Jame could answer, a sizeable number of riders bearing torches swept down on them, reining in only at the last minute. Jame found herself among the war horses. Their massive bodies surged around her, white-rimmed eyes rolling in her direction, iron-shod hooves dancing. She whacked one on the nose when it bared its yellow teeth at her.

'Behave, you!'

The beast reared back, snorting, astonished either at the blow or at a voice speaking Kens almost under its hooves. 'What in Perimal's name...' said its rider, but Jame had already ducked away through the press.

'Grimly!' a voice cried nearby. 'Have you seen either Tori or Ardeth?'

'No! Weren't they with you?'

'Well, yes, until we tried to cut through the woods to rejoin the Host. Then, somehow, w-we lost them both.'

'*What?*'

Jame was close enough now to see the speakers. One was the shaggy man who had attacked her, and the other, a young distraught-looking Highborn who apparently led these riders.

'Grimly, it was so strange,' the latter was saying. 'One minute they were riding ahead of us, then the mist came up and they were gone, except that we could still hear them for a while. Then their voices faded, too. I didn't think we'd ever find our own way out.'

Jame retrieved the sword, practically from under the Highborn's horse. 'Which direction is this forest?' she demanded.

'Why, that way,' Danior pointed. 'But who . . . ?'

She was already gone.

'This is ridiculous,' said Torisen. 'Somewhere in the immediate vicinity, the greatest battle of the millennia is raging, and I can't find it. Adric, do *you* have any idea which way we should go?'

'None, my boy. I'm completely turned around. Really, this is a most peculiar place.'

That, thought Torisen, was putting it mildly. The woods were even more a world of their own now than they had been the previous afternoon. Mist lay even thicker on the ground than before, glowing faintly. No sound of battle penetrated here. Lightning occasionally flashed overhead, throwing green leaves into relief, but only a whisper of thunder reached here below. The entire forest seemed to be holding its breath. It was almost as if through mist and misdirection it was trying to keep them from the battle.

No, thought Torisen, irritated with himself. That was pure imagination. He was simply worried about the fight, about Harn's ability to control it, about Ardeth's health.

'How do you feel?' he asked the old man.

'Oh, well enough, considering.'

Considering that he was still very close to a heart attack. Damn Pereden anyway. Nothing about this business, desperate as it was, would have upset Ardeth half so much if his wretched son hadn't been mixed up in it.

556

'Highlord! Torisen!'

A voice in the woods, calling his name.

Ardeth put a hand quickly on his arm. 'Don't answer.'

'But surely that's Holly.'

Brithany was listening, ears pricked. The distant voice called again, joined by another.

'No, that's not Lord Danior,' said Ardeth in an odd tone. 'I don't know who it is, or what, but as for that other voice...'

'It's not Pereden,' Torisen said sharply. 'I told you about the changers. Never mind who it sounds like. Damn.' He swung down hastily from Storm and helped Ardeth to dismount. 'Sit down, Adric. Steady, steady... there. All right?'

'Yes, yes... just let me rest for a minute.'

Torisen settled him back against a tree. He always forgot how old Ardeth was, how close to that abrupt slide into senility and death that marked the end of so many Highborn. Adric would probably prefer to die of sudden heart failure or even by his own hand than finish as Jedrak had; but it hadn't quite come to that yet, not if he could spare the old man any further shocks for a while.

Ardeth gave him a rather shaken smile. 'Thank you, my boy. You know, it's odd to think that when we first met, you were half the age you are now and I was already old.' He shook his head. 'Fifteen years ago. I think, on the whole, that we've done rather well by each other.'

'On the whole. That sounds like running water. Rest here a minute, and I'll get you some.'

He took his helmet from Storm's saddle bow and went to look. Mist drifted between the trees. Forest depths appeared and disappeared silently, grey trunks shining silver in the mist-glow, leaves a pale, luminous green. The liquid chuckle was almost underfoot now, although all Torisen could see was a feathery carpet of ferns. He parted them. The sound stopped instantly. Under the fronds ran a stream made up entirely of bluebells.

Lured.

He tried to find his way back to Ardeth, without success. This was really ridiculous. First he had misplaced a battle and now an old man and two horses who surely couldn't be more than fifty feet away. He called and thought he heard Brithany neigh softly in response, but which way was she? When he tried again, only the voices answered him, calling his name – six, seven, eight of them at least, eldritch and mocking. The one that mimicked Pereden was still recognisable, but the others made no attempt now to sound like anyone he knew.

If he couldn't find Ardeth, he must at least try to lead these pursuers away from the old man to some place where he could confront them. After all, it was the Highlord whom they wanted. This was his fight.

He raised his helmet to put it on, then hesitated, staring at it. Its polished back seemed to be glowing. No, it was reflecting some light, just as were the inserts of fine chain mesh on the backs of his leather gauntlets. But what possible source ... On the helmet, he saw the distorted reflection of his own face with something bright beneath it. The Kenthiar. He was wearing the silver collar and its single gem for the first time since Wyrden, and the gem had begun to glow. Had that ever happened before? He didn't think so, but then in all its long history, no Highlord had probably ever brought the collar to a place like this. Should he take it off before it decided to do something else? No. Better not to meddle. Besides, the damned thing might object to being removed. He put on the helmet, unslung his buckler, and drew his sword. There. Now, which way to go? The voices called again, closer this time, but he still couldn't tell which direction they came from. He set out at random.

The dreamlike quality of the woods grew. The mist itself drifted between glimmering tree trunks, silently, continually changing shape. Torisen was haunted by a sense of constant movement just out of his line of sight. His armour felt almost as if it were deliberately hindering him. Its outer layer consisted principally of rhi-sar leather, boiled, beaten, and finally shaped to his body before it hardened. Although excellent against sword and arrow, it had hardly been designed for sneaking about in a midnight forest. His right boot kept squeaking. All he heard beyond that were the voices, especially the one that sounded so much like Pereden.

'Torisen, where are you?' That voice was calling now in a jeering croon. 'Don't run away. Brave, sweet Blackie, wait for me.'

Blackie?

Ahead, the trees ended. Was he entering a glade? The mist made it impossible to tell, but he sensed the presence of something solid on either side. Beyond, the feeling of open space returned. The Kenthiar's glow grew. Ferns brushed his knees. Mist swirled, momentarily clearing overhead, rolling back. The walls of the bluff curved around him. At their heights, the stones seemed to shine faintly through the dirt and plant growth accumulated over centuries if not millennia. He was in the hollow at the heart of the wood.

Movement behind him. He turned as figures emerged from the mist – six, seven, eight of them wearing the patchwork skins and ivory ornaments of Waster elders, a ninth in rhi-sar armour stained blue. They surrounded him. So. He saluted the ninth and waited in silence, poised.

Afterward, Jame remembered little of her hasty trip across the battlefield. Visibility changed practically from step to step. Sometimes whole vistas opened up before her, sometimes she couldn't see beyond her own outstretched hand. The battle seemed to be raging in scattered pockets all over the field as the Wasters who had broken into the middle ground grappled with Caineron's forces above them and the rest of the Host below. She stumbled onto scenes of heroism, carnage, and horror beyond anything she had ever imagined. Here a ten-command under a randon cadet charged a force three times its size to rescue a fallen comrade. There a solitary Waster sat munching someone's arm while the battle surged about him. Her hand was beginning to blister from gripping Kin-Slayer, especially around the ring. This was clearly not a weapon to be wielded without cost. She had no idea how many Wasters she had killed and only a vague impression of the wave of startled half-recognition that followed her.

Here at last was the edge of the woods. Under the leaves, in the glowing mist, she stopped, amazed. It was so like the Anarchies, only somehow less deeply rooted and more awake. The Anarchies had been a sleeping land, thick with ancient power, difficult to rouse in any but a superficial sense. Beneath its surface calm, this place felt as twitchy as a horse's hide in fly season. Before she had gone more than a hundred feet she realised that she was already lost. Damn. She could wander around in here all night, unless...

She groped in a pocket and drew out the *imu* medallion. Waster blood still ran down the sword. She let it drop on the *imu*'s lips.

'All right,' she said fiercely to it. 'Do something.'

It just lay there. As she turned, however, it suddenly tugged at her hand. She went where it pulled her, walking quickly at first, then running. Trees, mist, and then suddenly a stone cliff soaring up overhead. When the *imu* pulled her left along the base of the cliff, she guessed she was moving southward. Distant voices were calling her brother's name. Jame saved her breath for running. She had gone about a mile when the cliff abruptly fell away to the right. Jame hesitated. Her keyed-up senses told her that she was on the edge of an area thick with ancient power. Like the Anarchies, this was no place for humans, and especially not for anyone with the Darkling taint.

From inside came a sudden shout, ringingly echoed, and the crash of steel. Jame ran towards the sounds.

A fight was going on very close at hand. One voice was shouting almost continually, shrill with rage and hate, against the rasp and clash of swords. Echoes rang from all sides. Sword in one hand, *imu* in the other, Jame crept cautiously closer. If the mist was this thick throughout this place, she could suddenly find herself too close to the combatants for comfort.

Ah-ha. Ahead it thinned and dropped to knee-level, leaving an arena of sorts a good fifty feet across. Two armed figures confronted each other in the open. One, clad in black and silver had a glowing jewel at his throat. The other wore dusty blue. Jame dropped to her stomach and wriggled closer under cover of the mist and ferns.

The blue warrior was making all the noise. His technique seemed to consist entirely of fire-leaping swordplay, fast, aggressive, and showy. Every time he shouted, his voice cracked back from the cliff walls and more dirt rattled down from them. The echoes were deafening.

In contrast, his opponent fought in silence, using mostly water-flowing and wind-blowing evasions. Jame knew immediately that this was her brother. 'Never make an unnecessary move,' Ganth had said over and over when Tori had begun his training at the keep in the Haunted Lands, and she had crept close to watch as she did now. Tori had learned well. His style was as spare and elegant as any she had ever seen and made her remember with some embarrassment all the thrashing about she had done with Kin-Slayer, getting here.

Just then, the blue warrior seriously overextended himself in a lunge. Torisen slipped out of the way, caught the other's sword hand, and jerked him forward even farther into a sharp blow with the hilt of his own sword that drove the other's nasal guard back into his face. The man dropped without a sound. The ground mist swallowed him. Jame almost gave a whoop, but just then Torisen turned directly to her, or so it seemed, and gave a formal salute. She was startled into silence – luckily, as it turned out.

Something moved behind and to either side of her. As she flattened herself under the ferns, the mist withdrew slightly to reveal eight figures surrounding both Torisen and her. She had apparently crept between two without noticing them or being noticed. They were dressed like Waster elders, but something in their eyes gave her pause. If she had been Jorin, the fur would have risen down her spine. The odd thought came to her that this was all a trap that the woods had set for these Darkling creatures, using her brother as bait; but he didn't know how to spring it and neither did she. She edged carefully backward through the ferns.

On the far side of the circle, one of the creatures stepped forward, and Torisen pivoted to face it. It saluted, clenched fists held at waist height, crossed at the wrists – a derisive challenge from superior to inferior. Torisen responded silently with hands holding sword and buckler held uncrossed chest high, the challenge response to one whose rank is unknown. The other gave a scornful snort and picked up its weapon. Worked metal of any sort was rare in the Horde due to its constant movement and general lack of forges. The most prized weapon was a stone-headed axe with a long shaft made from the femur of one of the huge shaggy beasts that pulled their tent wagons. That was the sort of weapon this creature hefted and swung with sudden, murderous strength.

The axe-head glanced off Torisen's steel buckler, denting it. He retreated step by step before the onslaught, using water-flowing and wind-blowing moves to avoid any blow he could. The other followed, snickering.

Just then, Torisen's foot caught in a tangle of ferns. Jame gasped as she saw the killing blow whistle down on him. Unable to sidestep, he caught it full on his shield. The buckler shattered. He was driven down to one knee, his left arm at least momentarily useless. Before the other could recover, Torisen lunged. His blade caught his opponent in the abdomen and ripped upward. He disengaged and staggered back. The other dropped its axe and stood there swaying, arms wrapped around the terrible wound. Why didn't it fall? Instead, it began to laugh, a crazy, giggling sound. It spread its arms. The wound had closed. Torisen threw aside the remains of his buckler and went back a step, sword raised. The blade had been almost eaten through by the other's blood. It fell apart in his hand. Soft laughter rose from all sides.

Changers, Jame thought, horrified. *They're all changers.*

She gave a shout and threw Kin-Slayer: 'Here, Tori... catch!' The mist closed around her as she ducked back into it, drawing the Ivory Knife from her boot.

He turned to see the blade flashing towards him, caught it, and swung. It caught the changer just under its chin as the creature rose. Its head flew off, bounced once and disappeared. Jame heard it some distance away, mewling petulantly under the ferns. The changer's body collapsed slowly, its gaping wound already sealed. Even as it sank under the mist and fronds, it kept moving like a swimmer slowly floundering. Its hand rose, clutched air, sank.

Torisen had sprung back, breathing hard. Now for the first time he looked at his weapon and saw with utter amazement not only that it was undamaged but what blade it was. He turned sharply to discover who had thrown it, but saw only the remaining changers, closing in around him.

Jame, hidden in the mist, heard the sound of renewed combat. She was neither equipped nor trained to help Tori out there in the open, so she must do what she could here on the fringe, in the shadows – like a proper sneak, as Graykin would say. But this sneak bit with the tooth of death.

A changer stumbled back into the mist, clutching a bloody sleeve. Before its wound could close, Jame slipped up behind it and drew the Knife lightly across its neck. The creature whirled, snarling. Then a startled look crossed its stolen face, and it toppled, dead. One down, seven to go.

She claimed two more, catching glimpses of the main battle each time. Kin-Slayer, reforged in Perimal Darkling, seemed as proof against the changers' blood as the Knife, but Torisen couldn't go on wielding it forever against foes who could heal themselves of practically anything. Damn her bungling anyway, to have got the sword to him without the ring.

Meanwhile, Torisen did indeed begin to feel his strength fail. He hadn't realised until now how badly that forced march had drained him. *No, don't think about that,* he told himself. *Concentrate on weaving the Senethar patterns of evasion and attack, sword against axes, and remember that too many direct blows will shatter already weakened armour.* Damn. There went his helmet, carried off by a glancing blow that made his ears ring.

'Good,' grunted his opponent, applauding his own strike, the Highlord's evasion, or both.

Torisen struck in reply and missed.

'Not so good.'

The sword was shaking in his hand now and the air burning in his lungs. He had almost reached the end of his endurance. According to legend, Kin-Slayer was supposed to strike true as long as its rightful owner wielded it. Ganth had hinted at some further secret to its use, but had been too jealous of his dwindling power to reveal it, especially to one whom he already suspected of wanting to usurp his position. A fine time this would be to learn that his father's curse actually had taken effect, that he really was disowned and not the rightful Highlord after all.

Lunge, parry, turn... too slow, damnit.

He saw the blow coming, a white blur of stone and bone. It hit him in the stomach. He heard armour crack, saw Kin-Slayer spin away, all in the split second before he found himself doubled up on the ground, gasping for breath. There was no blood, ancestors be praised: The chain mail byrnie under the hardened leather had stopped the axe's edge. Now, if he could just breathe...

Hands scooped him up. The largest of the changers was holding him aloft as one might a child and grinning up at him through freshly broken teeth.

'Come to daddy,' it said, and let him drop into its full embrace.

Torisen heard his armour shatter, felt the chain links dig into him. He struck at the other's eyes and ears, but the changer drew folds of flesh over them. Its arms tightened. He... couldn't... breathe...

Somewhere, someone screamed. The sound merged with the roar of his own blood until both faded into black velvet silence.

Jame saw her brother fall and rise again in the changer's grasp on the far side of the mist clearing. She started to run towards him, only to fall barely ten feet across the open space. Something had grabbed her ankle. It was the headless changer, still wallowing sluggishly under the mist. Its grip felt strong enough to break bone. The other changers were turning towards her but she ignored them. She saw her brother strike at his captor, first with strength, then more and more weakly. Pieces of his armour rained down. In near panic, she threw the Knife, but it wasn't balanced for such use and she had no skill. It missed. Torisen went limp, and still the other squeezed. Blood ran down from his nose and mouth.

Jame screamed.

The sound echoed piercingly off the cliffs, bouncing back and forth, seeming to grow – just as the rathorn's death scream had in the Anarchies. Almost without thinking, Jame pitched her cry to that terrible sustained note. The sound lanced through her head. The *imu* vibrated in her hand as if it too screamed, and perhaps it did. Above, other *imus* of diamantine emerged along the cliff heights, spitting earth from their frozen, gaping mouths. They were less well defined than the ones in the Anarchies but, it seemed, no less deadly.

The changer dropped Torisen and clamped hands over its ears. Its face distorted horribly. The others had already fallen and lay convulsed among the ferns. The hand gripping Jame's ankle let go. If this really had been a trap, she thought, lurching to her feet, she had just sprung it with a vengeance. She staggered towards where her brother had fallen, guided by the gem's glow under the mist. They must get out of here. The noise grew, shattering thought, and the *imu* exploded in her hand. She stumbled on – how far, she didn't know – until her legs seemed to melt out from under her and she fell into the cool ferns, under the glowing mist, into blessed silence.

All night, Harn had felt his berserker blood undercutting his random discipline. He had briefly lost control once when he had attacked Prince Odalian; but when the charge began, he finally, deliberately, let go. Better that than to consider too closely what would happen to the pale boy who rode beside him. Besides, the battle had gone beyond anyone's control now. There was nothing left but to smash and smash and smash until it was all over, one way or the other.

So Harn rode over the Lower Hurdles borne on the crest of his battle madness, seeing the field laid bare for a moment before him by lightning, shouting with the thunder. For a moment, he thought Torisen was galloping beside him on a white horse, but that was a hallucination: Blackie would never ride white, the colour of death. The pale horse disappeared, and Donkerri with it.

Death take you, boy. Go with honour.

Harn found the largest contingent of Wasters he could and smashed into it. His sword had gone with Donkerri. Now he again wielded his long-shafted axe, his Kencyr steel against the stone and obsidian of the enemy. The night stretched on and on in blood and thunder. All around him, lightning lined upturned faces, sharp teeth, wild eyes. He reaped heads. Hands clutched at him, and he lopped them off, too. His horse was splashed with gore up to the shoulders. It reared and plunged, striking, biting, finally screaming as Waster knives found its vitals. It crashed down. Harn rolled free and charged on into his massed foes until their sheer number stopped him. By now, he had outrun all but one Kendar, who had covered his back all the way. He fought on in savage joy, too deep in madness to count the odds. The Kendar behind him was chanting a war song full of the crash of steel, full of battle cries. Lightning and fire transfixed the night.

Then the scream began. It came from the woods to the right, preternaturally clear and piercing. Harn started, thinking it was the Knorth rathorn war cry, but it went on and on. A light shone in the heart of the forest. It seemed to spread. As that incredible scream continued, glowing mist drifted out from between the trees onto the battlefield. Where it went, the demon wind lost its strength, and the Wasters retreated. Suddenly they were all in flight. Startled out of his berserker fit, Harn watched them go in amazement. They scrambled out of the middle ground, into the lower meadow, onto the stairs.

'D'you see that?' he shouted to his companion. 'Look at the buggers run. Look!' Getting no response, he turned. The Kendar was leaning on her spearstaff as if too tired to move. 'Are you all right?' Harn demanded.

'No,' said the other in a curiously husky voice, raising the haggard face of a haunt. It was Ashe. 'I'm dead. I've been dead ... for at least three days.'

In the woods, the scream faded, and the mist began to disperse on the battlefield.

Just about this time, the Wolver, Lord Danior, and the combined war-guards reached the trees. They had been trying to get there for some time, but the currents of battle had swept them far south, almost into the lower meadow. Now they followed the Wolver into the woods, leaving their mounts, who still refused to enter. Here the mist still faintly glowed, lighting their way. The Wolver picked up Storm's scent. Not long afterward, they met Ardeth leading the war horse and riding Brithany, also in search of Torisen. The Highlord's scent led them to the hollow. The Wolver crouched unhappily on the threshold while Ardeth and Danior went in with a handful of their guards to look by the light of mist, diamantine, and torch.

One of the guards gave a sudden yelp. 'Something bit me!' He reached down under the mist and came up with the changer's severed head, which he held gingerly aloft by its hair. It made a hideous face at him.

They found other bodies under the mist, mostly by tripping over them, and carried them out beyond the hollow to where the ground had begun to clear. Of these, some were dead, some moving in slow convulsions with constantly changing faces and bodies. It was clear what the latter were, and also that their minds had been utterly destroyed. The Kencyr had collected two dead and three insane when Ardeth spotted the Kenthiar's dimming glow and followed it to the Highlord.

At first they thought he was dead for he lay so still. It wasn't until they had carried him out and laid him down under torchlight that they could see he was still breathing.

'But, my God!' said Danior, staring. 'What's happened to his armour?'

Ardeth wiped blood off the young man's face. 'Who knows? Most of his adventures recently have been beyond me. Life used to be so much simpler. Ah, he's waking.'

Torisen groaned. His eyes opened, and he stared at them, blankly at first. Then, 'What happened?' he said weakly.

'God's claws and whiskers. Don't *you* know?'

'I-I remember the fight and being grabbed and not being able to breathe. Then someone screamed, and I passed out.' He looked up at them, confused. '*Who* screamed?'

'Nothing human from the sound of it,' said Danior. 'Tori, you should have seen the Wasters run! I bet there isn't a clean breechcloth in the entire vanguard right now.'

Torisen struggled up on one elbow. 'The noise routed them?'

'Well, not entirely. They're on the steps again. We should have pressed our pursuit, I suppose, but, well, we were a bit shaken up, too. And now an attack is apt to bring them swarming back up. It's a stalemate of sorts. I don't like to think, though, what will happen when they realise we've got their precious founders, if that's what those things over there are.'

'That's it!' said Ardeth. He rose abruptly and went over to

look at the pile of changers, living and dead.

'That's what?' Danior asked, puzzled.

'Never mind, my boy, never mind. Let's just say that you've given me an idea.' He gestured to his guards and gave them a low-pitched order. They bent to pick up the changers.

Meanwhile, Torisen had been trying to collect his scattered wits. He felt, on the whole, as if he had just been rolled down a mountain in a barrel full of rocks. Then he saw Ardeth standing by the changers and one thought at least leapt into his mind with startling clarity.

'Pereden,' he muttered, and struggled to rise. Danior helped him. 'Adric...'

Ardeth put his hands on Torisen's shoulders. 'Now listen, my boy. Over the past few weeks, you've had insomnia, nightmares, bruises, cuts, bites, poison, and now probably assorted internal injuries as well. Let someone else have some fun for a change.' He bustled off.

Torisen looked at the changers as Ardeth's Kendar carried them off after the old lord. He saw no familiar faces.

'Holly, do me a favour,' he said to Danior. 'Go back into the hollow and look for a sword with a smashed hilt crest. I-I think it's Kin-Slayer.'

Danior stared at him. 'Your father's lost sword? But... Tori, are you sure you're all right?'

'I feel,' said Torisen, 'like something the cat threw up, but I don't think I dreamt either that or... Holly, while you're in there, look for the – the changer that resembles Pereden. He'll be wearing blue armour. If he's still alive, take him to my tent, bound and gagged. He's to speak to no one, understand? Not even to you. Swear it!'

'Yes, of course,' said Danior, looking bewildered. He signalled to the Highlord's war-guard. 'Now you'd better go back to camp yourself before anything more happens.'

During most of this, the Wolver had been snuffling around in the undergrowth beyond the hollow. He came trotting back just as Torisen was leaving in the midst of his guard, who had no intention of losing him again.

'Tori, there's another scent here...'

'Not now,' said one of the guards, pushing him aside. Torisen hadn't heard.

'Yes, but... but...' But the war-guard had already left, bearing its leader captive with it.

Meanwhile, in the hollow, Danior had found both the sword

and the blue-armoured warrior lying close to where Torisen had fallen. Danior bound and gagged the warrior as ordered. When he emerged, he looked rather sick. Perhaps that was because he had never dealt so closely with a changer before, or perhaps because for all his puppylike bumbling, he was an intelligent young man and had begun to suspect the truth about his prisoner. At any rate, he was in no mood to gossip with the Wolver.

'But I'm telling you,' the poor Wolver cried, 'there's someone else in there!'

'I know. I stepped on at least two more bodies. If you want them, Grimly, you can have them.'

'But this isn't a changer!'

'I don't care if it's the Witch-King's maiden aunt!' Danior snapped, and left with his own captive.

The Wolver paced back and forth at the mouth of the hollow, torn with indecision. This place was almost as dangerous for him as for the changers, although in a different way and for a different reason. His ancestors had been little better than the dogs of the men who had worshipped here. None of his kind liked to remember that or to admit the effect places like this had on them; but he also couldn't forget the stranger with Torisen's eyes whose scent he had been following until the tide of battle bore him southward. She had gone into the hollow and not come out. His keen nose told him that. He paced a moment more, almost whining, then bared his teeth and dashed inside.

Five feet over the threshold, he dropped to all fours. At five yards, he was padding through the ferns in his complete furs. At fifty feet, the human part of his consciousness had faded to a dim flicker. It was a wolf in mind and body that slunk through the fronds now, barely remembering what he sought, only knowing that this place was frightful. He found two twitching bodies and then, almost against the far cliff wall, one that lay still. The smell was right. Now what? His lupine mind held only the confused impulse to protect. He lay down close beside the motionless form, whimpering slightly until the cliffs caught the faint echo. After that, he lay still in watchful, frightened silence.

30

Blood Rites
The Cataracts: 30th of Winter

Torisen and his war-guard emerged from the wood into the lower meadow opposite the head of the Mendelin Steps in time to see Ardeth set his scheme in motion. The vanguard of the Horde was backed down the steps with some of it still spilling into the field. It looked a very compact, dangerous mass, black under the stormclouds that still hung over it despite the faint, predawn light gathering in the east. The Host faced it over a no man's land of about a hundred feet, as silent and keyed up as its enemy. One war cry on either side would probably have been enough to set them at each other's throats again.

Then the Host parted and Ardeth rode into the space between the armies. He stopped about fifty feet from the Horde and sat quite still. Behind him, his men came forward with the changers' bodies and laid them on the trampled grass. Actually, there were five bodies and six heads, the spare having been brought too, still fitfully grimacing. Then the Kencyr withdrew, Ardeth last, backing Brithany all the way to Storm's side. The entire Host fell back a short distance, waiting, hardly knowing for what.

'It occurs to me,' said Torisen softly to Ardeth, 'that it might not be exactly tactful to show the Wasters what's happened to their revered founders. Just what are you up to, Adric, besides maybe getting us all killed?'

'Think, my boy, think. If, as you guessed, the Horde is only attacking us because its founders have told it to, and if they realise now that their so-called forefathers are no such thing...'

'They might just turn around and go home. If they can still recognise their "founders" in that lot; if they know what changers are; if they object sufficiently to having been tricked...'

569

'And if you spin me one more "if," my boy, I'll... look!'

A Waster had crept forward to the pile of bodies. Several more followed him. For a moment, they formed a dark knot around the changers, then from their midst came sudden yells of rage and grief. A Waster broke away and ran towards the Host, still screaming. The spears of the first Kencyr line came down. The man charged into them, trying to twist past the points, but they caught him, and he fell. The Host went forward a pace, war cries rising in their throats, and so did the Horde. Torisen spurred in front of the Kencyr line.

'Still!' he snapped at it.

Simultaneously, someone by the changers also barked a command, and the Wastelanders checked themselves, startled. An elder rose, holding the spare, severed head by the hair. He was wearing a death mask that might have come off the changer's still-twitching face. He addressed the Horde's vanguard in *Ka'sa*.

Where the hell were Harn and Ashe, Torisen wondered, trying to quiet Storm. Was he about to get caught without even a sword between two colliding armies or...?

But what happened next needed no interpreter. The Waster elder suddenly raised the changers' head and spat full in its face. Then the entire vanguard simply turned, muttering, and withdrew. The elder dropped the head, gave it a contemptuous kick, and followed his people. They all went out of the field, down the steps, onto the plain. The stormclouds followed them.

A collective sigh rose from the Host.

'Is that all?' demanded Essien incredulously.

'It seems so anticlimatic,' protested Essiar.

Torisen turned in the saddle to regard the Edirr twins. They were wearing identical armour, riding twin stallions, and had both managed to get wounded on the left forearm. If he hadn't expected it of them, he would have thought he was seeing double.

'Haven't you two had enough excitement for one night?'

'Oh, never,' they said simultaneously.

Lord Brandan had ridden up. 'Just the same, be glad things ended now. The main body of the Horde is almost here.'

'Will it turn?'

'It's already started to, following the vanguard. I would say, Highlord, that you've just won a rather major battle. Congratulations.'

It hardly seemed to Torisen that he had been involved in the main conflict at all, but it wouldn't do to say so. Others would point that out soon enough. Speaking of which...

'What's become of Caineron? I would have expected him to be in the thick of things.'

'So he was,' said Brandan dryly. 'Rather more so than he intended, I think. For some reason, he was crossing the top of the middle field when his own riders came over the Lower Hurdles on top of him. I don't suppose he's stopped cursing since, although I couldn't swear to it because he seems to have dropped out of sight again.'

'The longer, the better.'

Brandan gave Torisen a sharp look. 'You had better do the same for a while,' he said bluntly. 'On the whole, you look as if you've been fighting the entire battle single-handed.' With that he rode away to look after his own people.

'Sensible Brandan,' murmured Ardeth, looking after him. 'He's right, you know. You do look like something hardly worth warming over. For Trinity's sake, my boy, go get some rest.'

'My lord.' It was one of Ardeth's Kendar, riding up. 'The Wasters left those... those creatures just lying there. What should we do with them?'

'That, I expect, was the final insult,' said Ardeth. 'The changers weren't even considered fit to eat. Tori?'

'Build a pyre and burn them.'

The Kendar was shocked. 'But, Highlord, three of them are still alive, and then there's that head.'

'Kill them and it with my blessings – if you can.'

He rode up through the meadows, through the dead and dying lying thick on the ground in the growing dawn light. His own people were here somewhere. For the first time, he hadn't fought beside them, and now every instinct told him to seek them out; but he couldn't, not just yet. First, he must keep his appointment with Danior. Here at last was his encampment, his own tent, and Burr waiting for him.

'Where's Donkerri?' he asked as they entered the inner chamber.

Burr told him.

Torisen sat down on the cot. After a long moment, he said, 'Does it ever strike you, Burr, that we have a very strange code of honour?'

'My lord?'

'Never mind. Just help me out of this gear.'

Burr gingerly removed the Kenthiar. Its gem still held the ghost of a glow, which lit the inside of its iron box with faint, opalescent hues until Burr slammed the lid on it. He unlaced what was left of Torisen's armour, both the rhi-sar leather and the chain mail byrnie. Under them, Torisen was wearing a padded shirt, which had prevented the mail rings from cutting into him, but he still had darkening bands of bruises where the changer's arms and the axe blade had caught him. It hurt to take a deep breath. Blackie's proverbial luck hadn't prevented him from getting at least a few cracked ribs this time, although Harn would undoubtedly point out that again he had got off very lightly indeed. But where was Harn? He had just turned to ask Burr when a guard announced Danior.

Torisen slipped into the soft black shirt that Burr had handed him, taking his time, bracing himself.

'Send in Lord Danior,' he told the guard. 'Burr, go tell our people to make a special search for Donkerri's body.'

Burr stood his ground. 'Lord, I already have.'

'Then go help them, and take the war-guard with you. I want this tent cleared, Burr. Now.'

Burr left reluctantly as Holly entered, bringing his bound prisoner with him. He had stripped off the latter's distinctive upper armour and put a different helmet on his head, visor down, over a gag. Noting these precautions, Torisen gave Holly a sharp look.

'As far as you know, this is one of the captured changers, right?'

'Yes, but Tori...'

'No "buts". Stick to what you know for certain and make no guesses. They aren't safe. Understand? Now I expect you'd like to get back to sorting out your people.'

'And leave you alone with this... this...' He gave up on the word. 'Tori, is *that* safe?'

Torisen sighed. 'On the average day, I usually do at least three stupid things before breakfast, but this isn't one of them – I hope. Now scoot.'

Holly started to leave, then suddenly turned back. 'I almost forgot,' he said. 'Here.' Almost reverently, he drew Kin-Slayer and handed it to Torisen. Even in the dim tent, the patterns on the blade shone coldly. 'No one will ever question who you are again, Gray Lord's son.'

'I suppose not,' said Torisen a bit dubiously, remembering how his father's sword had served him in the hollow at the heart of the woods.

Holly left.

'Turn around,' Torisen said brusquely to the prisoner.

He cut the cord that bound the other's wrists. The captive shook his hands to restore the circulation, then took off the helmet and spat out the gag. His was a young face that would have been quite handsome if not for a badly swollen nose. Touching it gingerly, he said in a petulant, nasal whine:

'I think you've broken it.'

'That wouldn't surprise me. Why did you do it, Pereden?'

'How did you know it was me and not another one of those damned changers?'

'Several things suggested it. First, you called me "Blackie" in the woods. Not many people outside of the Southern Host know that that's my nickname. Second, I recognised both your armour and your fighting style. Third, we were the only two to come out of that killing circle in anything resembling our right minds. But I wasn't really sure until just now, when you told me. Why, Peri?'

'Oh God. What else had you left me to do?'

'I?'

'Yes, you, damnit!' he said explosively. 'Taking my rightful place as commander of the Southern Host, turning my father against me. You reported every little mistake I made to him, didn't you? You deliberately gave me impossible tasks so you could tell my father how incompetent I was!'

'Peri, I never asked anything of you that I wouldn't have of any officer under my command, and I've never told Ardeth more about anything than I've had to, especially about you. Now I wish I'd told him more.'

'You lied to him!' It came out almost in a shriek. 'You stole his love! Now you're his son, not me.'

'Peri, that's not true . . .'

'True!' he began to pace. 'You want the truth? You never gave me a scrap of authority you didn't have to. You never trusted me, so neither did your officers. And when they became mine, when I finally got command, did they give me their loyalty? No! They still reported to you, still told me at every turn how the great Torisen would do this or that. Damn.'

He snuffled and drew the back of his hand across his face. His nose had started to bleed. Torisen silently gave him a handkerchief.

'Then word came that the Horde was marching north,' he went on. 'My randons said that the wise thing would be to harry and delay it. That was what *you* would have done. But I knew I could turn it, I *knew*, and I would have, too, if those precious officers of yours – yes, and the troops too – hadn't failed me.'

'I see,' said Torisen. Suddenly, he felt almost dizzy, both with fatigue and with knowledge that he had no desire to possess, but there was no stopping now. 'What happened next?'

'I was captured. The changers told me what a fool I'd been not to demand my rights from the first. They showed me how I could still take my rightful place. My place?' He gave a wild laugh. 'No, yours! The Knorths forfeited their power over thirty years ago when your father slunk off into exile like a whipped cur.'

'So they promised to make you Highlord.' Torisen sighed. 'Peri, you are and always have been a fool.'

'Maybe, maybe not. But I'll still have my revenge. How d'you think my father will react when he hears what I've done, and why?'

'It will kill him. And I promised to protect his interests.'

This time Pereden's laugh was distinctly nasty. 'Try,' he said. 'Just try.'

He dropped the stained handkerchief on the floor and turned, sneering, to leave. Torisen came up behind him in three swift strides. His left hand slid around Pereden's neck to brace itself against the other's right shoulder. His right hand caught Pereden's chin.

'I keep my promises, Peri,' he said in the young man's ear. Then, with a quick twist, he broke Pereden's neck.

The young man tumbled down into an untidy heap. Torisen stood staring down at him, breathing hard. Suddenly, there didn't seem to be enough air in the tent. The canvas walls moved... no, he was falling. Something dark moved in the chamber's entrance and strong hands caught him. He blinked. The cot was beneath him now, and Harn was bending over him, his broad face like a full moon incongruously stubbled with beard.

'All right, Blackie, all right. Don't fret. He wasn't worth it.'

'You heard?'

'Enough. He deserved worse. Now what?'

Torisen pushed him back and sat up. His mind felt clear again, rather like the ringing vault of a cloudless sky. 'Put him on the pyre with the other changers – and, Harn, make sure he's unrecognisable first.'

'With pleasure. There'll be no dirges for this one.' His expression changed.

'Now what?'

Harn hemmed and hawed, but finally told him about Singer Ashe.

'Sweet Trinity,' Torisen said heavily. 'If we won this battle, why do things keep getting worse? This is my fault, too. I should have made sure she had those haunt-bites tended to. What did you do with her?'

'Nothing. She's down in the lower meadow now among the wounded, helping to sort the dying from those likely to recover.'

'A haunt, being useful?'

'I don't understand it, either. She has the oddest attitude towards the whole thing – not glad it happened, mind you, but interested in what will happen next. A strange woman, that, and rapidly getting stranger. I don't know what to say to her. Ah!' He shook himself. 'Where's a helmet?' He picked up the one Pereden had worn and clamped it on the young man's head to hide his features. Then he slung the corpse over his shoulder. 'You get some rest, Blackie.'

'But what about my people?'

'A lot of good you'll do them, falling down in a heap every ten minutes. Be as stubborn as usual, Blackie, but for God's sake don't be stupid on top of it. Get some rest.'

He left.

Torisen sighed and stretched out again on his cot. Harn was right. A few hours of *dwar* sleep wouldn't entirely restore him, but it would certainly help. Trinity, but he ached. Senethar techniques controlled the worst of it, but not his restlessness. After about five minutes, he swore out loud and got up.

'Stupid, stupid,' he muttered as he found and put on the oldest clothes he could, including a dull red jacket of Burr's. Then he went out.

The sun was just coming up when a very tall man strode through the woods, following a golden ounce. The cat led him straight to the hollow and bounded in. The mist was thinning. Two changers, one of them headless, lay on beds of crushed ferns, writing slowly. Their flesh was as puffy as drowned men's and mottled with bruises, which even now kept appearing in new patterns. A third changer lay motionless nearby. The ounce skirted them all warily and darted toward the far wall, only to bounce back, all his fur on end, as a large grey wolf rose snarling from the ferns.

The big man hesitated. Then he advanced slowly and went down on one knee.

'You're the Wolver, I think,' he said, pitching his voice almost to a whisper because of the echoes. 'I heard you were about somewhere. Forgotten yourself a bit, have you? There, there, gently...' He reached slowly toward the still form the wolf guarded, but stopped as the beast held his ground, white fangs bared.

'Well, this is a bit of an impasse, isn't it? I'm Marcan, Marc to my friends, and that's one of them there. Friend. Do you understand?'

The wolf snarled.

'Oh dear. We came to Hurlen together, the lass, this kitten, and I. I was captured by Lord Caineron. Ah, that's a name you remember. Enemy, eh? Anyway, the battle began, and then suddenly everyone in camp charged out of it, my guards included. I found the kitten, and we went looking for our friend there in the thick of things, where she usually is. No luck. It wasn't until the battle was over that it occurred to me to look for her here. That was rather slow of me, because this is obviously just the sort of place she would end up. Now, if you'll just let me have a look...'

He spoke in a low, soothing voice, counterpointed by Jorin, who practically stood on his shoulders, singing defiance. When he reached out again, the Wolver went back a step, then suddenly lunged. His jaws closed on Marc's wrist. Kendar and wolf stared at each other.

'There, there,' said Marc gently. 'You don't really mean it, do you?'

The Wolver, if anything, looked embarrassed. He let go. His fangs had barely dented the other's skin.

'Now, let's see.' Marc parted the fronds. 'Hmm. Still breathing, no obvious wounds... what's this?' He picked up something white by Jame's hand. It was the Ivory Knife. The Wolver growled at it. 'I agree, but then the lass always did favour odd toys. It wouldn't do to leave this one here.' He

576

slipped it into her boot sheath. 'Now, let's get out of here.' He picked Jame up and carried her out of the hollow with Jorin bounding ahead and the Wolver trotting at his heels. By the time he crossed the threshold, a shaggy young man followed him, looking sheepish.

'Sorry about that,' he said as Marc put Jame down. 'I got a bit lost in there.'

'So I suspected. Ah.'

Jame had started to revive the moment she was out of the hollow. Now she sat up abruptly with a sharp cry.

'Where are they? Where... oh, Marc! Ancestors be praised. What a foul dream I was having, or at least I think it was a dream. W-was there anyone else in there besides the changers?'

'No, lass. Who else should there be?'

'Those... those men. They came when the scream ended, almost as if they were answering it. I couldn't see them very well. They seemed to be wearing leather collars hung with glowing stones and nothing else. They were very squat. I-I could see their mouths move as if they were chanting, but I couldn't hear anything. Then they started to do... things to the changers. Terrible things. You were there,' she said, turning suddenly to the Wolver. 'You saw.'

'I saw, but I hadn't the wits to make sense of it then, and now it's all slipping away.'

Jame shivered. 'I wish I could forget as easily. At first all eight darklings were there as well as Tori and that man in blue. There was a... a sort of dome of light around Tori and the other, centered on that gem Tori was wearing. The shadow people wouldn't come anywhere near it. Come to think of it, it looked like the stones they were wearing, only polished and bound to that silver collar with Builders' runes. Then, somehow, Tori, the other, and all but three of the changers were gone. The shadow people went on torturing the two changers who were still alive. I think they would have killed them outright if they had been strong enough. That would have been kinder. But they weren't kind. They made me watch, and wait. Maybe they were saving me for last, or maybe it was the worst they could do to me because you were there, wolf, guarding.'

The Wolver was staring back into the hollow, ears flat, half cowering. 'I couldn't have held them off long, not if they were the people of rock and stone who built this place. There are more kinds of ghosts on Rathillien than one. Now can we please get out of here? This place makes my teeth ache.'

Just then, a branch snapped close by in the woods. The Wolver spun about with a squawk, but instead of the squat men whom he most feared, Kendar warriors silently emerged from the trees all around them to ring them in. Just the same, his relief was short-lived.

'Ah, here you are,' said Caineron to Jame, stepping forward with a bland smile. 'You've led me quite a chase, my dear, but now I really think you will accept my hospitality at last.'

The light of a sun just barely up showed the middle and lower meadows strewn with battle debris, much of it human. Because most of the houses had kept their people fairly well together despite the confusion, each now had its own area to search for its fallen. The dead had to be gathered for the pyre, the wounded sorted according to who was likely to live and who to die. Highborn did much of the culling since, oddly enough, many of them had a better instinct for such work than all but the best-trained Kendar. Then, too, it brought more honour to the mortally stricken to be dispatched by the White Knife of a Highborn. Those with lesser injuries were either treated on the spot or sent back to the surgeons' tent in camp.

There were, of course, a great many Wasters still on the field. Most were dead. Searchers dealt summarily with the survivors when they found them.

There were also scavengers. Torisen came on a clutch of them stripping a dead Kendar, and a moment later was nearly trampled by the Coman's war-guard charging down on them. The scavengers bolted. One of them ran between the horses straight into Torisen's arms and struggled in his grasp, scratching and biting. It was only a child, one of Hurlen's tower waifs. So were the others.

'Names of God,' said Korey, staring at his captives. 'And what am I supposed to do with this lot?'

'Take them back to the city,' said Torisen, carrying his prisoner in among the riders and dumping it with the other cowering children. 'You'd better leave a ten-command guarding the bridge and another at the ferry or we'll be overrun.'

'And who in Perimal's name . . . oh, Highlord!'

'The same, getting underfoot and frightening the horses as usual. See to Hurlen, won't you . . . and Korey, I understand that your people were among the last to retreat when the battle line broke. Good work.'

Korey glowered and blushed at the same time. 'Thank you, Highlord. I'll tend to Hurlen.' He wheeled and rode off with his guard.

I really have been wearing black too long if no one can recognise me in anything else, Torisen thought ruefully, and went on.

Torisen found his own people not much farther on, the last to give way when the line broke. Now the lines of the dead seemed incredibly long. All those stiffening hands and still faces, most painfully familiar. Nearly three hundred dead, Harn's second-in-command reported, and perhaps a hundred more still missing. Even if all of the latter turned up, Torisen would still lead back to Gothregor a force more than decimated.

'Still, at sixty to one odds, it might have been worse,' said the second-in-command dryly.

Torisen sighed. 'I suppose so.' He did what he could there, and then went on down into the lower meadow to look for the missing Kendar.

The dead and wounded of all nine houses lay here where the vanguard's initial charge had rolled over them. Searchers moved among them, identifying, classifying. Torisen recognised Ashe. At a distance, she looked unchanged, but as he approached, she turned to look at him, and he stopped short, aghast at her pale face and lifeless eyes.

'Do I ... frighten you, lord?' Her voice was a husky, halting whisper.

'Yes. I didn't know haunts could speak.'

'Most of us ... probably have nothing ... to say. And yet your father ... spoke to you in the White Hills.'

Torisen looked quickly around, but no one was within earshot. 'How do you know that?'

'I find ... that the dead know ... what concerns the dead. It's the concerns ... of the living that we forget ... bit by bit.'

He came closer, drawn despite himself by curiosity. 'What is it like, being dead?'

'I ... hardly know yet. It's like ... a new language, heard for the first time. It will take awhile to learn ... the words, and then they may have no cognates ... in the speech ... of the living. At least, for the first time in forty years ... my leg doesn't hurt.'

'Ashe, I'm very sorry that this happened. Maybe Kindrie can help. Ardeth tells me that he's a powerful healer.'

'He would have to be ... to resurrect the dead. No, Highlord. And don't ... be sorry. Look.'

He had noted the gashes in her jacket without paying much attention to them because there was no blood. Now he realised that they really did correspond to wounds, some very deep. Of course: The dead don't bleed.

'I got these ... defending Harn's back. He never remembers to ... when one of his fits comes on ... which is why I followed him. Any one of them ... might have killed me – if I hadn't already been dead. I have time ... before me now ... that I would have lost forever.'

'But not an eternity,' Torisen said sharply. 'I grew up in the Haunted Lands, Ashe. I saw how haunts change. You belong to the shadows now. Sooner or later, they will consume you.'

'Ah ... but before then ... what songs I will sing!'

Torisen shivered. 'I wonder if the living will be able to bear them. But I'm not fool enough to interfere with a singer. What else can I do for you, Ashe? I owe you for Harn's life.'

'Then give me ... the child. Her brother ... is with the Host now. She should go to him ... and then ... to the pyre. This half-life isn't for one so young ... so defenceless.'

'I know. I've been selfish. But I-I seemed to need her.'

'You did. You don't now. Did you know,' she said, with apparent irrelevancy, 'that during the battle you were seen repeatedly ... both riding a white horse ... and on foot with a sword?'

'So I've heard. I don't know what to make of it.'

'Neither do I ... but it has something to do ... with why you no longer need the child. Let her go.'

Torisen still hesitated and wondered why. What was he really giving up with such reluctance – the bones and shadow of a Kendar child whom he had never known or, in some confused way, the ghost of his own sister, of the child she had been when he had stood by and watched their mad father drive her out into the Haunted Lands? He had let her go then and had felt guilty ever since. He didn't want to lose her again. But, damnit, this wasn't Jame. This was some stranger child with her own path, and he had selfishly kept her from it too long already.

'Yes, yes, of course,' he said, impatient with his own weakness. 'Let her go.'

'Good.' Death-glazed eyes regarded him with deceptive blankness. 'Highlord, this is going ... to sound strange coming from me ... but you look awful.'

He gave a sudden snort of laughter. 'So everyone keeps telling me. Let's just say I'm tougher than I look. It's a family trait. And don't tell me I should rest. I think I'll see what I can do down here to help. After all,' he concluded more bleakly, looking around, 'this was my party.'

The sun was up well above the east bank bluffs now. It would be a hot day. Already heat waves rippled above the lookout's stony point on the escarpment. Torisen brushed insects away from an injured Kendar's face. She was unconscious – a good thing, given the severity of her wounds – but as far as he could tell she was also on the edge of *dwar* sleep and so likely to recover.

'Another one for the surgeons' tent,' he said to the stretcher-bearers who accompanied him. They carried her away.

Torisen rose stiffly. Despite Harn's prediction, he hadn't keeled over yet; but he was beginning to feel distinctly lightheaded. In a way, he welcomed that. It took the edge off his perceptions, made the suffering around him easier to bear. The pain, especially of his own mortally stricken Kendar, seemed to draw him. Perhaps it was their collective suffering that had pulled him all the way here from his own camp, as if part of him lay dying on this hot field. Torisen shook his head impatiently. *Leave fantasies like that to the Shanir*, he thought. He didn't ask himself how he knew that all the dying Kendar personally bound to him had now been found.

Somewhere not far off, someone was whimpering in pain. That didn't sound like a Kencyr. Sure enough, in a fold of the meadow Torisen found a Karkinoran soldier curled up on the ground, arms wrapped around his lower abdomen. Half of his bowels had already spilled out on the grass. Someone in Karkinoran field buff bent over him. Torisen saw with surprise that it was Odalian. The Prince looked up as Torisen approached and shook his head. He drew a knife. The soldier saw and began to scream. He fought them both with a strength born of terror until Torisen pinned his hands, and Odalian delivered a heart thrust.

'Messy,' said Torisen as they walked away.

'What did you expect?' said the other with a sort of suppressed violence. 'They don't have *dwar* sleep, or Senethar techniques to control pain, or even a practical attitude towards death. They're like children, waking up in a slaughterhouse.'

Torisen shot him a surprised look. *And you're so much older?* At that moment, it seemed true. 'You hardly sound as if you think of yourself as one of them,' he said. 'For that matter, just now you've behaving more like a Kencyr Highborn.'

This time, Odalian looked surprised. 'How so?'

'Well, here you are – in common clothes, without your retinue, helping to cull the wounded...'

'Just like you.'

'Yes, I suppose so.' He looked around, shivering. 'So many dead. It wasn't this bad when I led the Southern Host, before anyone was bound to me personally. This was my first major battle as Highlord. And you?'

'My first – as prince.' The other's face indeed bore no lines of experience, but his silver-grey eyes looked old and sick. 'I didn't know they would suffer so much; but that happens in war, doesn't it?' Abruptly, the naive young man in Odalian was back – voice, face, eyes. 'Actually, I came down here looking for you. Have you thought any more about subject ally status for Karkinor?'

'I've hardly had a chance,' said Torisen, thrown off-balance by the other's sudden change both of subject and manner. For a moment, he could have sworn that he was walking beside quite a different person. *More fantasies*, he told himself, and dismissed them. 'You're still serious about that, Highness?'

'More than ever.'

'It isn't something I can just bestow on my own, you know,' he said, hedging. 'In theory, yes, as Highlord, but the rest of the Council would be furious, with good reason. I'll have to consult their wishes.'

'Yes, I can see that,' the other replied with quiet persistence. 'You said before, though, that it might impress them if I showed I was willing to undergo the full rites. What if I were to blood-bind myself to you now, as an act of good faith?'

The idea at first startled Torisen and then made him very uneasy. He had mimicked blood-binding many times before, as with Harn at Tentir, but never gone so far as actually to make the cuts. The blood itself didn't bother him or the scars. What, then? Because Odalian wanted him to play the Shanir in such explicit terms? Yes. He could feel all his mental defences rise at the very thought. But should he let that prevent a just decision? No, of course not. But... but... but...

'Damnation,' he said, disgusted with himself. 'Your people fought beside us and many of them died. We owe Karkinor something for that. Whether the Council will go so far as to grant ally status of any sort I don't know, but at least I can give you the chance to put your request in the strongest possible terms. If they say "no", I'll release you and no harm done. That, at least, is something no true blood-binder could do.'

'You'll go through with the rites?' The Prince's voice was eager. It must have been imagination that for an instant his eyes looked so bleak. 'Here? Now?'

'In the middle of a field with stretcher-bearers tripping over us? No. I suggest the lookout's point on the escarpment. At least there with the sentinel withdrawn we'll have some privacy.'

'That,' said the Prince, 'will be perfect.'

Jame circled the room one more time, looking for some way out. Actually, 'room' was probably the wrong word for it. It was an inner compartment of Lord Caineron's tent, which was the largest, most intricate of its kind that Jame had ever seen. She had been brought here in the midst of Caineron's war-guard nearly two hours ago. Marc, Jorin, and the Wolver were presumably prisoners, too. She didn't think Caineron would hurt any of them, but precious time was passing, and Tori was still unwarned.

The walls were made of strong canvas dyed yellow and orange. She might have cut her way out, if Caineron hadn't taken the Knife. She tried again to pick a seam, but her claws were too sore now even to extend. Attack the guard? Fine, if she could get at him. The room was laced shut on the outside, an arrangement that made her wonder if it had been used as a prison before, probably without that delicate table in the corner with glasses and a carafe of wine on it or these pillows scattered about its canvas floor. Jame kicked one in sheer frustration. Damn, damn, damn...

Someone was unlacing the door flap. A moment later, a guard held it open as Caineron entered smiling, respendent in a white coat embroidered with sunflowers and marigolds across the shoulders. In the golden light of the room, he seemed to glow. The guard laced up the flap again after him.

'My apologies for having left you on your own for so long, my dear. Have you been comfortable?'

'Why are you keeping me a prisoner?'

He made a slight face, as if silently deploring her lack of manners. 'A prisoner? Oh no. An honoured guest. But I see you haven't touched the refreshments my guard left you. Let me pour you some wine.' He crossed to the table.

'Where is my brother?'

'Somewhere in the lower meadow, I believe, ostensibly helping to cull the wounded. The Prince is there, too. Soon their paths will no doubt cross. How delightful for both of them.'

He was playing with her. He knew she knew about the changer, because Graykin had told him, but he didn't know that she knew that he knew. Damn these games anyway. There wasn't time.

'Torisen presumably has friends among the Highborn, if not on the Council,' she said. 'What will they say when they find out you've allowed him to be trapped by a changer impersonating the Prince?'

He turned to look at her. 'Ah. And who will tell them? You?'

Jame stiffened at his tone. 'No one has ever questioned my word or honour.'

'Honour doesn't come into it,' he said coolly. 'Not with the unbalanced. My dear, just look at yourself. No Highborn in her right mind would dress like that or disport herself as you have. Lyra has told me about some of your little escapades at Karkinaroth, and I've seen others for myself here at the Cataracts. You're patently unhinged, my dear. There's not a chance that anyone will take you seriously. Then too, you forget that eventually your brother or more likely something very similar to him will come back from the lower meadow. Who will the Council believe then, you or him? But do have some wine, my dear. It would be much better if you didn't repulse my hospitality.'

He held the glass out to her. Under the circumstances, it would be an insult to refuse; but Jame remembered all too clearly that last time someone had offered her wine. That in turn gave her an idea. She accepted the glass.

Caineron beamed at her. 'That's better. Now we can be more comfortable. You know, my dear, it would interest me very much to know where you've been keeping yourself these past fifteen or so years, and how you came by such an odd weapon as this.'

He was wearing the Ivory Knife sheathed at his ample waist. How like the man simply to appropriate it, just as he had Jorin – twice now, presumably.

'It has a very sharp edge,' said Jame, hoping he would try it and find out for himself.

'I daresay. But you haven't answered my question.'

Jame had turned her back. Keep him talking. 'First tell me what you mean to do with me.'

She heard him sigh behind her. 'I really must teach you the meaning of obedience, my dear . In fact, it will be a pleasure . . . perhaps for you, too. At least, I think you'll be pleased with the plans I have for you. It isn't every girl who is honoured with an alliance with the first blood of such a powerful house as mine.' He went on, happily describing the advantages of such a match, most of which sounded extremely trivial to Jame. At a time like this, he was trying to bribe her with toys, confident that they would delight her. She made noncommittal noises, her back still turned. Deftly, she unsealed the inner pocket that held the crystals from the Builder's house. If the river water had got at them . . . but no. She had taken them thinking that someday she might find someone to test them on. Well, no time like the present. She dropped a pinch into her wine. The crystals dissolved immediately, leaving no visible trace. As for a smell . . .

'What are you doing, my dear?'

She turned, the glass still raised to her nose. 'There's something in my wine. A potion? Was this what you meant by hospitality, my lord?'

'Nonsense,' said Caineron sharply. 'Give me that.' He took the glass, sniffed, drank. 'There, you see? Next time, perhaps you'll trust . . . hic! . . . me.'

For a moment, he looked uncertain, but it wasn't in his nature to doubt himself long on any point. He went on talking about the glories of his house, sipping absentmindedly from the glass, which he had forgotten to return, and hiccuping whenever he least expected it. Torisen's presumption figured in his discourse too; but now he seemed contemptuously amused by it rather than angered.

'Imagine that . . . hic! . . . man, thinking he can disguise himself simply by putting on a red coat, sneaking . . . hic! . . . off without his war-guard to the lower meadow. Why? All so he and the Prince can confirm a pact without the Council's . . . hic! . . . approval. Ardeth is going to spit blood when he finds out. He still thinks Torisen only jumps when he pulls the strings. Well, we'll see after this who jumps, and why. Hic!'

He poured himself more wine. His feet, Jame suddenly noticed, were no longer quite touching the canvas floor.

Caineron also noticed. He tentatively felt downward with one elegant boot, then cleared his throat and put down the glass.

'This is a rather potent vintage,' he said carefully. 'Luckily, I have a very strong head for wine ... hic!'

He went up another inch and began to look rather alarmed, but much more so when Jame darted in and whipped the Ivory Knife from his sheath. She jumped back. He began to shout.

'Guard, guard! Assassin! Sorcery! Hic!'

The guard could be heard frantically unlacing the door. Jame slashed at the rear canvas wall. The tough fabric ripped, half cut, half rotted by the Knife's cold edge. She wriggled out through the slit into a canvas corridor. Which way now? More guards were coming. She cut through the opposite wall, and emerged in a silk-draped bower. Lyra sprang up, shrieking.

'Just passing through,' Jame said hastily, and did so by the next wall.

Another corridor, another wall – Trinity, how big was this tent? – another room, and a guard spinning around to face her. He went down with a grunt under Marc's fist.

'I thought you'd be along sooner or later,' said the big Kendar tranquilly while Jorin rubbed against her knee and the Wolver yelped questions from the next compartment. She slit the wall to let him out.

'Look, I'm in a bit of a hurry. Can you two cause some confusion to cover my escape?'

'I'd say you've been doing pretty well on your own,' said Marc, listening to the shrieks, bellows, and shouts that followed in Jame's wake. 'But certainly. Our pleasure.'

'And hang onto Jorin again.'

She heard the ounce's protesting wail as she slashed into and dived through the far wall. Poor Jorin, always getting left. Two more canvas barriers, each brighter than the one before, and at last the open air of a sunny, hot morning.

People had begun to gather around the tent, listening with amazement to the uproar within. One of them, a Kendar girl, led a tall grey war horse. Jame seized the reins.

'But this is Commander Sheth's horse!' protested the girl, hanging on.

'And I need it. Understand?'

The other met her eyes and let go, gulping. 'U-understood, Highborn.'

Jame scrambled up onto the stallion's bare back. Trinity, but the ground looked a long way down from up here. She had played tag-you're-dead on the roofs of three-storey buildings and felt more secure. Behind, part of the tent collapsed to the sound of outraged shouts from within. Marc and the Wolver were evidently enjoying themselves. If they could just manage to breech the roof, maybe Caineron would float away, sunflowers, marigolds, and all.

Jame clamped heels to her mount and nearly shot off over his tail as he bolted. If she survived the day, she thought, clinging desperately, she simply had to learn how to ride. They thundered down through the camp, over the Lower Hurdles (fortunately, at a low point), and across the middle field. Searchers leaped out of the way and shouted angrily after them. The ground seemed paved with bodies, but this time she had a mount who knew where to put his hooves. They burst through the bottleneck between the woods and river into the lower meadow.

'Where is Torisen?' Jame shouted to a pair of stretcher-bearers, reining in as much as she dared. The stallion curveted, as if to test her none-too-secure seat. 'He's wearing a red coat.'

'Red? *That* was the Highlord? Then he's gone to the lookout's point, Highborn. The Prince was with him.'

Jame galloped on. She was below the battlefield now with no more bodies underfoot. The upper cataract roared below her in its gorge. Ahead some five hundred feet the world seemed to end at the edge of the escarpment with nothing beyond but sky. On the point stood two figures. One wore Karkinoran field buff; the other, a dark red coat. The man in buff knelt. The other gave him his hands.

'Tori, no! Don't...!'

The horse shied. Jame lost her grip and tumbled off. Earth and sky blurred together as she rolled over and over in the thick grass. Her cap flew off. Long, black hair whipped in her eyes. Then she had tumbled to her feet and was running. Ahead, the buff-coated figure seemed to be on the ground, and her brother was bending over him. What had happened? She was still a good hundred yards away, her shadow leaping on before her. Her shadow? But the sun rose in the east, not the north. Something very bright was coming up fast behind her. Even as she turned to look, it shot overhead, blazing. Sweet Trinity, the Dream-Weaver. What in Perimal's name was going on?

Torisen asked himself the same thing. The proper words had

been spoken, the cuts made, and the Prince had gone down on one knee to drink the blood welling up in the Highlord's cupped hands that would symbolically bind Odalian to their conditional oath.

'There. That's done,' Torisen had said, relieved; and the Prince had looked up at him with an odd expression.

'Yes. It's done.'

Then a tremor had gone through the Karkinoran as if the very flesh rippled on his bones. His look had turned inward in astonishment and growing dismay. Another tremor had shaken him.

'Odalian? Your Highness? What's wrong?'

But the Prince didn't answer. He was huddled on the ground now, hands over his face. His fingers seemed impossibly long and thin, stretching up over his eyes into his hair like the bars of a helmet, but the thing that he fought was inside.

A blinding light passed overhead. Torisen stared after it, bewildered. It arced out over the plain, shining like a comet as it crossed the blackness of the retreating stormclouds. The after-image of a woman's form burned in his mind's eye. Something about her made him catch his breath. Who *was* that?

The Prince gave a ragged laugh. When Torisen looked sharply back, a girl was crouching opposite him, panting as if after a hard run, her dark hair tumbling down about her to the ground. Surely, he knew her too, but it couldn't be...

'Binder,' gasped the Prince through his hands. 'Joke's... on me.'

Jame stared at him. Then her eyes snapped up to her brother. Binder? *Blood*-binder? Tori, a Shanir?

He was staring back at her with growing incredulity. 'Who in Perimal's name are... oh no. Don't tell me.'

'I'm afraid so. Hello, brother.' Growing light made her look sharply southward. 'Sweet Trinity. Here she comes again.'

'Here who comes? Who *is* that woman?'

The light was almost on top of them now. Jame sprang up without answering, shielding her eyes against the brilliance. The Prince caught at her, but it wasn't the Prince any more. This creature's face rippled like a reflection on stagnant pond water. 'Don't!' it croaked. 'Don't get in her way, either of you! One touch, and she'll reap your souls. She can't help herself!'

The light slowed, hovered just beyond the escarpment's edge. Its brightness hurt the eye. Torisen saw nothing staring directly into it, but when he turned away, eyes watering, the woman's image danced before him. Her shadow stood between her and the false prince. It held a white knife.

'Leave him alone, damnit!'

Jame's voice sounded shrill even to her. What on earth was she doing, coming between two creatures of legend? The Master had sent the Mistress to bring back his faithful servant, apparently not realising what a subtle, double game the changer had played. What was that to her . . . except that if it were not for Tirandys, she would never have learned the meaning of honour.

'Let him die in peace!'

She had spoken Master Runes more than once. For the first time, she heard threads of their power weave through her voice, but not enough of them. Never mind. She had the Ivory Knife. She could defend herself and the other two if . . . if . . .

The Dream-Weaver's beautiful face was still tranquil, almost masklike, and, this time, startlingly familiar. Jame glanced from it to the pommel of the Knife and back again in amazement. Yes, of the three faces carved there – maiden, lady, hag – the Mistress's was the second. But no ivory could catch the silver sheen of those eyes or the impossible black of their pupils, like the void between the stars.

As in the Ebonbane, Jame felt that darkness tug at her. She was falling into it, down, down. . . . But at the same time she felt the stones of the escarpment under her feet and sunlight hot on her left cheek. What she saw, though, was darkness, and an arch of rock spanning the unmade chaos that gaped at the very core of the Dream-Weaver's being. Winds howled into it. Jame could almost feel them. She had heard of the soul-metaphors used by healers and knew that this was the other's soul-scape; but if the bridge was a metaphor, the gaping emptiness beneath it wasn't. Through the abuse of her Shanir powers, the first Jamethiel had opened this breach into the void beyond the Chain of Creation, just as the Arrin-ken had said. Now the souls of those whom she touched fell shrieking into it, as Jame's would too if her namesake touched her.

But where was the Dream-Weaver? She had been scarcely ten feet away, just beyond the cliff's edge. Jame stepped hesitantly out onto the arch. She felt the grass between the stones of the escarpment brush against her legs and knew that she was walking towards the brink.

Light glimmered ahead. A figure danced on the arch over the

void, tracing with singleminded concentration the kantirs of the Senetha, which helped her to keep her precarious balance. In outward aspect, she had been a beautiful lady clad in dazzling white. Here at the centre of her being, though, the garments of her soul had faded to the colour of bone, with a glow that barely touched the surrounding darkness. Her long hair was also white, and her pale features bore a likeness more to the third than the second face on the Ivory Knife's pommel. Some shreds of beauty remained, however, saved from ruin by an underlying innocence that not even this personal hell had thus far managed to destroy. Jame took another hesitant step towards her.

'Mother?'

The woman turned. They were very close to each other now. Without thinking, Jame almost touched the other's pale cheek and saw that in a mirror gesture the Dream-Weaver was almost touching hers.

'Daughter?'

Jame stared at her. 'I-I hardly remember you,' she stammered. 'It's been so very, very long. Why did you leave us?'

'Because I could no longer touch you.'

There was so much more to say, so many questions and answers needed to span the years of separation that lay between them; but time had run out. The Dream-Weaver tottered, her eyes widening in sudden horror. She had stopped dancing. The rock beneath them had begun to crumble. Jame also staggered. She hardly knew if she felt the escarpment underfoot now or the metaphoric bridge; but whatever it was, it wouldn't be there long. If the other touched her now, she would surely fall; but the Dream-Weaver just might regain her balance. She saw the other's panic-stricken indecision. The Mistress had reaped souls before as if in a dream. To take one now, knowing what she did, would be the end of innocence, the true fall from honour, but it might also mean survival.

A sudden smile lit the Dream-Weaver's worn features. Her hand passed Jame's face in a phantom caress, and the span of rock on which she stood gave way. Jame gave a sharp cry and lunged forward to catch her, but missed. Sprawling on the edge of the broken arch, she saw the other's soul plummet away, white hair streaming, into the void. Pieces of stone fell after her. The bridge was disintegrating. Jame clung to it, too afraid to move, even though she knew instinctively that the brink of the escarpment was also giving way beneath her. Behind her,

590

someone was shouting her name over the winds' howl:

'Jamie, give me your hand! Do you hear me? Answer!'

'I hear you, Senethari,' she whispered. One of her hands released its grip on the crumbling rock and groped blindly behind her as if of its own accord, impelled by a childish trust she had thought long since dead.

Another hand closed on hers. Even as the arch gave way under her, she was wrenched back out of darkness into blinding light and fell face down on the hot stones of the escarpment.

The roar of wind seemed to fill the world. Jame felt the rushing air try to suck her off the ground, but something held her down. She could hear the trees of Eldest Island bend, groaning, and a great whoosh as tear-of-silver leaves rose in a glistening sheet from the gorge. What was happening? Even with eyes squeezed shut, she was half stunned by the light, as if the sun had come to rest just beyond the escarpment and everything was falling into the darkness at its heart. While the Dream-Weaver's soul had kept its uncertain balance, only other souls had plunged through the portal of her body into that void. Now her soul had followed the others, and all matter seemed to be rushing after it. By sacrificing herself, Jamethiel had saved both her daughter and her long-compromised honour, but had she also doomed all of Rathillien? For a moment, that seemed all too likely, but then the winds faltered and began to die.

Jame dragged herself free and turned to look. For a moment, her eyes were dazzled; but then they cleared in time to see a point of radiance as bright as a distant star dwindle and vanish just beyond the cliff edge. The portal that had been Jamethiel Dream-Weaver had collapsed in on itself and closed forever. If the destruction of the body freed the soul, then the Mistress was free at last – if such rules applied beyond the Chain of Creation. Jame found herself praying to the god she despised that they did.

She glanced toward the ground then and saw the changer Tirandys sprawling before her, his fingers dug into the very rock like pale roots. She had crawled out from under his left arm. Torisen still lay under his right. Hastily, she pulled her brother free.

'Are you all right?' she demanded as he sat up, looking distinctly groggy.

'Well . . . enough. Too many things caught up with me at once – including you.'

'Sorry. I didn't mean to be quite so dramatic about it... Trinity!'

Tirandys was moving. She had thought he was dead, had hoped it, at least, for his sake, forgetting how hard changers die. He rose on an elbow. His face moved as if secret things crawled at will beneath the skin. Then he made a choking noise and convulsed horribly. They heard bones break. Jame threw off her brother's restraining hand and dropped to her knees at the changer's side. The muscles of his back and shoulders writhed like snakes under her hands.

'Tell me what to do!' she cried in an agony of helplessness.

The seizure subsided, and for a moment he lay still, panting. Then he rolled over. The Ivory Knife was in his hand.

'You've already done it,' he said in a hoarse, nearly unrecognisable voice. An expression almost like a smile crossed his tortured face. 'We trained you well, Jamie. Some good does endure, it seems.'

Then, before the next convulsion could grip him, he turned the Knife's point to his chest and fell forward on it.

He was already dead when Jame turned him over. Even as they watched, his face changed one last time, settling into lines as fine-cut and tranquil as any on a Knorth death banner. Jame closed his silver eyes. *Goodbye, Tirandys, Senethari.*

Her own eyes were stinging.

'But I never cry,' she said almost defiantly to her brother, and then amazed them both by bursting into tears.

Epilogue: Moon Rise

The Lower Hurdles: 31st of Winter

Jame paced the small inner chamber of Torisen's pavilion, which had been set aside for her use. Light was fading beyond the canvas wall. It was late afternoon, almost thirty hours since the events on the escarpment. In all that time, she had hardly seen anyone. When her brother did return to the tent, it was only to collapse in the outer chamber and sleep as long as Burr could keep away the swarms of people who still surrounded him day and night, making requests and requesting orders. Just the same, she wished he would at least look in to say hello. She was beginning to feel more and more like a forgotten piece of luggage.

Jame eyed the canvas wall. It would be the work of seconds to cut her way out with the Ivory Knife, which Torisen had let her keep, apparently not realising what it was. For that matter, it wouldn't be hard simply to slip past Burr and take a little walk, just to see the sky and feel the breeze. Since Torisen had moved the tent away from the main camp down here to the edge of the Lower Hurdles, perhaps no one would even see her.

She sighed. No, that wouldn't do. Highborn women apparently did not wander around unattended. In fact, there seemed to be a great many things they didn't do. Again, she had a new game to learn, and she already hated the rules. Just the same, she would have to know what they were before she could find a way around them – if such a way existed. If not ... well, she wouldn't think about that yet. Once they found some 'suitable' clothes for her, perhaps she would at least be allowed out of this canvas cell.

In the meantime, at least she had Jorin for company. The ounce was napping on the cot now with his head under the pillow, pretending to be invisible. He had charged into the tent last night and scuttled under the bed, clearly determined not to be hauled away again. Then she had heard Torisen outside, speaking to Marc. It was curious that while the big Kendar had been looking after her, her brother had had charge of Marc's little sister Willow, or rather of her bones. She gathered from what she had heard eavesdropping, that Marc now had a place in Torisen's household whenever he cared to claim it. That was reassuring, as was the note she had found knotted in a scarf around Jorin's neck, written by the Wolver for Marc, who didn't know how. It seemed that her friend had finally landed on his feet. She wondered a bit forlornly if she would ever see him again.

She also wondered about Graykin. Just thinking about him made her uneasy, and yet she found that she no longer distrusted him. Accident or no, he was bound to her, and she believed that he would keep the Book safe for her – if that lay in his power. But Caineron must have realised by now that his bastard son had betrayed him. That put Graykin in great peril, perhaps all the more so because she had entrusted him with such a dangerous secret. In retrospect, she probably shouldn't have; but as with Kin-Slayer, there hadn't seemed to be much choice. The thought of Caineron wresting the Book from Graykin made her shudder, but somehow she didn't think Graykin had yet faced any such crisis. She would have to find some way to help him before he did.

Jorin's head came out from under the pillow, ears pricked. The next moment he had leapt off the cot and dived under it.

'Lady, may I enter?' It was Burr, in the no man's land of the middle chamber.

'Are you sure you want to risk it? Ah, never mind. Come in.'

He entered, his arms full of something pink and frothy. Jame eyed it with misgiving.

'What in Perimal's name is that?'

'A dress, lady, from Hurlen. It was the only decent one we could find for tonight's feast.'

'Feast? What feast?'

'To honour the dead, lady. The entire High Council sups here this evening. They also want to meet you.'

'Trinity. I think I preferred being a piece of lost luggage.'

'My lady?'

'Never mind. Let's see that thing.' She took the dress from him and held it up. 'Names of God. Did you say "decent"?'

Burr stared at it. His expression didn't change, but colour

crept into his face until, to Jame's amusement, he was blushing violently.

Dusk.

Torisen collapsed wearily into a camp chair before his tent and stretched out his legs. All the bodies had finally been gathered from the meadows, the wounded tended to, and the slain given to the pyre. That last had taken most of today. He could still see the glow out on the escarpment against the darkening sky. Tomorrow all the lords would start rebuilding their forces by taking *yondri* into their regular service, but that was a rite for the morning. Tonight still belonged to the dead, whose memories they would soon be honouring.

Burr emerged from the tent and offered him a cup. He took it, sipped, and made a face. Another damned posset. Oh well. If he objected, Burr was apt to say something scathing about his general decrepitude or, worse, about the barely closed cuts on his hands. He hadn't explained those yet to anyone and didn't intend to if he could help it.

Their sting reminded him of another pyre, down by the river, away from the others. Even if Jame hadn't insisted, he probably would have arranged full rites for the false prince. Odd that after their brief conversation down there in the lower meadow among the wounded, he couldn't quite think of the changer now as the enemy he undoubtedly had been. At any rate, he hadn't been prepared to leave any Kencyr to the outraged Karkinorans. It hadn't pleased them to learn an imposter had led them into battle; and Harn hadn't sweetened their tempers any by pointing out that between Odalian and a darkling changer, they had got by far the better war-leader. But then they had already been upset by news from Karkinaroth of the palace's collapse. Torisen suspected that Jame had come down the Tardy from that city. He shifted uneasily in his chair, wondering if she could have had anything to do with the palace's destruction. But no. Surely not even Jame could have that cataclysmic an effect – or could she?

She has power of her own, boy. Why do you think I named her Jamethiel?

He flinched away from the memory of his father's voice and remembered instead, despite himself, the strange events on the escarpment. All that light and wind and noise. He hadn't understood any of it then and wasn't sure that he wanted to now. It was confusing enough to have his twin sister back, not as the child he remembered, not even as the woman he had tried to imagine, but as this half-grown girl with a tentative smile and a darkness lurking in the shadow of her silver-grey eyes that frightened him more than he cared to admit.

Face it, boy, he thought glumly. *If she were strange before, when Father drove her out, she's ten times stranger now ... and this time she's your responsibility.*

He supposed that in a way that culpability extended to the damage the wind from the escarpment had done to the camp. Trinity, what a mess that had been. Panicking horses all over the meadows, supplies scattered, tents blown down right and left, all but Caineron's which, for some reason, had already been half collapsed ...

Come to think of it, Caineron himself hadn't been seen since. When Torisen had invited all the High Council to dinner tonight, Caineron had sent back word that he was indisposed.

'Not quite feeling in touch with things yet,' his randon commander Sheth Sharp-Tongue had added with a sardonic smile.

Torisen didn't quite know what to make of that, and he wasn't about to ask for fear Jame would turn out to be at the bottom of that mystery too, as camp rumour already hinted.

He looked out over the middle and lower fields, darkening now. Fireflies danced over them and glowing mist nestled softly in their hollows. After the wind had knocked over his tent, he had moved in down here away from the rest of the camp to the Lower Hurdles ...

'Putting me in quarantine?' Jame had asked.

... because it was so peaceful. Now below the tent Kendar were setting up chairs and a table borrowed from Hurlen. The fine silver and crystal had all been lent by Ardeth, as had been the cook. The odour of rich meat and spices wafted over the meadow. It was fitting that they gather to celebrate their victory, or at least their survival. The entire Host would be pausing to catch its breath tonight, to share the joy of still being alive and to remember the dead. Torisen wished he could spend the evening with his randon. If the Council didn't sit too late over its wine, he would slip upfield to Harn's tent to talk again with Commanders Elon and Lorey of the Southern Host, just to convince himself that they and their troops were really here.

They had come in early that afternoon, nearly two-thirds of

596

the Southern Host, exhausted and filthy after their desert campaign, but alive. It turned out that only Pereden's centre column had been virtually annihilated. The message found at Wyrden had come from Larch, its randon commander, who had had no way of knowing that when Pereden's ill-judged assault had failed and he had been captured, the right and left flanks of the Southern Host had fallen back, each unaware of the other's survival. They had continued to harry the Wastelanders all the way to the Cataracts and probably were the reason the Riverland Host had reached the battlefield first. So Pereden had a fair chance of going down in history as a hero after all. Ardeth must be very pleased. Torisen wondered, though, what kind of a song Ashe would make out of the whole affair, given her new perspective.

A faint light grew over the east bank bluff. The horn of the new moon edged up over the trees, the merest curve of ivory topped with pale rose. Torisen watched it rise.

'I thought I would never see that again,' said Jame behind him.

'Nor I.'

Her thoughts so closely matched his own that it took him a moment to realise that she was actually there. He turned. Finding Jame anything like proper clothes had been quite a problem in a camp with only one other Highborn lady who also, apparently, had arrived without luggage. She looked, he thought, like a child who had made a not very successful raid on her mother's wardrobe. She glowered at him from behind a makeshift mask.

'Go ahead. Laugh. I'd like to see how you would look in some three-hundred-pound courtesan's best street dress.'

He stared at her. 'How in Perimal's name do you know that?'

'Simple. This wretched thing is big enough for three of me.'

'No, no . . . the rest of it.'

'Oh. Well, best, because it's perfectly clean; courtesan, because it had slits. Fore and aft. Poor Burr nearly had pups when I pointed them out to him. They're sewed shut now. Wouldn't it be better, though, if I wore my old clothes? After all, plenty of people have already seen me in them.'

'Believe me, the High Council will find even a street-walker's gown less offensive than a knife-fighter's *d'hen* – although I sincerely hope they have no more ideas of whose dress that was than I did.'

Jame sighed. 'All right, Tori. I know I haven't had your experience with the world, but then,' she added, with a flash of pure mischief, 'you haven't had mine, either.'

'Oh, for God's sake...!'

'Sorry. But what *will* you tell them about me?'

'Just what you've told me. Nothing. Let them speculate.'

'Oh, I expect they'll do that, all right,' she said dryly. 'But Tori, do I really have to meet the High Council tonight? Isn't it a bit unusual to show off any Highborn woman in public?'

'It is, very. But you're a new player entering an extremely complex game of bloodlines and power. Our house has led the Kencyrath since the beginning, by our god's decree. The other Highborn thought they only had me left to deal with, but suddenly here you are, a new Knorth, a new possibility – or threat. After all the rumours that have been floating around camp, the High Council needs to see you, to be reassured that you're only a pawn after all.'

'And am I?'

'Yes,' he said, looking away, willing it to be true. 'What else?'

'I see,' she said in a expressionless voice, after a pause. 'Well, then, I suppose you'd better take this.'

She tugged at a ring. He had noticed its gold band before, but not the stone, which had been turned inward and wrapped with a scrap of cloth to keep it in place. The cloth fluttered down. The stone caught a flash of firelight and blazed back green as a cat's eye.

'Father's ring.' Torisen rose quickly. *The emblems of my power in her hands, boy.* 'Give me that,' he said sharply. 'You should never have put it on.'

'I didn't exactly do it to amuse myself,' she said, nettled. 'And I would have returned it before now if I'd had a chance. Here.'

She held it out to him. He reached for it, then paused involuntarily. She must have realised what made him hesitate for she raised her other hand and flexed the claws. 'Some things don't change, do they?' she said with a bitter smile. 'Yes, Tori, I'm still a Shanir.'

Torisen took the ring and put it on. He probably had her to thank for the return of Kin-Slayer too, he realised; but the words of gratitude stuck in his throat. He remembered Kindrie. There was another debt to a Shanir that he hadn't been able to make himself pay – yet.

'Perhaps I haven't changed all that much either,' he said

slowly, 'but I am trying.' He looked up sharply. 'What did you say?'

'I?' Her eyes widened, startled . . . guilty? 'Nothing.'

He knew that was true, but the ghost of a whisper still echoed in his mind: *'You had better try, blood-binder.'* He shook his head as if to clear it. After the past two days, it wasn't surprising that he had begun to hear voices, even if they didn't make any sense.

Jame had picked up his posset, sipped it, and made a face. 'You actually like this stuff?'

'No, not at all.'

'Nor I. It tastes as if something was sick in it. So now what?'

'Most of us will start back for the Riverland tomorrow. Only token garrisons at Kestrie and Kraggen keeps hold it now. Some will stay here until the wounded can travel. Ardeth will probably insist on going to the Southern Wastes to look for his son's bones.' Torisen suddenly felt rather ill. 'I suppose I'll have to go with him.'

'No. I meant what will happen to me . . . to us?'

He looked at her, then away. 'I don't know.' *Your Shanir twin, boy, your darker half, returned to destroy you . . .*

No. Those too were his father's words. But she *was* dangerous. He would have to control her, find some way to bind her energy and power . . . or was that Ganth talking again?

'This is going to be hard,' he said. 'For both of us. But we'll find some way to make it work. We have to.'

Burr appeared around the corner of the tent. 'My lord, the Council members are coming down from the main camp. I can see their torches.'

Torisen took a deep breath. 'So now the game begins again.' Under Burr's disapproving eyes, he deliberately emptied his posset onto the ground, almost as if pouring a libation. 'Ready?'

'Sweet Trinity. Of course not.'

'Nor I, but here we go anyway.' The Highlord stepped forward to greet his guests, whose voices now clearly sounded by the tent's far side. 'Oh, and by the way,' he said over his shoulder to Jame with a sudden, wry smile, 'welcome back.'

Appendix I

The Thieves' Guild

The thieves' guild is the most powerful professional organisation in Tai-tastigon, so much so that it usually has a representative on the city's governing council, the Five. Guild members obey both Guild and municipal laws (the latter rather peculiar, in some cases) and are considered respectable citizens – unless they get caught. Then the penalties range from fines to the loss of a finger for a first offense to the removal of one's entire hide, usually for a robbery involving undue violence or the injury of a guard.

The Sirdan is high lord of the Guild. Under him are five officials, each one in charge of a court where a certain type of stolen goods is assessed to determine the duty that the thief owes the Guild and also the period of jeopardy during which possession of the stolen object is punishable by law. These courts handle gold, silver, jewels, and glassware (a highly prized commodity in the Eastern Lands). The fifth court specialises in fur, fabric, and works of art. At the time of this story, the following officials are in charge of these courts:

Gold Court:	Abbotir *(Bane's foster-father)*
Silver Court:	Carbinia
Jewel Court:	Thulican
Glass Court:	Odalian
Shining Court:	Chardin

The Sirdan appoints these people, so they tend to support him – unless someone makes them a better offer.

Next in importance are the one hundred master thieves who each have been granted one of the city's districts as his territory. There are landless masters too, but they haven't the right to take on apprentices or to vote.

Every seven years, a Guild Council convenes on Winter's Eve to elect a new sirdan or to reinstate the old one. Three weeks before, the landed masters meet to select their two representatives to the Council. Each of these men has one vote. Four more votes go to the Provincial representatives, who come from affiliated thieves' guilds in Endiscar, Tai-Abendra, Tai-Weir, and Tai-Sondre. The real power, however, remains with the lords of the five courts, who have two votes each. Guild elections tend to be quite before the fact and violent afterwards, when the unsuccessful candidates for high office are no longer protected by law.

Appendix II

The Tastigon Calendar

Tastigon Dates	*Equivalents*
Spring's Eve (new year begins)	March 1
Summer's Eve	May 1
High Summer's Day	July 1
Autumn's Eve	September 1
Feast of Dead Gods (begins at midnight of Autumn's Eve and lasts until dawn)	
Winter's Eve	November 1
Mid-Winter's Day	January 1
Feast of Fools	February 29

360 days = a year (361, actually, but the Feast of Fools is never counted)

Autumn = 60 days
Winter = 120 days (60 to Mid-Winter's Day)
Spring = 60 days
Summer = 120 days (60 to High Summer's Day)

1 week = 10 days

The novel spans just over a year, beginning with the Feast of Dead Gods and ending a few days after the next Winter's Eve.

Appendix III

The Kencyrath

Some thirty millennia ago, the entity known as Perimal Darkling first breeched the barrier between the outer void and the series of parallel universes called the Chain of Creation. It began to devour universe after universe, entering each one in turn through a threshold world. These special worlds existed in different dimensions but overlapped each other so that parts of each extended into the two adjacent universes.

Whatever Perimal Darkling touched began to change. The animate and the inanimate, the living and the dead, grew closer together in nature. Good and evil began to collapse in on each other. Many men chose to serve the spreading darkness, and so became extensions of it. Others fled, or were enslaved.

The Three-Faced God stood in opposition to the dark invader. As inscrutable in his own way as Perimal Darkling itself, he chose three races from different threshold worlds to be his champions and forged them into the Kencyrath.

The original Kencyr – renamed (by themselves) the Highborn – became the leaders of this new people. They were quickwitted and proud, blessed (or cursed, as some thought even in those days) with an unusually close relationship with their god. Those especially affected were called the Shanir. These individuals possessed strange powers and had a tendency to go mad. They often became priests.

The warriors and craftsmen of the Kencyrath were the strong, easy-tempered Kendar. These capable, self-reliant men and women found that their god had altered their basic natures so that they must now either serve a Highborn lord or suffer great emotional distress. This ensured the Kencyrath's continued existence. Of all the ways in which the Three-Faced God manipulated his people, however, it was perhaps the most cruel.

In contrast, the Arrin-ken retained most of their independence. Not even a god would have cared to tamper much with these folk, who were themselves nearly immortal. Unlike the Highborn and Kendar, the third of the Three People resembled great cats. They served as the Kencyrath's judges, interpreting the laws that the Highborn priests pronounced when their god chose to speak through them.

These, then, were the defenders of the Chain, the champions of their god, whether they wanted to be or not. But when the first clash with the servants of Perimal Darkling came, the Kencyrath found itself fighting for its life, alone. The Three-Faced God had left his people to fend for themselves. No one knew why. The demoralised Kencyrath was defeated.

This was the beginning of the long retreat. On threshold world after threshold world, the Three People made a stand, defending each in turn until forced to withdraw again. As their fighting skills increased, their numbers dwindled and their bitterness grew. They felt betrayed by their god, but were unable to refuse the role that he had forced on them. Stubborn pride and a fierce sense of honour alone upheld them.

Then one man rebelled. Gerridon, Master of Knorth, Highlord of the Kencyrath, offered his soul and that of his followers to Perimal Darkling in exchange for immortality. He induced his sister and consort, Jamethiel Dream-weaver, to pervert the great dance used in the temple so that instead of channelling the god-power, it would suck out the souls of all who witnessed it. Two-thirds of the Kencyr host fell. The rest fled into the next threshold world, Rathillien.

On Rathillien, the remnants of the Three People struggled to re-establish themselves. They became obsessed with honour, feeling that Gerridon's fall from grace had somehow tainted them all. Much of their bitterness was taken out on the Shanir, whom many of them blamed for their current plight. After all, hadn't both the Master and the Mistress been of the old blood? Because of Jamethiel Dream-weaver, Highborn women also fell under suspicion. Their lords stripped them of all civil power and confined them to special halls.

The Arrin-ken disapproved of these changes, but their influence was dwindling as their number, too, declined. The handful of them that remained withdrew into the wilds of Rathillien to consider what should be done next.

During the long absence of the Arrin-ken, contention grew among the Highborn. By now, nearly 3,000 years had passed since the Kencyrath's arrival on Rathillien, and in all that time there had been no significant clash with Perimal Darkling. True, the barrier between the uninvaded areas of Rathillien and the parts now claimed for Perimal Darkling by the Master grew weaker each year and large areas near it, like the Haunted Lands, had been contaminated. But that hardly seemed as serious as the recurrent attacks by the native rulers, most of whom still considered the Kencyrath itself an unwelcome invader.

The Highborn no longer agreed on their priorities. They couldn't entirely abandon their traditional role as the guardians of the Chain, but they could divert much of their energy towards carving out a place for themselves on Rathillien – or so many of them argued. This debate came to a head when Ganth of Knorth was invested as Highlord. Ganth lead a great Kencyr host against its enemies on Rathillien, but he was betrayed and the host broken. Ganth Gray Lord presumably died on his way into exile.

A time of near anarchy followed as the remaining lords vied for power.

Then a young man came out of the Eastern Lands, claiming to be the Gray Lord's son. His name was Torisen. Although he had neither Ganth's sword nor ring to prove his identity, the war-weary Highborn proclaimed him their lord so they might have at least a season's peace. No one thought he would last longer than that. But Torisen Black Lord proved himself so superior a leader that his rivals lost heart. They would have been astonished to learn that while Torisen dismissed them almost contemptuously, there was one rival whom he feared, even though he had not seen her in over twenty years. Somewhere out there was his twin sister, Jamethiel – cursed at birth with the name of an arch-traitor, driven out into the Haunted Lands as a child by Ganth, their father.

But she would come back. She was already on the way. Torisen waited, wondering what would happen when he at last met her face to face.

Appendix IV: The High Council

Houses	Current Lords	Keeps	Standards	Kendar*
Caineron	Caldane	Restormir	A serpent devouring its young	12,000
Ardeth	Adric	Omiroth	Full moon	9,500
Randir	Kenan	Wilden	A gauntleted fist grasping the sun	8,500
Brandan	Brant	Falkirr	Leaping flames	8,000
Jaran	Jedrak	Valantir	Stricken tree	4,000
Coman	Demoth, then Korey	Kraggen	Double-edged sword	3,000
Edirr	Essien and Essiar	Kestrie	Stooping Hawk	2,000
Knorth	Torisen	Gothregor	Rathorn	2,000
Danior	Hollens (Holly)	Shadow Rock	Wolf's mask, snarling	1,000

* These numbers are only approximate and include both bound and the *yondri-gon*.

The above are all major houses, located in the Riverland. Minor houses such as the Harth of East Kenshold and the Mindrear of the High Keep are located near the Barrier and help to maintain it. Once all the houses did, but since they became concentrated in the Riverland, their attention had turned more toward the affairs of Rathillien. Some argue that this is why the Barrier has weakened in such spots as the Haunted Lands.

Appendix V: The Master's Generation

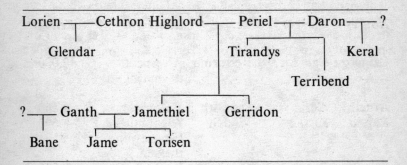

Lorien, Cethron, and Periel were all Knorths. Daron was a Randir. No one knows who Keral's mother was, or Bane's. Both were Kendar.

The Master's generation may look improbably complicated, but its mix of full and half siblings is fairly typical of Highborn families. Most lords have a number of consorts during their lifetime. Their contract specifies how long the arrangement will last and whether or not the lady is authorised by the head of her father's house to bear her consort children. If she does, they stay in their father's house even if she moves on. This has always been so, although before the Fall Highborn women had a far greater say in determining their own fates. They still have more influence than their menfolk realise. Now as then, they can usually control conception at will, which is fortunate because childbirth is often fatal for them. If they do die, their child and its sire are both more or less blacklisted as future breeding stock. The rare illegitimate child is considered as having no family and its mother again, is blacklisted.

The point of all this, of course, is to control the ways in which various houses are linked through bloodlines. At the time of this story, the aim is purely political. Historians suggest, though, that long ago the Highborn may have been trying to breed Shanir, from whose ranks the Tyr-ridan or chosen three will come to lead the Kencyrath in final battle against Perimal Darkling. The way to get the most powerful Shanir, however, is to inbreed, hence the custom of mating twins. But since the Fall, Shanir have become less popular and cross-breeding between houses has become more and more the rule. Now all the lords of the High Council have mixed blood except Torisen and Adric. The Ardeth have always had a special interest in the Shanir. As for the Knorth, because of their divine mandate to provide Highlords, they have always chosen leaders from among the purest of their blood. Now only Torisen and Jame are left in the direct line.